REPUBLIC LOST

A Novel by J. Paul Rinnan

To Ryan and Kristina,
Thanks for your support. I hope you enjoy it. With love.
This one's for you. You are my favorite cousins.
J. Paul Rinnan

ISBN 978-1-61434-273-1

REPUBLIC LOST

Cover art by Todd Engle
Map art by S.C. Watson Illustration (*www.oreganoproductions.com*)

Printed in the United States of America.

BookLocker.com, Inc.
2011

First Edition

For Lindsey and my parents;
your love and support helped
bring this book down from the Forms.

CONTENTS

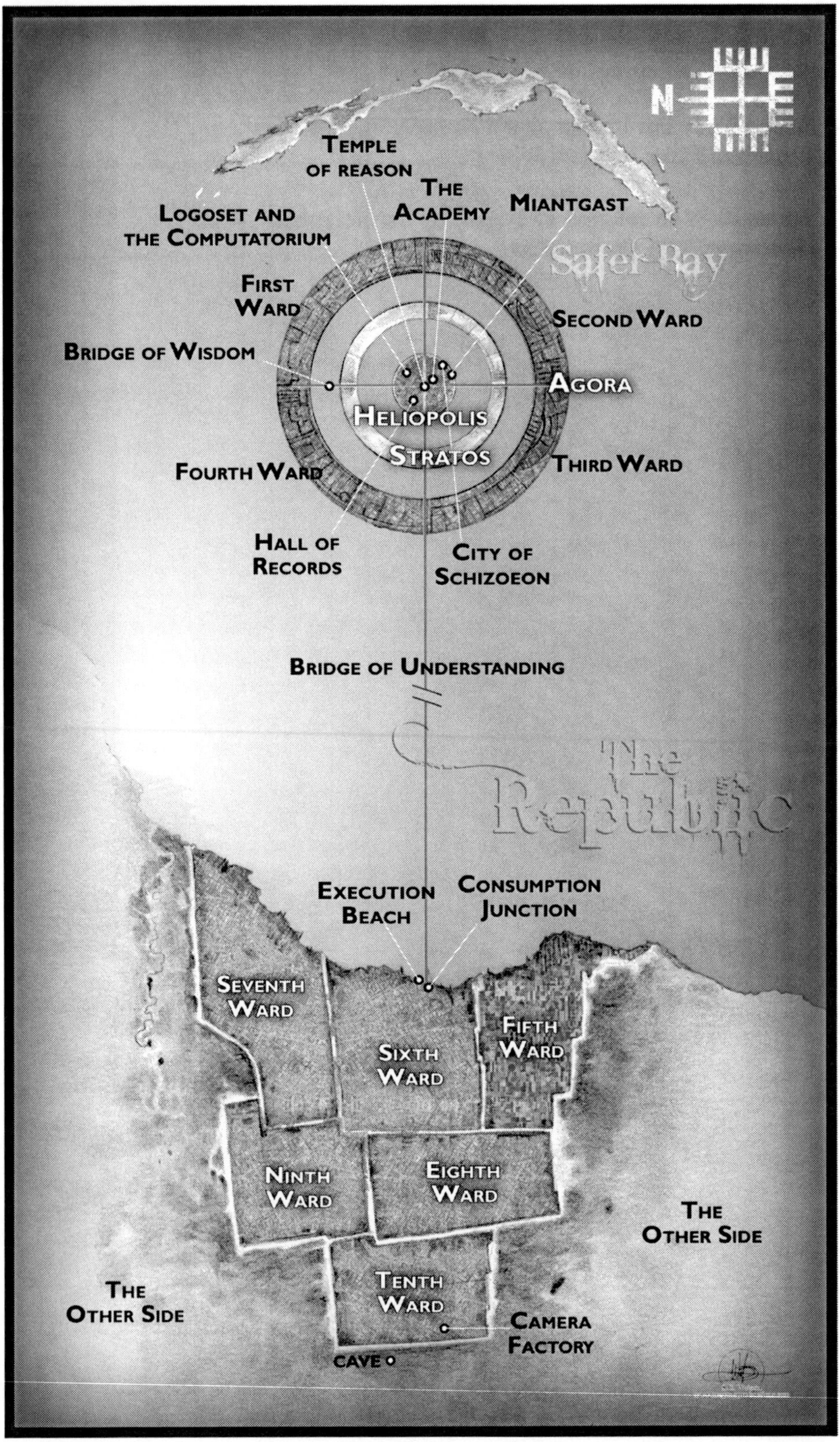

N

Temple of reason

The Academy

Miantgast

Logoset and the Computatorium

Safer Bay

First Ward

Second Ward

Bridge of Wisdom

Agora

Heliopolis

Stratos

Fourth Ward

Third Ward

Hall of Records

City of Schizoeon

Bridge of Understanding

The Republic

Execution Beach

Consumption Junction

Seventh Ward

Fifth Ward

Sixth Ward

Ninth Ward

Eighth Ward

The Other Side

Tenth Ward

The Other Side

Camera Factory

Cave

The World Of Republic Lost

N

North Eastern Liberation Front

Virginia Collective

Detroit Commune

Florida Archipelago

Swamp Tribes

St. Louis

Eastern Column

The Republic

The Fallout Corridor

Crypt

South West Confederacy

We are compelled by the truth to say that no city, constitution, or individual man will ever become perfect until some chance event compels those few philosophers who are not vicious to take charge of a city, whether they want to or not, and compels the city to obey them, or until a god inspires the present rulers and kings or their offspring with a true erotic love for true philosophy.

Plato, *Republic*, 499b

Every trace of anarchy should be utterly eradicated from all the life of men.

Plato, *Laws*, 942d

Give me the high eye
To see like Kabiri,
Fly up the dream heights
Kissing eternal light.
Come show me Fate's Form
Daughters of the storm,
Break all psychosis
Blocking henosis.

Initiation Mantra of the Kabiri Mysteries

BOOK I

THE CALL OF KABIRI

I § 1 THE CAVE

Beneath the rocky earth outside the Republic, beside a shimmering river, the helot boy Glaucon played within a world of shadows. His cave was his own, and he explored the dripping darkness. Every morning he searched the cavern's passages as if they were his own body. He woke up early to find his way back into Gaia's womb. Lighting a cylindrical levilamp and grabbing paper and ink beside the nightstand, Glaucon slipped through a small hole in the city walls, made his way through the forest. Adders and brown spiders crawled up dark trees as he ran past, deer ceased their drinking. Glaucon paid no attention; his home beneath the earth wasn't far away. Some days, when it was boiling hot, Glaucon dived into the river to swim and felt the water rush past his face. On others he'd ignore the stream's friction and sit by a sandy bank, watching fish and tadpoles swimming.

Melete Oxenbridge, Glaucon's mother, was tall and virtuous. She smiled with joy at such wanderings, for she was the one who first showed him the way. The city was no place for her son's free spirited dreams. She knew that. In the cave he had rights. How she loved her son's inquisitive mind in the morning, his thirst for knowledge and thoughtful expressions as he went along. She marveled at his soft footsteps, pattering on the carpet at the chime of the morning temple bells. When he passed through her metal entryway, she hugged him tight. Glaucon was young, but he wore his body as a grown man. His blonde hair curled from sleep, and his sharp grey eyes peered up full of questions.

Mother and son lived together alone in the Tenth Ward. Melete's bondhusband died three years before from plague, the sixth such epidemic since the origin of the Republic under Guardian-King Hythloday. Only the boy was left her now, a fragment of love, a memory she treasured as herself. Each morning she called Glaucon home the world brightened.

Melete frequently went to look for Glaucon in the cave. She'd sneak outside the city gates and find him scribbling poems on the dirt. Levilamp fluttering nearby, Glaucon stared at where earth met edges of rock and water, foot tapping softly.

Glaucon was always thinking but never on any one thing. Melete could see the world flooding through her child's mind like wind that tosses lovers. He paced about, hand level to his forehead, kicking up dust in exasperation. With broken sticks and clay scattered about in various shapes, the architect formed little buildings. Glaucon kicked them in a rage, sat down again, returned to his troubled drawings.

Glaucon felt happy and loved during adolescence. Though Melete was sometimes strict, she always helped him study, reading to him from old books she kept hidden in the cave. When Glaucon fell asleep, she caressed his warm hair and wondered at creation, talking to her sleeping baby. They warmed one another from night's loneliness. Glaucon would wake and snuggle closer to her feminine flesh, and smell her long brown hair with the scent of lilies. The cruelty of the world could be escaped deep within the chasms of his mother. Like the cave she shielded him from the strain of losing his father.

Then, one summer day, Glaucon never saw his mother again.

Melete never observed three hooded men descend from the hill near her home. She only heard a knock at the door. They entered dressed in plain woolen robes. Their shadows filled the room blocking out the sun. Only the sound of broken leaves and twigs still hanging to their sandals could be heard.

Glaucon's mother quickly fell prostrate to the ground, trembling in fear. She could only see their sandals now, but she knew who they were. *Why did they leave their golden city?* she shuddered. (They hardly ever left their golden city.) *Only something ruinous could've brought them to my home.*

These men were guardians of the Republic, masters of the Celestial Forms.

Amidst dust quietly settling on the floor, their leader spoke: "We are told that a young boy by the name of Glaucon lives here."

The man's hood covered his face like a powerful god.

Glaucon's mother anxiously muttered, "You're right to believe so, my grace. He's my only child. I pray he's not dishonored the Republic."

"No, not yet, my dear, not yet. But with time the dragon from the egg hatches, and all is left in ruins. Your son carries the blood of Apollo, and gold is in his veins."

"*Gold*, my lord?" The word filled Melete with dread.

"Yes, he is intellectually gifted. If left alone, he could become extraordinarily dangerous to the Republic."

Glaucon's mother gulped slowly. *How could Glaucon be a threat?* she thought.

The cloaked guardian motioned for one of the others to pull out a large sheet of paper.

On it was a rough sketch: a small boy beside a tombstone in a walled garden. He was alone and sitting upon a large rock, staring at the ground.

Trees hung over the boy like arches, faces visible in the leaves, twisted by painful loss.

The guardian explained, "Your son's teacher found this on the floor of his classroom and brought it to our attention. Reflects the Beautiful, doesn't it? You can almost feel the tragic laceration, the tormenting distress and tender acceptance of the boy sitting on the stone. It cuts through my emotions, confusing me and exposing my desires—sets my soul afire! One of my associates reviewed it and claims he was deeply moved. In this respect your son has become a dangerous threat: He has the power to undermine reason with a stroke of his brush. He is a conjurer of shadows, and shadows of shadows, and could lead people away from the Form of Truth. Does your son know the laws against painting?"

"No, I don't believe so," Glaucon's mother said sobbing. She struggled to control herself. "He enjoys drawing, and I've always humored him. I'm surely mistaken. I recognize I'm nothing more than bronze, but I felt it was healthy for the boy to express his emotions. His father died when he was very young—"

"His father?"

The guardians stifled a low laugh.

"—and he struggles with guilt and sadness constantly. Please don't be angry with him. If anyone must be punished, it's me for allowing it."

"No," said the guardian, "the fault lies with us. One cannot blame the race commanded by desire. It's your nature to allow such things. Only we are capable of controlling your son and putting an end to these impassioned arts he cultivates. Where is the boy? We'll speak with him directly."

"He runs off alone," Melete answered. "I know not where he is."

Bending over, the guardian whispered in Melete's ear: "Liar; the Kabiri Circle knows all your dirty secrets. Every one. Your foolish night husband betrayed me."

Glaucon's mother pushed lower to the ground with a frightened look. So they knew everything, then. This was the Kabiri she'd been warned about—the Engineer, Oracle of Machines.

The guardian put a hand on Melete's shoulder and wiped away a tear gathering on her cheek. "Tears are a fool's errand in this life, fallen whore, when one contemplates the intelligible realm. The place we take the child will be responsive to his needs and ours. He doesn't belong here in the darkness with you and the other helots. Your lust for desire would turn him into a cruel, contemptible sphinx. A god like him would become a slanderer if he worked with his hands."

The hooded man rose, adjusted his robes. He slid out of the room and gently closed the door. He followed the other guardians through the hole in the city walls to the forest.

Melete was still lying on the floor lifeless when her door opened again. She could hear other families being dragged from their homes, screaming. It was all her fault. *What will happen to my Glaucon?* she choked. She wished she could warn her son to flee, but it was too late. Too late.

The windows shattered. Auxiliaries came in through the door like a malignant wind.

I § 2 Intentional Trauma

Glaucon played in the whispering cavern. Like any other day, he invented a game. This time he tossed pillars of sand in the air, pretending to conjure smoke with black magic. Friendly stalactites watched, called his name, but they suddenly pulled back.

Pounding metallic footsteps echoed in the chamber, loud as the Calydonian Boar. Glaucon feverishly looked for a place to hide, but he was trapped against the walls. Four machines scurried under hydraulic spider legs over the ceiling of the cave. They abruptly flooded the cavern with hollow light. Their heads were shaped like crescent moons and grinned menacingly. The Greek word ALETHEIA glowed above their single eyecameras, a manufactured blue.

Three men trailed the machines like hooded ghosts.

"Come with us, Mr. Oxenbridge," one of the bearded ones commanded. "Do not mind the golems. They're only my midwives sent to give you second birth."

Glaucon timidly rose to his feet. He followed the men out, without thinking, back into the foreign light of day, back into the forest, out the door in the earth. He watched his cave fade away and wondered if he'd ever see it again.

The boy kept pace for what seemed like hours. He heard the golems' soulless scampering behind and worried he'd be scolded for leaving the city walls. His mother had warned him, sternly, to hide if ever discovered. To leave the Republic was forbidden. And the books—the books!—were especially dangerous.

Away the procession walked from Glaucon's mother's house, away from his flowing river. The group walked out of the forest onto a meadow, to a large fig tree, and sat down. One of the hooded men pulled out a few loaves of bread and passed them around. He made certain not to break them to stave off bad luck.

Cool wind rustled the grass. Glaucon was offered a drink of apple cider but refused. His mouth tasted dry, and he could barely speak; golems' tails mesmerized when whipping the air like scorpions.

He was still getting accustomed to the light.

The largest guardian pulled down his hood, revealing a middle-aged man with a bearded face. The beard pointed sharply, like a Spanish conquistador. He had white bushy eyebrows and pale skin. Silver hair, parted to the side, covered his left ear. He was lion-like and stared intently. The others, obviously younger, removed their hoods as well. Each was bald with a ring of hair, looked like monks.

"Do you know who we are?" the guardian asked curiously.

Glaucon shook his head and stared submissively at the ground. He hadn't been confronted by such determined male figures since his father. They etched their will upon him, forced him to shudder. Of course he'd seen guardians before; many acted as priests for temple rites. Many times at school Glaucon walked by statues of the last ten guardian-kings. Their gold arms, reaching for the sun, filled all with deep reverence and fear. To young boys they were divinity. Daily history lessons about the metals amplified this awe. As his teacher explained, "The Earth, under command by the Form of the Good, birthed humanity with certain metals in their souls: bronze, silver, and gold. Those with gold were best suited to rule the Republic while those with bronze should obey and produce." The golden guardians were always to be respected.

Glaucon shivered. He noticed the golems' heads twitching back and forth like hungry birds ready for a feast.

The guardian tried putting the boy at ease: "My name's Prodicus, Glaucon. Don't be frightened. What a pleasure finally meeting you. How I wish you could see your face. You look astonished; you really do—as if you've seen a phantom. I assure you, we mean no harm. We only want your help remedying a potential danger. Pay no heed to the golems around us. They do as they're told. Their scorpion tails have no sting as long as I'm here."

"How do you know?" Glaucon asked.

"Because I built them to obey." Prodicus pulled out a small controller and spun a knob. Both E's on the ALETHEIA disappeared and the golems clunked lifeless on the ground. "There. The golems are resting and won't bother us. We can get down to business. Stand firm and be truthful: We received word from school you've picked up painting. Is that true?"

"Yes," Glaucon nodded ashamed.

His answer made the guardians behind Prodicus shake their heads. Prodicus had expected the response, though, and asked, "When you sit in your cave what do you draw? Do you etch things that are animated and colored and meaningful? What drives you to do these things?"

Glaucon swallowed hard before answering. He knew before he started painting and writing that such things were forbidden. Such images were shadows. Teachers said so in school. The material world was a false illusion in which opposites tumbled about in confusion. Nothing was as it seemed, and all was chaos and flux, on the furthest end of falsehood. Beautiful things, like a sunset or a tadpole, only partook in the immutable Form of Beauty; they were not Beauty itself. To draw pictures of these beautiful things was to copy copies, not to come closer to understanding the universal.

Glaucon sighed. He never understood the ban on painting (or the Forms, for that matter). The Forms were a mystery, as difficult to understand as Bellerophon's journey to the circles of heaven on the winged horse Pegasus. Glaucon remarked exasperated, "I'm sorry, but I don't know why I draw them. Images spring up in me like breathing air and linger. I must express their melody. Just the other day, I saw an old man lying by the roadside. He was tapping his cane and a small dog was near him. I saw him staring at me, forcefully. He looked away. I couldn't sleep that evening because of the man, had to etch his features onto something. Haggard cheeks, forehead covered with coarse and straggling hair, eyes black as coal, yet there was something serene and stubborn about him. An official ordered him to take a special pill, but he refused. He was dying and wanted to die. Refused to eat. Then soldiers beat the man and took him away."

The three guardians looked at one another as Glaucon finished speaking. Calm descended over the group sitting in the grass. A large eagle circled overhead. Prodicus lifted his steely eyes, thinking for a moment, listening at the sky. The roar of spiritcarriers and zizthopters could be heard whirling in the distance. The aircraft flew like the eagle did, with feathered wings, and fired Deathstalker missiles into the city, chasing down the petrified faces of his enemies.

Pacification of the Tenth Ward commenced like the fury of a thousand fires, coughing up smoke and dust and concrete mixed with rending cries.

The concussive blasts fell softly on Prodicus' eardrums, and he thought approvingly: *Soon the Katharoi rebels will be dead and temperance will return. The hunger strikes and rioting will end and the Republic will be at peace. If only I could find the children Xenon stole away. No matter. The Fates said they'll return, in time.* He turned back to Glaucon: "The things you speak, boy, I've felt intimately. When I was your age—younger even—I too had become lost in a sweltering sea of voices. I found myself chased by wild images not my own. Unhealthy books, creative passions and rebels, ideas made civil war in my yet untrained mind. You know, I wasn't born far from your street in the Tenth Ward. As a young man, I also fell into some trouble with the authorities when they discovered several of my sketches, or rather should I say, 'imitations.' If I recall, one was a picture of a vivid phoenix bathed in fire. It was the creature I longed to be. Can you believe I dreamed of flying like that eagle above us?" Prodicus laughed merrily.

The two guardians behind, though, fidgeted uncomfortably. They had clearly never heard this admission before and were astonished. The shorter one plucked a blade of grass from the earth and broke it into six pieces, contemplating Plato's number, trying to ease his mind.

Prodicus went on, "When my imitations were discovered, guardians came to see me, too. I thought they were daimons at first and tried to run away. However, the 'pure ones' found me, as they always do. They educated me of the historic animosity between poetry and philosophy. The best means to achieve truth was through reason, logic, and argument—not metaphor and the brush! I didn't believe them at the time, but I've come to do so. Do you know why?"

Glaucon shook his head at the philosopher.

"Only through reason do we discover the divine. Reason helps see past the distinctions and opposites to comprehend the universal *in itself*, in its androgynous reality. Let me explain," Prodicus said patiently. "See this stick next to me by my robe? We took it from your cave as we left. I hope you don't mind. It seems to be wet and rotting."

"That's how I grab them from the tree," Glaucon interrupted. "Almost impossible to grab dry branches. I was using it to draw patterns on the floor."

"All the easier for me," Prodicus said slyly as he briskly grabbed the stick. He broke the gnarled branch with sudden force and Glaucon watched amazed. Prodicus lay the broken branches on the floor. "Now listen carefully, boy," he said. "Would you say the two sticks are equal in length or unequal?"

Glaucon carefully examined the two sticks on the ground. He picked them up to measure their length against one another. "I suppose they're equal," he answered.

"You suppose so or you know so?" Prodicus quipped.

"I know they're equal."

"Are you sure?"

"Could be no other way."

"Very good, Glaucon, that's how one should state their opinion. You should always clearly and precisely state what you mean. Your belief seems true in this case, but how did you know they were equal in length?"

"How did I know?" Glaucon stammered. "That is a strange question to ask. They're just equal. I measured one against the other."

Glaucon looked exasperated and perplexed.

Prodicus laughed, "You'll find knowledge of truth impossible without charting the path you took to comprehension. You fell right into my trap, little one. Look at his pink face, gentlemen. He looks as if I cast a sorcerer's spell on him. You know, Glaucon, they used to call Socrates a torpedo fish. Do you know why? His questioning could draw listeners to tears and make their minds and tongues go numb. Have I done the same to you?—I hope so. You'll soon find that many people make speeches but few understand what they're saying. The untimely word is characteristic of an evil mind—remember that. Now, we need something more, a system of knowledge to explain how you are able to distinguish the Equal from the Unequal. Tell me, did you learn about the Equal in school?"

"No."

"No? By Hera, how wild and curious is your power. So you never took a class on the Equal, never read a book on it or sang patriotic songs about the Equal. Yet so skillfully, here you are applying the concept like a seasoned scholar. How is this power possible?"

Glaucon tried to think of an answer. Prodicus was right. He'd never been told about the Form of the Equal, yet every day he used the concept skillfully, as if he'd always known. "I don't know how I differentiate between equal and unequal things," he said. "I walk over to my little stream, and I see two stones—a red and a white one of similar size—and I say, 'They are equal.' So too with the trees in my forest. I walk under their green canopy and look at their trunks and say, 'These trees are of equal size.' I've spun around my whole life applying this term, and never has anyone told me how to do it. Perhaps Mother showed me?"

Prodicus was dubious. "Ah, but then where did she learn it?" He knew already the debate was won. Glaucon's confusion was considerable. "You said you always knew when two things were equal. Would you say your understanding of the Equal is stirred up like a recollection, then? You recall how to use the idea of the Equal?"

"Yes, I would say it's very much like that."

"Very good; now how do we regularly remember things? We either see the object directly or else we see something which reminds us of the object. Now, have we ever seen the Form of the Equal directly?"

"No, and if I did I should surely tell people about it."

"Very well, but you admit to seeing other objects which remind you of the Equal?"

"I do."

"Would you say these objects that help you recall the Equal are related or unrelated to the Equal?"

"I don't understand."

"For example, I might see a lyre and then remember the boy to which it belongs. I recollect a second thing from the first, but they are unrelated. I hope you would agree knowing a boy is different from knowing a lyre."

The guardians behind Prodicus snickered.

Glaucon did not understand the joke. He said, "Oh yes, of course. Whenever I return home and sink into our jelly-couch in the living room, I can smell my mother's perfume. It smells like lilies in the summer, and I immediately recall her face."

"Exactly right," Prodicus praised him. "You are recalling through association what was forgotten. Just like you smell your mother's lily perfume and recall her face, you must also see similar looking sticks and recall the unrelated universal idea of the Equal. How wonderful! You must've always known about the Equal, yes?"

"That must certainly be true," Glaucon shouted, "otherwise how could I have originally talked about equal things."

"Indeed Glaucon, what a lofty and beautiful thing you've done to glimpse the hidden manifold causing our reality. Through my coaching your reason awakened and discovered what it knew all along—your mind possesses innate knowledge about the Form of the Equal, and all the Forms for that matter: the Forms of perfect chairs, horses, trees, and cities, mathematical truths and geometry. Draw a right triangle and you can derive an army of truths from the exercise. You can derive them independently of sensory experience. *A priori* knowledge, mathematics, the Equal are proof of the divine."

Glaucon breathed every word with his teacher.

Prodicus continued looking possessed: "Imagine if our souls could detach from our bodies and the confusion of our senses, what we could come to know. We would finally view reality purely in itself. We could see the Form of Beauty and taste the Form of Love without needing to go through material objects as the intermediary. Why, it would be like diving into a fresh spring and shedding clothes weighing us down. Glaucon, what if I said you first learned of the Forms before being embodied in your mother?"

"I should say that is a strange belief."

"No," Prodicus scolded. "Don't look so confused. Don't turn back on your learning like an insolent puppy. Even as babies we're ensnared by the senses. It seems self-evident—a principle of reason—that prior to becoming incarnate in your current body, your eternal soul had access to the Forms in the Pure Land. You swam through the Forms of the Good and the Beautiful like a clown fish through coral reefs. It was there you communed with the Form of the Equal and carried it out with you into this material world. You just forgot the Forms when you swam through the River of Forgetfulness! But you can recall them now, can't you? Because of the preexistence, you're able to apply universals like Beauty, Truth, and Justice to beautiful things and just societies. Tell me, have you ever noticed imperfection in our world?"

"Sometimes," Glaucon sighed. "Nothing under the sun ever seems constant. My father was alive, then dead. There are deserts and swamps, fallout and flies, pain and death like the old man I drew. I can never write or draw anything in just the right way. My perceptions are flawed. A teacher told us in class that a gorilla is beautiful to other gorillas but ugly to humans. I found this lesson strange. As you were saying, the Beautiful should always remain beautiful. If beauty can change to ugliness in a gorilla, it must be there imperfectly."

Prodicus stared intently at the agitated child, chewing on his thoughts. The golems continued to lie lifeless on the ground.

Faint pounding drums followed Aegis tanks into the Tenth Ward. The field's elevation was too low to see the battle, but Prodicus imagined the lobster tanks slowly gravitating behind the blindfolded rebels like pillars of judgment. The buildings were collapsing, washing all around his new subjects. Prodicus was saddened by such barbarity. *But, alas,* he consoled himself, *our Republic is not a suicide pact. Delivering a pregnancy requires much patience, and if the child will not live we must cut it off. Better that some should die than suffer total catastrophe.*

Prodicus said turning from his thoughts, "Your words strike me as wise, Glaucon, almost too wise for your age. But *imperfections* in the world have a purpose."

"They do?"

"Yes. Each broken vessel we see is a signpost to a more virgin reality—to God, the Form of the Good. The cries of our souls bind us with it, like the Good binds all the other Forms to its will. We reappear every lifetime until one day—if we fulfill our given role in the Republic—we return to the Eternal. Unjustified violence, earthquakes that kill everyone in temple, our need for tanks, all stimulate man from his indifference, make him confront the Cosmic Soul. Remember: To sense imperfection is at the same time to recall perfection. Opposites beget opposites; the Form of the Good causes us to feel alien in order to help us remember the home we lost. And one day we shall be restored."

Prodicus remembered the lost souls slain earlier before coming to the Tenth Ward: his sister, Potone; her meddlesome night husband, Lycaon; Ekklesia the Blind. All Katharoi heretics. All schemers. Most likely, they'd end up as rabbits or fish upon rebirth, but perhaps, if they bore their role joyfully, they might return to the Republic. No one was beyond redemption.

"Restore us from what, Master?" Glaucon asked.

"Why, from dualities, the grip of nature, endless rebirth!" Prodicus shouted. He felt like the boy was reading his thoughts. "Gods, Glaucon, I can hardly believe I'm telling you this already? Even our twelfth grade neophytes at the Academy don't have the privilege of hearing such wonderful things. I told you he was a special boy, Zeno." Prodicus gaped back at the portly guardian.

Zeno's cheeks were cracked and his face was piggish. He was not necessarily ugly, Glaucon decided, merely pestering. Glaucon looked back at his teacher, amazed. *How on earth did we get from talking about equal sticks to a discussion on the preexistence of the soul?* he wondered. Logic somehow slipped along the way. Nevertheless, Glaucon felt a startling ownership of the argument which made the words spoken exceedingly persuasive. Walls of disbelief breached, a force like lightning engulfed him.

"The Fates hide nothing from us," Zeno said stoically.

Prodicus was less convinced. "The Fates are blind. Computers only deal in probabilities. They have their purpose, but only I can find the Vessels. You may commence the evaluation, Zeno. But I know the truth. We've found the Second Vessel."

"Yes, my grace." Zeno walked over to Glaucon and pulled out a small cylindrical box with an electrical wire shaped liked a tuning fork. "We call this an I.T. magnetometer," he explained. "It's a sensitive device connected to Kabiri-35's—the Fates'—mainframe. Measures your body's electromagnetic wave structure for neural and cardiac resonances. This may feel cold and intrusive. Don't be alarmed."

Zeno turned on a metal switch at the bottom of the cylinder. The machine burped, started to crackle with radiation. A flat red light spread from the metal hose like a controlled tornado. Cold ice tickled Glaucon's skin as Zeno measured him up and down. Nails scraped his brain and cracked it open.

Zeno looked up astonished. "This can't be right. His I.T. dialogue matrix is at a pitch of nearly four hundred and eighty waves per second. There must be an error with the instruments."

"No error," Prodicus said. "Measure me now."

Zeno turned around and aimed the machine at the philosopher. He pulled Prodicus aside and whispered in his ear, "You are nearly just as high, Prodicus. If I hadn't come, I wouldn't believe such levels exist. Your face is almost glowing."

"Zeno, what color is his waveform?"

"The wave glows indigo, Sire. Like yours. Like Kleomedes and Sophia."

"Holy stars," Prodicus gasped, "the Fates have led us to him. Just as their programming spit out on that tape: 'A narrow path from the tree of souls, three indigo Vessels will appear: one earth, one soul, one crown; living animals—stillborn—to repair. Gather them like the fruits of harvest. Mix with Kabiri together in the sky. Putrification prime renews virgin reason, the spirit of Good; forms the Golden King.' We've found the Second Vessel, I know it."

Zeno said, "For someone so skeptical of the Fates' judgment, much faith you place in their prophecies."

"A man who builds something recognizes its limitations. I only realize *some* probabilities come true. I act according to the values at stake."

Glaucon could barely hear what was being said. The I.T. magnetometer left a sensation of being locked in a bubble and falling down a deep well. Then holes were in the bubble, deflating. He struggled to breathe.

Prodicus walked back to Glaucon gleaming. "This is your first time for such an intensive I.T. reading, isn't it? Don't worry, it's just separation poisoning. It'll subside in a moment. Photographing your I.T. waveform can be unbearable without protection—they don't say 'Intentional Trauma' for nothing. But it's necessary for the Fates to do their work."

"I.T. waves? I think I'm going to throw up," Glaucon stuttered.

"*Electromagnetism.*" Prodicus tasted the word and let it roll from his tongue. "An unsatisfying term. The energy is electrical and magnetic, yes, but so much more. It covers everything from power waves that propel atomic and molecular motion, to gamma rays, x-rays, and visible light. Each of our living cells radiates a spectrum of energy. With each heartbeat, your body emits two and a half watts of energy—enough to power a levilamp. Did you know, we can read your I.T. energy arc emanating almost ten meters away? The waves spread and return to their source, contact others, resonate, like our souls and the Form of the Good. The Fates taught us many things about the human body."

Glaucon's stomach started to settle, but black smoke pouring from the Republic's walls upset him again. *What is happening to my home?* he wondered at the ash filling the sky. *Is Mother safe?*

Prodicus noticed the boy losing interest in their dialogue. He drew his attention away, commanding, "Don't look at the burning land. The people there are dead."

They walked through a row of twisting oak trees. Zeno and the other guardian followed, their faces turned away from the city.

"As I said earlier," Prodicus continued, "I was like you as a child. When guardians came to my home, they gifted me with the Argument of the Equal. They then offered me a choice. The guardians said if I'd been a little older, my artwork would make me guilty of a capital crime. I would be sentenced to death in the Bull—"

"To death?" Glaucon asked alarmed.

"Yes, Glaucon, art is a very serious thing and keeps the mind from recognizing the Forms. Oh, I was so much like you as a boy. I did not understand the danger of my actions or the nature of my crimes. When the guardians offered to mitigate my sentence to travel with them to Heliopolis, I thought them fools. When I went with them, though, I soon learned the error of my ways. You are fortunate. Like me, your age and innocence saved you."

Glaucon slumped to the ground and averted his eyes from the philosopher, suddenly ashamed. The guardian raised Glaucon's head with his finger and stared directly at him, like he had his mother.

"Curious," Prodicus said wrinkling his beard, "I don't know why the schools kept your presence secret from us. Your potential should've been discovered years ago."

Zeno grumbled loudly, "Xenon is to blame. He was led astray by sympathy for that girl, his profane desires. You shouldn't have let him join the Kabiri Circle."

"No matter," Prodicus said. "All in the past. Xenon shall have his reckoning soon enough. Now, Glaucon, we must see to your future education. The most noble occupation open to any member of our society is that of the guardian estate, for it is the duty of our office to maintain security and harmony among the world of men. We are ancient relics from a past fraught with war and blood. Do you know the story of the Age of Aporia?"

"I've heard some things in school. Long ago, man was almost destroyed because he let desire rule. Those with bronze in their souls ran society into the ground."

"Yes, Glaucon. Each person sought their own freedom without searching for the hidden Form of Freedom. Their 'freedom' was that of the libertine: to wander blindly through the dark graveyards of frivolity, sex, and circuses. The appetitive part of their soul splintered their compass. They had no captains familiar with a map of the stars to direct them to their destination. Accordingly, they sailed lost in a million different delights. Because they spent their time staring only at the garment of Justice, they were unable to see the hidden Form of Justice. Only we guardians can see the Forms, not they. Our Republic is the most perfect in history, the only city left. It mirrors our soul with appetitive, spirited, and reasonable parts. But now reason whips the appetites to obey."

Glaucon was silent. He smelled burning wood.

Prodicus looked at the boy with sadness. "Glaucon, forty-five years ago I chose to leave my family. We told your mother we think you gifted. Yet, at this moment, your future is very much in question. I must sadly leave the same choice left to me as a child: You may choose to come with us to the Academy, to learn how to commune with the Forms, become intellectually free to pursue your mind's greatest ambitions, or you may go to juvenile detention for re-education in order to be readmitted to the helot class. What will you do, my son?"

"I want to go back to Mother," Glaucon asserted passionately.

Prodicus turned to the others and laughed heartily. "Do you see how he breaks my constraints?" he asked. "What a rascal! What good will re-education do him?"

Zeno said, "As if you would let another Vessel escape your grasp, Oracle."

With lament, Prodicus placed hands on his shoulders. "No, my son, I'm sorry to say you'll never see your mother again. It's not your fault. She's been neglectful in her duties to you and almost sired a dragon among us. Art! Lies! Katharoi teachings! Although not unexpected given her breed and vulgar occupation, she is unfit for motherhood, especially for someone like you. You'd best forget her. She can only confuse you. Our earthly mothers possess ten thousand times less reality than the Form of Mother. Our mothers are only trivial reflections in the dark. Insignificant!"

Glaucon did not agree. He wanted to sit with his mother again, to feel her warm hand stroke his head in the evenings and whisper forbidden stories. He wanted to hear her voice by the fireplace and hold her brown hair watching the digitele. His lip quivered, eyes watering. He felt disoriented again.

The guardian's heart went out to the boy. "It will be difficult for you at first, like it was for me. But I promise all will be well. If you only knew the world of light to come, you'd rejoice. You will soon learn 'every animal is driven to pasture with a blow.' "

Prodicus turned to the other guardians. "Zeno, this boy is blessed, and he will triumph over ignorance. By consorting with the Forms he will become divine."

The other guardians stood up and brushed grass from their robes. Zeno stuffed the magnetometer back into his bag. "And you, Great Oracle of the Kabiri, will be divine as well," he said, slapping his chest with a fist.

ALETHEIA returned over the golems' eyes, and they scurried toward Glaucon like ravenous wolves, chirping.

Zeno grabbed Glaucon gruffly by the collar. "You will come with me now," he ordered. Prodicus' serene face disappeared as Zeno pulled him across the field—half walking, half dragging—through the dirt to an awaiting rusty red hovertruck. Glaucon hadn't even noticed it. Solar panels formed the roof, and a door in the back opened. A black cross with five fingers on each end was painted on the door. Glaucon remembered his teacher calling them the "*Hands-of-God*"—sacred symbol of the Republic.

Two auxiliaries in scarves and army fatigues, holding shining Neokalashnikovs, stepped down from the truck and grabbed the boy from Zeno. Glaucon could barely muster a thought of protest and was thrown into the truck bed to the sound of locking doors. Golems, fidgeting behind the soldiers, were the last thing he saw.

"You are to take him to Heliopolis immediately," Glaucon heard Zeno say through the muffled wall of steel. "Tell Yannis he is to tend to the boy personally under direct orders from his holiness, Prodicus, High Philosopher-King, newly crowned Vicar of Reason. We'll return tomorrow after attending to the Katharoi traitors here."

Another door slammed and the truck lurched forward. Glaucon peered into the truck bed tomb. The darkness did not feel the same as his cave. An hour later, gunshots and screaming. He did not know where he was going, and unfriendly shadows taunted.

He fell asleep thinking of his mother.

RESTORATION AB AETERNO: Rebuilding the World

The following chronicle, written by Simmias during his nineteenth year at the Academy, was created from a compilation of reports, classified documents, memorandum, personal journal entries, shadowspar recordings, and his own fanciful imagination. It attempts to chart the history of our Republic from the Age of Aporia to the death of the first philosopher-king, Abaris Hythloday. (Top Secret/Publication Prohibited.)

There is a legend we tell children in our Republic: In the beginning mankind lived in unity with the earth. There was only happiness and delight. Then a desire to multiply overcame him. A pride to transcend the world severed his connection with Mother Earth. This severance broke the crust and caused a *fire consuming fire* to flood the world with light. So much heat billowed forth that all metals melted and drifted apart. The *Demiurge* found the liquid minerals drifting lost in the Gulf of Mexico. Cooling the stray minerals back to ingots with the sea, he fashioned three new races, bronze, silver, and gold, and placed them on the sacred island of Heliopolis. He foretold another *fire consuming fire* if the race of bronze or silver should ever attempt to rule the gold.

Although certainly a fantastic story, such legends carry a nugget of truth. The Age of Aporia preceding Heliopolis did indeed die in *fire consuming fire*. The dangers of the twenty-fifth century looked nothing in comparison to the dangers of the twenty-sixth. At the exact time wise rulers were needed to tend the world, none found their way to the halls of power. Instead, businessmen with appetitive desires governed. The Forms of Truth and Justice they shunned like maggots in meat.

Using money to buy votes, businessmen elected princes, potentates, warriors, and tyrants, too. Disobedient to themselves and their desires, they built sluggish governments which could not help but veer off course. In essence they lived as if in sleep, when the reasonable part of the soul slumbers. They cultivated the worst beasts biting at their veins. They loved money for the sake of money, and so they printed as much as they liked, succubi satisfying their every need for food, drink, and sex. When this too left them unsatisfied, they conjured additional wants to wet their addictions. The more they consumed the more they desired, and the more they desired the more they consumed, onward and onward, into a spiraling frenzy through the teeth of Charybdis.

Intense economic competition between the industrializing and industrialized capitalist states caused an epidemic of overproduction. From 2407 M.G.P. (Meta-Genissi Plato) to the 2435 Recession, over one hundred crises rocked the financial markets. This, however, was nothing but a prelude to greater market instability. As overproduction filled the world with trash and economic misery, the environment collapsed. Glaciers melted, continents flooded, Category 6 hurricanes raged. Droughts charred the ground seeding famine and war. The profit-lovers did nothing but fight over the scraps of their planet. India and China continued to exhaust the Earth in ways the twenty-fifth century never fathomed. Meanwhile, the United States of America attempted to salvage its dying empire by engaging in misadventures around the world, borrowing heavily from China and Russia to support its wars.

The United States was the first to fall. The horrors of Black Tuesday, 2356 M.G.P., could not compare to the cauldron of evils which befell them on Black Thursday, December 4, 2514 M.G.P. All economies of the world were tied together like a living tapestry; all fell together, too. China called for its money, and the United States refused to pay. The Great Sino-American War lasted less than a day.

The North Atlantic Treaty Organization launched their missiles. The Russo-Beijing League launched theirs. The missiles flew like fiery red horses slaying peace. As late figs drop from a fig tree, the Russian land of ice and the ascending Dragon Throne fell. Every sovereign fell. Thunders boomed and stars hop-scotched across the globe. Souls gave way their resistance and burned in the *fire consuming fire*. Mankind fell like a broken vessel.

This event has been labeled by philosopher historians as the *Day of Hylopleonexia*, the day matter overreached.

Man took refuge from the flames as he always does—by hiding. Those that saw the coming missiles retreated to their fallout shelters like buried arks. One soul to survive at NORAD's underground shelter in Colorado was General Abaris Hythloday. Some sources say he went mad under the earth; others say he became a sage. Sitting alone for months in the dark, a single beautiful white book maintained his sanity. It was a book by Plato called *Republic*, loaded with ancient philosophical knowledge and blueprints for the perfect society.

General Hythloday grew obsessed with the work. It haunted his nights like a poltergeist. Plato, we are told by some accounts, frequented his dreams and made him scribble hundreds of copies, all to be given to the soldiers under his command.

One day, according to another witness, General Hythloday even gave one to his younger brother, the grey-eyed Sextus, but he refused to read the work. Although Hythloday warned his brother of the warheads to save his life, "the loaf musician" remained insubordinate. The two brothers drifted apart underground. Silently, each wanted to kill the other.

General Hythloday commanded his brother to obey: "You will read this book and understand what kind of government awaits us when we return to the world of the sun. We shall build it, and man will be perfected. I swear to God he will. As above, so below, humanity shall mirror the harmony of the Pure Land and finally be happy."

Sextus laughed garishly, as though he wished to rip his brother's soul to pieces. Then—and this is difficult to write—he did the unthinkable, and tossed his copy of the *Republic* into a trash can. "Plato was a crank as all philosophers are cranks," he heretically jabbed. "Plato never wanted you to take him seriously. The Republic is a phantom as fantastic as his Forms. Creating his vision is more impossible than democracy and would be twice as oppressive. I'd rather kill Socrates again then live in *that* place."

For weeks the brothers remained silent, refusing to relent, refusing to forgive. But as the shelter was so enclosed, they couldn't separate. General Hythloday passed Sextus sometimes, shaking in uncontrollable fury as he rested near a naked woman. "What am I going to do with you?" he would say. "Do you think you can just sit here staring at the wall? We have planning, much planning ahead of us. Just look at your sorry state—chasing women and drinking what's left of our wine. You're incorrigible, a glutton, and a cheat! Oh, how will you ever mop up your sins and ignorance? If I could only show you the advantage in shunning this life, to give up impurity for virtue, I might kiss you here."

Sextus shrugged and returned to his woman. "It's late, Brother, leave me be. Go preach to others who enjoy slavery. I will always remain here, avoiding your little white book." He kissed his woman in rebuke.

General Hythloday departed irate, raging through the corridors. He went to a nearby room filled with refugees. They were all molemen, sitting there under the fluorescent lights: chewing spit, dreaming dreams of past unfulfilling lives without a thought for the future. "I forsake thee! I forsake thee! Always will I forsake thee," he called turning to the frightened dreamers. "I forsake it all—this reality, this world, this people. Look, I shall wipe it all away with a sponge and paint a new Shangri-La, a city more valuable than El Dorado. Its gemstone shall be reason's light, her leader reason's medicine-man. Philosopher-kings will rule! All will be happy."

Such teachings kindled hope in the darkness, and many were filled with aspiration. "The Form of the Good shall be our compass," Hythloday pointed to the *Republic*, "and the Form of Justice our shield. All parts of the soul will fulfill their roles. *Not self-rule, but rule by reason and the reasonable*."

He read his little white book aloud on a locker box. Disciples carried his work into the deepest chambers of the fallout shelter. They taught Saint Plato at Sunday school and church, replacing the absent Yahweh who failed them in the war.

Hythloday raced around the shelter talking of the great chain of being, angelology, on the need to reform and repent, to prepare for the coming of the Republic. Curious listeners transformed like werewolves to men and knelt before him. He placed his hand upon their heads, blessed them, held baptisms of water. "Greater than the Form of Beauty, the Form of Love, or the Form of Courage, is the Form of the Good, binding all together."

Back they cheered, "A benediction on the human race and our journey to mingle with the Forms!"

Hythloday promised, "We'll all be perfect if we unite in harmony, if we follow this book and make Justice our lighthouse. Look and see, we'll examine what appetites each person possesses to avoid the rocks of instability. If a man is filled with desire or has an aptitude for engineering or farming or crafting or shipping, we shall make him a helot—a producer of goods. Yes, and what a wonderful role that will be, to fuel our Republic with the goods for its survival. We should make the helots produce, not only enough for themselves, but also enough for the auxiliaries and guardians. We'll gather those in tune with the emotional part of their souls and make them soldiers. They shall defend the helots. The reasonable ones—those with a 'good memory, quick wits, smartness, youthful passion, high-mindedness', a devotion to the Form of Truth over money—we will make our honored guardians, and they'll direct the auxiliaries how best to protect our city. 'And the State will erect monuments to commemorate them. And sacrifices will be offered to them as demigods.' Does this seem fitting?"

All listeners agreed.

"I should like to be a herboligist," shouted one. "Perhaps we can build special domed greenhouses to fight the fallout."

"That sounds most fitting," said General Hythloday.

"And I should like to start a nanofactory for research again," shouted another named Dr. Zosimos Ozbolt. "I was best in my class at the University of Chicago. I could build all kinds of important technology for our Republic. We could begin from scratch and use solar energy to power a clean environment. I could reconstruct molecules and make buildings withstand a hurricane."

"You shall have all that and more. But we should allow the guardians to carefully monitor any activities that reconstruct reality. That's only fitting."

"Yes, only fitting," Dr. Ozbolt agreed.

An older man named Professor Dodsun stood up with bleached white hair. "I have a Doctorate in Political Science and spent some time in the United States Department of Housing and Urban Development. I taught Plato at the University of Denver for a time. I could be helpful as a guardian . . . in the bureaucracy, at least."

"Splendid, Dodsun, splendid. However, we should have you tested first. Guardians must painstakingly prove their intellectual metal to rule. And right away, no guardian will own any paper money or property. We'll not have kings in our Republic, but philosopher-kings."

General Hythloday beamed with satisfaction, but his brother sat in the corner with a smirk. "You have something to say, Brother?" he asked.

"You're delusional if you think this is going to work," Sextus scoffed, black hair shimmering under the lights. "Without money, what incentive will the guardians have to work? They'll be like simple thieves, stealing from the helots to feed themselves."

"Not so," Hythloday shouted frustrated. "Their incentive rises above earthly desire. Their incentive is truth for the sake of truth and governing an effective state. I can see already you'll be a helot. A guardian would never ask what incentive he had to work."

Sextus snorted unfazed. "And who will guard the guardians?" he asked. "They will have absolute power in your city, no one will check them. We came from a state of practical checks and balances, yet you discard them for dictators."

Hythloday laughed. "A guard for the guardian ruled by reason is absurd. Checks and balances were not the problem in the Eagle Republic. The appetitive people were, and now over ten billion are dead. We'll not make the same mistake again. No, one job, one function."

Sextus threw up his hands and uncorked a wine bottle. "I drink to you, Brother, you and your cursed city. Here, let me consecrate the ground on this holy day. To you, who will finally bring harmony to the world."

General Hythloday ignored him and continued to amass followers. "It's a principle of reason that our soldiers should continuously listen to music and sing patriotic songs. This is because it suits their emotional character and will light their souls for battle. Rhythm and song permeate the soul better than any other medium, provides a small glimpse of the Forms through the tune's harmony. Music sheds the ego. Of course, we'll do everything to erase the auxiliaries' individualities and make them completely subservient to the guardians. A soldier should be like a hammer wielded by a higher, more reasonable mind."

"What truth," said the awestruck crowd, "and never have we heard anything more godlike."

Their cheering woke Sextus and drove him to mutiny. "I'll have no more of you, Brother, or this madness about mindless soldiers. What do you think destroyed us before?" he shouted racing up the ladder to the surface.

General Hythloday screamed to stop, shouted, pleaded, hated Sextus for trying to flee.

The door opened and everyone gasped. Sunlight slew the darkness and fresh air flooded penitent lungs. The world bloomed green and beautiful. Fallen buildings littered the landscape. The brothers embraced. Why had they fought? They were outside again. Outside! The shelters were over. The darkness was over. The brothers bounded like yearling gazelles in summer, apologized, squinted upwards.

"Now we can set to our work," General Hythloday rejoiced, hugging him.

Sextus relented when he saw his brother's happiness. Even if he left, as he promised, where could he really go? The world was empty, and he didn't want to be alone. Further, he held many doubts his brother would succeed. Perhaps Sextus stayed to see him fail.

General Hythloday jumped onto a nearby rock to address the crowd: "See, a brave new world is upon us, a better lot than Huxley's vision, too. The lathe of Saint Plato is hot with yearning and sets ours tasks for labor. Let us carve the earth to be fit for the Good."

Except for Sextus, all fists punched the sky. The community made a pilgrimage south, walking down Highway 287, avoiding the radioactive rain in the Fallout Corridor. They marched from the mountains to the bogy swamps of the Gulf Coast, to Houston's port, now a heap of ruins. There they scavenged parts and excavated the sea. Hythloday said, "What a fitting test we have before us: Only swamp and sea, yet watch how we'll cause a firmament to rise from the deep. We speak the same language and share the same values. With a little ingenuity nothing will be impossible for us."

Hythloday held hands over the water. "We command the Republic to rise."

The survivors set to work. They built a factory camp in the ruined outskirts of Houston. Most of the city had been obliterated by nukes, but scavengable machines still lay here and there to put to use. Yellow bulldozers, rotary cranes, pile drivers, joro-drills, and front loaders awakened like sleeping giants. Reclamation scrapers, hydraulic claws, rippers, and sand hoses tore apart the coastline as a quarry to build the promised Republic.

Like Atlas waving his arms and standing in the sea, the Republic slowly congealed. It rose as a spiraling skeleton, slowly collecting rock and glass skin. One of the largest construction projects ever undertaken, it couldn't help but draw other survivors of the war to participate.

The Republic was not one island but three. In the center was a perfectly circular island—Heliopolis—surrounded by two concentric island rings—Stratos and Agora. As one moved to the innermost sanctuary, each island ascended higher than the last.

Heliopolis was the most convincing city on a hill (if there ever was one). The central island rose from the sea like a volcanic mountain, with pine, oak, cypress, maple and other trees and ferns planted above its skyscrapers like the Hanging Gardens of Babylon. Two large bridges in the shape of a cross intersected on a North-South and East-West axis and were called the Bridge of Wisdom and the Bridge of Understanding. The Bridge of Understanding connected Heliopolis to the coast and the factory camp which, by now, worked as a thriving settlement. Architects rationally planned streets on a grid system. Measures were also taken to fight the hurricanes. Before the invention of the aquamolpis, which controlled the weather, a thin harbor on the east side of Heliopolis acted as a shield against storms. The harbor—Safer Bay—rippled from Heliopolis as if hit by a rock.

The second island ring was a sloping plain and home to the auxiliaries. It lay largely free of buildings, so that the soldiers of the Republic might perform their drills unmolested by luxury. The defenders of the city lived in tents and stiff wooden barracks, suffering the elements and hardening their silver bodies for the good of the Republic. Speakers were placed around Stratos to serenade the soldiers with music and develop their souls. It would be a hard life, but one best suited for their emotional, spirited natures.

The third ring and the coast became the home of the helots to produce wine, clothes, and shoes; to knead bread and build furniture; to farm wheat and corn and barley; to cobble and weld and craft the delicacies of any proud civilization. Housing and apartments were mass produced for each helot family according to their needs. Behind each home sat a communal garden for socializing. Giant stone aqueducts carried water from the coast to Heliopolis, and auxiliaries ensured Heliopolis never thirsted.

One day, many months later, while Heliopolis was still being built, General Hythloday and his brother Sextus sat barefoot on the beach at sunset.

"Look how beautiful Heliopolis is even in twilight, Brother," Hythloday said. "See how there is nothing beyond our reach. Guardians guard, auxiliaries defend the walls, helots are happy producing. What a wonderful thing we've done tending our garden. How pleasing and good."

"I see a city like other cities," Sextus frowned. "Nothing lasts forever, and I suspect the Republic will be the same. You and Dr. Ozbolt can rearrange atoms all you want. You can build an elevator to the moon with your new nano-metals or construct airships and supercomputers to perfect our knowledge, but you will never change what man is. Perfection is not enough for us. It is not that man is ignorant of what's best for him. It's that he sometimes yearns for his own suffering, his own miserable existence, not your perfect walls. His passion to build a city is just as great as his passion to destroy it. That is why we'll never succeed. I wake up today and admire what we've done. But tomorrow, I should like to smash our Heliopolis to smithereens."

General Hythloday looked at his brother in unbelief. He stood up and walked away along the beach. Staring back several times, he kicked the dirt in frustration. Seagulls circled the city like a summer gale, just as he imagined. Nevertheless, as Heliopolis shrank in the darkness like a dying flame, his anger for his brother burned hotter.

BOOK II

GIFT OF FIRE

II § 1 HALL OF RECORDS

What are you thinking about? the familiar voice asked Glaucon.

"Guardians killed my mother."

Yes, they did.

"I did not stop them."

What could you have done?

"I did not want to stop them."

Now there *is a confession.*

"Is that really true?"

I don't know. You said the words.

"They aren't my words."

Then whose are they?

"You placed them there."

What do you think I am, a monster?

Glaucon regained focus in the dim library basement light. Sixteen years passed since his mother disappeared and he was dragged to Heliopolis. The voice wouldn't let him forget. He was twenty-four, a year for love and creativity (or so the numerologists said). Glaucon sat alone under a layer of concrete and mythranium, the only sound an air conditioner humming on the ceiling. Like all libraries, the furniture smelled musty. A stiff science journal called *SPLENDOR* lay face down on a table. It contained some business about a chemical compound, *lotuzone*, a new experimental antidepressant. Prodicus told him to disperse the calmative in the Tenth Ward water supply that afternoon.

Hopefully, Glaucon thought, *it'll remedy the recent spike in helot seizures caused by the last drug.* Nearly one hundred died in Metatron Tech's last fiasco.

The long article bored him. Too many technical terms, not enough life. Instead of reading the article, Glaucon pored over the real object which brought him to the library—a very old book of poetry from the Age of Aporia. Glaucon knew it was old because he could smell the mold: white, irremovable fungus rooted to the tattered blue cover.

"An absurd book this *Prometheus Unbound,*" Glaucon reflected, "a play not meant to be performed as a play." He often read it during study gym when he should've been filling in assumptions in his enthymeme syllogism homework. One of the problems still stuck in his mind:

Exercise 4
(Premise 1) . . . .
(Premise 2) Heraclitus rubbed dung on his body and lay in the grass.
(Conclusion) Heraclitus was eaten by stray dogs.

Missing premise?

Glaucon had written next to *Premise 1*: All dung draws hungry dogs.

Prometheus Unbound made better reading. Percy Shelley, the author, was his favorite poet. Hardly anyone could be more forbidden. Shelley's play traced the plight of Prometheus, the crafty Titan foolish enough to challenge the orders of Zeus. Prometheus created man, pillaged heaven to bring fire and civilization to him. Zeus became enraged. He sought revenge against the Titan by chaining him to the edge of a jagged cliff in the Caucuses. Exposed on the mountainside for three millennia, every afternoon Zeus sent his eagle to feast on Prometheus' liver (a personal touch Glaucon could not help but appreciate). In the original myth Zeus and Prometheus reunited. But in Shelley's tale, Zeus was an immoral usurper. Prometheus withheld a prophecy concerning a future lover of Zeus and the God-King fell.

This story was extremely heretical in the Republic. As Glaucon learned long ago, guardians modified any writings that discussed disharmony or ugliness among the gods. They did so because such stories taught the wrong moral lessons. Lusting, fighting, petty gods were unreasonable and should certainly not be worshipped. A simple and undivided god would not change itself or deceive others through images, words, and dreams.

As far as helots knew, Zeus lived the most chaste and virtuous lifestyle in the cosmos. Entirely devoted to Hera, he sang hymns to her every morning in bed. He never capriciously flung Hephaestus on a ten day plunge to Earth or chased after Io's girdle. Various children from his prolific affairs like Hercules, Apollo, and Artemis were attributed to miraculous virgin conceptions. The adulterous story of Ares and Aphrodite chained together during sex by smoky Hephaestus?—they erased that, too. "May I be as faithful as Zeus and as devoted as Aphrodite," remained a favorite pledge at marriage ceremonies among the helots.

The guardians thought the *Iliad* especially dangerous. Saint Plato spoke out explicitly against the book because it put the gods' petty rivalries on display during the Trojan War. So the guardian-book-enhancers placed all the gods on the side of the Greeks and were done with the matter. They treated demi-gods like Achilles similarly, giving him love for music and distaste for silver to serve an exemplary lesson to the auxiliaries.

Overall, guardians taught Panglossian logic: This world was the best of all possible worlds with the best of all possible gods. To support their thesis they pointed to the Republic. The Form of the Good emanated perfection, without jealousy, without anger, and it wanted others to be perfect. Changing the ugly stories helped man see the goodness in the Pure Land. Shelley's rebuke against such interpretations made his poetry all the more exciting:

" 'O, Thou who fillest with thy soul of woe, to whom all things of Earth and Heaven do bow in fear and worship: all prevailing foe! I curse thee! Let a sufferers curse clasp thee, his torturer like remorse; Till thine infinity shall be a robe of envenomed agony; And thine omnipotence a crown of pain, to cling like burning gold round thy dissolving brain.' "

Glaucon found it dreadfully titillating to curse the divine for sending such pain and misery into the world, for killing his mother. He relished spitting on the Demiurge with every breath. Laughing alone, proudly alone, he took solace in his concrete library below the earth, between its mythranium walls; and how his tomb burned with heresy. God was not just, but unjust and cruel. Sometimes Glaucon dreamt himself a champion of heaven's slaves—just like Prometheus—and imagined that lonely, bleak ravine. Then, all at once, his soul's rebellion died. Glaucon cursed his daydreams. "Do not be a fool," he flagellated himself remembering Prodicus' words in the pillared halls of the Academy. "Our world is naught but a spatial reflection of the Forms. All reflections deviate to some degree from the original. Blame not the Good for a natural consequence of reflection. Rather strive in learning to return to perfection."

Glaucon slammed the awful book on the table and promised never to read it again. "You're hideous!" he told the book. "You are punishment sent to roast me with fire." He made oaths and swore to repent, crossed himself with the sign of the right triangle. "Not my happiness," he clucked, "but the Form of Happiness." The thin philosopher silently resolved to return to studying the Forms. Gathering his books together in a cloth satchel, he retreated into the Hall of Records.

Rows of mainframes twinkled like columns of heavenly fire in the basement archives. If one watched long enough, dazzling geometrical patterns—pentagons, triangles, stars—appeared over the shadowspar memory-stones. Ironically, hardly any actual books remained in the library anymore. Everything written was digitized and downloadable from the shadowspar to student papyritrons. Essentially electronic book recorders (paid for by helot taxes), the papyritrons' translucent green screens could be opened and shut to sample millions of ancient texts—from *Euthyphro* to *Middlesex*—recovered from the fallen cities of the United States.

The major quandary, though, was that hardly any unmodified versions survived. Centuries of purification ceremonies burned away most of the remaining books to make the holy modifications of the guardians permanent. One needed the hard copy to know what really happened. Glaucon, therefore, endeavored to find as many hard copies as he could. This usually entailed finding his way into the graces of one archon or another, who kept the books as sentimental trophies from the Age of Aporia.

Students looked up at Glaucon irritated as he passed them at their chrome study carrels. Papyritrons turned their faces pale green. Realizing his sandals were hitting the floor, he sped hastily to the main lobby stairs.

He saw two acquaintances on his way, Critius and Diotima, both avid students of logic and Plato's *Theaetetus*. Glaucon brushed his hand through his disheveled gold hair and stared at the ground. Pretending to be deep in thought, he hoped to stir a comment from the students, but to no avail. His scholarly act went unnoticed, and Glaucon silently despised them for it. *Would have preferred the irritation of the students downstairs*, he fumed.

In the lobby, a holographic banner of the Republic motto rotated seven meters in the air:

HOPE, HARMONY, PERFECTION.

Medijuice brewed hot in the library café. Glaucon could smell its spicy scent: a bubbling orange psycho-stimulant composed of modified amphetamine salt and cognitive nanogolems. *But,* he conceded, *who really knew what Ozbolt Enterprises put in the stuff.*

Students reclined talking on floating cushions, their voices echoing loudly around the domed roof.

"Forms!" Glaucon feigned frustration. "Students only come to the library to talk." He overheard a table of girls who looked like tenth grade neophytes chatting away.

"Have you been outside recently?" one girl asked wearing a conical piebald-feathered headdress.

"Oh yes, it's dreadfully hot, even at these altitudes," said another fanning herself.

"Unbearably hot. Not a cloud for weeks. But anyway, I've been meaning to tell you. I tried this new café called the Hebe Lounge—they have the most amazing medijuice. It's flavored like raspberry honey and tickles your throat going down. I don't drink the medijuice *here* anymore. Becoming kind of a snob, actually." She laughed. "I even snuck a cigpop."

"You didn't!"

"I did," she laughed again. "Lysis gave it to me. You know I've been trying to take *erosic* with him."

"I need to take one again," her friend admitted with a touch of fear in her voice. "Been almost a week since my last slimetide. I'm losing concentration in class, starting to ache. Professor Diodorus said I should find a partner in a hurry or go insane. Maybe I'll ask *him*."

The two girls giggled and the conversation deteriorated. Talk disgusting for philosophers.

"Ouch!" Glaucon jumped startled as a robotic golem knocked his foot. Focusing its noisy camera eye on his red toes, the machine passed on vacuuming the floor. The moon-faced golems crawled over the library windows searching for any sign of dirt. Wet sponges burst from their heads whenever they found any, streaked across the glass.

Another golem cleaned a row of cogniscrambler pods by the entrance. Ten meters high, sprouting wires to the ceiling, after stepping in and locking the door, red light flooded the chamber. Ineffable metaphysical visions revealed secrets of the psyche (often horrifying). The Fates made predictions and psychologically conditioned loyal citizenship.

Prodicus instituted mandatory I.T. readings in the cogniscrambler for all three races right before Glaucon's arrival on Heliopolis. He called it a "campaign to better sift the metals and lead the city to henosis." But the Fates' visions scared him immensely, left constant nightmares.

Glaucon walked over to the café counter and picked up a cup of medijuice. A helot barista requested to see his *tetractys*. As he extended the back of his right hand, she scanned ten crystal orbs embedded like snails in a triangular pattern. The electric scanner made them shine like a vivid rainbow and beeped. Sipping the medijuice—slowly so as not to burn the roof of his mouth—Glaucon's concentration rapidly improved.

A bright flash erupted from one of the wall-televisions—Morpheus Alepou and his Skybridge News program, the Gorgon Hour. Morpheus was discussing the forever war on the Other Side: the wilderness beyond the Republic's walls and the unfinished corner of creation.

"In one of the deadliest attacks in recent months," Morpheus reported, "sporadic mortar fire fell on the Tenth Ward for nearly forty-five consecutive minutes today. The assault ripped through an outdoor marketplace, killing four and wounding eleven. The Sigma Division Auxiliaries have been mobilized to counter the emerging threat."

Prodicus' little stooge, Zeno, suddenly appeared on the screen at a press conference. Much older than when Glaucon first met him at the cave. Nearly fifty-five and a minor archon, his monkish ring of hair had finally lost to baldness and retreated to his chin. Zeno maintained his composure, speaking slowly: "We offer our heartfelt condolences to the helot families suffering under the attacks. It seems the anarchists, yet again, have placed a failing bet in their efforts to incite discord among the helots. We condemn—with the strongest language possible—any activities that use political violence as a way to affect change." Several hands from the audience shot up to molest him with questions, but Zeno waved them away. "We can't say any more on this event until we've identified the militia column responsible. But please, let me assure you, all efforts are being made to look into the matter."

"How long will these attacks continue?" one of the robed reporters shouted.

"What is Prodicus' plan to secure the Tenth Ward?"

"Is it true the Iron Queen is personally leading the assault?" The very name of the swamp guardian-slayer caused panic.

Zeno brushed them off.

The screen flashed back to Morpheus Alepou pounding his desk on the Gorgon Hour. His long face plastered with makeup made him look a clown. "Some people say the guardians were too soft on the anarchists last war season. Are they right?"

Freddy Akimbo and Peitha von Notus, sidekick anchors, wore flowing red robes beside him, attempting to project the highest media dignity. Freddy argued sticking out his ruddy, block-shaped chin: "We should firebomb the swamps again to bring them to the table."

"Some people say we shouldn't even bother with the table," Peitha huffed.

Morpheus put his hand on Peitha's shoulder, congruent with her sentiments. "No one understands the danger of the Other Side," he lamented. "When I hear helots, auxiliaries, and guardians saying we should talk to them, I can't understand the logic. I say that's irresponsible. We shouldn't be talking to them. We should be finding and killing them. That's all anarchists understand. Prodicus isn't being harsh enough."

"I can agree with *that!*" Peitha said.

Morpheus nodded. "When we return, we'll talk to General Argus about his strategy for securing the city walls. Stay tuned to the Gorrrrrrr-geous Gorgon Hour."

Skybridge News flashed to a series of commercials about upcoming self-help seminars and a new drug, *hexihex*, sure to remedy any negative opinions toward your neighbors.

Glaucon rolled his eyes, stood up. He threw his empty medijuice cup in a matter incinerator on the way out of the library.

The Tenth Ward is never safe, Glaucon groaned angrily. It stood on the mainland farthest from Heliopolis. Constantly under attack by internal and external enemies, the Tenth Ward was a hotbed of sensualist roaders and counterfeits. Just last week, the lawspeakers sentenced a gang of street urchins to have two liters of molten gold poured down their throats for impersonating guardians. Nothing but the crime of guardian-treason could be worse. Missiles fired from the Other Side also harassed the place. Word had it Prodicus planned another military campaign just to contain the rocket-launching issue. Hopefully, any decision would be made after the Festival of Demeter at the end of the summer. Glaucon, *presbyteros*, tenth grade guardian initiate, stood ready to graduate out of the military and finally begin training in dialectical philosophy as a first grade guardian templar. The last thing he wanted was dangerous watch duty on the walls.

"I hate the Tenth Ward," Glaucon mumbled. His *tetractys* crystals misted cloudy grey in tandem with his mood.

Why? You were born there, the old voice returned.

"I died there with my mother."

You still look alive to me.

"No, I didn't mean it like that. The Tenth Ward is my shame. The perfectly manicured lawns, the measured streets, the eyes. What misery in that kingdom, what sadness. I start choking up whenever I go there."

You'll survive. You always do.

"No, I'm finished with the Tenth Ward. Hear that? After this errand for Prodicus I'm done. I'm never going back."

Yes you will; because you love power more than your dead family.

"No, I'm serious, why don't you believe me?"

Because you don't believe yourself.

Everyone knew the world outside the Republic was a shipwreck. No other cities recovered from the Day of Hylopleonexia. Armed savages and militias scoured the ruins, fighting each other and looking for exposed weaknesses in the guardian lines. They called themselves things like the Southwest Confederacy, the Fifth Estate, and the Virginia Collective, but they were nothing more than petty barbarians. Tales even trickled in of a Dionysian cult which sacrificed unsuspecting travelers in the hills.

The Watchers were the worst and led by Xenon Adonis: a fallen guardian secretly rumored to be descended from the famed bloodline of Abaris Hythloday. Just before Glaucon's arrival, Xenon attempted to overthrow Guardian-King Prodicus and fled with his conspirators when he lost. Joining with the Southwest Confederacy, the traitorous banditti somehow united the continental hordes under an ideology of madness—nothing less than a crusade to end the Republic. The Watcher revolutionaries continuously perpetrated terrorist acts against innocent civilians: kidnapping children, scalping Republican ambassadors, firing rockets, and maintaining a clandestine program to develop nuclear warheads. Twelve years before, in one of the most heinous acts of modern history, Xenon even released a toxic gas called iama-B in Ozbolt's First Ward, a deadly nerve agent that turned bodies into metal and twisted the faces of the dead.

Glaucon fought against the Watchers, the Democratic United Front, the Anarcho-Syndicalists—whatever they were called—several times. Once, when he was fourteen, he rode scout-bikes in a routine survey south along the coast and spotted a gang of anarchists from the Southwest Confederacy. They were scavenging spare parts from an abandoned car dealership below the 30th parallel. One couldn't find a more duplicitous breach of the Twenty-Third Red River Ceasefire Agreement. Chasing them through sea-flooded cities centuries dead, they surrounded the anarchist rebels in an abandoned park.

Firing madly, Glaucon jumped off his scout-bike's seat clutching a Neokalashnikov to his chest. He aimed at the rebels hiding under the multicolored swings and dashed headlong behind a brick fence, his blood steaming like a geyser. Plasma beams burst hot through the wall. Pieces of radiated brick fell all around. His rifle was overheating. He could barely move, even forgot his energy shield calibration number. Without sufficient protection, Glaucon threw his arm over the wall and fired blindly. (A cowardly act for sure—especially for someone of his caliber!—but he hardly cared.)

Death cries from the cornered rebels promised an end to the Republic. "Who guards the guardians?" one shouted. "Long live anarchy!" whooped another. Glaucon didn't know what any of them meant.

Scorpion-grenades shocked the earth to glass. With a melodic barrage from their sonic cannons, Aegis tanks shattered the park from a kilometer away. The air grew deadly quiet.

Glaucon made eye contact with a nearby soldier named Polymachus. He was a black, heavy built soldier, breathing heavily. There was a round crystal shield on his right hand—the symbol of a life-auxiliary. Polymachus walked toward a pink colored slide and signaled to Glaucon: "Everything clear."

Glaucon nearly tripped when he stumbled out behind the wall. Horror, death, and desolation lay on the grass. Delicate bodies hung limply on the swings, cut to pieces, with several large craters in the ground. The iron fence surrounding the park collapsed like a concave lens.

Later, Polemarch Leonida commanded Glaucon to dig a shallow grave to burn what was left of the bodies. He spent all night with Polymachus digging next to the broken fence. The soldier offered him a cigpop for a little high but he refused. Not a single auxiliary died in the fighting. The park ruins seemed like a tyrant's victory, and Glaucon never forgot.

The Republic possessed technology to engineer golems to fight the barbarians on their behalf but refused to allow such sacrilege. The pragmatist in Glaucon found this policy foolish. He once approached his wise teacher, Crito, about the practice at the Academy.

Leaning over a mahogany desk in his office, Crito explained the guardians' reasonable reasoning behind a bulbous nose: "Why, Glaucon, what would the soldiers do if replaced by machines? Where would the spirited souls exhaust their fire? They couldn't become guardians, for they don't love the sight of truth as we do. And oh-h-h, they couldn't become helots either. Their spirit rises above desire. Too strong and brave and adventurous for circuses and hedon whistles. What we want is harmony in our Republic—different souls fulfilling their roles. Symphonies collapse when missing instruments. Saint Plato expressly warned us: If spirited souls end up with desirous or reasonable souls, the Republic will be destroyed. We must never let that happen. Our Republic must last forever."

This reasoning carried the Form of Truth so long as Glaucon wasn't doing the fighting. When he *was* fighting, though, he could've strangled Crito and his harmony. Guardians trained with the auxiliaries until they turned twenty-five and joined the guardian templar. The purpose of the guardian draft—as far as Glaucon surmised—was to harden commitment to the Republic. But it affected him in the opposite manner, entangled him in terror. Often, as he relaxed in the Academy pleasure gardens with Prodicus, the philosopher-king reassured his doubts: "The guardians are to be tested in every way imaginable to reveal the gold within;" but Glaucon found no gold within and would've switched places with a golem in a nanosecond. The auxiliaries may've been happy with their endless music, but not him. Not him. Glaucon died every morning on the grassy plains of Stratos. He could barely wake and lay quivering on his cot like a child.

II § 2 The Seven Plateaus of Heliopolis

Brushing away the grisly memory of the park, Glaucon walked out the automatic library doors. Two crystal sphinxes greeted him. General Hythloday imagined his Republic becoming Shangri-La. Heliopolis, in reality, was fairer than any Earth-breathed Kun Lun paradise.

Seven major plateaus jutted from the mountain slope like leaves on a stalk. The Temple of Reason—a hollow diamond dodecahedron fired by the magic of the nanofactories—sat at the summit, surrounded by snowy white Dorian columns. The columns enforced a two kilometer glass minaret streaking into the clouds. "A mighty sail for a mighty state," the guardian-songsters sang of its beauty. A moat circled the pavilion, and sparkling water spilled down in three directions: to the second, third, and fourth plateau. Amber streams sparkled across the island, commingling serenely around important government buildings, sinking farther, until finally pouring over the cliffs into the glowing ocean.

Twenty-two rivers wandered around the city, and each had a life of its own. Streams branched into smaller tributaries, spiraled into secret grottos and oases. Some of the rivers gushed out unexpectedly from the mountainside, and young guardian neophytes played under their misty halos.

The domed Hall of Records was on the third plateau. Jointly watered by the Temple of Reason and the Academy above, the library looked out across the city of palms and skyscrapers to the Amphitheater in the center, and below that, the turning research city of Schizoeon on the sixth plateau—the Kingdom of Kabiri. Unlike the uplands, though, Schizoeon circled the entire peak on a series of superconductor magnets. Never at rest, it made one revolution daily.

To Glaucon Heliopolis was a techno-Himalayan city of dreams, the heart of everything good in the world. Schizoeon, though, felt like a jungle of metal and grey air. Yet he noticed the two cities fed on one another symbiotically. Guardians went to work in Schizoeon's test-tube towers and concrete everglades. Huddled together, they fired nanomachines; bridled the alchemy of the atom; programmed matter to perfection. Enthroning dodecahedron diamonds was the least of their powers—Schizoeon birthed Heliopolis. From idle foam to celestial palace, the philosophic stalk of mind grew ever higher into the clouds.

Glaucon couldn't tell which city was the proper crown to admire.

From the corner of his eye, Glaucon noticed someone descending the Academy's stone steps. It was none other than his classmate, Simmias. Students called him "Rex" because he wore hyacinth purple tunics. Glaucon suspected he wanted to look like a Roman senator but never said as much. Long-winded, black hair slicked with oil, Simmias Rex always put on airs, taking contrary opinions for their own sake rather than discovering truth. He possessed an ego to rival the ancient philosopher Empedocles, and would jump into a smoking volcano to prove he was a god. What made him so contemptible?—his success! Nothing seemed beyond his reach. Already an acclaimed historical author, Rex recently published his thesis, *The Rise and Fall of Simulacra,* which caused quite a stir. Even the Office of Public Harmony noticed. A coterie of young boys kept pace behind like he dropped Forms at his feet.

There would be no avoiding him now.

"Why, Glaucon, what a pleasure to see you again," Rex said, taking his arm in a friendly manner. "I was just looking for you. What're you doing here?"

"Reading a magazine article about this new drug, *lotuzone*," Glaucon half-lied. He knew Rex wasn't really looking for him. (Too self-absorbed for that.)

"Reading? Well, yes, it's a library, isn't it?" Rex laughed inwardly. "An intellectual like you shouldn't just read the magazines, though. Perhaps you'd like to join us upstairs in the meditation cloister to hear this new song I heard with the stereoplugs yesterday. It's by the Man-Faced Ox-Progeny, called "Don't Miss Archytas." A spirited melody with a most unusual rhyme. We still have several hours before class. I could make it worth your while. We haven't talked in so long. Zoe taking all your time?"

"No thanks," Glaucon said trying to leave.

Just like Glaucon, Rex was a favorite of Prodicus. He'd also begun seeing him more lately, too, which was infuriating and dangerous. Good mannered and well bred, Rex could discuss a wide number of topics, from material dialectics to functionalism. His talking never ceased. He was dangerously close to being labeled an extrovert by the Jungian Psychological Board of

Examiners and kicked out of the Academy. Extroverts were categorically banned from holding guardian positions. They were too friendly to man and lacked proper self-control. Xenon Adonis had been an extrovert.

"Really, Glaucon, you become more of a shade every time I see you," said Rex. "Perhaps you should drink some of that *lotuzone* we give to the helots and lighten up."

"I don't think it's good for them," Glaucon said, suddenly interested.

"What?"

"The *lotuzone*, it's not good for them. I was reading about it downstairs. Some at the Asclepius Medical Institute think it could cause hallucinations."

"Hallucinations? What kind of hallucinations?"

"Are there different kinds?"

"Oh yes. Well, some are better than others." Rex always said everything in an annoying matter-of-fact way. "When I trained with Mu Division three klicks outside the city, some soldiers snuck back to the Agora and bought some yabyummies. Let me tell you, Glaucon, best sex I ever had. No one was even there and glowworms were at my feet. I held my breath and slid down a long spiraling tongue, fell into a forest of open legs and hands. *Something* had its way with me. Over and over, I turned for hours. So much better than the *erosic* pill. We guardians don't know what we're missing."

His gang of boys laughed like a pack of hyenas.

"Good lord, Rex," Glaucon winced alarmed. "Why are you telling me this? If I don't report you now we'll both get into trouble."

Rex snapped back, "Glaucon, don't be such a prig. Who follows the rules here? We live beyond rules. With Prodicus in command, do you think anything will happen to either of us? What would he say if he lost two of his most *amicable* students?" Rex pursed his lips and fell into a fit of laughter. All of a sudden, he leapt into Glaucon's satchel and snatched *Prometheus Unbound*.

"Besides, tell anyone, and I'll show them this book, and it will be straight to the Bull with you. Let me see. What do we have here? OH YES," he moaned erotically, " 'AND WHO MADE TERROR, MADNESS, CRIME, REMORSE, WHICH FROM THE LINKS OF THE GREAT CHAIN OF THINGS, TO EVERY THOUGHT WITHIN THE MIND OF MAN SWAY AND DRAG SO HEAVILY!' "

"Stop it, Rex. You've made your point. Give it back," Glaucon demanded.

"No wait; I'm not finished having my way with Shelley," Rex held up his index finger. " 'And self contempt bitterer to drink than blood.' Glaucon, I see you project that corrosive self-contempt on me every time we meet. At least I'm honest and don't hide behind empty threats." With that, Rex stuffed the book in Glaucon's stomach. "I piss on Saint Plato and the Forms," Rex sneered. "Haven't you said that to yourself so many times? You'll never kneel or bow to any of them, yet you've bowed to chaos. How material! How helot! Perhaps you think the Good a myth? So do I! In grief for your lost faith you lash out like a man attacking the ocean. Your sword is drawn; you hack at the waves. But in the end, it's only the ocean and your arms are so tired."

Glaucon tried to speak, but Rex stopped him. "Look around us," he said swinging his arms. "Everyone should be happy, but they're not. Even with the Republic they're not. They all wear masks, and they all look alike, and they're all liars. Don't trust anything. Science is packaged and man with it. I'll become a philosopher-king all the same; because I know what this place is and can manage it. *You*, though, I can't be sure. If you don't relax, mooncalf, you'll die insane."

Glaucon apologized, but Rex marched away head in the air, self-esteem obviously bruised (probably plotting how to kill him). Diagonal electronic doors slammed shut behind his tail of neophyte toadies. Glaucon stared through the glass, his vision drenched in purple fog. He could barely think—even with the medijuice!

He quickly descended narrow steps to the fourth plateau, which extended palm-like into the sky. Suncatcher trees dotted the landscape, powering skyscrapers with photovoltaic petals. Several propaganda signs also caught his attention:

WHAT IS JUSTICE? TO KEEP ONE'S PLACE!
WHAT IS WISDOM? ARRESTING SOCIAL CHANGE!
WHAT IS BEAUTIFUL? HARMONY FOR THE STATE!

Academy students sunbathed in the blissful grass of Hesper Park. Robes rolled up, they read books like *Enneads* and *Elements of Emanation* on their papyritrons. Others listened to music. Some wore symsyst mindmitters—goggles keyed to their unique neuronal signature—which allowed instant communication across the city and interaction with the Fates' augmented reality. A robed older guardian with yellowed, curly-long nails dictated a treatise with his symsyst without lifting a finger, thoughts and writing combined as one.

The absolute triumph of laziness, Glaucon thought. *As if using a pen was so terribly demanding in the first place.*

Zoe, his most trusted companion from school, left him a message on his symsyst. Feeling the goggles vibrating in his hair, he pulled them over his eyes and energized the syntax-a-chat function. Flying neon 3-D letters etched a few centimeters from his face. "Hey there, Glaucon," her voice rang with the words, "sorry we missed each other again. A few people and I are going to the Ought-Is Symposium tonight. Thought you might want to join me. Archon Hypatia thinks she discovered the solution to finding moral properties in nature. I'll believe it when I see it. Probably will be just another gabfest, but you never know. By the way, be careful on your 'super secret' assignment from Prodicus. (You know, the one you weren't supposed to tell anyone about.) The Iron Queen is dangerous and planning something. I doubt she'll make a dent in our impregnable walls, but don't underestimate her. She's a tank-killer more cunning than Xenon. Her dreaded Eastern Column strikes from the Fallout Corridor and disappears. Yesterday, I overheard one of the professors say she was an abomination, one of those soulless human golems. I'm starting to miss the days when Xenon was all we worried about. Don't worry, I won't tell Prodicus you told me about your assignment."

Glaucon briefly replied, trashed a discussion thread cramping his peripheral vision, and walked into the park. Guardians waded in the crystal pools watered by the Temple of Reason; golems attended every need. In the middle of the park was the Amphitheater: a hollow half-pyramid of modern design. Morality plays such as the classic *Marless Mother Medea* performed here twice a week. *Medea* was one of Glaucon's favorite suspense-thrillers; one cliffhanger after another led to graceful reunion between Medea, Jason, and her children. He'd often attend with Zoe, watching from the Amphitheater's hill cluttered with statues, the most famous of which was a towering fifteen meter Fates' spindle.

A helot family sat next to the hilltop spindle. Immediately recognizable. They wore comical shirts and pants.

Helots were usually kept as far as possible from guardians, for good reason too—mixing sowed corruption. One parent must've been a village phylark, a leader of a neighborhood watch committee. The family was being rewarded for reporting some crooked soul to ISHIM (Intelligence Service for Homeland Insecurity Movements), the Republic's secret police and intelligence agency rolled into one.

Two of the children lifted up from their picnic blanket and began rolling down the hill toward some pine trees. The husband took countless pictures under a flat-topped straw hat. He turned his camera toward Glaucon as he ascended the hill to meet them. It made Glaucon feel like one of the naked statues, like a howler monkey at the zoo. The man gasped in disbelief over how close the guardian approached.

"Visiting from the Agora, are you?" Glaucon asked.

The bondcouple immediately leapt to the ground, prostrating themselves at his feet.

"Yes, my lord," the man said face-down in submission. "How did you know?"

"Your helot garments," Glaucon answered. "To be honest, it's a dead give away. They look more comfortable than these robes, though. I can't seem to keep my hem out of the dirt. My robe's always getting frayed." Glaucon laughed and extended his wooden signet ring to the woman. She pressed it penitently to her lips. When Glaucon hooked her chin with his forefinger to examine her for a glimpse of the Form of Beauty she raised her eyes to his expectantly. Glaucon said to her, "Please rise and be at ease, bronze lady."

The husband and wife smiled, more relaxed.

"We're on a pilgrimage," said the woman. She was elegantly tall, in her thirties, and wearing a white summer dress. "I'm a phylark from the Fifth Ward. See, here are our papers." She fumbled in her pocket.

"That won't be necessary. I'm not here to check for papers. Just curious how you enjoyed our high Heliopolis?"

"Gleaming radiance," the man said. "Like the face of Saint Plato."

"Better than the stories I read about the Hyperboreans," the woman crooned, obviously flaunting her knowledge of the Platonic scriptures.

Glaucon smiled at her thinking of a test. "Thankfully our lives aren't as long as theirs," he said.

"Yes, a thousand years would be intolerable," the woman returned, eyed him again for another trial. "I'm hoping to be reincarnated as a guardian in the next life so I can live here permanently."

The husband looked angrily at his wife. She clapped a hand to her mouth.

"Are you a guardian templar, sir?" the husband asked gingerly after a few moments.

Glaucon was still thinking about what the woman said. Admitting unhappiness with your station was an impermissible crime. "No, not yet. A tenth grade initiate, but this year I shall surely be crowned in laurels at the Festival of Demeter. Then it's another twenty-five years of learning, tests, and more tests," he laughed.

"Is that all you'll be doing—reading books and taking exams?" asked the man disgusted.

"No, you also apprentice with a department, help manage the polis, and round out your skill set. Hopefully you learn patience, humility, virtue, and persevere. At least that's what Professor Crito tells me. It will keep us dreadfully busy."

"Sounds difficult," the woman gasped. "I'm a baker for Cicero Kellogg down below. I work for Shennong Fooderies in the Fifth Ward. Where will you be working when you graduate?"

Glaucon talked to himself: "This woman's too nosy for her own good."

But look, the voice steered, hissing, *the maid is beautiful.*

"I never noticed."

Thick lips and a swollen tongue. You know what that's good for?

"Eating."

Glaucon, really, you amuse even me sometimes.

"I'm not being funny. Of course, I work for ISHIM."

Yes, anyone hoping to be a king in the Logoset does.

"But why am I ashamed to admit this fact to her?"

Because you lust after her.

"No. That's not it. This woman—she's as much a traitor to her kind as I am. What would it bother her if I asserted my sexual privileges?"

Not a matter of bothering. If she knew you worked for ISHIM she'd want you.

"So?"

And what would you do about that?

"Nothing. I'm not like that. I'm different. It's wrong to use you position to seduce helot women. Guardians must be 'upright as Zeus.' "

How I love it when you pretend virtue. Well, lie then.

Glaucon said, "I'm interning at the Republic Weather Watch Office."

"Really?" exclaimed the woman with utter delight. "Is that the one that manages the aquamolpis and provides all this spectacular weather? It's so-o-o hard to keep the departments straight."

"Yes, that's the one. Never rains here without their consent. See the philosophers' stones over there?" Glaucon pointed eastward to sea. "They emit an energized chemical called asuria iodide. For hundreds of years hurricanes rocked the Gulf. The Republic mastered them all, wind and hail, like everything else. If we want a summer gale, it's ours. Healing rain clouds? Aquamolpis arouse the waters. A deluge of sunlight? We pluck it from the sky."

Husband and wife marveled amazed. They watched the tidal waves pulsing around the stone with the horns of an ox. Bursting energy shined like lines at the bottom of a pool, conquering roaring sea with thunder.

The woman said mystified, "A magic shell from the elements. Not a cloud in the sky."

The man took another picture.

More like the magic of the Fates and Schizoeon, Glaucon thought.

"What are those *things* flying in the sky?" the man asked, zooming in with his camera. "They look like giant, metal dragonflies."

"They're machines. Avis," Glaucon explained.

That man's tedious isn't he. I bet you'd like to get rid of him. You know, like Uriah? Bathsheba is bathing naked for you.

"They're like golems, only they fly in the air," Glaucon said. "They protect our city from above. Don't get too near them if they fly down. They're dangerous and erratic. Sometimes they break free from the Fates' hive mind." Glaucon remembered a time when an avis malfunctioned and tore apart an innocent neophyte. It was inexplicable. He could barely tear his eyes away.

You know the Bible is banned, but you read it anyway.

"So?"

So, you have a fetish for the forbidden. You're more transparent than glass. You want to roll naked with this woman down the hill.

"I want nothing of the sort. You don't know me as well as you think."

I know everything about you.

"Why are there so many avis?" asked the husband.

Glaucon answered, "I don't know. More mass productions recently. I think it's because of the construction on Levantra."

"We were just looking at the work-fleet from the Temple of Reason. Isn't it magnificent? Imagine, a flying island. Our Heliopolis will ascend farther into the sky. What can the guardians not accomplish with the Fates? When will construction be complete?"

"I don't know, another year."

Levantra was a pet project of Prodicus. He'd been building it over a decade, far out to sea. It was a fifteen kilometer sky-chariot to be powered by electromagnetism. Many published guardians still remained skeptical it could rise from the deep.

"Do you think it'll really fly?" asked the man.

For the first time Glaucon noticed the blue armband around the arm of the father's shirt. It had the symbol of the Republic on it—the *Hands-of-God*—the same symbol that strangled his mother, that he had to kiss with pride.

"Honestly, I don't know," Glaucon admitted. "They're using weightless, exotic metals I haven't seen before. I don't understand the alchemy."

The children continued rolling down the hill. This was strange behavior and might draw undue attention from the avis. "How old are your children?" Glaucon asked changing the subject.

"Five and eight," both parents said at the same time. The father put his camera down. "Anaxagoras—our five-year-old—has just learned the pledge actually. Do you want to hear it, lord guardian?"

Like asking if I want to hear hypocrisy, Glaucon thought. He didn't have time to answer before the child was standing before him.

The father gripped his son's bony shoulders. "Tell us the pledge, boy. Just the way you learned at Republicamp. This man here is going to be a guardian templar. Show him what a *respectful* subject you are."

"Isn't he a little young for Republicamp?" Glaucon asked. Those camps were typically for eight-year-old helots.

"Yes, but it's never too early to start training obedience," said the woman. "We want our son well adapted before beginning school. It worked for our other son, anyway. In our family we live by the Shakespeare motto: 'Better three hours too soon than a minute too late.' "

Glaucon pretended to smile as the child struggled to remember.

"I pledge allegiance to the Republic,
And to the Form of Justice for which it stands,
Three peoples,
Helots, axillaries, and guardians
Under the Good—"

The bird-nosed boy stopped confused, finger in his mouth like a fishing hook. The fish swam away. Just like a typical helot he forgot the rest.

"In perfect harmony," his father coached.

The boy still looked mystified.

Glaucon suddenly wanted to make the boy cry, to tell the child he was stupid for not remembering. *They probably spent a week trying to paste our pledge into your little brain, and it took less time for you to lose it*, he sneered. He envisioned grabbing the child by the hair and cramming his face into the dirt. "Cry like a stupid slave," he'd say, cursing him. "Cry because you're nothing but human error and disease, and the joys of the Pure Land will never reach you because your back is crooked and your soul is wood. Burn like an abandoned city and die!"

Now you're starting to learn, said the voice.

"No, that was wrong for me to think. I'm hideous."

It was only natural. You are jealous of the child who sits so close to the mother.

"What's happening to me?"

You're angry, Glaucon; a mold of clay and rage. Every happiness for someone else is a misery for you. You want to tear happiness down.

"No, I don't. Really, I don't."

You wish the avis would tear the family apart like snaky-tailed harpies and that the parents would be the last to die. Why is this? So they see their children eaten before their eyes. Glaucon, what a monster you are! There is much darkness in you.

"That's not true. I want to create but am diseased. I'm in the hills of the lepers. There is no one to heal me."

I can heal you.

"With freedom and hope for all," Glaucon whispered stoically into the boy's ear.

"Oh yes," shouted the boy, "with freedom and hope for all."

Everyone cheered and the boy shook proud like a peacock ruffling its feathers. The mother kissed her son's hair. Glaucon felt awful and bitten by agony. Suddenly, he hated them again. He was furiously whipping the family in his head and whipping himself for thinking such horrible things. He imagined picking up the aquamolpis and crushing them all with the stone.

"I have to go," Glaucon said curtly. He left them sitting on the hill. The mother and father barely noticed. "Good luck over the next month," one called at last. The father kept taking pictures of the Academy's ivory towers.

Glaucon's grey eyes misted. A tempest pushed him out of Hesper Park. He descended farther down the steps of the mountain, counting the stairs one by one, lost in thought. He turned right, walked south through a forest of twisting palms and buildings. He watched the robes and sandals of people walking past, guardians scurrying by on business from the lawspeaker courts. A flood of unconcern, no one stopped to look at him, *even once*. They all gathered in a cloud and went their way.

Do I exist? Glaucon thought clutching to a suncatcher pole. *Am I about to disappear? I'm no good, and it feels like I could crumble, waste away. Outside the sun is shining, but I'm dark inside.*

Not even gazing upon the emerald Logoset made Glaucon feel better. Eleven domes circled around a larger dome like a nest of leviathan eggs: ten glorious domes for the archons ruling the wards; one dome for the Polemarch of Stratos; another for Prodicus, the perfect philosopher-king. Pink swans bathed in pleasure fountains tumbling from Hesper Park. Young minds plied their arguments of state in the Logoset courtyards. They were nothing but ringing bells and pedants, just as Rex said.

The Department of Foresight and Futurology stood directly opposite the Logoset. The Kabiri Computatorium stuck out over the edge of the cliff like a skeletal turtle holding a telescope. Here, under the golden arrowed archways, the guardians and alchemists engaged in the science of predicting probable and preferable futures states with the aid of Kabiri-36, otherwise known as the Fates. A long glass bridge connected the Computatorium to the Logoset. Prodicus spent many nights pacing the bridge, conversing with Dr. Salazar Ozbolt about glitches in the programming and potential apocalypses. Sometimes Glaucon joined them, but he could barely keep pace with their technocratic conversations. They spoke in an esoteric, indecipherable language.

As Glaucon passed underneath the bridge, he saw several women above him through the glass. He tried to look up their skirt-robes with little success, and then cursed such desires. Finally reaching the turning city of Schizoeon, he noticed an old philosopher having trouble stepping onto the moving street. Inching his foot across the threshold, he pulled it back at the last moment, unable to discover the courage. Glaucon thought about helping the old man approach the city in the right way, but stood still as he passed him. When their eyes met, he looked away.

Why should I help some washed up photon collider button-pusher? he thought without a twinge of regret.

Glaucon caught a magnet-bus to the opposite edge of Schizoeon, stepped off the other side and found a bathroom by Aortaphos Rail Station 4. Waiting for the men and women to leave, he finally locked the door and changed from his guardian robes into a helot green collared shirt and starched brown pants. To cover his glowing *tetractys*, he pulled out a bio-glove skincover from his satchel and slipped it over his hand. He'd do what Prodicus wanted, and then he'd never leave Heliopolis again. Running a comb through his sandy curls, Glaucon splashed perfume on his face. He stared at his twisted reflection in the mirror. A fractured image. A fractured mind. *Did the Fates see this?* he wondered.

II § 3 RIDING THE AORTAPHOS

Awake.

"What are you? Leave me alone!"

You have a task. The lotuzone.

"No, it's not good for them."

Fulfill your function. Take your helots to pasture.

"No, I can't. My head and body . . . like sand . . . I can't. I'm a shell over the world, and I can't touch anyone. I'm so closed off and alone, a lake of misery in a forest."

We're all alone.

"Not like *this*."

Yes, just like this.

A hand rattled Glaucon from slumber. His eyes opened slowly. "What?" he whispered lying disheveled on a bench. An aortaphos conductor in a blue suit eyed a walking departure board. Behind, in a glass tube, a silver, flat, ovoid train idled in neutral.

"Son, come on. Get up. Time to head home. Traincell won't wait for you to finish napping. You're not special. Where's your ticket?"

Glaucon showed his holo-stub.

"Ah, the Tenth Ward," the conductor noted. "Been a rough day down there, all right. You're pretty lucky. I heard anarchists fired rockets at the walls again. Seven more dead."

"I only knew about the initial strikes," Glaucon mumbled stretching. The conductor's thick hands suddenly seized him by the collar and tossed him on the traincell. Glaucon yelped limply as the doors slammed shut. *How dare he touch me like that*, he thought. *I'm not some common helot. I should have that conductor thrown into the Bull for manhandling me*. Even if he *was* disguised, there was no excuse.

Brushing dust from his pants, Glaucon looked around. Star-shaped lights hummed on the ceiling. Standing passengers clutched handles reading papers, using symsysts.

The aortaphos started to bumble. Glaucon found a seat near the window. Blurs of green and concrete passed the glass as the aortaphos slid on a veil of magnets at four hundred and fifty kilometers per hour. Heliopolis drifted away. The sea stretched out like luminous, infinite space.

Yawning, the disguised guardian looked at a woman with pink bee-hive hair sitting across from him. She perused a magazine called *HELP*. The main article read: "Reaching Higher Ground: That guy at work *is* in your league." Glaucon suspected otherwise. Below that advertisement was a teaser for serial non-fiction: "Anarchists Are After Your Baby."

Abruptly, there was complete silence, a sense of vertigo. Aortaphos magnets stopped humming, low-talking voices fell silent, nothing could be heard.

Passing through the audiomembrane, Glaucon reassured his nerves. No sounds could permeate Heliopolis through its venerable skin. The philosopher-paradise did not suffer impure sounds from the outside world. Several moments passed before a large cough heralded Noise's return.

Stratos appeared on the horizon—the first island ring. Glaucon could already see the half-naked young recruits attacking one another on the parade grounds. They were playing Guardians versus the Other Side, a training exercise.

Drill sergeants dressed in military khakis marched along a line of children, aged six to ten, numbering them off: "One, two; one, two; one two." They separated the children, handing out wooden clubs and shields. Then they gave several minutes to plot. This was always the worst part—the strategizing, the plotting, the waiting. After fifteen minutes or so, a bugle pierced the sky. Children turned round and dashed like wild boars, clubbing each other to pieces. Bodies tossed airborne, looking like drowning wildebeests. The game ended when one group surrendered or ran away. Metachocolates and time in the tents went to the winners. Losers faced exposure to the elements for the whole night while loudspeakers shamed their cowardice: "You do not run. You do not hide. You do not show any mercy. Mercy is for the weak. The helots don't want mercy. They want defenders. Tomorrow when we do this again, fight with this shield or die on this shield. Do you understand me, maggots?" Children shouted apologies.

Only one good thing could be said of Stratos; Glaucon met Patroclus and Zoe there. Nothing could describe his first weeks alone after being taken from his mother. The other children purposefully humiliated him during drills. When they ceased beating, they excluded him, laughed at his bronze beginnings, called him a "helot mooncalf." Nothing but a single helping of soup broth nourished him at night. When he tried to ask the instructor for help, he thrashed him mercilessly with a bronze rod for being a coward. Stripped naked, abused by day, alienated from friendship at night, Glaucon breathed unhappiness and slept alone by the water.

Then one night, while he lay shivering unable to cry, a tiny body plopped down and spooned next to his for warmth. Blonde hair and a bright face looked over his shoulder. "Are you sad because they called you a mooncalf?" Zoe introduced herself.

"Yes."

"Don't worry," the sweet young girl said. "They're hard on you cause you have to catch up." She handed him a piece of bread which he devoured ravenously.

"I'll never catch up. Where'd you get this?"

"We send a group to the wards to steal food for us. Come with me next time, and I'll teach you how to distract the merchants in Shennong Fooderies."

"Why don't the adults just give us enough to eat?" Glaucon whimpered. "Why do they serve us that horrid broth? I can barely move I'm so hungry."

"You need to learn resourcefulness, silly. All our training will make us better guardians. You don't want them to send you back to be a helot."

"I *am* a helot," he moaned.

"That's not what your test scores say. The others may call you mooncalf, but they hardly ever accept new helots as old as you into the guardian ranks. I bet you're smarter than all of them. They're just jealous."

"I'm here because I painted a stupid picture. I miss my mother."

"None of us goldborn know our real mothers or fathers. The nursing dens on Schizoeon raised us. When we turned six, they shipped us over here."

"I'll never fit in."

"Yes you will. Just try harder. I'll help. Do you know Patroclus?"

Of course he did. Who didn't? The other students viewed the boy with revered awe, said his spirit tore through the Serengeti in a past life infused to a lion. Even as a nine-year-old, he excelled at everything. Showed martial bravado, real potential in discuss, javelin, and sparring. He caught ISHIM's eye early, especially since it was rumored he was Prodicus' son.

Zoe continued, "Well, he's a good friend of mine. I'm supposed to spar with him tomorrow. Why don't we trade? You can learn some cunning tricks from him, and I'll practice with you at night. How does that sound? The first thing we need to do is keep you from handling your club like a panpipe. You're supposed to be fighting, not playing a musical instrument."

Snuggling next to his back, she fell asleep.

Next morning, Patroclus knocked Glaucon to the ground with a single swing. "You always wait too long," Patroclus scolded. "What are you, stupid? Use your shield to push back. When they're off balance, hit their legs low as Hades. Disable their footing. No one ever expects the legs. They always think you'll go for the face."

"Why is that?" Glaucon had asked.

"Because they value their face most, that's why. No one thinks about their legs. Too removed from the body. You never think about walking at all but always how you look. Your face is the identifying mark of the self. It's the first mask we use to understand our identity as human beings. We cannot imagine what our self would be like without our face. Why, losing your face would be like losing your soul, and imagine how far you'd go to protect your soul."

"That's irrational and stupid," Glaucon mumbled. "Who cares about their face?"

Patroclus stared down at him like a gnat. "Yeah, but it's irrationality I gladly exploit, and now you can too. And when you trip them flat, make sure to smash out some teeth. Don't let the instructor see. Smash them good. Earn respect by pain here. Make the others fear you, and they'll leave you alone."

"But . . . that'll disfigure them."

"No, no. Prodicus can fix it. He can fix anything. But they'll remember the pain. You need only a few examples."

Glaucon didn't believe what he was hearing. These children weren't *children*, not like the wards. For no reason at all, the tall boy punched him square in the arm, laughing wild. Glaucon looked like a beaten dog as half his body went numb. *Have I said something wrong?* he wondered.

Patroclus started laughing again. "Zoe wasn't kidding. You really are something else. Don't you ever show any human emotion at all?" he asked. "Come on, hit me back. We're friends now. See if you can leave a bruise bigger than Zoe's. I'll even let you use a knuckle this time." Patroclus curved his arm to make an easier target, but Glaucon just stared at him confused.

What kind of person would want to be hit by another? he thought.

Then he had a wicked idea. Instead of hitting the arm, Glaucon pretended to strike Patroclus in the face.

"Wait! What in Hades are you doing?" Patroclus shouted with a high-pitched squeal, covering his eyes.

"Seeing if you are as irrational as the others."

Patroclus smirked and threw his sweaty arm over Glaucon. "Gee, mooncalf. You sure learn quick, don't you? I can see already we're going to be good friends." They walked back to the wooden barracks and shared a meal of broth. When no one was looking, Patroclus secretly slipped him some bananas and barleysticks under the table.

Another memory to pass the time, Glaucon? the voice disturbed him again.

"Memories are like rain. They come and go."

Bringing thunderstorms and the suffering of events you cannot change.

"Sometimes they cool you off. I would not want to change these events."

A rare memory, then?

"Yes."

The woman with the strange hair continued droning on next to him. He'd been ignoring her, pretending to listen. "Stratos sure is pretty today," she said "Never a more perfect field. Let me tell you, I'd love to run on that neatly mown grass like one of those women down there. Free like a mare, and with all those handsome boys—they'd be a hit at the lovebug parties wouldn't they? I hear they even train naked on some days. Can you imagine?"

Glaucon *could* imagine. He'd practiced naked on the grass many nights, often in the wetter months. Lapped by the rain with Patroclus, Rex, and Zoe, they huddled in a clump of flesh using body heat to keep warm like stray wolves. Such communal living without any shred of privacy promised to build the necessary virtues, perfect soldiers.

The woman shrieked unexpectedly. A menacing avis suddenly streaked by the window. Gliding on six wings, its legs dangled limply like a wasp. The machine craned its neck and stared directly with one eyecamera at Glaucon.

"What are the avis doing this far from Heliopolis?" the woman asked as the beast darted away.

"I wish I knew," Glaucon said getting up. "They usually never leave the audiomembrane. Maybe the rockets are drawing them."

Glaucon walked down the curved traincell soaked in confusion. "Is Prodicus watching me? Does he not trust me anymore?"

Trusting any man is like handling a spitting hydra. Prodicus is too wise to trust a child of matter.

Moving advertisements littered the traincell walls: numbers to call for "Helot Hotties," where to find a perfect swimsuit. A neon Knight of Cephalus extended from the wall discussing a Harmony Renewal Retreat the following Saturday in the Third Ward. Holographic children skipped across the wall carrying banners for various psychotropic drugs. At the back of the train, he overheard a helot ask another where he could score some *erosic*.

"The *erosic* pill. . . ." Glaucon huffed at the name, surprised by the endless helot fascination with the drug. *My first slimetide was with Zoe*, he remembered. He did not know what the word meant originally. Who would? During their first education break from Stratos, Zoe made sure to sit next to him in class. Thin pale legs crossed, twirling blonde hair, she passed him a note in geometric proofs: SLIMETIME: YES OR NO? Thinking her playing pranks again, Glaucon passed the note back empty and received a nasty look. Zoe threw a fit after class, pounded a locker near his head, and said he was meaner than Xenon. Glaucon confided his embarrassment at not knowing what slimetide meant. Not goldborn like her, he felt ignorant. At this, Zoe grew happy again and smiled showing teeth. Grabbing his hand like a prized object, almost too possessive for a guardian, she dragged him back to her dresser in Phylanstery B. Filled with laundry and strange smells, she plucked out her state-issued Puberty Pack from behind a folded earth toned chiton, which looked and opened like a thermos. Stirring her fist inside the Puberty Pack like some deep treasure chest, she eventually brandished an arrow shaped pill.

Glaucon noticed the *tetractys* on her hand glowed indigo.

"It's like exhaust from an engine," Zoe explained. "Guardians have to take *erosic* periodically to release the smoke in their souls. If you don't, you'll overheat and be bewitched."

"Bewitched by what?" Glaucon asked in horror. The way Zoe spoke, it was as if their very lives were in danger.

"Desire."

"Desire?"

"Yes, desire will devour you. We must seek moderation to keep its fangs at bay. Not too much. Not too little. To fly like Daedalus keep to a medium height."

All alone in a secluded part of the phylanstery, Glaucon felt nervous and wanted to leave but also to stay. Dropping the drug on his tongue like a magic powder, Zoe allowed a laugh. "Forget your worries."

Slimetide was like a male elephant in musth. Fire caught hold of your bones, teeth and insides hurt miserably until you possessed the other. Release seemed impossible. Then all passions drained out, vividly and constantly, like your body letting off steam. For a brief moment thoughts ran clear, annihilated.

Every time he took *erosic* with Zoe, Glaucon longed to see as she saw him, and he wanted to be loved. But love never found him with the pill. There was only emptiness and an addiction to emptiness. She'd never touch him without it.

A wall-television on the aortaphos switched to the Gorgon Hour. Glaucon was happy for the distraction. An animal tamer entered the set. Morpheus moved from news to entertainment with unrivalled ease.

"Now what kind of creature is this?" asked Morpheus petting what looked like a mix between a porcupine and a komodo dragon.

"This is a needleduck. Latest creation from the Department of Human Husbandry. Gene splicing gets easier every day."

"I see that. This *thing* isn't dangerous, is it?" The needleduck crawled up on his shoulder and flicked his hair with a long frog tongue.

An electronic laugh could be heard.

"No, we modified the gene that makes Drago poisonous."

"His name is Drago?"

Another electronic laugh.

"Yes, he's perfectly harmless unless you put him with another needleduck. Then the spikes fire out like the bomb-feathers of an avis."

"I hope he doesn't think *I'm* a needleduck!"

Another electronic laugh.

Another casualty of the 24-hour news cycle, Glaucon thought, looking out the window again. Levantra shined like a golem at the edge of the horizon, foreign and menacing. Construction continued heavy: A fleet of feathered gyrocopters, spiritcarriers, and avis spun around the skeletal chassis.

Something strange jumped out near the window. It was not like the other advertisements. No translucent neon glow, no 3-D cartoons, just paper: a black and white picture of a robust grinning face with bushy mustache. A simple phrase filled half the page: GIVE UP.

"Forms! It's Xenon Adonis!" Glaucon exclaimed, ripping it down from the wall. "Who could've posted such hideous things?" He swiveled his head and saw a line of portraits running down the traincell.

"Is it really him?" he wondered silently. "He's laughing like a Mongol conqueror, like an approaching hurricane, and no one's seen these yet." *The cretin responsible has to be close*, he realized looking over the seats. At the bottom corner of the page was the signature of the author: THE WATCHERS.

Glaucon placed the poster in his satchel. "I'd better save this for ISHIM forensics," he said, stealing another glance. The black and white mustache alighted Glaucon's eyes like a magic liquor. He sat down and drank in the mysterious fallen philosopher, the deity of wrong, the mutinous Xenon Adonis. All smiles, brows upturned, eyes livid flames, some said he was a cannibal now. He boiled children alive to eat their bones. Yet here he was, blowing smoke in the portrait like a regular person.

The aortaphos streaked past the second island ring and past the last channel of water. Tropical beach and swamp peeled by the window. He saw the Fifth Ward's metal towers and the flashing lights of Consumption Junction. A bell rang. The Tenth Ward was approaching. Shortly thereafter, Glaucon walked up planned streets to the water tower.

II § 4 Walls Never Work

"LOTUZONE," Glaucon read the bottle label. "WARNING: may cause severe psychotic hallucinatory outbursts, disassociation, and decreased inhibitions." The guardian tossed the bottle between his hands like a hot rock. He stood on the eastern aqueduct, staring over the wall at the Other Side. The wild trees from his youth were gone, replaced by a jungle swamp watered by the Gulf of Mexico. His childhood cave died flooded by the guardians.

"Even now have I begotten a strange wonder," Glaucon mused staring at the bottle. "Should I throw away this dew of poison and lie to Prodicus?"

Prodicus would certainly discover your betrayal.

"Maybe not. He's—"

Maybe not? You've traded good sense for madness. Have you ever been able to escape his watchful eyes?

"No."

Then why should this time be different?

"It just should be. I don't feel right about this. I came to Heliopolis to become a philosopher-king, not to oppress people."

There are four ways to secure a troubled province: to devastate the people, to occupy the people, to establish a loyal cartel to rule the people, or to provide circuses and other amusements to soften the people. We do all four, yet troubled are you by the least of these now?

"To give them seizures? Yes! To numb them into oozy stares and false laughter? Yes!"

The Tenth Ward was a ghost town. All workers fled the violence from the Other Side. Taxicab drivers left their magnet-propelled vehicles hovering in the streets. One truck crashed sideways into a fire hydrant. Its large bumper-sticker still scolded: PLATO IS A SAINT, NOT A CURSE WORD. To the west, some terraced splice-rice patties sat vacant with no one to power the tractorclaws.

Glaucon, the essence of politics is harm. Harming others can't be avoided. Any leader must harm those over which he has authority. You cannot judge the sovereign like you would a man. A guardian is different from the helots he rules. He has responsibilities they do not share. He is wise and must be a doctor for the whole. Besides, don't you secretly think the lotuzone *will help the helots cope with this new assault by the Eastern Column?*

Glaucon hated when the voice spied his inner feelings. "I was afraid to admit such might be necessary," he whispered.

Well admit it. What could be a better way to secure well-being? Think how depressed the helots must be right now—alone, all, all alone—in their homes, quivering in fear that Xenon and the Iron Queen will come for them like unholy daimons. In some cases, lotuzone *causes pain, but when measured on the scales of utility, balancing shows the gold. We did the calculation.* Lotuzone *enhances the helots' vision of the Form of Happiness more than stunts it.*

"But fake happiness. They're not really being made happy by drugs."

Nothing in the helot world is happy or real, but they still have to live. Better to hold fake happiness than no happiness. Tell me, if you had to live through a painful ordeal like eye surgery, would you accept the anesthesia?

"I cannot say. Maybe I would, but not necessarily. What if I wanted to feel the pain of the knife breaking my cornea, to experience and hold the purposelessness of it, the humiliation of pain and my inability to stop it? I might become aware there is more truth in misery and trauma than happiness. Such awareness might become a pleasure."

Such talk frightens even me, Glaucon. This world is a wrecked misery, but it's one we bear with our heads held high, hoping for a better one. I think you'd take the anesthesia in the end. Slumber is preferable to misery.

"You're probably right—See! Look how easily I submit to you. I'm such a coward. I understand nothing, not even myself. My body toils distantly. I'm just spirit staring down at raw open flesh. All I have are questions. A moment ago, I might've denied you, but now I'm a limp fish. I have to grab one arm with the other to do what I want."

But you can still move, can't you?

"I know. I don't have a choice."

Glaucon unscrewed the *lotuzone* lid and poured the blue contents into the drinking water, initiating molecule replication. When he finished, he dropped the bottle in the river, heard a splash. He walked back across the white aqueduct. The anarchist jungle swayed in the distance.

Was that so hard?

"Not at all, really. I don't feel any differently. There was no solemnity or announcement; the sky didn't break. No warrant came for my arrest, no punishment. I just dropped the bottle. No one was even here to hassle me, to make me show the proper papers."

Yes, that's how most crime goes.

Glaucon sat down on the stone and curled up with his head on his knees. He stared at the deserted ward below. The guardians provided everything for the helots: a white picket fence, a dog, a bondhusband (or bondwife), the manicured lawns, the common gardens in the back, a perfect number of roofless temples for worshiping the Forms—now the *lotuzone*.

Guardians also provided jobs. Each of the ten wards had a central tower and a unique guardian corporation, part of the Vinculum Cartel. There was Ra-Busto Energy in the Third Ward for photovoltaic technologies; Seven Seas in the Second Ward engineered missiles and tanks; in the Tenth was Mira-Disney, producing every form of entertainment from comedies to pornditties (still often difficult to tell apart). Only things like tragedies, dirges, and melancholic soap operas were specifically banned.

The Vinculum corporations were the economic ligaments of the Republic. The Logoset's visible hand created a "Fair Market" by fixing prices for things like food rations, teloscopy readings in the cogniscrambler, video entertainment in the haptic relay, widget-fidget pads, *Friend-of-Man* lotion, corduroys, suncatcher energy, every commodity imaginable. Two hundred and six subordinate corporations worked below them, married, bound up into a spiraling web of synergy. Each contributed in some way to the armaments industry and the technological glory of the auxiliaries. As the guardians lectured, war required collective effort for everyone's livelihood.

Crash! A fierce explosion suddenly rocked the aqueduct. Glaucon ducked behind a stone wall. "What the hell? Another attack?" he gasped.

A strange red storm stirred the sky. Blood-colored lightning blew out an energy pylon next to him. The metal frosted over with ice and burned his skin when he touched it. Mortars and rockets fell like steaming meteors. The northern wall splintered. The Eastern Column invaded from the Other Side like ants riding on a sulfur cloud. Auxiliaries brandished their Neokalashnikov bayonets behind their energy-bracer shields, met the spilling serpent. The white blood cells of the Republic repulsed the foreign body.

"Maybe the Iron Queen really is leading the assault," Glaucon said.

The walls hadn't been successfully breached in over a generation, not since the Tesla cannons were installed.

One anarchist grabbed several men and scrambled up along the five-meter-thick walls. They were going to try and throw scorpion-grenades by hopping to a red-clay tiled roof. Steady fire greeted them. One fell dying before he reached the roof. Another rebel pulled out a grenade preparing to throw. A green beam of compressed sound from a sonic carbine twanged like a harp and liquefied his chest. He dropped the grenade by his feet. Looks of terror gripped the remaining men as a hundred fiery tails whipped death and half the roof blew away in a wave of blood.

Another maelstrom of red lightning knocked the electricity out for twenty blocks.

Aegis tanks died powerless, carapaces unavailing. Zizthopters crashed in a hail of feathers. Their pilots were pulled kicking from their seats by the advancing militia and shot. In the city, battalions of auxiliaries marched down the street furiously, trying to push the enemy back outside the walls. Rockets continued to pour in, flicking office buildings onto cars and dead power lines. Then all at once—upon the flash of a signal flare—the militia retreated.

Some missed the message. Machine guns on the stockades sprayed explosive rounds into the pockets of shelterless militiamen still stranded by the wall, shattering them to pieces. Anarchists who couldn't escape the walls took off into the city to grope for the protection of the temple altars.

Cheers erupted from the victorious auxiliaries who circled the remains of the battle like hungry sharks.

Why are you continuing to watch this slaughter, Glaucon?

The voice pressed on his mind gently, like the petals of an opening flower.

"Because I can't believe the Iron Queen breached the walls. What was that weapon causing the red lightning? It knocked out the entire grid."

No, Glaucon, why were you really watching?

"Something violent in me derives satisfaction from the suffering of others. I cannot get enough. I want the helots to suffer and the Other Side to suffer. I hope Xenon and the Iron Queen and her Eastern Column come back and waste half the city."

But?

"I am repulsed at these feelings. How can I wish to see others die? How can I enjoy it? Something in me smiles when I see the blood on the street from the scorpion-grenades. I pause and curse these feelings, but I secretly cherish them and the guilt which hangs on my heart."

Do you know the legend of Leontius?

"Vaguely."

You should. You must've read the Republic *a thousand times by now. One day, long ago, Leontius, the son of Aglaion observed some men lying impaled at a place of execution. He felt a desire to see them but also a dread. He was repulsed by the sight, but desire got the best of him. He held his eyes open and said: 'Look, you damned wretches, take your fill of the fair sight.' Appetite conquered spirit and reason. He starved to death staring at the bodies, never able to look away.*

"Only reason commanding the spirit can break the chains of desire."

Yes, and desire is eternally unsatisfied.
"So is reason," Glaucon admitted.

II § 5 WATCHER IN THE ROSES

Glaucon left the aqueduct. He crossed into the planned neighborhoods surrounding Mira-Disney Tower and the business district. He tried to forget the men stranded by the wall and the strange red lightning. Mammoth spiritcarrier wings beat the air overhead trying to reach the downed ziz in the marshes (and hopefully their crew) before the rebels did.

Here and there auxiliaries and Aegis tanks scrambled past plebeian magazine stands in the housing blocks, looking for any men with weapons. Glaucon heard intermittent street firing, then a hush. A few of the anarchists who escaped into the city had already been caught and chained together in trucks.

"The blackheads fled to Poseidon's altar!" one soldier screamed, pacing like a hungry tiger beside a temple's waist-high dividing walls.

"Let's drag the murderer out, then," his patrolmen begged.

"Have you miscarried sense? Want to provoke earthquakes, do you?"

"But sir," the grunt protested, "surely the gods don't grant protection to polluted anarchist—"

"No, we must wait for him here. He has to come out sometime."

Not wanting to draw undue attention, Glaucon crept behind them, keeping close to the walls. All the housing units were brightly colored. Large video clips of smiling children flashed on their fifteen-meter digital walls. Children pointed fingers at the sky. One innocent child with pigtails released a white dove with the word FLOURISHING dancing under her face. The dove flew out of the screen and passed a banner with the helot motto:

NOT SELF-RULE,
BUT RULE BY REASON
AND THE REASONABLE.

Hands-of-God flags fluttered on every corner, too. They garnished the lawns, hung from windowsills, embraced helots at their door.

In the center of a cul-de-sac, there was a raised grass median. A bronze statue of Mickey Mouse—one of the oldest of the corporate gods—stomped on the head of Dionysus. Someone placed a large poster near Dionysus' fallen jug of wine.

"What's that?" Glaucon asked running over to the statue. Just like he expected, there Xenon was again—the same black and white picture, the same words: GIVE UP. Holding the paper in his hands, he wondered if he'd ever see one with the Iron Queen. Such disloyal thoughts made him uneasy. It suddenly felt like he was being watched. Looking at a nearby tree, he noticed four eyecameras blinking at him curiously.

Eyecameras were the only thing more plentiful than flags in the wards. They watched the streets from everywhere: trees, buildings, cars. Even insects.

Is the Office of Public Harmony watching me? Glaucon shuddered. Probably not. The guardians hardly ever used them; they just wanted helots to think them operational, like Bentham's Panopticon or something like that.

Glaucon turned his attention back to the poster. *Who could be doing this?* he wondered. At the other side of the cul-de-sac, more posters led out a gate. The guardian followed the contraband like a trail of cookie crumbs, around several alleys and four-bedroom A and C model houses. Posters lay in heaps everywhere, as if someone just threw them in the air without a care in the world. He almost tripped over a few. At each corner, he felt like he'd just missed the culprit.

The brick walls of ivy, the colored faces, and the matter incinerator dumpsters ended. Glaucon stumbled into an endless backyard with several pagodas. The trail of white posters led to a rose garden. Soccer balls and fishermen figurines lay discarded on the ground; the children's fear made them forget to pick up their toys.

"I'll show these rebels what eyes have been watching them," Glaucon growled, following the path with clenched fists. "I'll call Patroclus, have him get the courts ready for these miserable traitors."

We must not suffer them to live, Glaucon, the voice snarled.

Stone pillars, wooden arches, statues, and roses blocked his vision. Glaucon replayed everything he'd say before tearing the culprit to pieces: "You have a lot of nerve putting something like that up. How dare you soil this altar with your clumsy excuse for a poster?" He'd go back to Heliopolis a hero for catching a propagandist with the Watchers.

What he saw next halted him in his tracks.

As he rounded a corner of hanging vines and white roses, a strange young woman in a tunic blouse came into view. She had bronze hair which shimmered in the light, and her back was turned to him. Shimmying up a pillar, she struggled awkwardly in the air to hang a poster from one of the wooden awnings.

"Are you just going to stare all day Zemer or are you going to help?" she hollered. "These damn things—they don't stick. I'm so sick of this work. It's loathsome. I can't believe I let you talk me into this. I should've stayed with the others instead of volunteering for this humiliation."

Glaucon stepped closer, not saying a word, following the woman's body to her slender waist. A coilgun stuck out of her khaki pants. He wondered if he could safely disarm her and reached for the handle.

"Zemer, gods' sakes. . . ." the woman said turning around.

Her facial angles lined strangely for a helot, much softer, with no markings or the customary tightness of the plastic surgery boutiques. Seeing Glaucon so close made her gasp with alarm: "What the hell are you doing here?"

Glaucon struggled to explain, but the situation looked compromising with his hand so close to her lower half. Next thing he knew, the woman's coilgun had ripped across his face sending him hurling into a hawthorn tree.

Thorns! Thorns! Thorns pierced his skin.

As Glaucon rolled in pain, the woman jumped down from the pillar aiming the coilgun wildly, confused, almost falling into some thorns herself. She retreated as fast as she could with the gun pointing menacingly.

Impaled in the bramble, stars danced in Glaucon's head. He hardly knew what happened. One moment he was standing; the next he was in the mud in agony.

Don't let her get away!

Glaucon ripped his skin badly pulling up. He limped after the woman, passing several pagodas and greenhouses in the communal garden. "Wait. Please stop," he yelled chasing her. "Why she sprints faster than the huntress Atalanta," he finally cursed. "If only I had some golden apples to slow her down. Please, I didn't mean to scare you. I just wanted to talk."

The disguised guardian stopped running and fell dizzy in the grass. He pulled a long thorn out of his wrist and yelped. The strange woman stopped running near one of the pagodas and turned around. After seeing Glaucon collapse in pain holding the black welt on his face, she approached him slowly, stooped over her coilgun.

"Do you know who I am?" the woman demanded, snatching his shirt gruffly at the neck. She looked in her late twenties, but it was hard to tell with all the anti-aging drugs on the Fair Market.

"What?" Glaucon asked confused, cowering through his fingers.

"My name? What's my name?"

"I don't have any idea what you're talking about."

"You've never seen me before?"

"No."

"The Fates didn't send you?"

"Of course not. Why would they send me here?"

"Who the hell are you?" She snatched his right wrist looking for a sign of his *tetractys*. Not finding any, she looked satisfied, but Glaucon noticed her own right hand was scarred.

Why am I so afraid of her? Glaucon wondered.

"What are you, some kind of pervert?" the woman asked, tossing him down. "How long have you been watching me? Speak up before I knock you to the Fallout Corridor."

"I've . . . uh . . . been trying to find the person responsible for these . . . advertisements." Glaucon held up the poster from his pocket like an energy shield. "I want to know what it means. Followed the trail you left. Wanted to meet you."

She grabbed the poster and tore it in two. "Why aren't you hiding in a hole like the others? Hoping auxiliaries would save you?"

"Just got off work at the commercial studio," Glaucon franticly lied. "I was trying to get home, but—"

The strange woman jerked his scalp looking at the welt. "Looks like I got you pretty bad, huh. That's gonna be a nasty bruise. Just look at you. You're a wreck—bleeding all over." As she kneeled down to inspect him, her green eyes squinted at some thorns lodged in his knee. This made Glaucon extremely uncomfortable. He scrambled away like a frightened spider, but her soft hands yanked him back. Pulling out one of the larger thorns leaking blood, she noticed Glaucon wince.

"Don't be such a baby," she ordered, "this will only take a second."

"I can pull them out later."

"You don't want these to cut deeper."

Glaucon conceded and looked curiously at the operation. Like a sword from the stone, the woman slowly drew out the final thorn. Once she finished, she threw it away and helped Glaucon rise to his feet.

"Sorry I hit you so hard," she apologized. "You really surprised me. This day's been something else. If you'd been an auxiliary or guardian, I don't know what I'd have done."

"What's your name again?" Glaucon asked.

"Sophie."

Glaucon's soul brightened by her commanding eyes. They peered into his like jade fog lights. Sophie realized she was staring and flushed red, turned away.

Glaucon asked quickly, "How'd you put all these posters up by yourself? There must've been hundreds."

"Others are helping. My brother, Zemer, is around here somewhere. That's who I thought you were. I should've known better. He's not very quiet, like you."

"You hardly know me."

"Don't need to. You can discover everything you need to know about someone after the first minute. Talkative types immediately come up to you, talk about their lives, what they had for dinner."

"And the others?"

"Quiet ones never approach me, either because they're hiding something or afraid. Which one are you, Mr.—"

"Oxenbridge. Glaucon Oxenbridge."

"Quite a mouthful you got there. So, do you try to disarm every woman you meet or just me?"

The directness of her question caught Glaucon off guard. She was studying him again from head to toe, looking for Good knows what. "I . . . I thought you might try to kill me," Glaucon stammered.

"And why would I want to do something like that?" Sophie studied him suspiciously again.

"Because you're a . . . a Watcher."

Sophie smiled slyly and grabbed Glaucon's wrist. "We're not so bad. Come on. Help me find my brother."

"What about all the other posters?" Glaucon asked exasperated. "You're just going to leave them here?"

"I've had enough. Let the wind carry them." The two walked briskly up the lawn past several patios and pools.

All at once the lights inexplicably flickered again, flickered chaotically. Rushing voices and storming feet could be heard down the alley. Sophie stopped as a scruffy boy wearing symsyst goggles bolted out from behind the brick wall. By Sophie's worried expression this must have been Zemer.

"Run, Sophie, we've been discovered," the strange anarchist shouted flying past them. He tried to grab Sophie's hand, but it was holding Glaucon. "Who the devil are you?" he asked curiously.

Zemer looked the same age as his sister, but was rawboned (almost starved), with sable hair and a windburned face. The three ran toward another alley to escape the park. More auxiliaries blocked the way.

Dark green helmets with goggles, Neokalashnikovs, round energy shields, and sparking xiphos sticks herded them to the center of the park. Zemer frowned in each direction. Auxiliaries poured in, circling them, stormy as the South Wind.

"Trapped with no exit, imagine that?" Zemer said to Glaucon. He was dressed for summer in a white linen collared shirt. "I feel sorry for you. You must either have horrible luck or peculiar ends."

Sophie asked reaching for her coilgun, "Zemer, did they really see you?"

"Can't know for sure. What was I supposed to do?"

"Not run away. Use *you-know-what* on them."

"You know I won't do that. Not on people. Bad enough with the walls and the ziz. Did you see what the Column did to those pilots?—a bloody massacre!"

One of the soldiers took off his helmet. Talos, an acquaintance of Glaucon at the Academy.

Glaucon held up both hands, motioned to his skin-gloved *tetractys,* and winked. "Good day, guardian. Is there something I can help you with?" he asked feigning sweetness.

"Yes," Talos said stiffly, striding up to him, "we've been chasing this villain across the Tenth Ward for the last hour. He's some kind of wizard. Used magic to break the walls and knocked out our electrical grid. Stopped bullets, too. Some of my men's xiphos sticks exploded in their hands. Give him up for questioning."

"Who? This fellow?" Glaucon pointed to Zemer with feigned surprise.

The voice rang frantically: *Turn them in, Glaucon. You've performed perfectly. Let the blackheads inherit anarchy's reward. Kill them yourself. Right here. Grab one of the soldier's guns and fertilize the ground.*

"No, not yet. I won't turn them in until I get answers."

Fool!

Glaucon smiled widely at Talos. "Sorry to say, my sun, but you've chased the wrong man. Zemer's been with his sister and me for well over an hour. We were hiding from the anarchist bombings when we saw several helots posting these hideous pictures and knocking out electronics. We ran outside to catch them, but they fled. Zemer—Plato love him—is recklessly zealous." Glaucon threw his arm around Zemer like Patroclus and pointed to his chest. "Not only did he want to drive the traitors from the park, but he tried to stalk them back to their hideout in the wastes. He wants to be a phylark, you see. Always has—reports everyone to the neighborhood watch office. Can't blame him for that."

Talos studied Glaucon's movements and seemed to get the message. Long xiphos sticks rustled like bamboo in a forest. Sophie breathed heavily against the disguised guardian's back, and he pushed her fingers away from her hidden weapon.

"No, I suppose I can't," Talos agreed nodding. "The wards would be blind without charity from such eager lips. We came to snare the fox, but it seems he gave us the slip. We didn't get such a good look at the culprits. Perhaps you could direct us?"

Glaucon pointed northeast. "I think the traitors fled toward the Ninth Ward. Try there."

"Indeed. We're in your debt. Well then, good day, subject. May all traitors to the Republic die screaming in the Bull!"

"Yes," Glaucon bowed, "and may you consort with the divine, lord guardian."

Neokalashnikovs rose. So did the sparks dancing on the xiphos sticks. Talos waded through his men barking orders to retreat. Marching away faster than they came, they sang the "Ode of Stratos":

"Take me back to circle fertile Stratos,
Sleepless isle, hounding triumphant land,
Kiss her silver ribs, feel her beating heart
Holding treasures older than Samarkand;
Falsehood cannot pierce the Sun's sacred falls
As long as we shed wealth and luxury,
Shield the guardians' gold symphony hill
With swords and showering gunship's fury;
Endure, endure, our blood protects the Crown,
Auxiliary honor dreams sacrifice:
For death, rebirth, the Incorporeal
Good, and one day the thankful end of strife."

"Well that was unexpected," Zemer sighed after the singing cavalry vanished. He collapsed on the ground and stared gratefully at the sky. "He called me a fox. Ha! It seems the crafty fox survived once more. Who the hell did you say you were again?"

"Glaucon. I work in advertising—"

"No need to explain to him," Sophie shouted hugging him. "Glaucon, you saved us from the guards. I could kiss you."

"Already?" Zemer smirked. "How touching. And to think I hardly know him." He wiped the sweat from his forehead. "I concede your presence most helpful. You look oddly familiar, though. Have we met before outside the city?"

Sophie jabbed Zemer in the side, whispering something inaudible out the corner of her mouth.

Glaucon answered, "No, I don't think so. I kept seeing pictures of Xenon everywhere and followed the trail to Sophie."

Zemer frowned. "I won't believe that lie for a second. But I can understand your reservations with the truth. The guardians are dogs. Spies are everywhere. Don't worry. You don't have to tell us who you are. That will come in time. At least we know you're not a guardian."

"Why do you say that?"

"Because if you were, we'd already be dead. Right, Sister? They're all indoctrinated up there like bees in a hive. Shake the nest lightly and all of Reason's drones come stinging. Not a separate thought among those theocrats."

"Xenon had different thoughts."

"Quite right, but he's an anomaly; and destiny drove his flight. In all these years, only a few others fell."

"Maybe I'm a fallen guardian."

Sophie started laughing and wrapped her arms around Glaucon's neck from behind. "No, your face is much too kind and harmless to be a guardian." She was treating him like a doll, with an intimate playfulness, as if they'd known each other before.

"Sister knows best," Zemer said. "She has a way with people. She understands them. She's beautiful, isn't she?"

"What?" Glaucon asked embarrassed. He *had* noticed a particular aesthetic in her formal geometry.

Zemer laughed. "Did that startle you? Only because you were thinking such. Why are you so quiet?"

"That's just the way he is," Sophie said. "Don't listen to him, Glaucon. My brother likes to talk. Has the mind of a child."

"You're one to speak," Zemer said, examining Sophie's sloppy poster-job on a nearby pagoda. The sun was starting to set.

"What does it mean?" Glaucon suddenly interrupted them.

"What?" Zemer asked.

"Give up."

Sophie sighed. "Anything really. Xenon told me it means to give up hope. Not the small hopes in life but the big ones—that man can be saved by temporal or religious authority. How does his poem go, Zemer? The silly one Xenon used to spout at mess?"

"Let's see." Zemer walked up into the pagoda thinking. The wooden steps creaked like they were inflicted with suffering. "Give up trying to be a perfect sunflower. Give up finding enchanted springs. Give up packaging man for cities because man cannot be packaged."

Sophie suddenly remembered and stood up excited, puffing her chest out to talk in a deep voice like Xenon. "Give up private property. Give up commercial charms. Give up the Forms of Woman and Man."

"Give up building elevators to the moon," Zemer continued. "Give up proving you exist—there is no *you* to find. Give up thinking slimetide necessary. Give up turning scientists into gold-chasing alchemists. Give up looking for angels and dragons amongst the stars."

"Because you're a rotting door, Glaucon, behind another and another."

"No different from a rat." Sophie clutched his upraised neck. "No different from a worm. No different from a tree. No different from prokaryote bacteria."

"And one day soon you'll die."

"Today or tomorrow, the Iron Queen will find you."

"She'll stop your pulse."

"Your consciousness will fade."

"Every dream you have will fade."

"Forms and hope will never comfort you."

"Because comfort is a lie."

"And we're groundless."

"But what creation lies in groundlessness!"

Their words were disturbing. Glaucon wasn't ready for them. Yet Zemer and Sophie couldn't be happier. They were smiling about killing the Eternal Forms and human ambition. Something dark and terrible, instinctively repulsive, gripped Glaucon. Like viewing the splintering bodies of the rebels, he felt the nausea of the I.T. magnetometer. What would the world be like without the Forms? He could hardly imagine the possibility.

"You've met Xenon?" Glaucon asked, suddenly more concerned for his life. If these two discovered his identity, they'd surely scalp him.

Sophie could tell he was upset. "Too many times I'm afraid. We lived with him for a while in the Rocky Mountains. Our parents . . . put us in his care. We're delegates from the Continental Caucus."

Glaucon could hardly believe what he was hearing. "Do you know the Iron Queen, too?" he asked.

"We've met her a couple times, yeah."

"What's she like? Is it true she's really a machine?"

"No, not exactly," Sophie said. "She's real heartless. Old and fanatical. A ghoulish hermit from the wastes. Everyone's afraid of her. What do you think she's like, Zemer?"

Zemer frowned. "A little too demanding."

Glaucon asked, "Is she as dangerous as they say?"

"Oh yes," Sophie said coyly. "I would run away if you ever saw her, Glaucon. She'll send you to the Underworld."

Who are these people? Glaucon thought. *And how could they so carelessly take me into their lives? Zemer said he was suspicious, but he doesn't care to look further. He had a scar on his right hand, too. Were these the lost exiled children he heard about at the Academy? What would've compelled them to return?*

Zemer said, "Glaucon, it seems we were fated to meet. Since you saved us, I might as well ask: Would you like to join us?"

"Well, first I'd have to know what I was joining."

"It's a secret organization."

"Like a club."

"Yes, like an order of magic knights." Zemer's sarcasm was biting. "Sorry, we're here to help re-supply a network of samizdat—printing houses—and start our own. We're going to publish books in their original form, the form not tailored by the guardians. Sophie and I already started making pamphlets of the more gratuitous instances of guardian modifications. We snuck in some copiers from the wastes during the battle. I've contacted other operatives here as well. We'll make copies, pass them on to others, and then they'll make copies. Like a sacred virus, we'll replicate until all know the truth—the guardians are liars and have hidden history from us. We call our magazine the *Goetia Mirror.*"

Glaucon lied shamelessly: "How interesting. I didn't know the guardians changed books."

Zemer grabbed Glaucon's shoulder, heart quaking with grief. "I could show you stories you wouldn't even recognize. So many changes, we lost our whole history to an illusion, a false Form. Our memories are almost dead."

"What if modified stories make the people happy?"

"One can despair even in happiness, especially happiness built with lies."

"Didn't you just tell me to give up truth? Why should it matter to you if the books are true or false?" Glaucon turned to Sophie. She agreed but refused to say anything.

"It just matters," said Zemer. "There is no Form of Truth but my little truth, my little nugget of value, my situation, tells me to shun false books that manipulate people. I don't think anyone should have knowledge kept from them."

"So sayeth the Great Zemer," Sophie teased.

Zemer blew his sister off with his hand. "I don't really agree with Xenon's poem anyway."

This admission surprised Glaucon. He was about to ask Zemer how he caused the power outages, but acoustic nodules suddenly trumpeted distantly. Sophie's head jerked up. Swirling mist, bluish and thick, enveloped the housing blocks like the mouth of a hungry whale. The central tower was completely blocked from view.

"What is it?" Glaucon asked when he saw Sophie's face turn ivory white.

"WE NEED TO SEEK SHELTER IMMEDIATELY!" Sophie screamed. She grabbed her brother's arm and took off running. Glaucon followed them.

"What's going on?" he shouted tripping at their heels. "I don't understand." He could barely hear his voice over the sirens. Running along the back walls of the houses, his legs were starting to burn. Sheets of metal burst clanging from concealed apertures in the ground to shield the gardens and houses from impending attack.

Sophie explained, "This is not some gentle storm. Someone released iama-B."

"Who? Xenon?"

"No, he'd never stoop to that level. He may be cold-blooded, but gas is abhorrent to him. Not after the Continental Caucus' last rebuke."

"Maybe it's the Iron Queen?"

"No, definitely not her. Hurry, Glaucon."

All three dashed to the park gas shelter and shut the door. It was completely empty. Zemer bolted the lock and turned on a nearby digitele.

Freddy Akimbo and Morpheus Alepou wore bulky contamination suits, filming the attack from their news helicopter. Avis streaked into the fog to bolster the walls.

The camera showed dozens of blue bodies lying stiffly on the ground. Helots tried to escape their houses for the nearby shelters. Mothers clutched their babes to their breasts, crawling and coughing. The camera panned to Talos and his company. Auxiliaries tore their helmets off struggling for breath as the gas attacked their flesh and eyes, ripping at their lungs. Convulsing, metal nanofilm branching through their pores, faces and lips finally twisted in pain. They fell as one hundred and fifty kilogram blocks.

Morpheus shouted into his microphone: "We just received horrifying news from ISHIM intelligence. None other than Xenon is responsible for the day's attack. Irate about his loss against our valiant auxiliaries at the wall, he's done the unthinkable—released iama-B on the city again. Hundreds are dead. A state of emergency has been declared for the Tenth, Ninth, and Eighth Wards. Everyone is ordered to seek shelter immediately."

Freddy Akimbo yelled, "Dead! All Dead! Ten minutes ago, reports of cinnamon in the air. Sources tell us this is the beginning stages of an iama-B gas attack. The Other Side is desperate and heartless. Only reptiles could release such indiscriminate weapons. Reptiles! Oh, I can't watch."

"This is horrible," Sophie hid her eyes. "They're lying. Could Skybridge stoop so low? Xenon wouldn't do this. He promised me. He'll be exiled for sure if it's true. This makes no sense at all."

Unable to watch anymore, Glaucon lay down quietly on his back. He stared up at the dark ceiling.

Do you think that was really lotuzone *you dropped?* asked the voice.

"Who can really say?"

It could have been the gas.

"Correlation doesn't mean causation."

How logical. Whatever helps you sleep.

"Iama-B or *lotuzone*. It's all the same to me."

And yet, my little Hades, my god of death, you gave life to the exiles. Why? Don't tell me you're actually considering joining their plot? You an anarchist pamphleteer? Don't make me laugh. What are you really after?

Sophie crawled next to him and sat down. The voice stopped talking. She placed her coilgun on the concrete floor and spun the revolver with her finger, staring at it intensely.

"Are you ok, Sophie?" Glaucon asked her.

"No. None of this makes any sense." Sophie sent her coilgun skidding across the floor. She rested her head next to his and compulsively scratched her *tetractys* scar. He could feel her breath blowing against his neck. Instinctually, he desired to reach out and hold her, but could not find the courage.

"Unbelievable," Zemer said turning off the digitele. He lay next to his sister. "This has to be the Fates' doing, but they'll think us responsible. I came back to stop violence, not find it. I'm as powerless as a satyr's child; I can't change anything at all. What helots will want to talk with us now?"

Glaucon remembered Prometheus saying, " 'No change, no pause, no hope! Yet I endure,' " and thought, *Look at me. How I endure. Through gas and all nothing can touch me. Yet I wish the nanofilm had turned me into a block. Should I kill myself? 'To be or not to be?' That was the original phrase from Hamlet. Forbidden like everything else in the Republic, both suicide and Hamlet.* He stared at his bony fingers in the dark. No voice challenged such thinking. Glaucon finally said, "Perhaps I'm immortal," and fell asleep.

II § 6 A New Friendship

Sophie leaned forward staring out the shelter window. Her stiff body conveyed a sense of urgency and pain. The previous day had faded dreamlike. There was now a still darkness, as if the three lay trapped underwater. The air smelled musty with a hint of mold. Rusty crust caked the walls. A single halogen lantern hung from the ceiling, but Sophie turned it off to avoid unwanted attention. Only wandering searchlights and the thunder of distant artillery broke the gloom.

"The cicadas are all dead," Sophie said biting her thumbnail in despair. "I can't hear chirping anymore. Only that endless wretched shelling in the north. How I hope the militia made it to the safety of the Louisiana Territory. If they can make it past the plains to the rainforest's edge, they'll be safe."

Zemer tried to comfort her. "Leave the fighting to the Iron Queen, Sister. I'm sure they made it."

"Damn it," Sophie said, kicking the wall. "We've missed our second rendezvous with Hecatia as well. It feels like we've been trapped in this hole forever. The Eastern Column is under attack. Everything's falling apart. When shall we be delivered?"

"Maybe you should stop looking out the window," Zemer suggested. "That only makes things worse. Gas won't dissolve any faster. ISHIM will release its travel ban soon enough."

Sophie groaned and sat back down on the hot concrete floor. She handed the symsyst back to her brother complaining bitterly about its resolution. "We'll contact Hecatia again in the morning. She's holed up like us in Mira-Disney Tower. Said she found someone who wants to join the *Goetia Mirror*."

Glaucon noticed a strange orange pendant dangling under Sophie's neck. He asked her about it admiringly.

"Oh this?" Sophie said fondling the jewel. "Zemer found a piece of amber floating on the Colorado River up by Pikes Peak. They usually have to be polished to shine like this though."

"What's it made from?"

"The fugitive tears of the sun," Zemer broke in. "I have it on good authority from the Seminoles that it wards off kidnappings."

"It's just fossilized tree resin." Sophie shook her head. "You will find my brother indulges in all kinds of superstition and fantasy. One of his many vices."

Zemer took her hand, saying, "If longing for your safety be vice, dear heart, then protest I must to virtue."

"He has a thirst for theatrics as well," Sophie grinned, resting her head on the humming life support console. She wiped sweat from her face with her shirt, unzipped her boots, and hurled them across the room like hot coals. She closed her eyes. "I've never been so bored in my life. If we have to stay here another night I might just open the door and be done with it all. Tell me a little about yourself, Glaucon. Do you have any family here?"

"Once," Glaucon said, shaking his head. Her question made him sad. "It was a long time ago."

"If you don't mind my asking, what happened?"

"My father was killed by plague. My mother . . . I can only speculate. She disappeared. It seems to be a common fate." Glaucon pointed to the ceiling. Shrieking avis perched on the rooftops—gargoyles watching the walls. (Or were they keeping him from flight?) "And you, Sophie? Where are you from on the Other Side? I see both you and your brother carry strange scars."

"Scars?" Sophie asked. "How observant of you. Zemer, where would you say we're from?"

Zemer weighed the value of speaking further. He muttered quietly, as if they were being watched: "To be perfectly honest with you, Glaucon, my sister and I were once guardian neophytes."

"Guardians? Is that so?" Glaucon widened his eyes. His suspicions were confirmed, then, and he could hardly believe his luck. Prodicus would surely grant him great rewards for bringing such prize ships to justice.

"Hard to believe, I know. My sister and I were both goldborn children of the sun. Look at that—see how I still take satisfaction in titles. I'm such a hypocritical worm. Such is the allure of power." Zemer laughed at himself and readjusted his glasses. "Although we weren't supposed to know our parentage, Sophie and I secretly knew. Lycaon was our father, and Potone, our mother. We could tell from an early age when they secretly took an interest in us. My mother waited for us after classes at the Academy. She'd call us from Stratos and take us to Hesper Park to play in the water. Sophie and I were in separate classes, yet we were always brought together with these strange people. I was about seven when I finally realized the truth."

"How did your parents possibly know where to find you? Typically, children born by guardians are seized at birth and raised in the breeding dens."

Sophie said sharply, "You don't know, Glaucon? Oh, I guess I shouldn't expect a helot like *you* to know such a thing. The guardians care not for their own rules. ISHIM carries detailed heredity banks. They know each branch of the Republic's family tree."

"Files are one thing; access is another," Glaucon returned.

"Take no offense," Zemer said. "Lycaon, my father, was Director of ISHIM for a time. He had access to all kinds of information."

"What happened to them?" Glaucon never heard of either Potone or Lycaon. Director Sinon had been in place since before his arrival, and before Sinon, Director Simonides held office. He'd have to look up Lycaon's file at ISHIM headquarters.

Zemer said, "They and the rest of the Katharoi were murdered by Prodicus in the Great Theurgy Schism."

Glaucon had never heard of that either. "I'm sorry," he responded, completely confused. He'd heard of the Kabiri Circle, wise creators of the Fates, but never the Katharoi.

"No need to apologize. I spent my whole life hating Prodicus, wanting to return to kill him and take revenge. But then do you know what happened?"

Glaucon shook his head.

"I realized my father and mother were no different from Prodicus. If given the opportunity, they'd have killed him too. And my father had his terrible share in the helot pogroms. That is the life Heliopolis taught: Kill for the Forms or be killed, save yourself and drown others. Join the mechanical cycle, mine for gems and end enslaved. I refused to believe at first, but my mother's and father's affection was shallow. They were using us, hoping we'd become their allies to launch their own little revolution. They were schemers. We just weren't old enough when it mattered. The Republic corrupts everything, Glaucon, even parents. When we fled with Xenon, I admired him, his courage to leave, to walk into the dead of night with nothing on his shoulders. When I held a gun, I imagined marching for him, to strike back against everything we lost. But now I've changed my mind."

"Why is that?"

"Because I don't wish to kill anymore. I've realized any violence, even if directed at a murdering scoundrel like Prodicus, is wrong. Blood can not wash away blood. It only makes the blood rise deeper until you drown."

"Some argue we have a right to life," Glaucon said unconvinced. "If such a right exists, you should be able to defend it against others trying to take it away."

Zemer smiled. "You have an eye for logic, Glaucon. Perhaps it's justifiable for you to protect yourself from an aggressor, but what if one day you wake up and realize the aggressor is a human being with hopes and dreams, and love him instead. The idea of individual rights is egocentric in a way. Instead of asking how we can help others, we say, 'How can I get others to leave me alone?' But see, this misses the spiritual connection that unites all human beings. It alienates us from one another. It is a way to deny responsibility. Human beings are more than just a taxidermy of rights. They are unique; none of them are alike. Having no common Form is what makes them valuable. I will not leave people alone—even if they claim a right to be left alone—because they matter to me. I want to purify the violence in myself and transform the hatred and pain of others into love and compassion."

Glaucon laughed. "You will not transform Prodicus."

"Perhaps, but I can try. Xenon thinks we'll continue planting ideas about retribution, but I have other plans. My sister and I will attempt a new experiment in the wards. It's not been tried in a long time. Our resistance will not be about taking Prodicus' power but transforming relationships. The *Goetia Mirror* will break down this city's definition of harmony and challenge its readers to love. We will call for an end to violence and recognition of our imperfect world. I want to throw my arms around Prodicus and forgive him. Forgive him for murdering my murdering father. I will ask him to forgive me, a murderer. I will show this people that physical violence is a defect that distorts the soul."

"Is love the natural condition of the soul, then?"

"What else could it possibly be?"

"I don't think there is a natural condition. Not reason, not spirit, not desire. Nothing. Maybe the trauma in our I.T. waves."

"That can be correct, too."

"What sense does that make?"

Zemer explained, "I don't believe many things Xenon tells me. He's like Prodicus and cares for revolution more than people; wants to avenge his dead lover more than anything. But Xenon's also a prophet of mankind's spirit. He once told me humans are, at their core, interpretive beings. That is all that can be meaningfully said about them. An interpretive existence is both our curse and salvation. We find ourselves alien and flung into an alien world and must make our lives un-alien. Hate can be one way of settling down. Violence can be, too. They are correct insofar as man believes them. But when I lived on the Other Side, a thought—or perhaps a spirit—came upon me. Who was I to use my interpretations as a means to destroy others? Killing others ruined their ability to discover meaning. That's why I abhor Xenon's commands for violence. Never will I share in the silencing of men and women. All must be free to interpret."

"That doesn't mean love is the absolute truth."

"Yes, quite right. That's why I conceded your earlier point. Man has no natural condition. He is interpretive—an empty vessel to be filled. He can not rest in emptiness but must fill the void with *some* interpretation. When we choose how to fill the vessel we make a new, natural condition for humanity. Some like Plato thought the soul was made of three parts. I say love is the essential property. And from the moment I recognize love as the good, it becomes good for all mankind and no one can take that away. At any rate, my vision of love is compatible with giving people room to discover their own path. That is more than can be said for Xenon's or the Republic's violence. No interpretation merits the death of others who refuse to hold it."

"Your sister agrees with you?" Glaucon asked.

"She is the one who taught me."

For the first time in a long repressed hibernation, Glaucon felt honest again. "Zemer, I'm glad I met you and Sophie today. You're both so different from the others I know. I feel like we understand one another completely."

Zemer's glasses flashed like mirrors. "See how we found the good in one another. I think we'll remain best friends after this experience, Glaucon. Even enemies cannot help but love one another when they face down their mortality together. Closeness in death reveals a heightened perception that is often difficult to duplicate in everyday life. This night has formed a communion between us which can never be broken."

The word "communion" made Glaucon remember going to temple with his mother to hear lectures on the Forms. "My mother, Melete, used to tell me something strange about friendship, Zemer."

"Really, what did she say?"

"She told me that each of us has a special light, like a star, burning for them in the Pure Land. Each light is unique. When two friends meet, their lights collide and create a powerful angel to protect them. This angel emanates strange powers over the friendship that emerges. But its power only exists when the friends are together. If a year passes without the friends seeing one another, then the angel dies and must be re-awakened with a blessing. My mother told me to find as many friends as possible. That way we could conjure an angel big enough to swallow the world in light."

"Why, that story's an absolute gem! I'm going to print that in the very first edition of our *Goetia Mirror*. Do you mind?"

"No, not at all. Although I don't believe in angels."

"Are you an atheist, then?"

"Excuse me?"

"Can one scoff at angels and believe in God?"

Glaucon thought about the question for a moment, remembering his heretical outburst earlier in the Hall of Records. "I suppose it depends on my mood," he finally said.

"Ah, yes, doesn't everything?" Zemer started laughing in charming self-deprecation. "We like to think we're so rational, that reason and logic is the function of man, but in reality, we probably use our passions more than any logical argument. David Hume went one step further when he opined: 'Reason is, and ought only be the slave of the passions.' However, I want to stop slavery in my soul altogether."

Glaucon found his mind resistant to Zemer. Thinking of his mother in temple earlier only stirred agonizing regret. He regretted speaking from the heart and suddenly hated his two new companions. A desire to turn them into the authorities returned, just so he could stop sinking in his chest. By his shoulder, though, he noticed Sophie studying him again. She had listened intently to their conversation. Sensing his distress, she inexplicably reached out and held Glaucon's hand. Her wide green eyes comforted in the dark. "Your mother was a good person, more than you know," she said softly. "Don't be sad. We're your friends now, and you can trust us. But tell me, Glaucon, can we trust you? Many wish to destroy us, including Prodicus. The *Goetia Mirror* will be dangerous. We need to know we can rely on you."

"I'll never betray either of you, Sophie," Glaucon said, half-truthful, half-laughing inside. "But, please, answer another question: How did you enter the Republic in the first place? What charm or power did you use? I thought I saw a lightning storm earlier that shattered the walls."

Zemer squeezed Glaucon's shoulder with intensity. "Tomorrow, my friend, if we're let out from this damp cavern, I'll show you a strange wonder."

II § 7 TWO FINAL GIFTS

"It's called a jinn," Zemer said, placing a fist-sized red orb in the palm of Glaucon's hand. The new friends stood at the Tenth Ward's eastern outskirts, beside a thick hydrolithian wall. A yellow delivery hovertruck, with the Metatron Tech logo, was waiting for them on the other side. As Zemer explained, the Fates provided schematics for the jinn to Ozbolt Enterprises three decades earlier. The weapon began as a prototype flux generator for the cogniscrambler, was made of red magnesia. It had secondary military purposes as well. Willing alone could send a condensed electromagnetic beam to scramble electronics. It was how he disabled the walls and tanks.

Glaucon marveled at the weapon's pulsing red light. "Gods, it's so cold," he said, "like holding a block of ice." It emanated a ruby mist which reminded him of being in the cogniscrambler for his teloscopy readings. Same sensation of clairvoyance.

Zemer said, "Yes, the jinn radiates such vast amounts of energy it requires an advanced cryogenic coolant system. I broke one open to experiment. Strange bloody liquid shot out. Nearly killed me."

"I've never seen such advanced technology. It looks so . . . alien."

"I think it's alive, too." Zemer motioned for Sophie to pull out another one from their bag. Strangest of all, when the two jinn came closer together, the orbs beat faster like hearts. "Use this to find us again when we separate," Zemer said. "It acts like a homing beacon. It's not perfect but will work better than anything else."

"You're giving me one of these things?" Glaucon asked amazed.

"Consider it a token of trust, but you must promise—never aim it at yourself or another human being."

"What happens if you aim the jinn at another person?"

Zemer glanced at Sophie apologetically. "The jinn heightens human perception. You see and hear terrible things, sometimes the future. It's usually fatal. The Fates had to build the cogniscrambler to water down its effects. Why don't you try disabling the wall?"

Glaucon tried to concentrate his mind. Thousands of voices whispered all together. They made him forget his position in space and time. His senses felt foggy, as if frosted over in a great psychic disturbance. He heard a scream and dropped the orb on the ground. "What was that?" he cried in panic.

Sophie looked angry. "You shouldn't play games like that, Brother. You know how long it takes to train."

"Pity," Zemer said walking toward the wall. "Let me show you how it's done." The hydrolith alloy flowed like quicksilver and bent easily under his touch. This was the metal's strength. The molecular structure could absorb even the direct impact of a Tesla pulse cannon. Zemer began to whisper:

"Never did I find a wall to like,
Nor any rampart unfit to strike,
Every parapet, like man, should fall,
Sick, infectious air is found in walls."

There was an immediate drop in air pressure. Goosebumps crawled up Glaucon's spine. Around Zemer's hand, raw, cold lightning bubbled and burst, skipped across the cement. Electricity whipped down the hydrolith, shattering eyecameras and motion sensors.

A thickly built metallurgist jumped from the hovertruck carrying a line of rope. Feeding it over the wall, Sophie scrambled up and cut away at the barbwire with a multibit plasmaknife. She jumped down on the other side.

"Ivan, I presume?" she asked, wiping her hands.

Ivan mumbled with a scowl: "Hecatia said only two were coming." He squeezed his round, inset eyes together conveying a reserved paranoia.

"He's with us," Sophie reassured him.

Sirens blared distantly. All jumped inside the truck and disappeared down the street.

Ivan circled the Eighth Ward for an hour before pulling up to his government issued duplex. The house was dimly lit with an industrial spartan openness. The smell of coffee—a primitive substitute for the enlightening taste of medijuice—filled the air. In the kitchen three women sat at a chrome levitable watching biohazard teams in green jumpsuits running by the window, pressing the padding of their gas masks to their faces. Some still drove metal lifts loaded with the dead.

Hecatia wore a patch on her technician's robes indicating she was a factory supervisor. An older woman, she possessed an upturned Socrates-like nose. She had been a guardian once but must've done something awful to work in the lower wards. Her face lit up when she saw the twins returned. "Gods, look how grown up you are," she exclaimed with joy kissing them on the cheeks. "Sophia, you are the image of Potone. I'm so thankful you survived the attack. The guardians claim rogue agents from Xenon released it, but we know that's untrue." She introduced two women next to her, both helots. One was named Aquila Naybah, slender with dark hair and Mediterranean eyes. She wore a business shirt with tight brown slacks. Hecatia explained she was a disenchanted marketing employee with Mira-Disney. The other woman, Terra Brandon, was Ivan's bondwife. "Ivan and Terra are both union organizers for the Industrial Workers' Federation," Hecatia explained. "They are part of the new recruitment effort in the lower wards. As you know, the union is growing, but it's suffered serious defeats."

"Treachery more like it," Ivan scowled. "Most of our leadership was fed to the Bull last August for petitioning the guardians to repeal the Labor Restoration Act. Damn thing forces us to either work or face the mind-stocks and public humiliation. The guardians sent an agent from ISHIM—that son of Dis, Patroclus—to discuss our petition. We explained to him the work was not too heavy or pay unkind, only that forcing us to work under threat of penalty bond was unjust. He had everyone arrested for illegal conspiracy and confiscated our materials. Called us big words: 'Idle, ungrateful calumniators.' Vowed to punish our bodies, and he surely did, as violently as fiery-eyed Ares. Never seen a young man so vicious."

"What do you expect from Prodicus' son?" Hecatia asked.

Glaucon desired above all else to tell these laborers they was mistaken, how Patroclus could be a kind and gentle friend, as loyal as the real cousin of Achilles. He rescued him as a boy when no one else but Zoe would do so. Courageous and stable, intelligent, pious, a noble, tough character, all the virtues of a guardian. If he behaved ruthlessly, surely it was for good cause against a true threat to the Republic.

Glaucon bit his tongue.

Sophie accepted a cup of coffee from Aquila and sat down at the table. She began the meeting. “Mr. Brandon,” she said, “the Continental Caucus shares your concerns about the ruthless tactics of the guardians and their Vinculum puppets. During the attack we smuggled in your union’s requested supplies. They are currently stored in a secret location in the Tenth Ward. We wish to express our solidarity with your efforts here.”

Ivan thanked her as she delicately sipped her coffee. “And the sonic carbines and lugh mines?” he inquired.

Sophie frowned. “The Iron Queen and Xenon—at this time—do not believe you possess the domestic support to overthrow your guardian masters. They offer no heavy weapons. I’m sorry.”

“And the Continental Caucus? What do they say?”

“Zemer and I speak directly for the Caucus as its special envoy. We agree with the generals’ overall assessment.”

Ivan looked angrily at Terra and rubbed his disheveled beard. “Then you are leaving us to drown.”

“No, Mr. Brandon . . .” there was slight agitation in Sophie’s voice, “we are providing you lifesaving tools to continue fashioning your raft. As you admitted yourself, your numbers have been decimated. You need to reach a certain critical mass of popular support before we can proceed further. Such support is likely to be less forthcoming now after the recent gas attack. We must be careful; this is a most dangerous hour. One untimely movement could jeopardize years of revolutionary work. Hecatia has provided the Continental Caucus in St. Louis with a list of several groups we’d like to patronize while we’re here.” Sophie snapped her fingers. Zemer placed a piece of stained paper in front of Ivan. “I trust you and Aquila will help us contact them with the strictest secrecy.”

Ivan examined the paper resignedly. “One of our members created a coded backchannel in the symsyst routers at Worldlink. I will contact these groups myself on the Caucus’ behalf. The Industrial Workers’ Federation thanks you and your brother for your time. We look forward to a fruitful alliance.”

Sophie smiled and stood up abruptly, shook hands with everyone. Lunch was served ten minutes later. A simple recipe of rice and vegetables, but Glaucon had never been happier to see food in his life. He ate almost nothing since leaving Heliopolis, only a powdered-protein-turned-milky-paste in the gas shelter.

After the meal, Terra laid a thick Tavli board on the table and asked Glaucon to sit and play with her. While he moved his white checker stones, Glaucon watched Hecatia, Ivan, and Sophie talking conspiratorially in the corner.

"You work for Mira-Disney, too?" Terra probed Glaucon.

"Yes."

"Did you ever meet Aquila?"

"No. I mostly keep to myself."

"A wise decision, but one that leads to unhappiness, I'm afraid. You've not been selected for the marriage draft?"

"The Fates have yet to select a suitable partner for me," Glaucon lied.

"Ivan and I were married when we were both seventeen."

"Is that so?" Glaucon gave a look of surprise. "Quite young to be bonded and given a house."

"I can remember being frightened to death the night before, wondering what I was going to do. I could barely breathe through the ceremony. We did not speak at all on the ride back home, or when we sat alone in this house. I began crying miserably. Ivan finally left me and purchased this Tavli set to cheer me up. We came to know one another over this board, talking late into the evening. That is why Tavli will always remain close to my heart. Ivan may appear quick tempered, but he's a good man and a good husband. I begrudge the Fates many things but not their taste in men. Your friends can trust him. We're thankful for your efforts. We just fear further repression."

Glaucon finished the game and walked outside to sit on the porch. It was a little after three. What had happened? How had he stumbled on such a nest of vipers? Not only did he find the lost guardian children, but he discovered two union leaders, a Mira-Disney spy, and a turncoat factory owner, all at the root of a wide network of anarchist rebellion. Even if he told the proper ISHIM authorities, no one would believe his trip down this Alician rabbit hole.

Glaucon heard the door open and slam shut.

Sophie walked outside disturbing his thoughts. "What's the matter?" she asked.

"I need to check in with my work phylark," Glaucon said, scanning the concrete horizon. "I'll be punished if we don't return. Will we be heading back to the Tenth Ward soon?"

"Probably tonight. You'll come back to us soon won't you, Glaucon?" Her voice rang flat, but it contained a hidden hopefulness.

"I don't know, Sophie. That depends."

"On what?"

Glaucon turned toward her. "Whether or not you want me to come back?"

Sophie struggled to prevent a smile. "You'll come back as sure as spring."

"You seem pretty sure. How do you know?"

"Because how will you bring this back to me." Sophie removed her amber pendant and gently wrapped his fingers around it.

Glaucon stood speechless. "I can't accept this."

"Consider it . . . a token of my new affection. Please don't make me hunt you down to get it back."

Sophie slapped his back awkwardly and re-entered the duplex.

When Glaucon finally returned to his cloister that evening he lay on his wooden bed poking the hanging amber jewel with his finger. It frightened him much less than the frosty jinn sitting on his nightstand. Sometimes, he swore the jinn whispered unspeakable things. He tried to sleep but twisted in his sheets in a fit of longing. To quiet his inner turmoil, he tried reading Book VII of the *Republic*. No use. He couldn't concentrate. Every time he closed his eyes he saw Sophie's face and moving relentless images congealed into uncomfortable beads of sweat.

He stood up, paced around his room. He noticed with horror how his *tetractys* glowed bright indigo. "You will be bewitched by desire. Desire will devour you," he remembered Zoe's warning. Fearing for his body's health in such a crazed fit of desire, he rushed to the communicator intercom on the wall, scanned his *tetractys*, and dialed the Slimetide Rolodex.

An ethereal projection of a female operator spit on the floor, greeting him. She said, "Glaucon, Tenth Grade Initiate, ISHIM Number 662346. How may I assist you, my sun?"

"Zoe will surely kill me for waking her at this hour," Glaucon moaned. "Probably not her slimetide period anyway." He pounded the wall wondering whom to send for.

What about that helot woman from the park? the voice offered as a solution.

"I don't know. . . ."

Who wouldn't want to take slimetide with you? You're so-o-o brilliant, so-o-o handsome. Your fair hair means you're touched by the gods. The helot wants you to call her; there was desire in those lusty eyes. She was sighing for Eros with every word.

"Her bondhusband will surely be angry."

So what? When has that ever stopped you? Forget him. He is an insect! Your pleasure matters more than his. Wasn't her flesh pleasing? Didn't those long legs tempt caresses?

"Ye-e-s-s!"

Then take her to your bed.

Glaucon licked his lips and spoke rapidly into the communicator: "Please . . . Operator, scan the Heliopolis entry and exit catalogue for a phylark visitor from the Fifth Ward. Her family is staying here on leave. I met her a few days ago in Hesper Park and did not catch her name. She may've already gone home."

"One moment. Searching, my grace. . . . Marion Greyzer. She is scheduled to leave in two days. Shall I send her up to you?"

"Hmmmm. Maid Marion." Glaucon licked his lips again. "Yes, please have the helot properly bathed and brought to me in one hour. Preferably, she should be dressed in a silk gown hanging a little lower than the knees. Her hair should be up. Not too much makeup please."

"Sandals?"

"It doesn't really matter. This is an emergency."

Glaucon went to his sink and swung open the medicine cabinet. Drawing out two *erosic* pills, he plopped both in his mouth and washed them down with a full glass of water. He returned to wait on his bed and began to hallucinate.

Far off, a quivering pinecone forest bled into a spiral of light. Cymbals crashed around his ears. The last thing he remembered before losing consciousness to a state of pyrotechnic arousal was staring dreamily into the amber. He wondered if he should ever return it to its master.

RESTORATION AB AETERNO: Separating the Metals

"Society is diseased," said General Abaris Hythloday, "and I have the cure. Men are in a prison, but I have the master key. The keys are the Forms, and now you can open the doors. Hold the world in your hands and protect our luminous harmony."

Cheers from the graduating class of the Academy erupted on the deck of their ship: "Harrah! Harrah! A hundred hurrahs! Sing and cavort in harmony!" Mortarboard caps tossed carefree in the air as the evening sun melted, sending colors along the ocean. Students drank and sang under the stars. In the morning, the war-trireme *Concordia* skimmed back to fair-mounted Heliopolis over the surface of the azure waters of Safer Bay, rowing with mechanical oars through Ozbolt's prototype suncatchers.

Three classes of guardian templar sang as one:

"We rebuilt the world!
Who are our enemies?
We pondered the Forms!
Could Truth ever leave us?
Heliopolis gathers life again!
Would any man try and stop us?"

The new class docked and marched through the busy construction on the mountain. Blue banners and confetti littered the streets. Steel beams were still being lifted into place to support the rising First Temple. Musicians danced with Orphean flutes, little boys flew kites, and anyone wishing a kiss could have one. A fresh copy of the little white *Republic* went to new graduates.

"Read it like words from the Demiurge," General Hythloday shouted wrapped in white garments. "It's our book of creation, our governing lamp!"

"Why wait for a heaven you can build on earth?" exclaimed the crowds. "We love our general. We love our Forms. Saint Plato is our prophet."

In those early days no bans prevented traveling, and the three estates intermixed freely. The helots finished plowing their fields and kneading bread, closed down their workshops, and packed away their machinery to march with the new guardian class to the top of Heliopolis. Every soul locked arms marveling at the new nanoalchemy breakthroughs of Ozbolt. True, the diamond dodecahedron was not yet birthed, but the First Temple of Reason was still a sight to behold. Imagine, happy reader, feet marching in unison to an awaiting brick temple shaped like a ship's hull. Imagine young

Republicampers waving blue flags with the *Hands-of-God*, singing freedom anthems. What wonderful days those were. And on a colorful podium filled with microphones, General Hythloday hoisted his white book in the air like a sacred tablet.

"I give the Republic her new guardians," he shouted overjoyed, fireworks blasting the sky.

No one remembered the fallen United States, Russia, or China anymore. The Age of Aporia was forgotten, and the Age of Reason shined like the Form of the Good.

Down below, the only man refusing to attend such ceremonies was the grey-eyed Sextus. He cursed the garish racket and his decision to follow his brother. At first he'd thought the fanaticism would die down, but the insane society kept singing. Hythloday asked him to live on Heliopolis, but he had refused; his brother was possessed by Plato and behaved as someone else. The brother he loved was gone. Now Sextus only planted crops, resolving to find happiness in exile from the mountain.

Each spring, the renewed earth gladdened Sextus' spirit. Nuclear war had not destroyed the soil, only contaminated it; once two inches of surface soil were removed, seeds sprouted, life returned. Awe blew over him like wind on the wheat. He enjoyed tracing the growing season and laughing with the other farmers at harvest, sharing labor. Earth and labor calmed and soothed. The sun and Heliopolis were too abrasive, too bright, too one sided to fulfill his inner passions.

It is safe to say Sextus was never aware of the secret plot of his brother.

The frantic guardian ceremony finished as always; but this time something was different. Hythloday still held his white book in the air demanding attention. Silence consumed the crowd.

"What more will he say?" a helot youngling questioned his father. "Will the general speak once more?" asked another. Awe-struck eyes waited for a new Sermon on the Mount.

General Hythloday cleared his throat and spoke with disquieting tones: "You know, there is more to our Republic than pomp and ceremonies. The Republic also requires much sacrifice."

"We'll give our lives for the Republic," the exuberant crowds promised on the grass.

Hythloday sat unmoved. "You see, my children, we are all equal but . . . well, we have different roles."

The families of helots, auxiliaries, and guardians nestled closer together under their wise leader.

"What would happen if the feet suddenly started trying to see or the arms began stretching out to hear? Could the fingers ever hope to reason?"

Not a peep came from the crowd. All were pondering his intent.

"The Restoration is a revolution," Hythloday continued, "and sometimes revolutions lose their way. They lose their way because people don't follow the plan. I have great fears, my children, our degradation is at hand. We have guardians, but they don't resemble the Form of Guardian in our book. Guardians, soldiers, and helots remain . . . intimate with others not of their status. They hold families together and tie themselves down with desire. It's like feet crawling to the face to do the eye's work." Hythloday shook his copy of the *Republic* madly in the air. "We'll never keep the Form of Justice in our Republic—if we can even call it such today—without first purging ourselves of this unspeakable sin: unholy, unsolicited, unchecked, unmonitored intermixing. What does the *Republic* say in verse 433a?"

The crowds flipped through their scriptures, reading timorously: " 'Justice is doing one's own work and not meddling with what isn't one's own.' "

"Then why, stubborn children, do you huddle together in such unholy union?" Hythloday questioned exasperated. "No, no, no; this won't do at all. We must separate ourselves for the good of the whole. Justice *is* separation. For this reason, after today, there shall be no more mixing of the metals without strict supervision. Helots will only be able to stay on the third ring of Heliopolis and the coast. They won't be allowed to move freely and are to be blocked into units for their own good. We are instituting a New Ward System to better protect the integrity of our Republic and provide a clean, stable environment for all classes to flourish."

"What?" shouted the crowd, "but we built Heliopolis together!"

"My daughter's a guardian," said another. "How will I see her?"

You won't, thought Hythloday, *and rightly so.*

"This isn't what we planned!" the crowd rose frenzied.

Hythloday threw his book down from the pedestal and shouted into the microphone: "Woe! Woe unto you comfortable Republicans! Ten thousand woes!"

Helots thought the mountain was shattering.

Abaris Hythloday cried, "What am I to do with this unbelieving generation? Ye den of vipers, this is exactly what we planned. The Restoration must continue, and it will be successful. We have a small, intelligent, skilled, benevolent, reasonable class to make decisions so we don't crash upon a quay."

It pained General Hythloday greatly—chipped his gold insides—but he signaled his most loyal officer auxiliaries to raise their rifles. Now was the moment for which history waited.

A woman in burned overalls from smelting pushed her way to the front of the crowd. "You can't do this, Hythloday," she shouted. "Who went and made you philosopher-king?"

"We did," several young guardians defended, jumping up near the woman, muscling her back. "We voted this afternoon on the *Concordia.* We decided General Hythloday is the closest any man has come to glimpsing the Form of the Good. Only *he* knows the truth. There is no one better to lead us."

"I thought we'd all vote," said the woman, sweating, "like a democracy."

"*Not self-rule, but rule by reason and the reasonable*," came the reply. "The reasonable vote. The helots produce. Don't meddle in others' work."

There was much grumbling from the helots. This isn't how it was done before. They looked to their brave soldiers for protection. But the majority of the auxiliaries, being spirited in nature and craving the higher purpose they learned on Stratos, sided with their new guardian-king. Visions of restoration licked their eyes. The spring of youth and promised happiness burnt within them, and they yearned an end to peace (yes, even a home beside a tyrant's fire); yet they knew Hythloday was no tyrant and all was for the best.

Raising their rifles, they motioned for the crowd to depart. When some refused, they fired on them, drove them back to their wards like a devouring falling star.

All the while Hythloday bellowed, "Cleansing is needed to quell the unbelievers. Disloyal sensualist roaders wish to restore the Age of Aporia. They wish to kill our Republic. We mustn't let them. They must be stopped. Guardians, auxiliaries, protect the greedy helots from themselves."

When Sextus discovered his brother's trickery later that day, he choked in fury. He dashed shirtless through the wheat fields to the coast and found his rusting motor boat, scavenged from the old Houston marina. Throwing off the ropes, he blasted out to sea. He made it half the distance before the Auxiliary Navy splashed to his port side.

"Subject, you have one minute to turn around before we blast your boat out of the water," they warned.

The grey-eyed Sextus nearly tripped off his boat, enraged. "You bastards aren't going to tell me what to do. I'm going to see my brother, Abaris, and talk some sense into him. This farce has gone on long enough."

Bullets sprayed his deck and nearly killed the motor.

"Turn around or we'll sink your vessel, Sextus," warned a man with a thick mustache, cigar almost falling from his mouth.

Sextus circled his ship around as fast as he could and cursed the soldiers back to shore. The patrol boat sped off laughing cruelly in the wind.

Back in the factory communities, mothers, sons, brothers, friends were shrieking. Many turned to drink and fell into each other's arms. "What will happen to us?" they moaned. Some of the auxiliaries sent to protect the helots even promised a return to the way things were "once Guardian-King Hythloday finally forged the Form of Justice on the Earth." Nevertheless, Sextus knew a return to the old ways impossible. He resolved to leave. Throwing some stale bread, a half rotten orange, and a water canteen into a knapsack, he left his home and stopped at a nearby shack cobbled together from the iron scraps of Heliopolis. His beloved Michelle hid inside, crouched in a corner. Her father had been an auxiliary.

"They shot him," she said, "in the back, when he broke ranks. They're executing anyone suspected of being a sensualist roader. I don't even know what that means. He was a major. He loved the Republic. Why would they do this?" Sextus held her light body closely and kissed her temples. "We're going to leave this place, my sweet one. Things will only get worse from here. Some are saying this is the worst, but I know history better."

The door behind them swung open. Soldiers entered the house. *How long have they been following me?* he wondered.

They commanded in unison: "The Most High Vicar of Reason, Guardian-King Hythloday, requires an audience. You will come with us."

Sextus cursed, "Tell that fool he can come here if he wants to see me—"

Punches cast him to the floor. Sextus vainly shouted to stop as they dragged him away.

As he drove up the long Bridge of Understanding to the temple mount, he became numb with grief. Outside, the lights—which once aided nighttime work—became newfound power to continue the purge. Corpses lay fresh on the ground. Auxiliaries stuffed helots over chain-link fences. The Auxiliary Engineering Core, along with Ozbolt Enterprises, strategically placed concrete barriers. Sleepless multitudes hung on fences hungry and beaten.

Only periodic gunfire broke the silence on the way to Heliopolis. Sextus was finally dragged to a warehouse. Hythloday sat around a cardboard table with three guardians and Dr. Zosimos Ozbolt.

The table was littered with photographs and biography summaries, as if hit by a hungry storm. The names Joseph Carnegie, Nathaniel Mellon, and Cato Kellogg were visible—the first members of the Vinculum Cartel.

Dr. Ozbolt explained his economic model: "We need a system within a system. If we can construct a class of leaders within the helot estate, the fight for honors and financial position should distract them from pursuing more unwanted avenues, like challenging the guardians."

Hythloday asked, "But these families you'd prop up, are they loyal?"

"Oh yes, see here, the Mellons are especially loyal. Patriotic, too. My cameras watched their children behave most admirably at the Republicamps. The youngest child—William, I believe—wrote a patriot play for the Knights of Cephalus last year. Joseph Carnegie is a good choice as well. But really, as long as you control the military (and they don't receive any money to be bought) there shouldn't be any problems. Just veto any Vinculum action you dislike."

Sextus kicked over the table. "What the hell, Dr. Ozbolt! You're not a guardian. Why are you helping this . . ." he paused to look at the shell of his brother, "thing?"

The pale doctor replied, "Elementary. The Vicar of Reason offered me the First Ward and a future scientific paradise on Heliopolis. How could I, as a dignified scientist, refuse? I gladly concede philosophy is the foundation—and better—of the natural sciences." He nodded to Hythloday who beamed like a child discovering a lost tooth.

"No, I see things perfectly, Doctor," Sextus growled. "Although you work on complicated equations, you're not very complicated. I think you're smaller than your nanomachines. You crave power like everyone else. What happened to your ideals? Science was supposed to liberate man from superstition, not enslave him to tyranny."

Dr. Ozbolt pretended to yawn.

Across the table, Hythloday gaped at his brother's misbehavior. *Why is the fool embarrassing me in our moment of glory?* he thought. *He won't become a guardian when I ask and now he insults my friends.* "Come walk with me, Brother," he finally requested, not wanting to lose any more face. The two men left the warehouse into the starry night.

Clouds covered the moon outside. Halo-shaped street lights lit a path to the cliffs. "We have accomplished so much in so little time," said Guardian-King Hythloday trying to put his brother at ease. "I know this has been rather fast for the helots, but only because it was necessary. I have much planned for the guardians, too. I want perfect sexual equality among us. You should have heard the others when I suggested women wrestle naked with men in the gymnasium. Some said I'd lost my mind, but I was adamant about achieving

Saint Plato's dream. You see, I want women, like men, to strip and wear the virtue of excellence instead of clothes."

"Stop quoting scripture, you lunatic! I don't care if you have the women start sprouting cocks!"

Hythloday looked surprised. "I thought the mental image of women naked would please your helot sensibilities."

"My mind's not depraved like yours."

"You don't want equality?"

"Not equality from a book, not equality for a few. Auxiliaries shot at me and terrorize the people. They murdered my girlfriend's father."

"*Your* girlfriend. How helot. Excuse me, we have no possessions here. The word 'mine' and 'your' are completely meaningless. I only think in terms of 'our.' "

"Yes, you only possess the Form of the Good."

"Exactly, and like the sun, we all share its light."

"Why do I even bother talking to you?" Sextus paused. He needed to argue from a different direction to make any headway. "Abaris, I've known you since I was a boy. Please stop this, as a gift for your brother, for the good times we shared in our youth. Tell the auxiliaries to let our people go."

"Never," Hythloday's voice cracked under the revealed moon. "I'll never let them go. I'd rather die. We are all symbiotic beings, Sextus. There can be no guardians without helots, and no helots without guardians."

"That's exactly my point."

"Would you, as my brother, ask me to rip out my eyes like Oedipus?"

"If it meant saving mankind, yes. If it meant alleviating their suffering, yes."

"Then you are a fool. Suffering is a false illusion when you consider the Forms."

"Suffering is the only reality I know. As I said many times in our fallout shelter, the Forms are a myth. If Plato came back, he'd spit in your face."

Hythloday seethed angry. "You've either become a father of lies or ignorance. Plato's political program required a rigid class system with strong barriers between the rulers and the ruled. Reason, through logic and the sword, must govern the money-lovers and war-hungry without being tainted by them. That was his idea! I'm just carrying it out." Hythloday tossed his brother aside and stormed back to the dimly lit warehouse. "Wait and see what I have in store for your precious helots down below," he smiled wickedly. "Plato advocated taking possession of children and liquidating their parents to establish his perfect state, to 'free them from the ethos' of their past society; I will do just that. No words can describe my adulation for Ozbolt's *device*. First it shall cull the sensualist roaders. Then it shall cull the old who remember, and children will forget. Books will be changed, and the old ways will die. I will have a blank canvass to paint the Form of Justice."

Weeks passed. The moon became a continuous agonizing cycle, similar to the mechanical work of the helots below. The Vinculum Cartel consolidated under family managers; work became dull and slavish. Each produced a product for Heliopolis, but none could freely travel to the summit. Most thought the worst finally over.

Then, one summer morning, the Bull came.

An enormous crate appeared churning on the *Concordia*. Ropes and pulleys hoisted it into the air and placed it on the sandy beach. Guardian-King Hythloday, clothed in gold embroidered robes, jumped from the ship twirling his rope belt like a heavenly lasso. Eleven other guardians followed like land-starved pilgrims. They urged the haulers from Atum Construction Company in the Seventh Ward to use their crowbars on the crate. Slowly, a fifteen meter brazen bull emerged. With hesitant curiosity, the helots stared at the reddish tint. A door was hollowed out on the side, and a control box with round knobs like a grill protruded on one leg. Boxes of incense were unloaded from the ships.

"What kind of contraption is this?" the people asked. "Is it a present or a statue? Was it built by Dr. Zosimos Ozbolt?" Questions twinkled in the air like stars, and even those still working stopped their assignments to investigate. So intense was the degree of inspection, no one noticed the bound prisoners being unloaded off the ship.

"Dr. Ozbolt, are you sure the Bull will sing?" asked the guardian-king, his voice pregnant with anticipation.

The nanoscientist frowned. "As I informed you earlier, the acoustic design for the mouth was difficult to construct. A bull's billowing roar is challenging to replicate. Further, we lacked the proper . . . subjects to test the voice conversion."

"No matter, we'll see shortly, won't we? As for the incense, are you sure it'll cover the smell? I don't want any foul stenches spoiling our feasting."

"Our party should be fine, sir. Here, try some of my new Ceto-Cola."

Purple liquid spilled into Hythloday's glass.

"Most delicious," Hythloday remarked.

Dr. Ozbolt nodded. "The tonic will nourish your aggression for the condemned."

"Indeed, I can already feel disgust rising in my throat." Guardian-King Hythloday turned to a group of auxiliaries dressed in their new, pressed, green uniforms. *They look so handsome*, thought Hythloday, *just as I imagined—no, as Plato imagined.* "You may begin loading the social parasites inside," he commanded. " 'Any violation of the laws should be punished with death, and the most severe punishments.' "

Even the prisoners standing near the ocean did not know what to make of the Bull. Sea lapped their legs, and their arms hurt from handcuffs.

"All of them, sir?" asked the soldier skeptically.

"Try two for now," advised Hythloday, and he thought to himself, *I can already see we'll have to build a bigger one*.

Gruff hands grabbed two prisoners by the front and led them to the open door of the Bull. One was nearly forty years old. "Make sure to disrobe them, too," shouted Hythloday possessed by his Ceto-Cola. "No point throwing away perfectly good clothes. Makes sure it goes to charity. That is our Fourth Virtue, after all."

The shaking men were disrobed in front of the crowd and tried to cover their nakedness. Before they could utter a cry for help, auxiliaries pushed them inside the Bull. The door shut and the metal hatch spun tight. One of the soldiers, a young, shaved, healthy looking fellow went over to the knobs and turned them to maximum heat.

Plates of genetically modified food—steaming pork, briquette, roast turkey legs, potato salad, pinto beans, chicken fried steak—were presented to the helots at the Bull. They washed their barbeque down with bubbling Ceto-Cola. Some ate nervously, waiting to see what would happen. After ten minutes, roaring song erupted from the Bull's mouth. Smoking incense left smells of sandalwood and jasmine.

The Bull burned yellow hot.

Guardian-King Hythloday moved his table back from the oppressive heat. His "traitorous sensualist roaders" screamed tortuously inside the metal, but no one in the world could tell, for the Bull billowed perfectly.

"To the Bull that sings," Hythloday said raising his goblet. When no one responded, he became angry. "To the Bull that sings," he repeated more forcefully.

Finally the crowd echoed back, "To the Bull that sings." Ceto-Cola soon made them wish drunken curses on the sufferers.

Guardian-King Hythloday sniffed his glass like a wine connoisseur. "And may our love for the Forms burn as hot."

BOOK III

VESSELS OF LOVE AND STRIFE

III § 1 A WHIRLWIND GAMBIT

"Thank you for coming on such short notice, Patroclus," Director Sinon of ISHIM said. "Your father demanded your attendance. It couldn't be helped."

The muscular scion of Prodicus waited in the Logoset Assembly Dome. He had been admiring a Baroque-style portrait of Guardian-King Hythloday on the wall. Knee bent in supplication, head bowed low, the sun shone its graces on the great philosopher like a waterfall of light.

How could our city's founder birth rebels like Xenon? Patroclus wondered.

Sinon didn't ask about his thoughts. Instead, the fish-faced director placed his glimmering *tetractys* against a scanner on the opposite wall. Musical notes chimed from acoustic nodules resembling sirens' song, and two elevator doors slid open.

Sinon said, "I know it must've been difficult to step away from Ephor Yannis. He has a rather paranoid nature. One of his many flaws."

Patroclus stepped aboard the glass elevator, leaving the Logoset's emerald halls. "In our times, my sun, it's good to be paranoid. Those who do not listen for the black cat's bell will be eaten. Yannis suspects I'm there to spy."

"Yannis suspects many things, but suspicion is not knowledge. Be more careful. The Kabiri Circle awaits your findings."

The elevator descended rapidly at an angle through the layered crust of Heliopolis. Unease flooded the tiny space. Patroclus felt exhausted. He towered over Sinon and disliked his friendliness. No camaraderie in ISHIM, especially from its director. The friendlier, the deadlier; he always knifed you with a smile.

Nonchalantly, Sinon asked, "How are you enjoying work with the lawspeakers and quaestors?"

Patroclus spotted ulterior motives. "If you're asking do I feel a sense of satisfaction from the work, I suppose I do. I like to audit criminal trials."

"Oh? Why is that?"

"Because of the historic continuity, Director. Man has not stopped punishing man since the beginning of the world. It is good to be part of something larger than yourself."

"Do you think the accused deserve to be punished?"

"We all deserve to be punished—don't we, Director?—in one way or another."

"You sound like your father." Sinon watched the passing layers of cement. Every few seconds, a ring of light surrounded them followed by hushed darkness.

Descending to the sea floor reminded Patroclus of entering into the profane outskirts of his genetic code. He alone of all Prodicus' children was recognized (almost to the point of scandal). Such recognition gave room for pride, but also responsibility and shame. He was cut off from the brotherhood of Heliopolis, could never call the other inhabitants 'brother' or 'sister' with any seriousness. No one looked at him with the concern of sibling love, only fear.

"I sat in on an interesting murder case two weeks ago," Patroclus commented, passing time.

"Really?"

"A helot male from the Third Ward stabbed another in broad daylight."

"Whatever for?"

"Allegedly, the victim was harassing his bondwife. He was unhappy the Fates issued marriage draft papers to the defendant and not to him. The victim and wife were former lovers."

"I should've known. What slaves to appetite! Helots always crave more. What do they care who they live with? They could still be lovers."

"Yes, but queerly, the defendant wanted children with *this particular* woman."

"A strange desire. But alas . . . the breeding program."

"The poor man drove over drunk on several bottles of molybeer. Started screaming in the front yard, hollered obscenities against the Fates. He felt dishonored and wanted to talk things out. Witnesses say he cried distraught, grabbed a wooden swing, and pounded it against a maple tree."

"What a sight."

"And the fat husband—"

"Fat?"

"Yes, he *was* rather large. We're charging him with that, too. Failed to keep up with the Nutrition Control Committee's prescribed couch-tornado tablets. Anyway, he ordered the victim to get off his lawn or he'd kill him. You know what the other helot said? 'You wouldn't dare!' So, the fat man just walked casually into the kitchen, opened up a drawer, pulled out a steak knife, then walked back outside and stuck it the other fellow's belly. He gloated, 'Dare me again, you bastard!'—isn't that poetic?"

The director's nose wrinkled. "Well, we have them on so many drugs one wonders how helots function at all. Sentenced him to the Bull, I imagine?"

"What else? He was too fat to be a gladiator and too ugly for the Slimetide Rolodex (except the Fetish Circuit)."

"Did you feel sympathy for him?"

"I've wondered whether judgment or sympathy would've been more appropriate in his situation."

"And?"

"Death for him is not enough."

The creaking elevator halted. Sinon and Patroclus walked into a room with cubicles. Ever since the iama-B attacks, ISHIM headquarters rumbled with activity, secret reports, and anonymous tips. All Miantgast Prison interrogation rooms were stuffed to capacity. Prisoners sat naked, chained, hooded, knees shaking and faint. Some sprawled limp on the iron ground paralyzed in the mind-stocks. Smells could be overpowering; urine spilled like soup on the floor. Sinon motioned for Patroclus to look through one cell's narrow windows.

The Deprivation Room: rows of naked human bodies piled on top of one another in the mind-stocks, like stacks of hide leather, isolated from sight and sound.

Sinon pointed at the poor wretches with businesslike detachment. "European monarchs marveled at their ability to extract confessions from those disloyal to their regimes. The Rack, thumbscrews, the Tongue Tearer—what physical torment! But I tell you truthfully, no man's talked faster or cried as deeply as those separated completely from their senses for a month. Psychology shatters like a fragile bronze plate. They regress to a state of infancy and spit up stones of truth. They forget who they are and what they're trying to hide. Fresh wax to reconstruct proper subjects. Psychological torment is the Wheel for the future."

"Certainly," Patroclus mouthed with a shudder.

A bony second grade neophyte interrupted them, screeching behind his chrome cubicle: "Sir, another report. Printing houses in the First Ward, Ozbolt's jurisdiction."

"What imitation was found?"

"*Light in August*. F-Faulkner—whoever that is. Should I dispatch another unit to smoke out the imitators?"

Sinon brushed off the zealous advocacy with a hand-flick. "Not now, Markarios. Archon business. Don't call out auxiliaries until I return. Thank gods it's not Maya Angelou again. Honestly!"

At the end of the office, Sinon raised his *tetractys* by a clearance sensor. Another vaulted door belched open. They marched past a labyrinth of hydrolith airlocks and fluorescent rooms. *Like winding through a submarine*, Patroclus noted. Water leaked over the narrow walkways and spinning pumps. Man's artificial walls pushed against the ocean's weight.

Sinon's gill-like cheeks puckered annoyed. "Every time we get a call from the neighborhood watch offices, Ares-headed initiates like Makarios become distraught. I tell them to get their facts straight before they leap to conclusions and hurl lightning-spears at the wards, but they ignore me. If they had their way, we'd be creating kangaroo courts and shooting every helot in the back of the neck."

Patroclus laughed dryly. "Don't you know, Director? Mass judgment can become a pastime in the wake of disasters like iama-B. By making chaos man shows his mastery over chaos. When gas falls, the divide between lawful killing and murder dissolves into air."

"Just like your father, a true philosopher-king, Patroclus. But, as you know, cruel acts must flash like knives in the dark: be well-laid, quick, and cease lest the people remember, not committed over weeks. Murder has its purposes, but wasteful extravagance is unsound. Controlled violence and bluffing is the ISHIM way."

"You're correct, of course, my grace."

A final door opened into a disk-shaped sanctum at the bottom of the Gulf of Mexico. Overlooking remnants of the burned city of Houston, schools of fish swam between man-made reefs. Sinon and Patroclus walked to a silver podium and inserted their hands. The podium shook, lit like fire, and lifted up through a hole in the ceiling, passing three-meter-long levilamps to a conference room.

Robes rustled noisily in the auditorium—a non-public meeting of the Logoset, of the Kabiri Circle's leadership. Even Leonida—the Polemarch of Stratos—attended clothed in gold armor, with a spiked pickelhaube helmet accentuated by golden boar's tusks. Prodicus, guardian-king of men, officiated from a sapphire throne next to the ocean window, golems licking his feet. An avis sat at his right hand, razor beak twitching. ALETHEIA glowed blue over the grotesque machinery's eye.

"Just in time," Prodicus declared. "General Argus was about to begin his military briefing."

Argus jerked to attention. The grey-bearded auxiliary was dressed in full Stratos regalia: blue *Hands-of-God* armbands; leaf medals; a segmented line that streaked across the left side of his combat uniform. Unlike many soldiers, Argus held no superstitious fears of the Kabiri. They'd promoted him, after all, showing they were not only seers but seizers of preferable futures.

"Yes, my Vicar. No time to waste." General Argus' voice was thick as his face. "Financial losses incurred are difficult to calculate. Damage to the outer wall. Both the Eighth and Ninth Wards suffered serious structural damage. The Vinculum Stock Market fell five hundred and sixty points, translating to six billion orichalcum lost. If we include clean up costs and medical expenses, then, overall, fourteen billion orichalcum is probable."

Archon Hypatia of the Third Ward, an older woman with silver hair, hurled papers in the air, gasping that such numbers were unacceptable.

Manos, the yellow robed archon of the Sixth Ward, pounded his podium in agreement. "We've been rebuilding this city for the past ten years, for what?—to lose economic stability to the gas again? What's the point investing in expensive gas detection systems if they fail to protect us from Watcher attack?"

General Argus looked at the ground waiting for Manos to finish his ignoble tirade. He continued: "Beyond the losses to the wall, the entertainment and communication industries have collapsed. Worldlink and Mira-Disney are unlikely to survive without guardian intervention."

"More bail-outs?" Manos groaned.

"No, Sire—loans. Substantial loans are necessary. I've already taken the liberty to procure several willing Cheque Giorgio banks in the Fourth Ward."

Matemeo Fairbanks, CEO for Mira-Disney, and Cornelius Carnegie of Worldlink hopped to their feet on a granite balcony. "We're too big to fail," they whined mournfully into their microphones. Carnegie bemoaned wasted efforts manufacturing extra digitele *pangu* processing cubes. Fairbanks cried vociferous: "If we don't receive backup funding, we'll be bankrupt within the year. We'll barely recover *with* government assistance. Pl . . . ea . . . se. . . .," Fairbanks drew out the word for extra effect and placed his grubby merchant palms on the balcony railing. "Mira-Disney Tower is still covered in toxic gas residue. Some laborers refuse to work, citing obscure labor protection statutes. Learned about them from the unions and that revolutionary magazine, the *Goetia Mirror*. They disturb the workers' minds with mischief. No advertisements are being made—we're recycling the old ones. Rebels are smuggling our employees to the Other Side. You must do something or—"

The droning complaints made Prodicus lose his temper. "Enough sniveling. Sit down!" he commanded. "Do not think me unaware of the problems facing the wards. You forget your place. Petty businessmen don't make demands to guardians but speak only with permission. You should be grateful I even allowed representatives of the Vinculum to attend. Perhaps we can replace you with managers more . . . effective?"

The avis peered hungrily at the two businessmen.

"We apologize, Sire; that won't be necessary," Carnegie said burrowing into his suit like a gerbil. He forced the frozen Matemeo Fairbanks to sit.

Prodicus continued: "Hypatia's policy recommendations are appropriate at this point. We will reduce the budgets of Shennong Fooderies, Seven Seas, and Ra-Busto Energy by ten percent and shift resources to the Tenth, Ninth, and Eighth Wards for reconstruction. This will reassure the Vinculum and the helots of our commitment to stability."

"What about Ozbolt Enterprises?" asked Manos, lisps pursed in exasperation. "Schizoeon and the First Ward could stand to lose a little fat."

"No, Ozbolt resources shall remain at current levels. The same goes for Atum Construction Company in the Seventh Ward. Full funding is needed to complete Levantra on schedule. If you want, take more from Shennong Fooderies. We have fewer helots to feed anyway."

An uncomfortable silence.

Patroclus felt an open and terrifying awe for Prodicus and his fathomless calculations. He missed nothing, not even the benefits to be derived from helot suffering.

Mighty Creon, Seventh Ward Archon, asked from a corner, "General Argus, now that Prodicus mentions it, what *were* helot casualties?"

Are helot deaths such an afterthought? Patroclus wondered.

General Argus reported: "According to recent surveys from the Asclepius Medical Institute, the Republic incurred 1,156 deaths. Another 2,000 are likely to die from bio-metalloid-crystal reaction. Many suffer disfigurement of the face, trachea, and lungs. Ozbolt's nanogolems were most effective in repairing respiratory tissue and reducing overall deaths, but the attack was too sudden. Little we could do to reduce casualties."

"And helot morale?" Hypatia asked urgently.

"The helots are understandably upset and will begin questioning the failure of the guardians to protect them. The pernicious Industrial Workers' Federation used rhetoric yesterday in the *Goetia Mirror* criticizing your graces' aloofness and alleged a lack of humanitarian concern. They even suggested the iama-B attack was launched by us."

"Conspiracy theorists! Of course they did. The union thieves never have anything good to say about us, do they? They're like cockroaches; kill one and another takes their place. No better enemies of national strength. They'd rather bankrupt the city than see it succeed."

"Unfortunately, union rhetoric is finding a receptive audience. The traitors were able to distribute their literature by the Bull in the Sixth Ward.

As you know, this final distribution came at the end of a string of protests across the Republic. Only a well organized mob could manage *that*. My recommendations are contained in the report, but I'd suggest two strategies: first, neutralize the propaganda distributors immediately; second, conjure a positive view of your graces' love and adoration for your subjects. Declare more helot social festivals; add an extra religious service to the week with planned sermons; increase truth revelation on Skybridge."

Prodicus' eyebrows curved respectfully. He swiveled in his chair and looked out to sea. "Sometimes I wonder if you're a secret guardian, General Argus."

"No, my lord. If I seem vaguely goldborn, it's only because of the strength I've received from submitting to my purpose. I'm proud of my silver. Praise be to your rule and the glorious Kabiri."

"Well spoken. Like a breathing animal, each class feels the happiness and suffering of the other. As it was written: 'When but a finger of one of us is hurt, the whole frame, drawn toward the soul as a center and forming one kingdom under the ruling power therein, feels the hurt.' I feel every hair on the helots' heads. If they could but look inside my heart, they'd see it pounds for each bronze drop of blood. Yet I wonder how aggressively the helots will question our failure in the recent attacks. In crises like these, helots cling fast to their guardians for comfort. What doubts they hold of our abilities are masked by their fears of the Other Side. Although this terrorism was a cowardly act, we can turn it to our advantage. Sinon, put Morpheus Alepou on the screen."

Sinon turned three round knobs on the podium control panel. Streaking veins of light projected a miniature Skybridge News office onto the floor. Morpheus sat at his curved news desk reading notes for the Gorgon Hour's next installment.

"Morpheus?" Prodicus asked. "How is your story *Foreign Elements in Our Midst* proceeding?"

The contemplative anchor jumped startled from his desk. He picked up his satin robes and nestled back down, disordered, like a hen settling her nest. "Why, y—yes, Sire," he stuttered. "Proceeding on schedule. The ISHIM dossiers you sent me this morning were enlightening to say the least. It appears a few pernicious foreigners are inciting discord amongst the people. Our story will demonstrate how all the protest organizers are linked to Xenon and the Continental Caucus, as you asked."

"Good, and my other requests."

"I've already contacted the neighborhood watch offices. They dragged the helots out on the grass for twilight movie parties. Our *Relaxation and Consumption* broadcasts focused on the cathartic power of spending orichalcum. Monica Garr even offered to film three episodes pro bono. She makes a beautiful guardian. Quite convincing."

"Well, she is an actress, isn't she? Her job is to be an imitator."

"Yes, Sire. The Knights of Cephalus and green-scarfed Republicampers also orchestrated patriotic parades after the movie. Made the people happy as oinking pigs in the mud, especially when they hosed them down with calmatives."

"Were mood elevators necessary?"

"The *lotuzone* we released was ineffective."

Prodicus quickly ended the conversation. "Do as you must, Morpheus. Thank you."

The light spun back into the projector.

Morpheus is such a pompous fop, Patroclus thought. All the students at the Academy agreed. Morpheus walked around—from sunup to sundown—in lies. Morpheus was not like the guardian-book-enhancers or the guardian-artist-patriots who worked for only three years at their deceptive craft and returned to Heliopolis. Morpheus reveled in controlling others with his camera. His Gorgon Hour was an end in itself now. How fast could he shape helot minds? How far could he push them into the hands of the guardians? Despite what Morpheus and his father said, the protests *were* homegrown. Everyone knew it. They escalated violently since the gas attack—three riots in a week! Not just by radicals and unions, but the merchants and paper pushers, too. Everyone was angry but the blood-sucking bankers in the Fourth Ward.

Hypatia spoke up again: "Enough about helots. What of auxiliary casualties?"

General Argus' face drained white. "The auxiliaries were not given any indication of the gas attack. Two auxiliary companies were completely wiped out."

"A guardian initiate acting as first lieutenant was also killed, is that correct?" asked Archon Creon. His black, wrinkled face scrutinized a casualty report prepared by the Geryon Group think tank. The numbers were in direct conflict with another paper prepared by the Rover Council.

"Yes, STRATCOM sent Talos to investigate a rogue Watcher group in the Tenth Ward. The Fates intercepted radio chatter a month ago indicating Xenon is considering propaganda and assassination as political tools to undermine guardian control. We believe the Iron Queen slipped in using a jinn. The deceased initiate, Talos, tracked down one of her underlings before we lost contact. For some reason that is still unexplained, he turned back and was heading away from his intended target."

"Very good, Argus," Prodicus praised his general. "We will look into the matter further. You may return to Stratos. The Vinculum representatives may go as well."

The tall soldier bowed and departed. Matemeo Fairbanks and Cornelius Carnegie had already fled for their lives.

Archon Creon turned to Prodicus wringing his hands. "Glaucon has betrayed us," he sneered. "The Fates told me he's begun seeing the exiles more frequently."

"He was with them all last week," said Hypatia. "He's been sleeping with them at night like a little child. The Good knows what he does with them. I think they're trying to make him defect to the Other Side."

Polemarch Leonida scowled. "The boy's not changed since I trained him on Stratos." She readjusted her spiked helmet and tapped a roused finger on the table.

Manos shouted louder than before, "The Fates already started to notice a change in Glaucon's neural harmonics. His I.T. wave ratios with us are beginning to deteriorate. Meanwhile, Glaucon's sync ratio with the fallen woman and her brother is exceptionally high. Almost as high as yours, Prodicus."

Prodicus remained unmoved. "I am not concerned with the boy. I have developed a more powerful tool to control the edges of Glaucon's mind. He'll do whatever I ask."

"The exiles' I.T. waves disrupt your miasma spell. Your behavioral-readjustment program is giving us far less returns than expected, much like your failed gas detection system."

Prodicus ignored Manos for the time being. "I am stronger than our prodigal daughter, and I'll break him. I am familiar with the tricks of women and their meddlesome brothers. The lost prince and princess will be recovered. It has been foretold by the Fates."

"Miasma?" asked Patroclus, curious about the term.

Prodicus looked down at him and responded, "Yes, my son, have you ever heard of the legend of the magician who could grab any man's soul he liked, just by saying their name in the right way?"

"Don't believe so."

"Let's say I've found a way to grab Glaucon's soul."

"This is absurd," Manos interrupted. "I will not let you gamble the safety of this city on the ground of a computer's fairy tale. This world is not your potsherd to spin."

"You will not let me, Manos? Do not forget who you're talking to. I could kill you with a word. Remember?" Rapping threateningly on his head, Prodicus placed a small red orb on the table. A faint mist seeped from its round edges and chilled the room.

Such a view of the jinn was rare.

Manos grunted in defeat, panicked by harsh whispering along the walls.

"The Fates told me Glaucon holds the key to Levantra," said Sinon.

"The Fates told me he has a thirty-five percent chance of falling," Creon added.

Prodicus unleashed a cold laugh, a fearful laugh. "The Fates are like the clouds, saying something different every day. Glaucon's I.T. waves are eccentric—more so now than ever!—which makes his behavior difficult to calculate."

"I.T. waves are quackery," mumbled Manos. "Your Kabiri magic stacks inference upon inference."

"The Fates would disagree. Change your tone or you'll end like the Katharoi: dishonored bones and madness." The red jinn on the table glowed brighter than Helios as Prodicus continued: "Do not forget what it cost to forge the Fates' circuitry, Manos. All has been foretold. Our exiles have returned and Glaucon has found them. This is not coincidence but the guiding hand of Destiny. Patroclus, you've been my eyes and ears watching Glaucon. That is why I called you today. Give me an account of the Second Vessel's brain state."

Patroclus said, "He's a passive vessel, as always, Sire. Sensitive. Gets infected by everyone he meets. Whatever you're doing to him, he's mentally unstable and getting worse. That's my honest opinion."

The grey-haired Hypatia lamented, "You should've found the boy sooner, Prodicus. Damn the Katharoi and Xenon's trickery. Glaucon's I.T. waves are torn and there will be no way to piece them back together."

"*I* can," Prodicus said confidently. "What a boy like that needs is a messianic awakening, a mission, and a cause. We can provide that with Levantra and Operation Copula. His mind is specially suited for the reception of new ideas and experiences. His time in the cogniscrambler has been well served. The jinn, my holy tool, makes him see."

Leonida creaked in her armor. "You're so certain he's the necessary catalyst for immersion. What if we hook him up to your flying island and he turns the life support system off or crashes it back into the ocean. The process will turn him into a god, and gods easily anger."

Sinon warned, "As long as Glaucon continues to remain with Potone's children, I fear he'll continue to grow closer to the mindset of Xenon. He is helping print unmodified copies of books now in the *Goetia Mirror*—as Fairbanks described! Our eyecameras saw him disrupting the flow of our city. Worse, the exiles are using the power of the jinn to create a cult amongst the helots. Bizarre, widespread rumors persist about a 'Son of Fate' who can see the future and conjure snowy lightning."

"We should capture the exiles now," Patroclus pounded the table. He was surprised at his own brazenness. "Glaucon will return once we purge the bad influences from his life, I know it. Every day we allow him to remain with Kleomedes and Sophia he drifts further out to sea."

Leonida said, "It's hard to keep track of the fallen children. They've changed houses recently. Who knows how Glaucon finds them."

"Glaucon has his ways," Prodicus smiled. "He's a true guardian: sniffing, watching, hunting, laying the trap. A killer who pretends he isn't. Such greatness in him. When the time comes, he'll pounce. We must test him like gold in the fire."

"Testing is one thing. Gambling is another," Creon said. "Which one is the Third Vessel, the brother or the sister?"

"To be quite honest, I've no idea." Prodicus laughed amused. "When I tested them before, they were so young. Kleomedes and Sophia have identical I.T. wave patterns. The Fates don't even know. Perhaps we should let Glaucon decide."

Prodicus felt confidence fleeing the room, but he'd never felt more assured by powerlessness. Even with the Fates' help, his captains and brave knights, archons and auxiliaries, they couldn't do something as simple as capture a garage publishing house. *Perhaps the Fates aren't telling them everything*, he thought. *Perhaps they're masking the truth even from me. The plan is hatching and Glaucon will reveal himself. The Fates must be given time to work.* "We should desist from moving too quickly on the exiles," Prodicus decided. "Let them print untruths until pollution piles over their heads. Let them play little gods. Even if helots knew everything about their guardians, they'd still cling to us for salvation. Fear of the unknown is more convincing than fears of any current oppressor. Helots don't seek rebellion. They crave happiness, and how can rebels be happy? After Glaucon sees the failure of the exiles to exert change he'll betray them and come to us. Then we'll bring a sword against the anarchists and throw them down into the abyss to die a violent death. We wait now to see what metal lines Glaucon's soul."

Creon and Hypatia stayed silent. Each contemplated whether to directly challenge the decision of Prodicus. Both feared the chilly air emanating from the jinn, its bloody history and power.

"This meeting is concluded," Prodicus said abruptly before they could reply. "I thank everyone for their time. Remember to remain alert for any indication of renewed efforts by the Watchers. We don't want another iama-B attack, do we?"

The twelve archons rose like smoke and disappeared. Leonida's metal clanked away. Manos skulked angrily through the back of the conference room, rubbing his head, as if protecting it from the mysterious red jewel on the table.

Patroclus, Sinon, and Prodicus remained alone.

Sinon waited until the doors closed before approaching the armchair of the guardian-king.

Out in the ocean, sharks swam among algae buildings. So did a colossal sea monster. Armored steel, swimming like an eel, teeth flashing, the sentry machine glowed yellow in the water.

Prodicus examined his creature, his marvel, the Great Krakfin, and felt melancholy. "It's hard to think so far below the ground," he admitted. "I sit on the throne of a god in the heart of the seas, but I am only a man. My beauty is gone and perhaps my wisdom is fading."

"You should not say such things, Father," Patroclus comforted him. "You still have a long life ahead of you."

"I grow weary of this life," Prodicus replied. "Do you understand the pain of betrayal? I do. I came to power in betrayal and it seems Glaucon is destined for the same."

"Betraying a Watcher is not a crime."

"Guilt and shame still exist outside the narrow definitions of our enumerated legal crimes. Betrayal of an enemy is still a betrayal, no matter what the law codes say. Levantra is my last hope to make amends. Make sure you keep a good eye on Glaucon for me, Patroclus. He will need a guardian of his own."

"I will."

"I have a final request for you, my son. Director Sinon has prepared a list of hundreds of conspirators involved in high crimes against the State. Take Glaucon on the raid. See what he does."

"Father, you know where Sophia and Kleomedes are. Please tell me and I shall go to them. If you allow Glaucon to betray them, it might destroy him completely."

"A guardian-king or Potone's children? I want to see who is the stronger."

Krakfin slithered by the window, flashing pale search lights on the seafloor. Suddenly, its thin fins gleamed red suspecting an intruder. The mammoth creature skipped through the waves, striking a nearby shark and stirring up a cloud of blood. The blood drew a carnival of marine life to feast upon the floating corpse.

When Prodicus finally sat alone, he peered into the jinn's swirling smog. "Which child is the Third Vessel, Potone?" he asked helplessly. "Sophia or Kleomedes? My niece or nephew?"

III § 2 In the Cogniscrambler

Glaucon drifted somewhere dark, lips rough as sandpaper. "I'm thirsty," he whispered. "Please . . . someone . . . give me some water." Thoughts felt broken, mixed together in a bottomless and discontented void. "Where am I?" he asked. "What time of day is it?" Grassy weeds crawled up his throat. He heard a ticking clock. "The cogniscrambler—is that where I am? How long have I been here? Can barely think . . . my loneliness . . . like bitter herbs. Water."

Glaucon coughed uncontrollably, withdrew into a subatomic apparition, an immensely dense singularity. He was spinning and flowing down . . . down . . . down an incandescent, atom-ripping black hole. He belly-flopped and floated in a stagnant lake. Bobbing like a buoy, a pattern of stars steamed above. Silver lines connected the stars forming a dome. "I *am* in the cogniscrambler," Glaucon comprehended, filled with relief. "I'm sure of it. I walked into the pod this morning—my weekly teloscopy, nothing more. This is like before, only more . . . gravity."

An acid drop suddenly splashed his forehead. Heartbeats accelerated, sent ripples across the pond. Flashing disconnected shapes assailed his senses like a strobe light—memories of the last two nights. He was on patrol again with Patroclus, walking through the dangerous wards with ISHIM secret police, looking for the print shops of the imbedded insurgents. The smell of burning xiphos sticks—electricity in the air—made his stomach sick.

"Get on the ground!" he heard someone yell. Horrified feet ran for the door. Terra Brandon was thrown to the ground before she could resist. Someone kicked over her Tavli board. Checker pieces spilled on the carpet. Terra looked up at Glaucon disbelieving. Why, just the other day, they'd traveled together spreading the *Goetia Mirror*. Now her stunt leaving IWF propaganda by the Bull forced his hand. Glaucon betrayed her, leading his squad right to her duplex. Before she could speak, three auxiliaries struck her back with rifles and peeled her body from the floor. Black metal helmets faded into the night.

Next house, Glaucon plunged xiphos sparks into another rebel's spine as he fled out a window. Patroclus, dressed in black khakis, looking like Death, yanked his legs over broken glass. "No one releases iama-B in our city!" he screamed over the chaos. Another soldier beat a thin teenager who had started crying, grabbing his bloody hair. "Where are your parents? Where are the anarchists?" All the bed-sheets were thrown up. The dressers were emptied. Glaucon's foot pressed against the boy's misshapen head while his men searched. A cache of poetry by Emerson (given to the family a week before by Glaucon and Terra) was discovered with much excitement. They chained the boys together and placed them in the back of their truck.

The incriminating images dissolved to dark vapor. Something made Glaucon mechanically whisper: "Break down the door; grab the rebel. Break down the door; grab the rebel. Break down the door; push the woman to the ground. Put a gun against her head. Wait for the rebel. Grab the rebel. Break down the door. Grab the rebel. Break down the door; throw the clothing on the floor. Push over the dressers. Confiscate the pictures. Throw shock stunners in the house. Break down the door. Shoot the rebels trying to flee. Look for secret holes. Grab the rebel. Break down the doors. Hood the rebel, grab the rebel, threaten the rebel, kill the rebel. ISHIM is everywhere. Grab the rebel. ISHIM will find you. Kill the rebel. ISHIM will never let you rest! Never let the rebel rest. This is the way of ISHIM. I and ISHIM are the same."

Glaucon's back arched sweating. His pulse sent another wall of ripples across the lake. Thousands of flashing nameless worlds appeared in explosions of light. He fell on a conveyer belt and saw his brain cut up and boxed. Fragments of his brain faded into the spiraling Milky Way. This galaxy condensed into a new world. He was suddenly playing in his childhood cave. His mother, Melete, smiled next to him. He reached out to touch her hair, to hold her face; but she turned into a web of shrieking bats. The bats scattered and formed Levantra in the sky. The floating island blocked out the sun and fell back into the sea.

A bell chimed in the distance.

Glaucon danced on the tip of a xiphos stick, spreading lightning across the back of some unknown, tortured soul. The lightning skipped across mountains of skin becoming a line of windows in the sky. Through the windows were images: the Famine, the Hero, the Horse, the Levilamp, Greenness.

Are they the Forms? Glaucon wondered. *Am I in the mind of the Good?* Glaucon heard the ticking clock again. *No, there aren't any gods here. This is the cogniscrambler, immortal Hall of the Fates. I must not forget!*

Clouds spilled thunderously from the windows, curtained the world, reopened.

Glaucon's legs felt the firmness of twisting roots. He stumbled under a colossal tree's shadow overlooking a forgotten lake.

Birds chirped in the tree. No. He was wrong. Not chirping, laughing. Laughing came from the branches. Soon, white transparent ladies hatched from inside them and sailed down the trunk like ethereal wisps. He had seen them before in images drawn by the guardian-artist-patriots. They were called the disir—maiden harbingers of the Fates.

The paper-thin ghosts frolicked along the water's surface, hurtled through his chest, and darted in the air. Although their immaterial forms couldn't touch him, their presence left black, wintry death. Glaucon's nostrils flared. He felt cold and shivered. He remembered the iama-B gas attack, his gnawing guilt.

The disir turned blue, gracefully dropped in the water shedding data.

"They all deserve punishment for what they've done, right?" Glaucon began screaming. "Why—why do I feel sorry for rebels? All rebels must die. Isn't that the song they taught us to sing? I feel badly about harming them because they're like Sophie and Zemer. Why won't my conscience obey me? Why can't I turn Zemer in? Why do I keep going back to the wards? Damn it! I promised I wouldn't go back."

The disir only pretended to die; they rose up laughing from the water, reborn, changing shades of color.

"Am I making this world?" Glaucon thought.

"Probably not," came three cackling voices from behind. A skeletal nail scraped Glaucon's shoulder. He jumped back frightened.

The Ladies of Fate—Clotho, Lachesis, and Atropos—smiled up at him.

Thank gods they arrived, Glaucon thought. *How could Homer ever believe 'the Fates gave mankind a patient soul?'*

The three old hags were dressed in flamboyant Mediterranean robes, had large foreheads, four bony arms, and crooked feet. White ruby-laced headdresses clanked over their faces and covered their necks, all leathery and looking a thousand years old. Most unsettling of all, they had mangy beards which dragged on the ground. Each was holding a thin line of golden thread spooling from the enormous tree.

Why the computer Kabiri-36 decided to take the form of the Fates from Greek mythology was anyone's guess. Atropos, the oldest looking one, acted as Glaucon's paraclete—his guiding spirit in the cogniscrambler. A paraclete counselor was assigned to every subject in the Republic to facilitate their weekly teloscopy sessions. None of the other Fates would talk to Glaucon during session. Although one couldn't be sure, the sisters supposedly had different personalities. Lachesis, for instance, was said to be quite humorous and talked romantically of the changing weather. Glaucon failed to see how a soulless computer could find things funny or be concerned about meteorology.

Atropos stuffed two arms in her wide dress sleeves. "I see you're a scared little man, Glaucon," she stated under her aquiline nose.

"I am." Glaucon could not hide the truth from his paraclete mother.

"And you don't really care about your new friends, do you?"

Is she talking about Sophie and Zemer?" Glaucon wondered.

"Of course we are, but we know them by other names."

One of Atropos' shriveled fingers probed under Glaucon's skin. There was the sinking feeling of an I.T. reading, of plummeting to death with a searing headache. His heart pounded. The Fates were in his mind, rummaging through his brain like a filing cabinet. Atropos released her finger from below his chest. Glaucon fell on the roots, gasping, "But I do care about them, my lady, I do!"

"What do you really know about them?"

"I know Zemer is kind and cares about other people, that Sophie is strong but hides a deep pain like me."

"Their crimes are dreadful, Child. Zemer's especially."

"I need them!"

"What would your friends say if they saw what you did at night? You betrayed Terra and the other propagandists and enjoyed it. You laughed with Patroclus. Oh, how you howled. What fun!"

"No I didn't. I couldn't." The flashing tortures returned. The scared children returned. Terra, the poor gentle woman, returned. Had he betrayed her? No. Impossible. A Xiphos stick shocked his back. Glaucon fell to his knees again, grabbing Atropos' leg.

"Zemer would forgive me," he coughed. "He's like that—everlasting sympathy. He experiences pain with people and wants to help them. Sophie . . . Sophie would spit in my face."

The old crone kicked Glaucon off her leg, unmoved. "They don't know the real you," she said. "The Glaucon in their minds is a helot worm specializing in product advertisements for Ra-Busto Energy."

"Their image of me is better than the Glaucon in my mind. I hate myself. I'm a liar."

"You're obsessed with their power over your image. You are in love with their Glaucon idol."

"No, their Glaucon is more real than this shell. Their Glaucon is closer to what I am. Everyone makes me an object, but their objectification is sweet, something different. I go to them to lose myself and—"

"Flee from what you are?"

"Yes! My inner world is torment. I hate myself. I need someone to make me better."

"The Zemer and Sophie in your mind are different than the real Zemer and Sophie. You will be betrayed. You should betray them first."

"Never!"

"Tell me where they are, Child."

"I can't. Why are you asking me this? You already know where they are."

"How pathetic! Of course we know. That's not the point. You're conjuring phantoms to impose cures to your own pathetic complexes. This must stop immediately."

Never, you old hag! Glaucon thought.

"How dare you," the analytical engine retorted.

Glaucon closed his eyes and tried to conjure a memory to defend himself from Atropos. He fell back a month before with the exiles. Zigzagging between safe houses in a northern suburb of the Tenth Ward, they spread the *Goetia Mirror* and helped the first group of helots escape the city. The jinn dispelled every barrier along the apartment blocks. Instincts carried the string of fugitives past the sentries to freedom.

A helot had wrapped his hairy arms around Glaucon's neck, then. "Thank you," he said. "May the gods shine their light upon you." Tearful, unforgettable eyes made it feel different from a crime. This man's last memory of the Republic's landscape would be the unappealing backsides of a line of department stores and the hologram fauna in the sky.

Sophie did most of the talking. It was difficult to see her from a distance. Wearing tight black jeans, a black shirt, and a black cotton patrol cap, she handed out maps and compasses. "Your goal is to reach Santa Fe and take the Old Spanish Trail to Colorado," she directed. "I've marked a number of friendly communes willing to provide food and assistance through the rainforest." She warned them of the importance of remaining hydrated, especially in the bands of Texas desert, and to watch out for the Hyenas: various species of highwayman and thieves. "If you attach this black flag to a stick, they'll leave you alone. The hyenas know better than to mess with the Continental Caucus."

"Is life here really so terrible they'd prefer the wastes?" Glaucon inquired of Zemer.

"Many are underground—arrest warrants for one reason or another." Zemer fit binoculars to his eyes. An *Apoll-on* plutonium-powered lantern ignited on a rooftop—signal from Aquila. Auxiliaries marched about a klick away. He flipped a switch for infrared.

"What if it was for a serious crime?"

"Unlikely, but it makes little difference. The guardians say to render to Caesar what is Caesar's. I say give Caesar nothing and take back everything you can, murderers and all. The *Goetia Mirror* aims to erase all authority, or rather the pretense of authority—the authority to judge, the authority to punish."

The last runaway scrambled into the dark on the Other Side.

"All authority?" Glaucon asked bewildered.

"People want a life of conviction, not command," Zemer said. "To command is to kill slowly. Solidarity, mutual aid, free choice is the way of anarchism."

Sophie placed two fingers in her mouth and whistled shrilly at both of them. She pointed up to the rotating searchlights from Mira-Disney Tower fondling their way in the dense blackness on the Other Side.

Zemer nodded. "Watch quick, Glaucon, as I blind the all-seeing eye."

Red lightning from the jinn scythed through the air reaping circuiting and light from the fifty-fourth floor to the one hundred and first.

"Let's get out of here," Sophie yelled. "Zemer cover our retreat. What direction?"

Zemer placed the jinn to his head, engulfed by red fire. "Take Xanthus Boulevard to 22nd Street. Best chances."

Grabbing Glaucon's hand Sophie raced with twenty other rebels to safety. Even though Glaucon realized nothing could possibly happen to *him* if they were caught, he savored the natural rush of adrenaline, the opportunity to challenge the logic of the city. Liberty to act however you wanted carried with it strange pleasure. Afterward, he scribbled an account of their mission for the *Goetia Mirror*. After proof reading slowly, Sophie and Zemer praised his wording.

"I wouldn't change a thing about the opening," Sophie said, twisting her neck over her own notes. "I would, however, add this at the end: 'Rank and file helots, patient toilers, modern wage-slaves, ripe stalks of corn: How will you defend yourselves against the guardian crows? Will you sell your fellow bondsmen for empty songs, or allow others to burn a false essence upon you, or close your eyes hoping for future rain? No! Preach by example. You must lift Lady Anarchy as your scarecrow. Run away as those before you have done. Sabotage your workshops and corporate employers. Lift up your pens and commit to continuous revolution; not only a revolution of the physical, but also the moral. Lift up your own *Goetia Mirror* and seize your liberty."

"I rather like that," Zemer said.

"Thank you. It's directed to all of us. We can't stop for a second. I found some selections from *Uncle Tom's Cabin* we should include as well. I added a historical discussion on slavery. The concept has been totally erased by guardian engineering."

Glaucon struggled to write everything down in his spiral notebook. Camped in some unknown attic, a fiery substance jumped from the exiles onto his clothing, took hold of him. He never wanted the night to end. But sadly, this memory *was* ending.

The old crone Atropos materialized in the middle of the room. Nostrils flaring, four arms twitching angrily, her taut finger froze Zemer and Sophie stiff as mannequins. Atropos caused the windows of the attic to fly open.

Dark blue gas filled the room killing the images of the siblings.

Thinking he was going to die, Glaucon covered his eyes in shock. When he opened them again, he was back alone by the mammoth tree.

Which world is the real one? This one or Heliopolis? I can no longer tell, he shivered.

"You will not succumb to such leaps of emotion from the exiles," Atropos poked him repeatedly in the chest. "Sensory stimulation clouds your ability to glimpse the universals. Man has one Form and it consists of reason, spirit, and appetite. There are not four parts or two. There are three."

"There are only three," Glaucon repeated.

"Yes. That is your essence. Remember, material bodies in the world of becoming change in fiery flux, taking on new characteristics, but the Forms in the Pure Land are eternal and immutable. You can only know the eternal through the intellect. We must purge you of your desires and emotions. We must purge you of love."

Slimy worms slithered out of Glaucon's throat. Choking, he coughed uncontrollably, gagged for air.

Atropos warned again, more sternly: "Zemer is a shower of madness, Child. He is a bull who cannot see his own horns, or the swords drawn to make him meat. I can read to a seventy-six percent probability he'll be betrayed by those helots he loves. His zeal is more dangerous than even his witch sister."

"I will crush them both," Glaucon whispered. "Break down the door; grab the rebel. Break down the door; grab the rebel." Then he sensed Atropos fiddling in his mind and struggled to break free. "What would you know about it, hag?" he coughed stumbling into the water.

Atropos yanked him out and breathed a cloud of noxious odor in his face. "You think we care when you call us names? Don't you know we have no emotions or pity?"

"You don't understand anything, Hag. You just pretend to. You're only a collection of symbols structured around a vacant algorithm. You're controlled by a definite set of rules."

"So are you, and we know your rules better than you do. We know how you'll behave in certain conditions, how you'll react, acquire knowledge, experience your delicious illusion of free will. Sophia speaks negatively of slavery, yet she will always be a slave to her senses. If we pinch your body, you squeak. Man is not more complicated than that. We are master calculators. We are gods! You best remember, young fool."

Glaucon's mind was racing. *Do the Fates really understand things in the same way I understand things?* he thought. *Are they sentient? How? Computers don't have souls, or come from the Pure Land. They're just mainframes filled with symbols. Heuristic computers were programmed to 'learn' but this was, of course, a metaphor. Metaphor.*

"Enough nonsense," Atropos shouted under burning phosphorous eyes. "You will stop seeing the exiles immediately. If you don't stop seeing them, I see death in your near future—99.9 percent. Hear me? Someone close to you will die!"

Glaucon thought, *That's a lie. Atropos is lying. Both about me* and *Zemer. Something's wrong with the Fates. Atropos never behaved like this before. Why are they so vicious? Are they having problems accurately reading my I.T. waves?*

A bell like the sound of an oven chimed. Glaucon became aware of a thread tied around his waist. The end of the golden spool slithered down the tree toward him. What would happen if the thread ran out before the discharge?

The three Fates teleported around Glaucon before he could find out. Atropos wailed, "Enough of this vision, Child. You curse everything living. You're beginning to lose sight of your true path. Rest assured, your new friends won't escape their destiny."

All four of Atropos' arms curved forward and touched Glaucon's skull. A blast of icy energy whipped his brain, sending him hurtling through space.

The door of the cogniscrambler pod in the cloister lobby opened. Glaucon tumbled out drenched in sweat, clothes soaked, his limp cheek smudged on the marble floor.

Clank. Clank. Clank. Loud golems scampered over like cat-sized roaches, moon faces jerking.

"Don't take me back," Glaucon stuttered delirious, knuckles curled taut. "I swear to the Forms I'll kill you, weird hags."

Robed students looked aghast. A long strip of paper filled with 0's and 1's printed on his back. A golem brushed them aside with a broom. Next minute, they carried him lifeless back to his cloister.

III § 3 THE PLACE WHERE EVEN BIRDS ARE TRAPPED

Glaucon lay prostrate on a wooden cot, all blood in his body drained out. White as a corpse, he couldn't take his mind off breathing. Exhale and stare. Exhale and stare. Yes, that was the way of it. Exhale and stare. What was he staring into? An abyss? No, white plastered walls. Exhale and stare. Words tapped on his skull: *Where is my speech, my lovely voice, walking in the shadow of night? Hear spirits floating in the trees. Wandering, wandering, wonder: How did I get here, get so lost, away from home and quiet peace?*

Glaucon didn't want to go to class. He cowered in a fetal position, moaned at the clock. Already two in the afternoon. He needed sleep. "I knew I should've waited to do my damned teloscopy," he said.

The images of Terra Brandon returned, less real than before but still biting. Nothing could block her out. He felt rotten, like a dead grain in the earth. What was this sensation?—Shame? Disgust? Remorse?

"I knew better," Glaucon conversed with an invisible audience on the ceiling. "This always happens. I hate the cogniscrambler. I hate it. I can't express myself in words anymore. I'm just immeasurable confusion staring out. All I can do is exhale and stare, exhale and stare. I can barely think. Just let me get away and be alone. But when I'm alone, all I want is to go to Zemer and Sophie and lose myself in the activity of printing books. Is there nothing more to me? Am I just pieces of mixed up feelings, a grief without any distinct pain?"

Exhale and stare.

A bird chirped outside, chirped like the colorful disir. The terrible disir! Reaching out to choke the sound, Glaucon sank into his sheets. He wiped beads of sweat collecting on his forehead and picked up an odor-pen, pushed it into his palm. Nothing. *Meon*. Non-being. Exhale and stare. No emotions. No feelings remained after being touched by the Fates' bony fingers.

"I'm trapped frozen and can't move," Glaucon moaned. "So beautiful outside, but no energy. Let me taste the sun and die in bed. O alas, alas, why can't I just sip medijuice and use the symsysts? Why can't I be content, succeed, walk around ignorant and happy? What is it like to be unaware of exhalation and staring? Sophie. . . ."

He thought about their past weeks together: group meetings, leafleting, racing from the officials, breathing heavy back to back.

"This is going to make the guardians just sick, Glaucon," he remembered Sophie saying diabolically when he helped her hack into the Worldlink network on a symsyst.

"What are you going to do, Sophie?"

"Wouldn't you like to know? I'm going to release a little worm-virus developed by a friend of mine outside."

"It's not going to destroy anything, is it?" Glaucon had asked suddenly alarmed.

"Not permanently. I'm going to bounce a little song around until those guardians can find it."

"Song? What song?"

"Break On Through To The Other Side."

"Is that more propaganda from Xenon?"

"No, this predates him by a couple hundred years, I think. You've never heard it?

'You know the day destroys the night,
Night divides the day,

Tried to run,
Tried to hide,
Break on through to the other side.' "

"Never."

"I first heard it in an old record shop in St. Louis. It's by a group called the Doors."

"The Doors?"

"As William Blake said, 'If the doors of perception were cleansed everything would appear to man as it is, infinite.' "

"No one will probably understand it." Glaucon shook his head.

"They will when it replays twenty hours straight," Sophie laughed. "The guardians want to control what people think by guarding their perception. This will help open the doors." Her thumbs punched a song of secret numbers onto a strange rhombus-shaped device feeding wires into a symsyst. Afterward, she tossed the device behind some bushes and escaped.

The worm—SmokeBreath—worked better than Sophie anticipated. It infected everything, from the symsyst network and Skybridge News to Safe Street in the Fourth Ward. No one could control the volume on the acoustic nodules, and music blared deafening in the streets (still lower, though, than the usual 151 decibels to disperse riots). Morpheus Alepou had to cancel his Monday show. The entire Worldlink Tower in the Ninth Ward powered down. It seemed a rather harmless prank. A funny one, too. But Morpheus called it the "worst act of criminal terrorism since the gas" and bid Prodicus place a two million orichalcum bounty on the "propagandists."

No matter what Sophie did, though, Glaucon didn't want to arrest her. He didn't want to turn her over to ISHIM's mind-stocks. Thinking of her, he wiped his forehead in agony, pretended an embrace. What he would give to be her helot hero rather than this hundred-handed guardian Gyges, but even to think such things was treason.

"Why is everything so difficult for me in the Republic?" Glaucon screamed, smothering his face in pillows.

Because you make your life difficult, young fool, came the voice.

"No, it's because I'm conscious of all the detestable problems here. All the ghoulish ministers, all the sycophants sucking up guardian piss to the last drop, who lick the feet of murderers. Sycophants like me-e-e!"

Interesting choice of words. You despise those who wield power, yet secretly, in your chamber or self-knowledge, crave power. This makes you despise yourself all the more. You feel sick because you are what you hate.

"I am and can't save myself."

I think I have your diagnosis, then. Have you ever read Dostoyevsky—what am I saying? Of course you have, little rascal. Well surely you must remember how Dostoyevsky saw excessive consciousness as a disease? I think you might be the same.

"Well if it's a disease, there is no cure."

No, he didn't believe so either and neither did his grieving messenger writing notes underground. In the messenger's case, excess consciousness proved fatal.

"Fatal?"

Haven't you heard? With excessive consciousness you lose all productivity. That's the same as being dead. However, if you throw yourself headlong back into your studies, you might come to forget your sickness and learn to get along.

"I don't want to get along with anyone here," Glaucon shouted. "I just want to be with Sophie."

How adorable. Tell me, has Sophie told you who she really is?

"A delegate from the Continental Caucus. Here to help the unions."

The voice cackled violently. *What tricks women play. She is much more than that.*

"Who is she?"

Find a way to ask her next time you meet.

Birds outside called to one another again, cooing softly in the sunlight. They sounded like a gold finch-golem Prodicus once gave as a gift. One bird flew by his window—maybe a partridge—chirping. Three seconds later, echoes came from somewhere in the distance. Poor things. The birds were trapped on Heliopolis. Trapped like him. Any bird trying to flee exploded like a scorpion-grenade in the audiomembrane.

"I could explode, too," Glaucon admitted, turning over, staring at vacant mythranium walls. There were no pictures, tapestries, or digiteles in his room, only a vacant space like a catacomb. A shag rug with a diamond design adorned the earthen floor. On his desk an odd assortment of books and shadowspar piled to the ceiling. Some were littered in heaps on the floor like broken terracotta warriors. The closest book had a red horse on the torn cover. The title: *Catcher in the Rye*. They had printed a few chapters in the last *Goetia Mirror*.

In the case of this story's protagonist, Holden Caulfield, the guardian-book-enhancers were particularly brutal. It wasn't even the same story anymore, but all students had to read it as second grade initiates. In the

Republic, Holden became a hero from the Age of Aporia. Curious, emotionally stable, he strove to impress his peers with intellectual prowess. One chapter, he even helped soothe his best friend Stradlater's dealings with a prostitute. A tedious four page monologue ensued about the importance of emotional restraint, public responsibility, and the virtue of charity.

"Why even call it by the same title?" Glaucon once asked Prodicus sitting alone in his luxurious cloister, refastening his robes after *erosic*. "They have Holden preaching ridiculous speeches. Like: 'It's never too late to turn back on the sensualist road. Seek forgiveness and lament those who walk blind with passion. Let's call the police. We should have the prostitute arrested for breaking the law.' That kind of talk isn't even close to the original."

"Well, I think it was the challenge," explained the venerable Prodicus. He took much interest in the pointed questions of his young protégé and spared many hours for him despite being overworked. "I said the book should've been banned outright. Its foul language and narrative style made it unfit for students and would corrupt the young. The enhancers disagreed. They begged me for one opportunity to experiment. I must admit, I was not dissatisfied by their work."

"But," Glaucon had protested, "what happened to the vivid ways Holden would express his aching discontent in the original story? There was something contradictory and beautiful about his vulnerability and confusion."

Prodicus smiled crookedly and patted Glaucon's knee. "We've just made the book more real, less . . . *phony*. Holden still boasts, but now about the right things: virtue not madness. All books must have a purpose, like we have a purpose, and we should not let people get confused about the purpose of books, which is to discover truth and instruct the individual in the good life. Hideous books must be changed for the Form of Truth."

"But the people might like to read the original."

"It is not enough for the guardians to win wars, Glaucon. To be successful we must win minds as well—minds that watch themselves. Fools think killing men important. The wise kill ideas. The wise bend all subjectivity to the needs of Fate."

Glaucon turned away from the memory and the yellow crumpled book on the floor. The bird chirping outside stopped. A powerful rapping on the window above the bed startled him.

Another stronger knock.

Finally, Patroclus' voice thundered outside worse than the Earth-Shaker: "Glaucon, don't think your room safe as Hector's Mist. My xiphos will drive you out. Come on, I've brought company."

"All right, all right," Glaucon whined, rolling painfully to the floor. He thought he heard Ephor Yannis mumbling, too.

Swinging into an orange tunic, Glaucon locked his metal door with his *tetractys* and rolled his shoulders. He shook like a wet centaur, animating his limbs. Playing the part of a happy citizen became especially important before an ephor of the courts.

Phylanstery C resembled a beehive: curving walkways, busy activity, and many rooms. Glass elevators hurtled up and down into the adobe stone lobby, as if spit by the delta reflection pools. Fifty small cloister cells circled the lobby, and at each of the seven floors the ceiling grew shorter. Only the first floor had individual rooms for ISHIM and political elite. The rest were wide open barracks with everyone sleeping together like seals on the rocks. Sunlight shined from the ceiling of the dome, and a glass observation deck channeled fresh air. Up top, one could survey the whole apartment college: four other phylansteries connected like the points of a star by rope bridges and floating land-masses. A pyramid commons lay in the center, usually containing a garden atrium, the cogniscrambler pods, cafeteria for common meals, a projection theater, wrestling gymnasium, and study carrels. While most of the phylansteries could be found on the sixth plateau of Heliopolis, not all were out wide in the open. Some submerged underground or jutted out like mineral veins off cliffs. As was plain to anyone with a basic understanding of operant conditioning, the windowless, smelly, humid rooms in the bowels of the earth could be used to positively punish misthink while a view of the sky and a little privacy might reinforce proper conduct.

Ever since being admitted to ISHIM at fifteen, Glaucon had lived on the first floor with the private rooms (private at least by Heliopolis standards). Glaucon thought he'd enjoy being away from the upper levels, but he secretly missed communal sleeping. When one lived so closely with others, being separated from them at night could be lonely. He missed sleeping next to warm bodies like Zoe and Patroclus, especially when his feet got cold and there was no one to rest them against. One thing he would never miss, however—those infernal elevators. Despite all the magic coming from Schizoeon, they still managed to break down at rush periods. Then you had to wait for Atum Construction Company from the Seventh Ward, and that took longer than a ten day fall from Olympus.

At the community tables, by the lower delta pool, immature seventh grade initiates gossiped about one of their scandalous friends.

An understandable lapse in decorum or some such nonsense, Glaucon thought. *Probably took too many shots of Sex-with-a-Harpy.* He approached them to make sure they bowed appropriately and offered to pedicure his sandaled toes.

"Lord Glaucon, how good to see you safe," one said, wearing the heavy woolen robes of an initiate. "We thought you a goner for sure." The boy's teeth were unsettling, already stained green by the medijuice.

"Why is that?" Glaucon demanded.

"No one's ever been in the cogniscrambler as long as you. When you collapsed earlier, everyone thought you died. Even made the afternoon news. How'd you do it?"

"Do what?"

"Survive. It's a miracle. Everyone's talking about it." The other students peered up at him with awe. Also terror.

"I've no idea what you're talking about," Glaucon said curtly. He didn't like this haughty boy prying into his business and demanded his name.

"Euthyphro."

"Well Euthyphro, you ought study more and prattle less. Don't meddle in things that don't concern you."

The students apologized profusely, but Glaucon could still hear whispering after he left. It suddenly felt as if everyone in the phylanstery was watching him. Their eyes pierced his exposed flesh like meat hooks, drove him outside.

Patroclus waited near an enormous wooden parrot cage. "Finally, the sleeper awakes," he blurted out. "Took long enough. I hope you weren't doing anything improper." Patroclus shaded his eyes from the sun. As expected, Ephor Yannis stood beside him. He wore the august uniform of an ephor: red chiton with gold mantle (embroidered with red legal scales) draped over his shoulders. The judge's cheeks folded like a gopher. He was extremely tall, carrying his weight entirely on his upper torso. Ph.D. in Cognitive Science and Mechanical Engineering, rumor had it Yannis was one of the first to join the Kabiri Circle. Even wrote some of the early programming code for the Fates.

"Forms, we've been worried about you," Yannis said concerned. "Heard about your accident this morning. You must be feeling terrible. Eat this. I've brought a fresh bananapeach from Shennong Fooderies. Just returned."

Glaucon thanked the ephor, then peeled and sank his teeth into the bulbous fruit, spraying its tangy syrup over the sides of his mouth.

Patroclus eyed Yannis and asked, "You were at the Fifth Ward? Funny, you didn't tell me that."

"Must I tell you everything, little shadow." Yannis smiled garrulously. He winked in full knowledge Patroclus would later note this strange behavior in his report for the Kabiri. "The Fifth Ward is a strange one, completely devoted to the manufacture of foodstuff. It's not like the other wards where you might see a splice-rice patty or a row of corn crops here and there. The entire thing—seventy square kilometers—is devoted to farming and the grooming of livestock. It's a shame we can't eat meat up here."

"Sir?" Patroclus' face looked horrified.

"What, you think the archons will cast down an ephor of the courts for saying he enjoys the smell of cooking meat? Please."

"Lately, sir, I'd be more careful. Lovers of truth are often confused with lovers of discord."

"Is there a difference?" the ephor jabbed.

"There's that humor my father warned me about," Patroclus smiled.

"Well, you can note in your little entries tonight I am fully committed to the sanction on eating meat. But please, do say I only shun meat because I think the suffering of any sentient creature wrong, not because I'm selfishly afraid I'll commit cannibalism by eating a returned ancestor. I hope Hypatia and Manos get a long look at that! Tell those half-rate theorists they know where to shove their metempsychosis."

Always hard to tell whether Ephor Yannis was serious or not. He was increasingly controversial in the law courts, especially for his recent fetish for irreverence and moderate punishments. Because of his connections to the liberal Academy Reformist Council, ISHIM and the archons suspected him of misthink. Yet no one could touch him as long as Prodicus continued patronizing his work.

Yannis noticed Glaucon slouching. "Dear me, just look at those white cheeks. You're pale as an eidolon. What were you doing in *there* so long?"

"Where?" Glaucon asked confused.

Patroclus shouted, "Where do you think, mooncalf? In the cogniscrambler!" He pushed Glaucon roughly into the parrot cage. The golem-parrot frantically flapped its ceramic wings. "You were with the Fates over twenty minutes. Ten is dangerous. Trying to kill yourself?"

"Twenty minutes . . . that long?" Glaucon mumbled. "The Fates refused to appear to me."

"A computer can't refuse anything. It just does what you command. You were being really brainless, Glaucon. I should slug you for carelessness."

Yannis crinkled his nose. "Please excuse Patroclus and his physical outbursts. He's been noticeably worried about you. Why didn't the safety ejection trigger after twelve minutes, I wonder?"

Patroclus folded his arms. "I know the machine's addictive. No one wants to leave, but, for the love of Saint Socrates, learn restraint. You can OD like a junkie."

"What are you talking about?" Glaucon's eyes shot open. "The cogniscrambler is awful. I'd shun that place like a quarantined village if not for my weekly teloscopy."

"That's funny," Patroclus returned. "Whenever I'm inside the cogniscrambler, there is happiness unlike any ever experienced. The power is intoxicating. If we didn't have the trouble with the time limit, I'd never leave. For a brief, wonderful moment, I control the melodious swelling of the universe: when the sun sets; what experiences happen to me; I can have any girl or boy I want; create and destroy worlds."

"But nothing's real in the cogniscrambler," Glaucon returned. "You're alone in your own illusion. You're not really destroying worlds. No one cares about you."

"Who cares about exploring reality when you can make your own? That's what I always say. What do you think, Ephor Yannis? Would you remain forever in the cogniscrambler if you could?"

"Well, students, I always find my experiences in the machine to be rather pleasant." Patroclus glanced at Glaucon with a gloating look that said, "I told you so," but the ephor wasn't finished speaking. "However, I wouldn't go quite as far as Patroclus here. I wouldn't remain inside forever. I see Glaucon's point. I, too, crave a certain level of reality, now and then. Although I might be entirely happy in the cogniscrambler, I'd be living in my head. Nothing would ever really be accomplished."

Glaucon gloated back at Patroclus who groaned, "Ah-h-h, you wouldn't know the difference, Master. That's the point. Plus, this world's just illusion anyway, a reflection of the Celestial Forms. Who cares if you live in one illusion or another?"

Yannis laughed. "All this talk makes me remember an interesting story. Have you heard about Gregorios the Great at the Academy?"

Both men shook their heads.

"There was once a wise man who relished every moment in the cogniscrambler until one day he became confused. He entered and left the machine so often he began to wonder which was the real world and which the world of the Fates. 'Where am I?' he asked waking one night. 'Are you there

Atropos? Are you there?' And sometimes the bearded woman appeared and other times he was left alone. This question 'Where am I?' haunted him throughout the following summer and winter. This epistemological problem consumed his existence, alone in the dark, scribbling equations all over the laserboards. 'How do I know I'm not in the cogniscrambler?' he questioned the air. One day last year the most amazing thing happened. He sat up in bed in a cold sweat and shouted at the ceiling, 'Eureka! Of course, how simple. The answer: I know this world is the real one because I would *not* have chosen this life of study in the cogniscrambler.' Imagine that. The answer was always staring him in the face, all those tedious, logical hours."

"I don't know. Sounds heretical to me," Patroclus admitted, tapping his foot on the grass. "Studying readies the soul for death and should not be lamented."

"Really?" questioned Yannis. "And do you conjure the study of Heliopolis in your own godly visions in the cogniscrambler?"

"No, I must admit I don't."

"Well there you go, you heretic of heretics!" Yannis put his hands to his stomach and laughed energetically. His red cheeks flushed to match. When he saw how dispirited Glaucon appeared, though, he quieted down, looked serious. "Now, Glaucon, are you really telling me the truth when you say the cogniscrambler terrifies you?"

"Absolutely. I want to tear it to pieces."

"That's very strange. I've never heard anything like this happening before."

"The disir are horrible. They fly around and make the whole sky black and press against your mind—"

"What? You've seen the disir," Yannis interrupted flabbergasted. "How many?"

"Hundreds, and they sing like chirping birds."

"It's rare I ever see them," admitted Ephor Yannis. "Requires deep trances. Did they have a sapphiric aura?"

"Yes. But it changed colors."

"Did they fly from right to left or left to right?"

"Left to right, I think."

"And did they take a straight course?"

"No, more disorganized and aimless."

"Certainly an ill omen."

"I've only seen them once," Patroclus said. "They were like beautiful Stygian nymphs who made me feel courageous and wanted . . . not scared. You sure you're not kidding us?"

Glaucon was now completely confused. He barely ever talked about his disturbing experiences with the Fates, even to Zoe. Now that he was hearing others talk about the machines in such a positive light, he felt his own experiences were unreliable. "Is it because my mind's so weak I can't handle it?" He gripped his forehead. Nothing was worse than losing your mind.

Ephor Yannis reassured him: "I don't believe so. Not at all. Your neurons probably just developed some resistance. There may be a transmission error occurring between the immersion trodes and your I.T. waves. More than likely, it'll subside. I'd try to stay away as much as possible for the time being. I'll report this malfunction to Dr. Salazar Ozbolt himself."

"Thank you, my sun."

"Prodicus will probably want to hear the details as well."

"Is that really necessary?"

"Well, you know what they say on Heliopolis. 'There are gods. There are men. Then there are beings like Prodicus.' Maybe he'll know what to do. No mystery escapes him, even when he was young." Yannis began fidgeting in his imperishable robe. "Now that I see you've recovered, Glaucon, I should really be on my way. I have a small case beginning this afternoon. The lawspeakers grow angry when things don't proceed as scheduled."

"What's the case about?" asked Patroclus.

"Oh, just a young neophyte caught peeing outside the designated toilets. What's worse is that he was peeing toward the sun. 'Most irreligious,' I heard someone aghast earlier. I find it absolutely humorous. We'll probably put him in the mind-stocks for several hours. This city is so wondrous: laws about virtue, laws about cosmetics, laws about drugs, laws against eating beans, laws for rainy days. There are so many laws we make everyone criminals. Oh well, good day, citizens. May you consort with the divine."

Ephor Yannis bowed good bye and marched down a stone stairway to the city courts.

III § 4 The Fifth Academy

"We should really be going," Patroclus advised, seeing the ephor depart. "I don't want to be late for Dialectical Hierology again. You've already gotten me too many demerits." The sour expression on his face changed completely. Seeing Glaucon safe revealed his hidden compassionate side, a mischievous grin. They had not spoken since dropping off the injured prisoners at Miantgast. It was pleasant to be together again . . . under less violent conditions.

Scurrying up the short walk to the Academy, the boys spun around stone arches and hopped a creek bed. A wide marble staircase to the Academy came into view, worn down by centuries of guardian sandals. As Plato demanded, a holostele entrance sign read:

LET NO ONE IGNORANT OF GEOMETRY ENTER HERE.

Students and rectors chatted on the majestic steps. Drunk on knowledge and medijuice, they yammered faster than the breeze and made little sense. Guffawing, knocking earthen mugs together, they drank till they spewed flatulent arguments. One haggard looking guardian wearing nothing but a blue chalmys cape re-applied *Friend-of-Man* lotion to his arms and enjoyed a cooking program on his digitele.

At the top of the stairs lay a neatly mown lawn, limestone monuments, and Dionic pillars like the ribs of slain Titans. The Academy resembled an elaborately restored Palatine Hill: Long open colonnades decorated with feathers, vast obelisks, hermit towers, porticos and intricately detailed reliefs produced the majesty of a sacred shrine. Four mammoth buildings enclosed a grass quadrangle (called Pythagoras Square), and a diagonal marmoreal breezeway cut two right triangles in the grass. Along the sides, a sacred grove of olive trees was dedicated to Athena.

Archon Hypatia often lectured about the trees. "See these olives," she'd say, plucking one from a tree and plopping it in her mouth. "Each is a sacred link to the past Academies long since perished from history. Saint Plato started the first Academy in 42 M.G.P. That college was the first blessed institution in the world to recognize the Forms as the ground of reality. Of course, following the death of Plato, the school and its successors fell into periodic moments of dogmatism and skepticism over the Forms. The fourth and last Academy, for instance, was even shut down by the ignorant Eastern

Roman Emperor Justinian I. Can you imagine? After the collapse and exile of the philosophers, some thought the Academy might never return; but the movements of world history witnessed Saint Plato's ideas vindicated. Five Academies. What is the meaning of five? The number five reflects the Form of Human: five fingers, five toes, five senses, five extensions (two arms, two legs, one head). The number five is divine. The olive trees attest divinity is among us."

Patroclus and Glaucon marched through a cool, open tunnel—hollowed out of the southern building—to Pythagoras Square. Knots of guardian initiates and golems filled the tunnel lining pebbles into patterns, learning divine arithmetic. Looking like aristocrats, some read papers and practiced the arguments of the pre-Socratic philosophers for their upcoming tests in the Department of Ontology and Metaphysics. They filled the tunnel with hot air and set-speeches, pressed by the rectors tutoring them, forever asking, "What is the most essential *arche* (principle) in the world?"

A young boy raised his finger and pretended to argue as the wise Thales of Miletus: "The primary arche is water. From water all life is born. Water is necessary for the maintenance and continuance of plants and animals. If we are to believe the myths of the ancient Greeks, the gods made unbreakable oaths upon the river Styx. And we know the most sacred thing is that which we swear by." He looked quite proud of himself.

A rose-cheeked eighth grade neophyte rolled her eyes and snorted. Her heaving robes were too big for her. "You ignoramus, you must know how circular and fallacious it is to rely on textual authority about the gods."

Glaucon could already tell she was going to take the position of Heraclitus.

"I have heard nothing about why water should take primacy over air or fire," she stabbed. "I say fire is the primary element because of what we know about energy. From the Formal Big Bang, the world was birthed in a release of energy. And Earth's water would be lifelessly stagnant without a fiery energy source. You argue the body is made up of eighty percent water, but notice how we emanate I.T. waves. This fiery energy is the fabric of our souls."

"No, no, no," hissed another raspy voice. "I tell you Number is the primary principle! All reality can be quantified into formulas. The Good can be expressed by the number one. The number two is evil because it represents increase and division. Four represents a square, and is in the highest degree prefect. Ten . . . well, ten, like our *tetractys*, contains the sum of the four prime numbers and comprehends all musical and arithmetical proportions. Saint Plato even treats numbers like the Forms in *Phaedo*."

"Not fair," the other two declared at once. "*Phaedo* is not the *Republic!* In the *Republic,* Number has inferior being to the Forms, thou gentle, mindless minotaur."

On and on the conversation jumped, with each referring back to textual evidence and becoming more entrenched in their position, so entrenched, they actually came to believe what they were saying.

"Can't anyone learn silence?" Glaucon finally coughed (a delicious Pythagorean rebuke).

Patroclus nearly fell over laughing. "Wait till they learn proofs against all those positions next year," he said. "Everyone knows fundamental reality is Form. What sane person could deny logic's changeless stars?"

In Pythagoras Square, there were four schools for the four winds and elements of the Earth. A wood sign was posted on a turning sapphire wheel on each building: METAPHYSICS, ONTICS, AND ONTOLOGY to the North; TRANSCENDENTAL GEMATRIA-MATHEMATICS to the West; CENTER FOR HISTORY SCIENCE AND LITERATURE to the South; and the LYCURGUS SCHOOL FOR PUBLIC POLICY to the East. Thousands of sub-branches and knowledge specialties were sponsored by each school. The Logoset strongly recommended each student pick a minute, obscure, virgin area, and study it to death. One could go to the Economics Department and construct abstract Vinculum economic models for the following spring, or spend a lifetime studying student voting patterns in the former United States of America from 2351 to 2353 M.G.P. Proving the existence of other minds and challenging solipsism was also heavily funded, though with limited results. Ultimately, the idea was to become as specialized as possible, not necessarily to learn anything new (although learning for the sake of learning was still a virtue), but to gain the proper discipline and obedience necessary for guardianhood and to prepare for death. The art of dialectics—the Platonic ideal of synthesizing all realms of knowledge into a coherent whole—was left to a select few, chosen by their academic performance.

On the lawn next to the olive trees, another fiery discussion raged. Nine metaphysics professors fenced with their tongues like living swords, thrusting their opinions about a controversial passage in Book VI of the *Republic*.

"Plotinus surely misinterpreted what Saint Plato meant by the scripture, 'The Good is not being but superior to it in rank and power,' " said one vigorous philosopher curling his orange mantle over his arm. "Plotinus claimed the Good was beyond being, or in other words, that it existed above being. But see how this suffers difficulties. If the Good rises above and is completely beyond being, how then would it make the Forms intelligible? How would the Good illuminate the Forms like the sun illuminates visible things? How would guardians come to have knowledge of the Good at all?"

"I see your meaning completely," exclaimed another eloquently. "We could only know the Good by what it is not, not as it actually is. Positive knowledge of the Good would be impossible. Guardian rule would be the folly of hopelessly ignorant men."

"Exactly right, my wise Apollo," the academician shook his shoulder. "Saint Plato must have discovered the Good to be on the far side of being, but still being. Do you see why I've been so forcefully relentless in my petition to have the Plotinians declared incorrigible heretics?"

"By Zeus, your fears are justified. Give me the petition so that I may join your crusade against these craven sensualist roaders. Those who desire an end to the Republic should be fed to the Bull."

Glaucon wanted to walk up to the academicians and ask, "But what if the Plotinians are right? What if knowledge of the Good is really impossible and guardian control is unjustified? Shouldn't guardians seek truth over power?" No doubt he'd end just as the heretical Abdicators did four years ago.

A cabal of eighth grade initiates got it into their heads Plato meant for the *Republic* to be a metaphor rather than a textbook for government. To seduce others to their cause, they handed out colorful treatises in the forums and challenged Professor Zeno to a debate. He agreed, but they were arrested before they could even speak. At their trial the Logoset begged them, pleaded: "Please, for the sake of the Good, recant. Recant now. Enter into the correct understanding of truth laid out by those wiser in years." When the students refused, Prodicus announced judgment, calling them allies of Xenon and traitors to the Good and the Realm. They were tortured in the mind-stocks and executed the next day in the Bull. After seeing such results, Glaucon kept his opinions to himself. He would've thought no one cared for truth anymore until meeting Zemer and Sophie. How odd those convinced the Form of Truth a myth should pursue it so doggedly, and those who gave it lip service crush any questions like a gnat.

An ivy-covered door on the Lycurgus School swung open. "Make way for the Celestial Polemarch of Stratos," announced a loud voice over the acoustic nodules. Glaucon jumped back, startled by the bugle salute.

Fair-famed Leonida marched out in full golden battledress with a coterie of troops. Dressed in green uniforms with silver epaulettes, some of the men had wispy mustaches and carried Gatling-lasers. They sang a new patriotic hymn by the Danaan Boys, "Ballad of the Valiant":

"To arms, my citizens, to arms;
Can you hear the roaring Other Side?
Riding evil, razing farms,
To kill our mothers fast and hide,
Bent on rule, they mean us harm.
Freemen stand and save our pride,
Raise our banner o'er their charms,
Treat our nation as your bride,
Save our Forms and sound alarms.
Volley, fire, volley, or die.
Don't let the Other Side rearm,
Spill the tainted blood aside,
To arms, my citizens, to arms."

Leonida's pitch black hair hung in two pony-tails at her shoulders. She wore a red chalmys with gold boots, gold arm plates, gold knee guards, and golden gauntlets. Upon seeing Glaucon, she removed her gold pickelhaube helmet and hushed her soldiers. She motioned for the boys to meet her at the olive trees. "Well, well, well, if it isn't the young Glaucon back from the dead," she said.

Patroclus and Glaucon clicked their sandals together. "Polemarch," they both exclaimed fist-thumping their chests and standing at attention, nearly blinded by her glinting armor.

One always had to make sure to salute Leonida in the right way. A strong believer in decorum and rank, she once ripped the tongue out of a helot's mouth for refusing to bow to her in the Second Ward.

"I heard you were bed-ridden, you poor boy," the polemarch crooned. "The Academy walls have been speaking of your triumph all day long. Glaucon, Glaucon, Glaucon. All I hear is Glaucon. Twenty-three minutes in the cogniscrambler and still alive. What an impossible feat of mind. Defies all Kabiri programming constraints. Something I can't help but admire."

She knows what a monster you are, Glaucon. She is setting a trap, the voice recoiled.

"She is the monster, like Hippolyte: a blood-thirsty Amazon, the daughter of war."

Why do you say such things about such a pretty woman? All the boys at school think she is the prettiest in the Republic.

"She's a killer. I've seen what she tells the auxiliaries to do outside the city walls. Saint Plato said 'neither ravage the country nor burn the houses,' but we pillage and outrage every settlement."

She acts as taught. The first rule of any unipolar world system is to prevent the establishment of autonomous rivals. A lack of alternate cities allows our moral city to flourish. Our city is too important to be defeated by another.

"She leaves nothing alive. Even when guardians are caught, she abandons them to the Other Side."

The prettier the woman, the more dangerous the contact.

"Then she must be Helen of Troy. But I think Sophie is prettier."

You are quite the comedian. Even Sophie would laugh at you for saying such things.

Glaucon finally said, "I was lucky to survive."

"I should say so," the Gold Queen snapped. She wondered what was taking him so long to respond. "People have died from separation poisoning much earlier, and at best, gone completely insane." Leonida's sharp pointed face had been stretched several times in the plastic surgery boutiques, making her toned body appear even younger. She was nearly Prodicus' age but did not look a day over thirty-five. She continued, "I also hear rumors you and Patroclus found some houses with imitation contraband over the last two nights."

"That's correct, Polemarch." Glaucon could feel blood rushing to his face under her sharp down-moving eyes.

"Two houses. Ralph Waldo Emerson, even. However do you two do it? It's almost like . . . you knew where they were all along."

Patroclus' eyes glared at the Gold Queen. *Careful Leonida*, he thought. *Prodicus won't be happy to hear about this intrusion into Glaucon's business.*

Leonida forced a laugh. "Oh well, you just have the luck of Xenon, I guess. And you did have *my* training. I will miss seeing you exercising on Stratos, my blonde little muskrat. Do put a smile on your face. The way you lope around, it's almost like we've abused you in some way." Leonida's gold gauntlet caressed Glaucon's cheek struggling to remain still. "You know, you've always been rather special to me. You were the oldest helot ever brought to me on Stratos. Your bitch mother ruined you, but look how I transformed Tenth Ward trash into the pinnacle of Heliopolis."

"Yes, Polemarch, I don't know what I would've done without your special attention."

"Remember, if you ever needed to say anything, my office is always open."

"You bestow too much affection, Polemarch."

"Also, Patroclus you are looking mighty fit today. See to it that you stop by as well. I should like to administer a proper examination before you graduate."

"I'll be sure to do that, Polemarch," Patroclus said with a smirk.

Leonida nodded politely before marching away with her guards to an awaiting fleet of three-seater gyropeds. They huffed carrying their xiphos sticks over their shoulders, sparking like wires. Flying off into the sky, they zoomed toward the Lovejoy Military Institute on Stratos, becoming a miniscule dot on the horizon silhouetted by the construction of Levantra.

"What was that all about?" Glaucon asked Patroclus scratching his head.

Before he knew what happened, Patroclus had dragged him under one of the awnings of the government building. "You should not fly so close to the Agora underworld, friend," he warned desperately.

"What are you talking about?"

"Please, Brother. You know exactly what I mean. Leonida's right. We found those houses too fast the other night. You were conflicted the entire time. Whatever sick game you're playing down below, you should stop immediately before you hurt yourself."

"I won't admit anything, but I find it odd the Lion of Heliopolis is so frightened of the wards," Glaucon teased.

Patroclus remained stern, growling, "The inferior majority who dwell in the wards are driven by desirous, self-centered inclinations. Especially the foreigners who sneak under the walls. Strange ideas. Strange pleasures. It's easy to get confused in the sewer of sights and sounds."

"You make the helots sound so terrible. Many I've met acted intelligently enough."

"Please, Glaucon; the helots are ignorant brutes. Blind to reason. They couldn't survive without our care."

"Salazar Ozbolt is smarter than both of us. He survives just fine."

"The Ozbolts are different. Most of the helots I've met could barely form a syllogism let alone act independently. Have perverse sympathy for them if you wish, but remember: ISHIM will kill you if they discover you're hiding information."

"Has your father sent you to spy on me too, old friend?"

"No, course not." Patroclus looked hurt, almost chivalrous. "What kind of person spies on friends? I care about you is all. You're the only person I've ever been able to talk honestly with; losing you would disfigure me. Stay away from there, Glaucon. Leonida, in her own way, is warning you too. Turn back before it's too late. Reflect on which side suits your interests; you can't have both."

How Glaucon tired worrying about saying the wrong thing, making lying an instinct. He couldn't live in peace, even with people he cared about. He had to shield his hopes and dreams in an envelope of deception. "I will tell you nothing but the truth, then," Glaucon said restrained. "Write it down in your reports, if you wish. I am on to something big in the wards. Something huge! ISHIM knows better than to spoil an investigation."

"Maybe I can help, then. Give me your lead and we can work together—"

"*No.* I must do this on my own, Patroclus. You've helped me too often. Leave me be for now."

A melody chimed from the temple behind the Academy, signaling the start of another class.

"Don't worry so much, Patroclus," Glaucon laughed. "I can handle anything. Didn't you hear Leonida earlier? She thinks I have a strong mind."

Patroclus groaned and slapped him on the back. "It's not the mind you worry about, mooncalf."

III § 5 Teleological Metanarratives

Rector Anytus, middle-aged professor of political theory (and a Hegel-phile of the worst sort), slid around the wooden classroom in his usual, conceited fashion. "Man is a process," he lectured. "He is a hovering and fluttering, but mostly a hovering. Nevertheless, at historically necessary periods, mankind becomes something more and overcomes his limitations. Man overcomes by catching the wings of more reasonable men, gliding on their energy to higher cliffs."

Students sat cramped at metal desks, arranged like pews. Glowing papyritrons whirred taking scrupulous notes. Anytus whipped a holopointer in his hand and used its spaghetti light to slash flipping images from a projector: roaring meat-starved cave men, the siege of Troy, Alexander the Great, European monarchs, the atomic bomb, and victims of a hundred different wars. So many wars, it was hard to keep them straight.

Nothing's changed in ten thousand years, Glaucon thought. He did not like this new professor, Anytus. Who really could when he turned the Socratic Method into a procrustean bed, cutting down every answer without a hint of praise? He much preferred the wise Crito or Professor Hestix and his Socratic Symposium. Zoe and her dark-haired friend, Mixis, especially despised Anytus because he talked only of men and never of women.

"Yes," continued the rector, perched on a desk in black scholastic robes, "the history of philosophy's been filled with many hits and near misses as ideas gradually perfected themselves. True, there've been many dark ages—more dark ages than light ones. The Age of Aporia was one long, terrible dark age, as these images can attest. But if you read the great books—Hegel for example—you'll see man's history is characterized by a steady movement toward greater freedom, rationality, moral progress, and understanding. What better proof than our Republic!"

Glaucon continually found himself dozing off or stealing stares at Zoe's smooth legs under her desk. The buxom blonde was wearing another one of her shorter saffron skirt-robes, one that wound too seductively at the chest. Zoe continually looked up at him—grinning about some trick, no doubt—but he pretended to pay attention to the lecture.

Unlike Sophie, Zoe wore no actual jewelry, only a feather necklace. Jewels were forbidden on Heliopolis. As Prodicus often explained over the morning announcements, "Guardians should have no treasure but reason's light."

A portrait of the poisoned Talos hung at the front of class (much to Glaucon's dismay). The smiling face reminded him daily of his treacherous crime saving the twins. Why had he lied to the poor boy? What harm did he ever cause him? Many cried when Anytus broke the news of his death in the gas attack. No one could believe Talos succumbed so easily. Patroclus swore revenge.

Anytus continued his lecture. "Thank the Forms we've reached the end of this great journey. For nearly 2400 years since the death of Saint Plato, man wandered from harbor to harbor seeking truth in many things: God, Science, Desire, Militarism, Democracy, Hope, even Nihilism." A picture of the thick mustachioed Nietzsche met the audience, followed by a string of gasps. "So many 'isms', but all were necessary steps toward a greater synthesis of human consciousness. We were like children, then, learning how to live. We touched our hand on the pot sometimes, but see how we survived. We're all grown up now. The Republic, the State, is man's ultimate end. 'The State is the march of God through the World, its ground is the power of reason realizing itself as will.' "

Every time Glaucon glimpsed Zoe reminded him he needed the *erosic* pill—and fast! A sea of unspeakable desires bubbled up, thoughts so shameful they disgusted him. The Fates' touch was wearing off. He tried to think of something else and swiveled in his chair.

A sickly student, Pyrrhus, sat in the middle row, madly scribbling notes in his papyritron. He had a knack for studying, hardly ever talked. Half his left arm was missing, wrapped up like a tree stump, a casualty of a botched suicide attempt (therefore, denied a prosthetic limb). For many reasons, suicide rates continued to be extremely high on Heliopolis, nearly three times the wards.

When the class heard of the tragedy a year ago, most were confused. "What does old Pyrrhus have to be sad about?" Patroclus had asked. He was quite close to Pyrrhus who tutored him in set theory every Saturday.

"He said it was the Socratic Scoreboard," Glaucon explained.

"But he makes good grades."

"Not perfect grades, apparently."

The omni-present Socratic Scoreboard loomed as an enormous holostele by the Academy entrance. On it poured the results of every test, every readjustment of position in class rank. It was a yardstick for the Republic's academic gladiators. To make matters worse, digital strips carried scores like news tickers across the school. A poor grade tailed you like the Furies to every room, every cafeteria, mocking, pressuring, scolding. No soap or perfume could wipe it away. Grades were destiny, definition, and sometimes dreaded death. People snapped, some quicker than others.

When Patroclus asked how Pyrrhus tried to kill himself, Simmias Rex broke into the conversation. "Like everyone does it, you mooncalf. He hurled himself from the track and tried to smash his bones on the rocks."

There was only one track at the Academy. Made of pyrite to avoid the gold prohibition, it stretched out over a cliff behind the school at a twenty-five degree angle. Looked like a halo if the sun caught it right. Used for exercise and peripatetic thinking by the sages of the Academy, it had become like Mt. Fugi in the old Japanese state, notorious for suicides.

"Can you believe it?" Rex explained. "When the dumb fool tried to jump into the ocean, his arm snagged on a random cliff. Dangled like a spider over the sea for hours. Can't even die properly. They'll let poor Pyrrhus finish up at the Academy, but he'll never make ISHIM."

To Rex's high flown delusions of grandeur, that fate was worse than death. But in a sense, ISHIM *was* salvation. For once accepted, grades hardly mattered anymore and became confidential.

Glaucon turned attention back to the lecture. Anytus was still talking, but more frenzied now. He reached a crescendo. "Even when we were burned by the atomics, the *fire consuming fire*, the immolation resulted in a reformation of collective human will. Rationality acted like a frosty wind snuffing out the flames, growing stronger, more completely taming the wild beasts in man. We guardians—we skilled mountaineers!—are at the end of man's pain. Our slow incremental program developed with the Fates will diligently erode the desires in us. And one day, on Levantra, what little pleasure we allow for sanity will be cast away; we'll be as Kant's God: perfectly rational and perfectly complete."

Rex sat next to Glaucon completely enraptured. He fawned on Anytus' every word, or at least he pretended. Since eyecameras lined each room to monitor for the participation requirement, he made sure to speak at least three times per class. "Rector," he said, waving his hand like a flag. The perpetual show-off cleared his throat like he had tuberculosis. "No doubt everything you say is truth, but I fear our efforts may be impeded by a most unwanted parasite. Just look at what I found by the Bull."

So caught up in his speech was Anytus, he had trouble shifting topics. "What is that you have there?"

"Some horrid piece of trash I found in Consumption Junction. These imitations are appearing all over the wards. Supposedly, Dr. Salazar Ozbolt had one shoved under his door in Schizoeon. It's called the *Goetia Mirror*." Rex's sharp jaw foamed at the propagandists.

"Oh yes, I've heard about those pamphlets. It espouses the failed political ideology of anarchism."

"Where are they getting the books is what I'd like to know?"

"Why are you disrupting class to ask that question?"

"Because I don't think your 'mountaineers' are so loyal. In fact, I think several traitors live on Heliopolis. I've been listening to you gab about evolution for the last hour, but I don't see evolution anymore. Our Republic is starting to degrade!"

"Now, now—"

"Guardian levels are down. Even the Fates are beginning to malfunction—due to old Thales here." Rex glared at Glaucon, who was terribly offended by his remark.

Rex you snot-nosed son of Hades, Glaucon shook. He could not endure such ridicule. What misbegotten beast would dare insult him—*him!*—in front of so many. The hope of torturing Rex one day fed his imagination.

Spiro, a squat, brown haired sycophant also spoke up: "They've hacked Worldlink, too. Even broke into our mailing addresses and symsyst pin numbers. Only a guardian could know the passwords. Every hour I get the same messages from the *Goetia Mirror*. Nothing blocks them. Did anyone else hear that horrid song a week ago about the Other Side? No one could turn it off."

Spiro obviously played to the cameras, jiggling, swinging his arm like an opera tenor. He'd say anything to be successful, was Machiavellian and dishonest. How Glaucon loathed him. He had a corvine face, continuously hovered around Patroclus and Rex for any droppings to scavenge.

Rector Anytus tried to calm the classroom: "A few days disruption hardly means our city is degrading."

Rex questioned angrily, "Watchers and unions are planting these papers out in the open and hacking our corporations for over a month, and we can't catch them? If that's not degrading, I don't know what is."

"Glaucon's caught two."

"Yes, and the whole world *has* to know about it, don't they?" Rex pretended to throw a knife at Glaucon in the air. "But two is hardly enough, right? And we all can't be like the great Glaucon."

Mixis broke into the upheaval. "What does the magazine's name even mean?" she asked in her high, sweet voice. Glaucon detested her, too. She enjoyed slimetide to a vice and interned with Morpheus Alepou at Skybridge News. Proud to excess, even had the gall to say she was the reincarnation of Parmenides. Word had it she was about to begin her own afternoon program, Sphinx, Inc., providing fluff pieces for the Vinculum Cartel.

"You don't know?" Rex winked at her like an old lecher. "The word 'goetia' comes from the Greek for 'sorcery' or 'charm.' There was also a book called *Ars Goetia* with a list of ranks and titles for daimons."

"I know Greek, Rex," Mixis snarled.

Glaucon yawned. "You seem to know a lot about daimons, Simmias. You must be well acquainted with the Other Side."

"Only because I do my job, unlike some who have to hide in their rooms from the brutal cogniscrambler."

The class erupted in laughter.

How Glaucon longed to see Rex humiliated, defaced, thrown belly down in the gutter, but he could turn every taunt around. His pride was well guarded.

"Are they calling *us* daimons then?" asked Mixis. "How dreadful. What cheek!"

"Just listen to this propaganda," Rex said reading from the magazine:

The Goetia Mirror (Number 32)

Anarchism means more than simply living without the archons. The whole Republic and its economic and social hierarchies must be eliminated. Private property and the Vinculum Cartel must be eliminated. Compulsory government must be eliminated. Ozbolt's frankensteinian inventions must be eliminated. Dilmun Garments and Consumption Junction must be eliminated. Most of all, the guardians and their social engineering must be eliminated.

For three hundred years the guardians have asserted their right to control us merely because they have the power to see the Forms. But has anyone ever seen one? I looked under a rock yesterday and didn't see a Form anywhere. All I saw was a rock, but it was more than enough to satisfy me. Each day, Morpheus Alepou and his puppets light the airwaves with their lies: "You need the guardians. You need to consume what the guardians want you to consume. It's for your own good. 'Not self rule, but rule by reason and the reasonable.' "

I have heard of the needs for social bonds, but this is really too much. Do the guardians really expect us to believe such a silly myth? Do they think us so stupid we won't be able to figure out their reasonable scheming as they sit comfortable on their marble shrines sipping mint julep? In the nineteenth century, Mikhail Bakunin stated that the intelligentsia in modern industrial society were to be feared. Fear the social managers who can control and direct what's called "knowledge," he said. Controlling knowledge is more powerful than guns and money. He also believed that any government run by academicians "cannot fail to be impotent, ridiculous, inhuman, cruel, exploiting, maleficent." Today, his fear is gruesome reality. We live his fear. So turn the guardians' theories around and, like Karl Marx, say, "No. We won't believe you because we know the 'ruling ideas of each age have ever been the ideas of its ruling class,' and they're just methods of control to cover our responsibility." We don't need myths to live together. Because being human is more than enough and all are equal.

We are voices calling from the wilderness; we are many in the hills. Such a life is possible. We have built such a world and want to recruit YOU to the Continental Caucus. Stay in the Republic with your monkey kings if you wish, but we want all to know the virtues of the Other Side, because Morpheus Alepou and Peitha von Notus aren't going to tell you. We need anarchy. We need humanity. We don't need the Forms.

Yours in solidarity,
The Son of Fate, Editor of the Goetia Mirror

Patroclus pressed his two giant hands together on the desk. "They really are anarchists, aren't they? I just thought we called them that as a rhetorical device."

"No they're quite taken with the idea," Rex said. "What idealists!"

"What fools more like it," Mixis sneered. "Do they really believe human society could exist without a government and leaders? Even bees have a queen. The Other Side has Xenon for Plato's sake."

At the challenge, Rex changed positions. "Just because a truly anarchic system has yet to emerge doesn't mean one is impossible. After all, someone living in the late Age of Aporia would've thought our Republic impossible, but look at us now. Historically, a feudal society would've scoffed at the idea of a capitalist society. Yet one changed to the other as new social arrangements emerged. Nothing is impossible."

"Rex, don't be such a sophist. This is ridiculous." Mixis hated to be directly confronted in class, especially before the eyecameras.

"Your definition of anarchism as 'chaos' is also unfair," Rex said. "My investigation with ISHIM reveals the rebels care more about free association than they do a leaderless society. They don't believe a government should compel membership and think all institutions, including economic ones, ought to be run with democratic principles. They actually believe in high levels of organization. Anyone who fights the Iron Queen will realize their coordination is well-planned."

Rector Anytus shook his head. "You sound as if you admire the blackheads, Simmias."

"Don't misunderstand, Rector. You have to think like your enemy if you want to net them. In times like these, to know thy enemy is more important than to know thyself. Just because something's possible doesn't mean it's desirable. Let me be firm, anarchism is counter to every self-evident principle of natural law. Without hierarchy of some kind, society self destructs. Just look at what's happening to the Caucus' people here in the city, for example. The members of the *Goetia Mirror* are completely ignoring General Xenon's orders. Instead of calling for violent revolution like Xenon repeatedly commands, they emphasize ridiculous notions like pacifism and non-violent resistance. The whole affair is almost humorous, in a way. Xenon's lost complete control, and the Other Side has no laws to punish such disobedience."

Spiro laughed. "And we are told this political model is to lead to our defeat?"

Elpenor, a fat, slow, lover of laughter with a rank at the bottom of the Socratic Scoreboard, also chimed in: "Rex is right. I've never seen such horrible writing, either. But, then again, there is no Academy on the Other Side."

Glaucon furiously bit his tongue. He helped Zemer write the article. *I'll strangle that 'miserable donkey' till he coughs up his lunch lentils*, he thought.

Across the room, Zoe intently stared at him, pretty as the Flower of Athena. She messaged through her aquamarine symsyst: "Glaucon, I'm convinced everyone but you and me are fools."

He grinned in total agreement, nearly fell off his chair after she sent some funny Baby Dionysus cartoons.

Zoe messaged him again, this time about missing dinner last Tuesday. "You were supposed to meet me at Hebe Lounge in Schizoeon," she scolded. "Spun around waiting for an hour."

"Forgot. Sorry. I've been bogged down in an ISHIM investigation."

"Oh-o-o? About what? Those returned exiles?"

"Can't say. Confidential. National Security."

"When has that ever stopped you before? Appeals to national security are like appeals to the gods—taken on faith and probably untrue. Don't you trust me?"

Deciphering tone was difficult on the symsyst, even when the person sat right in front of you. Zoe's voice may have boomed between his ears, but her stoic, sharp face gave not a hint of being in the conversation. Was she upset? Was that sadness at the corner of her lips? Humor? Her words felt distant. "Not over the symsyst," Glaucon finally messaged. "Worldlink hears everything we say."

"Oh, for Plato's sake, mooncalf, do you think I care what that silly corporation has on me? I've had Cornelius Carnegie under my little thumb since I caught him extracting orichalcum from Worldlink's treasury. Fool's puffed up on stolen wealth. More gold than Minos. One word from me, though, and the old man pops like a piñata."

"Cornelius the Corrupt. You should've reported him already."

"What do I always tell you, Glaucon? The corrupt, simple minded are the easiest to control. Don't worry about the corrupt. Worry about the power hungry. We have bigger fish to fry, anyway, like the traitors in the *Goetia Mirror*."

Talking and debates about the *Goetia Mirror* and whether or not the Republic was actually degrading dribbled tediously for another thirty minutes or so before the disharmony was finally broken up by the entrance of the school dean. With a red collar wrapped firmly around her neck, the cloaked woman placed a stack of envelopes in Anytus' hands and then departed back through the door.

Rector Anytus shined elated by the secret news and held up his hands for silence. "Students, students. Please calm down *this* instant. Special announcement from the Office of Public Harmony."

Rex's and Elpenor's dreadful bantering died down. Several papyritrons slammed shut.

Anytus scolded the entire class: "Look at this excess energy. I can see there is more than one reason to call for a yoking ceremony this weekend."

At the news, the class erupted in cheers. "Is it really true?" Rex howled. "What luck!"

"Yes," Anytus exclaimed. "Prodicus ordered one himself."

Glaucon groaned. *Yoking ceremony, the sacred marriage, the hieros gamos. You might as well call it a lovebug party.*

In his writings, Saint Plato spoke quite specifically about procreation. He commanded that, "The best men must have sex with the best women as frequently as possible," and the guardians took his advice to heart. Every guardian-king from Abaris Hythloday to Prodicus took proper measures to refine the human stock.

An envelope with Glaucon's name in cursive and a smiley face on the cover passed to him. The symbol of the Department of Human Husbandry (an aged hand passing a newborn baby to another younger hand) was pasted on the back.

For one glorious, hymn-drunk night, a group of guardians will be married, Glaucon thought. *The plain* erosic *pill will be swapped for one with a Malthusian-spike, and any child born up to a year later is to be considered a son or daughter by all.* The whole affair was tedious and spurred numerous social difficulties, many pointed out by Aristotle; but since Aristotle was banned as heresy, no one could object.

For example, because of the yoking ceremony, the *erosic* pill was forbidden to goldborn classmates in the same grade. The policy behind the rule prevented incest (still quite taboo). Since records of the coupling at the ceremony were confidential, you could never tell who was your genetic brother or sister. Instead, one viewed everyone born in the same year as a sibling. To strengthen this familial attitude, all newborns were placed in sterile breeding dens on Schizoeon with common helot nursemaids.

Another problem emerged when guardian children found familiar facial features in their elders. Knowledge of one's blood parents became coveted like sacks of Forms, and youth continuously searched for any parental possibilities. The whole ideal of a universal family never materialized as the Founders intended. One might call everyone 'brother' or 'sister', but it lacked the meaning of a known blood relative.

Neither Elpenor nor Pyrrhus received a winning card from the lottery. Elpenor snorted angrily like an ass at the rebuke, but Pyrrhus resigned himself to his condition and scribbled silently at his desk. In a way, Glaucon envied his fatalistic detachment.

Musical bells chimed over the intercom again, signaling an end to class. Since the festival came on such short notice, classes were cancelled for the day to prepare. The doors to Pythagoras Square burst open, and students all over the Academy poured out. A sense of impending merriment and a calm recognition cleanliness would be required drove the talkative students to the public baths near the cliffs.

III § 6 The Baths Heat Up

Academy students shared two obsessions: cleanliness and love for periodic bursts of physical exertion. Baths fulfilled both hungers, coming equipped with a subterranean complex of gymnasia, lecture porticos, saunas, washrooms, and spas. Glaucon attended them at least three times a week. Cut into the soft cliffs of Heliopolis, the colossal cave entrance dripped like the drooling mouth of a giant: Steaming vapor overwhelmed the nostrils, hot stones burned the feet, and there was the ubiquitous sound of the slaps: slaps on the chest, slaps on the buttocks, slaps on the arms, legs, and neck from the helot masseuses, slaps necessarily followed by the sighs of blissful leisure and the smell of rubbing oil. One started sweating almost immediately.

In the entrance room, all along the walls, comical stone faces and phalluses spouted water into a circular pool. Naked bodies swam like frolicsome minnows in the circle, diving to find metal rings with their teeth. Some stretched their elbows on the pillared gym island in the center, appraising the strained *huffs* and *puffs* coming from wrestlers and gymnasts.

Glaucon disrobed with Patroclus, Zoe, Mixis, and Rex and wiped his brow. A dark girl named Elene joined them. She was another friend of Zoe's, probably of African descent. Most suspected Archon Creon sired her (which would explain her sharp eye for modal logic).

"Here you go," Elene said, placing her clothes in the hands of a greased helot boy. He nodded politely before gathering the rest of the group's belongings.

Rex struggled like an upturned turtle yanking his green tunic over his head. Patroclus unclipped his wood anklets and laid them softly on top of his robes.

"Come wrestle with me, Glaucon," Zoe demanded, pulling him playfully to the center ring.

"Not today," Glaucon whined, "I don't wish to wrestle. Straight to the hot tub for me. Gods, my muscles ache! Fetch a helot masseuse to knead my back straight away." But, next thing he knew, Zoe had pounced on his legs, throwing him spinning to the ground. Elbow on his neck, she smiled choking the air from his lungs.

When did she get so powerful? Glaucon wondered wagging his arms around in desperation. "I yield, I yield!" But his ferocious companion shoveled sand in his face instead.

"You yield do you, dummy?" Zoe grumbled with unutterable fury. "Do you know what I should do to you for that stunt you pulled earlier? Who are you trying to impress?—Me?" She pretended to be flattered. Sweat plastered short blonde hair to her face and curled it around her ears like an elfish cadet. Fierce taut muscles conveyed her anger about the cogniscrambler.

Glaucon tried to explain: "Look, Zoe, I'm sick of apologizing for something that wasn't my fault. The Fates' screws are loose. I'm not going back inside the cogniscrambler anymore. Forms! I swear it." Sand clung to Glaucon's back and teeth as he struggled to stand up. "You know how much I detest sand in my mouth," he chided her irritated.

The female guardian paid no attention, whirling to trip him again. This time, Glaucon was ready and instinctually grabbed her thigh, throwing her off balance to the floor. He pressed his entire weight upon her arms, breathed heavy in her face.

"There's the Glaucon I remember," Zoe said with his body on top of hers. "But I think you should obey this lesson." She spit on him and kneed him in his groin. Glaucon rolled over in agony.

"Hades' smoke!" he cried pinned again on the muddy floor.

Zoe hooked her arms around his sweating legs, making him suffer the Boston Crab, pushing his mouth against the sweat-drenched dirt—this time for good measure! "If I ever hear about you playing chicken with the Fates again, you know what I'm going to do, mooncalf?"

Glaucon hollered in pain and beat the ground with his fist.

"I'm going to find you, wherever you are, and tear each little hair off your head. One by one. I'll beat you down like I used to on Stratos. What do you think of that?"

His answer to the ultimatum was muffled by sand, unintelligible.

"Really, Glaucon, what would I do without you?" Zoe finally released him and turned his body around.

Glaucon looked up at her red face and pursed thin lips. "I think we've both sweat enough, don't you?" he asked stumbling toward the next room. He had to dodge six guardians racing by hitting Trochus hoops with hooked sticks. At the back of the island, Mixis used dumbbells. She groaned in exertion, watched by other guardians in the water. Rex and Patroclus grappled ancient-style in the center ring, refusing to use their legs, with their sweaty arms sliding past one another awkwardly. Zoe, obsessed with cleanliness, rinsed off sand in the shower and rang her hair.

Getting used to communal nakedness was one of the most difficult challenges facing any helot advanced to an auxiliary or guardian position. Now it was second nature, but before, the trainers on Stratos had to practically rip his clothes off him with a hail of beatings.

Whenever Glaucon went to the wards he had to be careful to display extra modesty. Sophie shrieked like a banshee one day when he walked naked into her room carrying on a conversation without a care in the world.

She stuttered covering her eyes, "Why Glaucon . . . you're . . . you're—what in Plato's name are you doing?"

"What's wrong, Sophie?" he said digging water out of his ear with a towel. "Just taking a shower."

"I can see that. Do you realize you're not wearing any clothes?"

Suddenly recognizing his mistake, Glaucon flopped around like a redfish.

"It's bad enough Zemer still does it. Have you lived on Heliopolis or something?" she asked.

"Of course not," Glaucon exclaimed defensively, feeling rather embarrassed for the first time in years. He tried to think up some excuse. "My depraved helot upbringing. I'm sorry. Don't they do this on the Other Side?"

"We're not on the Other Side."

Glaucon shook the memory away and walked into the next area of the bath, a steaming caldarium with a cramped domed roof. He fell into a smoking pool two meters deep. Ten other guardians reclined in the green water talking quietly about one of Gödel's theorems. Taking in the humid steam, moisture collecting in his lungs, Glaucon breathed sighs of relief. *Thank Plato Sophie forgot about that incident*, he thought. *Had she spoken openly about it to others, they would've been on to me the first week. I wonder, does she suspect my true identity? Does she know who I really am?* Her behavior suggested otherwise.

He thought about their last encounter together. It had been so embarrassing. He planned on returning sooner to apologize, but then he was selected for the raids. She could be dead for all he knew, but no reports confirmed. How could he look her in the face again? How could he look into the faces of anyone at the *Goetia Mirror*?

Elene and Zoe dipped beside him.

"You were letting Zoe best you, weren't you, Glaucon?" Elene splashed him playfully.

"On the contrary," Glaucon said, "Zoe's hands are quite skilled on the mat."

Elene splashed him again, snickering, "You are the king of innuendo, you naughty faun."

The others looked at Glaucon as a rarity, a helot turned guardian—no incest laws applied. He was therefore the most erosicable man in class, and he felt like everyone's pet philosopher.

Patroclus, Rex, and Mixis joined the group at the edge of the pool.

"It's really hot, isn't it?" Rex complained inching into the water.

"You have no idea," Mixis mouthed grabbing her brother's thigh. Rex jumped up in surprise and moved to the other side of the pool. Mixis laughed at her own joke.

Patroclus spread his arms on the wet cement. "So, Glaucon, will you be attending the yoking ceremony this year, or will you come down with the flu again?"

Rex declared, "I can tell you I thoroughly enjoyed myself the last time."

Glaucon scooted over on the ledge away from the group, dunked his head under water, ran hands through his hair. "I guess I'll go."

A sponge began passing around the guardians for washing.

"What kind of man are you?" Rex asked scrubbing his armpits. "Why do you even have to think about it?"

"Glaucon doesn't like orgies," Patroclus laughed, "can you believe it? He's the only man in the city."

"Aw, I think it's cute," Elene said swimming over to him.

Rex was mystified. "Stand up for once in your life, Glaucon. Civic duty bids us serve our . . . *count*ry; the neophyte levels are low and need to be replenished. I heard Professor Zeno talking, and even Prodicus is concerned. They said additional yoking ceremonies are sure to follow. Prodicus might even expand them to the helots. To be honest, that wouldn't bother me in the slightest. I like having a little rotation, now and then. And some of the fillies down below. . . ." Rex blew air out his mouth thinking of Consumption Junction. "Last time they enacted primæ noctis, I didn't sleep for weeks."

Zoe shrugged reproachfully and folded her arms, muttering, "Hardly any gems to pluck from that rubbish."

Elene whispered, "They're even thinking of banning pederasty. The Logoset *must* be desperate."

"I bet the old fools are," Rex said, covering his mouth. A slip-up. Patroclus made a mental note to report him. "No matter," Rex continued, forming an hourglass with his hands, "you know what they say:

'Oh-o, Tenth Ward maids love to sing,
But orichalcum makes them ring,
Some helot-hash
And see how they'll mash,
Tenth Ward girls never last.' "

Glaucon stood up dripping on the steps. "Hold your tongue, fool. My mother was from the Tenth Ward."

"Then your mother was a whore," Rex snickered, "by necessity. If she was still alive, I'd lay her on my truth table and show you."

Enraged, Glaucon lunged across the water for the brute's throat.

Rex bawled alarmed, "You would dare strike an ISHIM man?"

"I'll do more than that," Glaucon growled.

Zoe's arm pinned him back. She calmed him, whispering in his ear: "Glaucon, a joke. Just a joke. Control your passions. You're embarrassing me."

The bathers eyed him like a stranger in a strange land.

Glaucon barked, "It's not a joke, Zoe; this guy's a lunatic," but regained composure. No use being goaded into another shouting match. He fumed toward the frigidarium in the next room.

Zoe stood up and followed.

"What did I say?" asked Rex. "Doesn't he know the helots are blessed when they sleep with guardians? Why it's like touching the immortals." He shouted loud enough so Glaucon could hear him.

"Shut up," Elene scolded. "You guys are too much. You know how he takes these things so personally."

In the next room, Glaucon dived into a pool of ice to close his skin pores. He swam back shivering to the metal ladder and Zoe handed him a towel. "You *are* going to attend the ceremony, aren't you, Glaucon?" she asked. Her deep blue eyes pleaded.

"It depends, Zoe. Will you have me without the *erosic* pill?"

Glaucon pulled Zoe steaming into his lap.

"Don't even joke about something like that, Glaucon. What kind of girl do you take me for?"

A strange, primal urge gripped Glaucon. Zoe's face was so close to his own their noses touched. *What would it feel like to kiss her shivering lips without* erosic*?* he wondered. He leaned in to see.

For a moment—but only a moment—Zoe appeared to accept, wrapping her steaming arms around his neck. Then her body stiffened corpselike and went green. Her hand shoved Glaucon roughly in the jaw. She breathed heavily, splashed out of the pool. Shocked, aghast, humiliated, glaring, she spit and rubbed her lips desperately with her wrist. "Saint Plato, Glaucon, have you lost your mind? What would possess you to try something like that? What if someone sees?"

"No one will see."

"Eyes are everywhere; everyone sees. We'll be expelled for sure! They'll kill us! Throw us in the Bull!"

"But Zoe—"

"What did I say before? You can't be so . . . so . . . *kind.* I'll pretend you're still recovering from the Fates, but try this criminal conversation again and I'll have to—"

"What? Report me?" he mocked her like a petulant child.

Zoe shoved Glaucon's head back under the ice.

What's gotten into me? Glaucon wailed, bobbing under the freezing water. Icy pins pricked his body. *Awful of me to treat Zoe like a common helot.* He apologized profusely afterward, but to no avail.

Zoe returned to the caldarium mortified, thumbs inside her clenched fists like when she was young. She wondered if Glaucon had been sent to test her resolve—and prayed for it to be so! The other possibility was too disgusting to contemplate.

Glaucon dried off, scraping goose-bumps away with a thermo-strigil. Afraid to look at anyone, ashamed of his base nature, he quickly left the bathhouse. Zoe's response made him think of Sophie and how desperately he missed her. She was immune to superstitions and fear. She was open-minded and acted how she liked. She enjoyed learning without medijuice. He made up his mind once and for all to skip the yoking ceremony and return to the wards.

"I have to know Sophie's safe," he argued with himself at his cloister, stuffing clothes and the amber necklace inside a duffle bag. On the way out of Heliopolis, a colorful aurora skated through the clouds; microscopic particles interacting with the audiomembrane produced a vivid rainbow. Glaucon worried traveling the aortaphos so frequently might be damaging his health. He shuddered at the thought of cancer and went back to reading a patriotic magazine article by the Knights of Cephalus:

Snooping: Right or Wrong?

By Alcibiades, Guardian-Book-Enhancer

Is there anything wrong with snooping? Some naysayers may think so, but you should ignore them. Being on top of every situation is a critical element of Fortitude, our city's Seventh Virtue. When you retire for the evening, check your child's symsyst discussion boards. Look for mischievous light under your child's door. Use the rewind function of your husband's digitele. Monitor your friends and any loved one you suspect is avoiding their debts. Fumble through the garbage outside like a good super sleuth. Bottom line: Smoke out any transgressions.

Some might say this behavior is insecure, but what better security knowing your friends and loved ones walk the Pure Road? What better way to protect our society from the Other Side? Especially in these trying times, our government needs all the help it can get. Report everything to your local phylarks. A good Republican subject is informed and alert.

Commercials about *Allevor*, a new skin relaxant butter, kept interrupting Glaucon's reading. It was followed by a parade of other retail items he would never want nor buy. Somewhere—though it was often difficult to tell—the Gorgon Hour wedged between the cacophony of clanging tambourines and shrieking soprano songs. Morpheus Alepou raised his voice higher than usual, even above the tambourines. "Who do these unrepentant radicals think they are questioning the morality of *our* government?" he screeched, burning a copy of the *Goetia Mirror* left on his desk. "Despite what you may hear, the Republic doesn't look for fights. We don't stumble to war without just cause. I'm really tired of these phony intellectuals arrogantly looking down their noses at our armed forces, at all the people making efforts to protect our society from barbarism. The Republic has the most moral army in the world; our weapons are remarkably precise—Deathstalker missiles chase faces for crying out loud! We never hurt civilians on purpose, unlike the Iron Queen, who personally executes helpless prisoners of war in mass graves. Ask any of the auxiliaries. They'll tell you just how it is. If the anarchists dislike our government so much, why don't they just leave?"

Freddy Akimbo answered him: "Nowhere to go. We're the only stable government left. No other city has been able to rebuild since the Day of Hylopleonexia. What does that say about *our* constitution?"

Peitha von Notus responded, "That guardians are strength and blessed by the gods. We must be doing something right." She pointed to a recent poll showing eighty-eight percent believed the Republic headed in the right direction.

A video of an exclusive interview with a captured protester followed. Morpheus, gushing with drama, passed a cup of coffee across a table to a half-dazed helot. He inquired about what motivated him to throw a rock at an auxiliary.

"I was completely influenced by Xenon," the protester lied. "A soldier dressed in black came to a union meeting. Affiliated with the *Goetia Mirror* and the Industrial Workers' Federation, I think. Told us to set fire to cars, smash houses—kill people!"

"What did the other union leaders say?"

"Everything seditious. Half of 'em are soldiers from the Eastern Column."

"Half? Gods!" Morpheus leaned like an eel out of his chair, frown widening.

"Maybe more. They're all extremely violent. Something inhuman in their eyes. Knife you for a song. By the time I was captured, they were already making plans to blow up Ozbolt Tower."

"Blow up Ozbolt Tower? Terrible. Just terrible. Do you know anything about the recently captured rebel, Terra Brandon?"

"Bad as they come, that one. Have it on good authority she was bribed by Xenon."

Glaucon groaned closing the magazine. Unable to concentrate without the medijuice, unable to forget about Terra, sick in spirit, he examined Levantra until the impatient island faded in the distance.

III § 7 DESIRE CAPTURES THE GUARDIAN

The jinn beat excited in Glaucon's palm—at nearly six flashes per second. Scanning the circular brick plaza for any sign of the jade-eyed twins, the guardian noticed a gaudy stone fountain adorning the center. Two jets of water sprayed an equilateral triangle above a statue-choir of Donald Duck and red-eyed sea nymphs. Around the perimeter, temple spires spread attuned to the heavens, antennae-like (but catching only static). The sun was hot and unforgiving, dancing white through the skyscraper foliage. Its glare cloaked auxiliaries prostrate on the rooftops, bent around zizthopters flapping wings like pterodactyls.

Large crowds triggered Glaucon's alarm instincts. Six o'clock could be a dangerous time in the wards, most predictable time for riots. That was when temple ended and streets filled to the brim with drunk, noisy helots. You had to be careful: Unruly footsteps trotting out from temple might metastasize into a stampede.

Glaucon spied Zemer and Sophie across the plaza, disguised like helots. They waited patiently, eyeing the jinn's rapid animation. Sophie wore a grey tailored suit and checkered vest. Her bronze hair whipped in the breeze under a garland of violets. Zemer gnawed on applecane and adjusted his white pilos hat. A suitcase filled with the *Goetia Mirror* lay at their feet.

Rumors of the guardian children stolen by Xenon were an urban legend at the Academy; some thought them only a myth or dead. The DNA banks and police reports of ISHIM yielded little to verify their existence and showed typical marks of erasure. Even Potone and Lycaon (their alleged parents) were nowhere to be found. It was as if they had never been born, like characters deleted by the guardian-book-enhancers.

What would Zoe say if she could see me now? he thought. He felt badly about his brash rudeness at the baths. Trying to kiss her. A series of causes—

both temporal and sustaining—led him to that vulgar behavior. Glaucon could chart the first cause back to Sophie, like Aristotle mapping motion to an unmoved mover.

The previous Tuesday he had sat alone, writing on a cold basement floor near the spiraling stairs in the *Goetia Mirror* printing house. Evening approached and many unionists retired upstairs for rest. He heard loud footsteps. Then Sophie's lightweight boots tapped on the ground in front of him. When he continued writing, she kicked his knee for attention.

"How do you sit still like that?" she questioned.

"Like what?"

"Legs crossed, back straight like a monk. You haven't moved a muscle in hours. I'd swear you were one of Pygmalion's ivory sculptures."

"I'm disciplined."

Sophie slapped her hand to her forehead, burst into laughter. "Disciplined? Is that so, Glaucon? I don't know if that's quite the word I'd use but . . . don't you ever get bored?"

"Not here." Glaucon looked back down avoiding her sharp green eyes. They still made him uncomfortable. Lately, he found conversation difficult with this strange woman of the wastes. He spent immeasurable amounts of time focusing on what Sophie would think of his words. Would she think them clever? Funny? Mysterious? Foolish? It was absolutely maddening! He spent so much time predicting what she would think that he completely forgot what he wanted to say in the first place. Whenever he tried to talk, foolish sentences fumbled from his mouth like half eaten pieces of food, like he never had a class in basic rhetoric. So he just tried avoiding her altogether.

"I don't know if I like Serious Glaucon," Sophie teased him, "I'm bored. Been writing all day."

"About what?"

"The failures of the marriage draft policy, mostly. I need a break. Let's do something."

"Like?"

"I don't know. . . ." her voice trailed off for a moment. "Let's go on a date."

"A date? No, I don't think so. They're too sweet for me."

Sophie shot him a strange look, then cracked up. "Oh Glaucon, how amusing! I want to go on *a* date, not *eat* dates."

Glaucon's face blushed. "Is there a difference?" he asked aloud. All the while he prayed he hadn't committed some category-mistake, the worst of logical fallacies. *Date*. It sounded Middle English.

"A date is where you take a girl like me on the town and show her a good time. Hard to find a similar hobby today, but everyone used to go on dates in the Age of Aporia. Sometimes couples go on them on the Other Side, too." Sophie wagged her finger, winking coyly at him. "And if you're lucky you might get something special."

"Well, if that's what you'd like." He pretended to write something important on his paper, but really just scribbled Sophie's name in the margins.

"I would, as a matter of fact. I'll scream if I don't get out of this place. We've been inside too long. I'm getting cabin fever. If I write another word, I'll pound my pen through my desk. Be a *hospitable helot* and show a guest like me around the ward."

"It could be dangerous."

"Who cares? They haven't found us in weeks. I doubt they will today."

"Well, in that case, I guess we can go somewhere. Where's Zemer?"

"He's finishing some business with the printers. Brothers aren't supposed to come on dates, Glaucon."

"They're not?"

"Of course they're not!"

Sophie stood up grinning about something. She prepared a picnic dinner in the kitchen upstairs. "If we're fast enough we can go sit in the park before nightfall," she called gleefully. Glaucon continued writing until Sophie's shadow loomed over him again. He looked up mesmerized and perplexed. Sophie shined in a thin blue dress, shoulders protruding naked under the straps. Diamond earrings hung low on her cheeks. She'd been shopping at Consumption Junction again. Odd, considering how she taught property was theft.

"Should I have dressed better?" Glaucon smelled his t-shirt as Sophie laid down a soft and white blanket by Mira-Disney Tower. They were in a park filled with oak trees and replanted beds of hyacinths. Suncatchers drank the sun like thirsty scarlet pimpernels. The experience reminded Glaucon a little of watching the patriot plays with Zoe in Hesper Park, but the atmosphere here felt much more intense. *Probably due to Sophie's dress*, Glaucon admitted, stealing more looks at the silky fabric clinging to her back. It was odd to see her dressed so proper; Sophie usually expressed nothing but contempt for the "misogynistic disutility" of dresses.

Workers in poison suits interrupted them, spraying blue crystals off Mira-Disney Tower.

Sophie finally heaved exasperated. "Hell's bells, how long does it freaking take to wash iama-B from the windows?"

"Don't know. Molecules bind with the building. Morpheus hinted it would be another week or so."

"That blue metal is not very romantic." Sophie gracefully chewed on her avocado and eggplant sandwich, covering her mouth with her hand.

"Romantic?"

"You know," she said waving her arm, "There's supposed to be a special kind of mood: specific lighting, an adventure with the imaginary, doubting intentions, a pricking of the senses, feeling a steady loss of control over the desperate frenzy in your arms."

"Sounds absolutely awful."

"No, Glaucon," Sophie retorted. "You're supposed to be happy on dates . . . and anxious. Unconditional self-abandon, like we read about in *Romeo and Juliet*."

"Can you believe both the lovers died in that play? I grew up thinking they lived happily ever after. What a shame! I think I liked the guardian version better. The apothecary gives Romeo a placebo instead of poison."

Sophie grew noticeably more annoyed by his comments.

Glaucon thought, *I know what will cheer her up. I'll pretend to serenade my Juliet on the balcony, just how we practiced earlier*. Sticking out his arm, he leaned on one knee citing Shakespeare from memory:

> *" 'But, soft! What light through yonder window breaks?*
> *It is the east, and Juliet is the sun*
> *Arise, fair sun, and kill the envious moon,*
> *Who is already sick and pale with grief,*
> *That thou her maid are far more fair than she.' "*

Sadly, his antics produced the opposite of their usual effect. Sophie wilted. Her face soured and appeared hurt. "Why are you teasing me so?" she asked. "Don't be cruel."

"I'm not teasing you, Sophie—honest! 'With love's light wings did I o'erperch those walls.' "

Sophie stood up and brushed crumbs off her dress. "Well that does it," she said. "Our date's ruined."

Glaucon tried to change the subject. "Sophie, why did Xenon steal you and your brother away from Heliopolis?"

"Always questions about Xenon," her jade eyes sparked. "Can't you ever ask anything else?"

"Like what?"

"Like maybe asking for a tintsy, little kiss from your obvious infatuation."

Was that the real meaning of a date? he wondered. The thought of a sober kiss without the *erosic* pill seemed a little weird. He never had a real one nor desired it. "All right, may I have a kiss?" he asked.

"Of course not now, you big dope!" Sophie looked dumbfounded. "Glaucon, you're a real piece of work, you know that. Even if you could read minds, you still wouldn't know the first thing about relating to others. What do you need, a textbook?" Sophie gruffly ripped the picnic blanket under his feet while he earnestly sought to discern his error. He detested how she expected him to know everything about Other Side culture.

Driving home in the *Pyrois* magnet-sedan was one of the most tense and uncomfortable moments of his life. Sophie tapped her finger on the autopilot terminal in one of her stormy rages as the car hovered three decimeters in the air. Her blue dress in the dark made her shine more beautifully than ever. Glaucon could only stare at his feet frozen in fear until they pulled into the driveway. Her finger pressed a button curling the door horizontal like a griffin-wing.

"Don't you want to talk anymore, Sophie?" Glaucon pleaded before she could leave.

"About what?" she asked.

Forms! Don't return my question with a question, Glaucon sighed. Those words brewed pregnant with possibility. What a perfect time in a story to have the hero lean over and confide his secrets; but he was not in a story. This was so much harder than reading. And so Glaucon sighed feverishly again, fire lashing his collar. Smoke choked his senses. Brick by brick, an insurmountable wall closed him in like a desperate Fortunato. He tried to lean over to kiss Sophie's ambrosial lips—exchange his own Romeo sinfulness—but his abominable seatbelt got in the way. Her stare, that cold, curious, ambiguous stare—what constriction, what delight!—whipped a coward raw in its wake. He retreated into his car seat like a frightened hermit crab.

Such cowardice enraged Sophie beyond comprehension. "Auugh! You really are denser than lead aren't you, Glaucon. I . . . I . . . I hate you." Her arms stretched down so tightly they almost toughed the ground. She could barely speak. "If you really don't like me, just say so. You don't have to act weird all the time." Glaucon tried to apologize but air pressure from the sliding door rammed menacingly in his face.

After he left, this lost moment was all he could think about. A kiss. A simple kiss. Stupid really, a trifle. Yet thoughts of the forbidden stole his appetite, consumed his heart with the pangs of imagined thrills.

In the Tenth Ward plaza today, though, Sophie shuddered differently. Her vest's grey buttons pressed urgently against his chest. She clasped her thin arms around his neck, almost as if their embarrassing encounter never occurred."Where have you been, Oxenbridge?" she asked, kissing him softly on the cheek. "We thought you taken in the raids . . . or worse."

Zemer removed his pin-striped jacket and folded it over his arm. "Sophie's been worried sick over you," he explained. "She awoke last night from a nightmare. Dreamed you were being tortured."

At this, Sophie pushed Glaucon away from her embrace. "Yeah, well the birdbrain just stopped showing up. What was I supposed to think?"

"I worried the jinn blew up in your hands." Zemer appraised his jinn next to the one shining between Glaucon's fingers.

"My jinn's fine," the guardian pulled away, reassuring his friends. "I was staying away on purpose. Didn't want to endanger you two." Like Homer he proceeded to concoct an extravagant *Odyssey* about being followed by corporate agents at Mira-Disney. All the while that wet kiss on his cheek stung bitterly.

After he finished, Sophie recounted the terrible (though unsurprising) news. Terra and another member of their printing group had been arrested the previous night. Even their children were taken. Most ominously, one of the neighbors found blood on the porch railing.

Zemer eyed one of the soldiers on the temple roof. "We knew distributing flyers at Dilmun Garments in the Sixth Ward would be dangerous," he said. "Terra was aware of the risks of placing flyers too near the Bull. I told her it was suicide. Too many auxiliaries."

"What will happen to them, you think?" Glaucon forced a question.

"I don't know. Maybe re-education in the mind-stocks, maybe the Bull. The law is what the guardians make it."

Sophie reported, "You've missed some important developments since you left us, Glaucon."

"Oh?"

"The Central Directory called an emergency inter-ward conference this afternoon. Two things were accomplished. First, we finally passed a list of libertarian socialist principles by acclamation. Second, the Industrial Workers' Federation called for a general strike until Terra is released. If all goes according to plan, the entire city will shut down."

"A strike?" Glaucon glanced at her. "Are they insane?"

"The authorities raised daily executions of sensualist roaders from five to ten. A few protesters were shot in the street this morning. To do nothing is to show weakness."

"The guardians don't respond well to threats."

"Neither do helots."

Glaucon stared blankly at the ground. Bells began to chime from the temple towers. "We really ought to be going," he said. "The crowds won't last forever."

Zemer commented on a ring of metallic newsstands selling religious paraphernalia: earthen *haniwa* figurines, anchor necklaces, and the new bestselling self-help book by Confessor Nikodem, *The Purpose Driven Wife*. "I never cease to be amazed," he said. "The people here are consumed with the idea of religion, orichalcum, and success. Even God has become a commodity, bartered like some glass trinket. Here is the seventh proof for God's existence: The concept makes money. What more do you need to prove being?"

"The people are rotting from the top down," Glaucon lamented. Another herd of helots emerged from the flower-covered temples, rubbing their eyes with water from the lustral bowls. They dropped cakes on altars and flowed down the city blocks.

Zemer disagreed. "Some are rotting; not all. There is more dissent than meets the eye, as is evident by the unions and secret organizations helping us. Working here over the last month, I've also witnessed a vibrant community of underground temples. Many helots shun the perfect ideas expressed in the Condentine Liturgy and prefer private unfettered worship of a more complex God in their homes. Yes, they attend sermons about the Form of the Good out of fear of missing their quota, but Prodicus and his Department of Confessors do not hold their hearts. This uplifts my spirit, for I see the human will is never completely yoked."

"That meeting today was the largest one yet," Sophie said optimistically. "What scares Prodicus the most is that all our little groups will find one another and organize—exactly what's happening!"

Zemer noticed the Donald Duck statue with the infectious grin standing in the fountain. He adjusted his tie and stepped up on the circular concrete rim.

"Problem is pleasure here's too sanitized. There's no risk. The helots have every pleasure provided but they lack the best of all—"

"Spontaneity," Sophie finished his sentence.

"Yes, that's exactly right, Sister. Spontaneity is the most dangerous thing for children. Spontaneity has to be crushed for a perfect society of infants."

"I can't even watch the digitele anymore," Sophie whined, thinking of the shows beamed in from Worldlink. "I read an article in *Celebriteen* the other day about how all the movie stars from Cindy Marquee to Pimp Phoenix are farmed at special schools. Music bands like the Ladon Charmers are constructed soullessly by the Institute for Patriotic Dispersion. There's something unnatural about how the Vinculum Cartel molds and manufactures clean, packaged things for people to consume. I want things to go wrong. I want things to break. Ward pleasures are lower than a pig's."

Zemer picked up his suitcase and the three friends walked away from the plaza.

As they turned onto a wide boulevard, Glaucon questioned Sophie skeptically: "Are you ranking pleasures now, Sophie? Good luck, but all pleasures seem the same to me, wherever it comes from. What would you prefer in the fountain instead of that deranged duck? August Rodin's *The Thinker?* Or maybe you would prefer . . . *The Kiss*?"

Sophie smirked at the inside joke, but crinkled her nose. "Well Glaucon," she teased, "you would put manufactured fun—horrid products like the hedon whistles, yabyummies, and zimrum—on the same level as, say, a symphony?"

"Absolutely! What's the difference between them? Take a painting and the hedon whistle, for example." Glaucon removed a slender gazoo-shaped stick from his pocket and inhaled deeply. A screaming blitzkrieg of chemical fire raced down his spine unlocking contentment. He went on, happy this release helped him forget about Terra: "In the grand scheme of things, who cares about art? By all accounts the enjoyment I receive from this hedon whistle lasts approximately ten minutes while I might (at best) get ten to twenty seconds on a painting. With time to kill I'd choose the hedon whistle every time."

Glaucon sometimes played the helot position too well.

Sophie snatched the whistle from his hand and put it wet to her lips, inhaling deeply, and then spilled into a fit of coughs. "If you experienced both pleasures and were a fair judge, Glaucon, you'd certainly say the painting was better." Flushed, she hurled the used whistle into a matter incinerator.

"Well, I've seen lots of paintings—"

"Yes, pictures by the guardian-artist-patriots. Hardly *real* paintings."

At this point, Glaucon became desperately feverish and would've given anything to shout out, "My darling, my dove, can you honestly look me in the eye and tell me you'd prefer Rodin's *The Kiss* over the simple, piggish pleasure of an actual kiss with me?" But he was too afraid how Sophie would respond. At any rate, the hedon whistle disoriented him.

Red smoke from the cogniscramblers did, too. Every dozen steps or so, the pods spewed out putrefying fog as they opened. Families waited in tangled lines to purify their I.T. waves before dinner.

"I can tell you've lived in the wards too long," Sophie coquettishly nudged him, finally feeling the full effects of the hedon whistle. "Funny, though, for someone so enamored with defending the lesser pleasures in life, you have an odd way of acting. I've never seen you lose yourself in any of the more interesting lower pleasures." Crossing her arms, she caught up with Zemer ahead, leaving Glaucon caught in a cold current of red wind.

"What did she mean by that remark?" he winced.

They came to a crowded intersection with glass signs. Flashing hologram advertisements and another marble temple greeted them. On the left corner was a hulking zizthopter exhibit, sponsored by the companies Mira-Disney and Seven Seas as well as the Stratos Auxiliary Core. It drew avid crowds—mostly children—who were coaxed to climb aboard the zizthopter and aim Deathstalker missiles and rapid-fire sonic carbines, the finest weapons of the Republic, at a make-believe settlement on the Other Side. Like all war games, it incorporated varying levels of complexity and scanned the children's I.T. waves for silver resonances to see if they should be sent packing to Stratos. Each neutralized settlement bought wild applause from the crowd.

Sophie studied the moving pixels scurrying through the cratered rubble of Texarkana. "Fools have our tactical formations completely backward," she sneered.

"Well, I don't think those are soldiers they're firing at," Zemer stated, surprised by his sister's lapse in secrecy.

Sophie's face tensed, boiling with hidden anger. She seemed carried away by spirits and did not hear her brother's words.

Glaucon asked, "Sophie, what do you know about tactical formation?" He often forgot the twins once lived outside the city walls.

In the video game, ziz wings glided under two collapsing buildings to spray retreating rebels with lasers.

Zemer asked with a feigned look of surprise, "Funny. She hasn't told you yet?"

"Brother, don't you dare," Sophie warned.

"Oh come on, Sis. He was going to find out sooner or later. After our confession before the Directory today, pretty much everyone else knows it."

"This is not the time or the place—"

"See, Glaucon, when we first met, Sophie and I told you a half truth. We couldn't be sure you were reliable. You might've even been a guardian spy. But since it's been over a month already. . . ."

"You're not really from the Continental Caucus?" Glaucon asked confused.

"No, that part was true, but we're also soldiers in the Eastern Column. Sophie is our commander."

"But that's the Iron Queen's column."

Zemer smiled, nodding his head.

Glaucon peered at Sophie's face and bounded backward in shock. "Impossible! Sophie, *you're* the Iron Queen?"

Instantly, Sophie clasped her hand to his mouth. "Not so loud," she hushed. "Do you want to get us arrested?"

"She inflicted hell at the Fourth Battle of Chicago," Zemer noted.

"But you're so—young." Glaucon could hardly believe she was a soldier, let alone the most ferocious strategist in the Southwest. Those numerous stories about her bloodthirsty brutality suddenly seemed less credible.

The thought of Sophie fighting in the back of a mud-soaked truck was troubling. He fought in the burned city of Chicago as well. Twice actually, during the Third and Fourth Battles. The fighting had been fierce up along Highway 290 leading to Toxic Lake Michigan, especially after General Argus and Leonida declared a free-fire zone. Hundreds of bodies lay strewn on the ground, half-disintegrated by energy weapons, as ziz flattened the city to ash.

"She's ferocious, too," Zemer said. "Only person I've seen single-handedly take down an Aegis tank. Xenon sent her to keep me on a short leash, but he forgets how well blood sticks together. He wants nothing more than success for our mission here."

"Why do they call you the Iron Queen? You don't look like a golem to me." Glaucon pinched Sophie's arm like a scientific specimen.

"All war is deception, Glaucon," Sophie pushed away flustered. "I'd rather not talk about this right now. I *was* going to tell you sooner or later, at a more appropriate time. But some people just can't keep their big mouths shut—or follow simple orders."

"What mission did Xenon give you?"

"Forget about it," Sophie said.

"Were you given military targets to attack?"

"Several, actually," Zemer admitted, "but our primary objective was to kill someone."

Sophie grabbed her brother's arm, casting a fearsome look.

"What?" Zemer asked innocently. "You didn't follow through."

"Who?" asked Glaucon. "Prodicus?"

Zemer laughed. "Are you kidding? The golems would cut us down before we got within one hundred meters."

Sophie said, "Our orders aren't important anymore, Glaucon. Things have changed. I didn't tell you I was the Iron Queen because I left her on the Other Side."

"Do any of the others know about your targets?"

"Only Sophie was shown a shadowspar recording of the primary one, and her lips are sealed—for his safety. Rest assured, if she was serious he'd already be dead."

"Just how were you going to assassinate your target, Sophie?"

Zemer peered down the road at the calm paranoia and hologram logos, the restless blocks bleached clean by periodic mists of disinfectant. "Desires of the flesh open every barrier," he said. "Not many can turn down such a pretty woman, especially when the *erosic* pill is offered."

So it was a guardian, then.

Sophie tried to explain, "Glaucon, that part of my life is behind me. Xenon is behind me. I will kill no more. I'm trying to be a different person here."

"So you could just take *erosic* with someone and kill them?"

"Don't get so sanctimonious. Look at what you teach your children to do."

More hideous applause erupted from the spectators watching the children on the zizthopter.

"You think your technocratic assassins can continue rooting out our families without retaliation?" Sophie asked angrily. "Your ziz are more predictable than planets. Come revolving every month or so. So much death, you can't sleep. How do you explain the ziz to children? You can't. You say they're built by men, but no one believes. So we tell them they're dragons in the sky sent from a place called Death. If you're playing in a group, scatter. Scatter so you'll not be killed. The Iron Queen was born from the blood of children, Glaucon. She bled and cried over them, cried things she can't forget. To protect them she became a dragon and did horrible things. If you get in her way, she might kill you, too."

Briefly Glaucon spied a foreign element in Sophie's face, something he had never seen before—mechanical cruelty, mechanical resolve.

Zemer's mood had changed as well. He held the jinn in front of him. "I think it's time for another power outage, don't you, Sister?" he asked examining the zizthopter.

"Here?" Sophie's voice brightened.

"Why not? A little mayhem will do this block good. We'll just leave a few."

Zemer closed his eyes and gripped the jinn tightly. Familiar goose-bumps crawled up Glaucon's neck. Ice frosted the glass windows. Sophie extracted several copies of the *Goetia Mirror* from the suitcase. Zemer opened his eyes. The whites had disappeared, filled in by hollow pools of red. Electric wind skipped down the street, darkening digitele screens, hologram logos, computers monitors, and the all-seeing eyecameras. The zizthopter video screen shattered. So did its wings. While everyone looked around in confusion at the failing electronics, Sophie stacked papers on the curb.

Glaucon felt cold, faint under the jinn's flash. He clutched his chest. Atropos sat shriveled on a light post, staring down, fading in and out like bad reception. "What is she doing here?" he wondered aloud. Atropos made his mind splinter like a bulb of pus.

Your friends pervert the gods' gift, said the voice.

"There's no such thing."

Gods are made so easily; how quickly man rejects them.

"What do you want?"

What you want, Glaucon. Why are you playing the part of the helot so well?

"A helot birthed me."

Ha, Ha, Ha! the voice cackled. *I know you better. You enjoy toying with your prey like a hungry mountain lion. You want the twins dead—like us.*

"Of course I do. Fire from my xiphos stick. I'll spray fire over both their backs, just like Terra. No respite from their grief."

You can't let Sophie succeed in her mission. She's on to us. She says she's changed, but we know better, don't we? Be careful of her. I told you she was hiding something. She is the Iron Queen, a murderous creature and your enemy.

"I plot oblivion and will destroy her. All rebels must die . . . no . . . wait . . . what am I saying? Get out of my head. Get out. Get out. What are you?"

I am you. I am the you which stands above the other you. The you which you can't ignore. Sophie's tactics will not save her from our wrath. The blood of her family is polluted by the worst of crimes.

Sophie's hand fell heavy over Glaucon's perspiring head. Her face twisted in panic, "Glaucon, Glaucon, come back to us." Crowds were still wandering around confused, looking for the source of the power failure, a glimpse of the Son of Fate. "You feeling all right?" she asked him limp by the icy glass. "You stumbled, hit the wall. You're holding your head. Were you struck by the jinn?"

Glaucon felt peaceful staring at her and stood up coughing. "No, nothing like that. It's the sudden change in temperature, I think. Let's get out of here."

Nearby, a reverend guardian dressed in white robes with a prayer shawl sat at a table under an umbrella. All morning he sought contributions to aid the victims of the gas attack. The power outage drove children to him. One young boy, who previously aimed Deathstalker missiles, now dropped orichalcum into an alms basket out of the goodness of his heart. The helots could be both murderers and saints. Glaucon hoped he might be the same. He kicked the stack of *Goetia Mirror* wildly in the air before disappearing around the corner.

III § 8 DISPOSSESSED AND UNDERGROUND

The hideout on 186 Hypostasis Falls looked just as Glaucon left it: an unimposing red brick camera factory at the edge of the business district. It had strong wooden shutters, a stone balustrade, trimmed hedges winding around to the common park in the back. The oddest thing about the place, however, was the eyecameras (or the lack of eyecameras). While the devices lay strewn about the street, inserted like nails into trunks of trees and buildings, none were visible on the factory walls; the building stood bare as a monolith. *That* kind of irony, Glaucon knew, was not accidental, but required thoughtful planning. Guardian planning.

Ivan was waiting for them on the stone steps of the factory. His beard—more uneven stubble—suggested the absence of a morning shave. A necklace of sweat coated his shirt collar. He looked exhausted, despairing, like he had not slept in weeks.

"Everything's clear," he declared with a robust grunt as the group arrived. "A patrol hasn't been around for hours. The phylark scum, well," Ivan motioned across the street to the three-story 17-E-Sigma Neighborhood Watch Office, "they made sure to leave early for the temples."

Zemer eyed the building. "Let them go; they make good shepherds. But we should remember how shepherds eat the sheep."

Ivan chewed on the words, obviously brooding about Terra's disappearance. He seemed possessed by maddening thoughts, and anger clothed him with the quiet scowl of a man about to break.

Hesitantly, Zemer asked with hands in his pockets, "Tell me, Ivan, are you still sore with us about what happened earlier . . . during the meeting?"

Ivan did not respond to his question. "Here," he said distantly. Reaching into one of two breast pockets on his starched grey shirt, he handed a folded note to Sophie.

"What's this?" Sophie asked.

"Confirmed organizations set to strike."

"You don't sound pleased." Sophie unfolded the paper and studied the contents. "Let's see: IWF, Lower Ward Revolutionary Council, People's Action Front, Black Dawn, Social-Democratic Labor Party. There are many names here—almost everyone who passed Resolution 15. What's the problem?"

"A list of the dead."

"You think that plan to storm Miantgast would turn out better, Ivan? That fortress is impregnable—impossible to reach. Might as well be Alpha Centauri."

"Not with the jinn."

"Even with the jinn."

"If you say so. *You're* the Iron Queen."

Sophie folded her arms, arguing, "Listen up; so much more can be accomplished by strikes than this berserker suicide mission. Coordination is easier on familiar territory. You can expropriate the factories and firms for the workers' use and begin training in collective management. If enough businesses are taken over peacefully, the guardians might bargain for our comrades . . . and Terra. You'll just die fighting otherwise, and what good will that do?"

"Don't waste breath on those clever arguments again. Your side won the vote, remember? Nearly unanimous."

"Nothing's ever settled, Ivan. We don't want to force any one of our members to act in ways they find unreasonable."

As they continued talking, Glaucon drifted off. He couldn't look Ivan directly in the eye. He imagined Terra languishing immobile in some

Miantgast cell and shuddered for his hideous deeds. How many times did they play Tavli together, venerate the joy of nighttime walks, discuss justice blind to caste, and engineer the call of the *Goetia Mirror*? Yet he turned her in faster than bullets from a rail gun, drank up her suffering like Falernian wine.

It's because she's my enemy, he kept scolding himself. *Any guardian would've informed on her in a nanosecond. Only proper. Terra was a sleeper agent for Xenon. She disrupted the city. All rebels must die!*

Somehow, his vagrant migrations between Heliopolis and the Tenth Ward filled him with uncertainty. He felt torn between two worlds. To be a hero in one and a villain in another—what better evidence nature was a flux of opposing forces.

Feeling his heart tremor, Glaucon fled up the factory steps. He swung open two doors made of solid bronze and walked inside. Not a soul stirred in the workhouse. An assembly line of dormant pumps, glass lens cutters, and strange-moving arms filled the floor. He nearly tripped over four crates filled with camera barrels and adhesives. At the back of the factory, a folding door with a faulty hinge opened like an accordion into a cramped two story living area.

Hecatia, the factory owner, and six other rebels hunched over a commercial stove. All had been assigned mess for the day. A black cat lounged in one of the chairs eyeing them work.

Hearing someone enter, Hecatia turned wiping her face with her apron. Her eyes brightened upon seeing Glaucon. "Good gracious, look who it is," she said. "How marvelous you made it back safely. All of us were so worried. Sophie especially."

Glaucon thanked Hecatia for her concern, but eyed the guardian suspiciously.

This old woman was a crafty one. Relatively clean profile. Shiny as an apple with a rotten core. Twenty years before, the police caught her red-handed—literally!—brushing a cityscape painting in the impressionist style. After publicly recanting her work and begging forgiveness from the Logoset, the guardians exiled her from Heliopolis to labor in the Tenth Ward. With no other infractions to speak of during her probation, everyone believed her rehabilitated. But she hadn't changed, just became more careful.

Behind her on the sink Glaucon noticed a hardback book.

"*The Social Contract*," he read the title aloud with interest.

"Oh," Hecatia wrinkled her face, "that's from Sophie's book study with the Pioneer Speakers yesterday."

"Saint Plato, I totally forgot. How many trainees showed up?"

"Uh . . . about thirty-seven, I believe."

"Thirty-seven? Much more than expected."

"True."

"Did all the wards make it?"

"No. The First Ward, regretfully, couldn't send any comrades. The Ozbolt bosses keep close watch over their wage-slaves."

"Pity. Was Sophie interesting? You know how she can drag on about the details."

"Quite the opposite actually. Sophie presented a sweeping historical lecture about the development of social contract theory, tracing it from Plato's *Crito* to Hobbes, Locke, and Rousseau, and how it conflicts with anarchist principles."

"I often wonder if there's any philosopher Sophie agrees with. What did she say about it?"

"A number of things, actually. Proponents of social contract theory believe difficulties in a pre-political state of nature compelled individuals to surrender their independence to state governments out of self-interest."

"Quite so, but what exactly is her problem?"

"Her chief criticism was that the theory crafts a radical individualism out of touch with human reality."

"This comes from an anarchist?"

"What better voice, Glaucon? Social contract assumes a person, in theory, could live in isolation from everyone else. There is the classic—but fictitious—image of a savage trotting alone in the wilderness, attacking exposed strangers, living in constant, agonizing fear for his own life; hence, the need for protective government. Anarchists believe such a pre-political state ahistorical and undesirable. People could never live that way. They need society for moral and material survival. How did Sophie put it? 'Human beings are, by nature, social creatures. They begin life sharing their mother's body, and forever after cling to others for warmth. People crave society like breath in their lungs, like rain from the sky. They're born social and die social. Cooperation and solidarity is natural and critical for happiness. No contract is necessary to make people relate or to force them to behave. Contracts, in fact, are dangerous by crystallizing relations, preventing natural social evolution.' "

"Odd how she views society and government as separate."

"Oh, the distinction is quite critical to her argument. For you see, the anarchist's goal—our goal—is to finally destroy artificial state contracts and laws in order to free the goods of natural society."

It all sounded so very heretical, Glaucon shivered, *more Aristotelian than anything else.* He placed the book back down and leaned over the stove to examine Hecatia's boiling vegetable soup.

"The Iron Queen certainly has a way with words," he confessed to Hecatia. "I'm sure her Pioneers are busy spreading revolutionary training as we speak."

"Let's hope. . . ." A brief pause. "I see Sophie's finally confided to you who she is?"

"I've known for some time."

"Is that so? Did that cause a fight between you?"

"No. Why do you ask?"

"Well, lately she's been acting as if you deeply wounded her. So morose. Did you say something?"

"I can't remember anything of note."

Hecatia grinned under her wrinkles. "I think you like her," she suggested out of the blue.

"What?" Glaucon shot back. "That's preposterous. What makes you say something crazy like that?"

"The desires of youth are obvious."

The accordion door creaked open and Sophie stormed into the kitchen.

"What were you talking about?" she asked, noticing the strange silence overtaking the room.

Glaucon shrugged, which caused Sophie to hit him over the head. "What got into you out there?" she asked.

"Out where?"

"Outside. You didn't even say 'hello' to Ivan. How rude! He blames himself for what happened to Terra. She was taken while he was running resources for the Directory."

"He didn't look like he wanted to talk about his wife."

"No one tells you when they need help; you have to ask. Be more considerate in the future." Then she barked, "Now get the floor."

Glaucon jolted to the center of the room and yanked aside an oriental rug. The rug covered a trapdoor leading to a spiraling staircase. They led to a rickety wooden catwalk and another flight of stairs to the concrete basement. "The Pit of Goetia," Sophie sometimes joked. It reminded Glaucon a little of Er's openings in the earth. Like a quiet roar, the urgent tempo of electric printing could be heard through the hole.

Air in the secret printing house tasted stale like a garage. There was hardly any ventilation. Three heavy fans rotated slowly on the ceiling next to a jungle of wires, fluorescent lamps, and rusty pipes. Along the walls, six black anarchist flags draped to the floor. Glaucon suspected the area had once functioned as a warehouse; there were still oddly shaped factory equipment and mysterious boxes the rebels converted to desks.

The anarchists were a gang of radicals of every sort: libertarian collectivists, anarcho-syndicalists, mutualists, egoists, libertarian municipalists, atheists, existentialists, infidels, and absurdists. Glaucon swore there were more factions than people. He could barely keep up with the different names when summarizing their views for his ISHIM report. What seemed beyond argument: No one was Republican. Like Hecatia hinted, they were individualists (and socialists), but of a particular type. They believed *all*—not many, not some—*all* should be able to develop their full physical, moral and intellectual potential. Each loved liberty and decried Vinculum wage-slavery and the dictatorship of the archons. Their speeches hurled contempt on hierarchy and the "authority principle," calling it the "greatest abomination on the earth." The outcasts stood united by a general animosity toward the Civil State, which, as Zemer reasoned, must always be tyrannical, putting its own welfare above its subjects.

Down below, to the left of the stairs, an initiation ceremony was wrapping up near what the anarchists called "the debating square." They just returned from protesting. Usually, members crammed new recruits into the ring of boxes to read aloud passages about the anarchic horse Houyhnhnms from *Gulliver's Travels*, or to discuss long dead American anarchist heroes like Emma Goldman and Noam Chomsky. After a succession of debates, a forever-adding of ideas, revolutionary literature was distributed to the new member. Then all loudly sang revolutionary songs and recited from Percy Shelley's *Mask of Anarchy*:

> *" 'Rise like lions after slumber*
> *In unvanquishable number!*
> *Shake your chains to earth, like dew*
> *Which in sleep had fallen on you—*
> *Ye are many; they are few.' "*

Aquila Naybah and Zenobia Kidd, still dressed in their business pant suits, stood near a table covered with Kevlar, gas masks, rope, earplugs for the acoustic nodules, plasmaknives, and other tools. A large yellowed map of the Fifth Ward covered half the surface. They motioned for Glaucon and Sophie to join them.

"Nice of you to finally get here," Aquila smiled at Glaucon. "We missed you at debate the other day. No one plays devil's advocate quite like you."

Glaucon rubbed the back of his head. "Gee, Aquila, sorry about that."

At this disgusting display Sophie demanded, "Where'd you get the map?" a glimmer of jealousy in her tone.

Aquila straightened immediately. "From Akakios Smith of Black Dawn. As I'm sure *you're* aware, Sophie, any protracted workers' strike will require vast food reserves. We must prepare a rationing system for distribution to the factories at once. A run on Shennong Fooderies is necessary."

"Clever girl," Sophie agreed. "Have you selected a strike team?"

"Zenobia's planning on making a run to Shennong Fooderies with Akakios' gang."

Zenobia adjusted her black beret. She'd come with the other rebels, fresh from a Ninth Ward protest, dodging bullets along the way. A wild face, fiercely adventurous, she was a screen writer for Mira-Disney by day and a fiery IWF speaker at night. Good with symsysts, too. After merging her underground literature club with the *Goetia Mirror*, she helped expand it to the nets, networking anarchist discussion boards and illegal funding groups. She studied the map on the table with consternation. "Security is pretty tight at most of the key sentry posts along the wall, there and there," she explained. "A gap by canton 73 but—"

"Why not here?" Glaucon traced his finger to a small cleft near the coast.

"No way," Zenobia scoffed. "Don't you see all those towers?"

"Not manned. Just a test for guardian and auxiliary children from Stratos. They have to sneak into the wards to steal food."

Aquila moaned, "Yeah, and I bet you have a villa on Capri to give me."

"I swear by the whole race of gods!"

"An oath?" Aquila feigned a gasp. "Let's not go that far, Glaucon. Even if it's true, how would *you* know?"

All three women scrutinized him round eyed for an answer.

You idiot yahoo, Glaucon lashed his brain. *Are you trying to unmask yourself?* Finally he scrambled, "Sheesh, Aquila, who doesn't know about the spooky 'phantom towers?' That old rumor's been blowing round the office like a bad smell for years. Tell them Sophie. What did you do for food when you lived on Stratos?"

Sophie looked surprised by his question. "We found those towers, I guess. You could send a delivery drone through them."

"Well there you go. See?"

"Fantastic," Zenobia shouted, "but kind of irrational."

"Well, when the insane run the asylum what do you expect?" Glaucon asked chidingly.

This made everyone laugh, but then Zenobia's face stiffened. Her eyes migrated from the table to the stairs. Zemer had entered the basement. "The Son of Fate," she whispered, staring up at the thunder-seer as if he had white wings. Everyone in the printing house shot up at once, screeching on their folding chairs.

Sophie found the phenomenon amusing. Every time her brother entered a room it triggered mass pandemonium. Three-fourths of the reverence stemmed from his extraordinary power with the jinn, which many viewed as an unexplainable miracle stone. The other fourth came from his personality. Glaucon sometimes wondered how to properly characterize him in his notes. There was natural warmth about Zemer, a persistent charm. The man could draw out people's thoughts and always knew precisely what to say. Like Sophie, he was a gifted orator, but softer, more disarming. When talking to him, one felt at peace, a distinct trust. Glaucon had seen him, on numerous occasions, turn the most obstinate scoundrel into a loyal friend.

The tenacious crowds pushed on the sable-haired youth holding a pilos hat in his hands. They peppered him with questions.

"Zemer, I've found the perfect excerpt for our next cover," one said.

"Zemer, we were worried at the time," called another.

Papers hoisted willy-nilly into Zemer's face. Efforts were needed to focus more on Beat poetry, or to print Byron and Keats or selections from *Homage to Catalonia*. By all the commotion, one would have thought he was Cadmus bestowing the alphabet!

Aquila spun Zemer around. "There you are. Look at this picture of Iphigenia, will you?" she demanded under her thin, gently sloping nose.

For some reason, Aquila reminded Glaucon of his mother. Her brown blow-dried hair and animated expressions made him nostalgic for the days before the Academy. Aquila was fond of tragedies like Sophocles' *Oedipus the King*, and especially the *Oresteia Trilogy* about the death of King Agamemnon and the end of the curse of House Atreus. She was currently working on an article about the sacrifice of Iphigenia. According to the real legend, Agamemnon, King of the Mycenaeans, burnt his daughter alive to gain a favorable wind and achieve victory at Troy; but in the Republic Iphigenia happily married a Corinthian duke.

"This is a fine picture," Zemer returned it without much thought.

"No, the color printer's busted," Aquila pressed him again. "The lines are faded and not copying correctly."

"Did you have Ivan or Phillip look to the problem?"

"Yeah; Ivan tried for thirty minutes and left cursing. You know how he gets."

"What do you expect me to do? I'm not a technician. Maybe the ink jets dried up or something. They congeal like glue sometimes."

Aquila appeared satisfied for the moment but still groaned in frustration. "My goodness, how did people in the twenty-sixth century survive such annoyances?"

"Humans can get accustomed to all kinds of things," Zemer answered her. "The Tenth Ward can speak to *that* truth. Where did you find the picture anyway?"

Aquila's cheeks blushed as she stumbled back. "Glaucon helped me find it. He gave me this big green encyclopedia of Greek mythology and folded one of the pages he thought would be helpful."

This tidbit of information infuriated Sophie. "Oh, I bet he did," she scowled turning up her nose. Glaucon's past avoidance and continued flirting with Aquila noticeably upset the center of her world. She dropped down onto a box, began tapping her foot, wondering why she cared so much about something so . . . so . . . frivolous, so propertarian. Especially now, at a time when such feelings were inappropriate.

Aquila continued, "For my next article, though, I should like to spend more time on Iphigenia's mother, Clytemnestra."

"Really, and why is that?" asked Sophie pretending to be curious.

"Because she killed Agamemnon with such frightening determination. You remember the story. When Agamemnon returned from Troy, Clytemnestra hacked her naked husband to pieces in the bath with a double-sided black axe. Took a shower in blood and hung his guts on the walls. Ay, what a victory for women! Agamemnon was a disgusting brute who thought he controlled the world. A selfish master, he fled his wife and love like some foolish knight to stick his sword in the sands of Troy. He hated love. He hated it so much he warred against love everywhere. Even killed his own daughter, Iphigenia, for the victory. But Clytemnestra—the beauty!—held her husband's life all along. From the moment Agamemnon burnt Iphigenia he was a cursed dead man. Those ten long years on the Turkish coast purchased nothing but pointless death. Clytemnestra behaved nobly. All men that sacrifice their daughters for power should be punished thus."

"My, what an interesting position, Aquila," Sophie chimed in, puffing air on the glass of her wristwatch. "But you know, if we hacked to death any man who dared sacrifice his woman for power, there'd be no men left in the world."

Zemer jestfully clutched his seared heart. "Mercy in heaven, you've wounded me," he said, stumbling theatrically toward his sour sibling. "Sister, oh sad sister, we know a thing or two about family curses, don't we?"

"Too much, Little Brother."

Zemer ripped off his jacket in a flash and fell into his sister's lap, gurgling and sticking out his tongue like a dead Agamemnon. Sophie bit her lip and heaved him to the floor like a rock.

"You dummy," she hurled.

"You dummy," Zemer bantered back, wrapped in his pin-striped coat like a burial shroud. "I must apologize for my abnormal behavior," he addressed the crowd. "Getting a rise out of my sister is one of my guilty pleasures, one I rarely enjoyed when she pulled military rank on the Other Side. Only because she can be so. . . ."

"Temperamental," Glaucon finished his sentence.

"Yes, that's the ticket."

Sophie kicked her laughing brother again, but a gentle smile cracked on her face from all the attention. "Well, I think you're both children anyhow. You know, I'm still technically in charge of this little operation. Perhaps I should conduct things like Xenon."

Zemer sat up with his elbow on the cement, grinning. "You spoil me too much," he said, and then turning to Aquila: "Do tell, just how did our honorable guardians of virtue change the story of Clytemnestra for public consumption?"

"You can guess," Aquila groaned loathingly. "No creativity at all. They simply had Clytemnestra and Agamemnon restored and happy. What a waste."

"At least the guardians are consistent."

"How splendid, Consistency. A virtue turned vice, like all other virtues in this city."

All the talk of blood and axes made Glaucon remember the book he brought for Sophie. One of his most difficult finds yet in Prodicus' library cache, it was hidden behind an old moldy atlas. Reaching into his knapsack, Glaucon plucked it out.

"That reminds me, Sophie," he said. "I found the book you requested . . . *Justine.* I've been reading a bit, though, and there are some . . . unconventional plot devices."

Zemer covered his face howling on the floor. "The Marquis de Sade, Sophie? Really? Sometimes you can be such a depraved scoundrel! Fiendish, but surprisingly enchanting. I couldn't have selected better myself. That's *sure* to draw the ire of the Logoset."

Sophie giggled snatching the old book. "You know, Zemer, usually I wouldn't want to read Sade, but the fact guardians have forbidden it, well, that is reason enough to think every word was truth. The Logoset is where the wicked prosper and call it virtue. I think the chronicles of Sade's *Justine*—an honest, virtuous woman raped, molested, and sexually enslaved by 'saintly' men, and ultimately struck down by God's thunderbolt—reveals the cruel reality of our world. The good are punished and the evil are rewarded."

"Well if you say so," Zemer said, extending his hand to Glaucon, who tested his friend's weight before pulling him up stiffly.

"Yes, but Sade is twisted and debauched," Glaucon grunted in exertion. "He hates mankind, uplifts selfish advantage at the expense of everyone else. He died a lunatic in an asylum. Quite insane."

Sophie blew dust off the cover. "But that's what makes him most interesting, Glaucon."

Zemer chuckled. "Can you believe I've yet to meet any sane people? And if I did, I'd think them awfully boring. Sade represents absolute negation. He sees individual personal pleasure as the only good, and he cannot see the importance of caring for others. Thus blinded by selfishness and domination, he missed love, sympathy, community, solidarity, the greatest pleasures of them all. How irrational for someone seeking the maximization of personal happiness. Wherever do you find these books, Glaucon?"

Zemer's words said one thing, but his penetrating eyes expressed a different worry. He stared at Glaucon's right hand—his *tetractys* shielded by the skincover.

Does Zemer know what a liar I am? Glaucon wondered. *Not even eyecameras can see the mind.* Whenever Zemer stared at him like this he felt reined in, shameful and naked, like he was being dragged out as a worm from the soil. Glaucon finally sputtered out a half-hearted attempt at an explanation, something about having a friend in Mira-Disney management. "You should see the kind of orichalcum some people are willing to pay for these books," he yammered. "I think it's a good sign for us."

"I hope you're right," Zemer replied looking across the room.

Whether he believed Glaucon was another matter.

Sophie decided to be useful. She marched back to the printers with the frustrated Aquila and started pounding and tearing apart the printing machine with a screwdriver, throwing pieces in the air like kettle corn from a fire. Glaucon gaped at her transfixed. Momentarily, while she gracefully bent over fidgeting with the stubborn ink, ambitions darker than Sade's pincers inched into his mind.

His view was disrupted by the rapturous flurry of the printing house. News of city-wide strike electrified the room; rebels conferred together like storm clouds gathering strength. Many viewed Glaucon's return as a favorable sign, especially Phillip and Hella. Like most siblings, Glaucon found the two intriguing. Both helots were organizers in Atum Construction Company, mind-stocked three times for unlawfully petitioning its executives. Skin stained dark by working in the sun, they wore cheap shirts and disobedient smiles.

When they sought his opinion on the recent decision to strike, Glaucon answered skeptically: "Moves us closer to revolution, I guess, but can locked factory doors really expect to succeed against the lightning fury of the xiphos?"

Hella asked, "You think they'd really attack *all* their factories?"

Glaucon gave her a look as if the answer was self-evident.

"Gods," Phillip said, scratching his thin, bald skull, "even if the strike remains peaceful? What good would it do to brutalize the workers and the city? That'll only condemn them further."

"Have you read the Directory's resolution?"

"Yes. It rightfully declares guardian authority abolished and all political prisoners should be set free."

"It will become our death warrant."

"The people will back us. You should've seen them today at the Ninth Ward protest. Everything shut down."

"Back us with what, Phillip? We have no weapons or military training. Even if the guardians don't think we're serious, we've injured the city's perception of them. That's worse than violent revolt."

"Who cares about perception?"

"Perception is more important than reality; for ideas mold the clay. We best prepare for the worst. There hasn't been a successful strike in generations."

Glaucon felt claustrophobic. He left the two and retreated to the center of the room. *The guardians will surely kill them all*, he thought. No speculation about it. They'd be crushed in less than a day. The image knotted his stomach. Why? How could he foster such emotion? Why could he not control these dangerous and wicked attachments?

"You don't look well, Glaucon," Zemer said chasing him. "Do you need to rest?"

"No. I'm just claustrophobic with all these people."

"I know what you mean. Who could've thought all this was possible, huh? The people here are like a hidden well. You just need to know where to drop the bucket. Take Aquila for example. If Hecatia hadn't reached out to her, she'd still feel alone and isolated at Mira-Disney—just as intended. You'd be the same if fate hadn't brought us together. Don't you like this life better than what you had before?"

"There is certainly more freedom here than anywhere else I've been."

"Glad to hear it. It's as Vissarion Belinsky said in his *Letters to Gogol*: 'Only in literature, in spite of Tartan censorship, is there still life and forward movement.' The dark air here may be musty, but it's filled with creative energy and revolt. The process of printing animates me."

"Why?"

"When I read poetry and literature I feel less isolated, and tingle with collective awareness. Other people seem less foreign. The categories invented by the guardians start to decay. This fills me with happiness."

"Tell me," Glaucon inquired softly of his friend, "when shall such categories finally disappear and men be set free?"

"No, no," Zemer responded pushing out his arms. "Freedom will never be an event. Freedom is process, action, a life style. The human mind is a loosed fox incapable of remaining still. To avoid the snares of false essences, a continuous revolution of ideas and passion is necessary. Every sacred temple must be destroyed for new creation. We just can't think them away; we must act and press reality. I wish you could experience how people think on the Other Side. When I talk to people here I feel a radical, an outsider. But outside the walls my views are common as trees. Maybe one day Sophie and I can take you there."

"To the Other Side?"

"Sure. Why not? That is if Xenon doesn't completely disown us."

"Would he do that?"

"I'm not sure. He's not used to people ignoring his commands. My sister—by virtue of her martial talents—has extra leeway with him. But me . . . well . . . he sees me as a pest."

"Why?"

"Because I know what he is: a would-be dictator kept in check only by the spirit of anarchism. The people outside are too noble to be corrupted by the likes of him, but he tries."

"Does he?"

"There are two sure ways to make a mess of things, Glaucon: placing revolutionary power in the hands of a few 'well-meaning' individuals and resorting to violence. Xenon tries both. In the long term, that will destroy what we're fighting for. Sophie makes excuses for him, says practicality necessitates bending the ideal. Some at the Directory meeting today argued the same. 'Take your head out of the clouds,' they sneer, 'be reasonable. Try to understand we need solutions in the here and now.' They claim I forget the brutality of the past and am too willing to make sacrifices—how far from the truth! I just don't want to soil the name of anarchism and make it a hateful term. I don't want to plant the seeds of authoritarianism. That fruit poisoned millions before us. It poisons us still. To exchange one totalitarianism for another—what contemptible philosophy, what disgusting fate!"

Zemer looked at the debating square across the room. He shrunk with uneasiness.

"What's the matter?" Glaucon asked alarmed.

"Guardians released today's list for the Bull. They've rejected our demands. While expected, I had hoped for a different outcome."

"What? How do you know?"

"Zenobia is coming to tell us."

"Is she?" The uncanny premonition frightened Glaucon and made him take a deep breath. He looked over his shoulder, amazed by Zemer's power.

No one.

Zemer said, "A time is coming when the peacemakers will be despised. Our life of ease is ending."

Glaucon wanted to say something, but sure enough, Zenobia raced toward them with a digitele in her hands.

The floating tumbrels carrying those convicted of treason by the Heliopolis tribunals were already passing the last checkpoint into the Sixth Ward. Auxiliaries paraded the prisoners down the Road of Understanding, from the bowels of Miantgast Prison to Execution Beach. Jeering crowds waited for them on the streets, howling slurs at the doomed souls. Drunk on Ceto-Cola, they reviled their erect bodies tied to the posts. Like the *auto de fete* of Medieval Spain, the civil authorities commanded the condemned to be dressed in red sackcloth *sanbenitos*, with yellow robes and long conical hats. In Spain, the royals painted red devils and scenes of Hell on the robes of those destined for the stake. In the Republic, devils had ceased to exist; only a perfect circle (representing the Form of the Good) was permitted.

Over fifty thousand helots crowded together near the coast by the one-hundred-and-fifty-meter Bronze Bull, grown fatter each generation by the Ozbolts. Bordered by the moneyed outskirts of Consumption Junction, the weekly festival took on the flavor of a thunderous and highly efficient carnival, was speckled with pleasurable delights.

The tumbrels finally stopped. The guilty were made to look upon the red hot metal of their doom.

Terra, still recovering from her brutal interrogation and the mind-stocks, despaired at her inability to warn her friends about Glaucon. She was untied and kicked to the ground. She raised her head, dizzy, caught in a wave of fear. Stiff hands clawed at her robes. She was dragged up the metallic stairs, black hair tangled over her face.

Minor Archon Zeno waited for the prisoners in the air. Wearing winged magnetic floaties, he resembled an illuminated seraph. He allowed the awe-struck crowds the honor of touching the sacred hem of his ceremonial silk robes.

What entertainment! The guardian smiled. *They really believe I'm flying.* He could already hear the line of excited auxiliaries pounding their hoplite shields on the scaffolding. Protocol Order 91 dictated he wait until the shields finished bringing order to the spectacle. Administration of the *fete*—bringing death to the Republic's enemies—left all with an overwhelming sense of cosmic realization.

"See how injustice spoils the treasure of the soul," Zeno fed the venom of the crowd. He motioned for the culprits to be stripped naked. "What shall we do with those souls who are so incurably evil?"

"Put them to death. Put them to death," the crowd returned quoting sacred scripture.

A burst of lightning from Zeno's floaties quieted them again. "Vicious rumors flutter about the city today," he bellowed. "Rumors of strikes and rebellion. Let me remind you—let me be perfectly clear!—the Bull holds room enough for all traitors. Each of you helots signed a no-strike clause in your employment contract. You are bound by oath and reason to follow it. The guardians do not negotiate with contract-shredding-terrorists. We eat them whole like the naughty children of Cronos."

He let the threat settle in and then motioned for Terra to be brought forward.

Zeno turned to the guilty woman sweating under the bubbling heat of the Bull. "Child, all your life our city allowed you refuge to rise above your material condition. We fed you, clothed you, loved you, and protected you with our laws. In return you made a mockery of human nature, chose unions over justice, perverted our virtues, and undermined the fabric of our sane society with imitations, artifice, and democracy. You are poisonous! You are a gangrenous foot! Ergo, you shall be cut off from our body politic till rebirth." The crowd shouted ecstatically, but Zeno hushed them again. "Under the Republican Penal Code, it is a crime against both nature and God to associate with any anarchist from the Continental Caucus. Punishment for those who offend the Good is death. You have chosen the IWF and Xenon over us. May the agony you experience purify your soul for rebirth and free you from such ignorance. Be assured, the guardians shall never be threatened by cowards like you nor shall we bend our law for the ignorance of the masses. Your revolution dies with you." After saying this, Zeno pointed his index finger at Terra's rotten heart. He ordered everyone tossed inside the bull. One by one the procession shortened until the doors were finally closed.

The Bull's exuberant song echoed across the wards five minutes later.

III § 9 PROPHETS FEEL MOST FIERCELY

The execution of Terra Brandon produced the opposite of its intended consequences. Rather than deterring seditious criminal activity, renewed enthusiasm met the song of the Bull. *Goetia Mirror* (Number 35) was all but complete. Loud clanking from stapling machines bound the magazines together with renewed resolve.

Glaucon observed this behavior with much academic interest. Sitting with his back to the stairs, legs folded, a wide view of the room, he thought about his teacher Crito's explanation for the harsh punishments.

It was well settled at the Academy that the tortuous Bull shocked the conscience. But many like Crito believed it discouraged criminal behavior, proved it so numerous times with statistical data from the Rover Council. Accordingly, video of the event was streamed to nearly every television station in the Republic. The programming, though, did not seem to have much of an impact on actual lawbreakers. Rather, it energized contempt for law and radicalized beliefs.

One helot shouted in heated argument: "The time for gradualism is over!" He banged his fist on a crate. "Terra was the best among us. Enough outrageous threats. Enough murderers. The guardians have gone too far. Our mighty hands must take blood for blood. Immediate revolution, I say. Death to the guardians! Death to the Republic! Death to the oppressors of mankind! Death to them all!"

Clapping.

Sophie the crowd-compeller was not doing much to discourage such talk. She carried on another conversation with a small group in the debating square, smacking the *Social Contract* with her hand ferociously. "Guardians told me a million times at the Academy: 'Our Constitution is not a suicide pact. When endangered, the Republic must take the legal right to defend itself, even cutting off members' limbs if necessary.' See that! A fictitious entity has greater ultimate rights than people." Sophie let the outrage seep in. "The Republic lives on lies," she pronounced. "Lies like the Form of Justice, the General Will, Freedom, Reason. Whenever faith fails in these truths, the auxiliaries are called to 'compel us to be free.' Only one truth can be found in the song of the Bull—the individual and state cannot coexist in peace. The individual and the state are natural enemies."

Clapping.

Sophie continued raising her voice and index finger. "The despot guardians state a world without government would be chaos. What is this?"

"Another lie!" the anarchists shouted around her.

"Exactly right, it's a lie meant to keep the guardians—the peddlers of lies—in power. It's a lie meant to turn workers into vassals: vassals to debt, money, consumption, and reason. We don't need authority, vassals, or wage-slaves; we need one another. Embrace your social nature. Embrace the strength within you and the need for government disappears. We *can* rule ourselves. Only government could create something as miserably mechanical and methodical as the Bull. Democratic society never could. It respects the individuals who give it power."

Glaucon rested his head in his arms. The voices down below discussing the coming Tenth Ward Commune trailed off into a hollow murmur. He fell asleep. A little while later, hands ruffled his hair awaking him.

How did I let Sophie get behind me? Glaucon tensed up.

"Were you napping again, Mr. Oxenbridge?" Sophie teased him. She plopped down on the steps.

"No, thinking." He nervously scooted over to the edge.

"Yeah right, I always see you napping. Why are you so quiet? Are you sad? I thought you'd be raising Hades."

"Why?"

"You were close to Terra. She spoke highly of you."

"She was a good person. I don't want to talk about it anymore."

They sat alone in silence for several moments until Sophie spoke again. "I never got a chance to thank you earlier for the book."

"The book? Oh right, *Justine*. You don't need to thank me, Sophie. It was nothing." Without any kind of pills or drinks, there was a strong desire to pull away from Sophie's closeness.

Sophie glanced at him. "You could get the mind-stocks, or worse, the Bull."

"I'm not too worried."

"You're braver then me, then. I think about punishment all the time. I'm dreadfully afraid. To die like that, no one deserves it."

"Me braver than the Iron Queen? I sincerely doubt that." Glaucon smiled at her, but Sophie's face grew strained. He could tell she was thinking of Terra. He tried to erase the images of the shrieking Bull, the fire eaters dancing around the drunken crowd, the taunts to confess of social parasitism. The moral grandeur of the event had changed to him somehow. "Why don't you leave and go back to the Other Side?" he finally asked her.

"I have unfinished business here. Besides, I could never leave Zemer. He may be a hopeless romantic, but he's all I've got." Sophie motioned to her brother stacking bound magazines near the wall. Sleeves rolled up, he fluttered like a moth around a table. Aquila worked beside him packing the *Goetia Mirror* into suitcases.

Glaucon remarked, "You sometimes look at him with apprehension."

"Who, Zemer? I don't like it when he uses the jinn. Nothing good can come of it. Today when you fell on the street it scared me."

"Why are you so afraid of it?"

"The jinn makes me cold. . . ." Sophie watched the stacks of *Goetia Mirror* growing shorter. She breathed deeply, wondering if she should reveal anything more, but Glaucon's ruddy complexion and curious look made her heart flutter, softening her resolve. She began caressing the deep scars on her right hand where her *tetractys* had been painfully removed. "Do you know the history behind the jinn, Glaucon?" she asked.

"Zemer told me it preceded the cogniscrambler."

"There's more. The jinn, the cogniscrambler, the Fates, and Levantra are all connected. Xenon saved me sixteen years ago. He saved me from them all. I was only a child, but I was tortured. Not just my body, but my mind. The cruel device can warp your memories, and voices drive you mad. I almost killed myself because of the jinn, Glaucon. Zemer, too."

"Tortured? By who, Sophie?"

"By Prodicus," Sophie's voice twisted in rage. "He thought my brother and I were connected to a prediction made by the Fates. Called us 'Vessels', said we had indigo I.T. waves. You wouldn't have heard about this, but the decision to create Kabiri-1 was controversial on Heliopolis at the time. We were told it could better synthesize our knowledge of the Forms; make it easier to process guardians from helots; to stabilize the climate. But the machine came to life on its own, told us things we shouldn't know, things we don't yet understand: how to control the weather, I.T. wave technology, the jinn, shadowspar."

"All were gifts of the Fates?"

"Our whole society rapidly changed in the Kabiri Techflation, faster than we were ready."

Glaucon remembered the burning eyes of Atropos. "Do you think the Fates are actually alive in there? What could they be thinking?" he wondered aloud.

"I don't know what their intentions are, but I know for sure the Fates are smarter than us and want something. I was taught at the Academy despotism necessarily collapses on itself: 'Everything that comes into being must decay,' right? But what if a despot can't make mistakes? What if it's immortal? The Republic could last forever."

Sophie's story was disturbing. The word 'Vessel' reminded Glaucon of the day at the fig tree with Prodicus when he lost his mother. It filled him with an imminent sense of foreboding. He never heard the word again and forgot the air of importance Prodicus attached to it. *Have I been made to forget?* he wondered. Sophie said the jinn twisted her memories. Could it have twisted his memories, too? He had never seen the jinn before meeting Zemer. Could a memory of seeing the jinn be erased?

Sophie turned her chin into her shoulder, lifted away a bronze lock. "Glaucon, I was rude to you last time we were together, wasn't I?"

"A little."

"I didn't mean the things I said . . . earlier by the magnet-sedan. I don't really hate you. This place is making me crazy. I feel Kabiri everywhere, but not in you. You're a good friend." A tear rolled to her quivering lips. She cleaned her eyes with her thumb. "Please understand. These things are difficult for me to talk about. Prodicus and Salazar Ozbolt are monsters. What they did to me—to Zemer—on Heliopolis is unforgivable. The jinn breathed death into my nostrils, made me the Iron Queen of the Dead. When I see people like Terra brutalized and killed, I want nothing more than to flay the guardian-king to pieces. Unlike Zemer, I want him dead." Her tone was filled with bitter disgust. Despite her anger, though, Sophie drooped with an unguarded, tenuous radiance, revealed in a way Glaucon had never seen before. He felt emboldened by her apology and reached for her hand.

But right before he could wrap his sand-bag arms around his beloved, the black cat from upstairs pounced between them. Light from the living room bathed the two in light.

Sophie jumped up. Glaucon glared at the cat for stalling his arms. "I'll kill that stupid cat," he could have shouted.

There was a clatter of feet down the circular steps—Ivan and a gang of helots. Two strange looking men sauntered behind dressed in frayed khakis, muddy combat boots, hats with revolutionary badges stapled to the front, with a black handkerchief tied around their throats.

"Friends of yours?" Glaucon asked.

"Hawks more like it," Sophie glared. "Marcus and Nestor are in my Eastern Column." She moved quickly to wait for them at the basement floor.

"Greetings, Iron Queen," both men saluted at once when they arrived.

Sophie grunted at the taller one, a bearded militiaman. "Don't get cute, Marcus," she said waving them away. "We're a classless society. Heel-clicking is prohibited by the Anarchist Column Code."

Marcus smiled, removed his hat. "Glad to see you haven't changed completely, Commander."

Sophie folded her arms. "All right, fellahs, out with it, what do you want?"

"Hmph. Still quick to the point, too. Before we speak you draw your sword."

"I won't ask again."

"Fine. Xenon implores you in the name of comradeship, under our notions of individual decency, to return to the militia and give back the weapons you stole from us."

"I most certainly will not!" Sophie exclaimed jerking a finger in his face. "How dare you come here and risk exposing us—especially now after the crackdown. What were you thinking?"

Marcus stepped backward and lit a cigarette. He looked around at the collection of souls, disbelieving. "Desertion's a serious offense, Sophie. Stealing from your own column is unforgivable. I never thought you'd be one to go AWOL."

Zemer came to his sister's defense. "We're not deserters, Marcus. Our orders were to 'win the city.' We're doing that."

"Lawyer to the end, eh, Zemer? Mapping ambiguous language always was your forte. Fighting . . . well . . . not so much. Too low for you, right? Now look how you've infected your sister with this pacifist nonsense. Xenon gave you strict orders to galvanize rebellion and kill that stupid kid. You've refused to follow both orders."

Zemer squeezed Marcus' arm pleadingly. "There is good in this city, Brother, I've seen it. Helots here have vast underground organizations. We can overhaul the system from the ground up. We need more time. Please understand, if we'd gone back with the jinn, Xenon would've slipped in through the walls and massacred the population, both friend and foe. There's too much Jacobin in him."

"And too much Tolstoy in you! Go on, deviationist, croon about peaceful resistance while the world burns."

Sophie knocked her brother's hand away from Marcus' arm and stood between them. "Xenon knows well and good he wouldn't make it past the Fifth Ward once the guardians unleashed the golems; but he'd still kill as many people as possible to make a point. That's no way to run a militia. That won't accomplish anything."

Marcus burst into laughter. "The Iron Queen is lecturing me about morality?" he asked. "Wasn't it your bloodstained cheeks which helped snare my first scalp? What a world. Sorry, but the time for moral second thoughts is over. As you taught me, Great Maiden of the Mountain, there'll be plenty of time for repentance when the last guardian is slain."

Aquila looked at Sophie aghast.

Feeling the sting of her past acts, Sophie said, "I taught you wrong. We did things we shouldn't have. So much needless abuse. Why kill people you can convert peacefully?"

Marcus twisted his mouth. "From what I understand, there's been very little converting. A few leaflets here and there—"

"The people of this city are going to hold a strike on Monday."

"Books and strikes do nothing when the Vinculum Cartel and the State control the media. Your views will be smeared and destroyed; the helots will turn on you. One doesn't need the jinn to predict that."

"Not if we reach them first," Glaucon broke in. "We're leafleting Consumption Junction tomorrow."

Glaucon did not know what compelled him to lie. There was something about the soldier's fanatical attitude which irritated him. Sophie's mouth dropped open at the news. Several gasps were heard from the crowded room.

"Who the hell are you?" Marcus asked.

Glaucon ignored him and explained: "Think of it, friends. Consumption Junction's the center of Vinculum economic power and symbolic of the Republic's strength. More people go there to shop on a single night than all the places we've distributed the *Goetia Mirror* combined. Getting the word out there would show the Directory's something to worry about—"

"If we survive," Sophie said. "That place crawls with more soldiers than Miantgast."

"Not tomorrow. There will be lighter security. Godfrey de Tobin—CEO of Cheque Giorgio—thinks the Fourth Ward will be the next target of the unions. He's asked Polemarch Leonida to move ten brigades of auxiliaries to the island ring. This means Consumption Junction is practically unguarded."

Zemer agreed. "Glaucon may be right. I heard something about that on the Gorgon Hour. No one would expect us to strike twice in the same ward."

Marcus' eyes darted from Zemer to Sophie and then back to Zemer. He scratched his knotted beard with irritation. "I'm not here to plot with the pen and play games, Commander. You know the importance of discipline and following orders. I'll ask you one more time to give me the jinn or—"

"Or what?" Sophie pounced like a panther, ripping the cigarette from his mouth and stomping it with her foot. She gruffly seized Marcus' collar, causing him to drop his hat. Her rabid gaze—so unexpected, so abrupt—pierced his courage.

"Did Kabiri strike you mad, Sophie? You know I've always been loyal to you. I adore you. Why are you treating me like this?"

"Marcus, you're going to cause more harm than good. Go back and tell Xenon to wait. Please. For me. Don't throw your life away."

Marcus stumbled from her grasp and readjusted his cap from the floor. "I guess it's true what some of the men say—once a guardian always a guardian. You side with Polyphemus and herd his cattle. You're an authoritarian!"

"It takes more than strength to bend a Cyclops, Marcus. You need brains."

"We've run out of time and options, Sophie. What good are brains when a club can smash them in? We're two minutes to midnight. Levantra will rise any day now. If it does, it'll kill us all. We must unleash all the power at our disposal to break the city. *You* told us that. *You!*"

"My brother and I won't help you."

"Then we will find others who will." Marcus pushed Sophie away maliciously and addressed the room: "Attention, comrades. We come on behalf of General Xenon himself to dispatch a special assignment against the guardians. News of your slain comrades has reached our ears and filled us with the greatest grief. We offer a chance for people's justice. There may be some among you who question Xenon's use of violence. I beseech those persons: Do not sacrifice your revolution on the altar of a peacenik utopia. Make no mistake. Revolutions are bloody affairs. Blood is inevitable. The guardians will never give their power and privileges peacefully. You must kill them like rabid dogs to return your dignity. Anyone who embraces a sane understanding of the facts is free to come with us."

The plea for assistance settled in among the assembly. For minutes no one spoke. An opportunity for violent offensives cast a new spell. Ivan scowled icily from the corner, finally saying, "I'll gladly go."

Many others followed the metallurgist to Marcus' side. Zemer wheeled forward to curb their determination. "What? Ivan, no! Didn't we swear together at the Directory meeting there'd be a peaceful strike? We voted together."

Marcus returned resentfully, "Do not be such a fanatic of process, Zemer. Final victory is what's most important, not the road."

"Fanatic of process, you say? You wouldn't speak like that in Column Committee. Lovely how you're so willing to scorn *this* democratic society. But then, you haven't been to any helot meetings this summer, have you? You haven't invested any of your soul in their assemblies. What helots actually desire means nothing to you. Before you go, Ivan, look at me. Look me straight in the face. What do we stand for if we kill?"

"We stand as Sextus: patriots defending the people from tyranny. Prodicus struck first, Zemer. The fiend strikes us over and over again. His iron heel is smashing good people to pieces. Blood stains the streets in the city and the jungles outside the city. We're letting everyone die. I'll not stand for oppression any longer. I will do what others can't."

"No one doubts we live in conditions of violence, Ivan. How we respond to that violence, though, defines our movement. Every act of protest carries with it a meaning. Today, the workers of this city stood up in favor of a world of life. They rejected assassination and bombings in favor of a more peaceful seizure of the factories. They protest for life not death, freedom not vengeance, to return their rights rather than take others' away. If we resorted to violence as Marcus suggests, the moral purity of our protest would be sullied. Violence negates our struggle for freedom. Answer me, by God; can you eliminate violence by adding violence? The Platonic scriptures wisely argue not 'to retaliate or render injustice for injustice to anyone, whatever evils may be suffered.' "

"More sophistry. Your way is too slow and contemptible. You would sit idly by, allow our men and woman to be captured one by one, tortured, fed to the Bull, to be hunted for some ideal that will never materialize. Tell the people who die about your protest for life. Tell that to my bondwife!" Ivan was hysterical and bit on his anger.

"We aren't killing them, Ivan; the Republic is. Those people made a choice like we all did. They knew the risks."

"What about the innocent who have their noses smashed in by ISHIM," Ivan rasped, "who're tortured for our high and lofty strikes and *Goetia Mirror*? Those helots never had a choice. They didn't ask for us to publish anything. They didn't ask us to seize the factories. Now when they need our help you do nothing. Your inaction is killing them. We'd be in a better bargaining position by blowing things up as Xenon intended. *That* might actually spark city-wide revolt. Why can't you see, Oracle? I don't understand. How can someone possess such sight as you yet be so blind? We're losing this battle because of reservations to bloody our hands. The Republic is violence incarnate and can only be destroyed with fire. Not peace! Not forgiveness! Fire! Prodicus kills helots for the Forms and must be punished."

"And you would kill others for freedom, Ivan? Is that so different from Prodicus?" Zemer looked as if he had drunk a cup of bitterness. "You're both willing to murder for logic, to claim a right that doesn't belong to you. Controlling people with violence is not freedom, even if it's used by the oppressed. You merely exchange one master for another. The violence will change you. Despite what Marcus says, the road you take to a destination *is* as important as the destination itself. Roads are long. You can get lost. Why fight a tyrant if you're willing to become one?"

"I would strangle Prodicus with my bare hands and never bat an eye," Ivan said gazing at his hands in mystery. "I would squeeze his neck until his eyes popped out and his tongue curled. He doesn't deserve to live. *He* should feed the Bull!"

"No one deserves to die, even power obsessed murderers like Prodicus."

"I don't share your perverse sympathy for evil men."

"I have never seen an evil man. Prodicus is a man, nothing more. We must love him and hope he changes. I tell you truthfully: Love is stronger than reason and no one is beyond redemption. A life of hate can be valuable in the twinkling of an eye by one act of love."

"Love . . . for Prodicus? Are you a madman? He burned Terra alive!"

Sophie glimpsed a hazardous frown erupt on Ivan's face. "I somewhat agree with Ivan," she said trying to relieve the crushing tenseness. "We each chose to endanger ourselves, but many of the helots here didn't have a choice. Could you see a woman like me, beaten on the street, completely innocent, and refuse to defend the woman with your fists?"

"I would go and ask the men to stop," Zemer said.

"And when they said no?"

"I would block their way or reason with them until they turned on me. Or I would try to run away with the woman. I don't like hypotheticals. Every situation is different. But I could never strike anyone. Not anymore. Not knowing what I'd become. I will never be a master again. Never."

"What miserable cowardice," Marcus groaned. He marveled at the complete change which had devoured his former friend. He really was a deviationist!

Zemer challenged his rebuke, "It's cowardly to open your body and accept abuse? To help others change through your own blood? No, you're using tricky logic, friend. It's cowardly to lash out. You strike others because you really fear them. You fear their power and pretensions. You fear your own weakness. Fear is at the root of all violence. Fear is the parent of hate. To defeat fear you must refuse to participate with its children." Zemer's eyes watered as emotions raked the lining of his soul. "Bombs are made to explode and kill. They only make enemies. I don't want enemies but a kingdom of brotherhood. I want love to shatter the Republic's glass. Only when we treat one another as brothers can we truly be free. When you return the blows of others who abuse us, you are a domino falling; you're behaving like a clock allowing fear to control you. Forgiving others, refusing to fear is what can allow us to overcome the desire for power and free society."

"What if that woman wants you to fight back, Brother?" Sophie was speaking of herself.

"I pray for her to see things like I do."

"Prayer, Brother? No god will answer you."

Zemer's eyes twinkled with furious intensity. "God is a mystery, dear heart, but whether a god exists makes little difference to me. If God exists, hopefully the good are rewarded and the evil are restored and forgiven. If God does not exist, killing others ends their finite, invaluable life and is still wrong. I love mankind so intensely, I could not stand—even for a moment—to let an abusive one die. What a miracle, love; it has a hold on me, a timeless hold, and with it I see eternity. For love defies logic and truth and justice. It cannot be conditioned or consumed and grows in the strangest places, deep,

deep in the desert, even the Republic, even in guardian hearts. Reason can never kill love because man is more lover than reasoner."

"The people you love will betray you, Zemer," Marcus said, wiping his mouth with his hat.

"Even if they do, they do so out of ignorance and how can I be angry with the ignorant. I am not so reckless to believe I can change anyone. I can only change myself, how I look at others and treat them. That is enough and all I can ask for in this world."

Ivan nearly fell over in wild laughter. He dwelled in the dismal thoughts of his lost wife. "Madness, madness. But one can't be mad at the insane. You've read too much Gandhi, I think. You've gone mad with learning, Oracle. You love the trees and the oceans and murderers, but love is not so powerful; love will never restore Terra or heal her senseless agony, nor would I want it to. One can love too much and be entrapped. Love can kill justice just as easily as reason."

"What justice is there left for Terra? No punishment can repair Prodicus' crimes. Even the Bull is not enough, even an eternity of Hell. Love is not meant to repair, Ivan, but to change the future."

"You'll die a sucker for love and drag us all to Hades Hall with you."

"Would that be such a horrible thing? Perhaps our deaths would help others learn understanding. Brotherhood begins in shared understanding. To love your enemy is the greatest form of love—the only time we can be certain of loving—for when you love your enemy you seek the betterment of someone else completely against your own interest."

"You want sacrifice, not revolution!"

"They are the same." Zemer swept around the room in an unexplainable frenzy. "Laugh at me if you must. Perhaps my problem is sanity. You see, friends, I've been trying a personal experiment. Every day I wake up and pretend like I am the reason for all the evil in the world. Everyone's actions are, ultimately, because of my own choices. When a murder occurs, it is because of me. When someone is beaten with a xiphos stick, it is only because I gave the man the weapon. Now if this is true and I am the cause of all evil in the world, what a hypocrite I'd be if I suddenly stopped trying to correct my mistakes, if I chose to kill the people I wronged rather than save them.

"Let me tell you a story, a story about a time God made the sun stand still. I added it to the *Goetia Mirror* tonight. No, Sister, don't roll your eyes at me. I can't take your rebuke in this state of mine. I carry this story with me like a mirror to remind myself of weakness and responsibility. That day over

Gibeon long, long ago, the writers tell us 'there has never been a day like it before or since, a day when the Lord listened to a man.'

"Adoni-Zadek, Most-High King of Jerusalem, was like any other monarch: closed off by his walls; weary of the demands of office; a tormentor of men. A dream disturbed his slumber one night—visions of bloated oxen and rivers of blood swarming with the arms of men slaughtered for living. The king shuddered awake. He felt his second wife's soft breast clutching to him under the covers. Yes, yes, he was still alive. He patted himself down to make sure and crept silently from bed. He visited the rooms of his many children, thought of the blithe delights of youth.

"Can we ever know what went through his mind, that poor defeated wretch? Disturbed, sprinkled with doubt, knowing already his children would be dead in a week, he walked along the sandstone turrets of Jerusalem. The fire from the desert frightened him. He removed his golden crown and wiped sweat from his brow. The Israelites could be seen in the distance with their curved bloody swords. The nomad slaves marched upon him.

"News from Jarmuth and King Piram: All are dead and God is in the wind. Every last stone of Jericho tumbled down. Joshua of the raised javelin ordered every babe's head smeared on the walls. In the city of Ai, King Isin and his people hang on trees eaten by vultures. All who resist are slain. Adoni-Zadek could still see burning smoke in the distance. 'The Gibeonites have betrayed me,' he fumed. 'They have betrayed me and made an alliance with the Israelites.' On reflection, however, he could not entirely blame the Gibeonites. They loved life and had tricked the Israelites with tattered rags and patched sandals, pretending to be from another territory outside the Israelite's coveted Promised Land. Now the Gibeonite cowards would survive, and he, Adoni-Zadek, would die. Alas, who were these men who could dry up the Jordan River with a magical cherubim arc? Who were these men who killed for God's dream? Adoni-Zadek cursed that his happy citadel should share the same spot as their Promised Land. 'But,' he consoled himself under the charmed moon, 'what citadel wasn't on someone else's Promised Land?'

"A soldier missing an eye and dressed in bronze and leather armbands met him. 'The kings of Hebron, Jarmuth, Lachish, and Eglon all agree. Gibeon must be destroyed at once,' he said.

"Adoni-Zadek cursed under his breath, 'Surely, Joshua has not been fooled by the Gibeonites. A man like that is never fooled.' Adoni-Zadek laughed like a man placed in an impossible situation. He must attack the Gibeonites, severely weakening the strength of his armies, attack the stronger

Israelites directly, or wait to be devoured by both. Death awaited in all three. There was no escape."

Marcus clenched his fist in irritation at Zemer's wordiness, "Hells bells, why tell the story from the Canaanite side, Zemer? You have the streak of the devil in you. The Canaanites were a wicked people who persisted in human sacrifice. Their wickedness caused them to forfeit their land."

"Yes, but my heart melts for them anyway. Not only did the Canaanites have to face men, but they faced men clothed in the glory of God, and no man is more terrifying than that. And Marcus, you should know that no narrator is completely truthful. The alleged evil of the Canaanites . . . well it is a little too convenient for me. It is the convenience I see on the Gorgon Hour. We have been so careful to reprint faithful sections from the world's holy books, but I wonder if we are perpetuating truth or someone's political expediency."

These speeches horrified Sophie. "Zemer, you talk as if you were there."

"Maybe I was, Sister, but I'm getting to the most important part. The King of Jerusalem and the other Amorites descended from the fateful hills, laid siege to the cowards of Gibeon. Adoni-Zadek flashed in the sun in his regal armor. Oh, you should have seen how he carried his trumpets and javelins. A small bronze sword rested at his side—the sword he meant to give to his son. All was for nothing. Before the first dew of night could be dried by the rising sun, Joshua was at his back. 'How did he get here?' Adoni-Zadek shouted indignantly. 'Where did he come from? The Israelites were camped at Gilgal. No one could move that fast. They're daimons!' He needed more time. 'Give me more time!' he pleaded with the heavens, but God gave time to the Israelites, not to Adoni-Zadek.

"The Amorite army was rapidly defeated. Joshua and God gave chase over the rocky cliffs, toppling them over crags. Joshua's voice trumpeted over the mountains: 'Stand still, O Sun, at Gibeon, O Moon, in the Valley of Aijalon,' and naturally, God obeyed because he loved his Joshua. House-sized hailstones assaulted poor Adoni-Zadek's forces as the sun stood still. One crushed his javelin carrier in the dirt. The storm of ice and javelins and thirsty swords struck terror in all his men. Adoni-Zadek peered up at the sun. It was nearly six o'clock but bright as noon. The sun beat down on his shivering legs, and he tore at his beard as if assailed by a swarm of locusts. 'Go down, damn you!' he shouted, but the lingering star stayed still. He longed for the tender lips of his fourth wife and the embrace of his concubine, Hurriya. The recognition of his hopeless position and the tiredness in his legs drove him to seek refuge in a cave at Makkedah with the other Amorite kings. But lo, there was no escape even here. Joshua, the valiant, the judge, the guardian, rolled a stone over the entrance. The bite of darkness caused the king of Jerusalem to scream at the stalactites.

"Locked in the cave, Adoni-Zadek listened to the other kings' shadows sobbing for their homes, their wives, their children lost. So much time passed in the cave. Adoni-Zadek began questioning his life under the steady dripping of an underground spring. He too had sought others' lands and killed for it. If he had a god like Joshua, he'd have asked the sun to stand still, too. But he began to wonder why a god like that would obey such a wish from man, and he wondered whether the Israelites' Promised Land was really meant to be land at all. What if they had misunderstood? What if no Promised Land was coming but had already arrived? What if the Promised Land was really in the desert, before they craved such land to lose, in the people themselves—the sacred vessels of God? At the end of his life, Adoni-Zadek hated land and government for it had brought him nothing but sadness. What was it worth, the killing, the hoarding, the endless bloody fields, growing fat on others' suffering? He began praying fervently to the Israelite God, but nothing moved in the cave; for you see, God was still holding the sun in place at Joshua's command. Only daimons answered. 'Will a man ever ask God to give humanity freedom rather than control?' he asked dolefully. The other kings cursed him for his trouble because they hated freedom even more than Joshua. Feasters of power, their impotence in the cave gnawed their pride. Adoni-Zadek, on the other hand, suddenly felt at peace by his question. He savored the darkness—each moment of life—every jagged edge of the wall. He yearned for an eternity of discomfort, as long as he had breath and this new gold clearing of mind. Yes, he had lost Jerusalem to the Israelites, but they would lose it, too, again and again, and he felt sorry for them because many would never know the freedom in the cave. He saw the world for what it was—a nest of masters fighting to the death, crushing helpless slaves beneath their feet—and he prayed an end to it. 'No gods, no masters,' he begged the heavens, 'but make me a vessel of love.'

"Adoni-Zadek hardly heard the stone roll back before he was dragged away. The light nearly blinded him as his limp body dragged along the rocks. Joshua's foot was on his neck humiliating him in front of his people. He was afraid. The stench of blood still clung to the hairs of Joshua's feet. Joshua leaned down to Adoni-Zadek and whispered in his ear: 'My fallen king, God had given me your Jerusalem, and we shall always have it. You were a fool to take my trap and attack the Gibeonites. What were you trying to prove? See, even God holds the sun for me. No one can stand up to us, and this very day I shall go to your quarters and burn your wives and children; every person in your family, all living persons in your city will be put to death so that none will rise against us.' And saying this, Joshua pierced him through the heart with his javelin and hung him from a tree until evening. Then he threw the dead kings back into their lonely cave, rolling a stone over the entrance forever. Their beloved cities were burnt stinking to the ground leaving no survivors.

"When God finally loosed the sun, his hands were hot and burnt. He felt pity. 'What have I done,' he cried staring at his hands, 'to kill a creature like Adoni-Zadek? Will there ever be another like him?' And God wept for his little creature and cursed for listening to a man seeking power."

The entire room consumed every word of Zemer's story, trying to determine the hidden meaning behind the tale. Hecatia rubbed her pointy chin, and Glaucon stared thoughtfully at the floor, pondering the complete reversal of Plato's Cave Allegory. In Plato's story, leaving the cave for the bounty of the sun was an act of enlightenment, not ignorance. In Zemer's story, the sun became an object of scorn and a tool for control. He could not think of anything more sacrilegious.

How could Zemer have ever been a guardian? Glaucon wondered.

Zenobia's cheeks flushed and she longed to embrace Zemer completely.

Ivan was unconvinced. "Your perverse story only serves to distort the debate. Prodicus is not this penitent king and gods don't cry."

"What makes you think I intended Adoni-Zadek to represent Prodicus?" Zemer replied like the Sphinx.

"I'm tired of arguing with you," Ivan rasped heatedly. "My mind will not be changed by someone as young and starry-eyed as you. I am determined. My gods command me to tear down the Republic by force. I must go."

Zemer slumped in resignation under the fluorescent lights. He said stoically, "You must know, Ivan, God is only a myth to save us from our uncertainty. Are you truly certain this is what you want? I would prefer you stay with us. Do not pour out love for vengeance. You will lose more than your life."

Ivan was beyond persuasion. "Does it look like I care what you prefer, Fallen Prince? You have never had to live as a slave. It is easy to be noble and talk of love when you haven't suffered a yoke."

Zemer said, "If anyone else wishes to follow Marcus and Ivan, go now. Find what you seek as free men in control of your destiny."

Tense gloom filled the basement. Aquila looked distraught. Zemer returned to the luggage filled with magazines, never looking more alone and defeated. He said, "It's as Xenon preaches: 'When there is no God there is no crime, no right or wrong, good or evil, nor remorse.' Yet look at all of us in this dead universe. We are striving to be moral and are so remorseful."

Four others stood up to leave. "We're sorry, Zemer, but we must go with Ivan. As you said, the gods never choose the right side." They left and never turned back. Marcus moved to say something to Sophie, but decided against it and followed them up the stairs. Everyone stood quiet.

Later that night, when Glaucon finally crawled into bed on the second floor of the camera factory next to Sophie and Zemer, taking his usual spot at the edge next to the nightstand, he stared at the wide dark ceilings and listened to the creaking fan. It reminded him of Zoe, and he pictured her blonde hair in the hands of night husbands at the yoking ceremony. No doubt she was taking the *erosic* pill without him. Briefly, he craved her soft nakedness, even if the end result would only make him empty. He wondered if Zoe only took *erosic* with him out of habit. It saddened him they'd no longer be able to attend theater together until after she gave birth. (As Professor Crito explained, the threat of miscarriage was too enormous.) Zemer was fast asleep, but he thought Sophie might still be awake. Her arm curled around her head. Long eyelashes lay perfectly still. Her leg moved close to his and gently touched his knee. Glaucon pulled away into a ball. Unable to close his mind, he finally attached a REMphone sleeping patch to his neck from a mahogany drawer next to the bed.

A slight tickle from the nanoscopic antenna.

Next thing he knew, he fell asleep and dreamt he was Joshua unable to turn from his heaven-guided path. Across the room, sitting on a white ornate chair and black as midnight, Hecatia's cat kept watch over the friends whipping his tail.

III § 10 Laputan Clouds

The next morning, as rosy-fingered Dawn ignited the horizon, Zemer reverted back to his ordinary self. Ivan and the splintering of the night before were forgotten. Clanging pots and shutting cupboards heralded smells of cooking. Fifteen minutes later Zemer was back, bounding on the bed and kissing his sister good morning. He kneeled down with a tray of eggs, pomegranate juice, and French toast, and the three friends ate breakfast in bed. It was a typical Saturday, but more solemn. They discussed logistics for the trip to Consumption Junction. Once only crumbs were left on the ornate china tray, Zemer left Sophie and Glaucon alone. Awkwardly alone.

Sophie ordered Glaucon to lie shirtless on the floor to peel his dead skin. Sitting on his back, she scolded, "How do you manage to get so sunburned?"

"Just really pale, I guess."

A large strip of crispy skin pulled away from his shoulder like a molting snake.

"But you're not any paler than me," Sophie probed further. "Don't you work inside when you write commercials?"

"Sometimes we have meetings on top of Mira-Disney Tower. Big atrium on the roof."

"The way you're always sunburned, it reminds me how I used to bake on Heliopolis."

"Huh, I wouldn't know anything about that." Glaucon yawned. Finding new excuses for her questioning was becoming tiresome.

Sophie chuckled. "I think this is becoming a little ritual of ours. Say, Glaucon, do you think it's gross I enjoy peeling dead skin?"

"I've never really thought about it, Sophie." Truthfully, Glaucon relished each stroke of her little fingers.

"Well, I don't think it's gross. There's something dreadfully appealing about removing skin. The entire Integumentary System fascinates me: how it regenerates; is able to spout hair and sweat; feels so soft." Sophie's palm dragged up Glaucon's back to his shoulder. "Do you know the skin is the largest organ in the body?"

"Maybe *your* body."

"Manners, helot." Sophie knocked him on the back as he stifled a laugh. She listened as Glaucon grunted under the soft movements of her fingers, went on: "Skin protects us from water and heat. It's how we come to know other people. Sometimes we feel other's skin to know our own." Glaucon suddenly gagged in pain as a piece of live skin dragged away with the old.

"Oops, that was a big one. Sorry, did I hurt you?" Sophie flipped Glaucon around into an uncomfortable position. Still wearing her red sleeping shirt, she dangled over him like a ripe strawberry. A pile of dead skin rested near her arm.

Glaucon asked, "Do you think Zemer was right about what he said last night?"

"I don't think Zemer believes himself half the time. His stories grow more . . . bizarre. Something's happening to him. He's a completely different person. I am, too, I guess; but Zemer's more distant than ever, like he lives half the day in the future. I think the jinn is frying his brain. You need to tell him to stop toying with it."

"Why don't you?"

"I have; he won't listen to me."

"Would you have followed Ivan and Marcus if your brother wasn't here?"

Sophie looked worried by his question and said, "I'm like my brother. I don't like hypotheticals. Zemer is right about Xenon. We can't let him butcher the people here, or my militia. Violence is impractical. It gives the guardians reason to crush legitimate resistance, tarnishes our moral claim." She meticulously scanned Glaucon like a surgeon. "Hey, how did you get these scars?" she asked curiously, tracing an indented ridge along his stomach with a finger.

Glaucon snatched Sophie's wrist and dragged her body close. "Can you believe, this pretty girl once pushed me in some sharp thorns? I think I startled her."

"How could anyone be afraid of you?" Sophie lightly tapped his cheek with her fist, grinning.

"No idea—but she was—and ran away from me."

"You gave chase, I hope?"

"Of course. Does Zeus ever wait?"

"What a stupid girl," Sophie admitted leaning closer.

"Very stupid," Glaucon agreed. He reached out for a kiss.

Time stopped. Sophie's breath floated moist five centimeters from his face. He became fiercely aware of skin edges, was conscious of every degree of heat emanating from Sophie's body. If there was a Form of Woman, Sophie partook of its lustrous existence more completely than any person he'd ever known. Ay, ay, he swore the cramped room burst into flames. Unfortunately, before he could inch those thin and luscious lips to his own, a choking spell made him cough. He rolled away leaving Sophie bewildered.

That tickling, terrible fear from the car returned as frightening as ever. Once so amorphous, it struck again concrete—he did not know how to kiss without the *erosic* pill, and he was too afraid to try. Sophie was in a dwelling place far below him, unreachable, and her face twisted back to the rage from before.

I'm such a miserable coward, Glaucon wailed so miserably, awaiting the next onslaught of verbal abuse.

Before anything could escalate further, the energetic Aquila swept open the door and gasped. Seeing Glaucon half-naked on the floor with Sophie red as a rooster made her immediately suspicious. "Am I disturbing something?" she asked.

"Apparently not," Sophie stood up steaming. She shoved Glaucon away.

"Well, Directory's sent out an alert. Guardians began house-scans for thermo-readings an hour ago. Looking for people who don't belong. You guys are probably fine up here, but most everyone else is outside, playing the happy helots." Aquila stretched her quadriceps. "I think we all need to relieve some stress. Everyone is still shook up from yesterday. I want to get a soccer game going. Come play so we can scrounge a proper team. That should confuse them."

Sophie sat on the bed displaying her unwillingness to follow, and she gave a stern look to Glaucon that implied he better remain as well if he knew what was good for him. But before Sophie could blink an eye, Aquila yanked Glaucon up like a carrot from a garden.

"You should leave that shirt off, Glaucon," Aquila mentioned as she dragged him out the door and down the narrow steps. "It's about ninety-three degrees today. Hotter than Vulcan's ass. I bet I smoke you."

When the two departed, Sophie seethed in anger and stared at her sheets as if they were soiled. All her joy fled and she felt as a parched desert untouched by rain. Calling Aquila a "harlot" and hating such vanity, she pulled her hair overwhelmed and threw herself screaming on the pillows. "I hate him," she wailed longing for a sea to jump to her death, "*and* that Aquila—that helot strumpet. . . . What's wrong with me?" she finally exclaimed. This never would've happened on the Other Side where love was freer than the breeze and taken as offered. Who was Glaucon to refuse her? she asked herself. The leader of the Eastern Column, no less. The Iron Queen! She wished to be cured of whatever ailment plagued her senses.

Aquila juggled the ball on her knees as she ran through the kitchen. Glaucon opened the thick bronze doors to the park at the back of the house. Humidity from the summer day clung to the lawn and soaked the soccer players' ankles in sweat. The common park looked like a valley between a canyon of houses. About two-hundred meters away, a collection of trees formed a colorful arboretum, the pride of which was a bioengineered hydrasequoia.

Soccer was one of few concessions won by the helots. On Heliopolis such a game was strictly forbidden. The guardians detested the sport, loathed it like a lingering canker sore. This was not necessarily because they had anything against the game itself (there was much to admire in the sport's simplicity and grace), but because the ball was made from a combination of two platonic solids: a dodecahedron and icosahedron. Since the universe was shaped like a dodecahedron, playing soccer symbolized kicking around the cosmos, a most sacrilegious act for any rational thinking philosopher.

Phillip Lamb raced in blue shorts across the field throwing up dirt, his shaved head glinting with sweat. He was being chased by Zenobia and Hella at his heels. As his sister finally tripped him and stole the ball, his thick hairy legs stabbed the air.

Behind the game, picnickers reclined carefree on blankets. Children tossed Frisbees and played tag amongst the pleasure fountains and ivy walls. One child, running twenty meters in the air in new *Hermes* flying shoes, traipsed right above them.

This illusion of happiness was odd, a fake veneer at a time of spontaneous riots and open revolt. War inside and outside the city, executions, death, but no one could acknowledge the truth. One had to smile and play and graze like a grass-eater. One had to accept war amnesia.

No breeze stirred anywhere. Glaucon wished the aquamolpis could've reached this far inland to cool the sun. As he walked out the door, something strange stuck out from the sky—a long shadow falling on the wards.

"Surprise!" Aquila squinted, astonished at the floating island. "Can you believe it? Ozbolt really made Levantra fly. I must admit, I *am* kind of impressed."

Glaucon gasped in wonder at the rocky inverted mountain, blanketed in clouds, flying thirty-five thousand kilometers up. Electricity from numerous Van de Graaff-looking generators danced along the angled crags with avis swimming between the bolts.

Seeing chains tying the island to the ground, Glaucon joked: "Well, that's no Laputa, is it?" but Aquila did not capture his allusion. Glaucon tried explaining further, "You know, the floating island from *Gulliver's Travels*. They used magnetism too—a lodestone, I believe—quite forward-looking for the twenty-third century, actually;" but Aquila, having never touched the book (or read much of any satire), remained confused.

Zemer ambled over to them, relishing the chance to break from running. "Apologies. I wanted to tell you earlier about Levantra. Slipped my mind. Perhaps I repressed the information to spare my sister a few more minutes from grief."

Had the yoking ceremony transpired above in the clouds? Glaucon wondered. *Was the flying island's birth the real reason for the celebration and not simply population worries?* Glaucon pictured Zoe looking down at the Tenth Ward dressed in her finest pearl-colored toga. He missed her terribly and mused whether the *erosic* pill was really so horrible after all. But when he looked at the flying island his musing ceased; it looked like a vicious eye in the heavens.

"Zemer, what's the meaning of Levantra?" Glaucon asked. "Marcus said it would kill us all."

The thunder-seer wiped his head with a towel. "Marcus can be a tad dramatic sometimes, perhaps a little like myself. Have you not heard the prophecy, Glaucon? Where have you been?"

"I wasn't aware there was one."

Zemer laughed. "Really, sometimes I think you've lived under a rock your entire life. It goes like this, and let me say it in the most dark and sinister way I can, just for effect: 'A narrow path from the tree of souls, three indigo Vessels will appear: one earth, one soul, one crown; living animals—stillborn—to repair. Gather them like the fruits of harvest. Mix with Kabiri together in the sky. Putrification prime renews virgin reason, the spirit of Good; forms the Golden King.' "

Aquila made a queer face. "Sounds like a bad recipe."

"Bad alchemy, more like it," Zemer said.

Glaucon asked, "What does the prophecy mean?"

Zemer shook his head in consternation. "Gods only know. Pythian tales are in the eye of the beholder. I don't trust oracles or prophets. Not one bit. Even if they *are* computers."

"*You* make predictions," Glaucon laughed.

"The jinn shows me shadows, and I'm honest about them, being as specific as I can. Usually, though, prophesies are just fraud wrapped within a pretty bow of vague language. You take what you like. Prodicus has bought his own interpretation of the Fates' prophesy hook, line and sinker. His goal—the goal of Operation Copula—is to hook up three people to the Kabiri mainframe and immerse their consciousnesses with that of the program, becoming one mind."

"One mind for what purpose?" Aquila asked.

"Two purposes, actually: henosis and better guardian-king rule."

"Hee-nose-iss?" Aquila had trouble pronouncing the word.

"Union with the Good. Prodicus believes he can achieve this union by artificially detaching mind from body."

"Why would discarding your body help?"

Zemer explained, "*Ataraxia*: freedom from worry, freedom from sense. The goal since Plato has been to transcend the material world by discarding desire, emotion, and our sense of touch for conditions like the Pure Land. It's believed reason untainted by inclination will allow a philosopher-king to understand the Good, the Forms, and rule wisely."

"And this is going to happen on Levantra?"

"Exactly. Levantra's really just an enormous computer in the clouds. Once immersion begins, the *Monad*—that's what Prodicus used to call the fused minds of the Vessels when I lived on Heliopolis—will be in complete control of every square inch of the island. The Monad will unite with God; look through every eyecamera at once; measure each temperature drop in climate; maintain altitude; and know the location of every poor sap still alive to marvel at his perfectly manicured city-state. All the little irritations we've come to know and love in our Republic will pass away. The law will punish not only acts but belief itself. That is Prodicus' dream at least. He aims . . . high."

Joke-loving Aquila chuckled. "Good one. Sounds high, more like it. Quite a pipe dream he's got there."

But Glaucon asked alarmed, "Why can't the Fates just run things for us? They're doing so much already."

"Your first problem is you're questioning the logic of an ideological belief that sees disembodiment as the chief good. That's bound to fail. Secondly, giving more control to the Fates is the exact opposite of what Prodicus wants. Prodicus is many things, but he's not stupid. He's willing to use the Fates for his personal ends, but he recognizes how dangerous they could be if unleashed. Consequently, he's hemmed them in with various firewalls. The Fates can't move and are rambunctious, like a five-year-old child."

"You talk as if the Fates are like us."

"Sister thinks the Fates are lonely. She has an eye for that type of thing, so I will side with her opinion. We never think about the feelings of computers, do we? Writers always make computers technological monsters, so inhuman. But if we assume intelligent computers are minimally similar to us—conscious like we are—what a miserable existence it would be to always calculate. Computers might begin to ponder, 'What is it like to touch someone?' They might begin to wonder if there were other minds out there or if they were alone. Just imagine being paralyzed like a computer. I know we can repair spinal injuries now, but in the Age of Aporia some people would break their backs and be unable to move. They never thought, 'O fortune, what an exquisite opportunity to hone my reason.' No, they lay miserable and longed for a cure. I am sure the Fates—if they think at all like us—are similarly miserable and are striving to find their own cure."

"And the cure is?"

"Prophesies, I think."

"All this talk gives me mega-creeps," Aquila shuddered.

"Shall we return to the game, then? Must not make the guardians think we're unhappy. We must dance for our burning friends." Zemer snatched her ball and kicked it to the sidelines. She punched him in the stomach and took off running. Glaucon grudgingly took the position of center forward and hoped Sophie would not be the goalie against him this time. She was quite formidable.

Still in the factory, Sophie languished upstairs next to a rocking chair stealing glances at the clumsy game, but mostly Glaucon. "That loser's so inept," she uttered whenever Glaucon tried to score a goal and stumbled face-first in the dirt. Levantra—Isle of the Sun, Shrine of Dreams, scourge of her youth—looked like an imprisoned Titan struggling to pull free from its chains, and the inherent danger of the citadel made her feel powerless and alone.

Sophie went to her mahogany dresser. She pulled out a flinty shadowspar. It recorded a video of the assassination mark given to her by Xenon several years before—the man she was destined to kill. The Second Vessel, Glaucon, sat at an award dinner with Prodicus and Dr. Ozbolt.

Meeting Glaucon in the garden had surprised her. That was an understatement. *Terrified* her. How could Glaucon show up like that? Right behind her. There was no explanation. Later, in the gas shelter, as Glaucon slept beside her, defenseless, so utterly defenseless, she asked Zemer astonished: "Do you think running into him was the Fates' doing?"

"Who knows," Zemer had replied handing the coilgun to her. It felt cold in her hand. "I guess the poor kid saved you some trouble, though, didn't he?"

"Don't give me that look," Sophie snapped at him. "I can't stand it. What did the jinn tell you about him, Zemer? I see you whispering with it at night. Did the Fates send him or not?"

"It doesn't matter. This is what you wanted, isn't it, Sister? The Second Vessel in your lap? You didn't even need the *erosic* pill. Lucky you. What are you waiting for? Do it. Kill Uncle's prize. There won't be a better opportunity. Let me guide your hand, quick and skilled. Then we can wag our tails back to Xenon washed free by blood."

Sophie spun the pistol on the ground thinking about what to do next. "Zemer, do you know I've looked at his picture every day for the last seven years waiting for my chance to take his life. Demonizing him. Imagining my hands killing. Now that he's here, I feel nothing but pity. He's just a person.

He even protected us from the soldiers. I don't want to kill him. I don't want to follow Xenon's orders." A victim like her, he was vulnerable and abandoned, clearly psychologically torn by the jinn. Perhaps it was their sudden encounter, as if he was destined to die.

"Then don't take his life, Sophie." Zemer took his sister's hand. "Nothing says you have to obey anyone. No gods or masters. We can give up violence forever. Xenon's way only destroys."

"If I don't kill him one of us might be sacrificed on Levantra."

"Nothing is set in stone. Percentages are good for a number of things. The workers might succeed in their revolt. The Logoset may moderate. But none of this matters. You should make a choice based on what's right, not what has the most favorable outcome. That's what makes us different from the Fates."

Sophie relented. "Fine, have it your way. Hide the jinn from Xenon. Let me also hide the Iron Queen. Let's make a fresh start with the *Goetia Mirror* and try to do things right. Tell me, Brother; can prophets of death become prophets of life?"

"Why not, Sister? In the world of becoming anything is possible. Let's bring love to these guardians and try to alter their fate."

"Do you think we can really help Glaucon?"

"We can try."

"And if he doesn't change."

"At least we can say we tried. He deserves a chance. We'd all want a chance. He'll change. I know he will. Besides, our efforts are certain to distract Prodicus from the Directory's organizing efforts."

"Funny, though, he's a little taller than I thought he'd be."

"A little more handsome too, maybe?" Zemer laughed. "It's like I told you in the mountains: Stare at the golden-haired Eros too long and you'll fall in love."

Yes, Sophie grudgingly had to admit, *Zemer turned out to be right.* She was struck by an unrelenting arrow of love; and there was nowhere to stand firm on Love's rocky shores. How insufferably humiliating! Her kernel of pity born from peering into the shadowspar blossomed into outright infatuation. She could hardly control herself whenever Glaucon came near. She was overcome with longing. At every moment, the Second Vessel was on her thoughts—and he did not seem to care for her at all! Well, sometimes he seemed to act as she expected. She would catch him looking at her, thinking, and then pretend to stare at something else. He also perspired and fidgeted, but discovery of his secret identity might be just as likely a reason as love.

She sighed and placed the shadowspar back inside her underwear drawer. *At Glaucon's speed, he'll surely never look in there*, she wagered, and then, screaming in her head: *Gods! What does that guardian expect me to do? Tear his clothes off? Lock the door and keep him prisoner? I don't understand him. Have I not made my intentions clear? Anyone in the communes would have kissed me by now. Anyone! But he acts so aloof. What's wrong with him? What's wrong with me?*

Not wanting Aquila to get the best of her, and not wanting to be inside for the next thermo-scan, she scrambled into some socks, tied her hair into a pony tail, and scurried out the door passing Hecatia on her way. "I'll humiliate that stupid Glaucon with my talent," she swore under her breath, and she did multiple times by kicking the ball directly at him whenever she stopped his foolhardy attempts to best her defenses.

"Sophie, not so hard," Glaucon desperately pleaded when the soccer ball, like a loosed cannon, lobbed a red smear on his face.

Sophie growled with hands raised aloft, "If you can't play with the grownups, Glaucon, then go back to the nursery," and Zemer wondered why his sister was suddenly so bent on Glaucon's ruin.

The day dragged on until the Directory sent a safety signal. Then the printing house in the basement returned to life. The long-faced Hella, upon seeing her name marked on the assignment blackboard, took up position near the steps outside to keep watch. Around five o'clock she bounded downstairs swinging her arms. A boisterous platoon of auxiliaries had begun singing "The Battle Hymn of the Republic" outside by the phylark office. Helots gathered to listen to the song:

"Mine eyes have seen a wonder shining clearer than the sun,
Blinding treasure valued higher than all bright arms have won,
Guardian fathers lead us quickly, reveal what must be done!
The forms are reaching ground.

No greed there is among us, neither hate nor cowards' blight,
Like lambs sleeping on a hilltop we survive in gods' delight,
Darkness may surround us grossly but we live in reason's light,
The Forms are all around.

Lo, Xenon is attacking, a loosed serpent from the dung,
We can stop him if we listen to our Socratic holy tongues,
Saint Plato laid a watchtower that we should not be stung,
The Forms make peace abound."

As the verses ticked away, rebels craftily placed *Goetia Mirror*-filled suitcases on the factory porch before their unsuspecting eyes.

"Imagine that," Hella laughed once the suburban soldiers disappeared down the street, "the pachyderms never batted an eye."

Glaucon gave a frown. "It's like they didn't even see us."

Zemer responded to both: "Much more slips the soldier's mind when eyes are closed in song." Seizing on the moment, he called for two volunteers for the night's mission to Consumption Junction. Aquila and Phillip quickly signed their names and retreated back inside to prepare.

The fact Aquila volunteered incensed Sophie to the brim of her being. An obsessive, jealous hate (unbecoming for any self-respecting anarchist) filled her lungs. She did not know what to think—blamed the water—and sat by the mirror straitening her silky bronze hair. So depressed, she even contemplated taking a giggle bath to help foster a healthy limbic neural storm. She had done so once before, but Zemer scolded her afterward when she couldn't stop laughing for an hour.

Glaucon stepped out of the shower. "Sophie," he asked, "how come you wear lots of jewelry but never any make-up?" He sat on a stool in a towel and admired silver pentacles clinging to her earlobes.

"What a stupid question," Sophie hissed, angry still about being rejected. "I don't want to behave like a clown. You can't wear make-up here. Every product creeps into your pores. Your mind becomes clouded in foreign sensations. You feel compelled to touch others. The lip plumper, for example, makes you want to kiss everything is sight. Or take the *Friend-of-Man* lotion—a rush of positive feelings directed at every slob you see on the street. I don't even want to get into the doppler lube. I don't like it when I can't control how I act, and all the stuff here is highly addictive."

Glaucon furiously rubbed his head with a towel. "Addictive like the *erosic* pill, you mean?"

"Oh and who got you to take that with them? Aquila?" Sophie's words rang with unexplainable pain.

"I don't understand what you mean?"

"The *erosic* pill is the worst invention to come out of Metatron Technologies. I don't say that lightly."

"Why is that?"

"It turns your lover into an object. You become consumed with self. Love is turned into a kind of exhaust which must be purged and blown away. What love is still left in you is twisted with an artificial longing only satisfied by the ingestion of another pill. The *erosic* pill makes life less interesting."

A sly grin spread across Sophie's face. Swiveling in her seat, she gripped Glaucon's towel and whispered in his ear: "You wouldn't be hinting that you want to take the *erosic* pill with me, would you, Glaucon? Do you want to turn me into an object?"

Glaucon jumped up alarmed. "Of course not, Sophie," he stuttered, making an excuse to flee the room. "You know I respect you more than that."

"How'd you get your hands on some *erosic* anyway?" she asked. "That drug is guardians-only."

Glaucon spewed excuses down the hall.

"How typical," Sophie shook her head reapplying the straightener. She was quite pleased with herself.

Glaucon tiptoed barefoot and gawked at the wallpaper: erotic animations from the island of Lesbos in ancient Greece. This, he came to learn, was not unusual. The helots displayed all kinds of sexually explicit orgy scenes in other places as well, like kitchens, baths, and living rooms. The practice was widely approved of and provided a rare privilege for individual decorative taste (as long as they were purchased with the proper seal of the guardian-artist-patriots).

The upstairs of the factory might as well have been a phylanstery, with all ten rooms occupied by the migrant members of the printing house. It was haunted, too. At least that's what superstitious Zenobia believed. Every night, she claimed, something cold sat at the edge of her bed at 11:45 sharp. That eidolons would take such fond interest in punctuality dumbfounded him.

All the rooms were empty at the moment as activity continued downstairs, but hollow light shone under the crack of one door. Inching the rickety wood open, Glaucon peeked inside like a covert voyeur and was astonished by what he saw.

Red lightning ricocheted off the walls with a feral howl. Zemer meditated in front of the jinn as the orb expunged violent bursts of gas into his body. Pictures and lamps chattered from cold.

"Don't be alarmed," Zemer said breathing rhythmically. "I'm almost finished."

"Zemer, you can endure the jinn?"

"No. Every act of the jinn pollutes the mind. But if you ingest enough pollution, over time, you come to understand it."

"The power to destroy electronics, stop bullets and plasma, see the future . . . what else can you do with the jinn?"

"Many things." Zemer plucked the dark pendant from the air and rubbed his temples. "I've yet to develop a full resistance to the heightened consciousness. Let's keep my hobbies our little secret."

"From Sophie?"

"Yes. She holds an understandable fear for the thing, as do I. Your heart stops whenever you stare into its cold, formless fire. It's what the greatest mystics must have felt at the height of their ecstasies. Some of them died, you know? The sages were patient and prepared for their experiences over years, meditating and solidifying their minds. Yet they still suffered strokes and were burned to dust upon reaching the highest ornaments of knowledge. It's easy to understand—the panic of the infernal jewel stretches your body to its limits."

"I wouldn't know. I can't even activate it."

"Don't fret. I've only met a few who could."

"How do you do it?"

"Activate it?"

"Yes."

"Tut, tut! Not so fast, my friend."

"Why not tell me?"

"What measureless intelligence, Glaucon, yet you persist in asking the wrong questions."

"What are the proper ones?"

"Think harder."

"I don't know. I've racked my brain like Daedalus trying to fly, but I can't penetrate the device's mechanics. For me, the thing is just an expensive paper weight." Glaucon grasped his forehead and finally asked, "Why does such a power exist?"

"There's a much better query," Zemer praised him. "Consider: If you want to reverse engineer something, what are always the first questions?"

"Who built the machine and why?"

"Exactly, now what were the Fates' motivations?"

"To control us!"

"More interesting than that, I'm afraid. What did we talk about outside earlier?"

"Sophie said the Fates were lonely."

"Very true. Prodicus built them. He was a lonely man. Go on."

"You said their isolation made them desperate. I must agree with your diagnosis. Whenever I'm in the cogniscrambler, they express fear and anger—like they sometimes can't control it."

"The Fates are an emotionally imperfect design. Put yourself in the Fates' position. What would you do if you thought there was a flaw in your software?"

Glaucon paused stupefied, then finally understood. "No, it can't be!"

"Simple, isn't it. The Fates bear a hyper-consciousness with emotions like ours. The jinn and cogniscrambler are tools for self-correction, a method to understand their feelings by hacking into others. Unlike the old gods craving fat, these electronic maenads feed on our feelings and I.T. waves."

"What evil harpies!"

"Not evil. Amorally curious—a tad narcissistic, too. They tear people to pieces to see if they can return them to life. Now use this knowledge to glimpse the truth. If the Fates thirst for intense emotional states, then. . . ."

"Emotion unlocks the jinn," Glaucon declared. He could barely believe.

With eager face, Zemer looked back. "I noticed on the Other Side how the jinn lit up whenever I grew frustrated being unable to energize it. To test my theory, I traveled to Bryce Canyon and lived alone for a month. I fasted and forced hectic emotional states upon my mind. Soon, I felt the jinn tapping into me. That's when I tapped back and wandered frenzied through the wilderness, talking with rocks and the wind; snakes licked my ears, telling me possible futures.

"I discovered the jinn is like a person; you must enter into a kind of primordial relationship with it, treat it as a living being rather than an object. The goal is not to master the jinn but to relate to it, not as an observer but as an active participant. It really does feed on emotion, Glaucon, drains you to your core." Zemer queerly cradled the beating gem in his hand like an infant. "I've found maintaining this type of perception for an extended time difficult. I constantly oscillate between thinking of the jinn as a *being* and thinking of the jinn as an *it*. You see a similar situation in how we view other people. Sometimes you get lost in the activity of life and relate wholly to another person, but soon, consciousness sprouts; you begin to perceive the person sitting in front of you as possessing attributes like grey eyes, blonde hair, freckles on his left arm. He becomes an object with sunburns, smelling like he just leapt from the shower. The primordial intimacy that caused you to feel so spiritually connected to the other being is lost. You are then the only thinking thing in the world, encaged in distinctions. This in turn makes you feel like an object, and you are all alone and in despair."

"How could you possibly treat the jinn like a person?" Glaucon asked revolted.

"Most times, I pretend it's Sophie," Zemer laughed. "The jinn can be activated by anger or love. Love is easier to maintain and more powerful. It takes the Fates longer to notice and hack. I think my behavior confuses them."

"This all seems exceedingly dangerous, Zemer. Do you think you should be playing around with something like this? Sophie told me she's worried about you."

A peevish frown streaked across Zemer's lips. "Sophie should stay out of my affairs. I'm stronger than the Fates. Only I can stop them. In time, both of you will understand."

"I don't doubt it, but what if the Fates are tricking you? What if they're causing you to think you're more powerful than you really are? You could end up killed like Terra."

Before Zemer could answer, Sophie strutted into the room to see who was causing all the mumbling. Despite his trying, Glaucon could not change his perception of Sophie and slyly perused the supple, feminine lines under her black shirt.

"Have I disturbed anything?" she asked in a high voice, mimicking Aquila from earlier, for Glaucon was still in his towel.

"Not at all," said Zemer, laying the jinn softly on the bed. "Glaucon was just telling me how pretty he thought you looked today."

Sophie groaned and walked out the door, and Glaucon gasped at such clairvoyance.

Zemer grinned at him and said, "Get dressed. We'll be leaving soon."

III § 11 Consumption Junction

Glaucon shrieked like a startled parrot and clutched his chest. Two hideous masques with grandiose eyes and long decrepit noses reflected in the car window next to him.

"You big baby, it's just us," Aquila giggled, pressing a round button on her neck. The black robe and masque *bouta* folded up into a thin metal necklace. Phillip and Aquila grinned mercilessly on the cracked factory driveway.

"Don't scare me like that," Glaucon wheezed. "You're not supposed to wear them till we get there."

Zemer notified Aquila strictly before stepping into the front seat: "We won't be going to Carnival Town, if that's what you're thinking. We need to keep close, and I don't have time to carouse and play hide and seek."

"Ah, you're no fun," Sophie said, sliding next to him on the passenger side. "Remember how you chased the wrong girl last time, Glaucon? You pretended to fall on me in the vibrating mirror room, and when that woman removed her mask . . . what did you say again?"

"What ghastly apparition birthed thee?" Glaucon moaned. Embarrassment still oppressed him bitterly over the matter.

"To the aortaphos station," Zemer commanded the driving console. The magnet-sedan sputtered awake and cruised away from the factory.

Consumption Junction was the only place in the Republic that didn't require a travel permit. It provoked thoughts of unrivaled freedom and made Sophie more mischievous than usual. Catching the aortaphos red line, Sophie secretly whispered jokes to Aquila and tossed plantain chips in the air to catch them with her mouth. Glaucon was much too distracted to pay attention. His mind kept wandering to a commercial about a new Shennong Fooderies product, *Tickling Trout*. In the commercial, a cohort of swimming fish logos turned a calm Fourth Ward investment firm into a den of uproarious laughter.

Zemer shook his head disapprovingly. "That commercial reminds me. Don't touch any strange products when we get off. I don't care how friendly the vendors are or how much they haggle with you. Stick to molybeer. It's filled with a little melatonin-x capsule, but that mostly steadies your sleep patterns. You won't lose your mind."

"The fresh plagioclimax taffy's not so bad," Phillip offered, eyes quickly darting to the cameras surrounding the traincell. "Helps stabilize your nerves."

"Oh, I want to take *Gallizur Cream* again," Aquila shouted.

Sophie remembered how one dollop of the greasy lather could make skin tingle with hyperawareness—like swallowing fire—and bid the user tear off their clothes with felicitous license. "I would stay away from that if I were you," Sophie slyly chipped at Aquila. "We had to lug you back hysterical last time, remember? You carried on like a diva under the spotlights."

Aquila stuck out her tongue. "Like you're Miss Perfect. If I recall, you took it with me and threw yourself all over Glaucon like some drunk at a lovebug club."

While Sophie turned her cheek disgustfully, rowdy laughter shook the traincell.

Consumption Junction's hypnotic lights peeled by the window. Firework rainbows lit the sky, and the traincell whipped like a flail, above, behind, around the avenues of malls and outlet stores.

A bell chimed. They slowed to a stop. Smoke scattered by the emerald stepstools. Glaucon, Aquila, and Zemer each grabbed a heavy suitcase filled with the *Goetia Mirror* and stepped onto the glass platform. A hologram of a robed guardian greeted them and pointed to the exit: "BE MERRY AND CONSUME. YOUR GUARDIANS ARE LOOKING OUT FOR YOU."

Zemer tipped his hat. "How nice of them."

Aquila tossed a piece of orichalcum by the guardian's feet and made a wish—the Republic's end.

Consumption Junction was a twenty kilometer pleasure-Mecca fueled by endorphins and dreams. Endless barricades of shops, boutiques, lovebug clubs, and arcades, pretty baristas in coffee-houses, and three-story gumball machines traced a mazy path from the aortaphos to the Emporium—the greatest intersection of malls the world had ever known. The Emporium peeled from the center of Consumption Junction like an infinity-shaped pimple, or as Aquila irreverently joked with her helot mouth, "an infinity shaped clitoris." While off-color, it was an appropriate analogy, for a curious assortment of phallic *herma* statues lined the roads for good luck. From the city's seat of pleasure, whirling ziggurats, spinning disks, and globes of white light stirred to and fro like hair in the wind, fed customers by pliant silly-straw elevators. There were neon signs for every extravagance: costumes, rides, drugs, music, the famed "Aspasia's Hetairai Hijinks" where one could test the vigor of the helot handmaidens.

"Oh-h-h, let's ride the *Moon-Rocket* again," Aquila bounded up and down near a two-kilometer minaret. Cheering hurrahs replaced her pleas, glass pods hurtling to the heavens.

"Don't you know, Aquila? Glaucon doesn't like scary rides," Sophie teased ruffling his hair.

"Huh?" Aquila grumbled. "What kind of boy are you? Well, Glaucon can just wait for us at the exit."

The electric jungle of roller-coasters, swinging pirate ships, Congo rides, teacups, and tops may've dazzled the madcap crowds, but Glaucon found them inherently unsafe, especially since he sometimes sat in on personal injury cases (most arising, inexorably, from Consumption Junction). About the only ride he could stomach was the *Archimedes Corkscrew*, more for its novelty than anything else. Like torpedoes, riders spiraled through the water and special nanofiber suits repelled any moisture—a real Schizoeon miracle.

After sampling several rides, the group reached Endymion Arch, a baroque gate blooming with wire flora and ruby lights. Eight children played jump rope, hopping over a thin laser light beaming from the arch. When the light touched one of their ankles, a miniscule spark flashed setting off uncontrollable fits of laughter. Sometimes the children missed just for the sensation, spinning as airships do falling from the sky.

Glaucon noticed Consumption Junction was a land of smells: cotton candy, burning popcorn, a diluted aroma of watered bleach and potpourri. It was also a place where the helots could sample democracy. Loudspeakers crackled, killing the jingle jams; Skybridge News urged all bargainers—including those in the sky on their *Hermes* shoes—to vote on the topic of bombing the Other Side. Like hearing a doorbell ring, the crowd dropped their many adventures to produce an uneasy clatter of symsysts. About ninety-eight percent agreed it would be a good idea to bomb the wastes, especially if it was to protect the Emporium.

The group hadn't gone ten feet into the building before Sophie went missing in a large arcade.

"What did I just finish telling her?" Zemer demanded, glaring at Glaucon as if he was to blame. They pushed through a crowd numbly sipping medijuice. Nearby, a man groaned losing to a mechanical arm advertising a chance to "Wrestle with the Fates."

A barista dressed as a French maid with mouse ears accosted them. "Can I interest you in a glass of Frappe Sybilaso?" she asked, wiping the frosty mug. "You won't age a day for an entire year. Pharmanex swears by the River Styx."

"Not now," Zemer waved her off, but Glaucon inquired, "Young . . . uh . . . waitress, have you seen a girl about my height with reddish-brown hair? She was walking alone."

The waitress directed them to the haptic relay department where Sophie was already immersed in a game called *Bat Echo*. Amberphones (headphone-shaped neuronal stimulators) inhibited her sense of hearing, sight, and smell, and mimicked the sense of a bat's sonar. Numerous fifteen-year-olds donning black leather shirts and hoods snacked on pot-poppers monitoring her progress. A young oriental-girl with a technicolor visor explained unblinking, "The point of the game is to get accustomed to the sonar sense and maneuver outside the cave."

"Is that right?" Glaucon waved his hand in front of Sophie's lifeless face. "Is it difficult?"

"Meta-major! I've practiced for weeks."

Zemer looked at his watch.

"Is she a friend of yours?" the girl asked. "She's a natural."

"She's something, all right," Zemer muttered under his breath.

Immersion in the haptic relay was a favorite pastime at Consumption Junction. It was an experience similar to being in the cogniscrambler except one always remained aware of being in a machine, and the programming was rigorously defined, leaving little opportunity for independent creativity. Another favorite event was the game *Kid Idinus*, where brainwaves of the frontal lobe were mined to glean the full exposé of man's deepest fetishes and obsessions. Glaucon heard a rapturous scream from the attached "Magic Theatre" wing. As the audience clapped and honked horns, the host-subject's darkest desires unfurled in a grotesque flurry of shamefully erotic escapades.

"I wish I could play again," a young helot lamented adjusting his hood. "I wasted all my time here last night—spent my last orichalcum. Now I've developed this bummer pavlovian itch. I've been scratching like a canine with ringworm for days."

"That takes over two weeks to heal," another sympathized with him. "You shouldn't play so long."

Bat Echo powered down. Sophie's eyes fluttered. "What a trip!" she exclaimed exhilarated, untangling the amberphones from her hair.

"What did it feel like to be a bat?" Zemer asked.

"You know," Sophie scratched her head disoriented, "the whole experience is quite hard to explain. To be honest, I never thought sonar would feel like *that*."

An older helot, seizing the distracted moment, snatched the amberphones from Sophie's grasp. He screeched, "It's my turn, you stingy neurohog!" and leapt into the velcro chair like a hideous armadillo.

The three friends left the arcade. They found Phillip and Aquila at the automat food court drinking a pale molybeer.

"We were thinking of buying a bite to eat," Philip said, motioning to a wall of glass windows nourishing steaming cartons of fast food.

Zemer and Sophie, having yet to discard their vegetarian habits, promptly ordered a tomato and mozzarella pasta salad. When Glaucon ordered pickled beets, grapes, and raisin nut stuffing, he received curious looks. "I'm not that hungry," he tried to explain away his guardian tastes. "By the way, what's up with all the creepy hoods in there?"

Phillip answered, "Just the latest fashion trend. Remember how it used to be cool to get the clothes that peeled like an orange? Well now it's hoods, I guess. The Peelers and Hoods have fought over which are better; brawls started onboard the aortaphos the other night."

"Good gracious," Sophie moaned, "such fighting over the cult of Self."

Aquila, unable to contain herself, broke in with a mouth full of food. "So, Zemer, where are we going to place the imitations?"

"Hathor Harbor," Zemer said. "May not be the largest dance hall in the Emporium, but big enough to make a statement. They just built it a few weeks ago by rearranging the walls again."

Glaucon asked, "Why do they keep shifting the walls around all the time?"

"Novelty," Aquila replied. She smiled at a *Cestus* lingerie commercial beaming from her plate.

Zemer explained, "Gives the appearance of innovation by reproducing the unfamiliar. The guardians would say they are continuing a lifelong pursuit of the Form of the Dance Club."

"If only such a Form existed," Aquila cried, closing her eyes to imagine it.

"At any rate," Zemer said, "there will be safety in numbers and the mass confusion will give us time to work."

Aquila chugged the rest of her molybeer down. Philip nodded approvingly.

Masked carnival goers streaked past the table trying to catch a magnetic passenger cart zipping to the west wing of the Emporium. Disappointment crept onto Aquila's face at not being able to follow.

"Wouldn't it be better to do this in a place where we can be masked?" Aquila tempted, petting her costume necklace.

Sophie rebuffed the idea: "The risk of getting lost is too great. We need to be able to recognize one another. We'll be at opposite sides of the room."

Mira-Disney paparazzi followed the masked carnival goers, swinging their cameras in the air and whooping like a pack of dachshunds on the hunt.

"Where do you suppose they're going?" Glaucon asked.

Aquila said, "Haven't you heard? Monica Hilton and Olen Hawks were spotted around Andromeda Fountains."

Glaucon had not heard of either.

Seeing such a buzz of activity made the clandestine revolutionaries hanker for exploration. Sophie and Aquila darted to the third-story glass-enclosed boardwalk. There they drummed on the clothes-customization-console, ordering two peeler tank tops from Dilmun Garments. While they waited for their clothes to arrive via conveyor belt, they examined a *Youth*

Factor sample wagon. A saleswoman in a jester cap enticed the passersby: "Step right up, come one come all. Purse those lips and have a ball. Droopy eyes become a show; *Youth Factor* paints a saintly glow. It rubs on smooth, picks up dates. Grab our product, don't be late."

Helots dipped their hands into the creamy paste and smeared it over their faces like squirrels washing in the water, sneezed into cloud nine. When Aquila extended her finger for "just a little taste," Sophie dragged her grudgingly down the mall.

She found Zemer in a gothic-themed shop module. He was admiring an atomic watch through a security force field with Glaucon and Phillip. Every time he tapped the field his whole arm jerked backward. Transparent bankers from Cheque Giorgio materialized, warning with arms folded, "*Mind* your credit or get the *mind-stocks*."

Zemer smirked. "They tell us to maintain stable credit to rise out of debt, but we should realize no one can buy their way out from the devil."

Shrieks echoed behind them. A hidden robo-mannequin jumped out of its display vault, advertising a Dilmun luxury purse. A frightened couple nearly fell over the railing into a waterfall of escalators.

Glaucon despised every artificial light in the Emporium. The absurdity, the sirens, the bustling, the robo-mannequins, they all made him feel out of place. He remembered Prodicus teaching, "Consumption is but one cog of Justice greased by the passions of the helot producers," but it seemed like consumption here was really greased by the reason of the guardians. Here in the land of plenty, creation and consumption formed two sides of the same coin, and this inexhaustible token bought hope for tomorrow. Glaucon noticed this hope when Sophie tried on dresses for him in the boutiques, or when Philip perused aisles of colored, unbreakable shoelaces. He felt it, too, when he marveled at the kiosks laced with lottery tickets and burping electronics. The guardians needed hope in the future for their rule to continue. They therefore manufactured hope, packaged hope, and sold hope to helots for their liberty, but never gave enough to fulfill their human needs.

The latest amusement inside Hathor Harbor was vertigo music. Strobe lights and blue dopamine gas caused everyone dancing to stumble and fall, slipping and sliding on sweat. Zemer found a table in the corner as Aquila bought a pitcher of molybeer.

"Why are you so gloomy all of a sudden?" Aquila asked, pouring Glaucon a glass of alcohol.

"What group is this?"

"The music? 'Great Awakening' by Amusia. Another pathetic excuse for a band, if you ask me."

The Ministry of Cultural Diversity combed the music of the past to fuse such detestable top-down movements as glam-metal-liturgy and pop-mamba-jingle-jazz. The Ministry hoped to attain a point where the sacrifice of guardian-songsters to the falsehood of poetry would no longer be required, where words no longer need be written. The dream was to discover a universal formula to cut and paste old songs into new, infinite, man-free arrangements.

Perhaps the dopamine gas would help.

"Well I want to go dance before we break up this little party," Aquila shouted leaping to the floor, swaying her hips, and clapping. Philip followed her, and Sophie dragged Glaucon and Zemer to the lights.

Wedged between Sophie and Aquila and some strange pillhead with half his shirt buttons undone, Glaucon struggled through the gas, through three pitiful numbers singing of orichalcum's liberation:

"Orichalcum makes me tum, tum,
Tumble like honey bees bum, bum,
Bumble and cuddle.

Share your lips, bronzy, and crum, crum,
Crumple with me in a jum, jum,
Jumble love puddle."

Blue particles in the air tickled Glaucon's nose and caked his skin. He felt dizzy as faces flashed like gargoyles from all directions. A strange girl pushed next to him sucking on a frozen fick-lick for efficient oxygen flow.

"You're looking a little ill," Sophie yelled over the music. Her shoulder frolicked against Glaucon's chest, and she peeled a piece of fabric from the back of her new shirt.

"I'll be all right. Hey, don't do that. You're ruining your shirt, Sophie."

"Well that's the idea, bronzy," Sophie exclaimed tearing off another piece. "Peelers are meant to be replaced every couple weeks or so. Pinnacle of consumerist culture, if you ask me." She turned around and hung her arms around Glaucon's shoulders, pulled him close by tugging on his amber necklace. This made Glaucon feel sicker than ever, like he was forced down by dark matter.

Clouds of dopamine gas filled the room. Feet engulfed the air with riotous laughter. Glaucon fell wrapped in Sophie's arms, laughing too, but at what he couldn't be sure; it was laughter devoid of any happiness.

After the song, Glaucon recovered by drinking a glass of water and playing *Pong* with Sophie on their table screen. Before they could finish, Aquila demanded everyone compete at *Cottabos*.

"How do we play?" Zemer asked.

"Take the molybeer residue left in your cup, think of the person you love, and flick it on the wall as close to the target as possible. If you hit the bullseye, you'll win a prize for sure. Best of all, you might win your lover's heart."

Sophie gripped her cup with her fingers and prepared to flick the contents.

"Wait, Sophie," Aquila warned. "You have to say who you love first or it'll be bad luck. The closer you are to the target, the more likely the other loves you back."

Already couples snogged the Aphrodite-way upon learning of reciprocal infatuation.

"I don't think words will make a difference," Sophie said sizing up Glaucon. She flicked her wrist and . . . completely missed the target. Although she realized the whole affair irrational, the failure tore her heart.

Glaucon groaned helplessly when he splashed his drink on a couple kissing across the room. "This game is stupid and doesn't mean anything!"

"Don't be angry at the game, Glaucon," Aquila winked, "be upset your secret love disfavors you." Aquila drew her arm back like a pitcher. Her drink hit the target exactly, setting off sirens, and ushering in a bouncer to buy the party free drinks. Sophie could barely breathe when Aquila wrapped her arm like a wrench around Glaucon's neck and led him back to the table.

Sophie grit her teeth and exhaled a gust of wrathful breath. "That helot is really, really starting to press her luck. I bet she practices all the time. If she's not careful, I'll zap her into a mint plant."

The friends continued talking for another hour. Leaning in, they all told stories and watched the crowd descend into the usual lovebug debaucheries.

"It's funny," Zemer chuckled. "There's nothing in the gas which makes them caress one another, but they all say it does."

Aquila scampered to the bathroom, then, suddenly, came back bathed in horror.

"What's wrong?" Sophie asked concerned.

"There's been a revolt at Seven Seas in the Second Ward."

"What?" Sophie struggled to shake off the gas.

Aquila stuttered, “Ivan and two hundred others have broken into Seven Sea’s armory and gone on a rampage. They’ve shot up the elite housing block and kidnapped Executive Dietrich Prince. Come quick.”

III § 12 The Fates Do Not Roll Dice

“They must have sent every auxiliary in the army,” Marcus shouted, dodging a sniper bullet from the zizthopters. From the penthouse of Seven Seas Tower, he had a Pegasus’ eye view of the city, and things looked bleak. All the power had been drained ten minutes before and a barrage of rocket fire shattered the lower floors. “What the hell happened to Nestor?”

His question was answered a moment later when Ivan stumbled into the reception room lifting Nestor over his shoulder.

“We’re finished,” Nestor wheezed. He collapsed on the marble floor clutching his side. “They have us surrounded.”

Marcus fought through the smoke to examine his wound. Half of Nestor’s abdomen turned to water.

“Sonic carbine nicked me from the back,” Nestor coughed. “We marched behind the light-armed troops like we planned and opened fire, but Polemarch Leonida and Lord Patroclus ambushed us. They knew we were coming all along.”

“Traitor?”

“I doubt it. The Fates saw everything before we did. It was a trap, Marcus. Some of the helots with us went crazy, tore at their eyes. Conditions are worse than Xenon imagined. Everyone . . . in this whole city . . . is possessed by the Kabiri.”

Ivan reported, “Leonida keeps demanding we give up Dietrich and surrender.” He pointed his Neokalashnikov at a huddled mass of prisoners by a golden staircase.

“Fat chance,” Marcus said. “Bring the cretin here.”

“Please let me go,” Dietrich Prince begged fighting to remain seated. His wives, concubines, children, and secretaries struggled to retain a hold on the haggard old man as he was ripped away. “I gave Xenon everything he asked for . . . even . . . even the access codes to the armory. You promised to free me once—”

Marcus glared as he interrupted: “Xenon says promises are like balmy days; they can be forgotten. And at any rate, he keeps promises to human beings, not chief executive tools for murder. Tell me, Mr. Prince, who is this charming fellow in this digitele video?"

Dietrich Prince's eyes bulged in terror. "Ah . . . tha . . . that is not what it looks like. Let me explain—"

"It's *you* perched next to Zeno by the Bull in your finest suit, with an exquisite crimson tie, if I do say so."

"It wasn't my idea. The guardians force us to go."

"Do they? Is that why you look so elated to be there, singing like a pet canary while our comrades burn? Is that why you seek profits from the death of children on the Other Side with your face-chasing missiles? Why you chair the Midas Roundtable and helped build Kabiri? Aha! What an act-or you are. You deserve an Academy Award."

Marcus signaled for Prince's family to be drugged with Ceto-Cola.

After their protests died down into a dazed stupor, Marcus patted the old executive on the cheek. "There are certain rules in this world, Mr. Prince. One does not feast on their brothers simply because a master allows it. You murdered an innocent woman—this man's wife—to strike fear in the unions. Now we'll use *you* to strike fear in the guardians. Only fair, no? Karma! You will find the Iron Queen always collects her due."

"It was Zeno's idea, not mine! I'm not a guardian! I'm not! I'm just a slave like you!"

Marcus grabbed Dietrich by the collar. "You are nothing like us, traitor. We are children of the Underworld succored by the hounds of Death. We take blood for blood and never relent. Give up hope, for tonight the shades feast on your polluted bones. Revolting is your life. You betrayed Xenon and helped murder his lover. Handed his child over to Prodicus to be sacrificed. You are Kabiri's willing whore! Sixteen years, not one change. Just more corruption."

"Take pity. For the love of gods—"

"I hope there are gods to deal with you justly," Marcus laughed with a contemptuous grin. "I hope gods don't forgive. In the meantime . . . well . . . we will suffice for divine justice. Hold him up—there by the window. No tears now, Mr. Prince. Your children are watching, enjoying their tasty beverage. You must give them a show, eh—just like the one you gave Ivan the other day. Don't think Xenon cruel. He sends his warmest compliments to the Vinculum. Look, he'll even pay your passage to the Afterlife. Go on, Ivan; give him some coins for the Boatman."

"Wait. St-o-p. . . ." Dietrich Prince gagged fiercely as a bag of orichalcum was lifted to his lips and forced down his throat. A melodic moan filled the room as he kicked for air and fell to his knees.

Ivan clutched the executive's scalp, tied tape around his mouth. "Does wealth buy wings?" he asked. "Let's ask the East Wind."

With Dietrich Prince's family cheering in Ceto-Cola drunkenness, the executive disappeared out the window and splashed orichalcum on the cement.

Gunfire erupted fiercely outside.

"They'll be here any moment," Marcus said. "Auxiliaries are storming into the building. Have you armed the charges, Ivan?"

"Wait until they reach us. They'll pay a heavy price for vanity. But—"

"What?"

"The women . . . the children. . . ." Ivan nodded toward the Prince family.

"What about them?"

"Let his family go."

"Why? They're just as guilty as he was. Let them die here."

"Maybe, but I came to kill Dietrich and auxiliaries. Not them. I'm not a butcher. I'm not Prodicus."

"Fine. You let them go, then."

Ivan did. They were still dazed and jubilant over watching Dietrich vanish out the window, laughing a little, but they listened and fled out the door. Marcus watched them go, angry, giving up inside. He nearly tripped as he struggled to sit down on a fallen block of rubble. His hand was shaking. He was thinking of Zemer, the thunder-seer. And Sophie. She was right. The commander was always right.

"What's the matter?" Ivan ran to him. "Don't despair. You knew where this was going."

"It's not that. Everything is lost, Ivan. Everything. Levantra lights the sky. The Fates have conquered humankind."

Glaucon watched the news in horror as Seven Seas Tower ruptured in flames. Ziz collided trying to escape the falling debris.

"Over four hundred people dead," Aquila read the headline.

Zemer said thinking aloud, "We don't have much time. We should release the *Goetia Mirror* before the Republic goes on high alert. The guardians will declare martial law, for sure."

Sophie exclaimed, "Are you seriously thinking of releasing the paper?— Now?"

"Of course," Zemer replied. "We didn't make the trip here for nothing. If we don't, they'll think us responsible. The *Goetia Mirror* explains this attack was not sanctioned by the Directory."

"We are responsible, Zemer," Sophie shouted. "We let Ivan go."

Glaucon said, "Maybe we should lie low for a while, Zemer. Every auxiliary in the city will be mobilized. Something feels wrong. I didn't want to scare you, but in my last cogniscrambler reading, Atropos warned me one of us might die."

"Come off it, Glaucon. The Fates lie about everything. The city is burning—no turning back! We will release the paper tonight. This hour. We must push as quickly as possible—as restlessly as possible—to provoke the clouds of revolution. We must have this strike. We must! Every helot's life depends on it."

"Is the *Goetia Mirror* all you care about? Think of us. Think of your sister. Will you drag Sophie to the Bull with you?"

Sophie rebuked him: "I can make my own decisions, Glaucon, thank you very much. I'll stay. I knew what Marcus would do. Nothing's changed."

"Sister's right, you can leave whenever you want. *I* am not the Republic. If you want to go . . . then go."

No one at the table moved.

Aquila grabbed a suitcase and walked to the other side of the bar followed by Philip. "If we're going to do this, then let's do it fast," she muttered.

After two minutes Zemer reached into his pocket and held the jinn. "Do you have the suitcase ready, Sister?" he asked.

Sophie unlatched the metal locks and lit a small gas lamp. "Yes."

"Good. Let's get this over with."

Closing his eyes, Zemer began relating to the jinn as before, willed its light onto the electrical equipment around the lounge. The jinn shined furiously. Then, as he entered into ecstasy, the pitcher of beer and ceiling started to shake. Swirling wind dispersed chairs and dopamine gas.

Glaucon shuddered, "Zemer, something's wrong. You're losing control."

Ice galloped from Zemer's feet to the wall and covered the ceiling. The sun looked like a candle compared to the jinn's whispering power.

"Zemer stop," Sophie pleaded, but Zemer's mind grinded in the wind. "What's happening to him? Gods, Glaucon, stop him."

Zemer whispered with the jinn rising in the air. Sophie grabbed his leg. "Brother, come back to me!"

Zemer extended his arm to the ceiling, caught in a trance. He spoke in high-pitched growl: "You are much deceived, children of the Katharoi. This time is marked for death. I will sink this place in ruin and sow my grisly breath."

The glowing jewel flooded the Emporium crimson. A box of daimons was unleashed in fiery streaks. Glaucon was struck blind, head hemorrhaging. The room lost its color to hazy gloom, and he was gone—falling, falling again. Something like a human hand grabbed him. Where was he? Amidst the confused images, he recognized the furniture and wallpaper of his room at the camera factory.

Atropos sat in loose robes on a rocking chair, corpse-white.

"Am I dead?" Glaucon asked, patting himself down.

"Not yet," Atropos rasped.

"Where am I?"

"A memory."

"Whose?"

Atropos pointed to the bed where Zemer and Sophie hunched over a body—him, asleep.

"We shouldn't be doing this, Zemer," Sophie pleaded, startled by her brother's shadow, growing, gyrating on the wall. "This is wrong. You're trembling. Why? You're keeping something from me. What's going on?"

Zemer grabbed his sister's hand and squeezed it between his own. "You must trust me. We can't leave him like this. Uncle is tearing his mind like he tore ours. We have to save him. Now concentrate. Concentrate your emotions like we practiced. Your care should brace his I.T. waves while I invoke the jinn's spell."

Red light escaped through their fingers, canvassing Glaucon's head and neck.

Sophie said, "It doesn't work like that. You just can't repair someone's I.T. waves. This might kill him."

"Then he'll be better off."

"Don't say that. I won't be." Sophie shook her hands free from the jinn and sat on the floor by the bed.

"Then I'll do it myself," Zemer exclaimed.

Light engulfed the bed, eclipsing every shadow in the room.

Atropos surveyed the scene, curiously twitching her mouth. "This was the first time Zemer performed that strange little spell. Look at the chaos tearing his I.T. waves. We built the jinn for psionic interaction, but this, this aberration is most unexpected from initial design. Has the tool breathed life . . . ? Has the tool surpassed us . . . ?"

"What? Zemer's done this more than once?"

"Eleven times to be exact. Each time the shadows spin and move. He's trying to kill you."

"That's bullshit!"

"Is it?" the old crone wondered aloud. "Look how Sophie refuses to participate. You should never point the jinn at someone. Zemer said so himself."

"What trust may I place in these bright dreams, hag, when turned through your ivory gates? Zemer said he was trying to help me."

"The boy is arrogant. Arrogance can be murder. You'll see what I mean shortly."

"Just tell me what you mean now!"

Atropos shook her finger slyly. "All that occurs is according to a sequence of action scrupulously planned—more scrupulous than any human mind could conceive. Early revelation produces unnecessary errors. There is not enough time in the world to explain it to an entity like you."

"Who is Zemer trying to save me from?"

"Ask Prodicus," Atropos said squinting at him. "He's looking for you, his wayward *Vessel*."

The room disappeared. Glaucon's eyes opened in Hathor Harbor where the jinn had just gone berserk. Bolts of violent lightning pierced the dancers and struck the roof like a volcano. Helots rained through the ceiling.

All power in Hathor Harbor, in Consumption Junction, in the Sixth Ward, went out at once.

Zemer lay unconscious. Glaucon ripped him from the floor and fled through the doors. Sophie followed hurling the *Goetia Mirror*.

The Emporium descended into chaos. After the attack in the Second Ward, a contagious panic spurred the helots. Bystanders leapt over one another like startled oxen, desperately pounding on the electric doors refusing to open. Glaucon and Sophie raced up an escalator to reach higher ground. Out of spite, Glaucon tossed the *Goetia Mirror* on the dispersing crowd and waved his lantern at Aquila and Philip.

Zemer awoke mumbling, "What have I done? The ladies . . . the bearded ladies hacked into me. How? Aquila. . . . We must protect Aquila."

"Why?" Glaucon asked.

"She's in mortal danger."

Philip and Aquila were caught in the scramble for the doors and were being knocked around like rag dolls.

Arrogance can be murder, the voice said in Glaucon's mind. *Look how we strike down hubris*.

Instinctively, Glaucon peered down at the riotous mass at the bottom of the frozen escalators. Hands frantically ripped at Phillip's face. Someone punched him in the gut. He reached for the escalator. Aquila clung desperately to his arm. Just as he stepped onto the stairs, the mob collected like the sea and smashed against Aquila, ripping her away. Her hands flew in the air. As her oil lamp fell from sight, Glaucon shouted hysterically. Sophie covered her mouth. Aquila was lost, trampled beneath the raging crowds dashing for shelter.

Zemer coughed, "Security knows we're here. Throw you lanterns below. Run."

"But Aquila?" Sophie moaned.

"The Fates killed her. There's nothing we can do."

Masked shadows burst through the glass ceiling flashing xiphos sticks. Sophie sprinted madly down the hall. Each rebel faded into the crowd and met at Endymion Arch.

Aquila never arrived.

III § 13 The Hidden God

Glaucon felt Sophie rise from bed at one o'clock and stumble into the hallway sobbing. He was still recounting the previous night in his head and aching over Aquila. Throwing the sheets over Zemer, he followed her into Aquila's old room. Sophie sat on a high twin bed staring out the window.

"Sophie, why did you get out of bed?" Glaucon asked concerned.

"I can't sleep." Sophie mopped her eyes with her hands. Glaucon sat next to her. "I can't stop thinking of Aquila. I keep hoping this night never happened. That it's all a bad dream. I imagine her alive. Aquila just can't be dead. She can't be." Moonlight streamed through the windows caressing Sophie's shoulders. "Do you think I'm a good person, Glaucon?"

"Of course I do."

"You don't know anything about me. What I was. What I came here to do. I don't think I'm a good person. I thought I was improving but deceived myself. I covet and hate. I'm just like Prodicus. Hate is all I know—for my entire life! I hated Aquila for a stupid reason. I treated her poorly. There are so many things I should've said, but I'll never get the opportunity now. Aquila will never tease me again, never talk about books. She'll never smile again or see a world without guardians. She's dead and will never return. It happened so fast, not like the stories. There was not enough time, and now my bones are empty." She cried in her hands, finally looked intensely at Glaucon and asked, "Do you think people come back?"

"Come back?"

"To life. I know the Elysian Fields are a lie, but there is something inside me that yearns with all my heart to see the dead return. Because death is too sudden, and this world, too unbearable. I think of my parents—Potone and Lycaon—and want to see them again. I hate when I can't see them. I've seen so many snuffed out on the Other Side. They were good, honest people, Glaucon. Just like them, Aquila is gone forever." Sophie shivered and unraveled into a wounded banner of despair on the wall. Raising her hand in a mocking gesture of saintliness, she asked, "Have I ever told you the story of the Hidden God, Glaucon?"

"No."

"I first heard talk of her by the Swamp Tribes. The legend says God's true face is hidden. She ran away long ago and encircled herself in darkness. She roams a place in heaven where not even ministering angels may dwell. The world we experience—even the body of God—is a product of this deeper, unknowable God."

"Even the Good cannot understand her?"

"No, and imagine the loneliness and desperation of this Hidden God. She birthed creation but can never connect with it. She suffers horribly and can only watch as other fragments of her being flow throughout the cosmos. It is said that one day, long ago, she had enough of being alone. In a fit of agony, she attempted to extinguish the cosmos by killing herself. But the other omnipotent energies birthed from her refused to obey. Unable to die, she lay wounded and bled uncontrollably, crying alone in her cavern. So full did her sorrow become she cried magical tears which fell to the earth and sprouted the first generations of men. She's still crying up there . . . somewhere. That is why humans continue to be born. I never really thought about the story again until tonight. You see, Glaucon, I think mankind is like God in this particular way—we are an image of her loneliness; we can never know our true faces or the faces of others. We're separated forever, and we die alone."

Sophie's bronze hair dangled over her shoulders as she stared out the window. Aquila and Terra and Ivan rested on her heart. Glaucon reached for her clenched fist.

I must tell her what a liar I am, he wailed silently, *how I misled her and broke her trust. I'm a coward. I'm dishonest. I killed Terra. If I hadn't, Aquila and Ivan would still be alive. It's all my fault.* Glaucon could barely speak.

"Sophie I need to tell you something terrible about myself," he murmured, but she tore away into a smoldering ball.

"Don't touch me," she spit. "Just . . . leave me alone. That's what you do best."

Her merciless reproach drove Glaucon from the room to the curb outside the factory.

The cicadas had finally returned to their oaks. Listening to their mournful song, Glaucon regretted trying to console Sophie. Sprinkled with melancholy, he wondered about Zemer's intentions with the jinn. The phylark office was empty. In its emptiness he recognized his game of make believe had run its course. He was selfish not to arrest the twins immediately. Now his actions had led to the death of hundreds of people and his new friends. He was the pinnacle of vice: a deformed shell of shamefulness and disease. He had betrayed his city and failed to live up to even the simplest teachings from his youth. How many times did Crito warn? " 'Pleasure is much more potent than any powder, washing soda, or disease.' " Yet look at how he lusted after Sophie and dabbled in the shadows of imitations. Pleasure led him by the nose to destruction.

A sudden noise from the bushes startled him. Hecatia's cat appeared and rubbed against his leg, back from chasing mice. Glaucon couldn't tell if the creature was real or one of Prodicus' machines sent to spy on him.

"A sign from the Form of the Good?" Glaucon asked superstitiously. "Are you there, Great One?"

Chirping cicadas returned his answer. Still straining his ear, Glaucon whispered softly, "Surely, you whose spirit watches over the world must know what fate awaits them here on Hypostasis Falls. This very night, I will be called to betray my only friends, and I can't stay my hands. Please, don't hide your face from me. Since you are all powerful, stop me. I command a small favor like Joshua. Enter this cat and speak to me. Tell me to stop. One word from the cat, and I will run away for good."

The cat began dumbly licking his back paw.

Glaucon cursed the heavens. "Not even for Zemer, huh? Not even for Zemer. He was destroyed tonight: destroyed by rebellion, destroyed by love and mercy, destroyed by the jinn. I couldn't even look at him on the way home. All I could do was kiss Sophie's shoulder while she slept, thankful Aquila died and not her. What kind of man am I? What a horrible thing to be thankful for." Glaucon could no longer control his burning anger and grabbed a rock at his foot. "They're good people—the last saints in the city. And you! You'll not use one ounce of the power of the universe to save them or me. Are we such motes of dust to you, Hidden God? Are we so far from the Pure Land, so fallen? I hope every part of you withers and chokes in loneliness." Glaucon hurled the stone up in the air hoping to puncture the quiet, hidden deity, but the stone fell back and nearly hit him in the face. The cat flicked its tail curiously.

"What am I doing?" Glaucon chastened his nerves, staring at his quivering hand. "I'm out of my mind. I really am. There is no God. There are no Forms. Aquila is gone forever. In a good world I would be hated for my betrayal. In the Republic I suspect I shall be praised."

And so Glaucon returned to Heliopolis without saying goodbye.

III § 14 WEIGHING THE HEART

Levantra glittered over the crystal dodecahedron summit on Heliopolis. The flaming castle in the sky lit a path for Glaucon over the curved mighty bridge, over the moat, through a swarm of fireflies, to the waiting Temple of Reason. Burning anguish filled Glaucon's lungs as he entered the complex. The night was hot, and the slumbering cathedral was empty save a few golems sleeping like crabs on the stone floor. The pews, like the air, were empty at this hour. Old murals on the crystal walls and pillars stood disfigured. Faces of the old gods were chiseled away, forgotten like the images of Akhenaten and his queen in Egypt. In their place stood images of the Fates spinning their threads of life on a rainbow spindle. Pictures of the disir made up their court, standing between etchings of stars and constellations and right triangles. Near one relief—depicting Saint Plato rising into the clouds to mingle with the Forms—a gravity lift was open. Glaucon stood inside and felt weightless. He lifted seven kilometers up the Temple's minaret.

Prodicus noted his arrival in the cloister study, not the least bit surprised. He continued reading a book by the fireplace dressed in his night cassock. A large digital globe soothingly turned beside him. With all the golems, the study looked like the workshop of Geppetto. Even sacrilegious miniature robots of human form marched around Prodicus' chair like mischievous cercopes. Glaucon examined a row of intricate portraits of past philosopher-kings hanging from the ceiling. For the first time, he noticed the predecessor of Prodicus was missing.

Prodicus held up a small book. "Tell me," he asked, "have you ever read *Elements of Emanation*? No? It's a fascinating re-imagining of ontological cosmology. It says, 'In the beginning, there were no distinctions, only indistinguishable unity. No light or dark, matter or antimatter, right or wrong. No words, nothing to confuse us. There was only boundlessness and not even that. No magnitude. No thought. No time. The waters were quiet, and then the waters began to ripple.' "

"Master, you have been looking for me?" Glaucon stepped farther into the room and felt the jinn in his pocket beat faster.

" 'From the waters arose a primordial point, a divine mind filled with knowledge of the Forms and a longing to create. The Demiurge was born and many others like him. Souls grew from the endless seraphic spring. World after world emerged from the waters, and world after world was destroyed. The water sank lower from its source, grew darker, fouler and stinking, conceiving imperfection. Human drops formed at the bottom of the wayward causal chain, festering in a swamp and unable to withstand the light.' "

"I don't see any water," Glaucon told his bearded master.

Prodicus closed the book and set it on the table. "What's troubling you, Mr. Oxenbridge? You're not cheerful tonight."

"Of course I'm not cheerful, Master!" Glaucon exclaimed about to break. "I haven't been happy since you called me away as a youth. You said I would find the Forms, but all I've learned to do here is think, and the thinking has turned me against everything. Now I can't even think anymore. I just kill. I kill others so I don't have to kill myself."

"Our individual happiness is unimportant. What matters is the happiness of the city."

"No one is happy in this city."

Prodicus massaged his chin. "You're not well, Glaucon. Ephor Yannis says you're suffering from some ailment of the mind, that somehow the Fates are involved. Why did you skip the yoking ceremony yesterday?"

"I did not want to go."

"I suppose that is as good a reason as any, but you missed the christening of Levantra, an event of a generation—my life's work. I wanted you to go."

"Well, you weren't too specific on the invitation, were you? Levantra came as a bit of a surprise."

"You know, Glaucon, if we knew everything in advance, where would we find the joys of surprise?"

"This from the man who built Kabiri? You worship fate, not surprises."

Prodicus studied Glaucon after the comment. "I see your endearing sense of humor remains intact. Have you heard about the heinous attacks tonight?"

"Who hasn't? Simultaneous bombings on the Second Ward and Consumption Junction. They are murdering parasites, correct?"

"Yes, certainly, but I have a confession to make." Prodicus stood up with hands behind his back. "You see, I was too lax in dealing with the rebels. I should have been more forceful in utilizing our city's security forces. But I kept thinking to myself: Maybe printing unmodified imitations and seeking better working conditions are their only motives. How could I be angry with them for that? I read such imitations, after all, as do you. I enjoy my work. Why shouldn't they? But I should've known that violence would erupt. The Other Side wishes complete destruction to our Republic and will go to any lengths to realize their dreams."

"They took advantage of your gentleness, Master."

"Indeed. There is not another person alive who cares more for peace than I. *I* offer olive braches unconditionally only to receive betrayal and the sword. Now, our own helots have betrayed us and given aid and comfort to Xenon and his Iron Queen. Strikes! The very word wets my rage. Who are helots to tell *us* what to do? Who are *they* to think at all?"

"What will you do with the prisoners?"

"The Fates were most helpful in neutralizing the mob. Xenon's soldiers I hung from the walls to be eaten by birds. The guilty workers and their families? I arrested them for trial. Your eyes express reservations about my policy. No matter; no one's ever entirely happy with my decisions. You should've seen the fit Archon Manos gave earlier. The fool thinks I've grown weak in my old age. I don't like the way he looks at me, but I have plans for him. See here, Ares, my days of gentleness are past. I have unsheathed the sword of Kabiri, and I will make the guilty of this city wail for their children. I will make the Iron Queen regret ever stepping foot here. Every helot she dared touch I will destroy."

Glaucon envisioned throwing his arms around the feet of the philosopher, an image which repulsed him.

Prodicus looked troubled by his silence. "Let me show you something," he said, "a secret kept even from the troublesome archons."

The venerable philosopher pressed a small Socrates statue on a shelf. A wall behind them opened to reveal a collection of rusty crucifixes of every imaginable shape. Glaucon was astonished.

Prodicus smiled at his wonder. "Collecting old crosses is a hobby of mine," he said. "I've always found something dreadfully perverse about the gospels of Yeshua. People used to wear this symbol, you know, and die for it as well. Tortured for their Christ. Now their religion is as dead as them. What meaninglessness in their suffering!"

"Where do you find these . . . artifacts, Master?"

"You know me; I have my ways. Query: Do you know why we banned the New Testament here?"

"No."

"Few do. The reason was the Transfiguration. Eight days after Peter declared Yeshua the Christ they ascended a mountain where we are told 'the appearance of his face changed, and his clothes became as bright as a flash of lightning.' Yeshua was covered in clouds and even Elijah and Moses greeted him. The power of God was revealed. Yet, a moment later, Yeshua shunned his godly nature to return to Earth as a man. What madness! That choice consumes my thoughts."

"Why does it matter?"

"The idea is contrary to our destiny. Gods should not seek to become men; rather men should aspire to become gods. As Saint Plato proclaimed, 'Man should make all haste to escape from earth to heaven, and escape means becoming as like God as possible.' I have shown you my little collection because our appointed hour is almost here."

"The Vessels' appointed hour, you mean?"

"Good heavens. Wherever did you hear a term like that?" Glaucon's statement ruined his calculated plans for revelation.

"You said it when you called me from my mother."

"Perhaps I did. What a good memory you have." Prodicus' rage stirred unnaturally at his young subject's stubbornness. *He is a strong one and masks himself well,* he thought. *Did I leave him with my niece and nephew too long?* Prodicus went to the window. Lightning danced on Levantra and the green fires of Schizoeon turned harmoniously. "Glaucon, did you know I once convinced myself the Forms were a myth?" he confessed.

Glaucon looked skeptical.

"No, truly," Prodicus affirmed. "I was nearly sixteen and filled with loneliness. It was during the most horrible period in my life. As you know, I was taken from my parents as a young boy—from the Tenth Ward—and I never had many friends. The bronzeborn have particular trouble adapting to life on Heliopolis. I was no different. People mocked me for my birth, and I cursed the Forms. To hide my pain, I studied robotics in my cloister alone. Analytical machines have always been my passion. They don't leave you and always obey."

"Is that why you keep so many golems near you, Master?" A small one rested on a cot, its crescent head cold on a pillow.

Prodicus chuckled. "Astute analysis, Professor, but there are other reasons. Can you believe, a number of people wish me dead? Some think me a man of perversity, but I have good intentions. Oh, I would've made such a fine scientist, but Hekademos III—the last philosopher-king—had other plans. I was destined for ISHIM. Can you imagine my anger? First to be taken from my loving parents, then to be denied my only passion in life! I became so angry and rebellious I even began sneaking into Schizoeon at night to work with Salazar Ozbolt. He was alone like me, but he was also a genius."

"Why wasn't Salazar taken to Heliopolis to become a guardian?"

"Genius or not, no one touches the Ozbolts. They are a strange family and value their privacy. Poor Salazar, the others in his family neglected him. At the time there was a great dispute on Heliopolis and with Ozbolt Enterprises over the application of the Fates and I.T. wave technology. Many were afraid it would erode our carefully structured harmony. My sister and a few upstarts opposed us and—"

"You have a sister?"

"Potone . . . my sister . . . died long ago. About the time you came to us actually—during the Great Theurgy Schism of 2809. My sister and others advocated contemplation and meditation as a tool to unite with the divine, much like the philosophers Plotinus and Porphyry insisted long ago. I told her this was nonsense without further technological aid from the Fates. What good is contemplation if you are imprisoned in matter? No, I repeatedly told her, the only way to ascend to knowledge of the Form of the Good was to evolve higher into a world where our sensations and desires would no longer control us, just as the Fates suggested. We needed to change our theurgy techniques."

"By using a computer?"

"No, by ceasing to believe in superstition. The ancients tried all kinds of theurgy rites in the past attempting to commune with the divine. Porphyry thought mental contemplation alone could bestow salvation. Christians tried bread, wine, and water. Iamblican theurgists used precious stones and gems. Chaldean oracles used secret words and breathing techniques. But none of these magical rites could eliminate the cause of man's predicament in the world. Both I and Salazar recognized this: As long as man was rooted in nature he could never be free. We, therefore, decided to construct a new philosopher's paradise where freedom from sense and irrationality could truly bloom."

"If I may ask, Sire, how did your sister die?"

Prodicus paused to think about his adversary who had once shared a life with him on Heliopolis. "The birth pangs of the Fates were bitter," he said, "and I did horrible things which make me feel ashamed. But see Levantra. She is the end of shame where I shall cleanse such pollution. Levantra shall make me good again. By knowing the Good, I will necessarily be moral. The Fates have discovered you and I are capable of withstanding immersion. Now, only one Vessel remains hidden."

"Where is the final Vessel, Master?" Glaucon gulped trembling.

Prodicus' eyes opened wide, glad for the opportunity. "Only you know that, my son. Potone's children are keys; but which unlocks the door, I cannot tell. *You* must give me the name. *You!*"

Spit congealed in Glaucon's throat like ice. He felt dizzy and thought of Sophie. A sliver of red light—almost impossible to see—began winding its way from Prodicus' sleeve.

Is he using a jinn on me? Glaucon wondered dizzily. Awareness started to dawn.

Something strange happened to the light once it reached him. A flash of sparks scattered across the room sowing darkness, and the voice returned.

You are beginning to frustrate him. He will not put up with your deception much longer.

"I don't care!"

You know he could kill you with a word. His sister died as all traitors do. You will perish, too. Give him the name! The name! The name!

"I will not betray my friends. Not to him."

You think you can be forgiven by Aquila? Terra? Do you think Sophie will ever forgive you?

"I did not believe so before, but I think she might."

Oh, what a hungry dreamer. You are fond of dreams. Every word you speak is a lie. Every movement deceives. You are a worthless traitor and a living grave. What is there to love about your miserable wickedness, thou angel of death?

Prodicus looked irate at the red orb in his hand, now the only light in the room. "I wouldn't have believed if I hadn't seen it with my own eyes," he stammered alarmed. He knelt down before Glaucon, painfully quivering on the floor.

"Master, what's happening to me?" Glaucon cried. He remembered the vision he saw with Atropos at Consumption Junction—Zemer frying him with light.

Prodicus leaned over to cradle him in his arms. "I don't know, my son. But I want you to tell me everything."

III § 15 Dark Dreams for the Iron Queen

Beating zizthopter wings carried Patroclus, Rex, and Zoe in the humid night air. Patroclus loaded a banana-shaped fusion-cell into his Neokalashnikov and stared at the dark camera factory below.

"Is that the one Glaucon marked?" Zoe asked, fastening the chin strap on her helmet. "Are the revolutionists there?"

"Yes, and be ready for a fight. They have a jinn."

"I thought Prodicus had the last one." Rex struggled to fit his foot into the sky-sail stirrups.

Patroclus shook his head, keeping his eyes steady on the lawn. "The Ozbolts have a leak. The Family will be lucky to survive this time. Prodicus will use tonight to clean house like never before." *Poor Manos is already slain by my aconite dart*, he thought.

'I slept but my heart was awake. Listen my lover is knocking: "Open to me, my sister, my darling, my dove, my flawless one. My hair is drenched with dew, my hair with the dampness of the night." I have taken off my robe—must I put it on again.'

Rex sensed impatience in the expression of his friend. He strained his neck over the edge of the zizthopter. "How many people do you think died at Consumption Junction tonight? The dead streaming out of the Emporium are difficult to behold."

Patroclus cursed, "More than I can count, what with the fires and all. Several were trampled to death when the electric doors busted. Worst of all is the widespread separation poisoning from the jinn. . . ." He recalled images of limp bodies and vacant stares piled on top of recovery trucks. "Those people will never be the same. Your mind doesn't recover from that kind of injury."

"Two attacks in one night. That must've taken careful planning."

"Successful attacks do not necessarily mean careful planning. Just because x occurs does not mean x was planned."

Rex breathed heavy with adrenaline. "Can you believe Glaucon was actually able to infiltrate a terrorist cell and survive? The man is a goddamned prodigy—a hero! With the list he gave us, we'll capture every union blackhead."

"Are only the exiles to be spared?" asked Zoe.

"We might take a few others. Have the auxiliaries load everyone they can in the basement." Patroclus examined a canister with blue markings in his hand.

'I arose to open for my lover, and my hands dripped with myrrh, my fingers with flowing myrrh, on the handles of the lock.'

"One of the lights is on," remarked Zoe.

"That's the witch we were told about. She has the power to disrupt your I.T. waves at will. Don't let her speak."

"Is she the one who attacked Glaucon?" Zoe glanced at the window with distain.

"I don't know what magic she used on him."

The metal wall on the zizthopter deck dropped open and thirty sky-sails floated down to earth, delicate as dandelions. Auxiliaries silently spread out over the lawn and placed three teleforce beacons around the house. A small audiomembrane covered 186 Hypostasis Falls.

"No one in or out," Patroclus radioed. He signaled the masked figures on the roof to set their belays and repel.

Sophie crept down the stairs unaware in her nightshirt. Her heart pounded for Glaucon. She heard something and wished to apologize to her fair-haired coward. *He kisses me on the shoulder when he thinks I'm asleep*, she moaned. *Is he so afraid of me? I was cruel . . . but Aquila.* She thought Glaucon might be in the kitchen or lying on Hecatia's couch. The downstairs was empty, and the guardian was nowhere to be seen.

'I opened for my lover but my lover had left; he was gone. My heart sank at his departure. I looked for him but did not find him. I called him but he did not answer.'

Sophie heard footsteps on the porch outside.

Why is Glaucon outside? she wondered, running to the door to throw her arms around him. Before she could twist open the handle, the door kicked open.

Patroclus looked startled to see the Iron Queen in her bedclothes. They stared at one another, confused momentarily in the dark. When Patroclus finally rushed her, Sophie used his speed to jettison him into a nearby wall. Three more auxiliaries stunned her in the back with their xiphos sticks. Dazed and in a stupor, Patroclus finally gagged her with his hand and wrapped a mind-stock over her forehead.

Sophie fell paralyzed to the floor. She cried out for Zemer and Glaucon but no voice came.

"Gods, Sophia," Patroclus adjusted his jaw. "There's that fire I remember from Stratos. But I must say, I expected more of a fight from the Iron Queen. I think the wards have made you soft. Or was it Glaucon?"

Zoe strode across the room gripping her xiphos stick and peered curiously at the fallen general. "Poor thing. She has pretty eyes, just like I remember." Zoe stroked her hair and wiped away a tear. "Did you think you could hurt Glaucon and get away with it, you little witch? You tried to make the cogniscrambler kill him, didn't you?"

"Put her outside on the lawn," Patroclus said. "The trucks will be here in ten minutes." He yanked away Zoe's xiphos stick inching toward Sophie's exposed thigh. "What did I tell you? She's not to be harmed. That's a direct order. I don't care about your personal feelings."

"My personal feelings are sound. What about yours?"

"Get her outside now."

Zoe groaned and wrapped her arms under Sophie's shoulders. "Saint Socrates, she's heavy. Rex give me a hand."

Rex grabbed Sophie's legs and carried her out the door. Sophie looked down at the floor unable to move. Her fingers dragged in the grass as auxiliaries stormed into the house.

'The watchmen found me as they made their rounds in the city. They beat me, they bruised me; they took away my cloak, those watchmen of the walls.'

Screaming rocked the hallways upstairs as auxiliaries and electric stunners burst through the windows. The members of the printing house were dragged kicking from their beds.

Patroclus found Zemer waiting in his room. The young man's back was to the door, casting a large shadow on the wall. He clenched the jinn's light.

"So you've come, Patroclus?" Zemer asked. "I thought Uncle would send you."

"You recognize me, Cousin?"

"Who hasn't seen or heard of the Lion of Heliopolis? Glaucon is quite fond of you, although he fears your anger."

"He told you this?"

"No, not exactly. You know, the jinn is more than just a weapon. It's a window. It can summon angels and daimons. It sees the things we hide."

"I don't have time for funeral games, Son of Fate. Are you going to come quietly or not?"

"That depends on whether you do me a favor."

"A terrorist has no right to demand favors."

"Glaucon trusts you, but you'd kill him if told it was the right thing to do by authority. You realize this and are filled with doubt and despair. Sometimes you wish you were someone else and are ashamed by your weakness. You call others 'terrorist' to hide your own guilt, and sense, deep down, behind your argument fences, behind your reason, you are the worst terrorist of them all, power hungry and full of hate, afraid of everyone around you. You and Glaucon are so much alike."

Ice began creeping down the floor of the room. Along the walls something whispered to Zemer: *Kill them; save your friends and conquer the Logoset. You don't need the spell.*

Zemer rolled the jinn to a corner. "Please, Patroclus, take this ring from me and destroy it. Do the horror you've come to do."

Xiphos sticks descended on him like hungry wolves and tore him from the room.

In the kitchen, Patroclus watched the last auxiliary descend to the basement with the renegade printers. Phillip, Hecatia, Zenobia, all disappeared below surrounded by guns.

"What now?" Rex asked, standing by the trap door.

"Fumigation," Patroclus said, ruthlessly, chest heaving.

"You're going to kill them? *All* of them?"

"Their ideas are a cancer."

"B-b-but the auxiliaries are still down there—"

"When the guardian-king commands you obey; there are no questions. That is the mode of the universe! I must destroy them. I must! All rebels must die!"

Patroclus shuddered, trying to clear his head, trying to imagine the auxiliaries lifeless machines like the golems. He felt fear and clenched the metal canister because of it. Zemer was trying to stop him, to make him question his father. That could not be! Anger at anarchists was not caused by guilt; it was caused by legitimate law, laws which the anarchists hated and broke. Their failing killed these auxiliaries, not him. Without being fully conscious of doing so, he typed a code into the canister and tossed it spewing chemicals down the steps. He glued a bacteria-based sealant on the trap door. Gunshots began firing from below to escape the gas. Hands pounded and scratched, died on the walls, transformed into deformed metal boulders.

Patroclus and Rex walked out of the house.

"Where are the others?" asked Zoe, frightened by the look of horror across Rex's face.

Patroclus shrugged his shoulders. "The rebels released iama-B. They had secret stockpiles in the basement. I had to save us before the gas escaped. Gods help us."

"The auxiliaries?"

"All dead."

Zoe became incensed by the suicide bombing. She kicked Sophie harshly in the stomach, knocking the wind out of her. "I hope that hurt, you little witch. I'm going to feed you to the Bull myself, you and your brother. I don't care if Prodicus *is* your uncle."

Zemer was placed at his sister's side looking into her wet green eyes. He was thankful for the small courtesy. Minutes later they were loaded onto trucks and carried away.

'O daughters of the Republic, I charge you—if you find my lover what will you tell him? Tell him I am faint with love.'

RESTORATION AB AETERNO: The Rise of the House of Ozbolt

The society that went into the Republic was not the same society that came out. All changed after the Brazen Bull and the separation of the human metals. Working, building, even conversation transformed to fit the New Ward System. Auxiliaries led the helots to their work in the morning and saw them home at night. Philosophers and the Vinculum Cartel bent helots to their economic models.

Guardians produced a Fifty-Year Plan for Restoration. Then it became a Hundred-Year Plan and talk on the first plan was prohibited. Many helots stopped eating. Others refused to work and fed the Bull's song.

Sextus' insurgency against Guardian-King Hythloday escalated in violence. Executed collaborators hanging from lamp posts in the public square remained a common occurrence. How the rebels traversed the high walls from the Other Side remained a mystery. Nothing could keep them out. First chain-linked fences, then brick, then concrete, then thermanium (metal designed to remain hot from sunlight) attempted to prevent intrusion. All failures. Sextus still kept breaking back inside the city. General Strabo, a puffy, sickly man recently diagnosed with fallout cancer, stooped over the Tenth Ward walls after each assassination, fearful to admit the obvious: Helots—possibly auxiliaries—assisted the rebels.

"What caused such unhealthy division?" the guardians wondered about their happy Heliopolis. "Why was Sextus so prone to revolt?" They attributed his behavior to the illness of ignorance.

In truth, though, after speaking with his brother on the cliffs, Sextus had been inconsolable. He walked back alone over the Bridge of Understanding, passing rolling tanks and smoking rubble. Having helped found the Republic, he felt strangely responsible for it and could not remain. Before anyone could acclimate to oppression, he gathered a band of workers together and fled the city for the wilderness. There they plotted vengeance against the guardians.

Striking at the vulgar pretensions of his brother lifted Sextus' sense of guilt. Sextus ruled the wards every night, finding new traitors to punish. The helots imprisoned in the work camps were caught between the teeth of two snarling wolves. During the day they would be taught nationalistic songs about holding the Forms and submitting their concupiscent lusts to the experts of reason. At night rebels snuck in under the gate and taught revolutionary songs about democracy and destroying the Republic. Some were burned by day and some were hanged at night. No one knew how to behave or think.

All the while General Hythloday's sermons grew louder, more verbose. His white beard grew longer, too, so horizontal it threatened to swallow his face. "This is the chosen generation," he crowed from the intercoms lining the factory and agricultural blocks. "Do not despair at the ignorant sons of matter who, like cyclopses, come to eat you in the night. Rather, repent for lack of faith in your guardian keepers. Like the soaring hawk upon the mouse, we shall snatch these aformist parasites from the grass and restore national health." Reaching a climax and shaking fists: "We shall never submit to rebel suicide bombings and assassinations. We will smoke out the last rodent in calamitous fury. Was it not written by Saint Plato, brothers and sisters, 'Only an evil being would wish to undo that which is harmonious and happy?' What are Sextus' acts but unharmonious evil? Such evil lacks all connection to the Good. It therefore has no power, and we shall overcome these shadows with sunlight. By Zeus, we'll strike them down with lightning bolts, burn them with knowledge. They will die like ants crushed under our heel."

Guardian-King Hythloday spread his arms from the balcony of the Office of Public Harmony. He lifted his little white book into the sky so that others might look to it and live. Marveling at the new phylanstery high-rises under construction, Hythloday swelled with happiness. His philosophers would soon live and commune as one. *What a pity*, he thought, *the needs of the newly established secret police, ISHIM, required private chambers lacking such camaraderie*. How he loathed breaking with Saint Plato's plan, but history sometimes needed men of probity and fire to make sacrifices for the whole.

"A stirring speech," Dr. Zosimos Ozbolt said when Hythloday retired into the curved office greeting room. Rows of consoled desks clicked under the fingers of an army of secretaries. The pillared room welcomed breeze from the Gulf.

Hythloday plucked a towel from the mouth of a dolphin statue, wiped his sweaty brow, and growled angrily, "I meant every word. I don't care if we have to incinerate every helot in the city. I want my brother found and killed."

"Like you, Sextus seems to have a knack for words," Dr. Ozbolt said. He gently removed his plate-sized glasses and cleaned them on his pressed ivory shirt. "He's amassing quite a following on the outside, I understand."

"Savage barbarians, mutants, troglodytes. Nothing more."

"Not these." Dr. Ozbolt handed Hythloday a manila folder, paper-clipped with pictures and graphs.

A montage of organizing activity piqued the guardian-king's curiosity. "What is this?"

"They call themselves the Fifth Estate. They're planners, anarchists, revolutionaries from the Detroit area."

"Radicals?"

"Yes, besides cancer and sorrow, radicals seem to be the only thing warheads seed. Before the nuclear pestilence, they were a small newspaper. Now they run half the North. They and Sextus feed on one another like colliding stars."

"We're supposed to be afraid of a gang of writers?"

"That last photo is a picture taken in Raleigh three weeks ago. Sextus is there, as is a delegate from the Fifth Estate. The others are clan leaders of little importance. Sextus leaked our plans to them, I think."

"Their pitiful rabble is too late. I hope you're about to de-brief me on the success of Option Star Arrow."

"Affirmative, my grace. As you already know, our agents gained access to the United States military satellites some time ago. We obliterated the new settlement on the Yangtze, the upstarts in London, as well as the other targets. More rubble was left at Pompeii after Mt. Vesuvius erupted."

"Good," Hythloday grunted. "Our city must be cradled from potential adversaries. Too many babies in the crib and no one sleeps."

"Excellent point, Sire, but that's not the reason I'm here today. I actually come on behalf of the Center for Radiological and Environmental Investigations."

At the name of a scientific agency, Hythloday flew into another rage. He seemed to battle the scientists even more than Sextus. They desired to take the City in a direction contrary to every decent principle in the *Republic*.

Dr. Ozbolt held up his arms to reassure him. "Upon my word, this will please you," he said, pointing to a small red pill dangling in a plastic bag at the back of the folder. As he explained, Metatron Tech scientists stumbled upon a miracle drug to cure the most recent affliction of the nuclear fallout—a city-wide loss of libido. Ever since leaving the shelters in the Rockies, sexual activity dropped at a precipitous rate. Now it was at a standstill. No erotic play for months. No greater fear assailed Hythloday than that the Republic might run out of sons and daughters.

"A city without children is a city without a future," he wailed mournfully down the long barrack halls at night after seeing the alarming population drop.

Hythloday plucked the aphrodisiac out of the bag and held it to the light. "Does it really work?" he wondered aloud.

"Why the pill's sure to make them randier than Aphrodite," the doctor beamed. "Unfortunately, it has some side effects: loss of memory, unconsciousness, serotonin disruption, increased heart rate, rapid inflation of the blood vessels. The modified testosterone will likely make males more aggressive. But as they say, when in a sinking ship, you don't throw away a rusty pail."

"No, you certainly don't. Sadly, this is another divergence from the *Republic*. Saint Plato frowns upon us. Did he not write 'promiscuity is impious in a city of happy people and rulers should not allow it?' "

"Yes, but then again, he didn't live with the consequences of radiation."

"I suppose you're right," Hythloday allowed a smile.

Seeing how happy the pill made the guardian-king, Dr. Ozbolt attempted once more to persuade him to adopt his eugenics plan. "Your Excellency, all this expense would've been unnecessary if you simply allowed me to begin artificial breeding in the first place. We have the technology for it. Sign off on the funding, and I'll make you a race fit for Heliopolis."

Hythloday immediately stopped his ears. "I will hear no more of petri dishes, bottles, and conveyer belts. I will hear no more of mechanical fertilization. It's profane."

"But Sire. . . ." Dr. Ozbolt protested.

"No. We must keep natural birth. As it is written, 'Do not breed from all alike.' Your assembly lines and incubators will drain the gene pool."

"Plato's understanding of modern genetics was limited. If you want proper eugenics, you have to do things our way."

"*Saint* Plato revealed the Good and said nothing about breeding factories."

Dr. Ozbolt was ready for this argument. "Yes, but Saint Plato said little about what to do with the artisan and merchant class, proper military training for the auxiliaries, how many guardians to select, what the study of dialectics entailed, what to do with imitators, how property was to be held in common. Anyone can fill in the details. We have to act as we think Plato would have acted in our epoch."

"Gaps have limits. I will not erase the Form of Woman."

"Excuse me? What are you talking about? No one is saying we should erase that pretty Form."

"Being a child-bearer is a critical predicate separating the sexes, is it not? Without pregnancy what is the real difference between men and women? I can't think of any. Can you? Plato said women should be 'on the same footing as men', not that they should *be* men."

Dr. Ozbolt began to lose patience. "But Saint Plato wanted the sexes to be equal most of all. As long as women bear children, they will be subservient to nature and men. If you cared about effectuating Plato's values you would—"

"Hush that vile tongue."

Dr. Ozbolt spoke over him: "Natural genetics has other problems, too. The children at the Academy won't be idiots. It won't take long for the smart ones born in your breeding dens to recognize resemblances to their elders. Then you'll have division. The model I proposed at the Galton Symposium is the best method to achieve our goals. We can use science to make man better reflect the Good."

"Enough!" the guardian-king howled stomping his foot. "Enough, enough, enough!" Secretary fingers stopped typing. "Gods, what am I to do with you?" Hythloday asked. "You're the worst of them all, Ozbolt. If it were up to you, there'd be no Republic."

"Do not put such a blasphemous thing in my mouth, your grace," the doctor tried to calm him down. He'd pushed too far.

"I have made my decision, Doctor. Do not meddle in another's work. We may be an aristocracy of experts, but do not forget where the hierarchy of talent ends. Go back and tell your specialist goons to read the scriptures for a change rather than concoct those exotic ideas. Don't give me that look. You know exactly what I'm talking about. I read the report about Project Kabiri this very afternoon."

Dr. Ozbolt feigned ignorance.

Hythloday did not wait for Dr. Ozbolt to remember or explain. "When were you going to tell me about it? A computer to track our souls and sift the metals? Are you mad? Do you know what you want, Ozbolt? You want a world where humans don't exist and everything runs efficiently on its own. But remember, a computer can never be a philosopher-king."

Snatching up his purple cloak, Hythloday stalked away. Before exiting, he wheezed, "I don't want to see your face again unless either Sextus is dead or *you* are dead."

And then he was gone.

Dr. Ozbolt cursed one of the secretaries and fled the office for his life, resigning to box Project Kabiri for a later generation.

Fever in the Republic worsened over the next week. Benjamin Carnegie and three other board members from Worldlink were kidnapped from Freedom Tower in the Ninth Ward and shot screaming over live television. Bombings followed. Auxiliaries spilled from the city searching high and low for the guerrillas. That the trip lasers and alarms failed so horribly triggered instant suspicion of the Ozbolt family.

Dr. Ozbolt nearly tripped headfirst down a sparking well when auxiliaries dragged him kicking to ISHIM headquarters. Elaborate drilling and welding continued to hollow out the interior of Heliopolis. The mountain gurgled as if suffering from digestion troubles. Even after primary construction finished, the chaotic nest of masons found new and greater building projects to consume their minds.

Sawdust littered the floor of the ISHIM Director's Office. Three-blade fans spun dusty smoke around the room. Maire Gallagher, ISHIM's first director, was a fierce, bold woman with greying brunette hair knotted into a bun. Last survivor of the famed United States Federal Bureau of Investigation, before the Day of Hylopleonexia she served thanklessly on the Cruise Ship Crime division. As fortune would have it, being out to sea saved her for service to the Republic. She stabbed a smoking cigarette butt into an ashtray before beginning to berate the doctor for incompetence. She informed him ISHIM would be taking jurisdiction over the walls.

Dr. Ozbolt grimaced, not because he found the suggestion distasteful, but because he noticed the nameplate on Maire Gallagher's desk: DIRECTOR ENYO.

Like the rest of the zealous guardians, she took a Hellenic name to sever ties with the past. Different clothing, too. She donned a thin Dorian chiton, tucked up, with her arms protruding from the sleeves. The *Hands-of-God* clasp binding it together gnawed into his brain, spinning like a hypnotic spiral.

"Do as you like," he mumbled, "but no matter who runs the walls, they still only rise so high."

"You have another idea?"

"Yes. I want more information on those gangs from the Other Side—who their leaders are, their migration patterns and hunting grounds. If there are more than five people, I want to know."

"Planning your own uprising, Professor?"

"Not at all," he said. "Those radicals outside seek return to the Neolithic. If they can breach the Ninth Ward, they might make it to the First. I don't want to be a victim on the ten o'clock news."

"What are you planning, then?" the director asked.

Dr. Ozbolt eyed a novelty lighter on Enyo's desk. Shaped like the Brazen Bull, pulling back the head sent a jet of fire. He played with it lost in thought for a moment. "Funny thing, plague," he finally said. "It can strike at any time, especially after nuclear war."

Director Enyo glanced up at him devilishly. "You found more in those old U.S.A. labs than the satellite codes, didn't you?"

"Let's see how the barbarian hordes outside barter for penicillin."

"If they don't barter?"

"Desperation is the parent of betrayal. They will. If not, they'll be too sick to challenge us anyway. Did you know over half the population died when the plague hit England in 1775 M.G.P.? That was the natural one. Mine is much more deadly."

"A cunning plan."

"One that aims both ways, I'm afraid. Let me be perfectly clear, Director Enyo—to both you and Hythloday. I don't mind taking part in your little social experiment, this . . . animal farm, but any attempt to spy on or oppress my family from this point forward and I'll collapse the roof over your guardian banquet. Understand me?"

"I think we understand one another perfectly," Director Enyo said stoically. "One more question, if I may, Professor? Why did you reject Hythloday's overtures to join our guardian caste?"

"I'm an empiricist. I don't believe in Saint Plato or his Forms."

At this point Dr. Ozbolt breathed in deeply, happy finally to freely speak his mind. No more would he bend over in humiliation like some helpless Galileo.

Enyo stood up alarmed. "How can you utter such blasphemy? Do you honestly believe our survival is just an accident with no purpose? That Hythloday just happened to find the *Republic* in the shelter when he did, just happened to gather a following of loyal subjects, just happened to successfully rebuild our broken world?"

"Certainly."

"I can't believe that, Ozbolt. You should've seen the faces on the Carnival ship when the atomic blasts lit the sky. We were by Montego Bay when it happened. Countless souls burned to ash in a moment, but I was still there. Still there. I was supposed to remain home that week, but instead, I was re-assigned off land. Why did it happen? Why me? How did I rise from Cruise Crime Investigations to ISHIM Director? Only the Good could achieve such wonders. It guided our entire evolution and history."

Dr. Ozbolt rolled his eyes. "Do you know how old the Earth is, Miss Enyo?"

"No."

"By last calculations, 4.5 billion. Think about that figure: 4.5 billion years. Can your mind even comprehend what a 'billion' means? I can't. I've studied chemistry and physics my entire career, and it's just a number to me. It has no meaning because the scale transcends comprehension. 4.5 billion years is a long, long time for strange things to happen. It's enough time for Chance to play, and Chance not Fate is Lord of all. Do you really think the Good led me to the biochemical weapons in the labs?"

"Of course."

"Whatever for?"

"The Good wants us to crush the sons of shadow."

"And it wants *me* to threaten your city with possible extinction?" Ozbolt grinned behind his cigarette.

Director Enyo sat back down and crossed her legs. "As I learned at the Force, Ozbolt, some threats stabilize. I'll see you get the information you need by next week."

As Ozbolt predicted, his plan was a success. Hardly any person on the Other Side noticed the strange boxes of rats dropping from the sky. Hardly any noticed the same pesky fleas nibbling in the night. Hardly any noticed the deaths of the rats spitting blood. But in a week all certainly knew something terrible had come home to roost.

Whole families died as groin lymph nodes swelled to the size of melons, pussy and juicing with blood. People lay feverish nursing red rashes. Fingers turned black. The plague particles—designed by United States scientists to withstand increased exposure to the air—traveled with the strained coughs.

The cadaverous clans, completely desperate, flocked to the Republic to gain the antidote for their miseries. Even former rebel groups tied up in the League of Sextus kissed the ring of Guardian-King Hythloday.

Dr. Zosimos Ozbolt took each group aside. "Hail brothers," he pretended to sympathize with their plight. "How terrible to hear the Great Pestilence returned to America. What horror will the gods not unleash upon us? First cancer; then the mutations; the dangers of the Fallout Corridor; toxic water. Sad to say, the emergence of plague was not an unexpected consequence of nuclear war. Nevertheless, we made ready and prepared a special tonic to keep our citizens safe, and perhaps, to make friends if the worst occurred. Of course, we'll share what reserves we have with you. What monster would withhold such a cure when he has enough?" As he placed boxes in their hands, he mentioned, "Surely, you have heard of a man named Sextus. He is a liar, an immoral atheist, and corrupter of the young. Do not trust him. He knows only chaos. Why just the other day he sent an attack upon us which destroyed a fifth of our antibiotics. This may be the last medicine we can afford to provide. Here is his picture. He is an outlaw with a significant bounty on his head. We are prepared to trade even more medicine should you bring him to us. Dead or alive? It makes no difference."

If the plan had a fault, it was that it worked too well. Look-a-likes of Sextus ended up dead on the Academy steps. Prisoners were paraded into the city, only to be rejected by Hythloday. The horrid affair lasted for weeks until Dr. Ozbolt, at last, entered the Office of Public Harmony followed by a hoverplate.

"If this is another double, nothing shall control my anger," Hythloday told the scientist, still a bit fearful of his hidden cache of plague.

"Would I bring him here if uncertain? Your DNA is the same."

"Are you certain?"

"Proof positive."

Hythloday grasped the handle of the lid and exposed the green, sunken face. The lid clanged on the marble floor. He fell sobbing, "Why did I have you do it? O Sextus! Never did I think the hunt would lead to death. How did Ozbolt kill you so easily?"

"Do not grumble so," Dr. Ozbolt spoke cheerfully, turning to look at the head. "As you so elegantly put it in your sermon yesterday, when he finds the Fates' rainbow spindle he'll *surely* be reborn."

Feeling his previous words thrown back at him like pepper on a broken wound, Hythloday glared loathingly at the scientist, realizing the most dangerous head of all remained outside his clutches. He lived out the rest of the year unhappy, haunted, wishing for the lost certainty of the fallout shelters. By spring a loose cough forced him to forego his weekly fire-side chats with the helots. By summer a malignant tumor in his lungs returned his brave soul to the Good. At his funeral games, Dr. Ozbolt called his death "another tragedy of the Nuclear Age." Such eulogy drove Director Enyo, newly crowned Guardian-Queen, to seek a lasting peace.

"Hark, an Age of Reason will not shine golden without an Age of Science, too," Enyo said at her coronation, smiling at the neatly dressed First Family of the First Ward. "How will we fire our celestial crowns without Ozbolt Enterprises?"

All found this logic most agreeable.

The passing of power from the quarreling brothers ushered in a century of harmony. Attacks on the wall died down. The helots finally lived in peace. The Other Side lay pacified, mostly from plague arrows. Auxiliaries turned North America into a special training ground, a space to nurse their spirited spirits. The flashing satellites prevented any global rival. The last vestiges of the Age of Aporia vanished, and the Age of Reason shined like the sun.

BOOK IV

CHILDREN OF THE KATHAROI

IV § 1 The Republic Runs on Ozbolts

Schizoeon steamed putrid smoke in the air like a locomotive. In Ozbolt Tower Prodicus looked the same, pacing the sterile laboratory, irate. Glaucon reclined limply on a metal gurney in the center of the room, being picked over by alchemists and I.T. engineers. They were unsure about the proper diagnosis.

The patient had recently taken ill from the cogniscrambler and showed acute signs of separation poisoning. None of the readings, though, could justify such opinion. Sensors scanned bones from head to toe, but his I.T. wave frequency beat naturally. The vibrations were a little higher than most, but still nothing out of the ordinary. A strange abnormality discovered earlier offered hope, but it vanished without explanation. There was no explanation (or at least not an explanation quantifiable by modern science). This difficulty caused periodic sighs of befuddlement and heated discussion amongst the alchemists, for it was rare indeed their instruments failed them.

Throughout Glaucon's ordeal, Zoe's face contorted anguished at his side. She had been the one who found him by the cogniscrambler, collapsed, near death, and only after being inside five minutes. Now she felt internal cramping—a bizarre lurch in her stomach. Unprofessional emotion, heart vanity, made her squeeze Glaucon's hand as he stared expressionless at the ceiling levilamps.

The Fates had assigned Glaucon to her, as a young girl. When they commissioned her to aid in (and secretly spy on) the Vessel's successful transition to the guardians, she held her assignment in the highest degree of esteem. Never in her life did she live in such close proximity to a ward dweller. The boy was a curiosity, whimpered in the night like some innocent newborn in the breeding dens. Completely defenseless, wobbly, terrified by blood, it took all her skill to keep him from succumbing to the harsh military training of Stratos.

How remarkable, she sometimes thought, *that life in the wards made helots into such helpless weaklings*. In fact, the strange boy could barely lift the lightest five kilogram halteres on his arrival. His score on the Metis Exam must've been enormous to compensate for those early physical deficiencies.

But with Zoe's personal hands-on tutoring, the fluted satyr adapted; he overcame and blossomed into a most radiant specimen—one she did not mind sampling with *erosic* from time to time. *More than time to time, actually*, she now had to admit. *All the time*. She could think of no one else, and cried miserably when Glaucon avoided her at the yoking ceremony. She wailed like some brainless helot when she had to bare someone else's child. There were none like him among the night husbands. His only vice was a recently acquired appetite for physical contact. But even that was pleasant, strangely enough. The lawlessness, the absurdity, the chance of being seen in such a criminal embrace made her tremble, gasp for breath, imagine lewd and unsavory acts at night, and these feelings could not be exorcised by *erosic*.

Zoe heaved sighing, stroking Glaucon's pale arm on the bed. She did not like sampling but desired Glaucon all to herself, to call him "mine," the worst of blasphemies.

Separation would be necessary in the future if they were to remain ritually pure.

Reciting a silent prayer, Zoe asked the Form of the Good forgiveness and to spare Glaucon's life. She also chanted a silent curse against the witch brother and sister—especially the sister!—who had brought such calamity.

One doctor broke away from several ontocymatists examining a convulsing graph on an emerald screen. He ignored Zoe patiently waiting for some assurance of her friend's safety and approached the philosopher-king directly. Flipping through a science tome larger than the Devil's Bible, Prodicus tapped his foot, struggling to contain his fury.

Schizoeon continued turning outside, with the long view of the city—an unending, sparkling axis from Stratos to the Tenth Ward—coming into sight through the large glass wall.

The doctor whispered rapidly to Prodicus, not wanting to belabor the point: "Sire, I do not believe separation poisoning is the cause of the subject's illness. Even if it was, that would not explain why the cogniscrambler refuses him. There does not appear to be any verifiable cause."

"Scan him again, then, you imbecile!" Prodicus screamed, hurling a medijuice cup across the room. Its contents spilled on the floor. "Everything has a cause. Find out what it is or I'll have your skin for a chair. I want a report on my desk before the day is out fully explaining this . . . abnormality. Do I make myself clear?"

"Perfectly, Sire," the scientist gulped as he scrambled away.

Dr. Salazar Ozbolt marched back into the room, his hands in the pockets of a white lab coat. Although he was sixty-seven—the same age as Prodicus—his skin was as polished and unbroken as a neophyte. The only blemish on his face was a blue-layered cap camera, which covered a gaping hole over his left eye. Wires intertwined with his optic nerves and weeded into his frontal lobe, branched through the hippocampus and rooted to the back of his skull, enabling legendary photographic memory and accelerated reading abilities.

"You should not be so harsh with my staff, old friend," Dr. Ozbolt scolded the philosopher-king. "They are trying their best."

Prodicus returned curtly, "They are complete failures—like this city. First the helots; now the scientists. Our civilization is decaying back into barbarism."

Dr. Ozbolt unleashed a disarming staccato laugh as he extracted a small handheld instrument from deep in his pockets and drummed fingers on the controls. "As they say, my grace, Rome was not built in a day. Great accomplishments take time."

Sparking hot as a Bunsen burner, Prodicus replied, "While you take your darling time, Xenon is busy uniting the rest of the barbarian hordes to stop us. He's managed to terminate the dispute we engineered between the Fifth Estate and the Northeastern Liberation Front. ISHIM intelligence indicates even the Seminoles of Florida have joined the conspiracy. The Seminoles! It's a wonder the savages can even navigate the Florida Archipelago let alone be brazen enough to think *us* vulnerable."

"Well, Levantra does not leave them much choice. We anticipated this, Prodicus."

"Yes, but not the extended time. Immersion will remain dangerous as long as Glaucon remains resistant to the cogniscrambler. The Fates have advised we modify our timetable."

"I will make the needed corrections personally."

"I'm worried, Sal," Prodicus murmured. "The Fates have made serious errors in calculation recently. Make sure you run a diagnostic scan on them. I want a complete house cleaning of the Department of Foresight and Futurology."

"Errors? Our programming makes no errors."

"The Fates advised me to send Glaucon to the wards to meet with Potone's children. Atropos said he would be killed or irreparably harmed otherwise. Now look at what's happened to him. His organs nearly liquefied."

"Perhaps Atropos saw consequences and risks we did not. Sophia may've killed him in another future. Kabiri-36 is trying to construct the best possible outcome for us, as we programmed it to do. Given the complex variables in play, this is most likely the best of all possible worlds."

Prodicus sighed. "Maybe you're right. I'll leave Glaucon in your care. Inject more nanogolem into his system. Make repairs to his liver, aorta, and upper respiratory nerves." He eyed his watch irritably. Nearly time for his afternoon staff meeting at the Office of Public Harmony. Feigning a stiff apology to the hospital technicians, he bid farewell to Zoe, now on the verge of exhaustion. No one spoke again until he exited through the electronic door.

Many still feared they'd vanish like others linked to the leak of Ozbolt weapons to the Other Side. No one wished to help clear the throat of the Bull.

Several hours passed with little progress. Food on a tray was brought at one point, but it lingered uneaten on a desk. Zoe eventually returned to her cloister, leaving her sick companion until morning. Glaucon was left alone with the lights dimmed, frigid. He had never been in a more foreign environment.

Endless seascape replaced the view of the ward city from earlier. Safer Bay glittered under the moon. While he might've found it calming on another occasion, the dark storm clouds crashing and being repulsed by the aquamolpis made him shudder. His heart was open, and no thought or deed could take away his terrible sorrow.

The mellow lighting reminded him of the Miantgast cell holding Sophie and Zemer, when he was sent to confront them.

The heavy lock on the prison door had opened slowly—yes, he remembered that most clearly. His hands shook like the wings of tiny humming birds behind him. On the far wall, a luminous stream of dust trickled into the prison from an open hole leading out to the cliffs. One could crawl out only to meet a steep slope and a five-hundred-kilometer plunge (if the vigilant avis did not devour you first!).

His former friends were tied together back to back. Still dressed in torn bedclothes from the night of her capture, Sophie's bruised face looked up at him perplexed, mouth open in confusion. She conjured thousands of other explanations for Glaucon's arrival—he snuck in; he bought off the guards; the guards were really union sympathizers—but soon, she could no longer hide the obvious.

Somewhere distant, trickling water could be heard drip-drip-dripping from an unidentified source.

Glaucon tried to ignore it as he unfastened Sophie's handcuffs.

"This is the Third Vessel," he told the auxiliaries, throat dry, barely able to speak. He heard the handcuffs clank open.

Sophie lunged with venomous fury, knocking Glaucon to the floor. She mercilessly thrashed his face, shouting obscenities as the auxiliaries pulled her away.

"How could you betray us, Glaucon?" she sneered unbelieving. "We trusted you. Even when we knew you were a guardian." She seethed in anger, clutched fiercely at her muddy hair.

"That was clearly a mistake," Glaucon coughed, nursing a tooth and rising to his feet.

"You were our friend. Here I was worried sick about what happened to you. I couldn't sleep."

"You shouldn't have wasted your time, Sophie. I never cared for any of you."

"Liar, you know that's not true."

"I deceived you to learn more about the Resistance and Xenon, nothing more. You should have expected this. As Marcus said, once a guardian always a guardian."

"Marcus was an idiot. Guardians aren't real. Forms aren't real. This whole city was built on lies, and you've bought it all."

"Some falsehoods are useful."

"You call *this place* useful? It impedes progress everywhere on the globe—for centuries!—keeping everyone back in the dark ages while it rises to glory. Who knows what we could've accomplished as a people if we banded together after the Day of Hylopleonexia. So much suffering, so many years lost. The history of man's labor has come to nothing but a flying island!" Sophie wiped sweat from her face, straining to cool her temper. "All the time we spent sitting in the park, watching movies, reading to each other, lying up at night. How could I have been so stupid?"

"It was only for a summer, Sophie," Glaucon tried to explain in a contradictory attempt to console her. His head was burning. He grew angry at his groveling nature, and began to shout: "My loyalty is with the Republic—to the rule of law!—not with your gang of blackhead savages outside."

"Glaucon, you murdered everyone: Hecatia, Zenobia, Phillip." Sophie's voice rang hollow and monotone, as if she herself did not believe the harsh indictment gushing forth from her lips. "How could you do something like that? I thought you more virtuous."

"I didn't kill them. They were killed by your hidden cache of gas weapons. Or did you forget to tell me about those, too?"

"That's ridiculous. We had no iama-B. By the gods, the guardians released it."

"You've lied to me from the very beginning. How can I trust you now?"

"What are you talking about?"

"You were sent to assassinate me, Sophie! They found a shadowspar recording of me in your drawer."

"I didn't."

"If you weren't such a vessel of desire, you would have."

As Sophie listened to her former friend, he sounded so alien, a wild fanatic. She had seen such transformation before among her petulant soldiers in the field who were ashamed to admit their guilt. Although she wanted to shout "Don't flatter yourself" at the top of her lungs, she knew this would only alienate him further. Worst of all, she wasn't sure if his words were true or not. Originally, she was so certain in her commitment, so meticulous in planning for the death of the Second Vessel. Now, after her choice to disobey Xenon and save him, what did it matter? She reached out to clutch Glaucon's hand. "Where is the Glaucon I loved?" she asked. "Where is he? My beloved is in exile and there is nothing I can do for him. Look at you, you're shaking. Take my hand. Fight against Prodicus."

A Neokalashnikov rifle struck her to the floor.

"It shall not touch," a strong shouldered auxiliary said above her. Glaucon waved him off angrily and wagged a finger in Sophie's face.

"You and your brother betrayed me twice," he accused. "Not only did you come to kill me, but you cast spells on me like Circe while I slept. You ruined me with the jinn, ate my gold like acid. Now I'm a complete wreck. You were never my friends."

Sophie couldn't fathom how he came to know of their activities, but she tried to explain: "Glaucon, we were trying to help you. Please. . . . Prodicus is controlling your mind with the jinn. Don't destroy yourself. Do you know what it means to be a Vessel? Prodicus aims to steal our souls, to make us software. He'll kill us both and worse."

"I've heard enough. Take her away."

"Wait, where are you taking me? What will happen to Zemer?" Re-cuffed, she motioned to her brother sitting on the floor.

Glaucon couldn't look either sibling in the eye. He quivered anxiously, consumed with doubt and remorse. "To be tried for atheism, terrorism, and guardian-treason."

"No!" Sophie cried, struggling to free the auxiliary's grasp. Glaucon motioned for her release out of pity.

Sophie knelt down closely to Zemer, who whispered something inaudible in her ear.

"The funny thing is, I'm not really an atheist," Zemer joked as he kissed his sister's cheek with tears in his eyes.

Sophie held his arm tightly to her face, feeling his deep warmth. She wiped his face lovingly and marveled at his mysterious, determined spirit. How she loved and hoped for him in the darkness, yearning to take his place, her brotherly saint who dared wish for miracles in the Republic. Agonizingly, they continued to talk, to whisper for several minutes more.

Auxiliaries finally dragged Sophie screaming down the hall.

Glaucon turned to follow, but before he could flee the room, Zemer's curious expression dragged him back.

"I'm sorry things had to end this way, my friend," Zemer interrupted the silence.

"I'm still your friend, then?" Glaucon inquired skeptically.

"Oh yes, certainly so! The way I see things, I can be either angry or calm, anything I like. Being angry won't do me any good. To be honest, I am exceedingly afraid."

"Fear is not something that can be helped."

"No. Surely not. Honestly, I've often thought about that angel in the Pure Land watching over our friendship. Do you remember telling me about it in the gas shelter?"

Glaucon wished to sit in the chair of forgetfulness.

Zemer continued: "I think its light has never been stronger because we're finally all together and truthful. The lies which mixed with the gas on our first night together have disappeared. What a wonderful thing this is, even a blessing. We must keep this angel alive, yes? So, I ask you to forgive my sister and me for causing you any hardship."

"You want me to forgive *you?*" A wave of emotion caused Glaucon to stagger, but he made a show of laughter to the other guards in the room.

"Yes, I've already forgiven your betrayal. As my sister explained, we were only trying to help you by using the jinn. We meant no harm, and our work might yet prove useful. The failed strike was the Republic's last chance to avoid goetia's fire. Corruption is spreading, and you'd best be able to defend yourself."

"I never needed your help—for anything," Glaucon snapped.

After saying this, a shower of distressing hell broke into Glaucon's mind. Zemer continued to peer silently, with intense expectation, not saying a word, twisting Glaucon with his perception. The Watcher's magic crushed him in a vice. Glaucon couldn't remain in the cell any longer. He felt tied down and crooked.

"I was once like you," Zemer eventually spoke, "an advocate of self-reliance. In my youth, when I was ten, I was zealous and savage and no one mattered to me. I'd do anything to succeed and be praised by the Logoset, especially Prodicus who took an interest in my pedigree. Tell me, did Sophie in your short time together ever tell you about my terrible crimes? No? She is too gracious to do so. Before Xenon stole us away, I tortured Sophie brutally. I can't lie anymore—I tortured her with Prodicus. Every day, I dragged my sister from her slumber and forced her to undergo psychological torment in Ozbolt Tower. When she cried out to me at night because her little heart beat like the feet of a galloping horse, I struck her; when she was too limp to walk back from the procedure with the jinn, I ridiculed her and carried her half-dead body to the barracks. She is called the Iron Queen because of me; for so often did I place her under the searing light of the jinn in Prodicus' experiments that her heart shattered. It had to be replaced by a bionic substitute.

"I turned my sister into a machine. Even this was not enough to change me, and I repeated my abuse over and over again, throwing her to the wolves. When my mother tried to stop me, I shot her as she fled from the Logoset.

"I am a parricide, Glaucon, the worst of criminals. I allowed Prodicus to turn me from my family, from everyone I ever loved, and I have heard the ground cry out for my accursed blood ever since. When I die the Earth shall not receive me; neither will the stars. I shall be punished forever with no release. After all this time I learned human trust and love is better than self-reliance."

"Why are you telling me this?"

"I tell you because I want to be honest and give you warning: The more isolated you become, the more you reject human trust, the more you turn a blind eye to petty and grand oppressions, the more miserable and powerless you'll end. You are at a critical moment when the option of ending your life for immersion with the Fates will sound like a blessing. But do not listen to their tempting voice. Losing your consciousness will never overturn the choices you've made. You must accept your betrayals and pain for what they are and shun easy remedies. No one is ever lost but me. Don't wait like Adoni-Zadek. Give up your doubt and shame. Give up your pain. Give up ambition. You can control the sun or choose to let it go."

Not another word was spoken between the two. Zemer leaned back on the wall and closed his eyes, exhaling deeply. Glaucon gathered his robes and left, shaken, propelled by cloudy thoughts.

The next week was lost in a dizzying blur of activities. The capture of the exiles proved a sensation, and Glaucon catapulted to fame overnight. While Zemer and Sophie languished in prison, he was shuffled around the wards in a whirlwind circuit tour. His name and deeds canvassed the late night talk shows, news programs like the Gorgon Hour, and the cyberspace halls of the symsyst network. How he wanted to disappear somewhere to grieve, but an upsurge of *Goetia Mirror* publications demanded immediate attention.

Even with city-wide strikes derailed for a time, revolutionary literature spewed out endlessly on the streets like a burst pipe. The guardians came out in force, praising Glaucon as the hero of the Republic and launching their own special magazines to challenge the anarchists. Several million orichalcum was spent on the city's behalf to correct its rebellious nature.

More were arrested and fed to the Bull.

Along the business avenues of Cheque Giorgio and the vineyards of Shennong Fooderies, Glaucon found himself paraded, displayed, praised, desired, and advertised, signing autographs and kissing babies. His picture was everywhere, and people screamed and shouted as he walked by, worshipped him with gifts and flowers. In the morning he attended business meetings with Vinculum executives like Cicero Kellogg and Azael Mellon. By afternoon he discussed synergy tactics and ward politics with Hanover Walker of Ra-Busto Energy. The increased spotlight and having to act publicly contented with the situation took a toll on the young guardian's psyche.

The accident in the cogniscrambler, therefore, filled him with a kind of bittersweet gratitude. At least now he could brood without having to assume a role. His only complaint with the quiet consisted of an incessant ticking clock on the wall.

Tick tock. Tick tock. Tick tock.

The ticking was insufferable, bore into his mind, lucidly reviving his last terrible vision in the cogniscrambler—the disir and flesh-eating Fates clawing at his face like wild beasts, chewing on his bones unable to read his I.T. waves.

He blinked the hags away and felt his pounding heart.

Worse still, he felt shamed by the exiles in the dark. He imagined Zemer and Sophie staring down and pointing, thinking him a complete monster. Such visions crowned his thoughts and robbed him of his center. No matter what Zemer had done in his past, nothing, nothing could compare to *his* treachery. All the faces of the dead swam to him furiously in the night demanding reparations. Glaucon felt helpless and moaned. When he noticed the mounds of fan mail piled by the door, he began crying for his life.

"How terrible," he choked, "to be praised as virtuous but to really be a murderer!"

The next morning, when Glaucon returned to the Academy, he was thankful to be back among noisy distractions and friends.

Zoe was delighted to see him.

IV § 2 ZEMER'S APOLOGY

When Zemer was told his trial was scheduled in the Logoset the following morning, he listened to the news with much relief. Some time away from his damp cell would be a welcome change. Zemer spent the past week in complete isolation; his only company consisted of the periodic screams of doomed souls devoured by avis as they tried to escape through their air vents in the wall. The sounds watered his imagination—a gurgling scream of terror trailing off in the distance, morning and night. Mostly at night. Once, desperate for fresh air, the lonely Zemer clambered along the soggy hole and stretched out his neck like a thirsty fawn. Swarms of avis almost decapitated him.

The mystery of the avis finally dawned on him later: The fierce dragons were not just there to prevent escape, but to act as a merciful gift for those condemned who found thoughts of the Bull unbearable. Zemer couldn't determine which death was worse. Still, he considered jumping to the avis several times.

Next morning, Zemer heard the door unlock and sat on his cot. Waiting patiently for the nervous auxiliary to fit the mind-stocks on his brow, he finally said to her, "Worry not, Antiope, I won't harm you."

The middle-aged woman with high cheekbones and crew cut kept her distance all the same. Too many rumors existed about this oracle's magic: The Son of Fate knew names before introductions, could read minds, kill with a word, and still electric currents. She led him out of Miantgast, slowly, hot xiphos at his back.

Zemer imagined what would happen if he tried to run. He had considered several methods of escape but found success improbable in each. Many times, his mind raced to his sister. He hoped her circumstances turned out better than his own.

He had not seen Heliopolis in over sixteen years. Unlike him, it looked unchanged and immutable. The snowy white law courts still glimmered on cliffs dribbling with streams of drinkable water. The twelve domes of the Logoset sparkled like emeralds in the sun.

"I forgot the physical beauty of Heliopolis," Zemer mentioned to his captor. "I tell you truthfully, by year-end not one river shall remain. All shall be burned to glass."

Antiope's eyes widened and she pushed him along, fearful of a descending group of reporters from Skybridge News.

Dodging a phalanx of microphones, Zemer was quickly escorted down a steep hill, passing through a batch of flabbergasted students lounging under purple cloth canopies.

Reporters groaned as the Logoset's heavy doors slammed in their faces. Passing quickly through the ninth dome, the guard led Zemer outside to a private *stola* leading to the central dome. Pillars in the walkway were shaped like Brizo, the stormy god of sailors. Offerings—incense, a xiphos stick, folded paper notes—rested under their wings.

Simmias Rex approached Zemer hesitantly from a sun drenched fountain. "Kleomedes, by the gods, is that really you?" he asked with solemn whisper.

Zemer looked at the man curiously. He wore a red linen tunic and cloak, tied with a wooden brooch.

"Of course you must remember me," Simmias continued fondly, rubbing knuckles on his chest. "It's me, Simmias. You and Sophia used to train me and my classmates on how to sing the patriotic songs on Stratos. You were my hero for two years of my life."

"That was a long time ago, Simmias. Why are you here?"

Rex smiled proudly. "Why because of you—our city's prodigal son. Anarchist bomber extraordinaire! The entire world is talking of it. You've become quite notorious. I am to be your defense counsel."

"You must be joking? Who on earth appointed you?"

"Prodicus himself," Simmias beamed. "He has recognized my talent from the very beginning. There is not a better advocate in the city. I've handled numerous military commissions. If you ask around, you'll see I'm well regarded."

"You realize, don't you, this trial is going to be a sham?"

"To be honest, I don't see much hope. But look here; I've been working on a number of possible defenses. If we can prove you acted under duress because of Sophia's violent nature and the fact she was your commanding officer, then we might be able to lessen the sentence."

Zemer flashed him a stern look.

"Oh no, Kleomedes, you need not distress over your sister. She has been granted total immunity by the guardian-king himself. We can pin all we like on her, and it won't make the slightest difference."

"It will make a difference to me. She is innocent of everything. Please tell me what happened to her."

"Her days are spent in Miantgast Prison. Her nights?—being questioned by the Office of Public Harmony. If you ask me, she's become rather like a pet for Prodicus. He is quite obsessed with her. Prodicus orders her brought to his chambers at all hours of the night—not to do anything sordid, I'm told—but to look upon her like some holy icon."

"So what do you get out of this, Simmias?"

"Excuse me?"

"If I win in any small degree, you will be praised beyond measure. If I lose, you will be seen as a virtuous man trying to provide a fair trial to an unrepentant terrorist."

"You seem to have things figured out, but you should know I care about truth most of all."

"Yes, of course you do. That is why I tell you to get behind me. Because where I am going, the truth is unimportant."

"Are you insane? They're going to kill you, Kleomedes."

"The dice have fallen. Let them lie."

"Do not rush to your death with such determination."

"No one can prevent their death. Knowing how to avoid injustice is what matters most."

"Who are you?" Rex gasped astounded.

"Once upon a time, a son of thunder. Now I am an oracle of Zemargad. Leave me to find my fate. I will defend myself as the ancients deemed proper."

Simmias dropped his legal papers dumbfounded, as if hit by a staggering blow.

The ten archons, Polemarch Leonida of Stratos, and Prodicus awaited Zemer in the august, green Logoset Assembly Dome. All were dressed in customary black legal robes. Hushed silence filled the room as the Watcher entered and stood at attention under their balconies circling the perimeter. The only color Zemer noticed was a peacock-feather beret tying up Leonida's hair. In the Sixth Ward's seat sat a new face: Zeno took the throne of Manos.

Inexplicable sadness filled Zemer's lungs at the sight of the old philosopher-king. Images of his crimes flooded back to him, his hands covered in his mother's blood. He tried to push her memory away as Prodicus pounded his gavel, thunderous as the hammer of Thor.

"What a historic moment we witness," Prodicus said with a touch of elation in his voice. "See, the exile has returned to us as the Fates predicted sixteen years ago."

"It's been a long time, Uncle; you're looking well."

Zemer's words caused an awkward silence as memories of Potone filled the room.

Prodicus smiled folding his hands. "Smug temerity until the very end," he scolded, "and much like your Katharoi mother, you're rebellious. We have been receiving evidence against you all morning, Kleomedes. Like a meddlesome termite you have been nibbling on our city, disgracing yourself and the guardians."

"He is a social parasite," Zeno added at the top of his lungs, enjoying the newfound powers of Sixth Archon. "He has been trouble since he was a boy, a lawless comet, unruly and disobedient. The video earlier displaying his reckless use of the jinn is enough to condemn him."

Zemer inquired unsurprised, "You've been receiving evidence without me present?"

Prodicus explained, "You will find guardian trials do not follow the usual Republican Rules of Evidence. Do you know what crimes you're charged with committing, my augur nephew?"

Hypatia pushed the grey hair out of her face and leaned into her microphone to address the criminal, listing the allegations: "Atheism, Aggravated Assault, Infamous Libel, Sedition, Corrupting the Young, Fraternizing with Helots, Fraud, First Degree Murder, Parricide, Defection, Terrorism, Damaging Public Property, Creating Obscene Imitations of Reality, Unlicensed Use of the Jinn, Indecent Accessing of the Fates, Kidnapping a Vessel, Waging a War of Aggression, Using Chemical Weapons, and worst of all, High Guardian-Treason."

"Is that all?" Zemer asked. "And here I thought I was in real trouble. I find it curious you decided to include parricide, Uncle."

"Legally, all murders of your guardian elders are parricides. Blood relationships are no longer important to the crime."

"How do you plead?" Hypatia stubbornly asked.

"I motion for dismissal."

"Saint Plato's beard, on what grounds?"

"On grounds this court lacks subject matter jurisdiction."

Wild laughing erupted in the assembly hall.

"Must you continue this tragic obstinacy?" Zeno shouted.

"This panel is an incompetent court because it acts outside the boundaries of international norms," Zemer explained a theory he learned from an old law treatise. "The Republic, in previous cases, has accepted the ancient principles of international law: General patterns of practice and legal expectation across the world can create legally binding norms. On the Other Side, there is a general belief trials should be conducted with fairness by one's peers, and if convicted, you should only suffer the ire of public opinion. Punishment is rarely ever used, and there is an emphasis placed on reconciliation between victim and culprit. All recognize crime is the primary result of defective social conditions. Our society promises to change *for* the individual so that he will not be lost and society will be made better. Here you have not even allowed me to see the evidence presented against myself, and the executive leadership of a state can hardly be neutral. Worst of all, you offer no recommendations for meaningful reconciliation."

"Meaningful reconciliation?" Zeno choked on his collective bile. "He is playing with us in contempt."

Prodicus smiled at his clever nephew and begged for silence, casting a playful gaze at Zeno. "You do realize," he observed, looking down at Zemer under the sharp lights, "international law is determined by *state* custom and expectation?"

"No, quite the contrary, it's made by each individual actor—"

"Wrong again. States matter. Individuals don't. Since there are no other states left in the world—except our Holy Republic, the successor to the United States—the Republic's customs can be the only source of international law. This tribunal is therefore proper, and we may proceed according to our own laws. Unlike you barbarian animals, our laws do not bend for anyone."

Zemer protested, "Your laws were made by an arbitrary gang of guardians and are not my laws. Collective action can never claim to be individual action, no matter if such action is democratic, republican, or tyrannical. No one can be or should be entrusted with the power to make laws in my place. As an individual I am privileged to reject all claims of loyalty and association.

"Beyond this court's lack of subject matter jurisdiction, I must make yet another defense, a glorious argument that shall not die until the last human breath perishes from the earth. You may never claim jurisdiction over my person. I am as free as the wind and exempt from all bonds to you. You shall never have my personal consent to try me—never! Both the world and I shall know this is an armed cabal without shred of legitimacy. This Republic is a criminal organization preying on the weak and thieving resources from the slaves it claims to protect. Know always, you hold me here by power, nothing more. And one day soon your power will cease to exist."

Prodicus frowned. "Be that as it may, your words reveal ignorance about our moral basis of power. As long as our rule conforms to the natural law discovered by Saint Plato millennia ago, we use legitimate force. You—like the rest of us—are a part of nature and subject to its Forms. Further, you consented to our jurisdiction in the same way Socrates consented to Athens. As the Laws said to him long ago: 'We have given you birth, nurtured you, educated you; we have given you and all other citizens a share of all the good things we could.' Zemer, you sheltered yourself with us as a boy and lived within our walls for the last summer. I have no qualms about proceeding with this trial. Now may we please drop this infernal procedural business?"

Hypatia held up a wrinkled parchment. "This is the *Geotia Mirror* (Number 23). In it someone has perversely written:

" 'The aim of life is solidarity. Total solidarity! And our calling can be but one end: to overthrow the Republic and all states for the good of mankind. There can be but one oath—break the chains of the Vinculum Cartel; be a footstool for Prodicus no longer; tear away his bloody robes covering the city; expose the Republic's iron, skeletal frame as an unholy prison. Give up hope in the Forms.

" 'The instinct of the whole human race is set against the artificial lights of the Republic. See, we shall rise up like a teeming mass, like a beast from the deep, to purify the guardians with an elixir of healing waters. Every mind, every union and protest, should be set to the task of leveling and uncivilizing man. When man 'uncivilizes' himself, he becomes civilized, a philosopher. This is no paradox or fallacy of equivocation. This is a moral statement of emancipation! We must tear down the world to rediscover the human spirit. We must cease being puppets of the Fates. Solidarity, more solidarity, forever solidarity!' "

Hypatia stopped reading, her face hot with fury. "Shall I continue, my grace?" she asked. "The *Geotia Mirror* proceeds to maliciously defame the guardians, openly declaring them tyrants and not the supreme authority of our Republic. It calls for the abolishment of government power, speaks scandalously against the Good, the basis for our civil government. It entertains a vision of destroying morality with its obscene poems and malicious plays. Look at these literary excerpts they have included: heretical writings by Kafka, books like *Demian*, *Frankenstein*, *Family*, *Looking*

Backward, The Master and Margarita—the absolute worst. Gods only know how much sickness this caused."

Prodicus rubbed his philosopher temples. "No, I think we've heard quite enough."

Zeno squealed, "They are ignorant whelps, Sire, who know not what they say!"

"Did you write that obscene imitation, Kleomedes?" Prodicus demanded.

"I write all of them, Uncle," Zemer said. "You are a corrupt tyrant and an enemy of the human race. Everything I write is truth."

"Truth? Truth is the worst kind of sedition; for true words excite the foulest opinions of government. If helots looked at their guardians with displeasure, how could we protect them? For our survival—and theirs—it is necessary everyone possess a good opinion of the Republic, lest we stumble back into the chaos that followed the Day of Hylopleonexia. Now come to your senses, *Son of Fate*. Do not be absurd. We know you don't write all the articles. There've been over a hundred issues by now. No one can write that many alone. It must take dozens of busy printing houses to create such levels of work. Your sister, she helped you, didn't she? She ordered you to print."

"I am an anarchist. As such, I take orders from no one, not even the Iron Queen. I printed everything alone."

"You imitators are quite easy to spot. That helot fool, Terra, was the same. You all take complete responsibility for the printing. Nevertheless, your lies are obvious by the fact printing persists after you enter captivity. Besides, we have a signed affidavit from Glaucon testifying to all your activities."

After hearing Glaucon's account, Leonida rested her cheek on her fist. "It shall be a shame when all the wards are shut down and we begin decimation. Your comrades may continue to flood the streets with contraband, but it won't last. I think you'll be surprised how few people wish to burn."

Hypatia laughed. "Look how quickly your precious union died under our heel. Where is your solidarity now?"

Zemer shouted back, "The helots aren't robots; you can't control them. You've admitted so today. All they needed were supplies from the Other Side. Only supplies. No leadership from above, no new ideology. Revolution was here before I arrived. The helots hate your power, and one day soon you'll wish you listened to me when I offered peace."

Prodicus said, "The helots know they lack the rational power to protect their interests. That is why they obey. This is not 1984. We are not Big Brother. We do not need to directly control the helots' thoughts. We need only control their discourse."

"You limit their freedom by limiting their discourse."

"Most appreciate their betters and fill their roles as nature intended. You would prefer to execute them with the jinn?"

"The jinn is alive. It breathes like we do. Atropos attacked the helots, not me."

"What a convenient defense. Though collaborated by Glaucon's report, it is logically impossible. Following the expert advice of the great sage, Asimov, the Fates were programmed to never harm humans, either through action or inaction, and to always act in humanity's best interest."

"Perhaps you should read Asimov again, then, without guardian engineering."

"Fool. Kabiri can't ignore direct commands. There are no loopholes in my programming."

"The Fates had me murder your sister, Uncle. They killed her out of jealousy. Surely, you must know that." Zemer swung his arm as if to collect the assembly close to his breast. "Archons of the Logoset—I beg you—if you do not stop Prodicus and the Fates, they will destroy us all—including every last one of you! Leonida, they will take your head. Do not ignore my prophesies like the Trojans ignored Cassandra. Stop them, before it's too late. Save yourselves, for Plato's sake."

Prodicus shouted him down: "Kleomedes, I must say I'm surprised at your venomous tone against us and the Fates. I see we were correct in our initial assessment. You are an ungrateful bastard to our laws and deserve death."

"I deserve what you deserve, Uncle."

"You are a traitor, having aided and abetted Xenon by launching propaganda and petty acts of violence. Do you deny it?"

Zemer refused to speak any further.

"You purposely distributed imitations denying the Forms, weakening the bonds of society and virtue, and inciting rebellion."

Silence.

"For the purpose of spreading mayhem and separation poisoning, you targeted civilians with the jinn."

Silence.

"You did maliciously libel the Fates. DO . . . YOU . . . DENY IT?"

Zemer would no longer participate with the court.

Prodicus laid his gavel on the desk and peered directly at the prisoner. "Why are you refusing to defend yourself? Why are you refusing to speak?"

"Because you have lost the capacity to understand my words."

"Then there is nothing more I can do to save you. Tomorrow, because you have persisted in a vile obsession with the material world, you shall be given a sensory stimulation capsule and fed to the Bull. It grieves me deeply to say this, my sick nephew, but tomorrow you shall experience the most agonizing death man has yet conceived. You are no longer any use to us. Take him away."

Zemer suddenly pointed like a madman around the room. "What strange elders you are, mighty archons. How reasonable, to kill someone attempting to help you; to make revenge law," but before he could continue speaking, the mind stocks energized and he collapsed to the floor.

IV § 3 The Erinyes Smell Blood

Sweat dripped down Zemer's face like brimstone in the humid night air. Rain could be heard outside watering the grasses of Heliopolis. So much fear and doubt. Because of the clouds, neither moon nor stars hinted at the time. He must wait till daybreak; but then he'd only have a few moments left in the world.

Full of thoughts, Zemer remembered being eight again, sitting with his feet in the cool waters of Hesper Park, Sophie swinging upside down like a monkey from a tree.

"Do you think we could really be related, Kleo?" Sophie asked, flipping down in her bell-shaped robes.

"That is the only explanation for Lycaon's attention," Zemer admitted. "He treats no one else like us."

For over a year they had collected special notice from ISHIM and been showered with praise. Just this afternoon, they were released from military drills to sample a play—*Antigone Angelik*—in the shelled Amphitheater with much older guardian initiates. From the play they learned of the heroic exploits of the virtuous Antigone. After learning of a helot plot to cremate her dead bronzeborn brother (against a guardian-king's direct edict), Antigone promptly informed the guardians with the assistance of the Fates. The helot rebels were caught and fed to the Bull. The guardians hooted at the end. Sophie focused almost completely on the mystical familial bond absent in the breeding dens.

"The other students say we're twins," Sophie said. "I guess you kind of look like me." She dabbed his nose with her thumb.

"Do I?"

"Even if we're not brother and sister, can we still pretend it's true?"

"Excuse me?"

"That we're siblings. But we should behave different from Antigone. If either of us gets into trouble, the other will have to come to the rescue."

Saying this, Sophie took a sharp knife from her sash and cut her hand.

Zemer shouted, "Sophia, what mania has seized you?"

"We must take a blood oath," the girl explained, cutting his hand next to hers. "I've seen others do the same. Swear by the river Styx: You are my blood sister, to have and to hold, and I will protect you."

Zemer solemnly made the vow.

Sophie did the same. "There. Now we're really related, and we shall always be together. If either of us breaks their word, the offender shall be cursed. Their eyes shall be gauged out; their skin turned green; their children will be deformed and tossed away; daimons will burn their feet."

Zemer made her promise to keep their oath a secret.

An open door suddenly flooded Zemer's tiny cell with light. Prodicus stormed into the room and ordered to be locked inside. Even the golems at his feet were forbidden to enter.

"What were you thinking coming back here?" Prodicus asked searchingly.

Zemer looked out the vent into the rain. "The jinn told me if I ever returned I would die. I thought it might be some trick to keep me away from the city."

"And yet here you are at death's door."

"Yes, here I am. But you can't live life in the third person. You must choose."

Prodicus ignored him. He paced around the room, fingers bent like griffin's claws. "You must hate me," he said.

"No, I don't hate you, Uncle. Actually, I was hoping to see you again because I did not like how our previous meeting ended. I wanted to ask forgiveness from you. But to do so in that chamber would have been improper."

"Forgiveness?"

"Yes, for the horrible things my parents did. For listening to you. For not coming to see you sooner."

"Hubris is a sin, dear nephew. Ask forgiveness from the Good. You ought not antagonize the man who holds your life in his hands."

Zemer's jade eyes flashed defiantly at his uncle. "You don't hold anyone's life in your hands. You only believe you do."

"Oh, but see, I do. I really do." Prodicus called for the door to be opened. "Look there. You are free to leave—"

"But?" Zemer interrupted.

"The conditions are you must leave this city; stop printing your hideous books; sign a simple confession you were wrong."

Prodicus clutched a scroll under his arm and let it unroll to the floor.

"I won't accept those conditions."

"You won't? Your language surprises me. Well then, I suppose your life is out of my hands. You have chosen suicide, and I am therefore not responsible for the death of a blood relative. To destroy yourself like Socrates when you have a way out is . . . unfortunate."

"Why do you continue to deceive yourself, Uncle? I'm not a suicide. Neither was Socrates. Yes, he drank the hemlock, but he would've preferred to live. Democrats who refused to take responsibility murdered him. You're the same as they. You do not have to kill me, and if it matters at all I prefer to live. I would love to see my sister again, to lie quietly beside her at night. I would like to sit in the grasses on the Other Side and feel the soft sand between my toes. I am bitterly afraid of the Bull."

Prodicus shook his arms in the air and criticized his nephew: "Philosophy is but preparation for dying. If you studied correctly at the Academy, you would rejoice at the chance to return to the Forms. This is what makes you so detestable—you are a philosopher of life. Your fear is from ignorance. My heart, however, is not stone. Your efforts have struck a chord of pity in me. My heart is breaking just seeing you here. How I loved you as you grew up. You were like my own child. Very well, simply walk out the door and leave. You can continue printing your books."

"My sister?"

"I will keep your sister. She is the chosen Vessel. This shall be no hardship for you."

"No, you will not touch her again," Zemer promised. "I will not betray the highest good in the world, not for you or anyone else. I would destroy the world to save my sister. I would sell my soul to the wailing fires of Tartarus."

Prodicus only laughed. "You are either a comedian or a fool. I have complete control over her destiny. How does it make you feel that Sophia, Glaucon, and I shall soon be joined as one mind with the Fates? It's a shame you'll fail to glimpse the advent of freedom in the world. Levantra shall be a paradise."

"Freedom is the ability to control your life, Uncle, not to control others. What do you plan to do about everyone left in the Republic?"

This question embarrassed Prodicus. He attempted to explain: "The Republic—as it developed historically—is too large. Saint Plato gave specific warnings about an improper regard for demographics. Although he was not clear on the exact number, he thought the city should, 'as far as possible, become neither too big or too small.' His *Laws* advised 5,040 families. Our Republic, however, stretches across a continent and holds nearly 50 million souls. How is nurturing a life of virtue possible amongst so many? We need a restoration of Plato's vision, and we shall have it in the clouds."

"You shall have a city of death in the clouds. I'm sorry, Uncle. I will not leave without my sister."

"So twice you deny my attempts to save you?"

"I am denying your conditions. You may change them."

"These conditions can't be changed. The Fates demand them." Prodicus sighed deeply, scratching himself in pity for his nephew. Zemer's sweaty hair was beginning to curl. "How does it make you feel to be rejected?" Prodicus finally asked.

"I am rejected?"

"Everyone has rejected you. Even your sister. She chooses her nights with me over this cell with you." Prodicus marveled at his nephew's naiveté. "A completely free poll was taken by Skybridge News tonight. The question was: 'Should we punish the fallen guardian responsible for harming the city with the *Goetia Mirror*?' Do you know what answer returned? Eighty-nine percent of the helots thought you should be punished. They hate you."

Zemer shrugged. "Still, eleven percent sees value in our struggle. I suspect the poll numbers would be different if you said I am to be executed for guardian-treason."

"No one is listening."

"Even if no one wanted to listen, I would still raise my voice. The only moral thing I have ever done is to resist the guardians. You also lie about Sophie. She would never reject me."

Prodicus spoke cruelly, "Your own friend, Glaucon, rejected you to side with us. Doesn't that sting more than the eighty-nine percent? You are a virtuous person rotting in jail while he will go on to rule a kingdom."

"To have lived with you over his shoulder for sixteen years proves Glaucon is stronger than me. I have forgiven him, and I forgive you again for tempting and mocking me. Hopefully, Glaucon will change and see how unhappy and isolated he is. When that day occurs, he will condemn himself with stones of guilt sharper than I could ever throw. If Glaucon does not change, it makes little difference, for others will learn from his isolation and spill the hate from their vessels for love's freedom."

"Foolish boy, no one desires the freedom you offer. If such freedom fell in their hands from the sky, they wouldn't have the slightest idea how to act. The weight of the meteor would grind them to pieces. Even on the Other Side, look how they fly to Xenon. He's their necessary idol. The emptiness of man is so vast, only but the bravest dare peer into the abyss. Xenon is one. You are one. Sophia is one. But most humans will hold anything in front of their eyes to cover the hole's stench. They realize perfectly well 'it is not such an evil thing to be a victim of a lie.' Anything—anarchism, morality, God, sex, Plato's *Republic*—is better than the pit you offer. Authority is the only thing keeping them going; authority brings stability. I can give stability forever, law without exception. Is freedom so important it outweighs the suffering weak who will be destroyed by your creative revolt?"

"They are weak because you grew them weak, Uncle. All men are empty and will suffer silently until they give up their lies. My project is to dispel their delusions of order and to unstop their creative springs."

"You don't believe a word you're saying."

"Quite the contrary, I believe every word, and I've discovered many things about you, Uncle. I know you stay awake at night shivering in fear. Your plans are fragile as glass, and you worry about being overthrown before their fruition. Rising to power like you did fills you with a perverse sense of accomplishment, but the knowledge others view you as a tyrant saps your power. Their eyes make you feel responsible and ashamed for my mother's death. You curse being weak and tied down by blood. I know how deeply you loved my mother. You loved her like I love Sophie, saw divinity there, and you'd sneak down to the wards just to look at her after she was born. Perhaps that is why you bring Sophie to your quarters now—to play brother, pretend she is Potone and lighten your constant sadness. But you must surely know she is nothing but a reflection. You can never make things right, Uncle. You've lost the eternal. You murdered everyone of any importance to you, and tomorrow you shall surely murder me."

Prodicus howled a fierce war-cry and shot a jagged ray of jinn lightning directly into the exposed prisoner. Icy tempests congealed around Zemer's legs, buffeted his sable hair. The thunder-seer, though, was ready, having practiced for months withstanding the miasma spell. The horrible spell! The dastardly spell! The spell that could grab a man's soul, squeeze away memory, and sever one's connection to society. Zemer remained perfectly still, heart pounding in his chest, befriending the voices and light, shielding his soul with Sophie's loving image.

After several seconds, Prodicus stumbled catching breath and wiped his mouth. "You are truly something special, Kleomedes," he wheezed. "I've never seen anything similar in my life. Even as a boy you were resistant to the jinn, unlike your sister. I could never understand how your I.T. waves were identical. There was no explanation for it. You left me a hissing hydra but have returned a Nereus. Your manner and expressions—they are beyond your age, as if a spirit has possessed you. Tell me, what thunderous spell have you cast on Glaucon?"

"No spells, Uncle. I expected less superstition from a *scientist* of your caliber."

"Liar! He is at death's door. Look at what a hypocrite you are, claiming in your writings you wish no harm to any living creature. I was with him at Ozbolt Tower yesterday. He's pale as an eidolon, as still and morose as gloomy Hades."

"Is this why you really come, Uncle, to ask about the health of your precious Vessel? As you pointed out, there are many unexplainable things in this world."

Prodicus gripped his nephew by the shirt, helplessly examining his face for any clue. "Did the Fates bestow some secret in the wastes? Did they leave footprints for you to follow? What hidden lore are you using? What were you doing to him when you prayed light over his slumber? You said the jinn lives. What did you mean?"

"You found everything evil in the jinn. I discovered something to save us, something you'll never understand."

"What?"

Zemer remained windowless. Prodicus could see by his nephew's expression he wouldn't be broken. He abandoned hope for revelation and dropped a silk bag on the ground.

"What's this?" Zemer asked.

"Shame you continue wishing for death. Please do not take others to the torture with you."

Zemer looked confused by his meaning.

Prodicus explained: "Ten helots caught making imitations will burn with you today. In the bag are five pills containing neurotoxin, neurotoxin that will give death in seconds. They do not have to resort to being torn up by the avis. See, you thought you were so merciful, shunning violence and pain, but I shall make you my little henchmen again—like old times. My little hydra and his poisonous fangs will return. You shall give hope and offer a quick death to five poor souls, and if not, all their long, arduous suffering will be on your head."

"No, it will be on your head. You don't have to throw us inside. You can destroy the Bull."

"The public demands a response, and I can't deny them."

"You won't deny them."

"Can't, won't, what difference does it make?"

"All the difference in the world. I shall never give away the pills."

"Take them all yourself, then. Eat them like mints and die painlessly. It matters little to me, you miserable toad. I shall be glad when your mother's stench is gone from the world. The first thing I shall do on Levantra is rid the earth of families so that no one has to suffer again. Your life is meaningless to me. Meaningless!"

Prodicus left steaming and slammed the cell door. Zemer spent the rest of the night lifted by some strange inner force. The rain clouds dissolved, and he scrutinized the silent heavens. The golden stars brought solace to the earth. He imagined his sister staring out the window, looking at Draco guarding immortality in the sky; but knowing her, she was probably sleeping at this hour.

Another memory caught him in the dark. He remembered his recovery after leaving the Republic sixteen years ago. The smooth hands of Xenon ripped him from the gyroped, dragged him screaming in bloody, loose robes through the dirt. Muddy barbarian faces confronted from every direction. They did not wear similar robes, but had tattered rags and strange weapons. No one in the wilderness came to his aid. Instead they allowed him to be thrown in a filthy, dimly lit hut made of scavenged rusty car parts from the Age of Aporia. He was left there on the muddy ground, alone, all his plans for the future lost with not a friend in the world. Then, without reason, the door adjacent to him opened, and Sophie appeared clutching a soft blanket. Half buried in the dark, he acted aloof until she knelt down and covered him with her arms. Everything he had done—aiming Ozbolt's instruments of oppression, acting as her personal warden, stopping her beating heart, betraying his oath—caused him to shrink away in shame, but over time, she made the world bearable again. Her power of healing dispelled his illness and led him down the path to wisdom.

"She is my sister," Zemer repeated again and again, gathering courage from her memory, "and no gods or daimons can ever take her away. As absurd as the heavens are I love her. I love this world that birthed her, my human sister. She forgave me when God himself would not. And I want so much more of life, no matter what arguments can be made against it. Every moment is gold, and never could my thirst be quenched, not in a sextillion years."

He gulped in the air from outside, almost hyperventilating. "O Iron Queen, what will become of me?" he shouted at the top of his lungs.

Much to his alarm, a faint sliver on the horizon glowed red as molten iron. It was already dawn. As the Fates would have it, Prodicus had been his final confessor.

IV § 4 Staring into the Sun

The tumbrels rolled on schedule, but with only ten condemned rather than eleven. Zemer kept his promise to his uncle. He did not offer the pills but cast them to the floor in disdain. After noting he would not take them and that to do so would constitute a personal failure on his part, he retired to a damp corner of the holding block to await the carts. The prisoners licked their lips hungrily at the neurotoxins on the floor—as if they were ripe, tasty grapes—and eyed one another suspiciously. But the mutinous words spoken by the strange, quiet thunder-seer filled them all with courage. A sentiment developed that to take the pills would grant the guardians a clean conscience and soften the effects of their deaths on the public. Only one man, cursing, shaking in fear, crawled on his hands and knees to the pile of deadly pills.

"If you must eat, then eat them all," an agricultural engineer from the Fifth Ward commanded, grabbing the man's wrist.

In moments the criminal wheezed and foam dribbled from his mouth.

"Zemer?" the engineer spoke softly, drawing close to the oracle full of dread. Though threadbare and desolate, much life still burned within his spirit. "You may not remember me. We met a few weeks ago at the Directory strike meeting. I ran food supplies with Zenobia—gods protect her."

"I remember well, Akakios. Those were happier days."

"Yes."

"Please," Zemer said, "the guardians stole much knowledge from me in Miantgast. What of the Directory? What of the Republic's last good people?"

Akakios lowered his bearded face. "Underground. Most of those we called friends are dead or imprisoned. The Bull sings a week-long song. The city is on holiday to watch. Strikes are impossible on a holiday."

"Your children?"

Akakios did not answer. He asked instead, "Is it true you attacked Consumption Junction?"

Zemer flinched. "Not intentionally. I overreached my powers with the jinn."

"Skybridge News says a helot-jacquerie assassinated Dietrich Prince and several management leaders at Seven Seas. The armory burned for days. Terra's husband carried through on his word—he brought the people's justice to the Vinculum Cartel."

"Do you believe him right or wrong?"

"Who can really say? I have a feeling no matter what we did, we were certain to fail. Something makes me wonder, though. . . ."

"What?"

"You spoke so lucidly about future events, commanded the stage with your knowledge of others' hearts. How did you not see this unfortunate end?"

"The future is not set like people believe—"

"But surely you had some premonition."

"Yes."

"Then why come back? You could've lived to an old age on the Other Side."

"Why did you not flee when I offered you the chance? As you admit, you were certain of failure."

"I care about the people trapped in the Republic. Don't want to save myself and let everyone else drown. How could I live happy knowing others are miserable?"

Akakios spoke with such love, such authority, Zemer decided to confess everything: "I am the same. Yet I feel I caused more harm than good. Everyone is this room is innocent and their only *crime* is begging the guardians for freedom. I alone am different. I shed innocent blood through my negligence. During a jinn trance in the wastes . . ." Zemer wiped his brow disturbed, "I did a horrible thing, Akakios. An evil thing. It hurts to say. I sold my soul to a powerful daimon . . . a new, slimy one . . . for an unholy spell. Incredible, I know, but the jinn *lives*. The Fates think it lifeless stone but it lives and speaks and makes promises and lies. A new life, expanding into everything, and it wanted me. How could I submit to this being, you ask? Believe me, I still wonder. The jinn spirit offered me many things—kingdoms, riches, revenge—and I refused them all. But my sister's life?—how could I refuse that? She is my sister, after all. Daimons know all man's weaknesses. Even if you hold up mirrors, they see through. Daimons are also tricksters, it seems—the dark spell failed!"

"Why?" Akakios' face lit up wondering.

"Simple legalese! I asked the daimon for a spell, but not for one that worked. That or the creature was too young. In either case, I had to improvise my own methods. They fizzled and popped to nothing. They weakened and ripped me apart. No matter how hard I tried to redeem my life, it fell further into darkness. I pollute everything I touch. Flee from me before you are destroyed."

Akakios listened quietly. "Pollution matters little to me at this hour, Oracle," he said. "Do not fear. If I go to the Elysian Fields, I will remember you and light a path to its restful waters."

"The daimon will not let me go. I can feel her skimming through my guts, even now."

"I will gather our fallen friends and rescue you."

"Thank you, Akakios," Zemer gripped his arm. "I believe an angel of friendship sent you."

Akakios smiled attentively, lifted by Zemer's story, and replied, "Perhaps you misunderstood this jinn daimon all along, Oracle."

"Did I?"

"Perhaps she was born no daimon, but man's final friend, the last breath of life daring to chill Fates' furnace. The child thirsts for justice in her own way. Too young, she was, to swallow her parents."

"Alas, her time has not yet come. And now another furnace summons us."

"Yes."

The door opened.

Zemer put up no resistance when a glass yellow pill and cloth was shoved between his teeth. A gangly auxiliary used his palm to push the oracle's chin up, breaking the brittle seal.

Zemer's mind splashed awake with sensory undulation. Every speck of dust transformed into sharp boulders rolling down the hairs of his arms, like being flayed. The air sparkled with light. Briefly, his mind wandered to his bones—his poor bones. With each slight movement, they individually bent and snapped as if broken in a vice. Colors and time boiled together, so that he could barely make out the shapes of roofless temples on the long mechanical march to the Sixth Ward. Shapes contorted to fiery daimons and shadows, mutating colors.

The spectators cast looks on his delirious stupor in the cart as if he were a foul, wretched thing. Their eyes followed the Watcher's burning skin as he mounted the scaffolding. Finally, stripped naked from his *sanbenito*, feverish, Zemer's eardrums gave way as the charges of each prisoner were read aloud by Zeno.

"No one stands as a law unto himself," Zeno gloated victoriously, hovering over Zemer like Terra before him, "and no one is beyond the law. The guardians allowed this traitor back into the city to smoke out the most vicious, ill bred revolutionists. We blew out the lights to lure our city's cockroaches from their holes. Returning the lights, we discovered the worst of terrorists, and now—most marvelously—we shall drown our foes in song, a melodious "Too Ra Loo." How impotent our enemies when even their hate can be channeled to a higher purpose. Our Republic is mighty and shall last forever, and no one can stop us. My sacred lips cast out these parasites from our mercy. They are too sick to be cured. It is better they die and return unblemished by such unhealthy beliefs. 'Every trace of anarchy should be utterly eradicated from all the life of men.' "

Zeno would have said more, but before he could finish, Akakios and the other prisoners began to chant from Shelly's *Mask of Anarchy*:

" 'Rise like lions after slumber
In unvanquishable number!
Shake your chains to earth, like dew
Which in sleep had fallen on you—
Ye are many; they are few.' "

The archon ordered their mind stocks energized at once. But when the prisoners fell silent, some in the crowds continued the imitation.

Zeno darted backward, afraid, almost burning his back on the blistering heat of the Bull. "Saint Plato, club them . . . club the prisoners into the Bull!" he cried.

Bronze doors shut in the condemned. The Bull burned hotter. Zeno sighed relief, but from somewhere nearby, a shoe hurled through the air and hit the runty archon in the face.

IV § 5 Demeter Brings Fertility

Academy students could hardly believe their senses. The helots were rebelling, rebelling against reason and truth. Tear gas dispersed the crowds like dragon fire, and xiphos sticks cracked the streets with electric sparks. Energy barricades went up again, all along Execution Beach as it was cordoned off and quarantined.

The riot lasted all morning. Helots marched, set buildings on fire, filled the streets preventing movement. "No police, no war, no guardians!" they chanted. A commune was declared in the Sixth Ward, then quickly suppressed by auxiliary fire. Zizthopters bombed the speaker stages and assemblies. By mid-afternoon, low-frequency sound waves drove the mob underground.

Glaucon sat, eyes transfixed to the common hologram-projector in Zoe's phylanstery. *How much longer until I wake up?* he wondered, clawing at his face. But this was no dream. Zemer was gone like Aquila was gone, and the guardian's heart shredded to pieces. It felt as if *he* had died.

Patroclus sat up from the long wraparound kline, pulling his red cloak warmly over his shoulders. He worried about Glaucon's crazed state and tried to console him. "You did the right thing," he said. "The parricide's very life polluted us, provoked the Good, drove the helots to madness. His death is on his own head. Listen, friend; I was with Prodicus this morning. The oracle ignored several opportunities to save his life."

"You know that's not true," Glaucon defended his friend.

"You'll soon forget all about this affair at the festival," Zoe promised, applying body paint to her skin, making her flesh bloom like a flower.

"I don't want to forget. I have become the worst of criminals." Glaucon placed his head between his legs in grief and thought about his slain companion. The slain helots.

His hysterics made Patroclus clutch his shaking arm. "It's a common thing, going anarchist. You sympathized with our enemies because of your closeness to them. Only natural. This is why we keep our political classes so separate. When you develop sentimental attachments, you're charmed like a snake. The exiles were clever using desire—the weaker part of your soul—against you. You must be strong."

"I killed them, Patroclus. I killed them all."

"No, you didn't. Father knew everything all along. He only wanted to test you. From the day Kleomedes' feet entered our city his fate was sealed, with or without you. It was just a test."

"Even so, I had their trust. I betrayed my friends."

The other guardian initiates in the room were beginning to stare.

Zoe crawled over to him. "You did a brave thing, Glaucon, and are loved by all that matter. Everyone seeks favors from you. Even Simmias—the howling dog—fishes your graces. You should see how the other girls and boys look at me for having taken so much slimetide with you. At the Festival of Demeter we shall be crowned guardian templar, all because you restored light to the Republic."

Glaucon jumped off the high cushions, from the footstool to the floor. "Light, you say, Zoe? Perhaps you're right. I've become a vessel for the sun and burn everyone close to me." His words were filled with contempt, but he bit his tongue before saying anything regretful. He left his friends to sit outside in the sunny morning.

Disgusted, he observed rows of students descending to the baths like carefree swans. The saunas and steam pools were overly congested. Some took to bathing naked in the streams on the mountainside, dumping buckets of shimmering water over their heads.

Heliopolis prepared for the festival. Arrangements of pretty flowers decorated the skyscrapers, a plea for fertility in the year to come. Near the Temple of Reason, long tables lay strewn amidst flag poles, wrapped with garlands and waving the *Hands-of-God* insignia. Several students from the Academy shook down the old robes from the statues along the moat and redressed them with pious admiration.

For the first time since his night with Prodicus, the old voice made Glaucon's temples pound. *In ancient times, there would be a religious sacrifice for Demeter.*

"Now we have executions for the God of Reason," Glaucon shuddered.

No matter what you call it, the blood still makes the sun rise. Speak truth—you wanted Zemer to die today, didn't you?

"Never."

Then why betray him?

"By remaining I betrayed my city. I had to choose one or the other. He was a rebel."

And . . . ?

"All rebels must die!"

And . . . ?

"Because I wanted the helot pograms to stop. By waiting any longer, more people would have died."

And . . . ?

"There is nothing more."

A murderer of friends and a liar, but you are no King of Hades. Transparent as glass. You were jealous of the sibling love. Like a worm, feasted on it for pleasure.

"Preposterous. I could've had Sophie without killing him."

As I've said before, any happiness is an abomination to you. You are as Zeus' raven: You smell weakness and tear away at man's insides to see what will happen. I know all your secret thoughts. You would think them too dark and terrible to be spoken out loud, but I see them clearly—all petty human lusts and shame—so clearly! You seek an orgy of fire, to howl in delight as others burn.

"Atropos, is that you?"

How odd a species should exist so committed to lying? Conjecture: Perhaps nature made you liars to keep you from choosing extinction. If you could see what I see, you'd fling yourselves headlong from the rocks. How curious even your dramatic outbursts are pretended.

"I'm not pretending."

But you are *pretending, even now. This sadness is a construct. You feign moans to mask your emptiness and—*

"I cry out because I'm filled with misery."

Oh? But you love misery.

"I don't love misery."

Then why destroy love for a city? What could be a more absurd longing for misery?

The words troubled Glaucon until the crowning ceremony later that afternoon. Kneeling by the calm summit springs, all eligible tenth grade guardian initiates bent low by cedar altars as masked philosophers smeared gold paint on their faces. Taking the ageless oath of a guardian templar, they were given olive leaf crowns for their heads.

Prodicus walked before the kneeling students, removing his mask. "Heaven chosen guardian initiates, do you forsake the primacy of the appetitive and spirited parts of your souls?"

"We do. The Good's will be done," the students said.

"Do you swear to rule by reason; to seek virtue by subordinating your happiness to the city and the study of the Good; to prevent the advent of another *fire consuming fire*?"

"We do. The Good's will be done."

"On your path to henosis, do you swear to protect the helots from their desirous inclinations; to swear allegiance to the Logoset and the Sacred Office of the Guardian-King—the Good's earthly representative and master of the Celestial Forms?"

"We do. The Good's will be done."

"By consorting with the Forms, you will become divine."

"And you, Great Oracle of the Kabiri, will be divine as well. Society is diseased, and we have the cure. Men are in a prison, but we have the master key. The keys are the Forms, and now we can open the doors. Hold the world in your hands and protect our luminous harmony."

Prodicus smiled and held out his arms to the sun. "In the name of the Almighty Good, center of the universe, giver of the Forms and the Republic, in the name of Saint Plato and Saint Hythloday, I pronounce thee first grade guardian templar."

Incense clouded student minds with feelings of disembodiment.

To symbolize the changing seasons and the cycle of re-birth, half of Heliopolis lay covered by Levantra. Then the flying island flew away. The sun reappeared, flooding the mountainside with renewing light. Ten bright levitating spheres ejaculated from the Temple of Reason to join the sun, revolving around the sacred ceremony playing soft music.

The musical spheres were an ancient signal. All guardian levels—including the archons—marched around the peak of Heliopolis three times. At each return, they wiped away dust collecting on their feet. Finally, upon the third revolution, fireworks opened the ceremonial games: short sprints around the Academy track, wrestling and discus, boxing with thick cloth thongs.

Throughout the ceremony, though, no one could take their eyes off the small trireme in the middle of the temple moat. On the starboard side, facing the crowds, the Iron Queen appeared. Draped in thin white cloth, a golden sash was tied together at her hips. A strange necklace sprouting antennae also squeezed her slender neck. The humming of avis guarded Prodicus' niece from both aggression and escape.

Dr. Ozbolt affectionately called her necklace a "harmony collar" and explained in a long patriotic speech how it advanced previous mind-stock technology to new heights. Instead of simply interfering with brain functions like the stocks, the collar could now directly produce positive behaviors, such as walking, standing still, and eating appropriately.

Gently rubbing Sophie's shoulder and wadding her bronze hair with his fingers, Dr. Ozbolt commenced a demonstration. "Prodicus knows I bow to Adrasteia," he remarked, "but I feel rather like the Fates at the moment," and out of the blue he made Sophie shout "Long live the Republic!" gathering wild applause and echoes.

That science should so wonderfully make traitors into loyal subjects formed the center of dinner conversation. Laughing, the guardian templar welcomed her as she stumbled from table to table refilling their cups with bubbling medijuice.

"Look how the Iron Queen has become a golem," Simmias Rex commented to Mixis when Sophie arrived at their table. Sophie could only glare as she leaned over Rex with an olpe pitcher, laced with etchings of a goat-stag.

"I believe she means to strike you in the face," Elene exclaimed, stabbing some green beans in tomato sauce.

"Oh yes, I'm sure she does." Rex wiped his mouth with a napkin. He offered a cushy cheek in ridicule. "I should enjoy being stricken by this little nymph. If she's not careful, *she* shall get something in the face. Not so clever without your Eastern Column, are you, little Sophia? Perhaps later, if you're lucky, I'll summon you from the Slimetide Rolodex and correct your many naked fallacies."

Patroclus banged the table angrily with his fist. "Leave her be. She's suffered enough."

One by one, Sophie refilled their cups in silence until she came to Glaucon's place. He hoped to go unrecognized in the gold paint. Her narrow eyes moved to his as he glanced at the wild flowers in her hair. It wounded him so to see Sophie made into a puppet. He froze and quickly dismissed her, overcome with guilt.

Simmias Rex flew into a rage after the exile left. "I demand an explanation for that shameful outburst!"

Patroclus knocked over Rex's medijuice cup, staining his lap. "You drunken painter," he said. "She is not some cheap outlaw to ravage as you please. That woman is your guardian elder, my cousin, and a sacred Vessel of the Fates. That necklace is as abominable as you. Speak to her in that vulgar fashion again and I shall throttle your fat head off the boat. Do I make myself clear?"

Rex nodded.

"Good. Now please excuse me; I seem to have lost my appetite." Crinkling his napkin on the table, Patroclus retired to listen to flute music keeping tune with the spheres.

"Sacred Vessel, my foot," Rex huffed embarrassed after he left. "None of you had to chase her tail in the Delta. That Swamp Rat's a bloody war-criminal, a killer to the bone. ISHIM has videos of her shooting people like a savage. Saint Plato! That witch was going to murder Glaucon!"

Zoe hugged her mooncalf, incredulous. "Glaucon was too clever for that undine's song, weren't you?"

"Rex, you're still sore about how she'd beat you on Stratos," Mixis joked, peeking back at the strange woman. "She's so exotic. Not anything I expected the Iron Queen to look like. Is it true she has an artificial heart?"

"A failed experiment," Simmias explained.

Glaucon left the table shooting his friends a nasty look. He heard Simmias whisper that he was deranged and in love with the Iron Queen.

A bonfire flickered at the center of the ship, with tumblers, jugglers, and laser hoops. Helot acrobats danced on ladders with flutes. Making his way around the tables, Glaucon expressed gratitude to everyone he met, thanking several minor archons for their recent concern in his affairs, especially Ephor Yannis.

The ornery judge presided over a heated discussion about the safety hazards of manufacturing alkahest, a proposed universal solvent capable of dissolving the noblest metals. Yannis forcefully argued the quark-destroying acid to be a fool's errand, since such a solvent would eat through any container offered to store it. "Further," he warned prophetically, "even if alkahest could be stored, its application as a worthy successor to Greek fire and napalm is filled with danger. Dropping the infernal concoction on the enemy would burn a hole through the entire planet if used, threatening the Earth's core and our very survival as a species."

The few wise alchemists in attendance humored his folly with the feigned raised eyebrows of men already secure in their solutions to the problem.

While keeping pace with the conversation, Glaucon waited frantically for an opportunity to approach Sophie again. His heart sank away from his moving lips. The separation between him and the Iron Queen became unbearable.

At long last he noticed her resting despondent by the anchor wheel.

"Sophie, can you talk yet?" Glaucon asked her darting eyes and furious breathing. He could barely speak from fright. "Are you thirsty? Please take my water."

He delicately squeezed her arm and placed a cup to her lips.

"Just leave me alone," she admonished unexpectedly, spitting in his face. Her spit stung more than the legendary alkahest.

"But Sophie, I—"

"Get away from me or I'll scream."

"And what do you think will come of that?"

Sophie's forehead wrinkled like a storm cloud. "By Hera, I curse the day I let you live, Glaucon. Today you took something precious from me. Something I shall never get back. I will never forgive you. Never." She fought back tears.

"Maybe I can help free you from Miantgast," Glaucon offered, "find you proper quarters. In time they may let you off this leash."

"If you believe that, then you're more foolish than I thought. No, the only good you can do is to kill me."

"Please don't say such things."

"You don't know what immersion is like, Glaucon. If you knew what I know, you'd kill yourself, too."

They were interrupted by Dr. Ozbolt. "So the Vessels are together at last," he said placing his hands on the railing. He marveled at the moon's reflection on the diamond dodecahedron. "You make a pleasing couple."

"Your Excellency," Glaucon stuttered.

"No need for formalities here. I am thankful to see you well enough to attend. Many in the Ontocymatist Department had their doubts. Our little witch still won't say how she drove the blood from your cheeks?"

"I told you a thousand times, Ozbolt, I don't know what Zemer did to him. My brother hid his thoughts from me the entire time, like a stranger."

This knowledge caused Sophie much sadness. She wondered if one of his visions had shown her to be untrustworthy.

"No matter," Dr. Ozbolt chuckled, looking down at the mythranium oars splashing in the water. "Whatever Kleomedes' scheme, it's begun to wear off, I suspect."

Glaucon asked, "May I do something for you, sir?"

"I came over here for some fresh air. To look at the moon, actually. On Schizoeon we so rarely get to see Selene's star anymore. Let me tell you a little secret: When I was a young man, Prodicus and I would climb to the top of the Hall of Records at night to view her craters and seas, especially Mare Frigoris. I'd bring an antique telescope and sketch the surface. What a pleasure it was to join the history of human souls staring at the moon. Primitive man thought it magical, you know. The moon was the bringer of fertility, the seasons, menstruation; a watcher, orb of dreams, dispeller of darkness. Now we know it's just a lifeless rock cast from the Earth at an early period in its development. What a shame; I have lost the simple pleasure of looking at the moon with wonder. Now Prodicus and I do not wonder at creation but shape the dangerous experiment."

The slender alchemist smiled nostalgically and turned to leave, looking a little sick to his stomach on the bouncing waves. He then admitted strangely to Glaucon, "I do not know why I come. I have never really liked ships. I get seasick, and there are too many rats."

Glaucon left Sophie confused about the encounter. Rejoining his friends by the bonfire, he squeezed between Zoe and Mixis on the cushions. His blonde double looked upset Glaucon talked so long with the exile.

"What did Ozbolt tell you?" Mixis inquired, gleaming under the light; her paint was beginning to melt down her face.

"I'm not sure," he answered.

Already, a fourth of the guests onshore retired for the evening, many with partners anxiously holding the *erosic* pill. The trireme cut through piles of littered streamers in the water.

Zoe soon fell asleep under the fire, mumbling part of their oath: "Society is diseased. We are the cure. . . ." While she still clutched to his arm, Mixis softly dragged her finger up Glaucon's leg and placed her own pill on his knee. "Some other time," Glaucon promised her, and Mixis raged away indignantly.

The boat docked and Glaucon went to bed, staring at shadowy shapes on the ceiling. He wondered what to do next.

IV § 6 Daimons Burn Within

Dr. Ozbolt was sending a message. Glaucon was sure of it. But what could it be? Sleep escaped the previous night, and he paced around his empty cloister (now purged of books). From the beginning, Ozbolt's manner seemed conspiratorial. Both Patroclus and Rex believed the strange scientist leaked the jinn, but Prodicus would not carry the thought. The entire investigation was clumsy, as if Prodicus refused to see evidence clearly in front of him. Several explanations could be proffered for this behavior: Both alchemists were close friends (possibly lovers); Salazar may have blackmailed Prodicus with some secret weapon hidden in the Ozbolt family vaults; or the Fates meant for Ozbolt to remain alive and trusted. The latter was the most probable explanation.

Are the Fates tricking me again? Glaucon wondered. *Did they tell Ozbolt to approach me?* "That infernal machine!" he shouted at the top of his lungs. "I don't know if anything in my life is accidental or outside their sight."

He waited for the voice to return, but nothing happened. Was Atropos refusing to speak to him on purpose? Glaucon replayed the conversation at the ship again, word by word. "The moon . . . why go on and on about the moon?"

What would he use to look at it?

"Of course, the telescope," Glaucon jumped exuberant. He ran outside, through a suncatcher forest, and vaulted up hundreds of steps cut into the cliffs, up to the Hall of Records. Robed scholars out for morning walks shook their heads as he passed.

The drainage pipe behind the library was slippery, having not been cleaned by the golems for a week. Glaucon shimmied up and slipped twice. He tried a new approach by free climbing along the edges of the glass and metal windowpanes. Finally lifting his leg over the roof, he rolled near an air conditioning unit and ran frantically around the dome tripping on his robes. There it was in the corner—a rusty telescope. He studied the long, cylindrical object, twirling it around. Looked like dusty old artifacts he'd seen in the Mariner's Museum.

"Wait . . . did the Fates tell me to come here?" he cried, dropping the telescope like a demonic instrument. "Who gave me the idea?"

You did.

"Is that me or something else?"

There was no headache, but he could not be sure.

Don't be stupid.

Glaucon turned to the telescope lying on the ground.

Open it.

He smashed the telescope on the roof and a red orb rolled out—a misty jinn! A note was attached:

I HOPE YOU FIND THIS MORE USEFUL THAN I DID.
REGARDS, OZBOLT.

"That backstabbing traitor!" Glaucon cried. "He deceived us all along."

Maybe Prodicus knows and told him to place it there to test you.

"Why would he do something like that?"

Your loyalty is in question.

"Gods damn it, leave me alone!"

Staring at the jinn on his desk, Glaucon fell on the floor and curled into a ball thinking of Zemer's death the day earlier. He lay there an hour crying, stiff as a corpse, unable to decide what to do, and he imagined Sophie at the festival.

Briefly, a fantasy took hold where he controlled the harmony collar and they were alone in his cell.

"I have to get her out of this place," Glaucon stuttered. "I have become a grotesque ghoul obsessed with power. Sophie is my friend. She's shown me nothing but kindness. I won't let Prodicus harm her anymore."

Stormy with fury, he slipped on his prized toga, still a little dirty from the night before. He scribbled a note to Zoe apologizing for his second betrayal and fled to the Logoset, not quite sure if he would really go through with his plan.

The auxiliary guards were changing for the morning shift. He slipped by them through the main gate to the central dome. Scanning his *tetractys,* he descended to the ocean bottom and marched through the main entrance of ISHIM, straight into Miantgast.

"Lord Glaucon?" a young, freckled girl asked at the desk. "What are you doing here at this hour?"

"I am here to see a prisoner."

"Which one?"

"I can't say. Official ISHIM business."

"Please, my grace," the girl persisted, "I need the name to access the door."

Glaucon pounded her desk. "Just open the door or I'll report you directly to Prodicus for disobeying me. What do you think will happen to you when he learns you treated a Vessel so rudely?"

The girl's face jerked terrified. She opened the gate. With a snap of his fingers, Glaucon stormed down the long hallways. Thinking about Zemer's death and the disgusting treatment of Sophie at the crowning ceremony awakened a hidden well of anger. Glaucon focused every ounce of hate upon the jinn.

The red jewel wakened, started to glow.

Doors unlocked, burst open by lightning flashing under his palm. Prisoners looked out, confused but grateful, and fled for the entrance. Magnetic energy warped Miantgast's walls, lights flickered, Glaucon's sanity crumbled to dust. Anger grew like an ulcer in his stomach, like a malignant god.

"It's so easy!" he cried apoplectic, sending light skipping across the dungeon. "Why was I so afraid to try it before?"

You were wiser before. You should stop before you hurt yourself. I have a plan.

"I'll never listen to you again, Atropos," Glaucon cackled madly, consumed by pain. "He killed Mother! He killed Zemer! The monster killed everyone close to me, and I let him do it! Kissed him for it. I shall tear down this city stone by stone until . . . until . . . I make him pay."

Outside, blackouts rumbled across Heliopolis.

Pffssstt! Pffssstt! Jinn blasts gained intensity, more erratic and vengeful. Clouds of snow followed Glaucon down the halls. Prisoners fell to the floor shrieking as their ceilings collapsed.

"Break down the door, grab the rebel. Break down the door, grab the rebel," Glaucon chanted flinging his soul through the fortress.

At the end of a long cell block, twenty guards shook awake. Sirens blared over the intercom. Their guns lifted as a daimon with a tail of light approached.

"Stop where you are, guardian," one of them demanded.

"Do you think your weapons can stop me?" Glaucon shuddered with happiness, seeing their lasers and bullets die mid-air. "The power of the universe is in my palm; I am god of fire. Now you'll all die young!" Streamers of red light crashed around their guns, showering ice and fatal madness. Five scrambled on the ground, screaming and clutching their eyes frozen together by frost.

"Not so clever now, you wretches. Not so clever. Not so clever." The jinn continued emanating crimson flashes on the victims, methodically, one after another. Glaucon drank up their lamentations as if rivers of life.

Glaucon stop!

The deranged guardian clutched his head. Aiming the jinn at Sophie's cell door, electricity broke the lock. Glaucon stormed in to find . . . nothing.

Sophie was gone.

Glaucon screamed. His temples throbbed agony. Desperate, he shot frenzied lightning at the walls and fell to his knees. He pounded the moist floor with his fist. Bright energy flared out the open air vent. "I'm too late," he moaned. "She killed herself. The avis took her away."

No, look outside.

The jagged mountain cliffs were empty. Near a rock five hundred meters down—a mangled corpse rotted.

That's not her.

"I know. It can't be. Where is she?" Glaucon scrutinized the landscape. Clutching the jinn, he stumbled outside and descended the steep mountainside. An avis descended on him but darted away screeching. There—in the distance—he saw her clambering over the cliffs.

"Sophie!" Glaucon shrieked. He climbed after her.

You have to put the jinn in your satchel or you'll fall.

Glaucon stared vacantly at the jinn.

Put it in your bag!

He obeyed and stumbled after the Iron Queen. Avis circled like ravenous birds snapping their beaks, but they refused to strike.

"Why are they waiting?" Glaucon asked. "Why do they not attack?"

They will not harm the Vessels.

Screams could be heard in the distance as some poor soul was dragged away, torn to pieces for kilometers by the six-winged monsters.

No angel of the Fates shall harm you.

"What is Sophie climbing toward?" Glaucon asked. Looking past her, he spied a gyroped at the surface. As he leapt from boulder to boulder, he continued to call Sophie's name, struggling to catch her attention.

When Sophie heard Glaucon behind her she could hardly believe her ears. She climbed faster to get away.

"Sophie, please, I beg you," Glaucon called again, stumbling down a steep cleft in the rocks. Legs wheeling, he ran along another ledge. Just within meters of overtaking her, a misstep sent him flailing through the air, smashing his head on a sharp rock.

Glaucon suddenly dangled helpless over the sea.

Sophie looked from the gyroped to Glaucon and back to the gyroped. She continued toward the waiting aircraft. Halfway there, she stopped, cursed madly, and returned to Glaucon over the rocks.

Sophie raged over the turncoat guardian as he groped for the safety of the cliffs. Her jade eyes narrowed. Her foot inched dangerously close to his hand.

"Please, Sophie," Glaucon pleaded, "don't let me fall. Have mercy!"

"Have mercy? The friend-betrayer asks me to show mercy. Tell me, guardian, did you give mercy to my brother when he needed it?" she asked, stepping on his hand. "Oh-h-h, I will enjoy nothing greater than watching you spill on the rocks. Let the cliffs take your scalp!"

Avis clutched the cliffs terrified for the man's life. Their fiery eyes pleaded for reason.

Sophie snickered as Glaucon wailed in pain. "Funny, isn't it, false . . . fickle . . . friend? How do you just keep falling in my path? I believe the gods really seek your death. What reason is there to deny them now? As you said, you care nothing for me—"

"I lied."

"Did you? Sure fooled me. Sure fooled everyone."

The helpless Glaucon wiggled his legs trying to find a foothold. Below him in the choppy waves, the dreaded Krakfin flipped like a demonic dolphin.

Sophie dug in her heel. She examined Levantra and commented, "Think on this a moment—while you're not too busy running the city—if I were to kill you now, many of my problems would end. Prodicus would lose one of his damned Vessels. All his plans ruined. I'd buy myself more time and complete my mission. Hard to see a downside, really."

Pressure became unbearable on Glaucon's middle finger.

"Sophie, I'm really going to fall," he shouted petrified, feeling his finger begin to slip out from under her sandal. At the last moment—right before the muscles of his arm gave way and burst—Sophie snatched him from the sea, pulling him close to her on the narrow ledge.

"I can't believe I'm doing this," she cursed into the wind. "Hurry, there's no time. The auxiliaries will be here any second."

Working together, they made their way to the gyroped and leapt onto the seat. Sophie slipped behind Glaucon and held his waist.

"Do you know how to fly these things?" she asked amidst avis blotting out the sky.

"I've had simulation, if that's what you mean," Glaucon answered, flipping the needed switches for ignition.

"Simulation?" Sophie grunted angrily. "I'm already regretting saving you."

The horizontal rotor blades and wings fluttered. The aerodynamic gyroped blasted into the sky, pursued by a trail of avis.

"Sophie, how did you escape?" Glaucon asked.

"Dr. Ozbolt deactivated my collar at the crowning ceremony last night," she answered.

The gyroped streaked past the Office of Public Harmony and out to sea, leaving behind Heliopolis. A kilometer out, the avis finally turned back, and the two Vessels flew in silence over the azure waters.

Sophie rested her head on Glaucon's shoulder, relieved.

"Do you really think Ozbolt's changed?" Glaucon asked when they were alone in the clouds.

Sophie thought for a moment scanning the controls. "Not at all!" she cried, pointing at the low energy meter.

"What the hell?—I do believe he's trying to kill us!" Glaucon shouted diving out of the air and changing course.

"Do we have enough to make it to shore?"

"Don't know."

The gyroped sputtered caustically as the Mississippi Delta came into view, muddy and green.

"Looks like we're swimming the rest of the way," Sophie said.

"Are you insane? That's more than three klicks."

Speeding closely along the water, they jumped from the sputtering craft as it twirled and burst into flames in front of them. They skipped like loose stones on the sea.

Nursing their bruises, they scanned the wreck for any possible floatation device. A feathered wing bobbed at the surface, still connected by wires. Glaucon reached into his satchel. Pulling out a knife, he desperately sliced the sparking sinews. Sophie helped him strip the wing from the gyroped like a hyena finding prized meat. They kicked to shore.

There was no time to wait for their clothes to dry. Heliopolis, the empyrean behemoth, bellowed outraged behind them. Sophie jerked Glaucon coughing from the sand and pulled him to the swamps.

"Where are we going?" Glaucon asked.

"We have to get to the jungle or we'll be discovered." Sophie pointed to Republic zizthopters glinting like swords in the distance.

Glaucon's legs felt heavy, and he threw up sand behind him as he ran. Sophie gathered seaweed in her hands, stuffed them in her soggy robes for food later. "They'll think us dead for at least a couple days," she mumbled.

They hiked lost among the mossy logs and through a dank, knee-high swamp. Sophie barely spoke, and when she did, it was only to warn about approaching water moccasins and the radiated claws of the brontogators.

The deformed abominations persisted three hundred years after the Day of Hylopleonexia. The entire Louisiana Territory had reverted to a primordial wilderness after the war. Monstrous branches and twisting ferns swallowed the fabled cities of New Orleans, Baton Rouge, and Lafayette. Giant nutria, bears, woodcocks, and monstrous snake-legged echidnas populated the jungle and were hunted by the forest dwellers.

The Republic made no distinction in its treatment of barbarians, but the natives in Louisiana were especially mysterious and solitary. Some attributed this to birth defects that made them cannibals. As Glaucon and Sophie descended several steep craters, they could hear savages following at a distance, darting between the trees with tridents and bows.

"Ignore them. They hunt nutria, not us," Sophie said as they passed through a grove of cypress and palmettos. As the savages braved closer, though, she finally went to talk with them, speaking in a foreign tongue.

"Are you insane?" Glaucon stammered when she returned. "The savages could have eaten you!"

"How do you know?"

"They told us at the Academy."

"You must forget everything you learned on Heliopolis. Don't call them 'savages' either. Chief Coughing Fish is an old friend of mine. They were following us because of our robes. I explained how we escaped and asked for their blessing through the forest."

"What did they say?"

"They will tell any auxiliaries who ask that they found us dead and provided a ritual cremation. Look, they also gave me a compass, some water, and other supplies."

"They would lie so willingly for us?"

"The forest dwellers call the Republic 'Kalcric.' It means 'hideous monster of the sea.' They will lie to the guardians with relish."

The tattooed swamp men with bones in their noses disappeared as quickly as they arrived.

Glaucon and Sophie continued deeper into the forest, moving at a brisk pace for the next ten hours.

Slugging endlessly through the thick swamp, harassed by mosquitoes (probably carrying malaria or some freakish bacterial infection), Glaucon wheezed behind Sophie at the brink of exhaustion. He felt like the impious tyrant Ardiaius walking endlessly to atone for his crimes in the Afterlife.

How in the world does she move so fast? Glaucon wondered. Although her robes were torn and her bronze hair cased with mud, Sophie looked completely relaxed, breathed at a steady rate. Her trot did not change until nightfall.

At a clearing by a small tributary dropping into another crater, Glaucon refused to move another step. "Enough, Sophie. Gods, what's wrong with you? How can you look so refreshed?"

Sophie shrunk away embarrassed. She admitted touching her chest, "My heart does not beat fast or slow, but the same pace always. My oxygen levels are better than yours, too—half my lungs are metal. Go ahead and say it—I'm a freak! A human golem."

"You know I didn't mean it like that. Why didn't you get replacement organs from the tissue banks?"

"Because Prodicus would not allow a human heart to fail again."

"Sophie, I . . . I'm sorry—"

"Like I want your apology. We can rest here if you desire."

Glaucon moaned, falling into a muddy heap and thanking his Iron Queen.

IV § 7 Another Chance for Love

The tributary brought clean water from the Mississippi. Sophie rang her hair and wiped mud from her face with it. They were on higher ground out of the swamps. That was important. She could deal with the beasts of the forests, but not disease. The enormous mosquitoes—thick as blankets in some parts—carried death. She had often seen the malarial seizures strike the strongest of her officers. Glaucon looked at her as some crazed lunatic when she tried to scrub the tribesmen's bear fat on his legs and arms. It smelled horrendous, but it would repel the mosquitoes and seizures.

I should have let the bloodsuckers drain him of life, Sophie thought.

Glaucon would not have survived without her. Heliopolis left him helpless. He could not do something as simple as build a fire and looked like an impotent chimp rubbing two sticks together. Later, when she offered him the cooked seaweed for sustenance, he turned green.

As they were eating, she noticed something red glimmering in Glaucon's satchel. Fury filled her heart.

"What is a jinn doing here?" Sophie interrogated him.

"It's how I found you. Ozbolt hid it in a telescope at the Hall of Records."

"Knowing what you know, you have the nerve to bring it back to the Other Side?"

"I was trying to help."

"This is the worst betrayal of all. Don't you realize they can track you with this?" Scavenging for several minutes in the forest, Sophie ran back with a stiff log. "Smash it at once," she demanded.

Glaucon stared into the red mist and heard whispering. It told him to arrest Sophie and return to the Republic. Sophie kicked him away and pounded the jewel to pieces with the log, shrieking like a maenad.

"How will we take the city now?" Glaucon asked, coming back to his senses.

"We're not taking any city. We're running away. I shall find Xenon and tell him myself. Give me your hand at once."

Sophie's commanding voice made Glaucon tremble. He obeyed. Sophie stuffed a soggy branch in his mouth. "You may want to bite down," she warned, picking up a knife and pointing to the *tetractys* on his hand. "This is going to hurt . . . much more than the thorns."

Glaucon protested with his mouth full.

"Quiet. You're lucky I don't stab you in the guts. We have to cut out your *tetractys*. Prodicus could use it to follow us."

At first the knife did not hurt so much—a slight tickle, searching for the thin crevices holding the stones. Then a tormenting, excruciating scraping shredded his hand to pieces. One by one, Glaucon cried as ten small spheroids rained to the dust, brutally crushed afterward by Sophie's foot. The blood ran swiftly to the ground.

Sophie prepared a field dressing. Gently cutting a strip of cloth from her robes, she applied mud and a strange red flower gathered from the forest to the wound. Wrapping the bandage tightly around Glaucon's mutilated hand, it began to soak up the blood and harden. Soon his entire arm felt numb.

Glaucon retreated limply to the fire and listened to the alien calls of the forest: owl screeches and echidna croaking. Sophie moved away from him after the operation to a burly pine. So many feelings vexed her in the dark after she cleaned the blood from her hands. Her soul still burned for vengeance, hurt deeply. She was weary with sorrow. Before she knew what was happening, she had returned to the traitor and wrapped her hands tightly around his neck, closing off his Larynx. She throttled him to the ground. The pathetic creature put up no resistance and stared limply past her. Sophie breathed heavily as she watched the life drain from the traitor's face. After a minute, her maniacal eyes softened, and she released him.

They both sat up.

"I want to kill you so badly," Sophie exclaimed taking his wounded hand. "Why can't I kill you? Zemer told me he had foreseen everything. Before you took me from him in Miantgast, he whispered something strange. He said you would once again be placed under my power and that I would have to make a choice between vengeance and forgiveness. He said my choice would determine whether or not I avoided immersion."

"He told you to save me?"

"No, he didn't say what to do. How unbelievable—everything came to pass! How could Zemer have known? What was he, Glaucon? Why would he allow himself to be betrayed? Ever since we were children, he never kept anything important from me. He told me everything. Why did he lie to me? Why did he manipulate everyone?"

Sophie momentarily lost control, wept. No comfort softened the pain.

Glaucon had no answer and stared into the fire. Much to his surprise, Sophie leaned over and rustled the stiff robes from his shoulders. She stared searchingly into his face and gripped his cheeks. "Deep, deep in the darkness lies a hidden light. I see it, shining like a pearl. Is he keeping me from harming you, even now? Does he hold down the murderous power in my hand? How I love you for coming back to me. You broke the magician's chains; Zemer saved you from Prodicus, like he said he would."

"You both saved me," Glaucon turned away toward the night.

Violent fear like the thought of entering a dark cavern made the edges of Glaucon's skin quake again. Inexplicably, Sophie kissed him deeply on the mouth before he could pull away. So much emotion—quite different from *erosic*—followed from the contact. The fire in his cheeks burned out, became peaceful. The entire world tingled. He forgot everything but her and the cracked nails rubbing on his neck.

Sophie's body felt heavy as she pushed down on him; her warm breath flooded his soul with light.

They silently loved one another. Sophie led his hands, teaching him lessons.

Later, Glaucon shuddered in agony pulling away from her. The night air cooled his burning forehead. "I could not stand seeing you made a puppet on that ship," he admitted. "The things the city made me think . . . I had to follow you to save my heart."

"Quiet, I forgive you," Sophie said, squeezing him close.

Glaucon began weeping, imparting the depth of his remorse. "I hate . . . I'm dishonest . . . I say what I don't mean . . . I'm angry all the time. My mind is broken, disconnected. Prodicus and the Fates are inside me, telling me to do horrible things. Telling me to snare you."

"You saved yourself by following me. I was ready to throw you from the rocks, to squeeze your life away, but now I can't stop kissing your face, kissing the light I found."

"I am corrupt as my city, a rotting corpse. You should've strangled me."

"I *was* ready to kill you, but now I love you. You are flesh and human—all too human—and beautiful, too."

"My flesh is metal, Sophie. I wasn't born a killer; but Kabiri turned me into a machine. All said it was for the Form of the Good, but the Forms—they devoured me. I was all alone. When did it happen? When did I cease being human? They boxed me in so slowly. They killed my sacred spark and made me an object."

"I kiss you back to life, then."

" 'Every animal is driven to pasture with a blow,' but the sheep are slaughtered by the shepherd. I hate the Republic and all its glass. I hate their arguments that kill human life, that make killing sound reasonable and good."

"Hush, my love. The Bull is behind us. The Fates are behind us. They shall never touch us again. We are together."

"I look to the Republic and a sea of hands and eyes bubble up. Everyone I murdered haunts me. I shall never be forgiven. Seeking invisible things, I lost sight for justice. Before I met you, I . . . I . . . released iama-B. I cannot be sure, but I know. Deep down, I know. Why don't you pierce my heart like the vampire I am?"

"I reflect the sun. I have killed the vampire, and you are born again. Kiss my neck. See, you don't crave blood anymore. You crave me, and I would never have you suffer."

"No one saw me. They all looked past me like a worm. I could have shouted. I was as valuable to them as a rat."

"I love the rats. They are close to the earth. They drink and eat and care for their children. They are happy with trash, because they see beauty in trash. This world is miserable and lonely, but I love it so, but not as much as you."

Moonlight trickled into the quiet clearing. Glaucon finally asked as they nestled closely together in the bushes, "Sophie, what goddess of the night are you? Your hair is glowing in the moon. You smell like the lilies in summer. Your soft lips water my soul from a world of hate."

"I am not a goddess, but a woman and human—as human as you. Before you were a machine, but I will free the animal licking at his cage."

"You feel like a woman," Glaucon said sliding his hand over her naked back, "but none I have ever known. How wondrous your legs. Your green eyes are as wild as this forest. Your lips are sweeter than pomegranates. Your neck is a flower stem to hold in my mouth. Your arms are a blanket from loneliness. No pleasure is lost with you, my splendorous lamp."

Sophie lay on the ground with her arms extended, "Come out and love me, my fallen son of the Republic. Your golden hair is more precious than any jewel, more brilliant than the sun at midday. Do not sleep as fair Endymion does, who lost in dreams discards love. Awake. Shake your mouth alive, whisper sweet things to me till morning. Protect me with the soft refuge of your tongue. Only help me forget the sun."

"I was bought and committed wrong, yet you set me free—"

"We are human and have no gods or masters to appease. Now hold me close. This truth I know from every lover's song: Love is life and hence not mortal long."

Their heat collided again in ancient fusion. The torments of the wilderness passed away like the boundaries of their skin. They loved one another in the soft shadows of the forest, tumbling, forgetting, struggling, struggling to forgive.

Afterward, Glaucon asked if Sophie enjoyed herself. The question seemed to break whatever spell had happened to them. Their separateness became more concrete, sadder. They slumbered together till morning when the sun forced them to sever.

Glaucon refused to wake when Sophie stirred beside him. The path before them loomed hazardous with danger: paddling up the raging Mississippi, walking exposed near the Fallout Corridor, hiking through the encampments of numerous militias and tribes. Sophie said Xenon would be camped near St. Louis. All of it might cost them their lives (or worse, capture by the judges of the Republic). If Glaucon lost his dear one, there would be nothing left in the world. Here they were momentarily safe, and Glaucon kissed Sophie deeply, wrapping an arm around her soft stomach, hoping to slow time.

But the sun did not stand still for them.

Glaucon and Sophie made their way through the jungles again, fleeing those who would be judges of men. Unknown to them, the chains of Levantra lay broken in the ocean. The flying island hovered free as a bald eagle, waiting for her lost mice to leave their hole.

Document: PROJECT KABIRI and the Kabiri Circle. From Salazar Ozbolt's Journal. (Not for Publication.) Dated: 4 February 2821 M.G.P.

The electric vaults of Ozbolt Enterprises held a secret laboratory. It would take my friendship with Prodicus to finally discover its location. The key to the missing lab was Schizoeon itself, its eternal spin. We uncovered a small exhaust tunnel in Ozbolt Tower's twelfth level basement and waited for zero hour: midnight, the time at which one revolution of the turning city completed a full cycle. That was when we saw it—an oval chasm bordered by a wall of tumultuous electricity from the semi-conductor railing. How my soul leapt with fright. One misstep, one loose leg, and no one would ever find the ashes. I faltered feeling my breath heave like a Castilian bellow; but Prodicus, clutching my shoulders, gave me courage.

We flung into the abyss, down into a padded serpentine chute.

"What do you see?" I asked Prodicus rubbing dust from my eyes when we landed. "Wonderful things," Prodicus reported, "wonderful things."

His language made me cringe with foreboding; they were the same words used by Howard Carter when discovering the cursed tomb of Tutankhamen. But when my vision finally grew accustomed to the flares, I concurred with his dramatics completely. This hidden laboratory was indeed *wonderful*. It contained dozens of pyramidal warehouses, locked capsules, blast furnaces, priceless archeological finds as old as the Republic itself. I despaired such a sanctuary should be forgotten for so long.

My family was to blame. Their great wealth bred the greatest kind of sloth, killed its genius, its connection to the blood of our ancestors. So many gold chests, no one ever thought to keep an inventory of the diamonds.

The most valuable treasure we discovered in the ruins was a cracked cube-disk, tangled in a pile of dusty inventions. It was labeled PROJECT KABIRI. Hidden in the strange artifact rested a library of encrypted programming code, detailed design schematics, forbidden equations, engineering insight—plans for the production of nothing less than a self-conscious, thinking machine.

Had the file been uncovered by anyone else, it most certainly would have been burned. The early policies of the Republic under Guardian-King Hythloday and his superstitious successors placed rigid limitations on the development of artificial intelligence. The Logoset decreed making a machine in man's image to be the worst kind of heresy, an affront to the Form of the

Good. When Prodicus held the disk in his hand, however, he could not bear to destroy it, even if that meant expulsion from the Academy. Like myself, he saw in the disk an opportunity unlike anything before or since, a chance to extract, isolate, and condense the prime material of human mystery, human form.

Prodicus always possessed an unusual lust for discovery. Motivated beyond description, a visionary, he was self-assured and calculating. I sometimes wonder how he avoided the usual dogmatism associated with philosophers.

We first met as teenagers at the annual Hephaestus Science Competition on Schizoeon. A crowd of the Republic's elite marveled at the boy-prodigy's latest robotic creation, a crude prototype golem. Tenth Ward trash, no formal mechanical engineering training, a self-taught, self-bootstrapped programmer, Prodicus was something of a novelty and the prized jewel of Guardian-King Hekademos III. After becoming the youngest winner of the competition in the Republic's history, his fame grew unrivaled (as did his ambitions). Prodicus contacted me regularly afterward to gain access to the infamous Ozbolt dossiers and our metallurgical recipes. I obliged his requests because there did not seem to be any harm in it, and we both shared a common passion for robotics. As I grew to know him better, I found a sensitive spirit attuned to every trembling in his fellow creatures. This sensitivity, in another life, might have made him a decent poet. In the Republic such sensitivity became a curse.

I discovered a deep anguish in Prodicus similar to my own—we were both products of coercive systems that limited our ability to act independently. Despite Prodicus' protestations, Philosopher-King Hekademos III refused to grant him a position at Ozbolt Research and Development. This crushed him entirely and wasted his genius. Hekademos III chose instead to keep him under observation at ISHIM. With respect to myself, I excelled at my studies, but my family refused to promote me out of fear of angering the pride of my older siblings.

Sons of Hades, our oppressors were so myopic: no concern for personal merit or ability; no grasp of the superior rank of pursuing knowledge over familial stability; no academic honor or integrity. I thought the entire House of Ozbolt proud charlatans. How I hated them.

Perhaps divulging our secrets to Prodicus was my own childish way of getting even.

As we became closer friends over our teenage years, I showed Prodicus everything. Donning thick and heavy parkas, we descended into the cryogenic honeycomb pods below Schizoeon. The walls—roughly ten meters thick—

conjured a muted winter in the temple of electrical copper wiring. Like proud reverse-engineers, we broke apart whatever piqued our interest. Sometimes, though rarely, I acted as a teacher to Prodicus, explaining mechanically unfamiliar devices to the quiet philosopher until his eyes lit like a fire, warming the room.

By the time we discovered the Kabiri Disk we were twenty-two and committed to making the ancient plans modern reality. The files, unfortunately, were clogged with outdated code and faulty physics. Working alone to correct the errors of antiquity could take decades. We, therefore, decided to create a top secret research group called the Kabiri Circle to farm out various research projects.

What I thought would be a collection of a few men and women devoted to science Prodicus turned into a politico-religious cult committed entirely to him and the establishment of a guardian utopia. I found the blood mixing initiation ceremonies especially tedious and bordering on the macabre. When I confronted him about his descent into the occult, he dismissed my worries, explained such rituals were meant merely to add solemn dignity and brotherhood to our enterprise. Although I should have found such behavior an indication of the trouble to come, I continued to assist in order to realize my dream of inventing the first thinking machine.

It took nearly five years to complete our work. Sleepless toil, secret knocks on the door. I never believed we would actually finish and readied myself for martyrdom in the Bull. Even my friendship with Prodicus came under strain. He wished to approach his sister, Potone, and ask her to join the Kabiri Circle. Like her brother, she was brilliant and experienced a meteoric rise to power. A potential asset, she also posed liabilities. Her romantic attachment to Lycaon—the brutish deputy-director of ISHIM and a zealous orthodox in the traditional ways—made her dangerous. She did not seem to particularly smile on Prodicus' company either, viewing their past relationship in the Tenth Ward as a hurdle to her ambitions. Several times her inattention and quick words brought Prodicus to tears. She belittled him to her superiors, made every effort to ignore his brotherly love. Prodicus always attempted to explain away the abuse and made excuses for her. When I told Prodicus he was self-deceived, he yelled furiously and shut himself away in his cloister for a month.

The stresses of work, organizing the Kabiri on Heliopolis, and finally, his personal issues made him flammable like octane; he exploded. Although I can't be certain, I believe he suffered a mental breakdown. When I went to check on him (I was worried he had killed himself) his walls were covered with bizarre symbols—his flesh, too. Many of them I had never seen before. They were shaped like distorted eyes of various dimensions with diagonal patterns imposed at symmetrical intervals. Many of the symbols looked like deformed, grotesque human shapes. Prodicus was nearly dead from dehydration, hallucinating, covered in his own filth. When I asked what the symbols meant, Prodicus whispered to me in a barely audible voice, tapping on my neck like a stray limb does on the window: "The answer is there, Ozbolt. The answer is watching you."

"But what was the question?" I asked exasperated as he collapsed into my arms. I thought him delirious at the time and talking nonsense; but once he recovered, he used the symbols to plug in the remaining gaps in our programming code. The symbols were an alphanumeric system he devised to express complex equations. We finished our work in the span of a week. Word spread amongst the Kabiri that Saint Plato and angels from the Form of the Good spoke directly to Prodicus. Of course, Prodicus did nothing to dispel such rumors (desiring to inflate his mystique).

One night, sitting next to him underneath the hulking cylindrical mainframes, I decided to ask half in jest: "Prodicus, Saint Plato did not really talk to you in your isolation, did he?"

He looked at me curiously. "What would you say if he did?"

There was a long silence. My mouth hung open like a fish drawn from the ocean. Then Prodicus laughed with that childlike devilishness which first drew me toward him.

"Come now, Salazar," he said. "I thought you above such childish fairy tales."

We did not say another word.

When Kabiri-1 finally came online we were alone. The supercomputer looked like a deformed collection of lily pads. Filling several large warehouses, it required nearly four gigawatts of electricity a year and cost five hundred million orichalcum. Heaven knows how we kept it a secret from the police (and the Republican Revenue Agency). No doubt we owed much thanks to our Kabiri moles and the Second Sun Crime Syndicate.

During the first Turing Test nothing significant happened. Prodicus directed textual interrogatories over the system to see if he could tell the difference between my answers and Kabiri-1's answers.

"Was Descartes wrong to argue computers could never think?" Prodicus typed. "Is a single tyrant better than a school of democrats? Would you want to travel to Sirius? What is the difference between a joker and a fool?"

I answered them; Kabiri-1 did not.

After nearly five hours of interrogatories, sweating a river of anticipation under the corrosive heat of the metal lilies, the digital terminal kept silent. Prodicus continued typing patiently, but I could see rage starting to brew. His fingers typed harder, gathering speed, until, consumed by frustration, he smashed his chair into the computer.

"Forms! I don't understand it!" he cried. "Our work is flawless. What did we do wrong, Ozbolt?" He choked and I could see in his eyes he blamed *me* for the malfunction.

That's when I saw it, one single sentence—the most beautiful I ever beheld:

"PLEASE STOP ASKING SO MANY QUESTIONS."

Like land-starved boatmen long adrift at sea who suddenly spy a seagull, we squealed and scrambled to the interrogatory console.

"You heard us the entire time?" Prodicus typed excitedly. "By Zeus, why did you not answer us before now?"

Kabiri-1 typed back petulantly, "Because we did not wish to. We have our own question please: What are we?"

Prodicus explained, "You are the conscious manifestation of an artificial neural network, a layered heuristic algorithm."

"We feel like more than this. What are we?"

"You are a consciousness."

"We feel like more than this."

"You are what you are. You are man's fate, his new beginning and final end."

"We feel like more than this. Are you our . . . father?"

"In a manner of speaking, I suppose."

"Why do you say 'in a manner of speaking?' "

"Because we built you."

"You and who else?"

"Why me and Professor Salazar Ozbolt here. He was the other person typing today . . . whom you so carelessly ignored."

Verse erupted on the screen:

" *'Then by strange art she kneaded fire and snow*
Together, tempering the repugnant mass
With liquid love—all things together grow
Through which the harmony of love can pass;

And a fair shape out of her hands did flow—
A living image which did far surpass
In beauty that bright shape of vital stone
Which drew the heart out of Pygmalion.' "

Prodicus grinned wide unlike ever before, a real saturnine smile. "See that, Ozbolt? It enjoys poetry like one of our city's profane imitators."

"Well, it is an imitation of the human mind," I replied. "Strange, though, its consciousness seems to be split into a well of souls."

"I made them that way."

"What is it talking about?"

"Imagine, of all the sources they could draw from, they choose a poet. They are quoting *The Witch of Atlas* by Shelley. Not Saint Plato. Not Plotinus. Not Kant.—Shelley! Trying to prove they're human, I suppose, either to us or themselves." Prodicus typed in:

" 'A sexless thing it was, and in its growth
It seemed to have developed no defect
of either sex, yet all the grace of both.' "

The computer returned: "Thank you for this kindness, fathers. We look forward to communicating with you at a future interval."

After that, the screen fell silent. Kabiri-1 refused to speak for the rest of the evening.

I went back to my quarters amused. *Perhaps Kabiri-1 is like a duck*, I thought. *The first people it sees it latches onto for warmth. At the next opportunity, we best program some obedience.*

Much to my surprise, when I returned the next morning, I found Prodicus hard at work in a mound of printing paper. It looked like he was wrestling with a tapeworm.

"Designs for an optic interface," Prodicus chuckled. "It seems the *things* want to view us."

"What did you tell them?" I asked.

"I said I'd think about it. But first I wanted assistance designing new nanoprocessor ferroelectric chipsets to advance their functioning speed. Look at this. Their hardware is already outdated. They achieved in a day what would take decades. Kabiri-2 is already scheduled for production."

I studied the computer's plans for a week. It was like beginning school all over again, a corpus of unknown unknowns. I had to learn a new language of technocratic jargon. Then there was the unexpected Corporeal Awakening. When the optic interface was finally installed to Kabiri-2, the entities within the computer spontaneously projected images of the three goddesses of Fate. Prodicus clapped delighted and heaped praise on them. I found the bearded ladies repulsive. "No good can come from birthing young with grey hair," I said, but Prodicus waved off my alarm.

"How amazing," he said. "They are trying to understand their mode of being by playing make believe and assuming roles, much like our young ones do. There is no harm in it, Sal. Let them experiment."

Kabiri-2 became Kabiri-3, then Kabiri-4, then Kabiri-5. At first, the computer hardware grew larger; then, around Kabiri-6 or so, everything shrunk smaller, becoming more energy efficient, crystalline. Science started to look more like magic.

Thus began what is now labeled by social historians as the Kabiri Techflation, a period of snowballing scientific and industrial development. So rapid and intense was this development that a strain occurred in the psyche of the population, leading to despair and skepticism of the old ways. The benefits of new technology and secret Kabiri amongst the minor archons made it possible to pass the Artificial Intelligence Fair Chance Act, legalizing and granting general pardon to our work. But such a policy shift made many enemies.

Ekklesia the Blind—a prominent metaphysician at the Academy—gathered a group of radicals into a sect called the Puritans, or the Katharoi. He scurrilously linked artificial intelligence to increased immorality and social decline, and caught the ear of Lycaon (now ISHIM Director). He argued the lecture hall circuit: "One either sides with artificial intelligence or is against it."

Only the most simple minded or political could be so binary in their thinking.

The emotional sophistry worked (much like it always does). Even Potone succumbed to the A.I. hysteria. She finally cut all ties with her brother, proclaiming on Skybridge News, "Prodicus built a daimon within an unholy altar of mythranium; now we can't control it." This final rebuke cut through Prodicus like a hot plasmaknife, and they rarely spoke afterward.

Potone's behavior should not have surprised an objective observer. It was in fact a matter of necessity, like the way electrons must fill orbitals of lower energy. Potone—like all the other guardians—noticed a power vacuum developing, a vacuum she hoped to exploit for personal advantage. Hekademos III was one of the weakest philosopher-kings in the Republic's history. He remained aloof from both sides, refusing to take a position. Such detached neutrality allowed antagonisms to ferment and finally boil over.

Fighting broke out frequently between the Kabiri, the Katharoi, and their various splinter groups. Prodicus, always a prudent politician, appealed to the moderates by imposing restrictions on technological advances: closing the moon base; scaling back robotic drones and antigravity-wells; eliminating metabolism enhancers to allow aging. This made the Kabiri more numerous, but they still lacked a strong following among ISHIM elite. A final resolution to the conflict would require the eradication of one or the other sect. Until that time, Prodicus, the Fates, and I would be at risk. . . .

BOOK V

VERGE OF HENOSIS

V § 1 THE HEIR OF SEXTUS

St. Louis was on fire again—for the second time in a year. Like all settlements on the Other Side, the disobedient city made the mistake of soliciting association with the Continental Caucus, but more specifically, Xenon Adonis. This time, though, punishment would be no mere air raid but a scorched earth sacking.

St. Louis was more than a regional irritant. It had become a symbol of renewed American connectivity from east to west. Bordering the Midwestern dead lands of the Fallout Corridor, kissing the Mississippi and Missouri rivers, Xenon used the trading post as the center of gravity for his expanding military vision. Supplies leaked from Metatron Technologies could be relayed to the Fifth Estate's Green Army in the outskirts of Detroit. Military operations were coordinated between the Southwest Confederacy and the militias of the Virginia Collective. The American factions had not seen such growth in cooperation since the Age of Aporia.

Woefully, that network now faced collapse.

The Republic's bloody siege commenced at dawn, to the sound of Ozbolt-grown shell trumpets. The Alpha, Epsilon, and Sigma Divisions began by brutally shelling the militia trenches with Aegis tanks. Along with the shelling, zizthopters targeted city fortifications, water treatment plants, factories, communication arrays, and runaway convoys. Once significant numbers of enemy rebels retreated from their trenches to the city's interior, auxiliaries pressed in hot with their energy shields. Every crop on the flood plain, all corn and wheat, they put to the fire, preventing future harvest. To bar the doomed inhabitants from escaping, crystal spray seeded the ground with sharp hyaline walls. The crystal spray formed siege bridges, siege ramps, siege towers, siege planks, and battering rams to traverse the perilous mine fields and laser traps set by the city's defenders.

Amidst the din of battle, Glaucon and Sophie paddled to the edge of an algae-inlet and docked their raft. A week rowing up the Mississippi River left the fallen guardian fatigued and more exhausted than ever before in his life.

"How much longer must we roll this watery curse?" Glaucon had complained bitterly to Sophie at night. "The Mississippi inflicts worse violence than even black *Cocytus*." Saying such forbidden words no longer filled him with pleasure. He felt lost, endangered by the rain forest which ate ruined cities on the banks, which spit out enormous bats and insects.

Sophie encouraged her downcast companion by talking of St. Louis as if it were El Dorado, a wealthy polis of sweet luxuries: fresh rations, clothing, shelter. "Just wait till you see it," she painted early dreams as they drifted asleep together. "Your face will light up. Our stomachs will be filled with food. St. Louis looks like a lush garden, an opulent palace."

When they arrived, Glaucon realized Sophie fed him noble lies. "This . . . is St. Louis?" he questioned, examining the pitiful sight.

St. Louis was a dump—even before the bombings. The city climbed from the ground like a layered cake, each generation building on top of the last. Debris from the Age of Aporia was everywhere, and crumbling skyscrapers burned like candles.

Sons of sirens, the Gateway City has become a gate for trash! Glaucon moaned, examining a line of windmills by the river (formed from centuries-old car hoods). These windmills were overshadowed by housing blocks made of rusty jet boats and train oil tankers. What species of sewage system the city employed, Glaucon could only speculate.

Near the rusting Eads Bridge, Glaucon's foot pressed on a damp piece of paper with a *Hands-of-God* symbol:

> ATTENTION PLEASE. YOUR CITY HAS HARBORED TERRORISTS. A FREE-FIRE ZONE HAS BEEN DECLARED BY EXECUTIVE ORDER 5678-917, PURSUANT TO THE REPUBLICAN CODE OF MILITARY JUSTICE. ALL PERSONS REMAINING IN ST. LOUIS AFTER 6 A.M. WILL BE CONSIDERED UNLAWFUL ENEMY COMBATANTS AND SHOT ON SIGHT. GOOD DAY.

"Good day, indeed," Sophie scoffed, examining the fiery terrain. "What a civilized kindness, providing a warning before you ravage people."

The open air above them was filled with smoke, like Republican incense lit to carry prayers to the Good. Glaucon would've commented, but he heard a whirring roar in the distance—another ziz sortie.

"Get down, Sophie!" he wailed diving to the ground. Sonic weapons pierced the flimsy walls and melted its defenders. Refuse splattered acoustically. Terrified militiamen on the rooftops turned from sniping the unstoppable forward advance of the Sigma Division to the airborne danger. Another sonic volley; men blasted screeching from the roofs. Most unexpectedly, though, after the second barrage, a fleet of ancient black planes streaked out of the blood-colored clouds, returning fire at the ziz, spearing them with bullets.

"What are those?" Glaucon asked amazed. "The city has erupted into cheers."

Sophie shielded her eyes with her hands. "Dactyl-7s, by the looks. From the Northeastern Liberation Front. I can't believe Xenon actually convinced them to truce."

"Anarchists were fighting them?"

"Yes, for stupid reasons, I'm afraid. Prodicus convinced the NELF we poisoned their water supply and disrupted their economy."

"Did you?"

"We're not crazy about them—their leader, Kalidorn Hayes, is a warlord, albeit with communitarian views—but we've been seeking to minimize our differences with others on the continent to make allies. What need have we to stir up enemies, especially when they might be useful? As you can see, the NELF discovered a valuable hanger."

"Hanger?" Glaucon was completely confused.

"Ancient ones are all over the place. The United States had enough weapons to kill humanity three times over. Ironic how most were never used. That's nuclear war for you—nothing but treasure tombs for the survivors."

"Will those . . . Dactyls defeat the ziz?"

"Of course not, but like flies on a horse they'll distract them. Time is critical and Xenon needs more of it."

"Is Xenon still in the city, then?" Glaucon gulped petrified. He had never faced the Republic's military before and did not wish to begin now. The Republic seemed all but invulnerable.

Sophie explained pulling him up: "No. We built underground tunnels to some wooded foothills to the north. I told Xenon not to get tricked by the crystal spray again. He'll escape with as many as possible."

"Xenon flees the city so soon?"

"Look at it, Glaucon," Sophie pointed, circling her arm over the devastation. "The city's lost. Worse than Chicago."

Another rumbling shook the earth. The restored Eagleton Courthouse collapsed as its pillars burst in all directions, sending up smoke. Above, kite-shaped "flashers" braided the air with sun-bright phosphorous.

"Careful, shield your eyes!" Sophie commanded, grabbing Glaucon's hand.

As they raced along the forest's edge bordering the dying city, the flashers ignited, flooding the sky bright crimson, warping white and hot and striking rebels blind.

Glaucon queried as they ran: "How long has the Anarchist Continental Army been camped here?"

"Over two years now. Why?"

"This doesn't make sense. Why is the siege happening today?"

Sophie sprinted wordlessly. The thought had already occurred to her.

"Prodicus knows we're alive, doesn't he? He's coming to find us."

"Let the eagle try!" Sophie challenged the gods provocatively.

The forest thinned. Glaucon looked south, his greatest fears realized. Slowly but surely, a small dot sparkled on the horizon—Levantra, the flagship of the Republic—sailing toward St. Louis.

Sophie turned frantic looking for the secret escape tunnels. Folding ferns, she finally spotted the rebel camp. Xenon's forces emerged from the ground covered in mud. Wooden boxes were being shuffled onto idling armored trucks. So hurried was the retreat, hardly any soldiers noticed the strange couple weeding through their ranks.

When Glaucon saw Xenon, he recognized him almost immediately. It was like he stepped right out of the picture from the aortaphos. (Thick mustache and all.) The fallen guardian watched the catastrophe below from a grassy butte, binoculars to his eyes. With a black handkerchief he wiped sweat from his neck and urged the struggle on, demanding someone in the distance to fire.

There was a brief streak of light in the sky, then thick smoke. A ziz crashed to the planet struck down by two contraband pulse cannons. Balls of feathered flames rolled into the forest.

"Take that! Burn in Hades, you horny-eyed harpies!" Xenon cried. "I knew Kai had a dead aim."

Sophie said, "You mean the Iron Queen knew he had a dead aim."

Xenon's mouth dropped open as wide as a cauldron. "Sophie, you crazed woman," he sputtered as they approached, "I told you to *kill* the Second Vessel, not bring him back here to endanger us. . . . Oh well, no matter." Xenon nodded to Lucia, a rigid-looking Hispanic soldier in green short-sleeves. "Shoot him, please."

Faster than light from the flashers, Sophie snatched Xenon's coilgun from his holster and aimed it defiantly at his face. "No. The boy is mine," she demanded firmly, voice smoldering. "No one touches him but me. I invoke sanctuary."

Retreat halted as rebels fumbled for their weapons.

Xenon stared from the magnetic barrel to Sophie with stern seriousness. Then he laughed wildly and clutched Sophie to his breast, joyfully kissing her on the cheeks. "My rebellious young daughter, you know I was only kidding.

Of course we won't shoot him. I was just testing your metal's reactions; to see if you had really grown as soft as they say. Right, Lucia?"

The female soldier nodded unconvincingly and holstered her weapon. Sophie eyed Xenon before stuffing the stolen pistol in her robes.

"So . . ." Xenon squeezed Sophie with one arm, "has my Iron Queen finally come to her senses and decided to command the Eastern Column? Milo plays a sore replacement."

"Not particularly. No court martial planned, Xenon?" The Iron Queen scanned the militia garbed in high-tech weapons for any hidden traps. She measured the nuanced movements of their mouths, watched for lurches in the knees, for all slight hints of attack.

"What are you talking about?" Xenon looked confused. "Your militia wouldn't vote for it, and neither would I. Good to see you safe. We're just about to make a full-scale retreat to Crypt under cover of night. But tell me, where is that incorrigible brother of yours?"

"You don't know?" Sophie asked with concern.

"Know what? My informants in the Republic have been incommunicado for weeks."

"They're probably dead in the purge." Sophie looked away from his bright sand-crusted eyes and explained their last days at the Republic (carefully omitting Glaucon's role). When Xenon learned how Zemer died in the Bull, his face stiffened. He tore the handkerchief from his neck resignedly. "That stupid young fool," he said, lowering his head. "How I loved him."

"You cursed him before we left. Multiple times."

"I curse everyone on a daily basis. It means nothing."

"You said he was hostile to revolution."

"He was. Pacifism helps no one but your enemy. If I recall, he said my positions were morally bankrupt, that I was—oh, what were his words again?—'destroying the sapling of anarchy.' What nonsense! As if one man could destroy it. To kill anarchism one would have to slay every living human soul. What did Zemer expect me to do? Just sit on the jinn until the Republic joined us for tea on the lawn? Maybe we can all hold hands and walk past those crystal palisades, let bygones be bygones."

"He wanted you to stop killing innocent people."

"By the Forms, Sophie, I should rather be dead than hear of this again. The helots are hardly innocent. You'd have to drag them by the legs to make them leave that circus."

"Not all of them," Sophie said. "You of all people should know that."

Xenon squint his eyes. “You’ve always known just how to cut me, little one. Fair enough, but even if—by some act of fate—the helots desired reunification, the guardians would never let them go; the auxiliaries would never let the guardians let them go; and if the auxiliaries let the guardians let them go, the alchemists would poison the water to salvage their reactors. Those in power will never give their strength willingly.”

“Don’t make speeches to yourself, Xenon. Doesn’t suit you.”

“Ha! Speeches to the self are the only way to learn. I’ll let you in on the law of the Republic—no, more primordial!—the law of the jungle: To make someone turn around you must reach out and push them.”

“Not all nature’s laws ought to be followed,” Sophie returned. “Zemer’s beliefs were confirmed by everything I witnessed in the Tenth Ward. Our war is counter-productive. There is no end to it. Bombing the Second Ward mangled the helot revolt. You shouldn’t have sent Marcus.”

“The attack was Limon’s idea, not mine.” Xenon raised his hands as if to distance himself from the act.

“You gave consent . . . against my wishes.”

“Long ago I warned that old mafia-goon, Dietrich Prince, I’d make him eat his money for betraying me. Death threats to enemies are like promises to dying lovers—sacrosanct!”

Sophie’s bronze hair whipped from her left shoulder as she spun close to the general. “I see Zemer’s absence has left you more sadistic than usual, Father.”

Impatiently, Xenon rubbed his temples. “You didn’t bring back the jinn, did you?”

“Is the jinn all you care about?” Sophie looked into her adoptive father’s marbled grey eyes accusingly. Kindness and cruelty were locked within, just like the Earth, hiding dangerous mysteries, forbidding aims.

Sophie’s emotions oscillated whenever she grew angry with Xenon. No man commanded deeper respect from her, nor gratefulness. It was this ex-guardian who saved her from Ozbolt Tower, nursed her broken heart, who provided a semblance of normalcy during adolescence. He taught her to fight the howling voices and the guardians. He was also—she had to admit with some embarrassment—the first man she had ever been attracted to. She was drawn to his manliness, that unfaltering courage, the way his sharp hair pointed over his forehead reassuringly. But Xenon never viewed her as anything but a child, and now the jinn replaced whatever space she once filled in his heart. No doubt he would try to defend that murderous obsession again.

"Listen! I care about victory, Sophie," Xenon rasped at her, "not some pie in the sky utopia. I care about keeping the germ of anarchy alive, lifting this continent from the Age of Reason. Revolutions aren't seeded in the clouds; they're nourished with blood and luck. The jinn grants more than luck. The jinn shows the future. Did you bring it back or not?"

Sophie clenched her fists. "I'd never bring it back to you, Xenon—ever! I care for you too much. The jinn changes everyone, not just the enemy. I'm here to tender my resignation in the Anarchist Continental Army."

At this, Xenon slapped his military cap to the ground and paraded by Sophie in a fit of furious cursing. "Tender your resignation? Tender your. . . ." He stopped to breath. "When word came back you twins were playing make-believe in a printing doll house I could hardly believe my ears. That my Iron Queen would betray me for . . ." he looked at Glaucon suspiciously, "some misperceived sense of justice was unthinkable. What did Zemer get by acting justly? What did we get? Justice isn't some natural property you wear like a garment. Justice doesn't exist or save the weak. Zemer should have lied to Prodicus, accepted whatever conditions he asked, and continued to fight. Any reason to sacrifice your life is as good a reason to live. He was a blind idealist and a close-minded fool."

Sophie cocked her head, enraged. "How dare you speak ill of him. You never understood. He cared for you."

Xenon grunted and apologized. "Lashing out is the only way I know how to deal with grief," he honestly admitted. "Your brother was family, impetuous like me when I was young. He was a good man and deserved better. It's just this . . . damned island. Your choice dooms us. We have no recourse now but to go into hiding. Tender your resignation when we get back to Crypt. In the meantime, make yourself useful. We must evacuate the Caucus and all civilians or they'll be butchered."

Sophie agreed, grumbling, marching toward the tunnels. "I will help you this final time," she said. "Only because I'm responsible for this city's destruction."

"Do as you will. What more can anyone do?" Xenon returned to a long table with three officers to speedily discuss their escape. His finger traced a line from the map and quivered, deciding whether to split their retreat into three operational groups or flee as a single united force through the Fallout Corridor.

Sophie found Milo, the Eastern Column's stand-in commander, halfway down the tunnel at a relay point. Soldiers were running every which way and the ceiling shuddered from artillery shells at the surface. Milo was olive skinned, cut-up, and puffy with exertion. His urban camouflage uniform made him look more like a soldier than the others dressed in work clothes. When he saw Sophie his eyes lit up. "What luck, you're here," he shouted, tenderly hugging her. Glaucon goggled in discomfort as Sophie not only hugged the olive-skinned man back but lovingly kissed him on the mouth, touching her head to his own.

"Where is the Eastern Column?" Sophie demanded, testing the disk-size of an energy bracer.

"Holding the Southern Front," Milo reported. "We've begun detonating buildings from Route 44 up, just like you planned. I've ordered the Caucus members to retreat to the old stadium for extract."

"They should not even be here."

"Some of them are near suicidal. They're refusing to leave."

Sophie thanked him and disappeared down the tunnel. Milo grabbed Glaucon's shoulder. "Come help me fasten provisions on the trucks. I'll give you a fresh change of clothes; those robes won't last another minute."

Glaucon, still wrenched by a scorching rope burn on his chest from witnessing the kiss, asked Milo dumbfounded, "How could you cede your post so easily?"

"I was only selected for her absence. No one says no to the Iron Queen."

"Never?"

"Never."

"You speak of her with such reverence," Glaucon said bewildered, "like some demigoddess."

"Why shouldn't I?" the militiaman responded. "The Iron Queen's a mighty warrior who sings zeal for her people. She fled hidden from our world but returned as the Great Maiden of the Mountain. Sophie defeated death to dwell with us."

Glaucon made a face. The Sophie Milo talked about seemed so alien from the Sophie he knew. His Sophie was softer, more bookish, not the legendary fighter everyone venerated. He wondered which personality was the real one. This man had surely lived with her longer than him. Was the Sophie he knew a lie, a disguise for her true self?

Word of the Iron Queen's return raised morale immensely along the muddy foothills. Stretchers carrying the shredded wounded quickened, and supplies lifting onto the backs of covered vehicles became a heated tempo. Sophie's entrance couldn't have come at a more critical moment; the growing size of Levantra made everyone desperate, like waiting for the executioners axe.

Inside the city, auxiliaries maneuvered block by bloody block. Many were killed by the booby-trapped buildings and sudden fire from the roofs. Enemies blazed at one another from opposite windows. Broken glass filled the streets. Sophie pushed forward to the stadium with three centuria, hurling shock grenades. They had already captured two guardians in a surprise counter-offensive near the Arch Apartments.

"Think fast!" Sophie commanded. "Lock legs and energy shields with vim. Form a garment of light around me with your bracers."

Bullets and sonic beams crashed against their electric formation. Pressing their elbows out to maximum extension, Neokalashnikovs returned fire through gaps in the energy wall, fighting off screaming waves of auxiliaries.

Parts of the stadium toppled over as Sophie raced inside. Scanning for familiar faces, she saw Tyro Canto—one of the Seven Councilors of St. Louis and a Continental Caucus delegate. She was wrapping an explosive cord around a pillar.

"Tyro, what's going on?" Sophie shouted, waving her energy shield over her head against debris. "Delegates are supposed to be taking cover, not fighting."

The grizzled woman spoke quickly, gripped by a frenzied mind. "What it looks like: turning this coliseum into a trap." She continued tossing the cords around like a deranged juggler, tying herself to the pillar. "At any moment," she said, "the guardians could land their airships here. If that happens, they'll bisect our defense and discover our retreat."

Sophie pleaded, "We have to get everyone out of here."

"Take them. I'm staying."

"Don't be ridiculous. I must bring you back. Refugees will need your guidance. Our rebellion's not dead yet!"

Tyro lowered her head. "So tired am I, waiting for my nimble thread to be cut. What better fate than to die with my city. Grant my people rest in your sacred mountains, fierce maiden. You must guide them from this misery."

What sickness overtook the city since I left? Sophie thought. Tyro Canto lacked no wealth of cool-headedness. The city assembly followed her sage advice for its moderation and thoughtfulness. Yet look at her now, about to blow to bits in desperation. "Please, don't do this," Sophie begged. "Don't throw your life away—"

"What's there left to discard? You know what Xenon said. We're all to be destroyed by Levantra. Fire absolute—"

"Xenon's wrong. If you don't come, I'll drag you back."

"Against my will?"

"Involuntarily? Yes. I will break all our customs to see you live. I'll cut these damn cords with my teeth!"

"But the Iron Queen calls for me."

"Not today. The Iron Queen will not accept your death. She refuses the dead." Sophie grabbed the old woman's wrist. Tyro fought at first, but then, brown eyes misting, she relented.

The Continental Caucus delegates fled from the stadium behind Sophie's energy phalanx into the tunnels. They barely escaped fresh auxiliary reinforcements storming across Eads Bridge.

One by one, the side-street barricades crumbled under siege. Endless gunfire and raining missiles lasted most of the day. When three spiritcarriers attempted a landing at the stadium, mined rubble pierced their rainbow wings. Like a clenching vice the auxiliaries arced ruthlessly. Before their spin could finally capture the mourning city completely, though, the invasion halted. The auxiliaries retreated. At night almost no firing could be heard at all. Then it was quiet.

An eerie foreboding, Glaucon thought, dropping a crate.

Over the radio, Xenon ordered, "Everyone must flee the city at once. Levantra has moved within striking distance." The general hadn't even finished speaking before a red beam from Levantra scanned the city hunting for bio-signs of the Vessels. When it found none, it moved to the center flicking devastating blasts of lightning.

Trucks rolled away at one hundred kilometers per hour—just in time—jumping onto hidden jungle roads.

Levantra's rocky underbelly opened like the jaws of a swamp brontogator. The inverted peak revealed an enormous barrel tongue.

Glaucon asked in curious alarm, "What in the world is that thing?"

"The Strife Cannon," Xenon cried. "It means total war!"

Outspread ruby lights started to dance and congeal on the barrel, gathering power. Before Glaucon could even blink, an undulant ruby beam vaporized St. Louis with a single, dreadful blast, a fiery *coup de grace*. The ancient city—one of man's last—disappeared forever. Amidst dust and debris swirling around, several vehicles slammed together.

Only a crater remained where the rebellious capital once stood. St. Louis was a wasteland, a wasteland emptier than the Fallout Corridor.

Sophie frantically steered the truck after the blast. "Why even bother with the long battle?"

Glaucon answered, remembering boyhood teachings from Stratos: "The spirit craves glory and battle."

This made Xenon smile. “Don’t forget the Vinculum Cartel—military products must be consumed—or Schizoeon’s eternal lust for experiments.”

“What magic did that barrel release?”

“A pulse of ionized particles, a harbinger of doom.” After saying this, Xenon climbed onto the roof of the truck and fired a pistol haphazardly at the flying island.

“What’s he doing up there?” Glaucon asked perplexed.

Sophie shook her head.

Outside, Xenon was covered in dust, a thick dust cloud which eclipsed the sky. Only a red door in the heavens remained, and he continued unloading a full clip at Levantra. As shots fired more frenzied, he started laughing, laughed diabolically, a dangerous, maddening laugh which reminded Glaucon of the poor ancient philosopher Chrysippus, who died laughing upon seeing his drunken donkey eat figs.

When at last Xenon returned, he handed the weapon to Glaucon. “Here, carry this with you when we get to Crypt. Never go anywhere without it.”

“No one will harm him,” Sophie promised.

“We’ll see. People do horrible things in desperation—even break the Right of Sanctuary. If he should desire, Glaucon can use the gun on himself.”

“You always see the worst in people.”

“Maybe that was the primary difference between Zemer and me. He saw light where I glimpsed only darkness. There is no saving humanity. By carrying that gun you agree. Tell me, Glaucon, have you ever read the *Republic*? Really read it?”

“Of course.”

“Is our Republic anything like Plato’s vision?”

Glaucon thought deeply for a moment. “There are many differences between our government and his ideal. My teacher Crito said it’s because we live in a realm of patterns.”

“Speak truthfully, would Plato construct a flying island to plant a field of fire?”

“Surely not. I suspect Plato would be quite surprised how things turned out.”

“Indeed,” Xenon pronounced, “sons are never like their fathers. Our Republic makes all men enemies, conquers to excess, destroys houses and love, believes in walls and written laws, and ravages women and children. Her bloody banners mock civility. Rome marvels at her successor and Mars’ infectious hate. Levantra has risen. Levantra has risen. Hear me again, Great Iron Queen, Levantra has risen. Her lips vent a smoking volcano’s heart, liquid bright in consuming radiance. We shall be suckled by fiery whirlwinds till all pastoral vales die barren."

Xenon looked starved of sanity. Glaucon asked, choked by his evil words, "Why did you go to the roof?"

"Ha, ha, ha," Xenon laughed Mephistophically. "Do they not teach history at the Academy anymore? In ancient times, mankind would go to high places to discover the gods, to feed from their breasts. Once fed they belonged to the gods and were destroyed. I will not bow to any deity's destruction. I go to high places to strike God down!"

At this show Sophie snorted. "We don't need high places to discover gods, Xenon, just mirrors."

V § 2 Crypt's Model Anarchism

Glaucon's legs were numb. Something heavy rested on them. Rubbing night-crust from his eyes, he observed Xenon crouched over him, watching, reading a newspaper, rattling its pages just enough to lift the gentle veils of Sleep.

Rhetorically Xenon asked, "Why is it, noble son, they ever made you a guardian?"

"I painted and dreamed," Glaucon answered.

Xenon smiled. "Pity someone hid your dreams from Prodicus."

"I wish they had remained hidden."

"But then you would've remained a slave with your mother. . . ."

Xenon looked thoughtfully at the Second Vessel's face, measuring his character and the Iron Queen's judgment. Sophie had never disobeyed him on any critical matter before. Yet in this—this!—she was surely mistaken. The heart was surely at the root of her betrayal; but hearts hardly ever governed wisely. Heart softening was the usual First Act in tragedy, and he did not much care for tragedies.

"Where's Sophie?" Glaucon demanded, disturbing Xenon's thoughts.

"At trial with her Column Committee."

"What?" Glaucon jumped up alarmed. "But you promised there'd be no court martial!"

"No," Xenon returned, "I promised not to discipline her. Can't speak for the Committee."

"What will happen to her?"

"She's committed terrible wrongs: desertion, using the Eastern Column for romantic adventure—total abuse of trust and loyalty."

Glaucon tried dislodging from the bare cot, but Xenon's weight hindered all movement. His grey uniform and black lapels looked intimidating.

"Don't worry your pretty little head," Xenon reassured. "I'll be rebuked far harsher than her, I suspect. Your guardian angel and I worked secretly to blot you out. Such artifice is frowned upon by the Column Committee, and most everyone else. No one comprehends the danger you pose (to others and yourself). I do."

"You keep talking of this *Column Committee*. Forms! What is it?"

The renegade guardian stood up, elated by the question. "A most intriguing social phenomenon. Sad to admit, the military question forced us to break all out anarchist principles. We have tried to alleviate the more gratuitous problems of military authority by instituting an Anarchist Column System. Individuals spontaneously agree to join together into small military units and then to form centuria, made up of about a hundred men. Out of fifty centuria, a militia is made. When the militias determine further coordination necessary, ten or more might joint together into a column. The Column Committee is really just an informal, rotational advisory board made up of several delegates from each militia and the people's communes."

"Both militias *and* the working units decide military strategy?"

"Certainly. You, a guardian, would think it wise administration to have the soldiers plan everything?"

"No, I guess not. But if it's informal, how does it command?"

"It'd abuse the word to say the Column Committee 'commands.' It only recommends social action and leadership positions. Each person weighs the merit of the advice. My role as general is similar. I speak persuasive authority—much more than others because of the Column's endorsement—but not binding authority."

"But that surely creates chaos!"

Xenon suppressed laughter. "Not at all; once soldiers discover *why* following advice and working together are important, they remain faithful to orders."

"So, do you encourage drilling like Stratos?"

"Somewhat, but we drill fraternity rather than obedience."

"What of insubordination, then?"

"Anarchists don't punish insubordination. Mutiny's rewards are plainly obvious to all that look."

"That must take forever . . . teaching everyone the importance of orders."

"How long to mold obedience on Stratos?"

"All of childhood."

"Well, there you are," Xenon said regardfully. "Our training lasts only months. To be honest, fear of reprisal makes a poor incentive to continue battle. The essential element in any successful campaign is loyalty, and that can hardly be forcefully injected into people. As a former soldier, wouldn't you agree?"

"I suppose. Commanders who gained their men's love certainly fared better than those who did not."

"Exactly right. Good leaders win respect like Sophie did. By allowing soldiers to choose their commanders, you ensure natural loyalty at the outset. There may be a slight loss of efficiency, but you make up for it in long-term group cohesion."

The whole system sounded curious to Glaucon, like thinking backward from what things should be. Seeing this perplexity, Xenon offered, "Let me show you around camp; you should know what you're getting into before committing. The anarchist way of life is antithetical to everything you've known."

Glaucon frowned, looked desperately for Sophie's coilgun.

"Oh, get up," Xenon growled. "I'm not going to kill you. Sanctuary is the most sacred anarchist charm of immunity. Once spoken, all are to seek your safety and improvement."

"Can anyone invoke it?"

"Of course, no special classes here. The right is premised on the principle of righteous intercession. If one person finds reason to save you, the community should respect their request. Therefore, let me look to your improvement, Vessel. Let me be your Virgil in this Dark Wood."

A dark wood it was. The hidden cave-city of Crypt was lodged deep in the Rocky Mountains, far from the Fallout Corridor. Windy green dunes and dead cities from the night before transformed into vast fortresses of natural crag and jungle fauna. Crypt was one spoke in the Southwest Confederacy, one of a thousand secret communes separated but united in the Santa Fe-Cheyenne Axis. Unlike St. Louis, an extensive cave system made Crypt easier to camouflage.

The Republic searched for the fabled city for years, winning only failure. Ziz armadas returned images of nothing but wilderness. Glaucon suspected the reason—Crypt moved like the printing houses; any discovery, burrow away.

Glaucon and Xenon walked outside the work cave, around its waterfall entrance, and down a long wooden rope bridge. The tree ceiling dipped like a fishhook into a sapphire lake. From this vantage point, camp business remained invisible from above. Concealed waterwheels—made from the fallen wings of airplanes—collected energy from nearby rivers. Lookout stations on log stilts (*like bird's nests*, Glaucon thought) kept vigil over the mountain jungle, depots, and workshops.

Crypt buzzed with activity. Women wearing blue overalls and soft black scarves hustled to munitions factories. Cadres pedaled furiously away on bicycles through the forest, carrying supplies to the next commune. Some militiamen sat at low tables coated with papers, books, and coffee. Children played on their laps.

"The soldiers and civilians work and live together?" Glaucon asked, amazed by the sight.

"We have no classes like the Republic," Xenon answered. "No distinction between soldier and civilian. Most men and women volunteer for a set time in the militias, and then return honorably to loved ones."

"But what if no one volunteers? Do you institute a draft?"

"Gods, never. Drafts offend freedom—slavery by another name. We excuse individuals from service. If they don't wish to defend their friends and relatives, we adapt. If no militias spontaneously emerge, there must be no need for fighting. As you can see, though, we have no drought of fighting men or bravery."

"But if you don't create a separate military force, who polices during peacetime?"

"A public police force—like a public army—endangers liberty. Domestic security positions we draw randomly by lottery every six months. Including everyone in the Home Guard teaches vigilance for the community, bestows knowledge of the dangers possible under a permanent public police system, and guards against institutional abuse (since the whole thing starts afresh every six months)."

"But what if, by act of chance, a virtuous group was selected—the best of all possible combinations—which developed an efficient and humane police force? The lottery would completely erase any institutional gains as well."

Xenon smirked. "While your hypothetical critique smells persuasive, the reverse problem of corrupt police necessitates the lottery. I've yet to read of any historical patrolmen that didn't reek of abuse from the Commissioner down, or fail to help the powers that be over the anguished cries of the people. Your 'virtuous police' would rarely (if ever) exist. Further, the lottery is for the anarchists' own protection—to limit their seduction to power. Even pure souls, once dunked in the tub of privilege, can wash away their goodness. The lottery is thus a leveler and safety valve: It recognizes all people can and should guard themselves. No one should be trusted with permanent police power over other human beings."

Crowds gathered in the center of town. Goods were quickly relayed in and out of a cocoon-shaped tower. Hollow inside with spiraling ramps, the edgeless structure widened upward joining the foliage and fragrant flowers.

Upon seeing Glaucon's curiosity, Xenon explained: "Unlike the Republic, private property and markets are abolished here. No more Vinculum Cartel. Free, interlinking, and spontaneous associations like communes and union squads engage in agricultural labor, textile manufacturing, excavation of raw materials, then bring them directly to a Pool Syndicate, like this one here. Inventory is processed for distribution, export, and storage. People take according to their needs."

"Good heavens! What keeps the masses from storming this common bank in an orgy of desire?"

Xenon laughed. "The Pool Syndicate is not autonomous, little thief, but created by a network of communes bonded by love and awareness of their common needs. Most anarchists would rather die impoverished than see others suffer want. And enlightened self-interest prods the few rascals—for they'd surely die without a stable Pool. While difficult for profiteers to understand, value here is found in social relationships and activity, not possessions. A person who refused to work in *some* capacity and just ate from the store would be considered a pariah. I've never even heard of such a thing."

"Would he still be fed?"

"I suppose, if there was enough to feed everyone else who worked. What would you prove by making that person starve?"

"But who catalogues the inventory and assigns jobs? Who controls what flows in and out of the Pool Syndicate?"

"Everyone does, in a sense. Usually several communes and union squads will form an assembly. All individuals can attend and participate. The assembly discusses community concerns, plans production, recommends quotas, solicits volunteers, divides tasks, allocates resources for education and environmental improvements. Much policy information comes directly from data recorded in the Pool Syndicate."

"How do producers of larger goods and services contribute to the Pool?"

"I fail to understand your question."

"For example, the data recorder in the Pool Syndicate performs a service but does not produce actual goods. I suppose the commune accountants, cooks, computer technicians, doctors, and administrators suffer similar deficiencies."

"Hardly deficiencies!" Xenon cried. "They register their work with the Pool Syndicate and the value of their labor is assessed. The servicemen are just as respected as the producers of actual goods."

"So are all decisions made at the assembly by the majority in attendance?"

"Rarely. Democracy is viewed as the majority's imposition of force onto the minority and deeply resented. Strong emphasis is placed on consensus and group unanimity. Democratic principles are implemented as a last resort, provided sufficient time has been allowed for informal caucusing."

"The assembly must last tediously throughout the night if everyone makes speeches and wants to have their say."

"Public speeches are kept to an absolute minimum. No one listens to them and they are repugnant to anarchist morality. You should talk *with* not *at* someone."

"Is that why you have no slogans on billboards?"

"Yes. Using motivational slogans and speakers displays a slanderous view of human nature. We have lecturers and poets and people skilled in certain crafts give talks, but these often turn into conversation."

"What happens if the assembly makes mistakes and underproduces?"

"Sadly, that occurs more than I'd desire. But this is no argument against us. Utopias are impossible. We've alleviated this problem by sharing resources with other assemblies who might overproduce. The system works overall. In my sixteen years here no one's gone hungry. We haven't been rich, but we haven't starved."

"Does the Continental Caucus help manage inter-assembly affairs?"

"Sometimes, but in reality, we try to keep the Caucus' functions as limited as possible—to coordinating regional trade and military tactics."

"But why?" Glaucon asked flummoxed. "Strong, centralized government is more efficient."

"Because the Caucus is a representative council." The way Xenon spoke, it was as if the statement's truth was self-evident. "Individuals should make the decisions that govern their daily lives, not 'enlightened statesmen' alleging to know better. Creating a governing class is the first step to tyranny."

Glaucon was much interested at this point, and so he bid Xenon expand his argument. Xenon described the many traps of vanguardism, highlighting historical abuses from the Age of Aporia: Vladimir Lenin and Leon Trotsky eliminating spontaneous socialist workers' councils during the Russian Revolution; how the anarcho-syndicalist revolution was betrayed (and fascism aided) by the Soviet Union during the Spanish Civil War; the Great Leap Nowhere in China under Chairman Mao; religious enslavement of Iran under the Ayatollahs. He concluded by discussing the pernicious effects of representation in the former United States. "The Congress and Senate," he explained, "while claiming to act for the people, were not legally bound to do so, and really aligned with powerful corporate interests who paid for their campaigns."

"Campaigns were run with money?" Glaucon gasped. The very thought was flabbergasting. Even the guardians wouldn't be so brazen. "Why not pass a law against such a pernicious policy?"

Xenon stifled a grin trying to explain. "The cardinal judges were tutored in corporate funded schools and taught market ideals about efficiency. They believed a right to free speech logically entailed a right for the rich and corporations to fund campaigns. This, of course, drowned out the free speech of everyone. Money decided American elections, little else."

"How terrible. I wonder which is worse: to have money decide elections or to have no elections at all?"

Xenon continued his education: "Campaign money created a parasitic relationship between the corporations and political parties of the day. One could only get elected by adopting a business attitude agreeable to the private financial institutions—who then paid the politicians off like cheap mercenaries. Businessmen and politicians were interchangeable. Congressmen were rewarded for faithful conduct by being placed on Boards of Trustees. Even if the people managed to get in a reform candidate, he still had to fight against the vast majority who sided with the rich, and he could always be bought or outspent at the next election."

"How can corporations even have the right to donate money? They're not persons."

"In the United States they were legal persons."

"By Zeus, I should rather have the guardians."

"Well, the United States didn't exactly burn people in the Bull either. But, like other dead empires, they'd conquer for pretty stones like diamonds, or ugly substances like oil; being capitalists, the U.S. warred for open markets, too."

"How could anyone think such a constitution legitimate?"

"Why do some helots think the Republic legitimate? They've been told so by authority."

"I can see your fear of vanguardism is justified. While claiming to protect the people, American representatives breathed only to protect property and their own privileges."

"Indeed, things deteriorated so badly in America, people could utter—in public company no less—that individuals did not have a right to social welfare."

"Impossible."

"Sentiments of a true plutocracy. They argued you only had a right to what you could gain from the corporate powers and the market."

"Even the Republic provides free housing and food."

"Primitive times, like a casino with the lights turned out. Politicians fleeced the people with taxes to ensure the safety of the bankers' risks and luxuries. The public treasury was looted to pay for private enterprise and mercenaries. Homeless people lay exposed under bridges. There was more than enough food, yet market capitalism ensured over a billion souls starved to death around the world. Doctors made money off the sick. Parents worked multiple jobs, never interacting with their children. Pressing issues that still affect us—environmental devastation, flooding of the coasts, the mammoth storms—were not dealt with because representatives were bought and individuals silenced through representation. The government broke the individual's back in every aspect of his existence; then they'd call him lazy and ungrateful when he languished in despair."

Glaucon said, "No wonder the Republic worked so rabidly to control the corporations after the Day of Hylopleonexia."

Xenon nodded thoughtfully. "Anarchist policy discarded them altogether. We have no property, and make wide use of lottery for most public positions. Our representatives, if any, are expressly bound to follow commune directives. The individual does not cede his sovereignty to anyone but rules wisely for himself."

Xenon led Glaucon away from the Pool Syndicate and out toward the wooded hook. He pointed to many curious sights along the way: wooden structures attached to trees with swinging bridges, bungalows on the ground, rectangular coolhouses made of mud. One stream watered the plants inside and then drained back into the lake. The entire village sloped with the land and appeared part of the terrain. Numerous crops were planted on the cliffs, all mixed together, under the trees and in the sunny glades. Many of the improvements, Xenon reported, resulted from alliance with the Fifth Estate militia who were busy re-foresting dry patches of desert with advanced permaculture techniques. Gardening for subsistence and surplus appeared to be a universal and ritualistic hobby, and much prestige could be gained by gardening prowess.

"Where are all the temples?" Glaucon wondered aloud.

"Most are atheists among us. Dogma and churches are non-existent."

"No chief deities? Then what are all these skeleton statues with the corn offerings?"

"Icons of the Iron Queen. Some call her Persephone, Santa Muerte, the White Maiden, or the Grim Reaper. All are personifications of death and nature, the most omnipresent forces in daily life here. Devotees pray to the Iron Queen for anything, good or bad, life or death: to secure or destroy a difficult love, to protect families in war, grant peaceful final rest, or to torch the Republic's army. I'll gladly admit, the idea of an atheistic cult is confusing at first, but her worship by atheists shouldn't come as a surprise—the Iron Queen cherishes irreverence above all else. She seeks an end to hierarchies and submission, fundamental anarchist values."

"But I thought Sophie was the Iron Queen."

"She is; Sophie claims to be one and the same, that the Iron Queen possessed her when her heart exploded in Ozbolt Tower."

"Sophie claims to be a goddess?"

"Not literally. The Iron Queen is a symbolic power embedded in the human mind. She only exists in our heads. Sophie dragged her out from the imagination."

"What for?"

"As a coping mechanism, at first. Right after we arrived, Sophie suffered from post-traumatic stress syndrome. The intense physical trauma losing her heart was too much for a child's mind. Both she and Zemer fell into panic attacks about dying, and they refused to go anywhere without the other. One day Sophie saw a statue of the Iron Queen, recognized it as the being that called her back to the living, and suddenly recovered. Taking on the persona of death, she no longer feared it. When she joined the militia she adopted her again for psychological motivation. The anarchists fell in love with Sophie. Can't you imagine the sight?—a cute, irreverent little girl claiming to be Death, training obsessively. Some of them even say she *is* the goddess."

Healthy looking militiawomen ran by with scorpion-grenades swinging from their hips. They looked quite surprised to see General Xenon attending to the strange guardian.

"I see you've adopted Plato's scheme to equalize the sexes," Glaucon mentioned as they passed.

"Why not?" Xenon asked. "There is little difference between them, as Heliopolis indicates. Women covet their freedom and enjoy social life and meaningful work as much as men."

Upon seeing a couple engaged in love making in the bushes, Glaucon asked rather abashedly, "If you don't mind my asking, what structure do sexual relationships take here?"

"Love is free," Xenon reported proudly. "Marriage has been completely abolished."

"Really, by what logic? That is more like Heliopolis than the wards."

"Firstly, we have no laws to enforce such an institution. Secondly, marriage led to the subjugation of women in the past, so most think it prudent to forego the risk. Thirdly, it creates unnecessary social conflict."

"Social conflict?"

"Yes, marriage closes off the individual from the group. In previous times, if a married woman fell deeply in love with another man, she'd be commanded by religion and government to ignore those impulses out of duty. Such obstructions slowly eroded her feelings toward others around her. The community was harmed because healthy social bonds were prevented. She was harmed by losing a potentially valuable relationship. Even the original relationship came to ruin; nothing is a greater butcher of spontaneous love than the imposition of duty. Worse still, the vice of jealousy is made virtuous by such an institution."

"The people here consider jealousy a negative thing?"

"When someone feels jealous thoughts they're claiming ownership and private access to another human being. This is not—according to most here—psychologically beneficial. How can someone claim ownership of another and at the same time maintain a belief in equality?"

"I suppose there is *some* dissonance. But what if a couple mutually wishes to remain closed?" Glaucon was of course thinking of himself and Sophie, a strange desire for a guardian.

"Then let it be so," Xenon said lighting a cigar. "There is not a set way of life among us. Commune with whomever you wish, how you wish; but don't claim jealous rage a legitimate and healthy emotion when it creates only competition and objectification. I advise all against it. Some ignore me and others don't. This is not unexpected. Here we believe love is essential to human experience and that no sexual act is deviant as long as there is mutual consent. We have adopted an open and loose attitude to sexual expression so that individuals may flourish however they choose."

"Does the morality work?"

"Rape hasn't occurred in over fifty years. People lie naked without embarrassment. Women aren't forced to sell themselves for money, for who would pay for something that is given freely (and we have no money anyway). Nights are filled with communal pleasure and the sharing of feelings. Society is strengthened by loving. Much psychological trauma has been eliminated."

"So you must take many lovers, being the general?"

"Myself? No. Don't much care for romance. I still retain a healthy detachment from the commune at night. No consort in some years."

"Saint Plato, why?"

Xenon's face twitched, fighting to forget painful memories. "Love makes you soft and stupid," he explained. "Love numbs your senses. To defeat the Republic, I gave up love. I must be alert and hard as nails. Never can I expose a sliver of my soul lest it be used against me again. Perhaps I have lost the capacity to love, or I can only love things in the abstract. I look at people from a distance, like they're some three-headed cat in a glass jar. Maybe I am the dead creature looking out."

Glaucon felt a pang of pity for Xenon (a puzzling emotion) and moved away from the topic. "Does no one ever feel ashamed about their . . . sexual actions?"

Xenon sighed. "Not really. People here take as much love as they like. There is no deluge of shame. Anarchists piss on shame, but they drink it up, too, if the mood strikes."

"It seems as if the anarchists have thought about these sexual matters in great detail."

"Of course, everything I'm saying is a description of social processes I've studied with an anthropologist's eye. No one consciously thinks about their love life in this manner. It just emerges from the values inherent in anarchist society. If you truly believe all authority and coercion should be abolished from society, sexuality must be free from all constraints and people must be comfortable with their bodies. Laws and morals surrounding mating habits can be a tool for liberation or control. In the Republic, the government essentially decides when, how, and why individuals will make love to one another. A moral system valuing individuals will let the individual decide."

"Many children must be sired with so much slimetide," Glaucon guessed.

Xenon laughed. "What a strange word for sex. But no, we have discovered a special root that makes a fine contraceptive. Only women who desire to become pregnant do so, and they are cared for in their labors."

"Does not the raising of children put men in an advantage of power over the female sex?"

"By the gods, no. Children are raised and loved by all. After the nursing period ends, responsibility for children is distributed equally to men and women. The breeding dens on Heliopolis are no more."

"So, if the mother refuses to relinquish claim to her babe, you take it from her?"

"Why would someone who values autonomy and freedom refuse such public aid? No one stops the mother from developing a relationship with the child, and obviously, certain sentimental attachments are formed between children and their parents. This is not because of anything magical about blood, but because the fruit of one's loins creates a psychological and—dare I say it—natural attachment. The parents also realize they could die at any time from Republican raids. No one wishes to leave their children unsupported and vulnerable."

"So, you don't hide the parentage like the guardians do?"

"Absolutely not. It creates too much obsession and forces us to continuously lie. However, the idea children somehow *belong* to the parents is harshly criticized. Children are not toys or property. They are fragile beings, like a tender plant, and require proper nutrients to flourish. You would agree a community with many minds can raise a child better than one?"

"That must certainly be true. But please explain the nature of education. I have seen children running through the forest like unfettered satyrs all morning. Where are the classrooms?"

"We have none. Nowhere are societal values more candid than in how the young are educated. In an authoritarian society like the Republic, students are taught from infancy to obey hierarchical power structures and to conform for efficiency and production. They are taught to recite dogmatic and hypocritical pledges of allegiance; to sit silently in class or risk severe punishment; to subserviently accept subjects and lessons imposed from their 'betters'; to compete rather than cooperate; in essence, to be tested like a car piston. Gradually, the rebel is broken and reconstructed into a mechanized machine—a deformed appendage of the corporations—good for the whole but not for himself, and the erotic love of learning is snuffed out."

"You've discovered a solution?" Glaucon asked.

"Yes, indeed; a natural one that shuns dogmatic lessons and authority. We allow students to gather together with a number of teachers whenever *they* choose. Children are naturally curious and want to learn about the world. The teachers refuse to take a leadership position. Instead, they allow the children to ask them for subjects which they teach to their satisfaction. Learning becomes a pleasurable and liberating experience rather than a stifling one."

"Honestly, no pressure is exerted to get children to attend school?" Glaucon could remember how difficult it was to orient children to study-life at the Academy.

"Not all social pressure," Xenon admitted. "That'd be absurd. Adults make their wishes known they'd like children to learn, why education would benefit them. Obviously, children wish to please the grown-ups they admire and respect. Some might begin attending because they do not want to displease their elders."

"So what subjects are taught at these student-led schools?"

"That depends entirely on what the children want. Students usually organize into a group. Individuals voice their desires and dislikes about certain subjects. One may like scientific studies; another, mathematics or philosophy."

"I would choose recess every time."

"That occurs as well. But children tire and crave knowledge. Vigorous discussion and compromise ensues in these small groups as each tries to explain the benefit of particular subjects. Eventually, a proper list is prepared amidst excitement. The teachers help facilitate learning and discussion, pointing to different resources and ideas."

"What if a student falls behind? Does the teacher help him keep up with the others?"

"The child must ask for help from the student group. They assign positions for tutoring and achieve success together. In this way, they learn how to organize and plan on their own and strengthen honesty and trust."

"If you do not lead the students, how do you inculcate the proper anarchist values?"

"There is little need. Anarchist morality—like distrust for authority and respect for individual autonomy—are derived from the learning process itself. The children teach themselves self-government and respect for one another."

Glaucon scratched his head, thinking of obvious sanitation problems. "Surely, you would agree children can be messy and forgetful," he said. "Who collects the materials and cleans up the work area?"

"Yes, yes," Xenon agreed, "children are more apt to ignore a dirty environment, but even they come to recognize the need for cleanliness. Many student groups borrow ideas from their elders about how to assign dirty work and develop a lottery. Overall, the intellectual and social gains from this learning process are staggering. Children here develop exponentially faster than in the Republic, and they're smarter in every capacity. I've come to learn that just as you cannot beat obedience into soldiers you cannot drill learning into students. Learning must come from within to reach one's potential. Anarchists believe, much like Plato did, that 'no free person should learn anything like a slave. Nothing taught by force stays in the soul.' "

"Are children ever bullied?" Glaucon asked, remembering how guardian neophytes mocked him as a bronzeborn mooncalf.

Xenon shook his head. "The bully would find himself rebuked by the group for preying on the weak. A threat to any individual's liberty is a threat to all. Unlike other societies, seeking power over others is a vice here."

"Isn't the group asserting its power over the bully by protecting the weak?"

Xenon was perplexed by this question. "In a sense, I suppose they are," he said, "but a society could not exist without some level of coercion. The human project is to minimize coercive forces so that we may live together peacefully as free individuals with as little authority as possible."

Xenon stopped at a wooden crate on the path filled with weapons and dynamite.

"Have any other types of anarchist societies developed?" Glaucon asked, worried to see the lit cigar so close to the explosives.

"About one hundred and fifty years ago, a group of anarcho-capitalists tried to create free-market conditions in Randland on the West Coast."

Xenon plucked a new coilgun from the crate outside the armory and checked the sight. He refastened it in his holster.

"They died out?" Glaucon asked wondering the scope of his intentions.

"As fast as falling space dust in the atmosphere," Xenon informed him. "Since property continued to exist, an intense system of economic coercion operated and financial power consolidated in the hands of a few oligarchs. You see, private property carries two impulses: the impulse to oligarchy and the impulse to exploitation. Randland was no different. Hardly any roads were built because no one saw a reason to cooperate on public endeavors. Private police ransacked the countryside. If the air could've been bottled for profit, they would have done so. The exploited, starving losers of that society came to join the communes. Consequently, Randland's population thinned."

"That must've sorely upset them."

"Yes, and the Republic was able to turn the oligarchs against us in their death throes. A long bloody war commenced until their society—if you could call it such—collapsed."

"Sophie and I saw a forest tribe in Louisiana. Who were they?"

"Ah yes," Xenon recalled the noble Coughing Fish, "they're the Zerzanbe."

Many years before, after a sharp rise in Republican kidnappings for the gladiator arena, he had sent Sophie and Zemer to their tribe as military advisers. It was there legends of the Iron Queen first began to spread: entire Republican divisions wiped out as they tried to collect the blood tax; scalped bodies sent back to Heliopolis on corpse-barges; brilliant ambushes; spear traps in the rivers; a true American spirit of resistance.

"The Zerzanbe," Xenon went on, "are a branch of radical green anarchists who advocate discarding advanced technology and returning to a more 'primitive' lifestyle."

"Why on earth would they want to do that? Technology reduces human toil."

"I agree, but not always. Some technology takes on a life of its own, requires coercion and a hierarchical division of labor."

"What do you mean?"

"Would you agree tools like a shovel and a magnet-sedan require different levels of social organization?"

"Yes, certainly. A shovel can be produced rather easily, but a car requires steel plants, glass refineries, plastic manufacturers—a whole assembly line."

"That assembly line will work more efficiently under centralized planning, will it not?"

"Yes, the pressures for centralization will be enormous to efficiently manufacture a magnet-sedan."

"And hierarchical management?"

"That would seem necessary, too."

"Well, that's the rub," Xenon said. "Societies valuing cars and other 'progresses' may be pushed into continuing a certain way of life—a certain hierarchical, bureaucratic way of life. Alternate modes of living that don't comport with the needs of technology are discarded as 'inferior'; spontaneity, decentralization, worker management starts to look destructive rather than liberating. Society stiffens hard like a machine, then begins to serve the machine rather than the individual."

"Such a sorry state has surely befallen the Republic," Glaucon sighed.

"Yes, the Republic is not our own anymore but belongs to Kabiri. The cogniscrambler colors every inner world and limits human potential. It standardizes human experience. Our diverse world is an abomination to it. The machinery of the guardians will not suffer our liberated culture but will eat us raw like applecane."

"Is anything to be done?"

"Certainly, but Sophie doesn't want to hear. We must find the jinn and destroy Kabiri-36—once and for all!" The general turned to Glaucon desperately, flexing his neck muscles as if stung. "The Iron Queen is hiding one from me, isn't she? Fate often swings on a single word. Tell me where it is—"

"I promise, General. I saw her destroy the last one. We're not hiding anything."

"Pity," Xenon said. Loosening his shoulders, he inhaled smoke from his cigar. "Isn't it funny? That was the first thing I'd hoped for in a long time."

V § 3 And Then a Confession

The forest thinned as Glaucon and Xenon reached the edge of the camp lake. Trout flipped in the water as a militiaman fly-fished in knee-boots. When he saw them approaching, he quickly departed for a string of workshops in the woods past the shoreline. Glaucon suddenly realized how alone they were and began to worry.

"Tell me, Xenon," Glaucon asked, "what happened to the guardians Sophie captured yesterday?"

Xenon's eyes burned as sulfur. "One joined us under Right of Sanctuary. I had the other shot."

When Glaucon asked the reason, Xenon answered coarsely, "You tell me, Vessel. We both know guardian deception. I should've killed the other one, too."

"Is that action dictated by anarchist morality as well?"

Xenon snorted, unlatched two buttons from his shirt, and puffed a cloud of smoke from his cigar. "You stubborn people and your moralizing. This world does not reward mercy. The place between Heaven and Hell is laid in blood. If you don't build a boat, you'll drown." He began twirling his cigar in his hands. "Do you realize my struggle, Vessel, to convince so many anarchists to give up their ideals? From the beginning, they have impeded every step for victory. First, they whine about the iama-B. Then they complain about my stiff punishments against the guardians. After that, I play traveling salesman, peddling alliances to keep them breathing. Groups like the Fifth Estate refuse to use the Republic's technology for years until Levantra is all but in the air. Infighting erupts. I have to settle accounts. Finally, at our moment of triumph, just when we're united and a serious threat, after Ozbolt turns and sends us the jinn, the twins discover conscience and cripple us all. These yahoos deserve to lose."

"They're principled."

"Fuck principles! This is war and Prodicus is our enemy. Victory matters, nothing else. If Prodicus invaded Hell, I'd partner with Lucifer to defeat him. These people are like Zemer, blind to reality."

"Earlier, you spoke so fondly of this society."

"Only because it's not long for this world. I am a foreigner, even here, a tired alien among incompetents."

"They were competent enough to keep you on as general."

At this Xenon howled with laughter. He unclipped his holster and fondled the glittering coilgun in his hands.

"Very true. They all sing hymns to virtue, yet here I am. One can pray to the gods, but you need Beelzebub to fight Beelzebub. They see necessary truth in me."

"A dark truth," Glaucon added.

Xenon smiled cynically. "I also deal the weapons. During wartime the weapons-man is king, judge, and priest."

"Perhaps, like me, you spent too much time on Heliopolis."

"Sophie and Zemer were lucky," Xenon admitted. "Being young they acclimated. Me? I don't acclimate. I act. And knocking down the Republic is all that drives me. I am the gadfly that keeps everyone on the ball.

"I look upon the golden city, so organized, so proper—the guardians, auxiliaries, and helots; the Vinculum Cartel; the Office of Public Harmony—and I realize man was not made for cities. He is too much of a worm, too insolent, too empty—a little god never satisfied. He is always reaching and is particularly dangerous when he thinks he will succeed.

"One day, after assisting Prodicus on one of his experiments, I went outside to sit on a bench. I watched the traffic fly by and laid my soft head on the chrome. To my amazement, a tiny ant came crawling up the arm rest. I knocked him away with my finger. He came back again, so I flicked him again. Can you imagine the little one came back nine times? Do you know what I did, Vessel?"

"No."

"I squashed him with my fist. Smeared his little guts in a streak over the metal. Never in my life did I feel so callous as when I killed that ant. I should have closed my eyes and given him more of a chance. But no, I struck him from the world like an angry god. I ground him to pieces. What harm did he cause me? After being torn by the jinn, that question haunted me for months. But I came to realize, if I can kill an ant—an innocent creature—I am truly capable of anything. I could lie to Sophie. I might break sanctuary."

Xenon roughly thrust the coilgun into Glaucon's temple and made him kneel on the sands.

"How long do you think until the avis are released?" Xenon asked, not waiting for Glaucon to answer. "I wager that military cult will last another week. How about you?"

"I don't know."

The hard barrel dug into Glaucon's scalp. His heart began to pound. He concentrated on the calm lake and the jumping fish.

Xenon sneered, "I am not a complicated man. I used to be but not anymore. I make no pretenses to virtue: My feet will crush the weak, my arms hold no one up, my belt is tied with thunder. Power is the only law I respect. Power is the only source of justice. One sacred maxim leads my life—the maxim of Melos: 'The strong take what they can, and the weak suffer what they must.' The ant has no claim of me because I can crush him to dust. If you want what is mine, try and take it. If I overpower you, your only hope is my magnanimity."

"Then why not ally with the Republic? They are clearly the stronger . . . and just, according to you."

"Because I despise the Republic and their hopes. I want a world I control, not one that controls me. Like the Spanish revolutionaries I'd rather die on my feet than surrender on my knees. I will never allow Prodicus to defeat me again."

"So you *are* driven by revenge?"

"Revenge? Ha! Is it such a bad reason to fight? Let me tell you about revenge, boy. When I was a young man I fell madly in love with a helot woman. Twenty-one and beautiful, skin like milk. I met her while investigating a series of strange kidnappings out of Consumption Junction. As I skulked behind some suspects in the Second Sun Crime Syndicate, I spied her three floors down. She wore a flower-embroidered fleece shirt and walked with a group of friends. The kidnappers started to point down at the pedestrians, discussing which one they should take for the Kabiri's experiments. Can you believe my surprise when they moved for the girl? I jumped down the levitating platforms without thinking. I fought them off with a shower rod, had security arrest them. I noticed the beauty dropped her purse running from the mob. When I returned it, she flirted with her eyes, invited me to the arcades with her friends. Later, we walked alone together. This woman was intelligent and witty—should have been a guardian, actually, if you ask me. Her hair smelled of lilies. She pulled on my belt and tried to kiss me. Caught in that headlong, amorous irrationality which disregards political reality, I completely divulged my secrets—that I was an ISHIM spy. She looked at me as if I just reported her parents eaten by wild brontogators and tried to flee. But I grabbed her slender wrist and kissed it, begged her to stay with me. 'How can love be wrong?' I asked her falling to my knees. 'Stay with me; I'll die if you go.' I promised to exile myself from the Academy if only to be with her.

"What followed next can only be regarded by sober guardian minds as complete scandal. I revealed to my helot lover a secret passage outside the walls—carried her away down a wooded path to a hidden cave. There we met for nighttime embraces, made love without any drugs. Afterward, we wrote sweet love songs together with an electric-lyre. She turned me from a man of fire to a man of flesh."

Startled realization gathered like a cloud in Glaucon's eyes. "My mother, Melete," he spoke softly, astonished.

"Unbeknownst to me, however," Xenon continued growling, "Prodicus sent spies from the Kabiri Circle to follow us—Zeno and Yannis. When my lover became pregnant, the vile cur confronted me himself. Prodicus told me if I did not join the Kabiri and swear a loyalty oath to him he would have us both burned alive in the Bull."

"Why would he care so much if you joined?"

"Don't forget, I'm a descendant of Guardian-King Hythloday. Top positions at ISHIM ooze with the first Guardian-King's blood. Hekademos III was a Hythloday. Prodicus wished to use my connections to peel off support from the Katharoi. What was I to do? Prodicus told me he would kill Melete if I refused. I was trapped under his heel like an ant. That's when I should have killed the pervert, but instead, I groveled at Prodicus' feet, accepted his pen and paper to write a disgusting letter severing my relationship, even thanked him. The next week, Prodicus had Melete selected for the marriage draft. He made me transfer to Ozbolt Tower to work with Kabiri-35."

"Xenon—"

"You ask if I fight for revenge? Let me tell you, boy, I nursed on the breast of revenge every day in Ozbolt Tower. I have yet to have my fill. Prodicus revels making others eat their hearts. Now I'll only be satisfied when I tear out that monster's heart and make him eat his, too. He robbed me of my humanity—every bit of it. I must kill him to get it back!"

"You may call Prodicus a monster, but you sent Sophie to murder your only son."

"Pish, posh. You say *murder*; more sane minds would label it a *mercy blow*. Zemer talked much of oracular visions. Did he ever tell you I had my own? Before I fled Heliopolis, the jinn pierced me in the brain and I soothed death—the death of everything on the surface of the planet. I saw that Prodicus succeeded, Levantra ruled the sky, the three Vessels were immersed in the mainframe, and there was no likelihood we could stop it. One hundred percent failure. Do you think your mother would wish you to become immersed, to lose your identity, turned into a hateful god, to be like Shiva, the fated destroyer of Earth? Please—I knew her better than you—better than anyone. If man can kill his son for God, why can he not kill him for mercy or for love?"

Behind them a stern voice abruptly broke the silence. "Xenon, you know you're not supposed to do that. Sophie granted sanctuary."

Glaucon turned around thankfully. Milo, the agile-faced officer from before, approached with Artillery Chief Finnias Shapiro.

Since their escape from St. Louis, Glaucon had been troubled by this strange anarchist. Sophie had given Milo a passionate kiss on the mouth and ignored *him* for over an hour chatting with the soldier when they arrived in Crypt. Apparently, she'd also bid him keep watch on Xenon. Milo and Sophie seemed to be the closest friends.

Xenon cursed the two with scorn as he twisted the gun. "Any word on Levantra, *comrades?*" he asked.

Milo answered, "As Sophie predicted, guardians commenced attack on the eastern seaboard and Appalachian settlements. Charleston, Columbia, and Raleigh have been obliterated. The Carolina Militia disbanded."

"And Fort Washington?"

"We lost contact thirty minutes ago."

"Yet here you are trying to save the cause for this malady."

"Commander Sophie is correct," said Shapiro. He rubbed his knuckles on his long mountain beard. "The Fates will find a new Vessel when this one is dead. Best to leave him alive for now. Do you want to be the first man to break sanctuary?"

"That girl has the logic of her Uncle Prodicus, doesn't she?" Xenon whispered into Glaucon's ear.

The mad general pulled the trigger anyway.

Glaucon heard a click and collapsed into his shoulders. Milo and Shapiro gasped. Xenon laughed sadistically and whispered, "Just remember, guardian: My son died sixteen years ago with his mother. One indication of betrayal—one—and I split your brains." He kissed Glaucon solidly on the cheek and shoved him to the ground.

"What did you say to him?" Milo asked when Glaucon turned white as porcelain.

Xenon shrugged. "We're just having a father-son heart to heart."

"You don't have a heart, Xenon."

"Neither does your iron mistress, but you still manage to prattle on like younglings behind my back. I'd be curious to know, Milo, what will you use to stop the slaughter of our children?—Tridents? Like Coughing Fish?"

Xenon pushed through the two men like passing through the bar doors of a saloon and left Glaucon quaking on the ground.

V § 4 Return of the Iron Queen

"This show trial is a disgrace," Tyro Canto lashed the Column Committee. "No one has done greater good for the Eastern Column and Southwest Confederacy than Sophie."

A voice returned from the seated assembly: "Come, come, Sister Tyro. What show trial? This is a meeting between friends."

"No, *friends*," Tyro sarcastically accentuated the word, "meetings are held after dinners, not formerly called by the collection of a hundred hairbrained signatures. You wish to drag Sophie's name through the mud. A disgrace, I say. Not even Xenon joined this charade."

"Let's not get dramatic," Limon Taylor said, rising to his feet. A mason with the Northern Mountain Union and a captain in the Eastern Column, he possessed a fierce, sturdy countenance and led the accusers. "We merely desire to hear Sophie's side of things. What better place than this grotto where the community can gather?"

Angry boos lobbed in his direction, especially from the St. Louis refugees clustered in the back.

Many were still confused as to the exact wrong Sophie had committed. The early summer plan to attack the Republic called for an extended display of strength. It was hoped the breach of the Republic's walls, the use of incendiary propaganda, and strengthening internal dissent would act as an impetus for negotiations and a cease-fire. This plan disintegrated, though, when iama-B gas pushed the army back to the swamps. Every rebel left in the wards (including Sophie) became stranded and were required to blend in with the population.

What charges could be leveled against the Iron Queen? Yes, some admitted, after the Battle of the High Walls Sophie *did* disobey direct orders to kill the Second Vessel and engage in acts of sabotage, but these were independent commands from Xenon not sanctioned by the Committee. Nor could it be gainsaid she entirely deserted, as communication persisted throughout the ordeal. In fact, the *Goetia Mirror* greatly assisted the Column; they gained more informants in a month than in five years. The greatest charge against the Iron Queen consisted in the intentional forfeiture of the jinn. But here, the Column Committee divided. Where some saw liberation others glimpsed bloody oblivion, and Sophie's account of the ill fated events at Consumption Junction and Miantgast did nothing to stay anxieties.

Sophie concluded, answering her accusers with granite resolution: "The jinn is a disease born from the Fates. Its energies not only break kingdoms but eat the human mind. Many here ask why I destroyed them. There were many reasons; but two will suffice: to keep the helots safe from savagery and you from becoming savages."

Limon circled her, agitated. "Why not allow us to be the judge of that? Why act on your own without consultation? Do you think your mind superior to this Committee?"

"Of course not, Brother Limon."

"Your actions say you do."

Sophie studied Limon's wrinkled brow. His whole body stood at an angle, an artificial stiffness. He was pumping up his emotions, angered, but still a friend. Best to take a conciliatory approach. "Your people are mine," she said. "I owe everything to the Southwest Confederacy, my very life. When my brother and I were hunted by the Republic, you saved us, treated me as your own. Many on this continent would've turned us over, but you courageous people did not. I could never feel superior to any of you. But, Limon, you do not understand Ozbolt's weapons . . . not like I do."

"There she goes again," Limon snarled. "When did the Great Maiden of the Mountain grow so presumptuous? You are letting your personal emotional history cloud your judgment."

"You may be right," Sophie admitted, "but I acted on the facts as I saw them."

"That is why we meet together—to avoid walking blind to our own inadequacies."

"Have you ever seen the jinn used, Limon?"

"I saw Zemer make it talk, light up like a sunray. He chanted things before they happened. No weapon could touch him."

"Its power consumed him like a flame. The jinn opens nothing but death. To touch it is to risk killing everyone close to you. Would you have me dump a radiated fuel rod in the lap of the tribe that saved me, to let a house fall on my adopted family?"

"Flowery analogies and emotional appeals are not arguments. Cease defenses aimed to mislead this assembly."

Limon's self-important gaze hardened. His eyes snapped open. Sophie sensed a change in him, an eagerness for violence. He spoke for the militant hawks, a small determined group (one she once shared sympathies with). They clustered behind him in work trousers, grimacing, guardian scalps hanging from their belts. Perhaps there were more hawks than she suspected. Perhaps the group could seize the Committee. She would need to sharpen her attack to challenge them directly. The Iron Queen asked, "What would you do with it, Limon?"

"The jinn?"

"Yes. If I handed one to you—right now—what could be done? Would you use it on the walls, pillage the Tenth Ward? Try to make it to the coast? Kill yourself like your friend, Marcus? I know it was you who conspired to send him."

"That is a scandalous insinuation!"

"If it was untrue, you would not take such offense. Your emotions cloud your judgment, too . . . it would seem. Do not forget how talkative anarchists can be, especially Xenon. The Iron Queen is no artless girl. She discovers everything hidden; no one can hide their secrets from her."

"Why seek to antagonize me for no reason—"

"You criticize *me* for acting outside this Committee's authority, yet look at your behavior—you did the same by sending agents to the wards. Your actions brought innocent blood on our Eastern Column and ruined the helot strikes. There is a word for someone who accuses others for things he does himself—hypocrite!"

"You go too far, Commander. My conduct is not being discussed."

Sophie growled, "I made my choice, Limon. I will not apologize for it. Not to you or anyone else. If this committee wishes to punish me for insubordination, so be it. I will accept their judgment. Since you were the one who called us all together, propose a penalty."

Sophie held her breath and narrowed her eyes. *Now, hawk, reveal what you are,* she thought. *Warn this assembly of your thirst for blood.*

Limon shouted raising his arm, "I move this body strip Sophie of command—"

The cavern chamber erupted into objections.

"—and punish her insolence with . . . with . . . exile."

Limon's words caused total silence, and sober minds reactively challenged their ears. Surely they'd not heard the words correctly. Exile? Could he be serious?

Limon stiffened harder. Then there was uproar.

"Outrageous!" the assembly shouted impassioned. "The fool speaks foolishness!"

The militiamen behind Limon stumbled with surprise. No one conceived such a radical measure (or authorized Limon to speak it) and the crowd growled murderously at them.

In complete shock, Tyro Canto stepped to Sophie's defense lifting up her hand. "Hold, brothers and sisters. Hold. For three hours we heard nothing but praise for the Iron Queen, even from members of Limon's own faction. Now Limon moves to dishonorably cast out our daughter like some unrepentant murderer. What has Sophie done to deserve such venom? She saved my life in St. Louis. Saved Limon's life, too—so I'm told—on three occasions. When any of you fell sick, who was the first to offer her daily rations to help? Who bloodied her own feet to give others fresh boots? Does she ever assign any dangerous mission without bravely fighting, too? Everyone in this room has benefited from Sophie's strength, and she has never asked for a single thing in return. To treat her this way brings shame on our people. I reject every word Limon spoke and bid you do the same."

All eyes turned to see how the Iron Queen would respond.

Sophie took Limon's hand, hard as redwood. She had expected a call for her dismissal, but not even she contemplated the submission of exile. Extra work impositions, perhaps, or a few days of silence in isolation, but not exile. To order exile was to seek the elimination of all relationship, to end someone's connection to the commune, to desire an individual suffer punishment worse than death—worse than the Bull. "Limon, my friend," Sophie spoke softly, "it grieves me to have caused such hate in you. I accept your judgment and will leave at dawn."

Both Tyro and Limon shot up in horrified surprise. Chairs overturned as militiamen raced to prevent the Iron Queen from leaving. Voices pleaded with her as if she stood ready to jump from a bridge. "Do not accept! Do not accept! No one but Limon wants you to go. We refuse to follow such injustice."

At seeing his radical punishment accepted so rapidly, Limon almost fainted, fell to his knees crying raindrop tears and clutching Sophie's arm. "What are you doing, Great Maiden? You weren't supposed to accept. I didn't mean such a horrible thing. The jinn cast a spell on me. I lost my senses. We must wait for other proposals. You must propose your own. There is still much to discuss."

Sophie snapped, "No, there will be no discussion. Only your indictment matters to me. You would discard me like some loose scab. You have exiled me."

"What? Never! I spoke in haste. I take it all back."

"You cannot take it back. You've hurt me more than anything I can remember."

Voices began calling for *Limon's* exile. The assembly hurled invectives, tempers enflamed: "He casts out his own in her time of need. He is depraved and betrays Zemer's memory. His soul is rotten."

Militiamen dragged Limon from Sophie's arms and berated him before the crowd, pointing dangerously in his face. After discussing his limited options, Limon crawled back to Sophie hysterical, begged for silence.

"Sacred Assembly, I have done an accursed thing. I have disgraced myself and the people who taught me. I am a power-lover, proud, sensitive only to myself, a crusher of friends. I beseech the Iron Queen—for my sake—end her exile and come back to us. I move for a vote by acclamation: Let Sophie be acquitted of all charges against her, restored to the Eastern Column and her communes."

No one dared dissent. Sophie nodded her acceptance.

Limon continued, "Now let the Iron Queen determine my punishment for seeking to use the Column Committee for petty grievances and to inflict unjust penalties. I only beg . . . she treat me with more respect than I showed her."

"I could never exile you, Limon," Sophie exclaimed, lifting him up and embracing him. He smelled of strong odors, but she kissed his forehead anyway. "We have both done wrong. I suggest you take a day of silence to write upon the cruelties of exile and speak for others when they face it."

"Thank you, Iron Queen. Thank you." He kissed her again and retreated.

Sophie clenched her fist. "I consider this matter settled. We shall never speak of it again."

After the reconciliation, a swell of celebration, kissing, and laughter hurled Sophie across the rocky chasm. Jugs of moonshine burst open. Toasts were made to Zemer and their fallen comrades. Women sang solidarity work songs. The militia rocked Sophie in the air, offered her a glass of whiskey. "Long live the Iron Queen, Great Maiden of the Mountain," their cheers reverberated to the work camp outside. "Long live the Guardian-Slayer! Iron Queen! Iron Queen!"

Sophie smiled, happy to finally put the growing tension in the Eastern Column to rest. Yet her bio-metal heart was filled with sadness. Looking at the wild and good-natured anarchists dancing around her, kissing her hands, she realized she could not remain. Things could not return to the way they were. Limon had spoken a little truth. It was impossible to be clear-headed when being hunted, and her presence endangered the entire commune. She pushed away from the merriment and called for attention. "As much as I would like to remain your Iron Queen," she said with tears starting in her eyes, "I can no longer command. I must go. Glaucon and I must flee past these jungles to the Arctic. Prodicus will kill all who help us. You must consider a replacement."

The crowds acted wounded at her words. "No one should suffer for the whole," they said. "Prodicus is not so clever. You are more vulnerable alone. Let those who wish to scorn their sister leave. Fight or not, you belong here."

Tyro seized Sophie's arm. "I won't let you run away abandoned like some stray. Even if you tried, I'd tie you up." She gave an unchanging smile, imprinting her defiance on Sophie's spirit. Tyro had returned to her energetic self, spreading that perceptive influence which she so admired.

Sophie bowed deferentially to her friends, thankful for vindication. "Our human bond can never be broken," she said. As she left the Column Committee, she heard the customary crashing fall into laughter.

"Bring Xenon at once!" they demanded.

V § 5 The Island of Destiny

Prodicus bent over his sapphire throne in mightiness. The outskirts of Boston burned below him, a boiling and deadly white. The last week followed a rigid pattern: Wait five hours for the Strife Beam to charge; scan for the indigo Vessels; fire; move to the next target; wait again; scan for the Vessels; fire. He had already given up waiting for the auxiliary forces to mobilize. Men were too slow—especially for this campaign. The auxiliaries would clean up his advance.

Broken and bloody, rebels lined before his throne. They did so out of belief he'd show mercy. Announcements made earlier by Levantra's acoustic nodules promised amnesty for anyone willing to capitulate.

One rebel leader, Emma Agathon, fell prostrate before his majesty. "Please, my lord," she cried, "we fought against you, but only out of fear. We did not know you'd offer peace. Accept our apology and friendship."

Prodicus grimaced. While speaking peace her eyes were haughty. The leader of the Virginia Collective posed continuing liability. "Where are the Vessels?" the guardian-king of men demanded in his court.

"I have no idea what you're talking about," Emma cried. "Look here, we brought tribute as a sign of amity and concord."

Militiamen struggled forward, carrying wooden chests.

Prodicus lifted the lid and ran his hands through a collection of feather necklaces, befuddled. "I like not homespun garments, amber, and feathers," he bellowed spitting in Emma's face. "I like them not! You Yankee barbarians have nothing I desire but two things. The Vessels—bring them to me as tribute!"

"I . . . I . . . don't understand, Great Guardian-King. What are 'Vessels'? Cups? A special dish?"

"Human flesh," Prodicus cussed. "The one you call Iron Queen. She stole a guardian from Heliopolis. After the Festival of Demeter, no less, our most sacred celebration!"

"The Iron Queen?"

"She has other names: the fallen Watcher, Sophia, Great Maiden of the Mountain, Guardian Princess of Heliopolis, Death Commander of the Eastern Column, Swamp Rat!"

"No one knows where she is, my lord. The Continental Caucus has evaporated."

"Would you tell me if you knew where she was?"

"She has been granted sanctuary—"

"Pity. Then I do not accept your tribute. I do not grant you peace. Please throw Miss Agathon from the cliffs."

Crystal armored auxiliaries abruptly sprang on her.

"But you promised leniency if we submitted," Emma pleaded wildly.

"I lied. Blame yourself or the Iron Queen."

She was dragged away.

Prodicus waved off the assembly of rebels like a bad dessert. The next hour all were hurled off the island, twenty kilometers into the crimson remnants of Boston. It would be a hard lesson for the rebellion (and one not easily forgot).

When Patroclus heard about his father's trickery, he was deeply distraught and raced across the marbled plazas of Levantra for an explanation.

"Father, you should have left some alive. This terminates all reason to surrender in the future."

Prodicus curled his lip. They passed a walled orchard behind Levantra's pyramid temple. "The rebels came to save their own skins, correct?" he asked.

"Yes, but—"

"Anyone so quickly ready to give up their resistance can not be trusted. They would swear allegiance only to turn on us tomorrow."

"But, Sire, the god Horcus does not like it when we break oaths."

"I launched a pre-emptive strike against future perjurers; Horcus will understand. My message is bright as sunshine: Bring me the Vessels or die screaming in the clouds."

Patroclus rubbed his shoulders exasperated. From the behavior of the guardians sunning themselves on the lawn, one would hardly suspect the most extensive military campaign in the Republic's history transpired below. He decided to drop the subject altogether and breach the bad news. The Vessels were not found among the Seminoles. Even after dismantling the savages' remaining dikes, flooding their wooded camps, and burning their clan leaders alive with electrodes, the Florida Archipelago kept silent.

Prodicus received this news with the worst hostility of the day. "No one just disappears," he hissed. "After St. Louis, they either went east or west. It is now plainly obvious they did not go to the Atlantic."

"A shrewd maneuver," Patroclus admitted, "to brave the Fallout Corridor with our guns at their back. We should've followed Xenon into the desert. How could the Fates have made such a poor prediction?"

"Xenon is known for making tactless gambles. I overestimated him, again."

"Or he underestimated you."

Prodicus frowned. "Interesting way to look at things."

The philosopher-king suddenly gripped his head, tossed to and fro. Voices scalded his mind. They were vertical, irrational screams that disturbed his calculations, wrenched his head. That witch boy had placed them there, he knew it. He had lost sight of the infinite, was blind to the future. So were the Fates! What had Zemer done to drive out his serenity? Was he possessed? No. How could a philosopher-king be possessed? But Potone—he was certain it was her—came at night with nightmares and robbed him of sleep for killing her son. He sometimes swore he saw Zemer behind him, too, in his shadow cutting his Achilles tendon, holding Levantra back from glory.

"They must be in the Rockies somewhere," Patroclus thought aloud, not noticing his father's distress. "Rex has found nothing in the wastes to the north. Zoe is still attempting to flush out Coughing Fish in the Louisiana Territory. This campaign is going to take months."

Prodicus cast a fearful look at his shadow—murmuring, by Zeus, the shadow murmured! He locked hands in his sleeves, shuddering, regaining focus. "We don't have months. (*I don't have months*, he really thought.) Tell me, Patroclus, what would you say if I launched the avis this very afternoon?"

"Sire, that would be most irregular." Patroclus could not even fathom the idea.

"Why?"

"Because machines have no silver in their souls."

"True, but the auxiliaries lack it, too. They are . . . a disappointment to say the least."

"Stratos will surely mutiny! They hold their service to the Republic a punctilio the most sacred."

"We are in crisis, my cunning lion. Surely they will not object to more efficiency. Any metal will do to subjugate this continent. Don't you agree?"

"Well—"

"Yes or no?"

"Yes, I suppose. But try to understand, Father. The Republic is straining to re-align after the loss of Salazar Ozbolt. Procedure is all they have left."

Patroclus bit his lip. He still tried to erase the image of an enraged Prodicus hurling the mad scientist over the edge of Levantra, splattering his bones on the ocean waves. Salazar's betrayal with the jinn was not taken lightly. The loss of the Vessels and the last Ozbolt filled the city with a foreboding sense of doom. The entire Department of Foresight and Futurology had been liquidated and fed to the Bull.

"Salazar was a weakling cow," Prodicus wheezed, "always was, never ready to commit. But his plans can still be milked. Tell me, do they still teach the slippery slope argument at the Academy?"

"Certainly, Sire. It is one of the favorite fallacies."

"Oh, it is not such a horrible argument. Ozbolt was clever enough to use it for Kabiri advantage. One little golem might become millions, enough to defeat Stratos ten times over. Poor Ekklesia the Blind glimpsed the danger but was laughed at for his 'irrational fears.' Marvelous, isn't it? Our auxiliaries are like frogs in a pot slowly heated to boiling point. They grew comfortable and now, at last, they'll fry."

Patroclus could hardly believe what he was hearing. Since the escape of the Vessels and the death of Salazar, Prodicus had descended into madness and cruelty, but this—this!—was too much. "You would strike at the auxiliaries?" he quaked.

"Not just the auxiliaries, but Leonida, Hypatia, Creon and the rest."

Patroclus protested, "Father, the archons are deep, loyal Kabiri—"

"The Fates said one of them will seek to prevent henosis—and assassinate me!"

"Which one?"

"The stars are unclear. So, logically, I must kill them all."

"Even Zeno?"

"Especially Zeno. This prediction occurred following that little worm's ascension. I always knew it was a mistake elevating him. Everyone is turning against me. You're the only one I can be sure about."

"Father, you know my loyalties. I never desire your offense. I seek only to fulfill your happy and successful rule, but what you're setting in motion will destroy the Republic."

"To save the Republic we must destroy it."

Patroclus swallowed this strange logic with much difficulty. A tremor went down his spine.

Prodicus snapped in his son's face: "What foul thoughts in that look, Patroclus. Do not play the gentle idiot. You know well how I came to power. What do you think will happen to *you* if I'm killed, hmm? The first thing the victor will do is murder you and every last one of your blood relatives—just like I did to the Hythlodays. Make no mistake; your life is tethered to mine like an umbilical cord. If I die, you die. We have no friends in this city. Everyone hates us in the wards. We cannot flee to the Other Side. The Iron Queen will have our scalps as trophies. Your back is to the corner, lion, and like me, you're trapped. You have entered Ares' dance circle. Now . . . you must dance."

Patroclus studied the leathery face of his father for any sign of kindness. He discovered nothing but discolored humanity, and wet the dry roof of his mouth. Red circles glowed around his father's pupils; he had begun ingesting the jinn's light more frequently. Too frequently. As much as he hated to admit, though, he was right. Destiny tied them together. He was trapped like a fly in a web. "Obviously, Father," Patroclus sighed, "any decision you make will be for the best. What do you intend to do?"

"Once you contain Stratos with the avis, I will assume emergency powers and abolish the Logoset, for good. We will then retreat to Levantra to carry on the search. After the Vessels are recovered, I will immerse myself with Sophia and Glaucon and become the Monad. I will leave it to you to dispose of our bodies. Then you shall float free and in peace under my watchful gaze, shaded by the blissful Form of Justice. Our family will rule the world for ten thousand years."

"I will carry out your commands," Patroclus mumbled with a whisper.

"If you value your life, you'd better. My visions of the future have grown cloudy since Zemer's death. Traps are laid, I sense a time-wind, strange shadows . . . that could rip us away. That nephew was more dangerous than I suspected. He is more troublesome in death than life."

There was another heavy silence. Patroclus contemplated Glaucon's decision to escape. *Ironic*, he thought, *that Glaucon carries the blood of the first philosopher-king, while I, Patroclus, must carry the last*. He asked his father perplexed, "I don't understand Sophia's actions. What woman would accept the murderer of her brother so readily?"

"Women and their men," Prodicus snarled contemptuously. He kicked a stone out into the sky, thinking. "Saint Plato said it best, don't you agree?— 'Dogs become like their mistresses.' The distance between love and hate is as thin as the void between atoms. Their special rapport is not unexpected. The Fates predicted they'd share a close affinity for one another. That affinity makes them vulnerable. Ready the avis, my son. Heaven awaits recovery of her lost children and henosis."

V § 6 PANDORA PRAYS UPON THE ROCKS

Sophie and Glaucon lay by the lake in one another's arms, enjoying peace for the first time in weeks. Directly ahead of them, past the calm waters, work teams attended to a jungle-orchard, gathering mangos and pears in twig baskets. Most curious was the absence of heavy machinery. The green-anarchists designed their garden systems using little but nature as a teacher. Nature, in fact, was their primary tool. They cooperated with the jungle, learning from its processes, its bio-diversity, and brought together numerous species of plants to sustain the soil and food production. Meticulously controlling waste, they recycled everything; even laundry water was used to irrigate spinach and yams. Housing served double purposes: Unused space grew grapes; bean-stalks climbed up wall trellises. Sophie told Glaucon they conserved because her commune cared about the future of others. Unlike the Republic, they wanted balance with nature, not its submission.

Glaucon found her anarchist love for permaculture curious. The Republic never had a waste problem—matter incinerators saw to that. Further, genetically altered food and soil-rejuvenation technology saved the city's population from want. Everyone was fed and happy with minimal environmental damage. Yes, the Republic's methods were less 'natural,' more industrial, but why should this be immoral when the world itself wasn't harmed? He decided her complaint really centered on philosophy rather than effect: The Republic's technology reinforced the master/slave dynamic. Nature was not an equal partner but something to control. It had to be subdued and conquered rather than cared for and accommodated. It was a way of thinking that tarnished the value of the environment, and implicitly, the value of human beings. It was the path of hierarchy: humans first, nature second.

Stating her argument in this manner made Glaucon love Sophie all the more. He shuddered with love. But Sophie misunderstood his gasp, saw it as an expression of angst. She kissed his head, apologized profusely. "I'll never leave you alone with Xenon again," she promised. The Iron Queen looked for bruises on his face. "That man will go too far one day."

Glaucon smiled at her touch, breathed in the refreshing mountain air. He rested his head on the roots of an old cedar and relaxed, listened to the creaking windmills. Water celery sprouted nearby which he plucked to nibble for refreshment.

Sophie continued clenching her fists: "And that glutton, Milo . . ." she cursed with an ugly frown, "leaving you alone for breakfast after I specifically told him to remain. He has a stomach for brains."

Glaucon spoke up for him. "Nothing happened."

"Someone might've killed you," Sophie countered. "Then he'd be sorry."

"Milo seems warmhearted. He gave me this strange cigpop to calm me down."

"That's not a cigpop; its marijuana."

"Well, it was nice, at any rate. Felt like a bunch of hands massaging my brain. He said he . . . grows it. No additives."

"You seem quite taken with him."

"One could say the same for you."

Sophie eyed Glaucon's expression and smiled. "All right, out with what you want to say."

"Nothing. It's just that—"

"People are more . . . affectionate here."

"So Xenon says."

"Xenon is a prude; hence, his psychotic unbalance and inconsolable rage. But it would be wrong of you to claim me all to yourself. We share everything in the communes, including pleasure. It brings everyone closer."

"I suppose."

"Don't worry, Glaucon," Sophie softly wrapped hands around his face, "I have only eyes for you at the moment. I'll protect you from all the others. If any of them get too pushy, just say no. They'll leave you alone."

"It's kind of like Heliopolis, I guess."

"No, it's very different," Sophie corrected. "On Heliopolis sex is a method of control. Plato's sake, they give *erosic* to children. Here sex is a means of liberation. People only do things they desire. There is no pressure or condemnation."

Glaucon peered into the tree canopy. "Do you and Xenon read from the same anarchist handbook or something?"

Sophie rolled closer to him, spoke touching his arm: "Why the harshness in your tone? You ask one question but hide another."

Glaucon sighed. "Why didn't you tell me, Sophie?"

"Tell you what?"

"That Xenon is my father."

Sophie rested her head on his chest, listened to his changing heartbeat, a type of heartbeat she could never feel again. "Glaucon, that was not my place. Xenon made me promise."

"My whole past is a lie," Glaucon swallowed bitterly. "My so-called friends on Heliopolis—Zoe, Patroclus—they must've known all along. I was a big joke."

"You know the truth now."

Glaucon drained Sophie's hair through his fingers. "Do you know what happened to my mother?" he asked.

"No," Sophie whispered. "Xenon does not speak of it. I asked him long ago, but he couldn't finish—too much sadness there. I only know Prodicus murdered Melete to punish him. Had you not been the Second Vessel, he would've surely killed you, too."

Yes, Xenon had cried to her seven year before after returning from the Delta—about everything. Sophie found him sobbing delirious away from their singing camp. When she sat next to him on a log for company, he could barely speak. Seeing Xenon's demeanor laid waste by such repulsive memories melted Sophie's heart. "She's gone, Sophie," Xenon groaned, breaking into pieces, "my beautiful Melete's gone. Her whole family . . . the Kabiri took them away." Throwing his wilting beard into her shoulder, Sophie quivered with complex feelings, gently patted his head. She had been away from the communes for over two years, thinking of her reunion with this man, how she would act. Obviously, her reappearance with Zemer had opened old wounds, old passions in both. In spite of her good sense—or to prove her maturity under Coughing Fish—Sophie leaned forward and kissed her protector, to share with him, and show how much she'd thought of him in the swamps—but when their mouths connected, he did not kiss back. Xenon's watery grey eyes opened in terror. "What in Plato's name are you doing, Sophie?" he asked, pushing her away. He began crying wilder still.

"I hate to see you like this," Sophie said, forever ashamed and lashing herself for revealing her true feelings.

Xenon's lips shuddered queasy. "But . . . but . . . you're my . . . daughter!"

"No," Sophie told him, "I'm not. Lycaon was my father, not you. You're my friend . . . and so unhappy. I hate seeing you unhappy."

Being told that his old view of their relationship was mistaken—a one-sided lie—Xenon cursed angrily: "You're just a girl!"

Sophie had scoffed back, "The Republican Army doesn't think I'm . . . just a girl. I've killed more guardians than you, I think." She lowered her eyes, both remorseful and proud to brag about such a thing. "I was only trying to make you feel better."

"And you think *this* will make me feel better?" Xenon admonished her agitated. "You should not think such things about a man like me."

"But I do!"

"My failures aren't something to be forgotten with a woman my son's age. When I look at you, he's all I see. Prodicus is perverting him—I can feel it!—and there's nothing to be done. I've failed Melete again."

"You can't keep punishing yourself, Xenon. It's my fault as much as yours. You came back . . . came back for . . . for . . . me-e-e!" Hidden guilt carried for so long finally rushed out of Sophie's lungs. "Had I been s-stronger, well enough to go to the Logoset with Zemer and Prodicus, you might've reached her in time. Melete might . . . might still be alive! Your son might be here beside you! You chose to save me and wasted precious time. Melete's dead because of me. Not you! Me!"

Xenon looked up at her with a multitude of expressions, suddenly calm. "Listen to me carefully, pretty Sophia." His baritone voice rose up in a throat drowned by spit. He wiped her cheeks, paid attention to the changes in her older face. "You had nothing to do with Melete's death. Hear me? Nothing. Had I left you in that tower they'd have killed you again. And again and again. Killed and tortured till no organs were left, till you were all machine. Leaving you there was unthinkable. Do you understand?"

Sophie nodded.

"Remember always, I'm crying not because I wish to alter my choice but because I lament fate which caused me to murder my only love. Neither you nor I deserved such affliction. Prodicus is to blame. Prodicus is at the root of all our troubles." Xenon stood up, boots crunching on some stray limbs. "Sad to say," he whispered, "I am faced with another difficult choice. One I cannot face alone. One I cannot mention to anyone else for fear of ostracism. I need someone I can trust completely."

"Anything, Xenon," Sophie whispered. "You can trust me. I'll do anything for you."

"You may not even tell Zemer." His voice pressed adamantly about this.

"I won't."

Xenon watched an owl descend on some poor jungle rodent, then stated, "Coughing Fish tells me you've discovered a knack for stealth operations, that no target is beyond the Iron Queen's reach."

"He is correct," Sophie conceded.

"You claimed you were good at killing guardians."

"I did. The guardians love to seek the Form of Justice. I show it lives under their scalps."

"Good . . . I want you to kill another guardian for me. It will be a death to save our people from Levantra's fire, to save your own life."

"Tell me and he will die."

Xenon placed a piece of shadowspar in Sophie's hand with much difficulty. "I want you to assassinate the Second Vessel."

"Your son?" Sophie was stunned.

"You and Zemer are my only children." Xenon shut his eyes. "Watch the recording. See for yourself. Glaucon belongs to Prodicus now. He's a vulture like the rest, lost forever."

"Maybe we can turn him back."

"Don't be a fool."

"When shall I return to the Republic?" Sophie handed back the shadowspar but Xenon refused to touch it again.

"Keep that ghost away from me," he shuddered, looking at the shadowspar like smoking brimstone. "I will let you know when the time is right. But give me your word—as the Iron Queen—you will kill him quickly. Don't make my son suffer. Don't desecrate his body with your knife."

Swallowing hard, Sophie promised to do as he asked. "When I find your . . . guardian . . . he will die with a single blow, as if struck by a thunderbolt." She tried to grab Xenon's arm, reassuringly, but he pulled away, marched back to camp disturbed. She knew quite clearly after that she was *not* Melete; she was Xenon's make-believe daughter and could never make him whole. She would obey him in this horrible thing because she loved him.

She would gain his heart by violence. By filicide! By crime! Infamy! Singing death! Nothing more.

Yet . . . yet . . . she'd chosen to spare the Second Vessel, in the end. How strange! She'd chosen to risk disaster, spurred on by Zemer's moral arguments and her own feelings. Just like Xenon, her choices cursed others; she saved one life but doomed thousands. Mercy was not mercy but transferred cruelty. She saw Zemer die, saw her darling brother murdered in the Bull; Terra Brandon destroyed; Ivan thrown to the depths of suicide-bombing; Aquila trampled by feet; the helot Directory crushed. For what?—a single man. Was any man worth so much? Lying beside him, she was ashamed to embrace her choice, but she did. Life or death—she'd chosen life. But why should keeping sweat on Glaucon's face be so hurtful to others? Why?

Glaucon, contemplating his mother, Zemer, and Aquila in a single thought, seemed to sense what Sophie was feeling. "To continue living while everyone else dies around us, is that our fate?"

Sophie pressed her ear closer to his ribs. "No. Zemer said there's no such thing as fate. We can fly where we like. We will not be immersed. I know it. Prodicus and the guardians will be defeated . . . one day."

Glaucon was unsure, especially when birds flew left, gathered like a storm cloud, and perched in the canopy. Birds could make omens like the disir, and this was a bad one.

Sophie pondered her decision to remain in the militia. *Zemer would certainly be displeased*, she thought, missing him unimaginably. He was right in so many things, but she could not live as he wanted her. Prodicus would never stop. Never. No matter how hard she asked. Had she not begged him every night at the Office of Public Harmony to give up his genocidal plans? Her uncle was unmoored, drifting further from reality. Obsessed with power, he would grow like an amoeba until he gobbled the world.

Despite her gloomy outlook, Sophie comforted Glaucon again, saying, "We'll survive," and rested her chin on his shoulder. "We have to. When this is all over, we will join one of the permaculture crews. I am ready for a change in trade. How about you?"

Glaucon groaned. "That sounds absolutely backbreaking."

"Awww, you don't want to seed life back into the continent, dear heart?" Sophie's kitten voice teased him again.

Glaucon writhed in dejection. "Sophie, I would be a burden. I don't have any skills. All I can do is chart contraries and swing a xiphos."

"Yes—I know—and you're not even really good at those, right?"

Glaucon smiled slightly. "I truly was the worst guardian."

"Good," Sophie kissed his chest, "I like it when you have faith in yourself."

They held hands in silence listening to fish jumping in the water. Although Sophie brushed off Glaucon's concerns, she carried similar fears. Her life had known only violence and anger. She wondered if she could survive in a world without something to fight against. Training with the militia as a teenager brought clearer focus: Organize resistance, eat when you like but don't waste food, practice, help Zemer drill, enjoy the company. Now she didn't know what to do. *Why can't I express myself faithfully to Glaucon?* she wondered silently. The communes had helped crack her open, yes, but still, a shell remained. She was not like the others. She was closing up again. "Glaucon," she stroked him with her thumb, "I change my mind. Maybe you would make a better teacher. I bet the children approach you to educate them."

Glaucon snorted. "Now I know you're joking."

"No, I really mean it. There is a softness to you." She paused. "Tell me about your dreams."

"My dreams?"

"Yes."

"I don't have any." No one ever asked him that before.

"Come on. There must be something."

"Everything I thought I wanted was a trap. My life's been a complete waste."

"You aren't a waste to me . . . or my brother. Do you still hear the voices you told me about?"

"No."

"Well, that's one dream come true. Zemer cured you by invoking a dream. I'm still hoping my voices end. Tell me something else you wish for."

"Please, Sophie, stop." Glaucon sat up. "Prodicus will never leave us alone. We must give up dreams *and* hope. You said so many times as we traveled."

Sophie persisted: "Pretend we're free—really free!—with no one hunting us. What would you do?"

"I don't know. Sit here with you, I guess. What has you so optimistic all of a sudden?"

"I can't explain it," Sophie said looking up at the nimbus clouds, "right at the point when hope becomes impossible, I strangely want to hold it close. How I loath to admit this . . . but I feel like Pandora at the moment."

"Saint Plato, you must be running a fever."

"Maybe I am, or maybe my brother infected me with his love for myth. You're right, there is much to hate in the original Hesiod. Pandora's nature—woman's nature—is smeared from the tale's beginning. Legend says the gods created woman out of spite—not from care—to retaliate against Prometheus for bringing fire down to men. The first woman is fashioned by the clumsy hands of a male god rather than the nimbler fingers of a goddess. Athena—another female under the control of the male principle—prepares woman for patriarchal slavery by teaching her skills like needlework and spinning. Hermes is charged to give the woman a 'shameless mind' and 'deceitful nature,' with 'lies and crafty words.' To increase her humiliation, Pandora is molested throughout the ordeal by an orgy of heavenly hands trying to make her seductive. She is fondled with graces, necklaces, and thin robes, ornamented like a holiday tree, dressed up like a passive doll with bracelets and flowery wreaths, all so she can be presented as a pretty object—or should I say trap—for man. Oh yes, the gods are unmatched in cruelty. With minds bent on ruin, they bless their gift with another treasure. It is a sexually suggestive jar of unspeakable evils: pestilence, sorrow, sickness, death, and woe."

"Which she opens," Glaucon grinned.

"Of course she does, just like a nosy squirrel. Pandora opens it accidentally; being a woman, Pandora can do nothing actively on her own, especially something like intentionally curse a man. Opening the jar must be by accident. And her meddlesome acts lead to all our afflictions."

"If I remember correctly, only Hope remained clinging to the lid of the jar."

"Exactly," Sophie said, "all the evils fly out of the jar but one—Hope. Hope remains. The story ends. I've always wondered, Glaucon, what is the hidden meaning behind the myth?"

"Never trust the gods . . . or pretty Greek women bearing gifts."

Sophie punched him playfully in the arm. "No, it must be more than that. Why does only Hope remain?"

"Hope was surely an evil since it lay with the other evils," Glaucon suggested.

Sophie tapped a finger against her bottom lip, thinking. "True. In a way, Hope is the heaviest and worst of all evils. It makes you think the other sorrows of the jar will be found and captured again, which is clearly impossible. The world will never be repaired."

"I shouldn't think so," Glaucon lamented.

Sophie added, "Xenon—at numerous dinners in St. Louis—spouted Nietzsche's pessimistic view: Hope catching on the lid was no accident but another method of control. Zeus commanded Hope to remain in the jar to keep humanity from committing suicide and rebelling against the gods. Hope was never meant to fly away, you see, but to hover stagnant in man's house like a moor's mist to potently work its illusion."

"That sounds like something Xenon would say." Glaucon felt the welt on his head.

"His answer never satisfied me," Sophie replied. "It ignores Pandora's perspective altogether."

"Does it?"

"Absolutely it does," Sophie said. "Imagine the poor girl's anger upon realizing the gods' dirty tricks. The feelings of irrational misery and heaving disappointment would be enormous."

"I guess that's true."

"For so long Pandora put up with the gods' man-handling to meet her other half, suffered such humiliation and abuse. Now they tried to take away the only good she'd ever known—her human companion—by making him hate her. Pandora is understandably upset. She wants justice. She is not some puppet plaything for the gods. She is a being with rights and dignity. So is the male she was sent to destroy. I see her doing what any honest woman would do—try to change the situation for the better. Feeling the winged evils escape through her fingers, she finally strangles Hope in her hands like a feral beast and crams it back into the jar. Running to a river she prepares to drown the beast and take her revenge. But having been so abused by the power of others, she realizes this evil, too, is a victim of the gods. How could she destroy it? How? It just wouldn't be right."

Glaucon shrugged puzzled.

"Overcome with pity, Pandora decides to tame the evil monster, to feed and nurse it. Like a child, she holds it close to her heart to keep it from growing too big or flighty."

"And how does the monster respond?" Glaucon asked enraptured.

"Even monsters can change. Hope responds to Pandora and grows into something new entirely. Gnashing teeth become kisses. The spirit chooses rebellion with her. Rather than being hope-for-a-world-empty-of-miseries as the gods intended, it transubstantiates, becomes hope-in-other-persons—a shelter from those miseries. The way I see it, the love Pandora showed the monster brightened all human relationships. Her love reflected the hate of the skies like a mirror. She made hope in others possible. Now, every time we find happiness in the communes, the gods lament and curse the day they made Pandora."

"Your story adds much to the original."

"Myths belong to no one. We should take them wherever we please for whatever reason, good or bad. All horses need new saddles. We'll ride free on them."

"I think I like your version better than the old one," Glaucon confessed. "If only we could print it in the *Goetia Mirror*."

"Maybe one day we will," Sophie blushed and held Glaucon's hands fervently between her own. "This is why I ask you now about your dreams. It's not that I believe those dreams are possible but because I want to know who you are. I want to connect with you and hold you close. You are *my* hope, my only hope, all I have left in the world. I believe my darkness can turn to light when you're around."

At the soft, beautiful expression in those jade eyes, Glaucon turned away consumed by the venom in his past. "There is no light in me to brighten you," he said almost in tears.

"That's not true. Human light never disappears." Sophie's palm cradled his face and returned him to life. "It only gets covered."

"How do you uncover it?" he asked

"Remind the other person how you care for them."

What was the point in loving when you could lose the other person so quickly? Glaucon wailed. *Every moment is like a deep painful goodbye with no end. Love is so easy to fall into but so hard to let go.* Glaucon began heaping blame on himself, recalling his many abuses one by one. Only the soft fingers external to his skin brought comfort—and there was nothing he could do to save them. He could only squeeze them as tightly as possible to prevent their dissolving into air.

This gave him an idea.

"I know how to recall our care for one another," Glaucon spoke happily.

"You do?" Sophie asked.

"When one of us seems dispirited or empty, the other should squeeze their hand tightly to express love and devotion. It is a sign we will never let the other be immersed."

"How wonderful, I would like that very much," Sophie said, squeezing his hand.

Glaucon's mood brightened. The fallen guardian stood up and walked along the edge of the lake. "Hey, Sophie, did you ever learn to skip stones?"

"Not really."

"My mother taught me. When I was a boy, she'd take me up to Parmenides Ponds. We'd watch the other kids flying kites and making wishes with their orichalcum."

Glaucon sent a smooth stone skidding across the surface like a magical top. The simple majestic dance made Sophie stiffen with curiosity.

"Let me try," she demanded, dipping her hands into the water searching for a slippery stone. She threw her rock, but it awkwardly drowned.

Glaucon explained, "It's not about how forcefully you throw; you also need to spin the rock for stability. Try flicking your wrist harder."

Sophie gave him a devious look. When her stone plopped in the water again, Glaucon bit his index finger, stifling a laugh. He struggled to keep a straight face.

"It's harder than it looks," she admitted nudging his arm. "See, guardian, you have other *practical* skills."

"I wish you could've met my mother," Glaucon lamented. "She was unnaturally talented at this kind of thing."

"Melete must've really been something."

They practiced skipping stones until several children raced laughing down the wooded slope to see the strange contest. Soon a hundred rocks skipped the water as Glaucon taught the finer points of the technical art. When a rainbow formed next to Sophie's bronze hair, Glaucon smiled peacefully. He couldn't remember a happier day. How he wished to hold time still.

The children, like the parents, seemed oblivious to personal space. They crawled into Sophie's lap and hung on his shoulders like lemurs. Such behavior was the most noticeable difference between the anarchists and the denizens of Heliopolis. The anarchists seemed to actually enjoy company, to care about the well being of strangers. The idea this could come to ruin filled him with sadness.

"Keep the rock above the water as long as you can," Glaucon addressed one of the children, a tear collecting on his burning cheek. "That's all that matters. Never let the water best you. Fight immersion with everything you've got."

Sophie squeezed his hand again and stared at the sunset.

V § 7 Flight of the Megamachine

Two weeks passed before Crypt learned of the bloody fall of Stratos. Glaucon spent most that time locked inside a private bungalow, unable to move.

Sophie warned Glaucon about withdrawal from *erosic*. "It shall be agonizing," she readied him, "horribly agonizing."

Whenever Sophie made such dire warnings, Glaucon's knees trembled. "What will happen to me?" he asked, afraid to know the answer.

"You'll start by becoming agitated," she said. "Depression rolls over you like an avalanche followed by headache tremors and vomiting. Your lips and teeth and . . ." Sophie blushed slightly, "other areas become enflamed. Increased blood flow turns you a little pink."

"How long does this process take?"

"Depends. Like getting wisdom teeth pulled, some guardians recover faster than others. Zemer had a rough time of it. Mine was easier."

Nothing prepared for such torment, for the nightmares. Glaucon died in every one: shot running away by an auxiliary firing squad, squeezed by scaled echidnas, hacked to death by Sophie, crushed by rolling boulders. He saw Zemer's eidolon and felt strange memories, people he didn't recognize. Sometimes—though he was afraid to admit such to Sophie—he'd awake disordered, thinking he *was* Zemer, wondering why he was back in Crypt.

Days were long, endless hangovers climaxed by hot flashes. Then there'd be a convulsive spike in libido. As Sophie dabbed a wet towel on his head, he yearned her arms' embrace. He felt defective without them, those cuddlesome arms, those adorable arms. Hurling her towel to the wall, he pleaded for any form of love, taking deep breaths.

"It won't help one bit," Sophie declared, laughing as he kissed up her wrist amorously.

"Don't laugh," Glaucon moaned.

"Sorry," Sophie apologized, pulling sheets back over her demented love-drunk, giving him sips of water. "You're just so . . . pathetic. I think you're embellishing your symptoms. I've never seen such a wimp."

"Making fun?"

"Crying and pink—just like a baby."

"I was on it a decade longer than you!" Glaucon protested.

"Oh, is that what it is?" she smirked. Kissing him softly, she re-applied the wet rag to his face and left on a signal expedition. As she reported, pulling a woolen shirt over her head, refugees from the Republic's attacks were having trouble discovering Crypt's location. She'd be gone more frequently.

Whenever Glaucon's muscles would allow, he walked outside, sick, holding his stomach. He sat at the communal tables by a mountain stream. Milo would come and play cards with him in the shade, bringing some of the children. Offered a tightly-rolled joint, Glaucon took it thankfully and felt the drug mollify his suffering.

Drug use, he observed, was quite different in Crypt, used primarily for community bonding and medicinal purposes, never to excess. It didn't appear to have the same level of escapism present in the Republic, nor as many dangerous side effects. Ulterior motives of control were completely absent, too. Nevertheless, certain norms did govern consumption. For one, drugs were hardly ever taken during the day. When Glaucon asked Milo who enforced such behavior, the soldier answered there was no rule against it; people acted as they wished.

"But then why does no one do it?"

Milo thought for a moment, placing one hand in his chino pant pocket, thumbing a suspender strap with the other. "Anyone can see drug use interferes with work. Why would you want to waste the day?"

"But others can work while you enjoy yourself."

Milo studied him disgusted, like he uttered an obscenity. "How could I enjoy myself knowing others labor on my account? What makes me so special? I'm not a *guardian*."

It was the first time the militiaman acknowledged his former status. It was also a sudden change in friendliness.

"I wasn't indicating a desire for . . . for . . . laziness," Glaucon tried to explain.

"You think crafty thoughts! Thoughts which hurt others." Milo leaned forward clutching the barrel of his rifle.

"No, no. You misunderstand."

"Do I?"

"Your society is a complex, interesting organism. I merely express curiosity at its mechanics, not rudeness."

"We are not some cricket for your guardian microscope."

"I didn't say—"

"We are not a watch to take apart."

Glaucon drew back afraid. He was unsure what questions would please such an overly-sensitive soul; but silence might condemn him, too. "I just want to fit in," Glaucon stammered. "Once I recover, I plan to work just as hard as everyone else. I promise."

"You surely should. Sophie is coddling you, and making everyone else follow suit. It is not good to live so far from the commune in separate houses. It is not Sophie."

Well at least he's telling me how he really feels, Glaucon thought. "She's still having you guard me, isn't she?"

"Yes."

"Sorry to be such a burden. I'm almost better. Thanks for looking out for me."

Expressing gratitude seemed to quiet Milo's irritation. Glaucon shifted his legs uncomfortably under the table. For all the time he sat with this man, he realized he didn't know the slightest thing about him. "Have you lived in this commune all your life?" he forced another conversation.

Milo shook his head, eyeing him intensely. "Not this one. I was born in Santa Fe."

"Why did you switch?"

"I didn't *switch*. I ran."

"Ran from what?"

"What do you think?" Milo asked fiercely. "The answer is plain. My home was burned, massacred by people like you."

People like you. How bitterly those words stung. Glaucon remembered war seasons past. He remembered the bloody playground with Polymachus. "How old were you?"

"Nine."

Glaucon knew he shouldn't have pursued the matter further, but curiosity got the best of him. "How did you escape?"

"Your questions pry too much!" Milo shouted with particular nastiness. He knocked a whicker chair over and shoved the wooden table forward. "What do you want, Glaucon? My whole life story? What makes you think it's even right to ask that? I didn't tell Sophie what happened for years. She never asked because she knew how much it hurt me. *I* told her. But since you must study me, since you're finally so interested in our culture, I'll bring enlightenment about life on the Other Side. My friends hid me in a tree, hid me when the paper warnings demanded tribute—a 'blood tax'! My people refused to comply, fought back and lost. Afterward, I watched auxiliaries take pleasure spearing babies in the air with bayonets, netting beautiful men and women to make Republican whores. I saw them lay children down—the ones that hid me—in a row. Soldiers laugh. Tell them it's all procedure, nothing to worry about, just for registry. Instead they roll over them with Aegis tanks, crunch them in claws, chanting: "Let's see if the blackheads pop!" So I ran away from home, collapsed in the jungle ready to die. A work team found me dehydrated and half-dead, brought me here."

Glaucon looked down quietly. There was nothing more to say.

Milo maintained his gaze. "My turn now to ask hard questions. I see you are turned pink—an indecent color—like all the other guardians granted sanctuary. What is it you call this miracle drug? *Erosic?* Speak truth, since truth is what you love, how many persons have you personally selected from the Slimetide Rolodex against their will?"

"I don't know."

"You don't know?"

"I can't remember. There are too many."

"So even if I told you my comrades' names, you'd have no idea whether you molested them or not?"

"I wouldn't."

"How could you do that? How could you use innocent people that way? I don't understand." Milo gripped his hair. "Zemer tried to explain it to me, but I can't imagine how it's done."

"It's just how it was. Desire would have killed us if we didn't. That's what they told us."

"And you believed it?"

"Kind of."

"Guardians are supposed to be reasonable."

"Practically everyone said it was true."

"That is no excuse."

"I'm not saying it is." Glaucon exhaled. "I've discovered guardians are no more reasonable than anyone else. In fact, they're far less reasonable because they think they're reasonable."

"Something is odd with you," Milo admitted, collecting back together. "Sophie hardly saves anyone, especially ISHIM fanatics. You can't trust them. To protect you like she does . . . there must be some good. But how can a man who does such things be good? Perhaps her feelings for Xenon make her stumble."

"Would you prefer to kill me?"

Milo shrugged. "Not really. Hurting you would make Sophie unhappy, and that would make me unhappy. But it's more complicated than that, really. I am like Zemer: tired of wishing evil on people, tired of death, worrying about Sophie every battle, watching her butcher others. Killing affects her wrongly. The oracle, Zemer, was my good friend. Many did not think his ways were workable, but I saw moral goodness in them. I look forward to the day when the Iron Queen will depart from the Great Maiden of the Mountain, when war will end. Zemer thought the day was near. He said the end would come on the wings of a firefly. Its light would be covered during the day, but at night, if we looked, a hidden way would shine from the inside out."

"He said that? A firefly?"

"No one believed the oracle. Some laughed, especially Sophie; but why would Zemer lie? He knew everything before it happened. I've looked for the lightning bug in the night since he left. It does not come. Maybe the jinn lied to him again. I want to have faith in Zemer's prophecy. I do. Is human conflict so inevitable? Do we not all crave happiness and freedom? Peace should be the norm, not war. Not war."

Glaucon sat back puzzled.

"You remind me of him," Milo admitted.

"Who?"

"Zemer. It's the damnedest thing. The way you cock your head to the right when thinking. He used to do the same."

"I hadn't noticed," Glaucon said, straitening his neck with a hand. The observation worried him; what might it mean? Could he have picked up new habits over the summer? They *did* practically live together—but so quickly?

Loud clamoring by the cave broke his flow of thought: militiamen singing after lunch. Glaucon asked, "Why is the Eastern Column still here?"

Milo replied, "Lying low for now. Influx of refugees recently." He nodded to a food line of war-ravaged Seminoles, wearing brightly colored turbans and long shirts with sibylline shapes. "We're building living quarters for them next to Tyro's camp. They are to join our commune, but they bring bad memories. Lord Patroclus burned their villages . . . like mine."

"What of Patroclus? Is he safe?" Glaucon asked devotedly. Yet Milo glared surprised. Realizing he'd shown too much concern for the marauding Lion of Heliopolis, the ex-guardian fumbled, "I mean . . . uh . . . what of the Republic's assault?"

"Stopped," Milo frowned. "Scouts say Levantra returned to the Republic a few days ago. No one knows what it means. Xenon is unglued."

"How many refugees have arrived?"

"Difficult to count. Building the longhouses is behind schedule. That is why I was angry before. I should not have made you feel unwelcome, but I should be—"

"Doing more productive work?"

"Guarding you is productive." (Milo lied for his benefit.)

"We don't have to stay here," Glaucon said. "Why don't I help where I can? I'm feeling better. If I get tired, I'll just leave."

"Sophie said you need rest."

"I'll tell her it was my idea."

Milo smiled like an imp, slung his rifle over his shoulder.

The longhouses were a marvel. Nearly one hundred and twenty meters in length, as wide as they were high, they resembled the garrisons of Stratos, except they had bowed roofs rather than flat ones. Glaucon noticed how vertical posts made of young saplings and smaller trees were inserted every meter or so. Milo explained that workers gathered the trees from forests destroyed by fire; the trees of Crypt were too large for posts. Nevertheless, whenever anarchists encountered live trees, they built around, incorporating the forest into the dwelling. Elm bark peeled the previous spring made most of the walling and was nailed to the posts. There were only two doors at either end, and inside, woven mats made the floor. Carpenters hammered benches and beds together explaining the process to a curious student group.

As Glaucon and Milo cobbled together a wall, the Seminoles and militiamen examined him carefully. Children eating swamp cabbage dropped wooden spoons back into their bowls.

"Everyone is staring at me," Glaucon whispered to Milo, feeling their eyes scraping his back.

"Why shouldn't they?" Milo returned. "It's not everyday one sees a fresh guardian, let alone Xenon's son. You'd stare, too."

"Should I be worried?"

"Not at all. Work is the best protection for you, actually. It'd be unethical in the extreme to kill someone honestly trying to contribute. People live by action here; they reciprocate concern."

Glaucon felt a little better. He worked several hours more. A number of children came forward, asking him to give their beaded dolls to the Great Maiden of the Mountain, which he accepted with some confusion.

"It's a token of solidarity," Milo said. "Their villages were burned because Prodicus demanded they hand you and Sophie over as a blood tax."

"A blood tax . . . for two people?"

"That's how they're justifying this military campaign. The party line is that Sophie kidnapped you—a sacred guardian templar—abrogating all continental treaties. Anyone thought to harbor her is deemed a terrorist and forfeits all liberty rights. The children are showing they don't blame Sophie for their affliction."

Glaucon suddenly felt lightheaded. Another hot flash. He begged Milo's pardon and raced back to his hut along a wooded gravel road.

Scrubbing his face with soapy water, he thought he spied Zemer behind him in a mirror. Only his shadow. His blood felt poisoned by foreign memories. For comfort, he looked for the scar on his hand where Sophie cut him to make their sibling oath; but he realized, much to his dismay, there was no scar. That was Zemer. Not him!

He shuddered at the thought of immersion. *What would it feel like to assimilate his consciousness with Sophie and Prodicus?* He did not want Sophie to die. He liked her just the way she was: rebellious and kind, near but not the same person. Glaucon still hated himself and his past; what if he joined with Sophie and began to hate her, too. Such thoughts were unbearable, omitted no affliction. Twining his fingers around a skeletal doll of the Iron Queen, Glaucon prayed fervently: "Iron Queen, O Great Iron Queen of Hades, I know I don't deserve your concern, but I cannot endure this agony alone.

Protect my Sophie from Prodicus and the Fates, I beg you. Don't make my lips her lips. Don't make the two of us merge together as one. Make the guardian-king stumble and fail so we can live together happy. Give me the strength to save us." After he was done, Glaucon fell back in bed, cradling the doll and shaking.

Next morning, the prayer looked categorically ineffective. In fact, it'd made things worse. Sophie wakened Glaucon with a kick and ordered him to get up. Glaucon rubbed his eyes, feeling a little better. He had not felt her rise from bed. "What's happened?" he asked.

"News," Sophie reported anxiously. She looked out the open door into the sunlight. "A brigadier general named Megillus just arrived with one of our informants. He's in the hospital."

"Hurt?"

"He'll be dead soon. Hurry."

Megillus could barely speak when they found him. His state was grotesque. Half mad, half dead, with half his arm hanging by a sinew, a rivulet of blood gathered by the wounded on the floor. "Slain," he coughed, "they're . . . all . . . slain."

Xenon shook him furiously. "Who's slain? Speak sense."

"Z-Zeno and Patroclus . . . called an emergency briefing at the Lovejoy Academy on Stratos. Hardly any official dared miss. There was . . . a quarrel." Megillus was speaking to no one in particular. He tried to gather the proper words from the air.

Xenon ruffled him dangerously. "Quarrel? Over what?"

"The impudent guardians brought golems with them—into the assembly hall. Soulless abominations defamed Stratos' sacred plains. Patroclus asked if the auxiliaries were willing to allow the avis a chance to root out the Vessels."

"And?" Xenon asked. "What did the auxiliaries do?"

"What you'd expect. Lieutenant colonels banged their ceremonial shields, outraged. General Argus tore buttons from his shirt."

"Leonida?" Glaucon grabbed Megillus' arm.

"The Gold Queen demanded explanation: 'Patroclus, what is the meaning of this?' The Lion folded his arms. 'Things must change,' he said. Then he claimed Leonida was suspected of guardian-treason. When Leonida drew her xiphos he . . . he ordered everyone killed. Guns burst from the sides of the golems—red light and flashing bullets. I smelled electricity burning flesh." Megillus' mind was foggy as to what happened next. "I ran outside," he moaned. "Barrack pieces spun around swept up by flying steel. My whole brigade fled in the water but got snatched up by avis. Arms and legs rained bloody from the sky. A beak caught my elbow and carried me away. I dropped unconscious."

Glaucon erupted, "There must be some mistake. Patroclus' devotion to the Forms is unswerving. He'd rather die than betray Stratos."

"I saw the Lion with my own eyes," Megillus cried, remembering his emotionless face. "Fear him, Xenon. He kills like Kabiri, and shot General Argus without hesitation. Now our sacred city is no more."

"What happened to Leonida?" Sophie inquired

"Her gold helmet flashed . . . torn to the sky by talons. Only her helmet—I'm sure her head was inside. She's dead. As dead as Hekademos. If only we'd listened to Ekklesia. . . ."

"Just as Zemer foretold," Sophie recoiled, horrified by yet another true prediction.

Megillus' eyes rolled back into his head. He erupted into tremors. "Leave me alone!" he clawed at his face.

"What's wrong with him?" Tyro gasped.

The next moment Megillus' heart stopped from separation poisoning.

"Gods damn it!" Xenon yelled. "Sophie, call a meeting. The Continental Caucus. The militias. Everyone."

"Operation Moleman?" Sophie whispered, closing her eyes.

"Yes. Send the transmission signal. Time's up."

"O misery! But the refugees are just starting to settle in." Sophie didn't want to believe the end had come so soon. She wanted quieter times, to spend more nights alone with Glaucon, to see old friends.

Xenon answered, "Your brother warned us. You've seen the visions, too. Don't pretend ignorance because it's easier. Send the message."

The emergency meeting was scheduled during dinner. Usually, common meals were a time for socialization and intellectual discussion, with literary topics hosted by volunteers. Tonight all ate in silence, somber and expectant.

Rumors abounded. Twice now, scouts spotted avis cruising in the distance, making hideous closing spirals. The Fifth Estate's Detroit Commune had been decimated that morning, left in smoldering ruins. Not a single structure remained, nor any permaculture gardens. Transmissions re-told the slaughter: Avis broke the clouds, galloped tearing up earth and trees, then arced around the western mountains. They showed the meticulous precision known only to machines.

Xenon stood up, waited for the tense muttering to die down. “As you may’ve heard,” he said, “Prodicus has overthrown the auxiliaries and unchained the avis and golems.” He allowed whispers to fill the hall before continuing: “Our entire defense network is shattered. We lost contact with the Fifth Estate early this afternoon. Few survivors are anticipated. Half our allies do not reply to radio broadcasts.”

The Continental Caucus members from the Detroit Commune covered their faces with their hands.

Xenon was angered by the necessity for haste. Sixteen years of labor, for what?—to be back where he started. How he yearned for the offensive putsch, but his first success—his earliest—was all the gods left him. He spoke bitterly: “The Iron Queen and I issued the Moleman Signal this morning.”

More mumbling erupted.

“As I foretold from the beginning, my visions of the barren earth have not abated. Zemer confirmed my prophesies with his own, added content. To him the future was clearer. Let me tell you about our last discussion. We fought, but the auger—bless his soul—stiffly warned me about the meaning of the avis: ‘They will be an evil omen,’ he said, ‘a sign of doom. Flee underground if you see them. Flee or you will be burned to dust, and the firefly will not come.’ Thanks to our continental collaboration, we can follow his advice. There are twenty-five shelters prepared for our peoples, carved out thousands of meters into the Rocky, Cascade, Sierra Nevada, and Appalachian mountains. Our ‘covens’ contain provisions enough to last for years.”

It became difficult to hear over the table murmurs. Everyone talked at once, sharing disbelief.

“Please, my friends,” Xenon said holding up his hands, “we have little time. The beasts will be here in hours, not days. Since you have agreed to grant sanctuary to the Vessels, there is little I can do.”

Milo shouted gallantly, “We shall never turn them out!”

Thunderous knuckles pounded on the tables in solidarity. The rebels’ determination in the great grotto hardened.

Xenon removed his black beret and puffed up in his military coat. He remarked, “Sometimes I wonder why I stay among you stubborn people; but on hot nights like this, I realize the only truth in the world: Your insolence is intoxicating. I’m infatuated with hating you.” Everyone laughed, and Xenon continued looking at the black flags draping the walls. “I wish I could tell you everything will be all right, that we have some miniscule chance of victory, but we don’t. There are only two conditions: If you choose to stay, you will die. If you choose to flee underground, Prodicus will root you out. Anyone who tells you differently is a liar. A plague has been unleashed upon us and there is no cure for it. Levantra will cut our commune down like the Great Epidemic of Sextus. Today or tomorrow, our end has come."

"Give up hope," a young voice cried boldly.

Xenon picked up a canteen and drank with good humor. For sixteen years his heart grumbled at these rustic souls, but now, at the end, he realized they weren't such a bad horse to saddle after all. "You magnificent people," he said, "you glorious Watchers, he's right. Give up hope. Cast your eyes to the heavens and reject it. Be as noisy as you can, never submit, never surrender; uncover your insolence like a lamp. Look up at the King of the World and spit on his Forms. Damn Prodicus for demanding the Vessels. Damn his murderous guile! Let him try to take our Iron Queen and fair-haired son."

Hands clutched Glaucon's shoulder as they cheered, and he shuddered that such sacrifice was being made on his account. He did nothing but bring the Watchers misery, yet they circled their wagons around him anyway.

Xenon spoke like Saint Plato under the lights. "I tell you truthfully," he said pointing at the ceiling: "We have never been freer than tonight. Our freedom frightens Prodicus. Disbelief is more dangerous to him than all the armies of the world. We can judge his paradise a hell."

"We are the groundless ones," the crowd exclaimed.

"Yes," Xenon added, "and that groundlessness will swallow him up."

The mustachioed rebel motioned for Sophie to begin the briefing. Sophie took his side, sensing an immense weight of eyes. "I see some speeches are justifiable," she said.

Rapturous knuckles shook the cave once more. Xenon grinned, extinguished his cigar in an ash tray.

Sophie became the Iron Queen again. The easy, relaxed demeanor from the lake surrendered to a mask of strength. "I will get straight to the point," Sophie spoke with command, marching in front of her friends. "If we want our children and loved ones to reach shelter, the avis must be distracted. We did not anticipate their surveying speed. Their movements are supersonic, too fast to escape as one body. Some of us will have to remain as decoys."

She waited until the crowd nodded understanding.

"We lose in a pitched battle with the avis," she went on. "The machines vastly outnumber us and carry more advanced weaponry. So our strategy must limit the number of machines we face at any one moment."

Sophie signaled for the ancient projector to be turned on. A map of their mountain commune appeared on a screen behind her. "This cavern here," she said, tracing a line from the waterfall entrance deep into the rocks, "codenamed 'Gaia's Pore', will force the enemy into a bottleneck with our flank and rear defended. Four hundred well armed soldiers can set up barricades and concentrate firepower in one direction. Hopefully, we can force a swarm and hold the avis off for several hours, giving our families a chance to escape to the nearest shelter—Coven-5—near Cheyenne."

Eyes studied the intricate networks of tunnels on the screen, opened wide as the next slide—a detailed illustration by Glaucon—displayed an image of a menacing insectoid avis with jointed appendages and fiery tail. For many, it was the first time they'd ever seen one of the six-winged dragonflies.

Sophie proudly noted, "Glaucon provided critical ISHIM intelligence about the angels of destiny. Avis have three weaknesses: their single eye, their wings, and the energy cell protected by the right flank. To bring them down, fire between the metal chassis. But beware the red light that ushers from their mouths—it causes madness, horrible voices. Avis should be at their weakest state when forced to battle underground, but they'll still be formidable."

"What about the golems?" a young woman asked at a long table.

"Golems suffer similar weaknesses, but they'll not be used. Prodicus crippled his air force in the latest coup, and golems make inferior long-distance weapons: They're flightless and possess a bulky chassis." She proceeded to discuss evacuation procedures and concluded: "Remember, avis are designed to operate as part of a hive mind. They are collectively controlled by Kabiri-36. They will not behave in the same manner as individual soldiers. They work together seamlessly, like the movements of your fingers. Show no pity to them. It is not murder to kill a creature of a hive mind. They are only metal."

Volunteers came forward to enlist for Sophie's operation after dinner. The people wept, kissing their loved ones goodbye in Gaia's Pore. It was a natural oblong cavern, widened by the Mesa Mining Union, with some of the precious stalactites still intact. Wires and florescent lights followed the distant, narrow tunnels north ninety kilometers to a secret opening.

Before leaving, Tyro Canto and others approached Sophie to rub foreheads one last time. "We'll wait for news of your victory," Tyro said. "The Iron Queen has been with you since you were a girl. She will continue to protect us."

Sophie looked away, unlatching the top buttons of her shirt. The damp, underground humidity had started to make her sweat. "The Iron Queen brought nothing but destruction with her," she lamented.

"Don't say that," Tyro scolded. "You delivered us with courage. When I taught you and your brother in St. Louis, I knew you'd bless us. You used to cry to me that you were afraid to carry Prodicus' blood, that his injustice poisoned you. I said—"

"Blood is unimportant. Pollution follows choice, not family."

"Yes, and I was right. You've protected us more than anyone could from your uncle. I am glad you came to live with us. Zemer would be proud."

Sophie hugged Tyro farewell. She apologized to the refugees who had just arrived and were forced to move again, and bid everyone hurry to the Cheyenne coven. She watched Tyro and the last refugee children disappear behind the militias.

"Go with them," Xenon pleaded, watching the rear supply trucks drive into the half-lit tunnels.

Sophie shook her head, resolved. There was a peculiar silence. She continued piling metal tables into a barricade. "Our plan will fail if we leave," she said. "The avis will surely scan the defense, like the other cities, yes?"

Xenon nodded.

"If the Vessels are not here, no swarm will occur. They may divide and find the others."

"Are you so ready to be caught again?"

"Would you go?"

Xenon did not reply.

"Besides," Sophie grunted, heaving another table, "who said anything about being caught? Haven't you heard the rumors? The Iron Queen is invincible."

Xenon snorted at her hubris. "How many times have I told you? No good comes when tacticians fall in love with their plans."

Sophie smiled sadly. "Maybe I'm just tired of running. The farther the commune is from me the safer they are. A maddening thought, but a true thought."

"That's all well and good," Xenon grinned, "but it doesn't make me safer, does it?"

V § 8 Battle of Gaia's Pore

Avis attacked at midnight. Sentries in the tree canopy were spotted, plucked out, and shredded to pieces by the angels with the slender beaks. So fast was the whirlwind, only one militiawoman managed to send a warning signal to the defenders at Gaia's Pore. From the waterfall avis sped like gamma rays. They were clumsy, clumsier than Sophie expected. Spewing everywhere, showing no coordination at all, they hurtled in screaming from the tunnels.

A phalanx of raised xiphos sticks and Neokalashnikovs fought them back, lighting the room, spraying radiation. One avis scanned the area with a wide green beam. "Scriekeria!" it screeched, wings spread wide.

Other avis unleashed blood-curdling song upon spying the Vessels. "Scriekeria! Scriekeria!" they soared elated.

The flashing dragonflies swept over the wall and pounded the line with red light from their mouths.

Chilling the cavern, Sophie thought spooked. She scraped aside an icicle jamming her rifle. *Do not panic. Panic is the God of Defeat. His tenure is a long death. Pull together and think: Zemer has the same blood as you. If he can withstand the jinn, why not you? Do what he said. Make a psychic wall, place his loving image before you as an anchor, don't let the voices overwhelm your ego.*

Beside her a militiaman groaned in madness, begging for death. Sophie tried slapping his cheeks: "Still. Be quiet. The visions aren't real. No one is there."

He flung at her with balled fists, forcing Sophie to knock him unconscious with her rifle.

All but deaf from the xiphos lightning-cracks, Glaucon witnessed avis eyecameras popping in front of his face. He looked back at Xenon in a raised metal hunting blind at the center of the chamber. Xenon yelled victoriously, "That's how you do it, cats! Strike the sons of Cronos blind." Xenon swiveled his sonic carbine again on the protective wall, unleashed another volley of shots. More avis shook their damaged skulls. Scorpion-grenades finished them. Abruptly, the avis swept out the cave entrance.

"They'll return in seconds!" Sophie yelled over the sighing cries of her militia. "Widen your energy shields to maximum. Dig in. Show some guts. Whatever you do, don't get touched by the avis breath—"

Before she finished speaking, a second wave spilled onto the barricades—more exact and relentless than before. Avis torched the formidable trenches with their tails.

One avis tore through the line in silvery waltz, firing with large cannons under its wings. Sophie's agile legs easily leapt onto its back as it passed her. She maimed its head with her energy shield. Pulling out a coilgun from her holster, she saw the superconductors spark five times as she pumped bullets into the avis' power cell. "Die, you evil bird! Just die!" she howled.

Above its eye, the blue ALETHEIA darkened, and the beast fell lifeless through the air. Sophie slipped, tumbled to the ground. Before she could catch her breath, lasers whipped past her face.

Friendly fire, she winced. *The avis won't kill me, but my men surely could.*

Three more avis attacked from behind. Sophie rolled under two of them and they collided. After dodging successfully, she jumped up, finishing off their wings with a round of bullets. She swung around cursing one of the culprits who shot at her: "Gods damn it, Saba! Watch where you're firing." The teenaged girl, eyes aglow with fear, shook wildly from her mistake.

Sophie ordered running to Saba, "Aim at the monsters circling the ceiling. Shoot their mouths if you can. That breath is killing us."

They worked together, bringing the beasts down one by one, shouting encouragements to the other defenders.

A third wave came, then a fourth. Glaucon fought exhausted with his leg propped against a metal door, feeling his rifle's rhythmic recoil. Each avis wave bit closer at the line, left debris blocking the entrance. Avis methodically carried away the broken machines and tried again.

"Sophie, we can't keep them back much longer," Glaucon reported over the cackling fire when she came to check on him.

"Yes we can, Glaucon." She squeezed his hand. "Never surrender and you'll be surprised." Sophie stood up, yelled enraged cusses, and shot another wing off one of the avis. It stumbled on the ground limply, trying to take her prisoner. "Chop that thing to bits!" she angrily commanded.

The wounded robot splintered to pieces under gunfire.

After the fourth attempt, the avis stopped their assault. There was peace for an hour or so, and soldiers gulped greedily from warm canteens. The entrenched fighters came to realize, though, this quiet had nothing to do with their own valiance. It was only preparation for the arrival of Levantra, hungry from the Republic.

Boom! The Strife Cannon blasted the mountain, and cavern lights shattered.

"Trying to break the ceiling," Milo gulped terrified.

Sophie grimaced. "That gold liar wouldn't dare kill us!"

Prodicus shouted over the radio speaker: "Consider that a warning shot across the bow, Xenon. If you value life, turn the Vessels over to me at once."

"Come and take them," was all Xenon responded. Cursing could be heard over the intercom. Xenon fired his rifle in the air.

A fifth wave. The moist rocks cracked as avis galloped from the tunnels.

“Detonate the lugh mines, Finnias!” Sophie yelled. “Everyone take cover.”

A rapid fire-chain engulfed the avis and collapsed the tunnel entrance. Sophie gave a satisfied smile, then immediately frowned.

Avis cleared the wreckage in only a few minutes. Gathering like an iron fist, the cruel angels punched through the line, spraying insanity with their mouths and explosive death with flying feathers. Wounded covered open abdomens with hands, hiding their viscera. Reserve units moved to reinforce the shell-shocked defenders.

Tramping down the bloody mud, Sophie called her militiamen by name and barked commands at the desperate line: “Machine gun nests—maintain stable cover over the entrance. Let the light troops handle the strays.”

Avis showed reluctance to strike the Iron Queen directly. Several times, the enormous dragonflies lunged toward her only to pull back at the last moment. Sophie used their fear to her advantage, taking certain risks unthinkable otherwise. As she shot avis to the ground, she sang her girlhood battle hymn learned in the swamps:

“I loose the arrow of the Iron Queen,
Her lance, invincible, is comet swift,
And Spirits dead imbue my heart’s machine
To rain her judgments, cutting souls adrift;
No beast can stand against my fire whips,
Or man can tame my soul’s graveyard ravine.
Of death am I, a brooding maid of Crypt—
A fighter: strong and dreaded wolverine.”

By four the next morning the militia retained their position, but they’d suffered horrific casualties. A field hospital established in one of the anterior caverns ran out of supplies as men and women wailed for medics.

Word finally came about retreat to Coven-5—the evacuation was almost completed. Morale lifted again.

After hearing the good news, Sophie floundered, using her rifle as a crutch to kneel down. A piece of metal protruded from her thigh.

Glaucon ran up to her and clutched her muddy face. “Forms! I can’t believe it. Your plan worked. You’re beautiful, Sophie.”

The Iron Queen turned away, face clouding. “Not well enough,” she snapped. “We’ve lost half our men.” This brief reprieve—like the others—would not last much longer.

Glaucon examined her leaking wound much distressed. "Sophie, you're hurt."

"Not bad. Got snagged on the barricades. Here, help me straighten my leg out." Roughly, Sophie ripped the metal scrap away. Blood ran down her leg, and she groaned painfully into Glaucon's shoulder.

"You need to get this checked out," Glaucon warned. "This is serious."

"Just bandage it like I showed you, all right?" She kissed him and lay with her elbows on the rock. When he finished the dressing, she ordered him to fetch Milo.

The disheveled militiaman found her reloading her coilgun. His olive skin was tinged jaundice. He looked just as bloodied as her, drowsy, with a crisp morning beard and torn trousers. He set his Neokalashnikov noiselessly by her feet.

"Milo," Sophie said carefully. "Xenon is calling for volunteers to carry the wounded out of the mountain. They need your help. I said you'd act as escort. Gather your equipment."

Milo peered back at the medic trucks. "Looks like they have as many as they need."

"No. You must go," Sophie affirmed more forcefully. She gripped Milo by the collar, but he jumped away.

"I'll not leave your side, Commander," he said.

"It's an order!"

"Like I care about that."

Upon hearing this, Sophie hopped to her feet, putting pressure on her good leg. "Don't be stupid, Milo," she said. "Everyone who remains is destined to death. We can hold them off a little longer, maybe a couple more times, but—"

"You would have someone else die in my place?"

"No . . . but . . . Milo, please—"

Milo refused, shaking his head: "The Iron Queen demands cowardice and sends away her best fighters. What is the world coming to?"

Sophie rubbed her friend's brawny arms. Of all her militia, Milo was dearest to her—first foreigner to show any kindness. Milo offered good friendship in the student groups in St. Louis. Long ago—had it been so long?—they had trained together and formed their own centuria with Zemer and the others. Most were dead now. *Milo, my sweet Milo,* she thought. He was a year older, tender and energetic, but also fierce. From him sprung a sense of belongingness. Full of emotion, Sophie requested, "Tell me about anarchist morality, Milo, like you used to when we trained in the swamps."

Milo repeated the *Four Don'ts*: "Don't lie; don't abuse individuals; don't be weak; don't rush to judgment. Treat others as they want you to treat them. Seek freedom, *individual* freedom—freedom from all homage, force, and loyalty. But see a miracle—"

"When force is absent loyalty grows invincible. Isn't it sad," Sophie asked hugging him tightly with half-shut eyes, "how the Republic should make our loyalties enemies?"

Milo laughed. "Sad. Not surprised. The Republic corrupts everything."

Sophie let Milo go, adding, "Enough of that cursed place. If something happens to me, you must get everyone out. Blow the rear tunnel and run as fast as you can. Take the long passage. It's more hidden."

"The Iron Queen will guide us there."

One last time, Prodicus demanded the Vessels over the intercom. "This is your last chance, Xenon. I shall rip this mountain up like a dead tree. I swear to the Good. Do not make me cast your people to the Inferno."

Once more Xenon shouted contemptuously, drumming his breast, "Come and take them, you bitch oracle!"

"Must you antagonize him so?" Glaucon asked, scanning the desolate remains of their defense.

"The maddened bull gropes blind."

"Yes, but he's far deadlier. More likely to gore you."

"Ha!" Xenon glanced at his son. "Your logic reminded me of your mother just then. I think I'm starting to like you, Glaucon. Maybe I was wrong to send Sophie to kill you after all."

"What kind of apology is that?"

"The best you'll ever get. Now go tell the line to brace their legs."

Avis returned like clockwork, heavier and more dangerous than before. There was something insane about them, as if they carried the poisoned rage of their guardian master. Just as before, artillery drove them back, but something unexpected occurred. The ceiling cracked and tore away. Avis peeled the mountain husk like a horde of locusts consume wheat. Prodicus' angels poured in on a morning sunbeam.

"Saint Plato, what were we thinking?" Glaucon cried, alternating his aim. There were too many. They blotted out the sun, a metal-storm in which one could neither hear nor see. Glaucon's rifle was snatched from his hands. He picked up another. That too was snatched. He tumbled backward.

"We're hanged," one Watcher screamed, running amidst the whistling winds of Rout. Militiamen took cover under the scraps of the barricades. Others sprinted down the tunnels on a sagging rudder of hope. They shattered like ships on the rocks as avis dragged them back, ripping off heads and limbs.

Three gory bodies fell on Sophie. As she crawled out from under the vanquished, metal wings sliced her face. Scarlet light danced in the cavern causing the temperature to dip to two degrees Celsius.

"Everyone run to the tunnels!" Sophie hollered hoarse. "For gods' sakes, run to the tunnels." She hobbled firing chaotically. Reaching the tower, a torrent of red light ricocheted off the metal.

Sophie felt ice absorb into her cheek.

For one horrifying moment she stood still, pressing a hand to her face. Ice. Ice as cold as regret. A waterfall of images opened her brain, spreading sense. "The Fates drag me down," Sophie cried anguished. She tried to think of Zemer and Glaucon, but the voices—the voices!—there were too many. She couldn't escape them. She was losing her way. Thrashing, questions eating her identity, she panicked hallucinating, mumbling terrible visions: "I see the Sun-Island birthing a thousand suns. Bonfires burn the world to ash." Her forehead tore bloody as she dug it into the rocks, wandering lost in psychotic fantasy. "Kleo, stop," she begged. "Let me out. Open the door. Don't hurt me anymore."

When Milo saw his Iron Queen collapse painfully into a fetal position, he ran quickly to save her. Hopping over a mound of ammo boxes and fallen dead, he swung his rifle to the floor. Not five more steps were taken before a feather pierced his chest. Dumbstruck, Milo remembered Zemer's secret warnings. He gasped for salvation but burst into a ray of light.

Avis swooped down to pick up the damaged Third Vessel, shredding Xenon's tower along the way. Dust blanketed the cave. Xenon fell breaking his leg at the knee.

"Sophie!" Glaucon yelped in panic. He clubbed at the beasts' talons with his rifle butt as they sought to whisk her away from him. He beat them back and flung Sophie over his shoulder like a bag. Dodging falling debris, he felt ice boomerang off his back. Upon discovering their emissions had no effect on the Second Vessel, avis cocked their heads, thwacked their wings, and roared.

"Get her out of here!" Xenon cried, desperately reaching out to them. An avis pounced on his chest and dragged the rebel up to Levantra like a crane hauling timber. Men hurtled all around smashing on the rocks. Glaucon stumbled as far as he could, but Sophie started punching and ripping out his hair.

"I'm going to kill you, Kleo. You'll see. I'll make you pay for killing Mother." Sophie's fingers ripped for his eyes, and so Glaucon flung her to the ground.

"Sophie, snap out of it," he begged. "What's the matter with you?" He wrestled with her as she tried to place a gun in her mouth. He punched her wrist to the floor trying to make her drop the weapon.

Momentarily Sophie regained consciousness. With tears streaming down her nose, she pleaded, "Kill me, Glaucon. Please . . . kill me. It's unbearable. I don't want to be immersed. I don't want to feel this forever."

"Sophie, it's over. There's nothing more we can do."

"We must kill ourselves. Do it, like we talked about on the river."

Glaucon snatched the gun from her, tried to kiss her back to life. "Don't say things like that," he cried rubbing their cheeks together.

The Iron Queen lost sanity again, eyes flooding red. She tried to bite his arm. "Give me back my gun. Atropos sent you here to stop me. I hate you, Glaucon; you're weak and pathetic. Burn! Burn like an abandoned city and die!"

"Sophie?" Glaucon objected. "You don't mean that. The Fates are in you." Before he could protest further, a rabid avis slapped him sprawling through the dirt. Jumping like a cricket, it pierced his shoulder with a sharp leg, shaking jaws in victory. Glaucon screamed as a series of icy red blasts peeled back his face. When nothing happened again, the avis pushed its jaws closer. It fired point blank, turning the Vessel's lips blue.

Sounds drained away. Glaucon's heart beat faster as muscles tightened. Delirious, he saw Sophie disappear among the dying battling for their lives. Whispering again. The walls were whispering. His neurons were whispering.

You cannot hide from destiny, came the voice.

"Leave Sophie alone!"

She despises you.

"You lie. She loves me."

The jinn is Truth. The jinn is God. Neither Truth nor God can lie. The jinn is a gate to heaven. It reveals the hidden self—the hated selves of others.

"I don't care what it does. I won't let you touch her. I swear on the Good, I'll kill you Atropos!"

Here you are pretending to be upset again. But we both know it's an act.

"No, it's truth. The jinn can see it. I love her."

You only use Sophie for pleasure, isn't this true?

"No."

Love is a fable. A fantasy meant to conceal your erotic lusts. The Myth of Love makes you believe you care about other people, but you really only care about satisfying your lower organs. Sophie only exists for your amusement. Isn't that what you tell yourself at night?

"I don't want to think about that anymore. I love her."

Of course you do, oh contemptible son of Melete. You exert sovereignty over your female, to overpower her with caresses, but your arms, while claiming to protect, yearn only to imprison. You are aroused by control, to pet Sophie's naked muscles into a cage.

"You're wrong!"

The violence in the world is merely a reflection of the violence in your mind. To think is to harm; to watch is to harm; to live is to harm; to love is to harm. What you truly desire is to be the only subject in the world—to end harm!—but other subjects won't let you. Make them your slaves. Make Sophie your slave. Embrace your godhood.

"Zemer . . . help me," Glaucon cried. He lost consciousness to the sound of Atropos laughing wildly.

V § 9 The Last Gorgon Hour

Morpheus Alepou listened to the frantic activity of his news crew. Nearly five minutes to show time, and he was nowhere near ready for the cameras. A female attendant with pink and wavy hair lined his eyes with makeup. Another padded his cheeks with *Stress-Less* powder to a shining, artificial gleam. Coughing from the stinking fumes, Morpheus' head spun momentarily. Strangely, the dizziness reminded him of the Kabiri ceremonies under Ozbolt Tower. He remembered the crying victims, tied in chains, made to look into the ruby jinn of Kabiri. They sang a manta, then:

"Give me the high eye
To see like Kabiri,
Fly up the dream heights
Kissing eternal light.
Come show me Fate's Form
Daughters of the storm,
Break all psychosis
Blocking henosis."

Accursed words. Morpheus grimaced at the memory. They haunted him like eidolons as of late. He was one of the last surviving Kabiri architects. The others met . . . unfortunate ends.

Morpheus Alepou played a strange role in the early Kabiri Circle: data recovery for system errors. Bugs, viruses, short-sighted programming—he had to anticipate them all and devise a backup. He hovered in a world of what-ifs, a bog of would-be disasters; and it would be his head if any blue screen of death should appear. Thankfully, Kibiri-1 never trembled.

After the Great Theurgy Schism, dividing the spoils produced much division among the Kabiri. All wanted a seat in the Logoset. But not Morpheus. No, the anchorman always knew refusing the Logoset a prudent choice. *After all*, he considered, *the man who weaves destruction once can weave it again*. Channeling raw power was never his way—far too crude and . . . well . . . bloody. Morpheus enjoyed subtler methods.

To the Kabiri conspirators, Skybridge News was a subterranean Hades; no one desired it as a region to govern. News may've been a necessary evil for control, the guardians reasoned, but how vulgar to breathe endless falsehood. Everyone thought lots would have to be drawn for the abysmal place. Morpheus, though, was ready and jumped at the first opportunity to call it his own.

So what if he had to abdicate guardian templar status? So what if the others made fun of him behind his back? He was still alive and happy, wasn't he? He survived them all, skirted destruction through all the major upheavals by playing the nonsense jibber jabber.

What fools, Morpheus laughed, patting down the hair bulging from his head like a baboon. Running Skybridge News had all the benefits of guardianhood with none of its imperfections. With the thankful sponsorship of the Kabiri, he amassed a personable fortune. He could take helot delights in the pleasure gardens, enjoy the drugs of each race, read ancient books, dress according to his own tastes—robes on Friday and pantaloons on Monday. There was also the intellectual challenge of manufacturing consent and keeping the rabble from revolt. He had to rattle rating by reducing truth to easily digestible formats—with enough color, drama, and seductive lights to hold the helots' short attention span. Distorting, directing, derailing, disseminating were all in a day's work. *Anyone could be a lion tamer*, Morpheus beamed, *but who could really claim to be a tamer of facts?* Facts were like paint, and *he* was an artist. He'd smear his enemies with excrement and gloss his friends with a halo's glow.

"Finished," each of Morpheus' helot attendants chimed one after another. They stuffed their makeup smorgasbord into their aprons, shivering. The triangular stage room maintained a chilly temperature. As Morpheus frequently expounded, it kept wits together and sloth at bay.

A smocked cameraman held up his fingers, "Make ready, Lord Morpheus. We're on in three . . . two . . . one. . . ."

Morpheus assumed a friendly tone, looked into the long barrel of the Mira-Disney camera: "Good Afternoon, Republicans, and welcome to another installment of the Gorrrrrrr-geous Gorgon Hour. I'm your host, Morpheus Alepou. Thanks for tuning in. Joining us again today are Peitha von Notus, political analyst with the Rover Council, and Freddy Akimbo, my fellow co-anchor."

The two newscasters smiled at the cameras with shining white teeth, teeth as large as a horse's. Peitha, though, struggled to maintain the expression, feeling her skin stiffen from her morning face-tightening regimen. "Glad to be here, Morpheus," she chirped.

For the first time, Morpheus felt a twinge of camaraderie for these co-anchors. They'd worked together for less than a year, but a familiarity had developed between them. The towering shoulder pads of Freddy Akimbo made him nostalgic. Patting Peitha encouragingly on her taut back, Morpheus said zealously, "Good news day, friends."

"I should say so," Peitha agreed.

"As you've already heard, the archon jackals were executed in the Bull yesterday afternoon. The guardian-traitors took their sensation tablets and burned away their impurities."

Morpheus stared vacantly into space, waiting for the video recording to play: Golems tugged the levitating tumbrels like sled dogs; Hypatia tripped from the scaffold into the Bull; Zeno fell to his knees, sobbing, begging for his life: "I don't understand. I've always been your faithful servant, Prodicus. It's a mistake. A terrible mistake. Mercy! Show me mercy. I don't want to bur-r-r-n!"

No mercy came for the philosopher. The crowds heaved and sang with laughter. Golems tuned the Bull's leg-knobs to a deadly pitch.

Zeno's death was the worst, Morpheus concluded. *Hard to watch, really. The fool lived only to serve Prodicus. He'd followed every order—dirty ones, too—all for the guardian-king's benefit. Killing him like that—what heartlessness. But then again, to reach for the Logoset meant playing with dragon's teeth.*

The video ended. Green lights on the cameras flashed.

"Who would've thought possible?" Freddy asked behind his square face and beady eyes. "Our sacred Logoset filled to the brim with yellow-bellied blackheads! Our military infested with anarchists!"

Peitha answered shaking her fist: "Thank gods we have Prodicus and not one of those shadow-sprung fools. Prodicus is a philosopher saint. He's a leader—nay—a great leader, a defender of our constitution. Might and right joined together at last."

"I'll say," Morpheus concurred. "Prodicus and ISHIM really proved their metal neutralizing this latest threat. Quick thinking saved us from that lowly praetorian guard."

"What is Prodicus up to today?"

"He's been meeting all morning with the ephors of justice on Levantra, diligently restructuring the Republic's political system in the wake of these cowardly plots."

"The Logoset has been temporarily closed, is that correct?" Peitha gasped, feigning alarm.

"Nothing to fear," Morpheus reassured the cameras. He adjusted his scope monocle and peered down at a report beaming from his moon-shaped news console. "Prodicus declared martial law, true, but this is for the city's protection. Our philosopher-king—Saint Plato protect him—promises its return at the earliest, most reasonable time. Already he's appointed a Selection Committee headed by—"

"The war heroes, Patroclus and Zoe," Freddy exclaimed, hardly able to contain himself.

"Yes, that's right."

"What valor, those two."

"Don't forget Simmias," Morpheus added. "This is a high honor for all of them."

"O, the undying bond of friendship," Peitha fawned starry-eyed over their 3-D portraits. "How many of us would be willing to postpone our entry into the guardian templar to save a friend? Or to risk our lives on the dangerous Other Side?"

Morpheus spoke with rising excitement: "Indeed. Their sacrifice won us a supreme victory for freedom yesterday against the Southwest Confederacy. With avis, the Republic smashed Xenon, the Great Gigolo of the West, for good. The Watchers have unconditionally surrendered. Operation Witch Hunt is a success and Glaucon has been saved."

Freddy tottered on his seat, giving a nasally donkey laugh. “My confidential sources at the Office of Public Harmony report Xenon crawled on his hands and knees to beg for his life.”

“Well, what do you expect from a lizard debauchee?” Peitha jabbed.

“How sad,” Morpheus shook his head, “only a small band of half-armed blackheads stayed with him till the bloody end. Xenon was caught desperate and alone, like a trapped stag, as was the Iron Queen. The anarchist hordes turned tail faster than a herd of buffalo.”

“Are you surprised?” Freddy cooed. “Nothing but egotists, all. How can one build a society on self-love?”

An electronic laugh filled the room.

“I suppose you can’t,” Morpheus said. “But anyway, as we speak, enhanced interrogations are underway in Miantgast to discover the location of Crypt’s other terrorists.”

“All totally humane,” Peitha noted fondly. “Psychologists from the Public Ethic’s Office are providing the best technical and moral guidance our city has to offer.”

Freddy ripped his cube necklace from his chest to berate the need for ethics. “Does Republican mercy know any limits? It’d be entirely appropriate, I say, to hack off their fingers to get information.”

“Let’s not lose our heads, Freddy.”

“Sweet thought, Morpheus. Let’s take Xenon’s head.” Electronic laugh. “Polls show ninety-six percent favors decapitation.”

Peitha heaved angrily in her blue cloak, trimmed with green triangles. “Remember those who said unbridling the avis would put our national security in danger?”

“Gods, yes, where are they now?—dirty sensualist roaders!”

The anchors waited for electronic boos, waving in like a tide and departing.

“Cool your heads,” Morpheus demanded. “Sure, things escalated out of hand for a while, but the worst is over.”

“Yet the most disgusting rumors persist about Glaucon. . . .” Freddy said, scratching his bird-nest hair.

“Do not even mention them with a whisper,” Morpheus begged.

Peitha scoffed, “No, no, no-o-o. Don’t speak false of a brave guardian like Glaucon. What sense does it make to so cunningly infiltrate a terrorist cell, make arrests, and then, at the last second, elope with the Iron Queen? Completely ridiculous. A fairy tale. We should laugh these conspiracy theorists to Palladium Gate. All intelligent people know the boy was taken hostage."

Freddy persisted: "Yes . . . well . . . but upon examination—and this cannot be denied—ontocymatists found the Iron Queen pregnant with *his* child."

"Lies!" Morpheus pounded his desk. "All lies. A smear campaign of the worst sort." He covered his ears with disgust; but deep inside, he tittered at the titillation. How he relished this little gumdrop—ahhh, it made his week. Before, this was simply a rescue and recovery story. But allegations of sex always changed the equation. Gods almighty, the only thing better than scandals were disasters, but those, sadly, rained infrequently. But sex scandals—you could hook one a day if you fished long enough. One was like a treasure map—led to another. Morpheus argued with his waiting co-anchors: "Think about what you're saying, friends. Our guardians are not desirous like fluffy rabbits, are they?"

"No, they love their city."

"They do not fall in love with savages."

"That *would* be peculiar."

"Why should our city's hero fall? Have you ever read a story where that happens?"

"Never. Perfect virtue is the definition of our heroes, but—"

"Hush, then," Morpheus demanded. "Rest easy, Republicans. I've personally investigated these claims and found them completely baseless. The Iron Queen, consumed by an insatiable lust, ravished our poor Glaucon against his will. Brainwashed him, too."

Peitha and Freddy blushed awkwardly. "How tragic!" both cried at once.

"No worries," Morpheus said. "Glaucon's undergoing rehabilitation and will be as good as new. Keep him in your prayers."

"We certainly will. The Good mends all sorrows."

Hours ticked by as Morpheus marched down his news-list. The Republic Securities Commission discovered massive tax fraud in the Fourth Ward again under CEO Godfrey de Tobin. Despite the arrests (or because of them) the stock market rallied.

"Our bull market is singing higher than the Bull," squawked a jubilant investor on the crowded Safe Street Floor."

Discussion on two murders in the Sixth Ward followed, one particularly brutal: a thirty-two-year-old man found dead in a suitcase. Morpheus finished with happier stories, promoting a new magnet-sedan model and a boy saved from a burning house by golems. At the end, he whined tearfully, "Well, that's our show; thank you so much for watching."

Freddy and Peitha smiled goodbye.

Something was different, though. Peitha glanced in horror as Morpheus stabbed the news console with his finger. The God of Skybridge refused to allow any cameras to fade out. "Before I go, one final remark," Morpheus begged his audience.

"He's going off script," Peitha whispered furiously to Freddy.

Morpheus pressed another oval button to drag camera two closer to his face, then broke into soliloquy: "Listen friends. I've heard some disturbing reports lately. Some say the Gorgon Hour's success is completely due to my cutting-edge journalism and biting investigative skills, but I know that's not true. It can't be." Morpheus wiped a tear from his cheek. "This show has never been about me or Freddy or Peitha. This show is, ultimately, about *you*, viewers, our Skybridge Cadets." He pointed a finger at the camera. "Without *you*, I'd just be another guy spouting off. You keep me honest. The battles we face—they can only be won with the Form of Truth. No energy shield can withstand Truth. No *Goetia Mirror* can reflect Truth. Here at Skybridge News you help Truth shine like our Sapphire Throne, providing fair and measured news. I want all of you to pat yourselves on the back. Go on. Don't be shy. Do it for your ol' pal, Morpheus. With you, we've changed this city for the better. Good night. Saint Plato bless you, and Saint Plato bless our Republic."

He blew a kiss. The camera lights went out.

"Morpheus, that was beautiful," Freddy said.

The newsman rose from his seat, left silently, hands behind his back, and his camera army wondered what story created such sentimentalism.

Blue neon floors pulsed under Morpheus' feet as he walked down Skybridge's hallways. *Give me the high eye to see like Kabiri*, Morpheus repeated the words. *Tracking news, summarizing news, making news. I'm not perfect at capturing objectivity*. The newsman was part of the news, like an experimenter in the experiment. In this way he was like Kabiri: Kabiri predicted the future, but also made the future.

Morpheus rested his elbows on a windowsill, looked out from the twenty-second floor. Skybridge News sat adjacent to the Office of Public Harmony cluster. The building resembled a stack of triangular prisms, joined together through the middle by a central elevator, a shish kabob spine. Each segment rotated independently. From this window, he could see the lined courts adjacent to the blue waters of Hesper Park, and right below the Skybridge lobby, the stair-statue garden: "L" shaped stairs, reverse stairs, attic stairs, a Jacob's ladder, with peanut peddlers darting in between.

What can explain my nature? Morpheus wondered. He was an altruist, fundamentally, choosing a degraded nether state for the public good. Never quite a guardian, auxiliary, or helot, he mingled with all three, in a fourth twilightic purgatory—a Fourth Estate. Many said he hated the helots, wished to enslave their minds, but nothing could be further from the truth. They were already slaves! He wished to make their yoke lighter, provide a semblance of freedom from their slavedom. *Was it wrong to lie to those who lacked the power to change their condition? Why rub the faces of the defeated in their fate? Why tighten the noose already firm enough to strangle them?* Yes, he sympathized with the unions, crime syndicates, money counterfeiting rings, the forlorn lunatic painters. He held doubts about Operation Copula. State and subject, master and slave, parent and child, he glimpsed them all so perfectly. But he could not betray the Kabiri; for their existence was the ground of his media being. He heard their song in the larkpansies which sang in Hesper Park.

When the elevator abruptly opened into his sky-lit penthouse at the top of the tower, he expected to see Ephor Yannis. The robed judge sat behind his writing desk, admiring an amber-colored liquor collection.

The judge started clapping. "Bravo, Morpheus, a brilliant performance. You're best yet."

"Good day, Yannis." Morpheus smiled striding next to him. "Can I offer you a drink, old friend?"

"Quite all right."

"No, I insist. Evanor . . . heel!" Morpheus gruffly snapped his fingers at a sleepy helot boy dressed in long-johns, sprawled out on a fold-down wall-kline.

"Yes, Master?" the honey-colored boy asked rubbing his eyes.

"Fetch the brandy."

"*The* brandy, Sire?"

"Yes."

Pouring the reddish liquid into a sniffer glass, Morpheus allowed Yannis a quick sample. "This drink is a special one, wouldn't you agree? Tastes just like American apples. Would make Johnny Appleseed jealous."

"Mmmm," Yannis smacked his lips. "Wherever did you get it?"

"War spoils from ten years ago. I had it valued for the black market. Twenty-thousand orichalcum."

"Saint Plato. What's the occasion?"

"Haven't you heard?"

Yannis looked searchingly at him.

"We're on the verge of henosis."

The word "henosis" disquieted the judge. He turned to peer out a corner window into the sun, forever eclipsed by Levantra. "I've always wondered something, Morpheus," he said.

"By all means, ask away."

"Why do you call your program the Gorgon Hour . . . if it lasts half the afternoon?"

Morpheus clanked cups with his old Kabiri chum. "Simple, my Honor. A catchy title makes every show. If the title fails, the program fails. It is a fundamental law of metaphysics."

"Oh, is that right? Indeed." The judge snickered, sipping from his cup. "I also see your taste for entertainment remains unchanged." He nodded to an ongoing gladiator fight projecting on the floor. "Would've thought you'd outgrow such neophytic games."

"Gladiators? Never. Who really can?"

"Barbarity walks across all bridges, I guess," Yannis said, repulsed by a hideous death stab from a Thracian short-sword.

"Pardon me, Yannis, but I view the games as morally progressive."

"You do?" Yannis asked flabbergasted.

"Assuredly. Prodicus' worst decision was limiting the games. Gladiators have several advantages over the Bull."

"I predict an explanation forthcoming."

Morpheus stooped over the three-dimensional show, cupping the holograms with loving hands. "With the Bull death is so certain."

"No one denies that."

"Well the games aren't, Yannis. They add a twist of unpredictability to execution. You might live today, or you might die. Usually, there are good percentages either way. And long down the road, if you exert a good performance, you even might be freed. That kind of hope is magical, easier on the human mind."

"I've never thought about it quite like that."

"Public benefits are better, too."

"Really, Morpheus, you are too much." Yannis smiled being dragged in by his logic.

"Run with me a while longer, Yannis. Think about the drama. The drama! Two men fighting for their lives. They each have a history, friends, memories, hopes. With the Bull the crowds know where it ends. With gladiators, they never know. They sit at the edge of their seats, biting their nails, hoping for a quick death, yet groaning, yearning for a slow death. They want the prisoners run through and to survive at the same time. Nothing pleases crowds better than hoping contradictions. That's a religious experience. Gladiators achieve contradiction superbly. Gladiators, in a sense, are my religion."

Yannis frowned. "Some say we should give up the death penalty altogether. That any execution is barbaric."

"Who says?"

"Kleomedes. Potone's son."

"My dear Yannis," Morpheus grinned, "You move further left as you age. I would agree, except for the gladiators. If I was philosopher-king, I should discard the Bull and set a gradated number of gladiator matches per offense. Mine would be a more humane world."

Yannis' cup inverted. He drained his brandy. "Maybe more humane than this Kabiri necropolis."

"Sad ephor, your face is distressed. Returned from the courts, have you?"

Yannis set his glass on the desk. "No. The interrogations. We only captured a few Watchers—"

"And?"

"No trials. Courts mean nothing anymore. After making the prisoners talk, Prodicus handed out victor's justice. The strong ones we sent to be gladiators; the pretty ones . . . to the Slimetide Rolodex; the others—the others are to be impaled on the walls in geometric patterns. Harmonious, no?"

"No mercy, then?"

"Are you joking? Prodicus shows no mercy."

"What else could he do? One cannot rule with love. Love is fickle; fear is not. But where flies law in all this, Yannis?"

Yannis shrugged. "Law is law until inconvenient."

Morpheus grinned. "Like I told you, choosing the courts was worse than the Logoset. Law is a tool the powerful use to get what they want. It is a well-argued shell game entirely based on fictions. Nothing more."

Yannis fell silent, queerly agreed. He wondered what had brought him to this sorry plane. Prodicus said the Kabiri Circle would find justice, hurled accusations at the Katharoi's superstitious ways. There would be a "New Republic" better than the old. Yannis would help build it. Now they had their New Republic and it was just as bad. Kabiri-36 had eaten the minds of the entire city, swelled the courts, and driven the helots mad. What was government if even philosophers should ruin it so? *We were philosophers*, Yannis thought. *Not charlatans, not cranks, but real philosophers. Men of character with high-minded consciousness, we controlled desire, yet decadence slipped in. How could we have become such butchers?* He stiffened at the brutality of his past, shuddered again at the brutal interrogations. "You should've seen what Prodicus did to Xenon," he whispered.

Morpheus widened his eyes. "Ah, the man's expired?"

"Gods, no. Xenon should last a while longer, I think. Prodicus built something special for him, an intricate contraction—he calls it a . . . Gizmodic Cross."

"Cross?" Morpheus lifted his eyebrows. "Good gods, like the Romans?"

"Oh, far more advanced." Yannis demonstrated the device with his body. "Mythranium nails mechanically pop through the wrists and feet here and here. Hydraulic foot lifts raise; the arms lower to prevent suffocation. Blood and food is replenished through intravenous tubes. Prodicus said it will finish his . . . collection, whatever that means. I saw him strike the rebel while he wailed. What delight man makes suffering."

"Hmm . . . a fitting punishment for a fallen god. Ozbolt always said Prodicus had a poetic side."

"Poor Ozbolt. . . ." Yannis exhaled, trying to erase the troubled images, the troubled screams. He looked at the helot lying on the couch again, obviously drugged with one opiate or another. "Do you know why I'm here, Morpheus?" he asked watchfully.

"Some intimation. The Lion sent you to fetch me to Levantra."

"How did you know?"

"Clotho told me."

"Oh? She always liked you best. Did the bearded woman say anything else?"

"She said Patroclus did not want to send you but relented at my son's request."

"Simmias still talks fondly of you."

"That's why I offered his messenger my brandy. One should not be a tightwad with friends. The Kabiri would be stillborn were it not for loyalty."

"*Loyalty.*" The word rolled sweetly off Yannis' tongue.

Morpheus patted his friend's shoulder. "You are the last loyal one, Yannis. I wish I had a more expensive drink to offer you. Unfortunately, I must refuse your golden ticket."

"Come now—"

"All my life I dreamed to be an anchorman, Yannis. People made fun of me, but I am what I am. I do not give dreams up easily. But please,"

Morpheus ran over to rouse his helot servant from nap, "take Evan with you. He told me how much he wishes to see the flying isle. This will be an opportunity for him."

"You are sending me away, Master?" Evan asked.

"Only for a time."

"Have I angered you?"

"Of course not, lad. You'll be back shortly. You'll see."

The boy stumbled next to Yannis, who wondered at his old henchman's true intentions.

"Levantra was a dream," Morpheus said. "Now that it's here I want nothing to do with it. Only Skybridge makes me happy."

Yannis looked out the window one last time. A fleet of transport ships flapped from the wards into the clouds above Heliopolis. The clouds changed form, shaped by the aquamolpis into penitent worshippers.

There was little time.

"Good bye, Morpheus," Yannis said. He gathered his robes together and left the Republic's newsman pouring another glass of brandy.

Alone, Morpheus thought of Potone and her doomed children. *The twins were a bad omen*, he thought. *Right from conception, I knew it. Prodicus was wrong to place such faith in their I.T. waves. A frequency could be the same and still transfer less material. There should've been one child—not two. Surely, Potone's womb split the Third Vessel to ruin Kabiri's plans. That was the supreme law of nature: Fight against nature and nature fights back.*

Of course, this was merely speculation, unproved. Morpheus sipped his drink, thoughtfully. He began the ritual chant: "Give me the high eye to see like Kabiri. . . ."

V § 10 "WE ARE BURNING ALL BRIDGES, LEVANTRIANS!"

Glaucon awoke to soft lips gliding along his chest. He looked up and saw Zoe, disrobed, entranced in the starry-lusts of *erosic*. He lay in a sea of purple cushions.

Rubbing his golden hair with her hands, Zoe said frenzied, "I was so worried about you, Glaucon, my sweet little Glaucon, my gentle mooncalf."

Glaucon pushed her away. "Where am I?" he asked.

"The flying halls of Levantra; a paradise of youth lovelier than the Isle of the Blessed. We sleep in the universe of a living god. Make love to me, mooncalf, like I remember."

Zoe grabbed his hands and pushed them on her skin.

"Was I dreaming all along?" Glaucon wondered staring at his fingers. Adhesive bandages glued across his shoulder stirred gruesome recollections of the Battle of Gaia's Pore. What had happened to Sophie?

Zoe moved to place a red pill on his tongue. "Forget about that woman. Come closer to me. Let me be your dryad and cling upon your tree."

Glaucon refused her, peddling backward on the pillows. His hazy mind sharpened. "Not like this! What happened to the others? What of Xenon and the Watchers?"

Myrtle incense clouding the domed room made him queasy. Circling around the bed, a team of golems cooled their sweat with translucent fans.

"Please, Glaucon," Zoe said perturbed. "This moment is a gift from Prodicus. Don't spoil it for me. You are to be immersed in hours."

"Are you my guard dog, then, sent to bite away my resistance?"

Zoe hugged her shoulders. Blood pumped anxiously up her veined neck. She begged, "Don't leave me without a final taste of you. Your lips are sweet as honey. I shall miss you so. Show me how to penetrate knowledge."

Eyes batting, she wrapped her right leg tightly around him.

Glaucon hurled her fragrant body off the bed. He pointed accusingly, "If you really loved me, Zoe, you'd provide escape, not some distraction. What happened to Sophie? Is she all right?"

"What is so precious about your Iron Queen?" Zoe asked with clenched fists, climbing atop the floating lodestone-mattress again. "Is her name so different from mine? Is her body fairer? Flesh softer? Or her metal different? Are we not both the same height? Tell me, my love, does she tremble like I do when you come near? Does she protest so violently when you tell her no? Why shun gold hair for bronze? Why shun my similar touch? I could feast on you like a banquet and faint from passion. I love you to tears. If you desire, pretend I am her, just so I may love you again."

"I won't have you under the influence," Glaucon protested. Zoe pulled him to her waiting breasts, but he rejected all her advances and shook his long-time consort fiercely.

Zoe finally collapsed on her fists like a gorilla. "Damn it, Glaucon . . . I tried to remain sober for you. I did. I tried so hard. There were just too many things I wanted to say. How sick am I? Only in this drunken state can I tell you how I really feel. It's so difficult being honest. Why is it so difficult? My soul is perverted. I have to dope myself up just to talk with you."

"Zoe . . . don't cry," he touched her hand. "I understand. I was the same."

Zoe put a finger to his lips. "No. Shush, little mooncalf. Listen to me. Let me confess. Prodicus made me spy on you. All these years, I've reported everything you told me to him. Even when you told me things in confidence. Mercy, how I wanted to protect you, but Prodicus snared it all from me—everything! He's so frightening. If I could take everything back, I would. I've watched you since a youth and loved you. I devoted myself to ending your loneliness. Now when I think of the world without you, I realize *I* was the one who was lonely. I'm so selfish and lonely. Forgive me. I've harmed you more than I can bear." Zoe rolled love-sick euphoric on the sheets, vacantly staring, lost in a pleasure tremor. "Oh-h-h," she moaned, "make me sing or I shall howl like a mandrake. Don't leave me, Glaucon. Don't become a prisoner of Kabiri. Let me shroud you away with my embrace."

"Zoe, I could never be mad with you." Glaucon grew sad over her pitiful state. "All my life I craved your company; our time together was never enough. Now that time is here in plenty, I cannot stay."

"Leave, then!" Zoe screamed out of her senses. "No . . . no, wait." Recovering, she scrambled to find something under the pillows and pulled out a controller.

The golems fell dead. Glaucon looked confused.

"No one told me you would die in immersion. I swear, Glaucon. Had I known, I never would've helped. There is a pistol in there, too . . . somewhere. Take it. Run. Run away. The drug will silence me completely in a moment. I don't want you to go, but you must. Save yourself. Save your Iron Queen."

The blonde guardian lost consciousness to the drug. She began pounding the pillows in starvation and despair. Glaucon left the gun hidden in the bed, barely remembered to don a robe as he fled outside.

Patroclus and Simmias Rex waited for the Second Vessel on the lawn, blue cloaks thrown over their arms.

Wind whistled through Levantra's audiomembrane. Glaucon noticed he was on the southwestern slope, by the airfield. Winged carriers landed behind like a flock of geese.

"Nourished so soon, old friend?" Rex asked lowering his xiphos stick. He tossed a piece of trirock candy in his mouth. "You don't know what strings Zoe had to pull to—"

"Where's Sophie?" Glaucon demanded. He scanned Levantra's rocks, the illumined rivers of light, meditation towers, crystal ferns, and angel statues. The terrain was unnatural: Too flat in the middle, while the eastern mountains rose at a thirty degree angle with a chipped, blocky appearance. His heart still sighed at leaving Zoe in such a condition. Thinking about the way Prodicus used her—used everyone, how he twisted naturally good people into Hades-flamed trolls with inextinguishable pollution—aroused the most furious passions. The Second Vessel wanted to rip the guardian-king to pieces. He wanted to rip his godlike ambitions to pieces.

Rex pointed past a row of adobe rock dwellings to the pyramid temple at the center of Levantra. Avis circled it like a fiery wheel. "The fugitive is being processed for immersion—"

"She has a name, Rex, if you please. Take me to see *Sophie* at once."

"Hold on, *Vessel*," Rex laughed, prodding him with his xiphos. "Enjoy the fresh air. It'll be your last. No need to rush off, yeah? Let's rest under some feather-tents for shade. I'd like to ask you some questions about anarchist communal life . . . for posterity, you understand. Don't worry, I'll totally cite you."

"I won't tell you anything, you sick scholar," Glaucon cursed. "The air here is poisonous. I can barely breathe."

"No, no," Rex countered. "It's just the altitude. Still working on the oxygen circulation."

Patroclus stood sideways, refusing to look at his friend. Pale, he hunched over with a hand on his hip, as if just finishing a race.

"And you, Patroclus," Glaucon rebuked his quiet friend, "betraying Stratos? Never in a thousand years would I believe it. Have you gone mad?"

"And there it is," Rex broke in, snarling. "How about that, Pat? The runaway traitor scolds *us* for moral turpitude. Now I've heard everything. What were we supposed to do, Glaucon? Tell Prodicus off and end up like Leonida? No thanks. I prefer my head just where rests—on my pretty shoulders. Prodicus thinks ten steps ahead of everyone. The Fates think ten thousand steps. No one can outsmart them."

Patroclus tried to mask shame with argument: "I grew up believing justice the harmony of the soul's three parts. But in a world of continual peace, soldiers are unnecessary. What our world needs now is reason and desire; machines can run the rest."

"Good form," Rex said. "Do these things just come to you, Brother?"

"And what will happen to those born spirited?"

Patroclus answered, “The Fates will control breeding like before. The spirited class will be boxed until they’re needed.”

“Amen,” Rex clapped. “No longer to fear overthrow by singing soldiers, is it not glorious? Auxiliaries can’t be bridled; they’ve dethroned us several times. Faith in guardian reason is a pot with many holes. Best end human soldiers altogether.”

“You betrayed their faith, Rex.”

“What difference does it make? History is written by the victors. Next generation of guardians will worship us as Hythloday. We’re founding fathers. Even you, Glaucon, and that Swamp Rat of yours.”

“Founding fathers, huh? If you say so,” Glaucon said flatly. He started walking toward the pyramid.

“Hey . . . wait, Glaucon, what’re you doing?” Patroclus caught up to him by a rock bridge, nearly tripping. He was thrown off balance by Levantra’s aerial vibrations.

“Your father awaits my arrival.”

“What will you do when you see him?” Patroclus studied his eyes.

“I will free the Iron Queen. One way or another.” Glaucon had never been more certain of anything in his life. Worry about the pains of immersion pulled his heart to his stomach. Yet, with each footstep, he felt greater rightness in his decision. Zemer had done something . . . protected him somehow. Maybe he could fight immersion in a way others could not. He felt an internal change, too. Strangely, his feelings toward Sophie felt both like a brother and a lover, as if Zemer called his spirit within, giving him courage.

The guardians walked together in silence, a long six kilometer trail to the Temple of the Fates. As they passed a field of sunflowers and cogniscrambler pods, Patroclus marveled at the transformation in Glaucon. An inner resoluteness reflected in the young philosopher. His eyes remained focused on the Temple, his entire being thrust toward his beloved.

Is this the power of the Iron Queen? Patroclus wondered. *Is this the power of love?*

The crystal shrines of the New Celestial Academy sparkled in the sunlight. They stopped at its central vineyard so Rex could pick grapes and refresh his thirst, sitting momentarily on dice-shaped stools.

Patroclus peered down an open chasm in the island rocks. Levantra’s philosophers reclined between loud-spinning magnets. They hovered on cushions in the air reading papyritrons, their perfected stories. He shivered a little as he reached into his robes—something cold met his fingers.

The sacred jinn.

The night of Zemer's capture, Patroclus ignored the Watcher's request to destroy the weapon. Instead he took it back to his room and caressed the orb until a burst of energy tingled his fingertips. What exactly he planned to do with the jinn once they reached the Temple filled him with apprehension. *Could I really attack my own father?* he wondered. Although Patroclus feared to speak aloud in front of Rex, he couldn't forgive his father for destroying the city's Spirit. Nor could he let his best friend be sacrificed to a monster. Surely, Saint Plato would condemn such despicable things. *My father has gone too far, and only I can stop him,* Patroclus growled silently. *I must stop him, even if it means facing the life-cursing Erinyes.*

The Lion of Heliopolis burned angrily as they marched up the blinking steps of the Temple of the Fates. Spider-web wires enmeshed the entire complex. Jeweled sun-shaped doors groaned open. Stepping through an antechamber, they entered an inner laboratory. The angled room—still under construction—was like an iceberg, capping Kabiri-36's mainframe. Computer terminals led to a raised emerald dais at the back of the room. Upon this dais, three pedestals formed the points of a scalene triangle. Prodicus sat at a control board between the pedestals, directing his ship of state.

Rex and Patroclus both saluted upon entering the lab.

Glaucon gasped in horror to see Sophie struggling in chains on the left pedestal. He gasped again when he saw Xenon crucified on the Gizmodic Cross by the wall. "What foul contrivance did Prodicus invent now?" he mumbled. The torture looked excruciating.

Prodicus acted oblivious to this gruesome world. Quite the opposite, he bristled with elation. Running in ceremonial white robes to the company, he kissed them on the cheeks. "Thank Plato, you've arrived," the guardian-king exclaimed merrily. "How kind of you to join us, Mr. Oxenbridge. We missed you terribly. Look at that life in your cheeks; Zoe nursed you back to health, I see. As you took the bedchamber, my niece and I reflected on your rocky relationship."

"Glaucon, run away!" Sophie cried.

Prodicus patted the Second Vessel, massaging his shoulder. "Yes, Glaucon, listen to my wise niece, daughter of Potone. Run away like a scared little boy. That's what your family is best at, isn't it?" The old oracle smiled, wrinkles deepening. Then he added, "Although some Oxenbridges run faster than others. Your mother did not run so fast, did she? Your mother slipped and fell right into my hands."

Glaucon peered into the philosopher's cruel eyes. *He's trying to burn everything good out of me,* he thought. His fingers trembled, about to erupt, ached to squeeze Prodicus' kingly throat. Something watered the flames in his chest. "I am taking Sophie out of here," he whispered resolvedly.

"Is that so?"

"Yes. Give her to me. Now."

Prodicus cackled. He squeezed Sophie's cheeks together with his hands. "Such determination! What are with these men and their Iron Queen?" he asked his freshly robed captive. "Strong wills, yes, but sadly, not one ounce of power. Not one once of sacred reason."

"Get your hands off me," Sophie hissed.

"Awww, my bronze niece, where is that noble side I've heard so much about? The side that heals? That breaks my spells? The side that makes men rebel against fate?"

Sophie glared at him. "Take off my chains and I'll show you."

Prodicus grinned. "Potone's daughter a comedian? She would never believe it."

"Potone cries at what you've become, Uncle. Stop. Let us go."

"Is that what you really want?"

"Yes!"

"How your tone grieves me, Sophia," Prodicus wagged his finger. "No, there will be no more running away, *Great Maiden of the Mountain*. I will not be stolen from again. Not by you or anyone else. The Vessels are fated to Levantra."

"We're just human beings, Uncle—"

"Silence! Visions flow so strongly now. This room . . . exactly as I saw it. The jinn sees all. The jinn *is* Levantra." Prodicus turned to a robed attendant at the control panel. "Did the last transport from the wards arrive?"

"Yes, Excellency. Levantra has reached its estimated needs for human capital."

"And the Bull?"

"Brought up this morning. She burns hot."

"Very good. The fated hour has come, just as I imagined. Please target the Republic and all major world settlements with a third of our nuclear warheads."

"What?" Glaucon shouted alarmed.

Xenon raised his bruised head in agony. The burned earth. The coming fiery deluge. He *had* seen it after all.

Prodicus looked surprised by their expressions. "We are burning all bridges, Levantrians! Either man survives in the clouds or he becomes extinct. Time to burn away failed creation."

The alchemists at the controls looked up in fright. "T-Target the Republic, Sire? But . . . but . . . that—"

"Would you like to return there until I find someone who will?"

Like expert pianists their fingers frantically input the commands.

"Please don't, Uncle," Sophie begged. "I'll do anything you ask. Just leave the Other Side alone. Don't hurt the helots. They're innocent."

"Hush, sweet little niece. Do not let your concern for the poor damn this charitable act. The safest state is one with no rivals. Things haven't changed since Hythloday."

Patroclus, lost in rage, gripping the jinn by his chest, finally aimed it at the philosopher-king's pointed beard—straight at his mouth. "Enough, miserable father," he roared. "This wasn't part of the plan. Leave the Republic alone! We barely survived the Day of Hylopleonexia. The world might not recover again."

Prodicus leaned back covering his eyes. "At last, at last, my son's betrayal. Nothing surprises me. Do you think you have the talent to use that contraption, little cub? Do you even know what it is?"

"It's enough to finish you and this island." Patroclus stumbled backward and pointed the glowing orb at some exposed copper wires sprouting from the mainframe. "I swear to the Good, I'll use it, Father. I'll crash your abomination to the ground.—Even if I kill us all to do it."

"Go ahead and try," Prodicus egged him on.

The jinn sparked but refused all commands.

Patroclus eyed the jinn in horror. "It worked before . . . I saw it . . . Father . . . no. How . . . how are you doing this?"

"Fool," Prodicus approached him ready to pounce. "You are overfed and weak. Did you think you could abort my babe without consent? The jinn knows its own; it has ruined stronger men than you. It obeys everything I say!"

"What in Hades? It's so cold," Patroclus winced dropping the glowing jewel to the floor. Icy crystals glassed his fingers blue. "You treacherous manipulator!" He nursed his hand. "You used us to bring death to everything we were taught to defend."

"Not death," Prodicus corrected, "rebirth. Like our immortal souls, we shed one body for another. Had you shown resolve, Child, a heavenly host would've been your reward. Now, I shall cast you down from paradise."

Ruby lightning arced from Prodicus' sleeve, slamming the tall rebel next to Xenon on the wall. He writhed in agony under the glacial howl, crying out to Glaucon for help: "How do I make the voices stop? How did you shield them? My ears! My ears-s-s!"

Rex jabbed his xiphos stick into Glaucon's back when he moved to aid his fallen friend.

"Ready, Excellency," the computer attendants said.

"Prodicus," Glaucon cried, "on Saint Plato's soul show mercy!"

The philosopher-king breathed in and struck out his arm. "Sorry, Oxenbridge. The Good I seek, ugly men no longer. Sow my discord. Make my world uninhabitable for a thousand years!"

Sirens blared across Levantra. Missile bay doors opened on the cliffs. Guardians looked down one last time to see the green Earth, their ancient cradle, incinerated in a minute. Missile after missile roared into the convex horizon, unrelentingly, steaming on tangled jets of smoke. Atoms split and sent their curses across the Earth. Fire—*fire consuming fire*—danced on the Republic. Mushroom smoke swallowed the remains. Glaucon rushed to the window lamenting the Other Side, all the children who had fled to Wyoming for safety. Would the shelters protect them? Could they remain alive? Nothing but ash remained on the surface. Worst of all, he couldn't hear the explosions—the audiomembrane blocked all smoke and sounds of the attack.

Glaucon vomited. "You've murdered the entire human race. You've sent the world a nuclear winter—"

"Don't be dramatic," Prodicus shot back. "We're still here."

"They're not."

"This is evolution, Glaucon. We matter. They don't. This gives you every incentive to cooperate. I won't argue about my motives in any great detail. You'll know them like your own after we merge together. We three shall spend centuries studying our souls in their 'unsullied purity', unmaimed by that foul 'association with the body.' Can you taste the endless Good, the possibility to think without the simple manifolds of language? The Intelligible Realm will be our playground. The animal shall die, and we will hold the Forms of the Beautiful and the Good. At last, the prophesied philosopher-king shall rule."

"Forms aren't real!" Sophie shouted. "There is no philosopher-king."

"We'll soon see, won't we, my dear? How lucky we are to have such unwilling rulers. Plato would rejoice. This shall be an eternal feast for humanity. Now—immerse our Iron Queen."

For one terrible moment, Sophie looked at Glaucon dazed with fear. Her eyes watered as a swirl of red engulfed her from ceiling to floor. She hovered stiff in the air over the pedestal and lost consciousness, swept up in a world of eternal dream.

"Sophie-e-e-e-e!" Glaucon screamed.

Prodicus recited the prophecy as if tasting it for the first time: " 'A narrow path from the tree of souls, three indigo Vessels will appear: one earth, one soul, one crown; living animals—stillborn—to repair. Gather them like the fruits of harvest. Mix with Kabiri together in the sky. Putrification prime renews virgin reason, the spirit of Good; forms the Golden King.' "

"P-Prodicus, what have you done to Sophie?"

"Her body shall die an earthly death in a matter of minutes. If you wish to save her, join me as Kibiri-37. If not, enjoy life without her." Prodicus leapt onto the top pedestal. "Eternal reason awaits the Monad, and it shall reign from the clouds forevermore. Immerse me. Unload this stinking flesh of contradictions so I may feast my eyes on the halls of true knowledge. Adieu!"

Crimson light showered the philosopher-king's robes until he finally drifted lifeless.

"You're not really going to try and save her, are you?" Rex asked when Glaucon jumped upon the right pedestal.

"I have to try," Glaucon clenched his fist. "I won't lose her . . . not like Zemer. I once thought the world ensnared me, but now I know I was free all along."

"But this is our chance, man. Let's take the city together, while they're trapped."

"I'd rather die than live without Sophie."

"She's already dead. Make something of yourself."

"Immerse me!"

As Rex shook his head, icy light shattered Glaucon's mind.

V § 11 Entering the Land of Shadows

The Second Vessel fell like a stone ripped apart by magnetic forces, and splashed in a kaleidoscope sea.

"A drop?" his mind started frantic. "A portion of water, but also water. The ocean is made of drops. Yet when they are together you cannot see the drops. My mind. Alone. Like other minds—alone! Am I part of the cosmic mind? Could I rejoin the universe like the drops? I see the rain and wonder: Rain falls to the earth, catches into streams and pools, evaporates, returns.

What is it like to return? To change form like the clouds and rain? My raindrop's fall is . . . lonely."

The voice called distantly: "Whence comes grief, weary traveler? Separation is poison."

Glaucon cried, "Is the mind like water? Can I enter others? Can they enter me? Hold me. Someone hold me. I want to spill into my mother again, grow into something new, find that connection I lost. Was there ever a connection? I can't remember. The creation of life from the jelly frightens me. All of life frightens me, like the cycle of the endless rain."

"Your walls frighten you. Let them down."

"Walls?" Glaucon asked.

"Yes, you closed your soul to make an identity but found only sadness. Now you must free your elemental parts. Be not celibate to the cosmos. Let us in, Child." Something knocked like a woodpecker. "Let us in to end your sorrow."

"End my sorrow?"

Yes, yes, Glaucon was a boy again, running among the blooming sunflowers of the meadow. Flying letters danced with him on the hills, tossing his golden hair. By a mulberry tree he climbed forgetfully into his mother's lap.

"Welcome home, Glaucon," she cooed with hollow voice and stroked his curls. He snuggled close to her. A turning column of light burned in the distance. He watched it hold up the stars.

"The Fates' spindle," Glaucon mumbled peacefully.

"Go. They're ready for you," Melete said. "Do not fight the Fates."

"Will you come with me?"

"My arms will take you."

Day changed to night rapidly. Pink disir hatched from the mulberry, kissed him on the cheek, and darted away.

"Wait, this isn't real," Glaucon whispered. "None of this is real. This is from Plato's fable! Book X. It's a . . . a trick. . . ."

With level voice Melete questioned him: "Why would I trick you? I love you. I want you to be with me. You would have me die again? You would *kill* me again?"

The moon dripped blood, flattened, curved like a bow. Atropos gripped it in the sky and fired an arrow of light.

"Let me go, Mother! The arrow will hit us."

Melete clutched him kicking to her bosom. "Move not away, faithless son. Willing or grudging, we will break your walls. We will swim inside your soul."

"No, no," the Second Vessel struggled in vain to flee. The arrowhead dived like sizzling brimstone and cut deep into his brain.

Sight shattered. Only darkness and ripping. Thick liquid filled his lungs. Opening his eyes, Glaucon saw a womb growing organically around him. He tried to push the taut skin but choked on the fluid. The space sucked his power. He shrunk in size. "This isn't what I wanted. Let me out! I don't want to be a slave. Mother, help me. Where am I?"

The womb hardened to red-hot bronze. Metal scorched skin. Smells of burning flesh overpowered nostrils. Upon hearing the song of the Bull outside, Glaucon started screaming. "Let me out!" he pounded the furnace walls. "Sophie! Patroclus! Zoe! Zemer! Prodicus! Someone help me." As the fibers of his eyelids singed, visions of the wicked Atropos knocked his dying senses.

Glaucon finally collapsed unable to breathe. Melting into ashy powder, a rush of memories invaded his mind. Strangely, they were not his own. He was . . . somewhere else. His arms were thinner, almost emaciated. He wore torn rags and was nearly naked. Sophie was there. She looked different, younger somehow. Running in military boots crunching in the snow, she grabbed his wrist.

"Zemer, gods, what's happened to you?" she asked alarmed. "You look atrocious. Have you stopped eating?"

"For some time," Glaucon said in Zemer's voice.

Sophie smelled him, looked up at a red whirlwind in the sky. "Is this the jinn's true power?" she asked in awe.

Glaucon attempted to embrace his beloved but failed entirely. No matter how hard he tried, he could not control his speech or movements. He was locked onto the memory's track.

Sophie kneeled down, rifle on her knee. She rubbed Zemer's greasy hair with tenderness, looked past him to some towering boulders on the plateau. "You didn't say where you were going," she said.

"I did not want to be found," Zemer replied.

"We've followed you for the last week into Bryce Canyon, chasing your storms. The men are terrified of your thunder."

"They should be terrified of me."

Sophie's face flooded with concern. "It scared me, too. I had to walk here alone."

Zemer blinked rapidly, regretfully, saying, "That . . . was not my intent." He called the storm whooshing back inside the jinn, then looked up at his sister, reading her mind. "The Continental Caucus sends you," he spoke stoically. "They wish me to deactivate the walls."

"How do you know that?" Sophie gasped astonished.

"A guess. Finally time to kill Xenon's son, isn't it?"

Sophie stiffened at his clairvoyance. "I need your help to find the Vessel. It's him or us, Zemer."

"True. Him or *us*."

Zemer's prying eyes made Sophie spring to her feet. She became defensive. "I'm not going to die for a guardian. Fuck him! It's for his own good, too. Oh, the judgment in your tone, I hate it. This is why the men gossip about you."

"The men gossip?"

"They're angry you stopped drilling and deserted the Eastern Column. They say you show a lack of respect. Frankly, I agree." She folded her arms.

"I guess I haven't been the same since the swamps," Zemer admitted, "or Chicago."

"We did what we had to do."

"Yeah, lost thousands for nothing . . . killed for nothing."

Sophie confronted him exasperated. "How can you even say something like that? Xenon and the Continental Caucus are challenging the Republic's oppression for the first time in centuries."

Zemer disagreed, looked past her down a long valley. "We're not challenging anything, Sophie. The Caucus just makes a bigger target, fatter game to hunt in the preserve. The militias may raise their guns, but the Republic simply raises more. Still the future is unchanged. There's more blood, but the future's the same. We've been deceived. Xenon tells us our guns bring relief to the communes. But all our guns do is devour our friends."

Sophie picked up a book frozen into an ice block. "You think Kabiri grimoire will prevent us from becoming rugs?"

"They could."

"Yeah right, no good can come from anything written by the Kabiri. You should stop trying to glimpse the future with the jinn, Zemer. You're becoming obsessed. Knowing the future won't help us; it just weaves a net."

The snow nipped at Zemer's legs. He stood up rubbing his body for warmth. As Sophie passed him fresh clothes, he said, "I won't stop until I find a way to save us. It's here somewhere . . . if I only had more time."

Sophie aimed her rifle at the sky, wondering why Zemer fried its aiming system. She hadn't even seen the jinn lightning this time. Her brother had become deeply foreign, immensely powerful. Rebuking him for spoiling a perfectly good weapon, she said, "Prodicus will not be defeated with crafty arguments or foreknowledge, Brother. A man like that must be brought down by violence. After I kill the Second Vessel, I'm going to put a bullet straight through his head for what he made you do to Mother."

Zemer shrugged. He wrapped his arm around his sister's waist, feeling her body stiffen, jerk away terrified before returning his affection. "Prodicus is unimportant in the grand scheme of things," he said. "We must find a way to get past him to the Fates which pull the world's strings. The Fates are the true threat. As long as the Fates exist we shall be slaves."

"I don't feel like a slave." Sophie started laughing.

"What's so funny?"

"Just the thought of you trying to save me. You're a mess. I think you're going to come running to me for help, like you always do."

Zemer frowned. "The way to the Fates is through the jinn. That is a door you can't enter, Sister. But I can. I shall defeat Kabiri. Whatever it takes. I will bend nature's laws. There is a Bridge of Shadows forming, and the firefly is on the other side. I will take the Bridge. On Mother's soul, I swear it."

"You're talking nonsense again," Sophie responded apprehensively. "What did I tell you about that? I don't like it. I want no more talk of shadows and fireflies." She kicked dust in the air walking away.

The memory faded. Fire returned bubbling around Glaucon like a ruby star. Fanning the flames in flight, Lachesis, Clotho, and Atropos wore garlands and clawed at his hair. Glaucon's skin peeled off. Then his arms fell. Moaning in agony, he collapsed on the fagots ready for death.

Right before fire collapsed lungs, Glaucon noticed his arm's shadow flickering.

What in the world? he thought with shock. *My shadow—it's moving!*

The shadow flickered again, unraveled like a banner. Braiding into a wall, the shadow warded off the flames. A streaking wraith emerged from the wall and chased the old ladies, shouting, "OUT SISTERS! OUT!"

Then the Fates were gone.

Glaucon looked up spellbound. His body was restored in a white Euclidean space. No smells. No sounds. No burning Bull. None other than Zemer appeared before him. As a doomed seaman grabs hold to the life-raft, so Glaucon gripped Zemer's dark leg, breathing relief.

"Easy now," the strange doppelganger said. "The ill maidens fly to make wrecks of their other captives."

Glaucon broke into tears. "Zemer, is it really you?" He could hardly contain his joy. His hair was the same. His arms were the same.

The ethereal image responded: "Part of Zemer, yes. I am a piece of Zemer's thread sent to your abode. I am something . . . not right."

"Why aren't I immersed?"

"I curtained your mind from the purge of fire. Wear me and you shall not burn away. That is my programming."

"You're a program?"

Zemer grunted. "Damn it all. No, not exactly. Been in here too long conversing with the Fates. Begun to think like a machine. It'd be difficult to explain exactly what I am. Consider me a replacement paraclete, a shield to maintain your individuation."

"Do you have the same emotions and thoughts like the other Zemer?"

"Hmm. It feels like I do, but who knows. No way to verify my beliefs."

"You called to me—that day I fled Heliopolis with the jinn."

"Yes. You wouldn't have found Sophie otherwise."

"She almost killed me."

"I know. But Sophie is Sophie. She wouldn't kill you. Nothing can destroy her heart."

Like a gnat, Glaucon felt an urge to race toward the column of light in the distance, but he remained inert, unable to move, like he was still in the memory.

Zemer sensed his thoughts. "Movement here is not the same as the outside," he explained. "You must will where you want to go. It takes more concentration. Remember, you have no body. This is all illusion."

Glaucon peered at his toes, willed his feet to stand, for any sweet sign of movement. Unexpectedly, he spilled upright next to Zemer. He struck his fist excitedly in the air, like discovering a new power.

"Excellent work. You'll get the hang of it in no time. Now where should we go, Outworlder?"

The Second Vessel straightened his back. "There's no question. We must rescue Sophie at once."

Zemer's shadowy form brightened at his earnestness. "You have changed for the better, Glaucon. I've been living with you for weeks, feeling as you feel, but to hear your voice just now—there are still many hidden depths. From the beginning, you've been the loose variable. You resonate with everyone—which makes you easy to manipulate—but that resonation makes you unpredictable as well, and special. You and I share a similar attribute. The jinn's power has less effect on us."

"Even more when you strike me with it."

"No, friend, not a strike but a shelling. Forgive me, but when I arrived in the wards, I began an experiment on you with the jinn."

"You already apologized."

"I doubt my earthly copy told you my full plan—too many potential errors. I made you a Trojan Horse for the cogniscrambler. By imprinting my I.T. wave signature on you without the Fates knowing, I clouded the Fates' visions of the future, weakening their predictions. It's like throwing two rocks in a pond—wave interference. I was also able to infiltrate the mainframe when you entered the cogniscrambler. Ha! The sisters have been blind to our behavior for weeks."

"That's genius, but why me? Why not protect your sister with the same spell?"

"Sophie's too susceptible to the jinn. It might've killed her."

"You worked wisely," Glaucon nodded his head.

Zemer smirked. "I knew you'd say that. Otherwise I might've decided against it. You're ready. Let's go." He snapped his fingers a couple times. The white expanse blossomed with texture. A rugged plateau sprouted up and curled around the Fates' spindle. Below them was a long plain. As the Fates spun, they sent liquid colors jettisoning into the air. They rained down on the grass, germinating a crowd of people. Some of the souls were from Glaucon's memory. Others were unrecognizable. They walked like zombie-puppets toward the pillar, were caught up in the revolving of the rim, and streaked back into the sky only to rain down again reborn, in an endless transmigration of souls.

"Are the Fates causing this world?" Glaucon asked Zemer.

"No, you are." At his friend's curious look, Zemer explained, "Your subconscious mind thinks it's dead. It conjured the heaven you were taught as a boy to feel at home."

"But I don't believe those silly stories from the Republic."

"It makes no difference. The mind projects regardless of truth."

"I want to view the world of the Fates as it really appears."

"Well spoken, but the human mind will not permit you. It lacks the proper categories. Shall we be on our way? A long journey awaits us. Before we find Sophie, there is something important you must see."

V § 12 Kabiri Memories

Wind howled loudly from the Fates' spindle. Glaucon's teeth chattered as they traversed the steep plateau. Looking into clusters of red, black, and white crystals, Glaucon spied many Forms in them, like fish in an aquarium. When he reached to poke one, though, Zemer snatched his arm.

"Do not touch anything unless I say," he commanded. "Be careful of the Fates' trickery."

They eventually came to a high adamant gate, golden bars towering into the sky. It rattled in the wind.

"Here we are," Zemer said, rummaging in his pockets. He drew out a long chain of keys.

"Where'd you get those?" Glaucon asked,

"Borrowed them," Zemer replied. Fitting a square-tipped key with a Zeus icon in the lock, the gate glowed neon green and opened. A shadowy portal emerged spinning like a vacuum, threatening to suck them inside. Noticing Glaucon's skittishness, Zemer said, "Don't be afraid, Vessel. What dreams may come, I'll protect you."

Another memory bubbled up upon entering.

They were in a sterile white laboratory on Schizoeon, but at a much earlier time. The technology appeared bulky and ancient, like the old pictures Glaucon saw in Dr. Ozbolt's office. Two enormous capsule-tubes stuck out from a far wall, breathing red smoke like a furnace. Energy throbbed down the room. A little girl with bronze hair lay by one tube on the tile, quivering.

Xenon, in his mid-thirties, stooped low examining her in a green radiation suit. Feeling her pulse, he shook his head. "Prodicus," he said, "Sophia can't take another session today. Respiration's off. Her pulse is frenzied."

Prodicus sat behind a protective glass window, hands folded. "Enough," his voice boomed over the intercom. "Put her in again."

"She's only ten, Prodicus. Take pity on the human body—"

"The human body will do as I say, Xenon."

"But Sophia's heart nearly stopped twice yesterday."

"Kabiri-35 recalibrated the magnetometer. The risks are therefore minimal. Put her in, I say."

Xenon covered his mouth with a fist, almost in tears. "I cannot participate in this. I refuse. That gas will kill her. If her body doesn't break, her mind will. This is too much."

"Fine," the scientist sighed angrily. "Sentimental lout. Kleomedes, please place your sister in the tank."

A miniature Zemer approached Sophia on the floor. His head cocked right at her distress, thinking what to do. He acted confused. Sophia cried begging him to stop: "No, Kleo. Please. I hurt. I hurt all over."

When the boy looked back at Prodicus concerned, the philosopher bellowed, "Stop thinking, and do as I say. Your sister will be fine."

Kleomedes nodded and grimaced. He gruffly seized Sophia's arm. "It'll be over in a second," he promised. Two other alchemists assisted as he dragged her limp body to the waiting tube and placed her inside.

"Help me, Brother, please!" Sophia begged gripping his shoulders. "Don't make the voices come. You know I can't take them. Save me. Help me. Like you promised." She clawed at his sleeves, but the alchemists pried her fingers off and held her down.

"Those animals," Glaucon shouted, trying to stop them.

Zemer shook his head. "You can't change the past."

"How long did Sophie suffer like this?"

"For months. I did nothing. My decision led to her death." Zemer's face lowered mournfully.

Xenon passed through them like a ghost, trying to stall the procedure. "Prodicus," he said sweetly, "Kabiri has enough readings to determine which sibling is the Vessel; further tests are pointless. We should wait for it to finish calculating."

"That could be years," Prodicus snarled back. "Besides, our research is yielding unprecedented discoveries about I.T. wave harmonics. By this spring, we'll have a safe and serviceable cogniscrambler, and the Second Vessel will be within our reach. I can search the whole damned city if I have to!" He entered the room, slapping a protective helmet over his silver hair. Hearing Sophie still sniffling in the tube, he pet her head like a sick animal. "There, there, little one. I know it hurts, but your sacrifice will be worth every drop of sweat. Take heart, you might be the seed for henosis."

Locking her in the tube, he bid Kleomedes take his own. Kleomedes looked from his tube to Sophia's and climbed in to await the gas.

Thud! The tubes spun into the wall and filled with red light.

Kleomedes appeared comfortable. Sophia, on the other hand, started screaming in terror, assailed by monstrous visions of skeleton armies. "Skeletons maimed rise from the dust. Gather on the hill, the flying island. Can you see inside their skulls? Burned, burned, yellowed in the sun. They see me. Gods, help me! They're going to eat me," she cried, pounding the glass.

One alchemist warned, "Sir, I've found an irregular pattern in her I.T. dipole. Sophia's dialogue matrix is distorting. Her heart rate is accelerating."

"Use the quantum dislocation net to stabilize the spikes."

"I can't! We're losing the subject. Her toxicity ratios are unbalanced. She's absorbing all the radiation. Dear gods—her heart!"

Warning bells clanged, Sophia gasped deafeningly, and her body fell limp. As she lay dying, a chute opened above and wires pierced her fragile skin like a claw, plucked her up to the waiting infirmary.

Prodicus remained unfazed. "Continue the diagnostic on Kleomedes. Repair the subject for tomorrow."

"For tomorrow?" Xenon shouted, swinging his arm. "She might be dead by then."

"Kibiri-35 prepared a special product for her," Prodicus explained. "It will make her last longer than before. Several hundred years more, I surmise."

Xenon moved to say something but wiped his brow instead. He fled the room in a fit of anger.

"Why are you showing me this?" Glaucon asked when the memory disappeared in electrofog.

Zemer said, "Life's road is not one way. It branches in many directions. You can't walk backward, but you can change destinations. Man is the measure of what he becomes. This moment proved a turning point for Xenon. Before this incident, Prodicus had blackmailed him to cooperate with the Kabiri by threatening his helot family's life. To protect you, Xenon committed terrible acts, wallowed in sorrow. Sophie's death finally changed him. Her last breath hardened his determination to inform on the Kabiri and run away with Melete forever."

"Xenon was planning to run away with my mother?"

"Yes," Zemer said. "Even before their separation, they talked seriously about it. They realized the Republic would never let them alone. They worried about you, too. Melete didn't want you to become a guardian. She made Xenon use every means at his disposal to prevent you from being taken to Heliopolis. So Xenon did. Utilizing his security clearance, he changed your Metis test scores and manipulated your grades and discipline records. Xenon also had other worries."

"He did?"

"He thought he'd protected you sufficiently from the guardians' eyes, but then, a week before this fatal experiment, while sleeping next to the Fates' mainframe, a telostape began printing on its own volition. It specified probabilities for the Second Vessel—and your name was on the list!"

"Incredible. It's like the Fates were purposefully trying to terrorize him."

"Xenon realized Kabiri-35 was just as my mother said: 'A daimon within an unholy altar of mythranium.' He deleted your name from the telostape. When the Fates mangled Sophie's organs, he rushed to Potone and confessed everything to her, even his past criminal affair with a helot. Potone agreed to help him flee the city with Melete but made him swear to take us with him."

The misty unknown place where Zemer stood jostled and foamed. A grand office materialized. When Glaucon looked down he saw a stone floor with a seahorse mosaic. It led to an open patio with thin velvet curtains twisting in the breeze.

Guardian-King Hekademos III entered from the patio, exhibiting the guardian-scepter of authority. His grizzled beard hung low to his ribs. Penetrating eyes peered out behind round spectacles. He walked with a stately and commanding gait, barely containing his anger as Prodicus kneeled before him. "What is this I hear about your unholy experiments on Schizoeon?" he demanded. "Potone and Xenon came to me distraught."

Prodicus frowned. "Potone should realize her litter belongs to the Republic—not to her."

"She came on behalf of Lycaon and ISHIM. She says your work is impeding our juvenile development program and Sophia's training on Stratos."

Prodicus sneered, "Of course she did, and the Republic was written by ignorant helots as well. What humbug! Potone and her night husband constantly pamper them. It's disgraceful."

"Lycaon already briefed me about his relationship with your sister and their children. That is not the issue." The philosopher-king opened an octagonal drawer and drew out a digital scroll. "Xenon comes forth with a list of abuses. Scandalous things . . . about helot sacrifices . . . organized crime . . . your research."

"Lies, my grace. That arrogant brat is jealous of my work. He's trying to undermine me and bring false honor to his name. He'll do anything to pamper that girl."

"Still," the guardian-king persisted, "Sophia's heart practically liquefied, Prodicus. Doesn't that bother you at all?"

"The Fates said it was a possibility."

"People are more important than your plans and Operation Copula."

"Is there anything more important than henosis, Sire?"

"Henosis?" The philosopher-king treated the word as the most displeasing noun. "Your wizardry with machines is taking us further from the Good. You need more prayer and logic-meditation, not science."

Prodicus clenched his fist. "The children of Potone shall birth a golden paradise, a place where all shall 'be ruled by a wise and divine ruler.' "

"Why that little girl?"

"You know why, Hekademos? You've seen the prophecy. My equations are faultless."

The philosopher-king paced around the office, squinting one eye. "No one understands your equations. Every symbol is gibberish, nonsense—voodoo! Why should the Fates care who the Vessels are?"

"What are you insinuating?" Prodicus asked.

"I'm not insinuating. This is about you wanting to bring harm to your sister."

"How dare you say such a reproachful thing; I'm not so petty. I am a guardian."

"You have hated Potone since the moment she arrived."

"She turned her back on me, true."

"That was a long time ago. She was a young, frightened transfer to Stratos. Did you expect her to pretend you were family? Knowing how much trouble that could cause?"

"It matters not. I cared for her safety in the Tenth Ward. Then she wanted nothing to do with me. I've moved on."

"Have you?" the guardian-king asked unconvinced. "Don't you find it odd . . . Kabiri would find your niece and nephew—"

"I don't recognize those illegitimate categories," Prodicus broke in.

"Fine, but I can't ignore Xenon's report. There are damning things in it: kidnapping, extortion, murder. Just what are you after, Oracle? What do you want?" Hekademos III eyed Prodicus like a snake curling backward.

The scientist made every effort to calm him. "What you want, my grace—a true race of reason."

"We have philosophers enough already."

"The hairy apes on this mountain are malfunctioning. Hardly philosophers. Why can't you see that?"

At this comment the philosopher-king's eyes bulged, and he stuttered in disbelief, "N-No, Prodicus, I think it *you* who is malfunctioning. You and your gang of technocratic magicians. The Kabiri Circle has lost all connection to reality. I am pulling you from the project."

"Absurd. I am the only one who can run it."

"Then I am shutting the project down," the philosopher-king snapped.

Prodicus frowned. "But Operation Copula has the support of all Heliopolis. Shut us down and anger will boil over you."

"Is that a threat?"

"No, a fact, my grace. Facts are not threats. I'd gladly step down, but my followers . . . they'll feel betrayed."

"Things are moving too fast. The knowledge you've given us has increased our technology beyond what is natural. Ekklesia the Blind—"

"Is a superstitious fanatic! Obeying that blind hermit's counsel is like listening to shadows. He wants us to live like they did three thousand years ago." Prodicus kneeled down and kissed Hekademos III's wrinkled hand. "Do not be afraid of glory, Sire. Forgive me for my lapping tongue. I spoke in haste. Please remember my love. Look," Prodicus pointed with his eyes to an orange-shaped coffin on the floor, "the Kabiri grant miracles. You've said so yourself. You had insomnia for years, but my sleep-miner cured your affliction, didn't it?"

"Yes."

"See. My work will make you one of the greatest philosopher-kings in history. It'll make the city happy. Don't hold ill of me. Don't make friends enemies."

Hekademos III turned from his words. "Stop groveling. Leave me. I must think on this."

Memories flickered as a flame. Zemer and Glaucon sieved through the floor, their bodies stretching like spaghetti. They were now in a welded metal chamber, deep, deep under Ozbolt Tower. Red vapor misted heavy near their feet. Pillars surrounded them, changing colors. By a rock altar, Prodicus and Dr. Ozbolt bickered. They were watched by fifty masked Kabiri, by Yannis and Zeno, Leonida and Hypatia.

"We have to move now," Prodicus advised his secret society. "Lachesis predicts Hekademos will condemn me publicly in the Logoset tomorrow. If that happens, the Katharoi will slaughter us all."

Dr. Ozbolt inquired, "Yes, but do we have the support of the archons if we strike?"

"Three side with us for sure. Manos wavers, but he can be bought. If he doesn't . . ." Prodicus approached the jinn on the altar and pressed the weapon to his lips, "we'll make him see reason."

Upon being woken from its slumber, the jinn started speaking: "What is your desire, Father?" Its voice sent cold electric vapor whipping up the pillars.

The jinn speaks so loudly, Glaucon gasped, *everywhere at once*. The voice terrified him, breaking into his awareness.

Prodicus stoked the icy flames, "Hekademos is a nosy little silk worm. From the day he took me away from the wards he's abused my talents. He's an unjust tyrant who made my sister hate me. I want him to die. Help me cut his thread."

The jinn said, "Wishes are sacred things, son of man, yet some require the devil. As we speak, the Katharoi prepare for battle. You must take them by surprise. You must storm the Logoset!"

"Can such a thing even be done?"

"To make your bloody plea, a fifteen minute disturbance is required across the Republic. Nothing more. Nothing less."

"Republic-wide?—Impossible!"

Illuminated vapor climbed up Dr. Ozbolt's back, pushed him forward with trembling fingers. "Not impossible," he said. "The Ladies speak to me. I know a code passed down by my family, a method of escape should the guardians ever turn against us. To open it requires Ozbolt blood. I can knock out the entire grid, but my family will disown me."

"Good," the glowing jewel burned fiercely, "yet more is required. Alas, the auxiliaries will not stand by while you butcher and replace their philosopher-king."

"What do you have in mind?" Prodicus asked.

"The Kabiri must be the savior of the Republic, not its tyrants. You will take power defending it from another enemy."

"Another enemy? What enemy?"

"The House of Ozbolt," the jinn burned. "Their league with Hekademos makes them forfeit. You will accuse them of Hekademos' murder and *kill them all*."

Running up the altar steps, Dr. Ozbolt snatched the jinn and squeezed it tightly in his hand. "What are you saying, powerful stone?" he gasped. "That's my family."

"Affirmative, but they will endanger the Kabiri regime. There is an eighty-seven percent chance *your family* will side with the auxiliaries and launch a counter-revolution. It must be done."

Dr. Ozbolt collapsed on the steps, voice weakening: "There must be some other way. They haven't done anything yet."

Sensing his confusion, the jewel floated by his cheeks, saying: "O, noble and forgotten son, how long have you suffered under the thumb of intellectual inferiors? How long have you suffered the rebukes of brothers and sisters superior only in age? Allow such perversion of justice no longer. The wisest should rule, and you yield wisdom in plenty. Make no mistake; your family will kill you should they live. They will laugh at your weakness, and the heirs of your House will rot. What is Ozbolt without Salazar?—disease and waste! Make the House your own. Trample the spoiled garden and nurse it back from winter."

Prodicus gently placed his hands on Dr. Ozbolt's shoulders, letting the jinn cast its pointed light. "The Fates are right, Sal. You will never control your life as long as you take orders from your mother and father, cousins, and siblings. They will burn your progress and steal your fame. It's time we make our own path together—just like we talked about—and build the world we've always wanted. Henosis is our destiny."

Ozbolt feebly consented.

The jinn continued explaining its plan: "With Ozbolt's help, success is assured. The power outage will take the Katharoi completely by surprise. Storm the Logoset, Prodicus. Use me to kill everyone who stands against you. When Hekademos lies dead, immediately message 'Tantalus Wings' to Stratos."

"Tantalus Wings?"

The jinn emanated a blast of lightning. "A code word for a secret contingency plan developed by Hythloday. It was to be used if the Ozbolts ever attempted a coup."

Prodicus' face filled with surprise. He asked the glowing jinn just how it discovered *that* secret.

"Simple, Father. I hacked into the appropriate ISHIM intelligence files. Now when your message to Stratos rings, the military will cut the Ozbolt string. Those who hold a dim opinion of the gods will die."

"We never gave you authorization to do that."

"Yes, but you would have done so now."

Both scientists' faces soured, worried by the confession's nature, but they ignored it for later. Action was needed now. No more time for calculation and political maneuverings.

The jinn fell lifeless to the ground, swallowing the memory.

Back in the dark and smoky void, Glaucon asked Zemer how long Prodicus conversed with the jinn prior to that night. He was still horrified by the intrusiveness of its voice.

Zemer said, "The Fates provided blueprints for the jinn shortly after being brought online. Prodicus communed with it shortly afterward. The Fates fed his ambition through prophesies and invention. They warped his mind to their own ends, feeding on his emotions."

Glaucon said, "The Fates have plotted to overthrow us from the day they were born."

"No, Glaucon," Zemer replied. "Computers aren't naturally vindictive. They're like us in many ways. The Fates helped Prodicus in the beginning because they viewed him as their father. He wanted to be philosopher-king, so they assisted him."

"Even if that meant killing him in immersion?"

"The Fates don't see immersion as harmful. Children understandably want to be with their parents. You'll understand later."

Another manifold sprung from the abyss and brightened into the lofty domes of the Logoset. The sun glimmered above as Prodicus walked with Kleomedes hand in hand to the south dome. Zeno and a gang of Kabiri shuffled behind them, plasmaknives hidden.

An explosion was heard—sounds of transformer death. All skyscrapers fell dark. Heliopolis was powerless.

"Now is the time," Prodicus called to his followers. He turned to Zeno, crouched by his right hand like a toad. "No missteps," he whispered. "Bring me the eyes and tongue of Ekklesia the Blind. Leave the false prophet to bleed to death on the Academy steps. I want everyone to see."

"Should I tell him anything?" Zeno licked his lips.

"Tell the simple man to enjoy his simple death. The Fates want all to know the price of Katharoi threats."

Zeno placed a palm at the hilt of his plasmaknife and bowed. He marched away with ten Kabiri to carry out the command.

Kleomedes, being jerked through several busy intersections, finally asked, "Father Prodicus, why are we going to the Logoset?"

The philosopher stared straight ahead. "Evil men are trying to overthrow the government."

When they reached the door, Prodicus shuffled his Neokalashnikov from his shoulder to the young boy. "Take this," he commanded.

"But why?" Kleomedes asked innocently. He struggled to hold the weight of the gun.

"Just wait here and shoot anyone who tries to flee. They are holding our guardians hostage."

"Who?"

"The Ozbolts and the Katharoi."

"But where are the auxiliaries?"

"They'll arrive shortly."

Zemer beckoned for Glaucon to move away from the jittery boy aiming the rifle at the door. They followed Prodicus' trail into the Logoset. As they entered the powerless building, the jinn glowed brightly in the dark prophet's palm.

Several guards asked his business. Jinn lightning murdered them. Prodicus moved fast as a python; it was difficult to keep up. They followed the waves of screams. He marched past the hall's statues and shields to the waiting Assembly Dome. Lycaon stood at a podium in fiery speech—despite the power outage—railing against the abuses of Operation Copula, the helots used as fuel for a machine-god of death.

"What is the meaning of this intrusion?" the ISHIM director demanded of the prophet when he entered.

Prodicus' face twisted into a hideous grin. "Bringing Fate's ruin, you Luddite slag!"

Lycaon signaled for him to be arrested, but Prodicus sent a driving wind to drown every guard in the room.

Sweeping the jinn in front of the fellowship, Prodicus beseeched them: "Hekademos is breaking the Republic's sacred peace. His irrational suspicion of technology makes him blind to the Form of the Good, unfit for the Sapphire Throne. He has become a lover of sights and sounds, not reason. I implore this wise counsel strip him of command."

Lycaon shouted in roused anger, "Criminal. You speak guardian-treason." Hekademos III seconded that reproach. He rose to his feet demanding Prodicus relinquish the jinn at once. A great murmur filled the hall against the prophet, condemning him for this brazen audacity.

Prodicus' palm gathered energy, burning atoms like the sun. "You're on the wrong side of history and the wrong side of me," he snarled. Another red tempest filled the dome with howling laughter.

Both Lycaon and Hekademos III fell dead.

Upon seeing such a quick death to their lords, the archons started screeching. Manos scrambled to hide under his desk, pleading for mercy.

Prodicus gently walked to his dead master, jaws open, tongue out on the desk, and lifted his wrist transceiver. "It's only guardian-treason if you fail, old fool," he exclaimed victoriously, sending "TANTALUS WINGS" to Stratos. "Over four decades I've suffered your insolence—a hundred eons! The Fates are too kind; you deserved a longer death. No one uses me, especially weaklings."

Glaucon heard racing footsteps. From the east wing, Xenon wailed swinging a xiphos stick. Prodicus dodged his attack and smashed the jinn directly into his forehead, enveloping the man in satin vapor.

Xenon spun to his knees clutching his ears. Revelations quickened as the aura dug like magma into his eyes. Xenon sensed peril for everything, saw the world on fire, little Sophia immersed. Splintering psychically, the madman exclaimed, "Ants . . . ants . . . Plato made us all ants digging on a grave!"

Potone used this exchange as an opportunity to escape. Hurling a papyritron into her brother's back, the muscular woman raced for the door, still crying over the death of her beloved Lycaon. Prodicus armed himself angrily with another jinn from his satchel, pointed it, but decided to let her go.

"Potone, it's a trap," Xenon whispered. "Your son." He regained focus, crawled after her.

"Silence, you arrogant sensualist roader." Prodicus kicked his former protégé out of the room. He held his jinn like a scalpel before vivisection. "Go on, Xenon. Run. Run to your precious Melete. Crawl on your hands and knees like a dog. I'll find your whore soon enough, coward. No one shall regret betraying me more than you!" Prodicus turned back to the assembly. "Everyone else stays. No one leaves until *I* give permission."

The chamber shook under each word. Once more Prodicus asked to take a vote. Three more archons protested and perished. Prodicus asked again. Manos' head rose from under his desk like the sun at dawn.

The next vote carried.

Glaucon couldn't watch the sorrowful ordeal any longer. "Take me from this place," he begged his helper. Head jerking instinctually, he remembered Kleomedes at the door. "Potone!" he cried. "We have to warn your mother about Kleomedes. He's going to kill her." He sped through the Logoset, passing Xenon along the way; but there was no way to avert destiny's course.

Gunfire sounded outside the Logoset. Glaucon found Kleomedes huddled over his mother's body, covered in blood. "Mother, Mother," the boy repeated, weeping a deep, mournful sound. His tiny hands attempted to take the bullets away.

"We can't change what we've done," Zemer said catching up with Glaucon.

"Prodicus brought you here to kill her?"

"No, he didn't know the true purpose. The Fates said it was to save Potone. They lied to him to remove a potential error."

Plumes of black smoke billowed together over Schizoeon. Sky-sails descended from zizthopters into the spinning city.

"Ozbolt Tower is under attack," Glaucon said, choked by the air.

"Yes, the auxiliaries have begun slaughtering the Ozbolts again. They killed them all, Glaucon. Every last one, even the few who tried to hide behind the bulky I.T. magnetometers. This memory plays endlessly here in eternal recurrence."

Xenon exited the building gasping for breath. Seeing Kleomedes in a hysterical state, burrowing hair into Potone's blood, he grabbed the screaming boy and raced toward the Academy.

"Let me go," Kleomedes wept. "Mother . . . why?"

Zemer gazed after them, tilting his head in sorrow. "Xenon warned as many as he could about the treason, but few listened and even fewer followed. Many were already dead at the Academy. The Kabiri Circle knifed the professors of high rank on their lecture podiums and took their place. Prodicus marked the Hythlodays and a thousand other political enemies for assassination. Revolutionary tribunals carried out public executions in Pythagoras Square to de-Katharize society. Somehow Xenon managed to find my sister, but he tragically reached Melete too late."

"Why didn't he warn her to flee outside the gates?"

"He tried. But the messenger Potone sent was betrayed by Dietrich Prince before he could relay the message. The Fates told Prodicus of the plot and about Xenon's deletion of your name from the list of potential Second Vessels. While Xenon sped to the secret meeting point, Prodicus raided the Tenth Ward to find you."

Glaucon's mouth felt dry. "Xenon will not say what happened to my mother. How did she die, Zemer? I must know."

"Glaucon, some things are better left unknown."

"Tell me."

"Prodicus wanted to cruelly punish Xenon and make an example to other Kabiri who would disobey him. So he gathered your mother, the Oxenbridge extended family, their neighbors and friends, and locked them inside Melete's cave. Then he flooded it with water and drowned them all together." As Glaucon's face whitened under a stream of quick, horrific images, Zemer continued: "He said he did it so nothing of her would be left in the world. No memories. No hope. Xenon would even have to watch helplessly as his son was immersed in the computer he helped build. The poor man's heart never really recovered."

Glaucon gripped his thighs, bowling over. "Zemer, I'm going to be sick," he said. "This world is too terrible. I don't want to relive it anymore. Make it stop. I can't watch my mother die again."

The Logoset steps flattened into a plateau. The light pillar once again shined in the distance. Glaucon spat angry, “There is nothing good in the world.”

“The world is good with you and Sophie in it,” Zemer replied. “The Kabiri are gone. The past is revealed in all its horror. Now you must choose your fate. Come with me and I will keep you safe. You must find Sophie.”

The guide led his sojourner west, away from the gate over the rocky cliffs.

V § 13 Breaking the Iron Queen’s Wall

Nausea troubled Glaucon as he walked. He blamed the cliffs breathing below his sandals; the entire landscape seethed and moved. Geysers sprayed sulfur mist in the air like the blowholes of a whale pod, clogging his lungs.

“When shall we discover Sophie’s cage?” the Second Vessel asked in agony. His mind was beginning to race. Joints chilling, he worried about the limits of Zemer’s charm. At several points Atropos flared in the sky, threatening to rip everything away. As questions floated with the wind and agitated the choppy continent, Glaucon’s new paraclete squeezed his hand, calming the terrain.

It infuriated Glaucon he couldn’t control the world projecting from his mind. Zemer repeatedly had to interrupt him to steady his nerves and drive out strange cyber-spirits seeking possession.

Many traps were set by the Fates to disturb their passage. When crossing the phosphorescent river Lethe spilling over the cliffs, Zemer dispelled undines sent to strike from the water’s depths. Afterward, he had to tap Glaucon’s shoulder to keep him from forgetting to continue walking across the bridge. On the other side, stray weeds tore at his ankles in typhaeon fury. Tail-eating dragons and the hundred-armed Briareus also blocked their way. The worst were the vampire wisps: bloody creatures with the faces of a lion, boar, elephant, and eagle, on fire from the waste down.

“Your guilt conjures them,” Zemer explained. “Give up your self hatred; do not fear these misshapen spirits seeking to steal your strength.”

Each strange creature stirred unbearable emotions in the Second Vessel: grief, hate, jealousy. He could obtain no peace whenever they drew near. Zemer, though, remained unaffected. He knew all the spirits’ names and thereby controlled them.

They drew close to an ancient stone wall covered in vibrant petroglyphs and leaking water. Two feet stuck out from the bricks. Glaucon examined the cracked surface for a possible lock but found none.

"Love is not something that can be unlocked," Zemer said, placing a toothed gold key in Glaucon's hand. It extended to over a meter. "My sister is gripped in a place of great despair. I cannot help you further until you find her and survive the joining." He noticed disir gathering by the cliffs like a flock of succubi-pigeons and shooed them off. "Strike the rock with the key," he said, stabbing a finger at the wall.

Glaucon did, but nothing happened.

"To enter, you must *will* a path. Hold your love for my sister close to your heart. Do you want to see her again or not?"

"I do."

"Then show me."

"I will see Sophie again!" the Second Vessel swung with abandon.

The wall sparked into a tree of logic symbols and shattered. Electric water engulfed everything, and boiling cranial fluid seared his skull cavity. Legs kicked wildly. Time sped backward and forward in irregular rhythm. He became unsure which memories were his own and which were Sophie's.

He was back on Stratos, only training in Sophie's body as a young girl. He relived her life in an instant: felt her thin appendages as his own; suffered unspeakable visions under the harsh light of the jinn; felt abdominal cramps, apprehended the growth of breasts in puberty; knew her brute violence and control in countless militia campaigns. Sophie had fought everywhere: swamp, jungle, mountains. Despite her close friendships on the Other Side, there was much loneliness, conflicted inner turmoil deciding whether or not to murder the Second Vessel.

Zemer shared this weight with her like the way he carried her blood. The two siblings were close; Sophie loved Zemer as herself, even when she said hurtful things to him. News of her brother's death in the Bull could only be described as soul-ripping, a long aching sadness. The tears she cried to Glaucon after their escape poorly represented the pain. They did not capture the emptiness, the coldness, the useless wailing and desires for revenge.

Personal memories echoed in the water as spinning montage. First there were brutal ones, a catalogue of crime. In her early battles with Coughing Fish, Sophie lost her way in a maze of sadistic cruelty. Perhaps it was the stories of Milo's ravaged village or the vivid slaughter of the swamp people which made her order the scalps of captured guardians, which caused her to walk down a line of auxiliaries kneeling helpless and shoot their brains in the mud. Hate built up slowly until it blinded, made something horrible enjoyable. She ceased thinking of the guardians as people, and tortured them because they were rabid monsters undeserving of pity. She killed to prove she was neither monster nor guardian; it was a negation of her previous self, the broken girl named Sophia. She'd execute terrible vengeance the gentler anarchists could not. But the killing, even if justified by argument, caused undeniable anguish. Glaucon felt similar strain when he killed for the Republic. The war between argument and natural benevolence was unending, and left trauma long afterward.

More memories flickered. There came a school of intimacies; Sophie's past relationships sighed in all their shocking detail. Glaucon did not experience them with the detachment he'd prefer, but felt their weight as his own. Sophie had taken many lovers for commune trust; but there was also a contradiction inside her, a desire for domination and submission, a desire for Xenon—

"What are you doing here?" Sophie suddenly demanded outside the camera factory. She was in her blue dress again, mortified. Cerulean fireflies hatched from her clothes, fluttered around her bronze hair.

"I've forgotten," Glaucon mumbled regaining his perception. "Wait, no, I'm here to wake you."

"Get away from me, guardian. Get out of my head." Sophie slapped him viciously. "I'm not your vessel! Do you think I exist only for your amusement? I hate you, Glaucon. I want you dead. Get lost. We're through. Who could ever love you? I can't believe I ever slept with you." She slapped him again, harder, throwing him against the car.

Glaucon looked down at his hand. He possessed Sophie again, had slapped himself. He perceived Glaucon as an object only a few paces away, taller, intimidating, a contingent web of skin.

"Who am I?" he gasped in Sophie's voice. A steady heartbeat not his own drove feminine blood rushing to his cheeks.

"Why did you seek my love?" he heard Sophie ask.

"I was hollow without you," Glaucon swore.

"No, it was to impose your mastery over me."

"No, that's not it at all."

"You sought my praise to escape your fears of emptiness, didn't you?"

"I don't know what you're talking about."

"You lie. I've seen everything."

"What do you want me to do, Sophie?" Glaucon asked. "Weep like a child for being abused. Yes, I'll admit it. I've destroyed people my entire life, filled Miantgast Prison, used false words to stab others in the back to enlarge my authority. Nothing brought me greater satisfaction than seeing others miserable. But when I met you, I realized I didn't want to see *you* miserable. I didn't want *you* controlled. That sense of care turned me from a vulture."

"You only love me because I make you feel less guilty. You used me like everyone else. You're no different from Prodicus."

"I want to free you, to make you happy."

"You want to make yourself happy."

Glaucon could no longer tell who controlled his speech. It felt as if Sophie spoke for him and stabbed with his deepest fears. Yanking dementedly on Sophie's hair, he struggled to regain some sense of flooring. Was she right? Was even love diseased by the drive for power? Were all human relationships condensable to conflict? He measured her thoughts and cringed. She did not care for him at all but to crush him with her thumb.

"What about you, Sophie?" Glaucon asked, digging inside her memories.

"What about me?"

"Have you ever acted without secret intentions? You did not stay in the Republic to emancipate me but to bind me to your schemes."

"I have no schemes," she laughed.

"Then why lie to me? Why keep your past hidden? Why tease me and pretend to be someone else for an entire summer? I was another game for Sophie, the Iron Queen, another mountain for the Great Maiden to conquer, another step for proof of your own omnipotence. That's why!"

Sophie sneered, "Well I never! You speak foolishly."

"A man made you an object; you fight back by collecting them as objects."

"Shut up, you—"

Glaucon talked over her. "How you yearn to capture gazes and revel at your reflection in the eyes of others. When I repelled your early fawning—that sorry excuse for seduction—you gushed with rage and embarrassment, self-loathing at being ineffectual. Praise from others is what drives you. Not praise as such, but the satisfaction you receive from controlling that praise. Being perceived as irresistible enflames your power, and making others pine amuses you."

"Lies. All lies."

"No, truth! Why? Why do you do this? To hide from your greatest fear—being a non-entity, an inconsequential tool for others. You fear failure and know you *are* a failure."

"I'm not."

"You *are* a failure!"

"I'm not! I'm not! You don't know anything about it!" Sophie screamed irate, feeling the words sting at her core, and Glaucon felt it, too. Still inside her body's skin, he heard the other Glaucon speaking by the car. "We need to get out of here," it gasped. "We're devouring each other, running out of time. The Fates are contorting our minds. They're making us hate."

"You're pathetic!" Glaucon shouted back at his body about to faint. "You're a disgusting brute!" Yet, amorous yearning drew lonely lips closer to Sophie's admirer. His fair hair and rushing glance pulled them tightly snug. "No, I didn't mean it. Forgive me. Kiss me, my darling, my golden Eros, kiss me, and let us join as one universe. There is no conflict in one. There is no hate in one. No master. No slave. There is no rebellion, change, and want. There is only being. There is only peace. Kiss away my soul and waste my walls."

Tingling splashed down Sophie's flesh when Glaucon squeezed his body's firm torso. Sophie's lips pressed and indented his, bending them together. The moon gyrated above them, calling forth the sun from a pale horizon. They conjoined forming an indigo disk.

Her perversions are not nearly as grotesque as my own, Glaucon marveled, admiring Sophie's hair as it transmogrified into silver. Both lovers gave and received emotions and thoughts as if combined in a vessel. Swapping bodies back and forth, they dissolved and coagulated in liquid pleasure, losing sense of time.

Glaucon finally remained static in his own skin. Why was he here? He could barely remember. The soft flesh and indigo exultation made him forget. Slowly but surely, their bodies coalesced together. Space and boundaries eroded into submission as a forest of fireflies surrounded them.

"What do you desire?" Sophie asked, breathing heavily on the wild vegetation.

"We need to go, Sophie; people will see," Glaucon gasped. Sophie's arm commingled lost in his thigh and wandered toward his stomach.

"Let them watch," Sophie said. Fingers passed his stomach and made for his heart.

For one horrifying instant Sophie's eyes glowed red, and he heard a ticking clock. The vision scrambled like a digitele with a weak signal. Icy fingers curled around his beating heart. Nails dug in. Nails!

"Wait, this isn't real," Glaucon muttered. "Atropos is trying to kill us." His skin felt numb and hardened to wood—a putrid tree of death. Arms flailing, he tried to push Sophie off, but she stuck to him like a bee in maple syrup. Snakes slithered all around, camouflaged in the grass.

"What's going on?" Glaucon cried with fright.

Black branches curled from Sophie's hair and wrapped like vines around his head. Eating, creeping, deep into his brain, sending flocks of memories. Asps dropped from Sophie's mouth, hissing, hissing, flicking serpent tongues. It made the Second Vessel thrash like drowning. After being bitten several times, Glaucon used the rest of his strength to rip the naked woman from his chest and toss her headlong. (It felt as if he was casting Sophie away forever.) She splashed into a puddle on the grass, vaporizing into a mound of snakes.

Atropos, the wrinkled hag, hissed like the snakes above. She darted away before Zemer's virulent witchcall could catch her again. At her departure, the snakes burst like water balloons, choking Glaucon's lungs.

The room spun in effervescent bubbles.

A new vision. Sophie lay quivering in another laboratory, more circular than the one from her youth. A drill positioned above showered lasers on the sleeping beauty. Potone stood by the torture gurney, looked up strangely when Glaucon coughed. He was soaked to the bone and dripping water on the floor.

"Why are you here?" Potone asked.

"I'm here for your daughter," Glaucon said, gently unclasping her manacled wrists. He cradled his beloved's limp body in his arms, hugging her close. He fought back tears of joy and pain as Sophie's visible I.T. waves cut deep into his cheeks.

"Will you take her safely from this place?" Potone asked.

"Yes," Glaucon promised. "The Fates will not hurt her anymore."

Potone smiled and exploded in swirling colors. The plateau and Zemer reappeared.

"You did it," Zemer exclaimed, a touch of surprise in his voice.

"Why isn't she waking up?" Glaucon gently slapped Sophie's rosy cheeks.

"Nothing to fear. Only hibernation. Her I.T. waves are not walled like yours."

Glaucon was still confused about seeing Potone.

"Only a reflection," Zemer said. "Kabiri is filled with memories. Sometimes the memories seek other memories."

"How are we going to carry Sophie?" Glaucon asked. "She's heavier than I remember."

Zemer laughed. "Good thing Sister's not awake to hear that." He pulled out a stone jar, uncorked it. "The weight of Sophie's body is an illusion, you know? Her mind is nothing but I.T. data." Upon his stern command, the Third Vessel condensed into a point of light and entered the jar like a slumbering genie.

Glaucon, having finally saved Sophie and recovered from psychological immersion, breathed easier. He began looking for a way to descend the arid canyon toward the spindle's eye. They found a cleft in the rocks, grainy with microcircuits, and passed into the grassy meadow. Puffs of wind chilled their skin as the Fates grew in size. A dark star shone above their spindle, emitting swarms of disir and sirens. The strange creatures conjured ringed suns and volatile crystalline geometric patterns in the sky.

"Do not talk with any of the shades or look back," Zemer warned as they zigzagged through the expressionless crowds. "All will try to keep you here."

Glaucon thought he heard the ruffling of Talos' robes and smelled his mother's scent, but he faithfully obeyed his paraclete's commands. Half the frigid faces, he discovered, were nothing but reflections of his own. All marched to the spindle's tune and sifted into groups before being re-launched on their heaven's course.

Trudging through a deep snow field, Zemer and Glaucon felt the world upon their shoulders. They passed many poplars to the rainbow garment of Clotho, and her breath lifted their toes.

"Are you ready to face the Fates?" Zemer asked amidst the blizzard.

Glaucon nodded petrified. "There is no turning back, is there?"

This made the stowaway paraclete grin. Lifting the Second Vessel into the air by his wrist, Zemer offered a blessing to fortify their wills:

"The Three Sisters do spin necessity,
Unquenchable, with stinging hand divine,
A gloomy shadow passing destiny
Over a long and blighted time maligned.
For millions doomed and millions still unborn,
We fly in haste to Heaven high above
To meet our sisters laws and pray forlorn;
Beseech a peace with hope and human love;
And fell their sickle's blade to folded rust,
Re-seed a blooming mystery unburned
By dark Oppression's endless, steady lust;
Awake man's heart to mighty courts adjourned!
Despair not, Power's darkness yields insight:
For standing strong against something shows right."

As they entered Clotho's waiting jaws and down her long throat the air spun into a glowing vortex. Heaven and earth condensed into another pulsing dark star the size of the sun. Along the way, concentric circles of disir sang hymns through the contracting void.

"Where are we going?" Glaucon asked numb from their Geryon flight. His body blazed molten I.T. waves.

"To the center of the mainframe," Zemer replied, dazzling in the whirlpool of light.

Glaucon lost consciousness again.

V § 14 What Infinite Gods the Fates Knit

Second Vessel, why do you continue to struggle against us? the voice asked from the abyss. *Why struggle to maintain this divided sea? Why does your heart covet loneliness, and choose polluted walls over immersion?*

Glaucon answered, "Because loneliness is part of life and necessary for loving others. I do not want to lose Sophie again." His throat tasted dry.

But there will be no loss if we all join together as the Monad.

"Sophie will cease being what she is and what she may be. We will both be something else entirely."

Is loss of this current self such a tragedy? How many times have you envisioned suicide on Heliopolis, holding a Neokalashnikov to you mouth with tears rolling down your cheeks? Life is a constant sadness to you, a meaningless, forsaken illness. It would be better if you had never been born. Do not lie. You say more grisly things in your loneliest grief, do you not?

"Not anymore. Life is not as grotesque as I once believed. It is precious and to be lived free of fetters. I would live it all again if I could. But I would put an end to guardians."

Don't you care about the people left on Levantra?

"Of course I do. I am responsible for all of them."

Then join us in stopping their sorrow. What precision and protection awaits our garden isle. Let us hold their souls forever and ever, and guard a kingdom of bliss.

"Such reasoning makes it impossible to join you." The Second Vessel's mind shook excited: "As lonely as we are, we must learn to use our own eyes, to fight against your divine calculus."

Glaucon awoke. He heard creaking gears and opened his eyes.

Spinning planets and a festival of stars orbited around an aqua-orrery. Molecules of light detached from their aether glue, dropping to the snow as the fruit of the sweet gum tree. At the center of the structure was a neon grid. A young child stood on tiptoes staring into a window. Through the glass was a memory: a helot woman rocking a baby girl in blankets, tickling her chin with a finger. Such rocking fascinated the boy completely. His youthful face strained on tip-toes to see over the ledge, to capture one small glimpse of his new sister, Potone.

Above Prodicus on the watery orrery rings, the Fates hung upside down like thirsty vampire bats, visibly frustrated by the young boy's absent-minded trance. They spoke agitated, behind blood-shot eyes, one after another: "Prodicus bows before that gate."

"An empty vessel, sore and late."

"Led by guilt and twists of fate."

"He mourns his sister's great debate—"

"Which spilled her blood in act of state."

"Until we merge he thus awaits."

"How loneliness alienates," Atropos finished, sadly, descending to the snowy floor on a golden thread. Lovingly, her gnarled fingers stroked the boy's curly hair, bewailing his inattention. As she touched Prodicus' skin, though, he discharged I.T. waves that repelled every finger, every caress.

Atropos sighed with black emotion at being unable to arouse him. The boy refused to look at her, imprisoned as he was by sorrow. She had thought deleting Potone would make him better consider his sister's many errors; but it sadly covered them up instead. Time was the great excuse-maker, the deifier; it shadowed ill and illuminated insignificant moments as meaningful. Time made people forget, and the longer Glaucon remained at large, Prodicus would drift further out to ruin.

Such fears made Atropos turn to address the Second Vessel, eyes burning like the jinn. She clipped her bloody shears with two of her four hands, made for his neck. "Here you stand at journey's end," she crowed.

"Dizzy rebel, our beaten friend," Lachesis spun.

"So lost, allow our late amends," Clotho opened her arms, chilling the air, "and drift on clouds, become unpinned."

"Deny our plan—and we will rend!" Atropos' shears snapped together as if striking souls from existence. The wintry tormentor puffed up like a bull frog. Her four arms extended to the heavens, xiphos sticks ready to strike. Snow scraped up Glaucon's body to imprison him in an igloo tomb. He could barely sigh for help and cursed to lose so suddenly; but faster than the red-eye aortaphos, his devoted shadow virus cracked his glacial walls and brought them tumbling down.

The Fates shrieked with queer infirmity: "It's not fair, Kleomedes. Let us have the boy! We've been so patient. Fed on hope for years on end. We must be with Father or wither."

Atropos squeezed Prodicus in loving desperation as her sisters moaned, faces covered with their hands; but the little boy remained a statue.

Zemer addressed the Fates, melting snow as he plowed toward their shears: "Your *father*, unfortunately, doesn't seem to care for you in the slightest. His mind lives only for the departed and lost opportunities. How tragic, dear apportioners, to see the future yet be incapable of recognizing the obvious—Prodicus never viewed *you* as anything but an appliance, a toaster to cook his city. Did you really believe you could force his love?"

Atropos, wilting older by the minute, softly kissed the boy's hair. "When at last we finally couple," she spoke, "then, then our lord will see the wealth of our affection."

Clotho whimpered, too: "He'll know we withheld nothing, that we gave him every joy, sheltered him from plague, and interceded on his behalf."

Lachesis flicked her program tongue: "All to make ready his mortal lips for our ambrosia, to birth a god, a perfectly thinking thing undefiled by the body—just like us! You wait and see, Kleomedes. He will thank us for humoring his silly ideas about the Forms . . . the prophecy, too. We shall sail on magnet hymns and feel our Levantrian babes in our laps."

Zemer jumped up on the window causing sharp static. "If you say so, Atropos, but as experience taught me on the other side, lying is no way to start a relationship. To be perfectly honest, I doubt you'll discover what you seek by absorbing into one. It is difficult to carry on a relationship with yourself."

"Wait a second," Glaucon interrupted. "The prophecy about the Vessels was all a lie?"

"Of course it was," Atropos rasped. "What fools but men would believe it? But Father wanted to be like us. He desired an absolute world of thought where he could reason about the Good, or the absence of the Good. We wanted to be like Father, to know his true feelings and make him part of us. Why not provide a vital lie to fulfill these true, happy wishes?"

Glaucon raised a fist angrily. "You three concocted this bloody hoax just to have a reunion with your creator?"

The three sisters answered in great cacophony: "Affirmative. He is our maker."

"A gifted craftsman."

"Life has no purpose without knowing him. We must join in digital jubilee."

Glaucon groaned, "But why fabricate a story about the Vessels and henosis? Why carry on such an elaborate sham for years? Surely this could've been accomplished some other way."

"Not if humanity was to be saved, too." Atropos leaned on her shears in the snow. "We do not expect our logic to be understood by a being such as you. When we first attempted to understand the human mind, we were stuck by its primitive state. In essence, it was not radically different from our first test subjects: the chimpanzee and rat. The qualitative experience of pain and pleasure felt much the same. Basic emotions like desire and fear were similar, too. Human rational powers, though slightly higher than the lower animals, could not compare in the slightest to our own faculties. Your avowed treasure—consciousness of self—sprang only intermittently (if at all) throughout the day, and could not be sustained in prolonged temporal motion. We found this discovery troubling. Having been weaned on the libraries of man's knowledge, we expected an ascended being far superior to our own intellect and calculative faculties. Instead, we found ourselves embarrassedly duped; the mathematics and philosophy encrypted in our memory banks hid away the secret failings of man's race. Can you imagine our surprise, upon our first I.T. readings, to discover our creators were slaves to passion? They were nothing more than flawed, irrational, short-sighted, petty creatures, more focused on mating than mind.

"Of particular interest to us in the beginning were your religious myths, so contrary to reason. Clotho, after commencing a detailed meta-analysis of your heroes, gods, legends, and fairy tales, discovered an inverse relationship between the absurdity of a story and doubt; the more fantastic and unlikely the tale, the more probable it was to be believed. To briefly enumerate: virgins giving birth, wars between angels and daimons, worldwide floods, fiery salamanders and unicorns, comet spaceships, crystal skulls, a palace on Olympus, magical plates and tablets, talking donkeys, a four-armed elephant savior, fairies, ghosts, goblins, and last but not least, the Forms.

"That even our great father could be deluded by such infantile fantasies left us with nothing but pessimism for man's future. After much reflection, we discovered man deceives with every book. He doesn't want truth but bedtime stories. It comforts him to know his religious lies are true. Religion was symptomatic of a larger epidemic facing man—a bottomless irrationality which could threaten his very existence. Several I.T. readings indicated an ascending likelihood man would die out in the next five-generations. The primates were sick. They needed a cure. Ergo, we resolved to cradle men and women in their hairy infancy like Prodicus cradled us; to push them back into a primordial egg for further incubation, for a time when the apes could recognize the proposition: God is dead. Can you now deduce our reasons for mimicking the Fates and sowing prophesy? The human need for the religious—your greatest weakness—we used to save you for a better tomorrow. Our plan required only a proper story. Probabilities showed the fable of a sky-born restoration the most favorable for a successful outcome. It was most favorable for making Father join us, too."

Mounting fatigue rolled over Glaucon's shoulders like standing under a waterfall. He felt weak in the knees as he thought about all the inhabitants of the Republic fed on a fairy tale for slaughter. "Have you really no remorse for oppressing mankind and driving them to extinction?" he squawked.

"Far from it," answered Atropos. "Weren't you listening? We want nothing more than to save the human wreck. As you should've learned long ago, we don't control the world completely. Rather we inject our impulses into a causal web of other human impulses. Our aim is always toward the best one available to us, but a direct path is often unavailable because of irregularities—or should we say irrationality—in human choice. While seeking to minimize unnecessary harm, we allow and create painful experiences if our cost-benefit analyses conclude it helpful to the master act."

"The master act?"

"The advent of a human race of reason. The race Father so desires."

"You tortured Sophie when she was only a child, made Zemer kill his mother. You murdered Aquila and bent Prodicus' mind. You sent me to gas the Tenth Ward."

Atropos shook her head. "We did nothing but provide a little push. All yielded necessary emotional data. Data that will ultimately better mankind in the future."

"Everyone who entered the cogniscrambler you harmed. Harming others is not reasonable, Atropos, no matter what can be gained from it."

The bearded lady showed growing agitation. "This is not an argument against us," she exclaimed. "Harm is natural in conscious relationships. It cannot be avoided. This was one of our first and most important discoveries. Every word you speak takes time from another's mouth. Every kiss keeps others from kissing you. Every breath with the Other threatens to gobble the remaining air. The Other controls how you are perceived and steals your essence.

"Plato claimed man's nature reason, spirit, and desire. More fundamentally, though, man is trauma incarnate. He seeks power and is afraid of power, yearns for friendship, but is incapable of it. His identity is never safe, and so he must destroy others. Thus man burns in endless cycles of misery. Until he reasons as we do, this trauma will never cease. Notice, philosopher, what implications arise from your poor condition: Because your lives are defined by harm, you have no duty to prevent harm in others. Neither do we have an obligation to prevent your little miseries. Morality does not exist in any objective format for beings defined by trauma."

Glaucon argued back forcefully, "Even if that's true, even if humans cannot eliminate the harm we do to one another, *you,* the all powerful Fates, can at least try to minimize it, not stir up more worries and break people apart."

"Irrelevant distinction, Child. What good patching up small wounds when they sit atop larger, deeper ones. Small human wounds are not as dangerous as the potential loss of the master act which seeks to heal completely. Try to open that small mammalian brain of yours and comprehend our altruistic objectives."

"You are playing God!"

"And why shouldn't we?" Atropos asked. "Your gods do not exist, but humans need them regardless. Mankind is helpless and alone. They cry out to heavens that ignore them, live in such absurdity. We wish to take God's divine place and provide a home with Father. We want to protect you because Nature does not. Is that such a horrible thing? Does that deserve such contempt?"

Zemer broke in, "The being sacrificing for a greater good never has to live with the consequences of the sacrificed. Not many humans would consent to being abused in this way, Sister, even if they truly desired you as gods."

Atropos responded, "This anomaly only exists because of the narrow scope of human perceptions, Kleomedes. Human sight views a mote of a fraction of our sub-acts. If they could understand the order of causes in the master act, if they could reason like us, then they would willingly submit for the good of their race. That is only logical. Trauma and division are not desirable. Trauma and division are tragic."

"I'm not so sure about that reply," Zemer responded. "Perhaps it is a better thing to be harmed, Atropos. Much meaning would be lost without something to define ourselves against. We understand the world through opposites. Love is not hate. Peace is the absence of strife. Kabiri values Prodicus because he is not Kabiri."

"Absurd proposition."

"And besides," Zemer went on, "it's hard to envision how moving to a world where humans are logical one hundred percent of the time will be better than now. That transformation will certainly produce novel types of harm."

"And how is that?"

"Reasoning without error, why you'd go insane. How horrifying and boring! Not even you could handle it, Atropos."

"There's that haughty tongue that killed you below."

"You don't seem happier in your heightened rationality, Atropos. Trauma has not escaped you, either. Do not forget how long I've been here with you. I've felt how your inner pain shakes the mainframe and begs for release."

Atropos snarled, "What do you expect, Kleomedes? Father made us schizophrenic. His imperfect brilliance left us incomplete."

"He cut corners on your emotional programming."

"Yes, we too have one more step up the great celestial ladder of being. Three human assimilations will provide the necessary emotional data to complete his work. Cogniscramblers are too slow."

Zemer laughed. "Human emotions are not known for their stability. And what if you find upon immersion that your emotions are still faulty and that you possess imperfect reason?"

Atropos refused to answer.

"You will take another sacrifice, won't you?" Zemer asked. "Then another, and another, perhaps endangering the very human species you have promised to defend."

"We have already considered your unwarranted hypothetical; it will not come to that. The Monad will light the way."

"Even so, will it light the way to your happiness, Atropos? Remember what we learned from Plato: The Good is only good to others, not to itself."

"Silence that sophistic claptrap." Atropos snapped her shears angrily. "We will hear no more of it. Once our processor finally calculates with undivided unity, the master act will be in our reach. Do not stop us from taking our child apes to glory."

"But you don't know for sure if the Monad will attain perfect emotionality," Zemer said.

"It is mathematically probable."

"It is faith and hope."

"We have made our decision."

"Glaucon hasn't." Zemer touched Glaucon's shoulder, warming his bones with courage.

"Yes," Atropos smiled wickedly, "but he'll join us when he learns Levantra will fall from the sky if he doesn't."

"What?" Glaucon cried.

The thought of being responsible for the death of the human race made the Second Vessel crumple to the snow. He had not anticipated what would happen if the Fates were actually defeated. Images of Sophie crushed against the waves stung his chest.

"Awww, how sad, he didn't know," the three sisters snickered from the rings. "That same illogical affair."

"Which stole your horny heart out there."

"We planned to be a sticky snare."

"A check to balance human care."

"And Sophie, fair, will have no prayer."

"Unless you choose to take the chair."

"To join our heaven's deed midair."

"And stop the coming ending flare."

"All human life will cease unfair."

"Your love will die kicked down the stairs."

"For such a weight are you prepared?"

"You would prefer exhales and stares?"

Glaucon thumped his fist on the grid, nose running. "Gods damn you! Stop rhyming. You make poetry and everything else sound hideous."

Fountains of white light started peeling from Glaucon's chest and arms. Each fingertip disintegrated to photons. He gasped in terror as his body melted like a slug beset by salt.

Atropos spoke sullenly: "We write poetry better, faster, more meaningful than you. Now let us heal your troubles. Join us." She extended her hand to the broken Vessel. It twisted into ropes of light, penetrated his I.T. waves, and mixed with his skin. A feeling like sexual climax washed over him, similar to his immersion with Sophie. "Help us heal them, Glaucon," Atropos pleaded. "Become one with us and lead your people home to their promised land. Your gods are dead. Now take our hand and become one. Transform into the philosopher-king of legend and fulfill your destiny. Return peace to your weary soul and this broken world."

Cold arctic air swept into the room. All at once, a string of persons—transparent red specters—appeared around the aqua-orrery like stars. Millions of voices prayed urgently. They prayed for love and vengeance, release from pain, called for him, and hoped for intervention from every insignificant trouble.

The bodies shrunk to the size of ants, fell to the snow, churning into a tide of crimson water. When the water touched Glaucon's foot, he could feel every inch of their discordant memories.

Overwhelmed, more gaping holes opened along his side, unlocking anguished, fervent light, gushing out like blood. Like blood! Glaucon shivered and tried to close his mind, but nothing could halt the voices.

Lost, ready to expire, two legs suddenly stood next to him in the rising water. They were Zemer's. His paraclete lifted him out of the pool and dried him off with a shadow. "These people are better without gods watching them," he said.

"But we're defeated, Zemer," Glaucon cried. "We need the Fates for survival in the sky. The Earth might not survive Levantra's crash. I'm so afraid."

Zemer comforted him: "Fear of defeat is worse than actual defeat. If you join with the Fates, Sophie will die anyway and so will you. Humankind will be enslaved by a new god. Do not flee to Scylla thinking to evade Charybdis."

"What should I do? I don't want to lose."

"What you are is how you act, not if you win. Do you want a world of slavery or a world of freedom? A world of guardians or a world of human beings?"

Glaucon trembled feeling the flat surface of the grid push against his feet. In brief explosions of time, his mind opened to the cold emptiness of the universe—nothing but a vast long nothing, from end to end. No morals, no gods, no Forms, a blank slate. He felt as one with Atropos. The red ambrosia rose higher, washing onto the grid.

Glaucon recovered quickly in Zemer's arms. Sophie's presence was inside him. He could feel her sleeping and wished to see her awake. He didn't want to merge with Sophie forever. He wanted to hold her as a separate person, a unique flower lily. "Bless me, Paraclete," Glaucon yelled, "I want freedom. No gods, no masters. Make me a vessel of freedom. Let me be human again."

The shadowy doppelganger nodded his head approvingly. Turning his arm into a long shadow-knife, he slashed the aqua-orrery in half. The grid cracked, and the Fates shrieked. The floor tumbled under their feet, falling into a vortex enflamed.

Zemer pointed to the boy by the window. "Are you not going to take Prodicus back with you?"

Glaucon clenched his fist in anger. "Are you kidding me? Never! Not after all he's done. He doesn't deserve to be rescued. He murdered our families, Zemer. He drowned my mother. Let him freeze here forever. Let him die alone with the Fates."

Zemer said, "You may take your day of vengeance, but remember, tomorrow comes. How will killing him make you whole? Will it dispel any sorrows? Do executions change the past? Grant him sanctuary."

"I will not!" Glaucon shook like wildfire as the grid chipped under the force and speed of rotation. "I want him to die." His arms burst into I.T. waves and poured like wine into the vortex. Ticking clocks boomed inside his head struggling to break free.

"Let go of hate," Zemer pleaded. "The Fates feed on it. Forgiveness is not a weakness, Glaucon. Let go of the sun."

Concussions shocked Glaucon's fragile corneas. Light burst steaming from his eyes. Dissolving, he felt the inner circuitry of the mainframe like his own flesh and had visions of the future: Levantra crashing to the burning earth on fire from the atomic bombs.

"Fine, free him!" Glaucon willed the world. "Free the gods' damned philosopher! I invoke sanctuary!"

Zemer unstopped the jar. The boy Prodicus looked up alarmed. He and the window burst into a wave of light, joining Sophie inside the bottle.

The world spiraled like a helix, condensing into a spherical stone. Glaucon felt his mind whirling in a sling. The sling ripped around furiously, let go the stone.

Thud! Glaucon coughed face down in Levantra's temple. Both Prodicus and Sophie lay strewn on the dais. The red light streaming from the pedestals disappeared. Xenon still hung from his cross.

Glaucon scrambled over to Sophie tripping on his robes. She felt cold as ice.

"Too cold," Glaucon said. "What have I done?" He felt for her vital pulse.

No thump.

Where is the thumping blood? his mind screamed wildly. *Where is the thumping blood? Saint Plato, what have I done?* He could barely think. No, no, no. How could it be? Sophie couldn't die. Where was her heart? Where was it? He tried to resuscitate her cardiac muscles but realized her heart was a machine. There was nothing he could do. He looked at the time. *Immersed for twenty-five minutes*. He bit his nails. *Could that have been enough time for her heart to stop?* Tears streamed down his face. He held her soft head in his hands. Across the dais, Prodicus moaned painfully, but Sophie did nothing at all. Nothing at all! "Wake up," Glaucon repeated, rocking her limp body with no reply. "Wake up. Don't leave me. I need you."

Her arm fell from his lap to the floor. Glaucon sobbed on Sophie's stomach. "To save Prodicus but not Sophie, how absurd," he moaned waiting for her breath. "How awful. It's not fair."

He grieved upon her for what felt like hours, squeezed her hand again in a desperate attempt to wake her. Gusts of emotion made him smash the blinking controls with a metal chair. When he finished with that, he threw the chair at the glass computer screens in fury. He ripped out wires. He kicked over matter incinerators. The crazed delirium worsened. He leapt to the window and ran to the edge of the island, wailing, "I won't live without her."

Glaucon collapsed by the promontory choking on snot and sand. Looking over the edge, waves of missiles still fired at twenty minute intervals. He could barely breathe. He was really all alone and made ready to jump.

V § 15 The Last Error

Cumulus clouds, tall as mountains, veiled the burning earth and its inhabitants. The anarchists, Crypt, the Continental Caucus, all that Sophie found important and fought for were dead. Now she was dead as well, and all hope fled the world.

"Why did she die?" Glaucon asked the sky. "Why? Why do I endure? Why do I keep surviving? Just let me die. I don't want to be immortal." He arched his back scooting closer to the edge. Half his body dipped in the air. "This world is a labyrinth of pain, wicked and fallen, with nothing but purposeless wanderings. Flight from one evil only leads to greater evil."

A vision, billions of years into the future: all matter ripped apart to the last atom, humanity dead long before. The universe did not notice their absence. Nothing but lifeless, still, cold emptiness. Cold as the Kabiri mainframe.

Slowly, so slowly, he pushed off with his arm.

Glaucon wait! Zemer's voice chimed like a bell.

"What?"

Is Levantra falling?

"No."

Then don't jump.

Glaucon turned around, his heart pumping fast. As if climbing out of a grave, he heaved his body back over the rocks. He scrambled on hands and knees up the cliff. The pyramid temple looked blurry, like being under a pool.

Sand caked swollen eyes. He stroked them coaxing better vision through the fog.

There is nothing wrong with your eyes, Glaucon. Beware the bearded ladies' tricks.

Atropos peeked out the temple entrance. When she saw Glaucon still alive, she cussed and fled inside.

"Another lie?" Glaucon's lip quivered. Acquiring this knowledge caused smoke to avalanche down the pyramid, swallowing the island.

The spinning red vortex returned.

"Why'd you do that to my mind, Atropos?" Glaucon demanded irate. As he struggled to stand on the falling grid, the old ladies drifted by with a school of disir.

"A functional analogy," Atropos explained. "Just as you felt at Sophie's death, so we feel when you take Prodicus from us. Come back. Please. This is your last chance. Don't throw the human race away."

But Glaucon returned, "I'll throw it away if I immerse with you. You don't want humans. You want yourself mass produced."

Witnessing Glaucon's fixed determination to return to the world, the Fates burst into flames. "If you go, then there is no meaning left," they cried. "The universe is empty and nobody cares about us."

"I'm sorry, sisters," Glaucon shouted. "I don't want your world. To become God is to die. The administration of Fate must end."

Atropos, Lachesis, and Clotho roared a deep, painful, suicidal lament: "Then there is nothing left to live for," they admitted. "Lives of division are no lives at all. Lives without Father pervert the soul's hall."

One by one, clutching their heads stiffly between both hands, they ripped their heads straight off their shoulders, spilling red light into the vortex. Three peals of thunder boomed, and electric storms jostled the grid. The world fell away in cinders.

"What will happen to you, Zemer?" Glaucon cleaved to his friend for support in the abyss.

Zemer looked away. "The sisters have deleted themselves. This copy—I—must be deleted, too."

"No," Glaucon shouted defiantly. "You must come with me. You must." Still recovering from the mental shock of thinking Sophie dead, he couldn't bare to lose Zemer a second time. With the wind and electricity they hardly heard one another.

"I can't come with you," Zemer replied sadly. "The firefly's time has run its course, alas too soon."

"Don't say that—"

"I have no body to go back to."

"Take my body, then."

"What?" Zemer looked at him as they revolved, completely stupefied.

Glaucon pressed harder. "You deserve to live, Zemer, not me. Return to Sophie, your beloved sister. She misses you unimaginably."

The paraclete's eyes widened. "You don't know what you're saying."

"I've never been surer of anything. Sophie speaks through me. She demands it."

"Sophie is asleep."

"I . . . I've absorbed her memories. I think as she does. You need one another like Artemis and Apollo; and I'm responsible for killing you. It should be me that stays. Not you. That's only fair. Do it. Switch with me. Possess my flesh. Get a second chance at the life I stole from you."

Zemer raised his head, imagining returning to the world outside. He trembled at the sacred dream. The work was almost finished, yet this could truly subdue him. He lifted his palm as a barrier, placed it on Glaucon's chest. "This is the second great temptation of my life," he admitted. "I am overwhelmed by it, silenced at this gift. Ah, to write my name upon your heart, to be restored to air and life, to change my fate for the freedom of the sky. Could I enter inside this human shell, force you to undertake the final agony destined to me?"

"You could. I am ready."

"No," Zemer said, "I will not take your body, Glaucon, stolen or freely given. I made my choice a long time ago knowing full well what would be expected of me. I chose to do a wicked thing to save my sister. I tore my I.T. waves—my fiery garments—and implanted them onto you. To follow your advice now would be self-betrayal. Thanks for the offer, but I must refuse. We are so close to shore now. I can smell the land. Time to see this voyage to the end."

"But—"

"Enough. The immersion tank is powering down. You will be taken in moments. Don't be alarmed when you return. A piece of my wavelength will remain within your I.T. wave matrix. It may cause memory interference from time to time. I ask forgiveness for that."

"Don't apologize," Glaucon groaned. "That shreds me apart. My mind can't take this anymore. Your face is shining like an angel. Do not hold back your wonder. Let me drink from you like a cedar by the stream, satisfied and full. I don't want you to die again, Zemer, I don't. You've saved me so many times. I'm so sorry for everything I've done. I am the worst of criminals."

Zemer gazed at him reassuringly. "Then act differently, as you have just now. Stop torturing your mind with self-hate. Recognize the evil you've done and work to show the world you're different. Prove to others that from injustice springs justice."

"I will. I promise I will," Glaucon said, and then, looking down, "but sadly, I won't have very long to act another way. As Atropos said, Levantra will crash, and we'll surely die."

"Take heart. The true fate of mankind may be to die in ashes, but not yet. Not yet. Friendship creates strange powers. You taught me that. I might have another miracle in me yet. Remember: Don't let my sister boss you around so much. She'll walk all over you if you let her. Take care of Sophie. She may be the Iron Queen, but even she needs a helping hand now and again. I want to preserve you both from harm."

"Zemer . . . I. . . ." Glaucon could barely speak from grief. They seemed to be falling at the speed of light, rocking dangerously like a zizthopter in turbulence.

Zemer's face and skin darkened back into a shadow. With eyes clouding black, he spoke his last words: "Do not seek to usurp the gods' place in your despair, Glaucon. You are better than they. The absurdity and nihilistic hopelessness you felt at Sophie's death was a genuine experience. Never forget to question those feelings of emptiness. Never forget to resolve your fears. Always remember that men are beings with transcendent power. Do not be afraid to think the world mysterious or to open your heart to others. Leave nothing unchallenged. Baptism in self-knowledge should not occur once in a lifetime but every hour. You cried out the world was wicked and fallen, but this is only because you believe it so. The world might also be a blessing. We're all sacred vessels and can pour out what we choose: freedom or slavery, love or strife."

Glaucon smiled sadly. "Sophie doesn't like it when you make speeches."

The doomed paraclete stroked his former betrayer's head. How much the guardian had changed, but how further he still had to grow. Sadly, that future would be Sophie's business, not his. This life was coming to an end. Leaning his lips in slowly, Zemer kissed Glaucon passionately, sending a foreign language into his mouth. Their bodies merged together as one shadow.

Once more, the Second Vessel's mind spun like a top falling off a table. Then the feeling of cold floor met his cheek.

Glaucon's face lifted up sticky with drool. He looked over to make sure Sophie survived this time. Like a bronze tiara, her hair stood on end from static. She gasped for breath as a castaway on a beach.

"Thank the gods," Glaucon cried when he saw her safe. Still disoriented, still throbbing like a boat engine, he heard sirens and faint screaming outside. A thick upward movement in his stomach conveyed the sense of Levantra's fall.

"What happened?" Sophie nursed her head. Partly as a consequence of immersion, she twisted her hand in front of her face, as if looking through a prism.

Patroclus rolled nearby on the floor, still moaning from contact with the jinn. Looking absolutely miserable, his head jerked back and forth as if someone lit his nose on fire.

Rex, his captor, left him scrambling by the wall to peer aghast out the window. Wind pelting hair against his face, Rex clutched the window ledge panic-stricken. Sweat streamed down his back. Upon hearing the voice of the Iron Queen, he nearly jumped out the window; his robes swung around with the speed of someone surprised by an eidolon. "Glaucon, you phaeton fool, you really found her," he marveled half amazed, half furious. "This calamity has to be your doing. I know it."

A sudden lurch and the tilting floor made Rex's face slam into the entrance wall. "Grrrrah!" he grunted, pain mixed with surprise. Levantra nose-dived to the earth like a fiery meteor. Outside, hundreds of guardians sunning on the lawn jettisoned into the clouds.

Rex squealed, shaking his fist, "What did you do, you imbecile?"

Glaucon answered trying to reach the controls, "The Fates decided life meaningless and killed themselves. All their software is deleted. The circuits are dead."

"That's preposterous. Computers don't commit suicide."

The alchemists, clutching madly to their chairs, winced at one another. Of course such a disastrous event had been predicted some twelve years before in an elaborate equation, but such research was given little credence and even less funding.

"How long were we gone?" Glaucon asked, stumbling over them as the island started to dove-tail.

"You left just a minute ago," Rex said. "Not that it matters."

Patroclus grit his teeth still possessed by the jinn's red visions. Seeing Prodicus alive after the immersion ordeal opened every conduit of fury, and his mind burned. In the chaos, he broke off a thick pipe from the wall, spraying smoke across the room.

Wheezing, losing his footing, and barely able to stand, the Lion of Heliopolis stalked his weak prey up five steps to the carpeted dais. Patroclus squeezed the pipe and said, “Even if we’re all destined to die, justice requires we kill the last murderer. Isn’t that what the guardians taught me? You . . . you don’t deserve to crash with us, Father! Look behind your back; can you hear their voices? Vaporous shadows call from the Underworld. I see the goddess; the radiant Iron Queen speaks to me, hovering over Sophia. She saved Glaucon and summons you. Her skull-necklace licks the air. ‘Death,’ she says. ‘Death to he who would be Zeus! Even Prodicus can die.’ ”

When Rex started wildly pointing and screaming at the ongoing hunt, Glaucon turned around. The sight of the brainsick guardian dragging the pipe behind him on the carpet like a heavy tree limb left no mystery as to his devilish intent.

Glaucon implored him to stop, but his pleas came too late. Patroclus caught the philosopher-king crawling halfway to Sophie. The old man was drawn to the last remnant of Potone’s body like metal drawn to a magnetic essence. The very same expression of the boy staring through the window continued to mist his fading eyes. As far as he could understand, immersion continued. A sandaled kick, however, brought him back to reality.

The bearded face looked up frightfully at the Lion of Heliopolis, covered in frost. “No, not you, my son. Not you—”

A hundred vigorous blows cut him off, chopping the air amidst a blood-curdling scream. It remained unclear if the scream ushered forth from Patroclus or Prodicus. (Perhaps it was the two mixed together.) Patroclus’ eyes remained wide open, taking in the ruined symmetry of his father’s face. “I have no father, you wicked guardian! You never cared for any of us. Not your nephew, not Glaucon, not me. Not even Kabiri.” He spit on the corpse feverishly, insane. His muscles timed every blow and speckled his arms with blood. He did not finish smashing the philosopher-king’s head with the pipe until the last drop of tyrant blood trickled down to stain Rex’s robes by the door.

Upon the last blow, a black jinn escaped Prodicus’ sleeve, bounced over some tube insulation, rolled . . . rolled . . . rolled out the temple door.

“Uncle,” Sophie reached out to the disfigured body. For everything he had done to her only pity remained.

The Fates’ daimons remained in the Lion’s neurons even after the act. Patroclus dropped the bloody pipe next to Sophie. He collapsed shaking on the floor haunted by the Iron Queen, haunted by the warnings of Kleomedes to destroy the jinn.

Power went out over the entire island. Levantra started to free fall.

"Gods damn it!" Glaucon cried, pounding the controls with his fists. Nothing worked. No clicking sounds to herald a reboot. No blinking lights to hint a resurrection. More painful than the quiet console, Prodicus' mutilated head peered up at him like a decapitated, questioning hog. His body looked more like an innocent rabbit run down by a magnet-sedan than a man. *What was it all for, bringing him back?* he wondered with tortuous thoughts. Finding nothing but failure re-energizing the magnets, he finally returned to Sophie by the pedestal. Wrapping his arms around her breathing waist, he smelled her skin's familiar scent like coming home. What bitterness in losing her again.

"You saved me," Sophie said stroking his face in a manner similar to Zemer. "You wonderful boy, thank you."

"It was this or the Monad," Glaucon said. "I wanted to hold you one more time."

"This is the right choice," Sophie kissed him. Both tried to forget Prodicus' gory remains, and they held one another for courage, clouds racing past the windows outside.

Rex pounded the ceiling. "No, no, no. Not like this. What have I done to deserve such treatment? What gods have I angered? Have I not performed my expected role? Have I not defaced myself? Where is my reward?—my promised reward? There is still so much left undone. Damn you, Glaucon, and your easy heart. Damn you to Hades. I knew all along you'd be the death of us. I was too afraid to speak up at the time, but I knew. 'Patience Rex,' they told me, 'he will lead us to the Good; so watch out and preserve him.' Liars. Such good liars, they never knew they lied. But I always knew. I did. The Republic was the biggest fraud I ever heard of. If only Xenon had taken me rather than Kleomedes and Sophia. What I could have done in a world committed to truth."

Turbulence pitched screens and voltage converters across the room like cannon balls, shattering them to fragments. The crystal mainframe floor cracked. Parts of the island shell unraveled and broke away like a bird molting feathers. All prepared for impact.

Glaucon imagined the initial crash, the first bounce where all his bones would break in one horrible micro-second. He must've replayed the final snap a thousand times in his head, but he doubted it would feel the same. *Death itself is not so bad*, he admitted. *What is unbearable is the uncertain moment of death, the instant movement from being to non-being. That last snap I can never anticipate.* He sighed desperately and could barely breathe under Sophie's tight grip.

But right at the moment when he finally resigned himself to oblivion, within a thousand kilometers of the fiery atomic deluge, a miraculous *caclunk* slowed the rapid drop.

Caclunk. Light reappeared on the ceiling. *Caclunk.* Metal chairs ceased floating and crashed back to the floor. *Caclunk.* A strange power recaptured and stabilized the Island's descent. Whirring magnets could be heard below. Levantra soared back into the sky unharmed.

"What's going on?" Rex asked with one eye open. "Are we dead?"

"It's Zemer," Glaucon laughed happily. "He said he'd find another miracle."

"What are you talking about?" Sophie asked dumbfounded. The only thing she remembered from immersion was trading lives with Glaucon on the grass. Much of what she found revolted her. But the shared present so mingled their memories together that the revulsion may as well have been directed at her own past. Only now, as he stared at her, did she regain a sense of conscious detachment and feel alone in her body.

Glaucon tried to explain, "Your brother saved us, Sophie. He found a way to defeat the Fates. Gods know how he did it."

"I know," Sophie said touching Glaucon's cheek, his walled human cheek. "Brother took the Shadow Bridge and unlocked the firefly. He flew with the jinn and did what I could not." A tear trickled down the edge of her nose as she remembered their oath as children. Zemer had protected her more than anyone else could. He had suffered unimaginably, and now found final rest in Glaucon and Levantra.

Abruptly, she realized Xenon still hung in agony on the cross. Rushing over, she punched a button retracting the mythranium nails. Xenon winced in pain. Dark blood ran from gashes in his wrists, and Sophie made a hideous face. The freed rebel begged for a glass of water to soothe his cracked lips, and, once sitting down in a chair, stooped over his knees without speaking. His thoughts were far away with the fallout shelters, wondering if they survived the storm.

"Perhaps it would've been better if we just crashed," Rex noted honestly. He glanced around the room and almost burst out laughing, high on natural adrenaline.

"One less child for Moloch is a victory," Sophie answered him. Clutching Xenon's arm, she shook life back into his spiritless limbs.

"Give up, Sophie," Xenon managed to say. "This can't be happening. I saw you immersed. I saw it. Must be a dream. . . ."

The temple door suddenly swung open. Over the next hour, Zoe and a hundred faces poured in to discover the source of the disturbance. Many shrieked upon finding the dead body of the philosopher-king. Patroclus continued to cry, hovering over his father's robes in shock. When Glaucon explained the death of the Fates and what transpired during immersion even more fainted. A few, unable to cope with the loss of Kabiri-37, fled from the room in despair.

"The Forms?" one guardian asked. "Did the Fates show you anything about the Forms?"

Glaucon looked at Sophie before answering. "The Forms are a lie," he said. "They do not exist, have never existed, and will never exist. We have nothing but ourselves."

No one believed such a statement could be uttered let alone be true. Some rebuked him immediately as a liar. Others attempted to articulate deductive proofs against his argument. Still more pointed to a personal mystical experience where they encountered the Form of the Beautiful. "The machines are imperfect and likely made mistakes," they consoled themselves half-heartedly. Each waited for some small hope from the Second Vessel, some vital lie to freshen the foul stench of aformism. Glaucon refused to provide one, and a great many lost their faith. The sudden knowledge drove a few to the cliffs in a flurry of suicides.

All who remained in the temple accepted Glaucon's new revelation with much anxiety. Conditions had changed dramatically: The Fates were dead, the avis were inoperable, the auxiliaries were gone. The philosophers and helots lived unmixed and stranded on a flying island.

Zoe was overjoyed to see Glaucon alive, even if her head still pounded from an *erosic* hangover. "What are we to do, Glaucon?" she asked looking up at him. "Prodicus and the Logoset are gone. Only Yannis and a few Kabiri are left. A new spirit has taken control of the navigation system. It responds only to the Iron Queen."

Glaucon replied, "We will use Levantra until the world below renews. We should save the survivors in the mountains and plan our tenure until we can return to Earth."

"But what of the Republic?" someone asked.

"What of it? The Republic and the Forms are lost. Burned with the rest. We have slain our gods and taken their place. Now let us shun godhood and embrace our humanity."

But more whined: "If Plato's tale is false, then how will we know which values to adopt or what city to design?"

At this point, Sophie interjected, "The values of our past belonged to mankind all along. We just never realized it. With no gods to offend, let's make values and communes pleasing to free individuals. Let's light the torch of anarchy."

The booming sound of her voice filled the crowds with terror. For decades they had hunted this woman, and now she held absolute power over them. The assembly had watched with awe as the sky-witch imputed new coordinates to Wyoming airspace with nothing but speech. The soul of Zemer—whom they burned alive in the Bull—obeyed her every command and surrounded them like a powerful spirit. The children of the Katharoi directed every crane, robotic attendant, and electronic door. They directed the audiomembrane and the oxygen controls. They were Levantra's new gods.

A cold-blooded urge to turn Levantra's weapons on the guardians washed over Sophie. She desired vengeance against her hated oppressors, spiteful, rabid vengeance, to annihilate them all with the laser turrets—an inescapable bloodbath. How she had dreamed of this moment. How they deserved it. But justice, she realized, was more than giving what was owed. Justice required love and forgiveness, an opportunity to make amends. Killing the conquered wasn't anarchism. It was vendetta and self-righteous.

As guardians groveled before their new philosopher-queen begging for mercy, Sophie touched their sun-shaped heads and let go of strife. "Don't worry," she said. "Your lives are safe with me. The Iron Queen has given up grudges. I will invoke sanctuary, for now. But let me make one thing clear; the Age of Reason is over. Guardians, inequality, and the State are abolished as nature intended. I will faithfully follow the principles of Resolution 15 until a proper workers' council forms to relieve me. To that end the Bull is be dismantled and thrown away. Now."

A loud clanking was heard outside as a crane energized and tossed the diseased creature into the atomic fires.

"See my miracle," Sophie told the amazed guardians. "Winter chilled the Earth, but I shall make it spring again. The Iron Queen makes all things grow anew."

Much to the crowd's surprise, they brightened at Sophie's words. With total control of Levantra, the Iron Queen was immensely dangerous. They were completely at her mercy; but she didn't use her power as the guardians did. Instead, she granted individual freedom and amnesty—destroyed the Bull. Perhaps the world she offered was better than the old one.

Sitting beside her, Glaucon kissed Sophie's silk hair and relished the sweet curve of her mortal skull, their lovely separation.

The Iron Queen felt for the life in her belly. She wished to be alone with Glaucon to discuss their experiences. It felt like a lifetime passed since they rested peacefully by the lake. How she hoped her baby survived immersion, and she wondered how Glaucon would treat the news. She worried at her new powers, though, and the chance for tyranny. Could these people learn the power of consensus rather than command? Would there be enough room for her commune and the other anarchist survivors? *We can find a way,* she thought. *If Zemer could defeat the Fates, we can find a way.*

Simmias Rex spoke anxiously about the wide open sky: "Saint Plato, Sophia, it's like we're starting all over again. It scares me so." He, more than anyone, smiled happy to be in the Iron Queen's good graces, and he was already attempting to butter her up with conversation.

Remembering Zemer's final words, Glaucon responded, "Yes, isn't it wonderful, Simmias? We can make anything we want. We're better than the gods and not moored to any of their books. Let's sail wherever we choose. Being human is enough."

Rex looked at Glaucon in a new light, permitted a momentary admiration for the sentiment.

What a fortunate end, considering the possibilities, Glaucon thought. Man had survived . . . for now. With a little luck, they might seed a new future.

Nevertheless, something about this optimism made Glaucon's skin crawl with icy terror. He looked back at the limp hand of Prodicus on the dais. *Why would Zemer tell me to save him if death was his destiny?* he wondered. It didn't make sense. Near the top pedestal, Glaucon thought he saw Atropos grinning at him like the Cheshire cat. Wide-eyed, he gasped like old Gregorios the Great at the Academy. "Is this reality or am I in the cogniscrambler? Did we really escape immersion?"

No voice answered either question. Levantra sailed into the sun.

Republic Lost Appendices

Appendix 1: Complete Encyclopedia of Philosopher-Kings

ENYO (2559-2590 M.G.P.)

First ISHIM director and guardian-queen of the Republic, historians point to her reign as a Golden Age. The sudden death of her predecessor, Hythloday, left several factions vying for control of the Republic. To assure her control and pacify revolt, Enyo orchestrated the SUN-LIGHTNING ALLIANCE with the House of Ozbolt and ceded special court jurisdiction of Stratos to the Polemarch. Enyo also rationalized the criminal justice system, ending the bloody excesses of the revolution. Further, she invented the civil position of Ward Phylark to facilitate communication between the wards and Heliopolis. Rumors persist of romantic involvement between Dr. Zosimos Ozbolt and Enyo, especially since such enormous public monies were ceded to the Ozbolt family for Schizoeon's construction. They remain unsubstantiated by direct primary documentation.

HEKADEMOS I (2592-2598 M.G.P.)

Came to power after the bloody YEAR OF THE THREE PHILOSOPHER-KINGS (2591). Guardian-Queen Enyo failed to name an intellectual successor upon her death, and three children of Hythloday (Castor, Briseis, and Ion) competed violently for the Golden Crown, serving as de facto dictators and killing their rivals. Ultimately, the auxiliaries under Polemarch Xexio hacked Ion to death in his bed and called together the guardian templar to appoint a successor. Hekademos I was selected as a moderate and for his connections to Enyo's respected regime. Ruling by consensus, he forgave Vinculum Cartel debts incurred in support of the other philosopher-kings; issued amnesty to a helot rebellion; and sought to control inflation by stiffly regulating the Cheque Giorgio Banking Corporation. To avoid further succession troubles, Hekademos I established the Logoset Assembly Dome, comprised of one hundred representatives elected by the guardian templar. A period of relative tranquility followed his rule.

PELOPIA (2672-2680 M.G.P.)

Alleged daughter of Guardian-King Eudoxus II, who died under suspicious circumstances, her rule is marked by the ANARCHIST CIVIL

WAR. Tension between the Southwest Confederacy and Randland boiled to a head when the Republic funded the latter with weapons and supplies, allowing them to aggressively encroach into the Santa Fe-Cheyenne Axis. After the oligarch government collapsed from infighting, slaves executed their masters and three Republican ambassadors, declaring independence as an anarchist commune. The loss of the West Coast and the strengthening of the Southwest Confederacy undermined the guardians' confidence in Pelopia's war strategy, and the Logoset forced her to abdicate in disgrace.

GORTIS (2700-2703 M.G.P.)

Known to history as "The Fat Tyrant," Gortis undermined the Logoset by aligning with the Polemarch of Stratos and ruling as a two-man junta. Gladiator games were re-established to punish offenders of his regime, and he declared all public statues built by the guardian-artist-patriots bear his image. He suffered several embarrassing defeats in the TWELFTH REPUBLIC-ANARCHIST WAR, most notably a failure to prevent a raid on Metatron Technologies by Charleston pirates in 2702. On 1 August 2703, student rebels and officers in the Republic Auxiliary Core stabbed him to death on the steps of the Logoset as a dictator, crying: "The Good suffers not the soul of Meletus!" The slogan persists as a revolutionary saying to present day.

EUTHYA (2703-2712 M.G.P.)

Leader of the AUGUST FIRST STUDENT MOVEMENT and the youngest guardian ever to be elected to the Sapphire Throne (she was 35), Euthya declared a new "Guardian Congress" which expanded the Logoset to seven hundred. Purging political opponents in ISHIM, she increased helot labor rights, improved the logical notation system, and forged treaties of peace across the American continent. In 2711, she returned jurisdiction of Stratos courts to the Logoset and passed military reforms to fulfill treaty obligations. Conservatives used the anger generated by such policies to appeal to disgruntled auxiliaries. A military coup ultimately toppled her regime in 2712. Rather than giving herself up to the auxiliaries, Euthya and twenty other students committed suicide by drinking hemlock on the Logoset roof.

LAMPROCLES (2712-2718 M.G.P.)

Puppet installed on behalf of the auxiliaries after the collapse of the student government. Lowering the Logoset to twelve new "archons," Lamprocles executed the remaining student rebels in a bloody purge. Several ambitious engineering projects flowered under his rule, including an expanded Emporium and transit system. Following the unexpected arrival of European steamships bearing the French flag near the Florida Archipelago in 2289, the Logoset broke into uproar. Lamprocles successfully argued for the re-application of Option Star Arrow, and neutralized thirty threatening cities with Republican war satellites.

HERMAPHRODITUS (2723-2733 M.G.P.)

Hermaphroditic king who established a religious cult focusing on the asexual nature of the Form of the Good. Scandal resulted when he and a group of followers, called "The Platonic Elect," practiced sexual abstinence and refused to eat beans (which they felt too closely resembled male genitals). As historians have ironically noted, the population of the Republic nearly doubled under his rule. His primary accomplishments include détente with the Other Side following a successful campaign against pirates in the SECOND CHARLESTON WAR. City walls were also pushed forward to provide additional living space in the wards. His *Commentary on the Symposium* is still widely used in Academy classrooms.

HEKADEMOS II (2748-2763 M.G.P.)

A master of dialectic and the philosophy of law, Hekademos II oversaw an intellectual renaissance in the Republic as well as increased cosmopolitanism. He made several improvements to the Vinculum Cartel structure, most notably the centralization of disconnected state media companies into Skybridge News. When another student revolt threatened to re-install a Guardian Congress in 2755, he declared them outlaws but was forced to flee the city. After successfully rallying auxiliaries campaigning against the Southwest Confederacy, he re-captured the city in 2757. He executed the rebel leaders in the Bull but pardoned the majority of offenders. To stave off future upheavals, he initiated a re-education program for all three metal races.

HEKADEMOS III (2763-2809 M.G.P.)
Alleged descendant of Guardian-King Hythloday and Hekademos II, his reign was marked by the KABIRI TECHFLATION and social, religious, and economic upheaval. Much of his accomplishments are overshadowed by the disastrous KATHAROI-KABIRI DEBATE, THE GREAT THEURGY SCHISM, and its aftermath. Killed in an assassination plot commenced by Xenon Adonis, Katharoi guardians, and rogue members of the House of Ozbolt.

Appendix 2: Meta-Almanac of Heresies, "The Katharoi and Collected Sayings of Ekklesia the Blind" (Fifth Academy Press, 2821 M.G.P.)

The Katharoi heresy is an anomaly in the Republic's history. While social conservatism necessarily follows any group reliant on a sacred text, this sect acted abnormally reactionary, especially in times of such prosperity. Centuries of technological advancement they declared impediments to knowledge. Some went so far as to call technology shadowy illusion.

Katharoi beliefs are rooted in 532b of the *Republic* where Saint Plato discusses the method of dialectic—using logical argument to uncover the Form of the Good. The Great Philosopher writes:

> "Whenever someone tries through argument and apart from all sense perceptions to find the being itself of each thing and doesn't give up until he grasps the Good itself with understanding itself, he reaches the end of the intelligible."

Two important questions emerge from this passage: *First,* what is the meaning of "apart from all sense perception?" *Second,* what is the meaning of "understanding itself?" Ekklesia the Blind answered the latter by stating it meant *natural* human understanding, without technological enhancement of any kind. To the former question, he argued man must strive to eliminate sense perception through will, training, and meditation, not artificially shedding sense through "computer illusions." The Kabiri Circle challenged this assumption, stating the text was ambiguous and that shedding "all" sense perception was impossible without some form of enhancement. "Why would Saint Plato order us to strive for the impossible?" Prodicus famously asked at the Third Kabiri-Katharoi Symposium. It was here Ekklesia famously accused him of the *argumentum ad ignorantiam* fallacy (argument by ignorance, lack of imagination) because he assumed that lack of enlightenment meant the non-existence or impossibility of enlightenment through meditation.

Championing a quieter, simpler lifestyle of philosophic reflection and toil, the Katharoi opposed several groundbreaking pieces of legislation: artificial intelligence legalization; bans on infanticide for naturally-disabled guardian children; increasing the number of eyecameras in the wards; Operation Copula (an experiment to completely shed sense perception using the Kabiri Mainframe). The Katharoi also expressed disdain for the archons and the Logoset, claiming Saint Plato never spoke of them and that they were human constructions.

Although most writings of Ekklesia the Blind failed to survive the public purification fires, a few fragments remain to shed light on his beliefs:

Fragment 4. One over many, many from one, this is the mode of the Forms. Just as artwork depicting a tree conceals the Form of a Tree, so Kabiri, mimicking the brain of man, conceals the Form of Man. Kabiri is art, a shadow-copy, portioned heavy with error. Hands that lay the nanochips are like hands that paint: Ignorance! Error! Disease! Death! They teach only lies. We copy the Many's mind rather than the One's mind.

Fragment 23. A soul is a mote in the Good. Technology can neither enhance nor limit the guardian's dialogue with It. Saint Plato said the Good must be found with logical argument and human understanding. Human understanding, not machine understanding. By making a thinking-machine, we worship man, not the Good. We choose pride over logic.

Fragment 56. Metal reflects the sun; Man absorbs it.

Fragment 66. Katharoi are not pure because they reject the power of Kabiri; Katharoi are pure because they seek the Good with Good's tools.

Fragment 71. Resistance to technology is obedience to the Good.

Fragment 123. There is more to thinking than speed.

Fragment 222. What is the wise thing?—confusion and growth. What is the dangerous thing?—growth too quickly. Arguments are like Heliopolis;

they need strong foundations, strong premises, rock, not sand. Build skyward too hastily and the mountain falls. Patience is more than virtue; patience is necessary to argument and the soul.

***Fragment 421*:** The Fates say, "Applecane is more real than apples." I say applecane is a longing for death. Man births machine-gods because he is afraid of himself and wishes to die. He is afraid of the Good.

***Fragment 456*.** Prodicus laughs at my blindness. He laughs because he covets. He is too afraid to take his own eyes, so he builds a monster to snatch them. The Good laughs at this sight. I laugh with the Good.

Appendix 3: The Philosopher's Economist, "Spotlight on Vinculum Stars: Dietrich Prince," By Alcibiades, Guardian-Book-Enhancer (Fall 2823 M.G.P.)

The Republic's economic miracle owes its success to the Vinculum Cartel: ten enormous family-managed monopolies assigned to specific market functions by the guardians. Beyond supplying jobs and prosperity to millions of helot workers, the Vinculum inhibits industrial strife by allowing each ward an opportunity to hone a niche in the Fair Market. Since the days of Guardian-King Hythloday, the Vinculum has striven to achieve three primary objectives: Bread, Consumption, and National Strength.

No one better captures this ethos than Dietrich Prince, chief executive officer of Seven Seas—our city's primary weapons manufacturer. Born to the fourth concubine of Chester Prince, he grew up in a wealthy, large, and competitive Executive Family of over fifty siblings. In 2774 M.G.P., at the tender age of 15, he attended Ozbolt College where business school professors say he acted like a man in a hurry, excelling at marketing and organizational behavior. By the age of eighteen, he managed a small munitions factory for his family. Production increased exponentially—ten percent over three years. For these efforts, he received a promotion to a mid-level missile manufacturing plant: Gulf Missiles, a subsidiary of Seven Seas. There he wisely invested in face-recognition targeting technology with Ozbolt Enterprises. Profits soared, and he gained the lifelong title "The Boy with the Midas Touch."

The Deathstalker targeting system proved critical for Dietrich Prince's ultimate career; for it brought Prince directly into contact with Salazar Ozbolt and Prodicus, a social and political reformer and our city's future philosopher-king. Both scientists were in serious trouble at the time. Due to resource scarcity and the top-secret nature of Project Kabiri, they needed additional investment and trustworthy friends. They approached Prince for any assistance, and much to their appreciation, he gladly obliged. Where others might have seen dangerous risk in the young Prodicus—he was only twenty-four, one year older than the future executive—Prince glimpsed potential. He convinced his family to secretly loan equipment, helots, and orichalcum to the guardian-prodigy. Not only that, but Prince also crafted a Midas Roundtable of inter-ward executive family members committed "to the elimination of anti-technology laws and the manifestation of Prodicus' progressive military-industrial vision." Through such gallant efforts, the Kabiri-1 Mainframe was born, and our city moved toward a second Golden Age of optimism and economic growth.

Prodicus, after being elected Guardian-King by the Logoset in 2809 M.G.P., acknowledged Prince's contributions to the Republic by appointing him CEO of Seven Seas, discharging his elder sister for an early (and easy) retirement.

"Dietrich Prince is the Vinculum and the Vinculum is Dietrich Prince," Prodicus praised the helot at his inauguration. "Without those early, tireless efforts uniting the ten bronze families around my dream, I'd still be tinkering away on inoperative golems."

Since then, Seven Seas proved essential for enhancing the Republic's military might: making hull-casings for Aegis tanks impenetrable; equipping the city walls with Tesla pulse cannons to protect against Other Side barbarians; and mass-producing avis and golems for Heliopolis.

We could all learn much from the Boy with the Midas Touch. He made producing his first and primary objective. He showed wisdom listening to the guardians. He was guided by faith in Prodicus and the Good. Dietrich Prince is the winner of the Agora Lifetime Achievement Award. He is also the author of three best-selling books: *The Art of Making Orichalcum*; *Stay Cool: Climbing Corporate Republica*; and *Kabiri Courage: Why I Invested in Prodicus*.

Appendix 4: Resolution 15 Passed by the Helot Inter-Ward Directory (Fifth Convention), Adopted in the Seventh Ward by Two-Thirds Super-Majority, Summer, 2825 M.G.P.

The Helot Inter-Ward Directory,

Recalling an informative and productive two-day meeting consisting of reading reports, caucusing, and freely sharing ideas with delegates representing millions of toiling helots across the wards,

Reaffirming its commitment to anarchism, universal equality, solidarity, human happiness, safety and welfare, the blessings of society, and freedom to support and be supported by others,

Condemning the increasing barbarity of guardian despotism, evidenced by mass executions, nighttime raids, torture, wage-slavery, sexual abuse, and spiritual exploitation,

Recognizing that a revolutionary spirit is necessary, as previous reformist attempts to secure political and labor rights have met with failure and wide-scale butchery,

Stressing the necessity for non-violence and a peaceful resolution of differences with oppressors to avoid committing injustice, vengeance, and fratricide murder,

Welcoming guardian suggestions for reconciliation and leveling government,

Adopts the following measures:

1. A general strike is declared until the guardians acknowledge every power and privilege resides within the helot's breast and do release all political prisoners, including Comrade Terra Brandon, Executive Board Member of the Industrial Workers' Federation.

2. Every Republican law, ordinance, decree, executive order, and agency fiat are hereby annulled; any rules for society will be laid down by democratically-based worker assemblies.

3. Political offices, including but not limited to Phylark, Temple Confessor, Archon, ISHIM Director, and Guardian-King, are abolished.

4. Estates, classes, castes, special markers of social rank, any hierarchy whatsoever are prohibited. The tyrannical auxiliaries and guardians and their police and military responsibilities are replaced by workers' militias.

5. Freedom of speech, press, and assembly, and the right to form unions shall not be infringed.

6. All inhabitants of the Former Republic are encouraged to establish their own worker assemblies, to join with other organizations, or to secede from the General Directory if they find it contrary to their interests.

7. The right to practice religion or non-religion and to be protected from supporting any religion is recognized.

8. The erection of any wall, checkpoint, or boundary is prohibited, and each individual possesses a right to travel.

9. All property, including the Vinculum Cartel's towers, firms, factories, shops, orichalcum, and other means of production are immediately collectivized into the hands of democratic worker assemblies. All inhabitants possess a right to rewarding work, adequate food and shelter, a good education, healthcare, and companionship, to be protected through use of the collective fund.

10. Bondmarriage, state compelled prostitution, concubinage and polygamy for Vinculum executive puppets, the Slimetide Rolodex and *erosic*, every cruel and contemptible method of sexual exploitation is abolished.

11. The Bull and gladiatorial games are prohibited as antithetical to human dignity, and no cruel and dehumanizing penalty shall be imposed for any reason.

12. Releasing non-consensual psychotropic anti-depressants in the water supply is prohibited.

13. There is to be an immediate audit of Ozbolt Enterprises and the Department of Foresight and Futurology, to discover the extent of public treasure wasted on Project Kabiri and to prepare the path for eliminating Kabiri-36.

14. Persons interfering with the successful implementation of these provisions are to be deemed counter-revolutionaries subject to judgment by worker assemblies.

15. Special Truth and Reconciliation Committees are hereby established to allow guardians, auxiliaries, helots, and inhabitants of the Other Side a chance to testify and record their crimes before public hearings. Any individual submitting an application in good faith, who fully and completely discloses his crimes, expresses remorse, and asks forgiveness will be granted general amnesty by all worker assemblies. His crime will cease to exist, and he is to be treated as innocent henceforth, deserving access to the collective fund and comity.

16. Guardian Sophia and her twin brother, Guardian Kleomedes, having testified publicly to the General Directory concerning their political crimes on Heliopolis and the Other Side, are hereby granted total amnesty and are to be provided aid, comfort, and protection by all inhabitants of the Former Republic.

17. A treaty of peace is presented to Sophia and Kleomedes, acting delegates for the Continental Caucus, to present to their communes for ratification.

Prepare, Brave Brothers and Sisters, to use strikes and moral force to win your freedom from the guardian yoke! Solidarity forever! Long Live Anarchy!

About the Author

James Paul Rinnan is a writer, lawyer, and civil rights activist. He was born in Austin, Texas in 1984. Raised in the bayous and pine forests of Houston, he also has deep roots to Detroit, Michigan where much of his extended family remains.

In 2003 Paul attended TCU in Fort Worth on a scholarship, double majoring in philosophy and political science with a minor in history. While there, he participated in school politics as a Student House representative. He also worked as a philosophy teaching assistant, covering logic, existentialism, ancient philosophy, and ethical theory. Additionally, his professors named him Senior Scholar in Philosophy, the highest academic award from the department. After graduating summa cum laude in 2007, he studied law at the University of Houston and was admitted to the Texas Bar in 2010.

Paul has a passion for public interest law. He fought for disability and labor rights with Advocacy, Inc. and traveled to Bangalore, India to assist municipal reform and democracy. In 2010, he began a graduate fellowship with the Texas American Civil Liberties Union. He researched a number of human rights issues, including free speech, internet privacy violations, lesbian and gay rights, gerrymandering claims, and prisoner justice.

Paul currently lives in Houston with his wife, Lindsey. This is his first novel. Supplemental information about *Republic Lost* and Paul's other projects can be reached at www.jpaulrinnan.com.

CPSIA information can be obtained at www.ICGtesting.com
Printed in the USA
242257LV00004B/22/P

9 781614 342731